IN BORROWED LIGHT

Barbara and Stephanie Keating grew up in Kenya.
One sister now lives in France and the other in
Dublin. Their first novel was the bestselling *To
My Daughter in France* . . . This was followed by
the acclaimed novels *Blood Sisters* and *A Durable
Fire*, which along with *In Borrowed Light*, make
up the Langani trilogy.

ALSO BY BARBARA & STEPHANIE KEATING

To My Daughter In France . . .
Blood Sisters
A Durable Fire

BARBARA & STEPHANIE KEATING

In Borrowed
Light

VINTAGE BOOKS
London

Published by Vintage 2011

2 4 6 8 10 9 7 5 3 1

Copyright © Barbara & Stephanie Keating, 2010

Barbara and Stephanie Keating have asserted their right under the
Copyright, Designs and Patents Act 1988 to be identified as the
authors of this work

Map drawn by Thomasina Sawyer

First published in Great Britain in
2010 by Harvill Secker

Vintage
Random House, 20 Vauxhall Bridge Road,
London SW1V 2SA

www.vintage-books.co.uk

Addresses for companies within The Random House Group Limited
can be found at: www.randomhouse.co.uk/offices.htm

The Random House Group Limited Reg. No. 954009

A CIP catalogue record for this book
is available from the British Library

ISBN 9780099520634

The Random House Group Limited supports The Forest
Stewardship Council (FSC), the leading international forest
certification organisation. All our titles that are printed on
Greenpeace approved FSC certified paper carry the FSC logo.
Our paper procurement policy can be found at:
www.randomhouse.co.uk/environment

MIX
Paper from
responsible sources
FSC® C016897

Printed and bound in Great Britain by
CPI Cox & Wyman, Reading, RG1 8EX

FOR OUR CHILDREN

Savage stars pit the night
And I walk in borrowed light
To seek, to feel, to fear, to fly . . .
                    T. Ryan

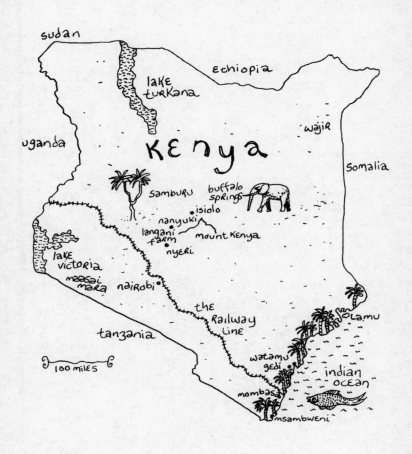

Chapter 1

It had started well, the day that Hannah's world shifted on its axis to spin out of its familiar orbit. It was the day she had left Langani Farm to travel to Europe for the first time. The day that her daughter vanished for the first time. The day that doubt crept into her sense of belonging for the first time, to gnaw at the core of all she held dear.

She rose before dawn on that morning, leaving the bedroom with unaccustomed stealth, not wanting to wake Lars who was snoring lightly through the last hour of sleep. He had held Hannah close during the night, unable to quell his excitement, although he was not a man to express extremes of feeling.

'We're leaving tomorrow, Han,' he said. 'There have been times when I thought you would never see the place of my origins. I know it was hard for you to choose between Norway and Italy, but I think Lottie understands.'

'She does.' Hannah burrowed under the bedclothes to warm herself on his body, understanding the pride he would feel as he introduced his wife and children to the land that had nurtured him. 'We can't afford the time or the money to travel to both places. Ma was with us at the coast last year, and we have promised it will be Italy next time. Besides, we never thought about a holiday anywhere in Europe, until now.'

'We will have the best times,' Lars said. 'Seeing the other half of our children's heritage, the farm where I grew up, and a different set of mountains rising out of such blue water.' He pushed his fingers into her thick, blonde hair, loosened from the braid that hung down her back during the daytime. 'You are going to fall in love with Norway. And the children will think they are in heaven.'

'They are pretty close to heaven right here,' Hannah said. 'I don't know

1

how we will persuade Suniva to behave like a normal European child. She could look so pretty now that she is eleven years old, but she is a wild tomboy. It will be a battle to convince her that she should keep her shoes on and comb her hair and wear a dress sometimes, instead of running around in those tatty old shorts and *tackies*, like a *toto* from the labour lines.'

'She can wear whatever she likes.' Lars was smiling. 'Her feet will sink into the softest grass you can imagine. I can see her walking through the wildflowers in the meadows. She will meet her grandfather's cows and pick up some more Norwegian. Piet can learn to row and to sail, and we will have the best shrimps you have ever eaten.'

'Yes. Of course we will.'

'What is it, Han?' Lars propped himself up on one elbow. 'You're not worried about leaving Langani, are you? Mike has stood in as farm manager for years, when we have gone to the coast or on safari. And David is a true professional with the guests up at the lodge. Sarah will look in, too, now that she seems to be well again. It's going to be fine.'

'Poor Sarah. I suppose a visit to Langani might help her, but she has been so depressed that I don't believe she is capable of doing anything much,' she said. 'But it's not the farm. It's only that I worry about Piet having a problem on the plane. He has had such a bad time with his ears, and I hope it's not too soon for him to travel. I keep wondering if we should have delayed everything.'

'Piet will be fine,' Lars said. 'Dr Markham says there is no sign of any remaining infection.'

'Yes, but this is the third time he has had trouble with his ears lately, and we have to be extra careful,' Hannah said.

'He is more likely to pick up another infection here, than in London or Norway. It would have been very difficult to change our dates and leave later. And think of the children's disappointment. They are so eager to be off, to see that big new world.'

'You mustn't spoil them too much,' she said, smiling up at him. 'Get them used to things we can never have here.'

'It is their first trip outside Kenya,' he said, running his fingers lightly over her face, across her mouth. 'And your first time in Europe. So I am certainly planning to spoil you all. *Ja*. Starting right now.'

'Go to sleep.' She pushed him away, laughing, as he reached

underneath her pyjama top to touch her warm breasts. 'I have to be up early in the morning to check the packing. I'm sure I've brought all the wrong things, especially for London.'

'If you need different clothes you can go shopping with Camilla,' he said. 'Take advantage of the fact that your friend is the queen of London fashion.'

'I can't afford to shop anywhere that Camilla would go. But I'm glad she will be there. We haven't seen her for months, and last time she was only at the farm for a few days. It's lovely that we can stay in her flat instead of a hotel, although I think she is a little crazy taking on us hayseeds, and the children too.'

'It will bring her back to real life,' Lars said, chuckling in the darkness. 'Make a change from all the pictures we see of her with the rich and famous. Instead she will be with us, looking at the sights of London from the top of a red bus.'

'I'm a little scared of the big city and the crowds and the pace of London,' Hannah said. 'And the cost of everything.'

'We've had several good years on the farm, with the wheat and your success in the dairy and the way you have run Camilla's workshop. The lodge is making money, too. We should enjoy a few luxuries while we can, so we will remember them when there is a drought, or the cows get sick, or there is rust or worm in the wheat. Come here, Han,' he said, kissing her earlobe, feeling her resolve evaporate under his knowing caresses. His voice was pitched at the special tone he used for lovemaking as he brought her closer.

'Ach, Lars, I don't know what you are thinking of,' she said, putting her arms around his neck as he began to whisper into her ear. 'Sometimes you have no sense at all.'

Hannah was warmed by the memory as she made her way through the silent house and into the garden, with its scent of jasmine and the sighing of the wind in the trees. The dogs followed her expectantly, whining softly as she opened the door onto the verandah, disappointed when she shook her head and left them behind. Outside, the night watchman murmured a greeting and she heard the call of a nightjar in the chilly darkness. The last stars still glittered in the sky, and the smell of rain hung in the air. She hoped another downpour would not turn the road into an ooze of red mud, sucking at the tyres and causing the car to sway and slide into a hidden pothole, or even a ditch. They would have to leave as early as possible, in case of unexpected delays.

She started the Land Rover and backed slowly out of the garage, keeping the engine noise low, not turning on the headlights until she had rounded the curve in the driveway. Then she changed gear and picked up speed along the track that led to the ridge. The sky was stained with scarlet and gold, and the beginnings of blue had appeared by the time she parked at the foot of the rocky incline. As she climbed the last few hundred yards, the distant silhouette of the mountain stood before her, dark and high and ragged against the glowing light, and she sensed that the Great God N'gai was watching her solitary pilgrimage. The earth felt ancient and familiar beneath the spring of her footsteps. In the distance she could see the glimmer of early morning fires, as men and women appeared from the thatched huts of the farm's labour lines to prepare for the day. Below her, on the viewing platform at Langani Lodge, two of the guests had come out to watch a group of elephant at the waterhole.

Three generations of her family had passed this way before her, scrambling up the loose scree to the ridge that had been her brother's favourite place. Piet had come up here to dream, looking out over the farm that his great-grandparents had carved from the devouring wilderness, planning what he would do when his turn came to tend and protect the land. It was on the ridge that he had asked Sarah to marry him. It was here that he had died, under the cold, pitiless eye of the African moon.

Sarah was the one who had suggested building a cairn in his memory, the one who had chosen the first smooth stone and set it in place over the ashes of his funeral pyre. Hannah had followed and then Camilla, the three friends taking their first steps towards broken-hearted acceptance, as close in their grief as they had been in the joys of their shared childhood. Over time Hannah had learned to look upon Piet's memorial as a refuge where his spirit remained to guide and comfort her. When her son was born and named after the brother she had adored and lost, she and Lars had brought the child up here on the day of his christening, to turn the ridge into a place of peace and renewal.

The air felt charged with beauty and purpose and the sounds of the bush began to swell around her. She sat down on the cool stones of the cairn, beneath the tortillis tree that Lars had planted on the place where Piet's funeral pyre had flared in the obscene brightness of that terrible morning.

'We're leaving today, Piet,' she said, aloud. 'On the visit to Europe that we've talked about for so long. Lars and the children and me. I can't believe it's happening – that we're going to London and Norway. I'm a little nervous, though. Even in Nairobi I sometimes feel like a real bumpkin – a plain, Afrikaans farm girl in the middle of all those fancy people. But it will be a wonderful thing for us, and I can feel the thrill of it already. So I've come to say goodbye for a while. To say that I love you, and I know you'll watch over the farm while we're gone.'

His answer came to her in the hum of the wind, through the bird calls that he had known so well, and from the sounds of the animals grazing on the plains beneath her. She drove back to the house with her mind at rest, taking the track along the bright coil of the river, passing herds of zebra and gazelle and a pair of jackals trotting across the plains after a night's hunting.

She had spent two hours at the Langani Workshop on the previous afternoon, supervising the Kikuyu and Maasai women while they cut fabric and sewed beads and ornaments onto Camilla's latest designs. They chattered and sang as they threaded their needles and set the machines whirring, and they had all laughed at her when she suggested that they, too, might one day make a visit to the faraway land where their work was sold in shops even bigger than her house. Hannah hoped that nothing would go wrong with the sewing machines in her absence. Mike Stead was a good farm manager and he could coax the tractor or harvester into grudging life, but she did not think that his expertise or interests ran to small devices that created handbags and belts and embroidered clothing for distant fashion boutiques.

Now, in the morning's pearly light she called in at the dairy to see her cows, and to admire the calf that she had delivered recently with Achole who had looked after the herd for several years. A few minutes in the stables made her regret that she did not have time for a brief ride before departure, but she had to content herself with putting her arms around each of the horses' necks and stroking their velvet noses. By the time she returned to the house she was ravenous, anxious to get the children dressed and ready, and to put the last things into their suitcases. She climbed out of the Land Rover and frowned. The promise of a fine day was fading, and a drift of cloud had hooked itself around the mountain's sharp summit, stealing the blue from the sky and bringing a tinge of gloom to the morning. She stood on the lawn, breathing in the scent of rain in the last moments before everything changed.

'Hannah.' Lars was standing on the verandah with Piet beside him.

'This young man is up early.' Hannah ruffled her son's blond hair, her heart skipping a beat as she saw her brother's mirror image in the boy. But Piet did not respond, and on closer inspection she was surprised by his sombre expression. 'What's the matter? We're going to London tonight, to see the horses, and the soldiers guarding the Queen in Buckingham Palace, and—'

'We can't go.' Piet's tone was flat. 'Not without Suniva.'

'Of course we're not going without Suniva,' Hannah said, puzzled. 'We'll wake her up right now. You can both have breakfast in your dressing gowns, and then put on your new clothes for the journey.'

'Suniva's not in her bedroom. She's not in the house, Han.' Lars stared at his wife, willing her to remain calm.

'So where is she?' Hannah tried to read the signal in his eyes.

'Suniva has run away!' Piet blurted out the words. 'Because she won't go without James. Not to the other farm, or on the aeroplane to London. And we can't go without her.'

'Oh, for heaven's sake,' Hannah said, exasperated. 'I can't believe she'd pull this kind of stunt on the morning we're leaving.'

Piet balled his fists, steeling himself against tears. Lars placed a hand on his shoulder, understanding the child's fear that the great adventure they had talked about for so long might now be cancelled. But Piet turned and ran towards the sitting room, colliding with Mwangi.

'What is the matter with this boy?' The old retainer looked at Piet, his wrinkled face full of concern.

'Suniva has disappeared,' Lars said. 'She is not in the house.'

'Piet thinks his sister has run away,' Hannah said. 'Have you seen her this morning?' When Mwangi shook his head she turned to Lars. 'When did all this start?'

'He came running into the bedroom a few minutes before you arrived.'

'She must be with Esther and James,' Hannah said, annoyance rising. 'I'll go out to the staff quarters and bring her back. Mwangi, please give Piet his breakfast. I asked Kamau to come early this morning, so he's probably in the kitchen already.'

In the staff compound she stepped over several broody chickens and knocked on Esther's door. There was no response and she rapped again, loud and impatient. She was shivering in the cold air, shaking the first drops of rain from her hair, aware that several of the *watu* had come out of their houses and were watching, curiously. When Esther appeared she was tying her headscarf back behind her ears, and her cardigan hung open over the flannel nightgown that had been a Christmas gift.

'Mama Hannah?' Her voice was still thick with sleep. 'It is very early. Is there something wrong?'

'I've come to fetch Suniva.' Hannah brushed the question aside. 'You shouldn't have let her stay here, Esther. I've told you before that the children can be together all day, but they must sleep in their own rooms at night.'

'I have not seen her since yesterday.' Esther was bewildered and indignant.

'Well, she's not in the house, so I thought she must be with you.' Hannah was frowning, a worm of disquiet curdling her stomach. 'Is James here?'

'*Ndio*, Mama.' Esther's mouth was turned down with displeasure. 'Of course he is here.'

Hannah put her hand on Esther's ample arm. 'I'm sorry,' she said. 'But Piet says Suniva has run away, because she does not want to leave without James.'

'Ehh, ehh.' The ayah nodded. 'That is what she said, yes. She has told you the same thing.'

'I don't pay attention to that kind of rubbish.' Hannah could not disguise her irritation. 'She must be hiding somewhere in the compound, or in the garden. It's beginning to rain and we must leave for Nairobi early, in case we get stuck in the mud somewhere. We can't be held up because Suniva wants to attract attention. Bwana Lars is already angry.'

Esther let out a soft grunt. 'Those two are always playing bad games,' she said. 'Piet not so much. But the others do not obey me because they are too big now. They are always making some *matata*.'

Hannah was not listening. She strode across the room to James's bedroom and opened the door. There was a mound in the centre of the bed.

'Wake up, James.' Hannah pulled back the bedclothes to reveal two lumpy pillows pushed into the shape of a sleeping form.

7

'Aie ya!' Esther's exclamation was one of frightened astonishment.

'Where the hell are these children?' Hannah's alarm sharpened her voice.

But it was obvious that Esther had no idea. James had gone to bed at the usual time, she said. And she had eaten her food and retired early, to be ready for the last preparations in the morning. She had not heard any sound during the night.

'Where the hell could they have gone?' Frustration overtook Hannah's effort to remain composed. 'They must have left in the dark. It's only three nights ago since a leopard took one of the dogs. Think, Esther.' She grabbed the ayah's hands. 'Please.'

'I do not know. They like to be in the forest, looking for birds or following a spoor.'

'That is the worst place they could choose. And why would they go there in the dark, anyway? Send someone to the dairy to find Achole, and ask everyone here in the staff quarters if they have seen them.' Hannah's anger was stifled by dread. 'You had better come and look after Piet.'

Hannah ran back to the house, taking the verandah steps two at a time. Lars was waiting, pacing the living room. 'She's not with Esther,' she said. 'And neither is James.'

'Christ! Maybe they're at the dairy. Or the stables. What has got into her?'

Hannah shook her head. 'I've been to both places this morning.'

'What's this Piet has been telling me? About Suniva not wanting to go away?'

'Ach, she is always fooling around,' Hannah said. 'Trying to play me up. You know how she is – full of crazy schemes. And she winds you round her little finger so easily.' Her voice was dismissive but the panic in her eyes belied her tone. 'Here's Esther. She will take Piet and organise him.'

'Tell me about Suniva's crazy schemes.' Lars put his arm around his wife, seeing her torment, trying to conceal his own apprehension.

'She made a big fuss a few days ago,' Hannah said. 'Wanted to know which was James's suitcase. When she realised he was staying here, she burst into tears and started shouting at me. Said she wouldn't go, unless James was coming too.'

'I suppose we might have expected something like this, sooner or later,'

Lars said. 'Those two are inseparable. And we haven't discussed the question of James and his place in the family, now that he is old enough for it to matter.'

'What are you talking about?' Hannah brushed an impatient hand across her forehead. 'James is protected and secure, he has a roof over his head and he knows that we love him. That is his place in the family.'

'Yes, but—'

'We provide him with everything he needs, he goes to school with the other boys from the farm, and he spends all his free hours with Piet and Suniva,' Hannah said. 'He is a normal, bright, happy boy who has no inkling about his parents' history, or the horrors of the past.'

'But he doesn't really fit into either world,' Lars said. 'He's not a full part of our household, even though he never spends any time in the staff compound except when he goes to bed at night. So he doesn't truly belong in either place. It hasn't made a difference up to now, but he is about thirteen years old, Han. It's surprising that he hasn't ever questioned his situation, or asked about his parents. One of these days the other boys on the farm will bring up the subject and that will be awkward for James. I think it's a priority—'

'You didn't consider this a priority until a few minutes ago, any more than I did.' Hannah cut him off. 'Right now our main concern is that James and Suniva are playing some stupid game, and we need to find them. I'll phone the lodge in case David has seen them, but it's unlikely that they would have walked such a distance. Achole should be here any moment. You had better go with him to the forest, although I can't believe Suniva would venture out there at night. God knows, we've warned her enough about buffalo and elephant and leopard. And she cried all day when the puppy was taken. It's not as if she doesn't understand how dangerous it is up there.'

David answered the telephone at the lodge. No, he had not seen either of the children. He would ask the rest of the staff, but the lodge was almost four miles from the house and they would have had to walk across the plain, or along the edge of the forest. He did not believe they would have ventured so far.

Hannah shuddered, terror gnawing at her as she pushed away the horrible images of an attack by leopard or buffalo. Or a pack of hyena. A rock lodged itself in her throat and her ears ached as she swallowed tears. She tried to determine whether she should join Lars and Achole or set off in another direction. Uncertainty rooted her to the spot and she stood there, biting her lip, racking her brain for some clue as to where she might begin the search. Trying not to think of the forest, of her brother and his monstrous end. Outside a steady rain had begun to fall, realising her fears of a slippery road and slow going later in the morning. If they ever got away.

'Achole tells me that Suniva and James have built a shelter made of sticks and leaves.' Lars had appeared with the grizzled herdsman. 'It's in a clearing just inside the forest, above the second bend in the river.'

'It is their special house.' Achole was sucking his gums. 'But it is a bad place to be at night.'

'They may not have gone that way, but we'll look there first.' Lars saw his wife's consternation. He reached out to squeeze her hand, and caught a movement on the edge of his field of vision. On the verandah Mwangi was holding James by the scruff of the neck, and Hannah gasped and ran towards them.

'I have found him, coming back to Esther's *numba*,' Mwangi said, pushing the boy forward. 'But he has told me nothing.'

'James! Where have you been? Where is Suniva? You know it's not safe to be out of the compound at night.' Relief and rage coursed through Hannah, leaving her unable to stop spewing out irate words. 'You deserve a bloody good hiding, both of you, and you had better watch out because Esther is also—'

'Hannah.' Lars spoke in a low tone as James backed away. 'We need to go slowly here.' He turned his attention to the boy. 'Now James, you must answer me. You are not in trouble, I promise you, but you must tell us where Suniva is.'

'I have not seen her.' James's words were barely audible and he stared at the ground, sullen and defensive, twisting his fingers together before stuffing them into the pockets of his shorts. His clothes were plastered to his skin by the rain and he had begun to shiver.

'Well, she was not in her room last night, and you were not in Esther's house. So I think you do know where she is.' Lars tried to sound encouraging as he led the boy inside and stood him close to the fire. 'James?'

'You must tell us the truth.' Hannah adopted a more conciliatory tone. 'She should not be away from the house at night. You know that.'

James remained silent, his body stiff with resistance, his expression anxious.

'Did you promise Suniva that you would keep this a secret?' Hannah persisted. 'If that is the case, then it's not your fault. But we need to find her.'

'Tell Mama Hannah what you know.' Esther had appeared in the doorway, her eyes blazing as she shook a fist at her charge. 'You are a stupid boy, James Karuri, and you should not have promised anything. *Mbaya sana,* stupid in the head. Causing trouble now.' She grabbed him and shook him lightly, but Hannah made a gesture of restraint.

'Come on, James,' she said. 'You were together all day yesterday, and she always tells you her ideas.'

Kamau had emerged from the kitchen to join Mwangi and Achole, and the night watchman who was still swaddled in the ancient greatcoat he wore in the cold hours of darkness. Everyone wanted to know what kind of *shauri* had erupted just as the family was going away to visit relations in a distant land. They stood together, placing themselves at a respectful distance that would still allow them to hear all that was being said. But James remained stubbornly mute.

'James. Help me, please.' Hannah's mind filled with the bloody memories of past years, and she was close to screaming. She stood back, clutching at an armchair, trying to think of some way to prise the information out of the boy. 'What will you say to me if Suniva is found dead? If she is attacked by hyena or buffalo. What then, James?'

'She wants to hide until everyone is gone. Then she will come out.' He was looking at her now, guilt filling his dark eyes. 'Because she does not want to go away from Langani.'

'You, boy, tell Mama Hannah what you know. *Sasa hivi.*' Achole stepped forward, his face thunderous. 'If Suniva is killed by a *chui,* or another animal, you will be responsible.'

'She made me promise, but I do not want her to be harmed.' The tension in the room heightened as James fell silent once more, staring out at the rain and the drifting fog that now obscured the hedge that separated garden from wilderness. Then he hunched his shoulders and glanced up briefly at Lars. 'She is at our house in the forest.'

'All right. You and I will go and collect her.' Lars turned to Hannah, flashing a warning look at her livid face. 'You see to Piet and finish off the packing. Kamau, we will have breakfast as soon as we get back. Plenty of hot porridge, and bacon and eggs. Achole, you keep a lookout, in case Suniva comes back to the stables or the dairy.'

Moments later Hannah heard the sound of the Land Rover roaring away down the drive. She made her way to Piet's bedroom and sat down beside her son. He looked at her, his face solemn.

'Is Suniva coming back?'

'Your pa has gone to fetch her,' she said, sweeping him into her arms. 'So let's get all washed and be ready for breakfast when they arrive.'

Lars parked the vehicle at the edge of the tree line and waited as James scrambled out of the passenger seat. The damp ground rose steeply, disappearing into the mist a few yards above them. They laboured up the narrow path, grabbing at the limbs of trees that loomed like bent giants in the dim light. The going was slow and torturous and they were often unable to prevent themselves from sliding backwards on the muddy track. Rain dripped onto their shoulders from gaps in the canopy of leaves. High above them a troop of monkeys screamed and chattered in mockery as they leapt, without effort, through their aerial world. Turacos and wood pigeons called, and then Lars heard the sound he had feared most – the rasping, sawing cough of a leopard. He turned to James, an unspoken statement in his eyes, and the boy's face turned grey with alarm.

'She made me promise,' he repeated, but his voice was trembling. 'I said I would not tell, but I am sorry.'

'How far?' Lars's question was harsh as he heard the crack of breaking branches, and the lumbering of elephant higher up the path. He released the safety catch on his rifle and repeated the question. 'How far, James?'

James pointed and then ducked sideways, vanishing into a wall of vegetation, making a sobbing sound as he moved forward at a faster pace. Lars pushed forward, thick bushes snapping and lashing his face as he forced a passage for his large frame, the prayers of his Lutheran childhood on his lips.

Old memories flashed through his mind as he followed the boy whose father had once hidden deep in this same forest, after the savage murder of Piet van der Beer. Seeing James ahead of him, uncannily attuned to the environment of his forebears, Lars felt a deep surge of misgiving. He had tried to forget but he had never been able to forgive. Unlike Sarah who seemed, against all odds, to have laid the barbarous vision to rest. The thickly wooded area was a place of haunting, terrible beauty and unspeakable revenge, and Hannah had never been able to set foot on this part of her land, where Simon Githiri had hidden after killing her brother.

As James led the way into a small clearing, the shelter came into view. It had been roughly woven together from branches and mud, with a narrow opening on one side and a roof made from the surrounding foliage. A shaft of murky light fell on the fragile structure that offered little protection from heavy rain or prowling wildlife. Suniva was squatting on the ground outside, her blonde hair tangled, her sweater and dungarees spattered with mud. An attempt to coax a fire of damp twigs into life had been unsuccessful. She leapt to her feet at once, glaring at the two figures before her.

'You told them. You broke our pact. Our promise.' Her voice was cold and flat, more deadly than any tirade. James looked away, wiping the back of his hand across his eyes to disguise oncoming tears as she turned her attention to her father. 'I'm not going away. I told Ma I wouldn't leave without James. I hate the other farm and I don't want to go there.'

'I'm taking you home now, Suniva.' It was a statement with as much authority as Lars could muster. Conflicting emotions battled in his mind, but he recognised that this was no time for coaxing or tolerance. 'You were wrong to frighten us by disappearing, and you will apologise to your mother the minute you see her. I thought you had enough sense to know that the forest is extremely dangerous at night. I'm disappointed in you. And very, very angry.'

'I'm not coming with you,' she shouted, turning towards the hut. 'You can't make me leave Langani. We never leave James behind when we go on safari or to Mombasa. I'm not going to London, or to your stupid farm in Norway, without him.'

Lars strode forward, and Suniva yelped as he took hold of her arms and spun her around, forcing her to walk in front of him, and to struggle down the muddy slope to the Land Rover. When she fell and tore her trousers he helped her up in silence, ignoring her protests, keeping close behind her in case she should bolt into the thick bush. James followed them, without saying a word. He climbed into the back seat as Suniva took her place beside her father, an expression of pure rage on her face.

At the house Hannah came out when she heard the sound of the vehicle, running to open the car door and to take Suniva into her arms, sinking down onto her knees on the driveway, weeping with relief as she hugged her daughter before leading her into the house.

'Esther, please make sure James has a hot shower and dry clothes,' Lars said. 'We don't want him to catch cold. And don't be *kali* with him. He has been punished enough.'

It was some time before they reassembled in the dining room. They sat through breakfast, Suniva pushing her food around her plate, mute and defiant. Both children looked self-conscious in their new clothes. When the meal was over, Mwangi brought the suitcases from the bedrooms and set them down on the verandah.

'I need to put the last things in my cabin bag,' Hannah said.

Lars nodded. 'I'll get everything else into the car, and keep an eye on these two.'

Half an hour later they were all piling into the old Mercedes and the staff had lined up on the driveway to say their farewells, faces beaming now that all had turned out well at the beginning of the great family safari across the sea. There was no sign of Esther or James, and Hannah did not know whether to be relieved, or to expect some further act of rebellion from her daughter who had not spoken a word since her return.

Suniva climbed into the car, withdrawn and pale, but instead of sitting down beside her brother, she knelt up on the seat to face out of the back window. And then she saw him, writhing in Esther's grip, breaking free with a triumphant shout, running forward, waving frantically.

As they rounded the curve in the driveway, the only sound in the car was Suniva's wild, primeval howling as she pressed her face to the glass, beating her hands on the window and screaming his name in desolation.

'James! James! I'll be back soon. I swear it. James . . .'

Chapter 2

London, July 1977

The novelty of the long flight to London did nothing to dispel Suniva's rebellious frame of mind. From the moment of departure from Langani she did not utter a word, other than an occasional monosyllabic response. In the aircraft she stared ahead, refusing to look out of the window, to eat, or to open the package of puzzles and games offered by the cabin steward. Piet tried to talk to her, but after a time he gave up and left his seat to explore the interior of the jumbo jet with a shining awe that increased tenfold when he was taken to the cockpit to meet the captain. He gazed, mesmerised, at the banks of flashing lights and knobs that controlled the huge beast, and it took a while to persuade him that it was time to return to his place in the main body of the plane. After dinner both children slept, Piet with his head on his mother's lap, and Suniva curled in a defensive ball with her head hidden underneath a blanket. But Hannah and Lars remained awake, enjoying the luxury of champagne and quiet talk, holding hands, looking out at the accompanying stars and a pale moon that offered glimpses of dark, empty lands below them.

Streaks of dawn flooded the cabin with the promise of a new continent. Lars placed his son in the window seat and pointed out the green fields neatly framed by hedges, and the lines and squares of small houses butted up against each other in towns and villages, appearing and vanishing through the banked-up clouds. And then they saw the city itself, spread out for inconceivable miles on either side of the Thames. The river glittered, brown and silver in the early light of morning, spanned by bridges, flanked by ancient spires and towers and tall, modern buildings that stood side by side on the hallowed ground below.

'I feel like crying,' Hannah said softly. 'It's a new world for me, and yet I know it so well from the poems and books we read in school, and the films I've seen. I feel as though I'm dreaming, but you've brought us here for real, Lars. To see it for ourselves.'

Camilla met them on arrival, her face alight with pleasure. Looking at her, Hannah was struck again by her delicate beauty, and the way she seemed to drift rather than walk from place to place. Her skin was pale and luminous and her blonde hair fell into perfect shape each time she turned her head. She took only the most prestigious modelling assignments now, but her photograph was one of the first things that Hannah saw on a large billboard in the airport arrivals hall, in an advertisement for a new French perfume.

'It's been too long,' Hannah said, moved by the tears in Camilla's eyes.

'I flew in from New York nearly three weeks ago, but I've had a punishing schedule since then,' Camilla said, hugging the children, laughing and crying at the same time as she led them to a waiting limousine. 'I wanted to clear my diary for the time that you are here, so that I could show you London myself and we could spend our time together. I've missed you so much, and I've promised myself never to stay away from home again, for so long. I can't believe you are really here, or remember when I've looked forward so much to anything.'

In her Knightsbridge flat the children wandered from room to room, enjoying the view from the large third-floor windows over the leafy square below. Soon there was the aroma of coffee, and they were consuming flaky croissants from the patisserie around the corner.

'It's like living in a tree-house,' Piet said, and even Suniva stood gazing out of the window with the hint of a smile on her face.

'We should probably rest for a couple of hours,' Hannah said. 'Especially the children.' But she knew that it would not be possible. She wanted to be where she could blend in with the pulse of the place, with the incessant drone of traffic, the horns and sirens, the growl of taxi cabs and the squeal of brakes at the bus stops on nearby Brompton Road.

And so they set out to conquer the city. At Lars's request they travelled on the top of the double-decker buses, with Piet and Suniva in the front row as they lurched forward and sideways, seemingly about to topple over, or to collide with the cars and taxis and bicycles that swarmed below them. They stood outside Buckingham Palace and watched the Horse Guards coming up the Mall on their gleaming mounts with the sun glinting on tall, brass helmets, and hoped that the Queen would appear on the balcony of her palace. Later they lunched beside the river, carrying sandwiches and Pimm's and lemonade out into the sunshine, and sitting at a trestle table to watch the slow barges go by and the crowds crossing Westminster Bridge.

'You should have seen it during the Queen's Silver Jubilee,' Camilla said. 'The atmosphere was wonderful, but it was mobbed and very difficult to get around.'

'This is more than enough for me, in terms of crowds,' Hannah said, sitting back in her chair, a little drunk from the Pimm's. 'I'm beat. I can't do any more, except hope that I'll make it back to the flat.'

'I'm amazed you have lasted this long, having just stepped off a plane,' Camilla said. 'Dinner will be at home tonight. Just for us, although Tom may drop round for a drink. He hasn't seen you for two years – not since he came to visit the new workshop at Langani – and he'd like to welcome you to London.'

Hannah was secretly disappointed at the thought of having to see anyone on this first night, least of all Tom Bartlett with his sharp wit and smart clothes and sophisticated London ways. He had become very close to Camilla over the years, offering loyal support as both agent and friend. But Hannah was sure he wanted more. She suspected his many girlfriends were a sham, as he waited for Camilla to realise that she belonged with him. Permanently. Now she wondered if Tom had finally become the main reason that Camilla had remained in London and New York for such a protracted length of time.

'I'm looking forward to seeing him, but in the meantime I need to collapse for a while.' Hannah was smiling, but her heart was filled with trepidation. It would not be a relaxing evening. 'You have to rest now,' she said to the children as she made her way to the bedroom. 'Otherwise you can't stay up for supper.'

'Put your feet up and I'll take care of these two,' Camilla said. 'I can be very stern when necessary.'

'It's hard for me to communicate with Tom.' Hannah fell onto the bed beside Lars. 'Even though he started Camilla's modelling career. He has been consistently successful in promoting her line of clothes, and the things we make in our Langani workshop. But there's something about him that doesn't ring true with me.'

'He's a wheeler and dealer in a big city, and we're a couple of farmers from the African *bundu*.' Lars had already been felled by jetlag. 'Still, I believe he's genuine. He delivers on his promises to Camilla, and to us. We speak a different language, that's all.'

Tom arrived with champagne and flowers, and gifts for the children. Piet crowed with delight as he unwrapped a model London bus with a remote control, and Suniva received bell bottomed trousers in lime green, with a matching tank top. She folded them carefully and returned them to their box, before sitting down opposite Tom to inspect him more closely, taking in his shoulder length hair, wide, flowered tie and flared trousers, and the polished boots with high heels. He had his arm draped around Camilla who sat beside him on the sofa, her head touching his shoulder. She had changed into a blue caftan, embroidered and decorated with beads and crystals by the *bibis* at Langani. Her hair had been tied back and she wore blue topaz earrings that mirrored the colour of her eyes.

'Here's to you,' she said, looking at Lars and Hannah. 'It's been a wonderful day. I feel as though I've seen London for the first time, all over again.'

'I love it even more than I had imagined,' Hannah said. 'It reminds me of school. Of learning "Westminster Bridge" and reading about the Great Fire of London and all the kings and queens. Do you remember Miss Moss? She used to read to us in English and history classes, trying so hard to make the words come alive. I wonder now if she was also trying to re-create it for herself. To keep it sharp in her memory. She'd been away from here for so long, but she still called London "home". What do you suppose happened to her when she finally came back here, after Independence? Do you think she found it had changed, and was disappointed? I wonder if she was able to adapt, after thirty years in Africa.'

'We weren't kind to her,' Camilla said. 'We used to laugh at her, with her frumpy dresses that were all the same. She had that permed hair, dyed black like an old crow, with a tortoiseshell slide to keep it in place. And that dreadful dog. He looked like a sagging sausage, and farted and leaked all through the lessons. We didn't understand, at that age, how dedicated she was. How could we, until we'd been thousands of miles from our own homes, to discover for ourselves what it was to long for another place and a time.'

'Lucky I was here to console you, then,' Tom said. His smile was sardonic, but he touched Camilla on the cheek with gentle affection.

'You're like people from a story book.'

Everyone turned to look at Suniva, who had spent the day trapped in her self-imposed, stony silence. Hannah gave a small sigh of relief at this first sign of a thaw. She stretched out a hand, but her daughter turned away, rejecting close contact.

'We are story book people,' Tom said. 'That's the fun of a big city like London. You don't have to be the same person or do the same thing every day. You can decide who you would like to be when you wake up in the morning, depending on how you feel. You could act like the Queen, riding through London and waving at people from your car. Or you might want to be someone who sings and dances on the pavement. Or a fat pigeon that struts about waiting to crap on the tourists. Who would you like to be tomorrow?'

'I'd like to be myself. At Langani.' Suniva lowered her eyes, her expression sulky once more. There was an uncomfortable silence before her next question. 'Are you Camilla's boyfriend?'

'No, I'm not.' Tom's laugh was forced. 'I'm not that lucky. Right now I'm sitting next to her and happy to be her friend. And I'm celebrating the fact that she has come back from New York for a while. She doesn't spend enough time in London any more.'

'She doesn't spend enough time in Kenya either,' Hannah said.

'I've already made a resolution to change the second thing,' Camilla said, her face flushed. 'Come and help me set the table, Suniva.' She stood up, creating a distance between herself and Tom. 'You're welcome to stay for dinner, if you stop talking about me as though I'm not here. Is that a deal?'

He grinned and nodded, and Hannah was sure that he had become an ever-present figure in Camilla's private life in London as well as being her agent. And perhaps more. She wondered how Anthony fitted into this picture. It was difficult to gauge whether he really mattered at all. His name had not been brought up all day, except for a brief enquiry on the way in from the airport.

'Did you see Anthony before you left? Has he been at the lodge?' Camilla's tone had been light and it was impossible to see the expression in the blue eyes, shuttered by dark glasses.

'I spoke to him on the radio the day before we left,' Hannah said. 'He was camping up in Meru, but he plans to drop in at Langani when he moves south with his clients.'

There had been no further mention of him, but the day had been so packed with activity that neither Hannah nor Lars had thought it strange.

They came to the dining table within a few moments, the children over-tired and unable to smother yawns or to resist rubbing eyes that prickled. Hannah had gone beyond fatigue, and after the champagne and a second glass of wine she found herself more at ease with Tom who sat across from her, separated by the flicker of candlelight on stemmed glasses and silver, and bowls of summer flowers.

'I've arranged a newspaper interview for you,' he said.

'For me?' Hannah was astonished. 'I don't think I could—'

'There are readers out there panting to know about the woman who turns out such exotic bags and belts and jackets from an old farm shed in the middle of darkest Africa. It's unusual for ethnic things to hold their own in the fashion world for so long, even though there are such broad influences today.'

'That's because of Camilla's changing designs,' Hannah said, offended by his description of the workshop. 'She is so well known, the embodiment of glamour. If she has made it, or she's wearing it or carrying it around, then it must be right. I only supervise the cutting and the embroidery. I wouldn't have anything to say to people involved in high fashion.'

'Ah, but you're the hidden light,' Tom said. 'In the workshop every day, keeping the quality high. That's what Camilla says, and now that you've finally come to London we want to show you off. It's a good angle in terms of press coverage. I've lined up a feature article in one of the glossy magazines – the *Tatler* will do a piece about you and Camilla, that will also feature the wildlife on the property, and Langani Lodge. And the *Daily Mail* will run an article too.'

She was about to protest when Lars clapped his hands in approval. 'That is great news,' he said. 'She deserves it, my Hannah. It will be good publicity for us and for Kenya generally. When will it be, this interview?'

'It's a lunch party' Camilla said. 'With a tame reporter from the *Daily Mail*. Afterwards we'll go to the *Tatler* offices. I've already sent round slide photos of us with Anthony at the lodge, and some pictures of the workshop that I'm sure they will use.'

'I'll take the children sightseeing on that day,' said Lars. 'There is no point in bringing them to lunch in a fancy restaurant.' He saw the flash of relief on Tom's face and resented it, even though the suggestion had been his own.

'I'd rather you came to the lunch,' Hannah said, panicking.

'No, Han. This is a business opportunity for you.' Lars was firm. 'The children would love the Tower of London and the Beefeaters. They've read all about them, and they want to see the Traitors' Gate and the Crown Jewels. You said it sounded too sinister for you, and you didn't really want to visit it. This way is better for everyone.'

'Are you going to fit in Camilla's country hideaway? If you want quaint, traditional England you ought to see her cottage in Gloucestershire.' Tom glanced at Camilla. 'I don't know why she hangs on to it, since she hardly ever goes there. As far as I know. But maybe she uses it for secret trysts with one of her many admirers.'

'What's a secret tryst?' Suniva directed her question to Camilla. 'Can I have one?'

'We'd love to do everything,' Hannah interrupted. 'But there's so little time, and we have decided to ration ourselves to London and Norway.'

Over the next three days they fed the ducks in Hyde Park and admired the blaze of flowers that bordered the velvet grass. On the Tube their only disappointment came when the train surfaced briefly into daylight, and they were no longer cocooned within the dark rattle and excitement of being underground. On the King's Road Lars gaped at the punks in studded leather clothing, appalled by their spiked hair and tattoos, the heavy boots and pierced faces and metal cuffs. More disturbing to him were the pale, scruffy girls in black who hung around, sometimes empty-eyed and sad, but often aggressive and noisy. Camilla laughed at his reaction, but he could only hope that his children would not want to emulate this particular London fashion. They saw the Planetarium and Madame Tussaud's and enjoyed the boat ride on the river that took them past Westminster and the Houses of Parliament. Even Suniva sat daintily on her gilded chair for afternoon tea at the Ritz Hotel. And then there was Trafalgar Square where she was forced into a grudging smile when a pigeon dropping landed on her father's square shoulders, staining his new tweed jacket.

At night, the children were tucked into bed, or allowed to watch television with Camilla's housekeeper who taught them Cockney rhyming slang. Hannah thrilled at her first experience of London theatre and a visit backstage. Late, candlelit dinners were followed by taxi rides to the most famous clubs where Lars was stunned by the roaring, thumping sound of the music and the instant availability of a table for Camilla in every place she chose to take them.

It was in the National Gallery that the change in Suniva came at last. Her brother was clearly bored, tired and fractious.

'Maybe I should take him back to the flat,' Lars said. 'Or we could wait for you in a café somewhere.'

Hannah's head was throbbing and her neck ached from gazing up at the endless walls filled with paintings. She decided they were all ready for a break and looked around for her daughter, only to realise that Suniva was nowhere to be seen. 'Where is she? Oh please, God, don't let her get lost here.'

'Hannah, don't panic.' Camilla was reassuring. 'Stand here and wait for me – she's probably next door and just as bored as Piet.'

'You don't know her – how wilful and stubborn she has become lately. She has no fear of running off alone.' Hannah pressed her lips together, quelling alarm, banishing images of a search in the vast city, suppressing a vision of accidents and ambulances and hospitals.

'I'll find her. Don't worry.'

It did not take long to track down Suniva in a nearby room, standing rapt and silent before a Rousseau painting.

'Can we stay here a while?' She turned eyes of supplication briefly away from the canvas.

'Of course we can,' Camilla said. 'I'll tell the others we'll see them at home later. Then you and I will be free to go through every room slowly. That's what I used to do when I first came to live in England. I was older than you but I had to go to a dreadfully boring school, and I spent all my spare time in the museums and galleries. I'll take you to as many as you like.'

'Did you really go to a boring school?' Suniva was doubtful. 'I thought you were always busy, wearing beautiful dresses and having your picture taken and being famous.'

'That's how I ended up,' Camilla said. 'I went to study art history while my parents were in Italy, and that was magic. But afterwards they sent me to a posh secretarial school here in London, where most of the things they taught were of no interest to me. Now, let's tell your parents to take Piet home.'

Two hours later they emerged from the Gallery clutching several books about the world's greatest painters. Camilla hailed a taxi.

'Do you want to stop and have tea? I know a place where they serve the best French pastries, with cream and jam and almonds and chocolate.'

'Just you and me?' Suniva could not contain the smile that had started in her eyes.

'Absolutely,' Camilla said. 'Two's company.'

'OK.' Suniva nodded. 'But I don't like almonds.'

The owner greeted them in French and made a fuss of settling Suniva into her chair. A waiter appeared with china cups and saucers, and heavy silver knives and spoons and when he winked at Suniva she blushed with unaccustomed confusion.

'Tell me what you think of London, so far?' Camilla asked, pouring tea.

'I like all the places we've seen,' Suniva said. 'And it's nice staying at your house, so high up off the ground with the branches around the windows. But I want to go home now.'

'You'll be home in three weeks,' Camilla said. 'And then you'll wish it hadn't been so short. In the meantime you are going to Norway, to see your grandparents and their farm. The place where your father grew up. Don't you want to do that?'

'No. I want to go home now.' Suniva's face had resumed its truculent expression. 'Because we left James behind. It wasn't fair. We always do things together, and I cried and I hated it that he had to stay there.'

Camilla was silent for a moment. It was the first time that Suniva had spoken more than a few essential words since her arrival in England, and it was important to proceed carefully with such an unexpected confidence.

'I know how that feels,' she said at last.

'No, you don't. You can go anywhere you want, anytime,' Suniva said. 'And you can take whoever you like with you.'

'It's never that easy,' Camilla said. 'I have to leave Anthony behind when I come to London or go to New York, and that always makes me

23

sad. Even though I've had to do it so many times, and I know I'll see him again soon.'

'It's not the same.' Suniva stuck out her lower lip. 'He could come with you if he wanted to. Anyway Ma and Pa say he doesn't deserve you.'

'Well, I have to make up my own mind about that.' Camilla tried to bury the hurtful truth in the remark. 'Maybe there is some special reason why James couldn't come with you this time. Something you don't know about, or might not be able to understand now. You can put that right, though. So that he won't feel sad without you.'

Suniva rubbed her hand across her eyes. 'How?'

'Here's a plan,' Camilla said. 'Let's go and buy post cards of everything you have seen here, and stamps to put on them. You can write messages for James on the back, and on the way home we will put the first ones in the red letter box near the flat. And from now on, you can send him another one every day. I'm also going to buy you a box of paints and a drawing book, so you can make pictures of your own to show him. And a diary to write in.'

'What kind of thing would I write?' The idea elicited a frown.

'You can make notes about all the places you see in London and Norway. That will help you to remember every single thing clearly when you get home and want to describe them to James. Then he can share your holiday, even though he isn't here with you. And he will also see that you were thinking about him. That you missed him. Isn't that a good idea?'

'Yes,' said Suniva, setting aside her cream cake. 'It is. Can we get the cards right now, so he will know soon that I haven't forgotten him?'

'Let's go,' Camilla said, waving a hand for a bill. 'We'll find some of those really big postcards, and you can write on them and put them in the box on the way home.'

'I'm a little nervous about the lunch and the interviews,' Hannah said. 'I hope I won't disgrace you.'

'You're amazingly full of shit.' Camilla was laughing. 'Considering that you're such a practical person. It's going to be fine. Editorial for our workshop and the lodge is worth far more than any paid advertising, which we couldn't afford anyway. We'll get in a mention of Anthony's safaris, too.'

'It was good speaking to him on the phone last night,' Hannah said. 'I'm

24

glad he has been in touch with Mike Stead, and that he will drop in at Langani soon.' Her next words came out in a rush. 'We haven't talked about him, but what is the situation between you now? I mean, does he really see how much you have done for him, bringing in so many clients from Europe and the States, going out on safari with him when he has some famous person that needs entertaining.'

'I'm a shareholder in his company.' Camilla's reply was brisk. 'It's in my interest to see that things run well. Besides, I love being out in the *bundu* when I get the chance.'

'Yes, but does he really appreciate the way you've made his camps so glamorous, with carpets and candle holders and proper silver, and so on? Anthony Chapman Safaris have been written up as the height of luxury, and I'll bet most of the journalists are friends of yours. More importantly, he would never have pulled through after the accident, except for you.'

'That was largely due to his own bravery. And his safaris are successful because of his knowledge and love of the bush. He also has an exceptional relationship with his staff in the office and in camp.' Camilla had turned defensive. 'Those things kept him going too. Gave him hope.'

'It's nearly seven years since Anthony lost his leg,' Hannah said. 'And it must have been hard to block out the memory of that burning helicopter, and the months in hospital. But now he is living a normal life that he could never have achieved without you, and he doesn't seem to understand that you are the most vital part of it.'

'I helped him through,' Camilla shrugged to make light of the subject, but her smile was too bright. 'And I'd like to remind you that it was you and Sarah who told me that I should stick with him after the crash, no matter what, if I really loved him.'

'That was a long time ago.' Hannah folded her arms, frowning. 'I'm asking about now. I'm asking if you still love him, or whether there is someone else in your life, when you are here or in New York? Someone you see from time to time. Flirt with, sleep with. Haven't you ever fallen in love again? You're thirty-two years old. You surely can't be living like one of the nuns we used to laugh about at school.'

'I don't want to talk about this.' Camilla concentrated on applying mascara. 'Show me what you're going to wear for lunch.'

'You spend months at a time away from Kenya these days.' Hannah would not be sidelined. 'Then you fly in to Nairobi, and from that moment

Anthony seems to rule your life. I'd just like to know what he is giving you in return.'

'He needs me.'

'But what do you need?' Hannah still would not let go. 'Yes, he lost a limb trying to rescue your father from a burning plane. But that's not why you keep coming back to him, Camilla. It's because you love him. Don't you think it's time he acknowledged that?'

'I'd somehow forgotten how brutally straightforward you are,' Camilla said. 'It's not your most endearing attribute, by the way. And I haven't got the time or the inclination to discuss Anthony right now. If you want to sort out someone's life, you ought to be thinking about Sarah.'

'I haven't seen Sarah since she took off on her own into the wilds. Shit. My two best friends are in a bloody awful mess,' Hannah said. 'And I can't seem to do anything for either one of you.'

'Maybe you could try a more subtle approach.' Camilla was smiling again. 'You might be surprised by the results. How was she, when you left?'

'We only saw Rabindrah, who drove us to the airport,' Hannah said. 'Sarah was still up at Lake Turkana. I hope it is the right place for her to be – it's so isolated there, and she has been gone a month at least. She could be brooding, becoming even more depressed. Do you remember how totally off the rails she was, last time we saw her? I honestly wondered if she would ever recover. What did you think?'

'Unfortunately there's no time to talk about her either, or we will be late for lunch.' Camilla began to put on her own clothes. 'Our priority right now is to remind ourselves that we're young and good looking and successful, otherwise we'll never convince a newspaper reporter to believe it.'

'Ah yes, and that's another thing,' Hannah said. 'What are you going to do about Tom?'

'Don't you ever let up?'

'Are you sleeping with him?' Hannah persisted. 'As a substitute for—'

'I'll pretend you didn't ask that.' Camilla had turned pale. 'And I'd prefer that you didn't turn our remaining days here into the London Inquisition.'

'Ach, Camilla, I'm so sorry. I have no right to pry. And you're right, I am too direct, not sensitive enough. I never have been able to erase that part of my character, and I'm still hopeless when it comes to keeping my big mouth shut. We're having a wonderful time, and I'm looking forward to the lunch today – doing something that will help Langani and our workshop, and Anthony's safaris. I just want you to be happy.'

'I'm not sure I trust happiness, except as a transitory thing. It fades too fast. It isn't reliable. Come on, Hannah, you're not even dressed.'

'All right, I'll drop the whole subject for now. But when we are back home, I think you and I need to get hold of Sarah, and the three of us should go somewhere and spend a few days together. We haven't done that for the longest while. Now, which of your handbags may I borrow, so my outfit doesn't look as though I bought it in Patel's *duka* in Nanyuki?'

'Yes, this is my first visit to London,' Hannah said to Graham Lance, the journalist from the *Daily Mail*. 'Although everyone is familiar with the most famous sights, it's impossible to grasp the true impact of the city until you see it for yourself. It has been more of a thrill than I ever anticipated, for my whole family.'

'So you were born a British citizen in Kenya,' Lance said.

'I'm a Kenyan,' Hannah said. 'A third-generation Kenyan, and proud of it. After Independence in 1963, people like me had the choice of retaining their British passports, or putting their faith in the country and applying for citizenship. I did the latter.'

'A white Kenya citizen, though.' The reporter wanted an acknowledgement of difference.

'I'm the same kind of citizen as everyone else,' Hannah said. 'Black, brown or white, we are all working to develop the best from our diverse origins. The spirit of *Harambee*, President Kenyatta calls it.'

He did not press her further on the issue of racial identity. After a while she found herself talking easily about the farm and her determination to set aside part of Langani as a wildlife conservation area. By the time the main course arrived she was enjoying the atmosphere of Langan's Brasserie, and was unabashedly thrilled when Michael Caine stopped to greet Tom and Camilla, and even shook her hand. They were all decidedly tipsy by the time dessert and coffee had been served. Hannah refused a liqueur, but Tom ordered brandy for himself and the journalist. When he rose and pulled out Camilla's chair he was definitely unsteady on his feet.

'One hack down and one to go,' he said, his speech slurred. 'They're nice to you at the glossies, though. Come on, Hannah, you're doing well and you'll love all the posh nonsense at the *Tatler*.'

'You're totally plastered,' Camilla said, taking his arm. 'I think you should go home and sleep it off. Hannah and I can deal with the *Tatler* interview on our own. We don't need a drunken chaperone.'

'I may be absolutely rat-arsed,' Tom said, staggering out of the restaurant. 'But no one will guess, I promise you. I have to be seen to be earning my corn, darling.'

As they waited for a taxi, Camilla's blonde hair was flying loose around her laughing face, and she looked like a celestial vision that had dropped out of the afternoon sky to tread the grey pavement for a brief, beautiful moment. Her eyes widened with surprise as Tom pulled her towards him and kissed her hard on the mouth. Taken unawares, she leaned into him for a second before pushing him away. There was a sudden flash that made Hannah spin round and come face to face with a photographer who raised his camera again.

'You want to comment on this?' He gestured at Camilla. 'No. Right then. No skin off my nose, darlin'. It don't need no words. Cheers then.'

'Oh God, what a bore,' Camilla said, watching him stride away. 'Who the hell was that?'

'No idea, but don't worry.' Tom was unrepentant. 'Always hanging around restaurants and hotels looking for a chance to make a quid or two, but he'll never sell a picture of you and me. There are bigger fish to fry. Look, here's our cab.'

In the panelled boardroom at the *Tatler* things were more formal, and Hannah was somewhat daunted as she shook hands with the features editor, Joanna Williams. The interview soon moved away from any political theme, however, to focus on the diversity of Langani Farm.

'There are large parts of our property where the soil is unsuitable for growing crops,' Hannah said. 'Areas that are home to elephant, buffalo, lion, giraffe and zebra, and various species of antelope. We have turned this section of our land into a wildlife reserve because the game needs to be protected from poachers and from encroaching settlements. Our conservation programme also provides a corridor that allows the wildlife to move between Langani and other grazing or watering places, without damaging the surrounding villages and smaller farms.'

'How on earth do you achieve that?' The journalist was smiling but a little sceptical. 'I can't imagine a traffic policeman directing herds of elephant away from the nearest vegetable patch.'

'Not quite that simple,' Hannah said, enjoying the idea that one of her *askaris* could be put in place on a podium with a whistle, to carry out the task. 'We do it with a series of fences and grids, and by leaving traditional game trails undisturbed, so that there is a natural flow of movement. There is no sense in telling people they have to protect wild animals, when an elephant or a buffalo has just trampled their crops or even maimed or killed a member of their family. Unless African smallholders are convinced that wildlife can be managed as an asset, and that we will do our best to protect their *shambas* as well as our own farm, then we cannot expect co-operation.'

'How do you get this message over?' Joanna asked.

'We are there to help, if a wild animal is destroying property or threatening a home. Last month, for example, Lars had to shoot a rogue buffalo that was rampaging through a settlement nearby. Luckily it had not gored or killed anyone, but it would have been only a matter of time. Our game rangers are also on patrol along the Langani boundaries, to protect both sides of the fences. We employ local people on the farm, as well as in our workshop and at the game lodge. I also run a clinic for the women and children. Plus a small nursery school.'

'You and your brother took over Langani Farm, when your parents left Kenya after Independence. Is that right?'

'Yes, that's how it was.' Finally Hannah was confronted with the subject she had dreaded.

'Have you created all this as a memorial to your brother? I understand that he built the original Langani Lodge, but he was murdered on the farm soon afterwards, and the building was later burnt down. What was the reason for those events? And were you not tempted to leave the country yourself, after such a tragedy?'

The journalist's tone was neutral, but the question tore through Hannah like a bullet.

'The man who killed my brother had worked for a short time on the farm. He must have been unstable, or he may have had some unknown grudge that resulted in his terrible action.' Hannah's voice was steady. 'Later he gave himself up and died in prison, while awaiting trial. The fire was judged to be an accident. When there isn't much rain and the bush is dry, these things happen. We rebuilt the lodge, however, using the original design, and it has been a huge success. So I suppose it is, in part, a memorial to Piet's vision and his life.'

'You're there to stay, then?'

'I'm Kenyan born and bred, and I want to play my part in the country's development. I would never think of leaving Langani.'

'Tell me about the lodge. I gather it's small and exclusive.'

'Langani Lodge was Piet's dream – a way of bringing guests to see the game from a small, private viewing point, and using the revenue to protect the animals. He built it into the existing rocks and trees, using materials that were on our land – thatched roofing, local wood for walls and furniture, polished stone for floors and shelves. There isn't a straight line in the place. Fabrics are all local and hand-dyed, made into curtains and cushions and rugs in our workshop. And a great deal of the food we serve is grown in my vegetable garden, or raised on the farm.'

It proved easy to turn the conversation away from Piet's death, and to focus on the lodge and the workshop in which twenty Kikuyu and Maasai women had been trained to produce embroidery and beading for Camilla's clothes and accessories.

'Well, your vision and courage certainly make for an inspirational story.' Joanna Willliams looked at her subject with undisguised admiration. 'I would love to see Langani Farm. It sounds irresistible in every sense, with all its complexities.'

'What a terrific day,' Camilla said, as they curled up on her sofa after dinner. 'The interviews went exceptionally well, and Lars seems to have had a great time with the children, even if it has sent him to bed early. Amazing how little stamina a big man has, when it comes to spending time with two energetic offspring. Are you ready for Norway, Han? It will be a peaceful contrast, after all the rush and commotion of London.'

'Yes, I'm ready,' Hannah said. 'Lars is so proud to be taking us there and it will be great, I'm sure.'

'I'm hearing a note of something else buried in those words.' Camilla poured two glasses of wine.

'They are kind and generous, Lars's parents, and they love Suniva and

Piet. It's harder for me, though, to make a real connection with them,' Hannah said.

'Because of the language?'

'Mostly, yes. Jorgen speaks English quite well, but Kirsten can only manage a few words and she is shy about using them. Their holidays in Kenya have been a bit of a struggle as far as I'm concerned,' Hannah confessed. 'Sometimes I've felt like an outsider in my own home, when they chatter on in Norwegian as though I didn't exist. On days when Lars took them to the Aberdares National Park, or on some other outing, I often stayed behind. And then I felt guilty about the relief of being on my own instead of making that extra effort for them. For Lars.'

'Everyone has mixed feelings about in-laws,' Camilla said. 'How much Norwegian can you understand?'

'Not enough for real conversation. I've never set aside the time to study it seriously, and I'm ashamed of that. The children have picked up words and phrases quite well and Lars talks to them in Norwegian sometimes, but it's a strain for me. Now that we are all going to be together for almost three weeks, I'm afraid I will be the odd man out again.' Hannah looked back at the times when she had been unwittingly excluded from conversations between Lars and his parents. 'I don't want to feel regret, resentment even, when I'm left out of the family talk, and the memories of things that Lars did as a child that make everyone else laugh.'

'Maybe it will be different there,' Camilla said. 'Perhaps they will try harder to include you, because this time they are the hosts and they will want you to feel part of all that they have to offer.'

'I hope so.' Hannah was unconvinced. 'In any case, it is Lars's dream come true and that is the most important thing. More wine, please. It puts iron in the soul, and I'm sure that's all I need.'

Their last night in London was a triumph of planning on Camilla's part. *Star Wars* had recently opened. They took their seats in the largest cinema they had ever seen, armed with bags of popcorn, dazzled by the enormous screen on which they watched the adventures of Han Solo in his battered starship, and the heroic space battles between the forces of the Galactic Empire led by Darth Vader, and the Jedi Knights armed with their light sabres. Afterwards they strolled through the arches of Chinatown, admiring the coloured lanterns, the carved dragons and the exotic displays of oriental statues and jars and fans crammed into small shop windows. The restaurants were noisy and crowded, with steam and flames hissing and visible in the cooking areas. Both children were amazed by the selection of food, staring at rows of dried ducks hanging on hooks, at slippery octopus tentacles and chicken feet in metal dishes, and steaming dumplings in bamboo baskets which they selected from dim sum trolleys that rattled through the narrow aisles between the tables. Suniva wanted all the strangest dishes and quickly learned to ladle the food into her mouth with chopsticks. Piet was more careful, restricting his choices to items that seemed familiar and could be attacked with a spoon and fork. Later Camilla led them through the bright, neon lights and the snarl of traffic that sped round the statue of Eros in Piccadilly Circus, and they walked along pavements crammed with people pouring out of theatres and clubs, immersed in the city's throbbing nightlife. They rode back to the flat in the comfort of a black taxi, laughing and storing their memories for retelling in the wild, empty spaces of their African home.

In the morning Suniva waited until Hannah was occupied with last-minute packing, before holding out her final London postcard.

'Camilla, I've run out of stamps.'

'If we go to the post office now, and stand in line, we might be late leaving for the airport,' Camilla said. 'I'll have to get a stamp later, and put it in the box for you. Or we can try to find one at the airport.'

'No. I'd rather you posted it here.' Suniva said, her expression guarded. 'As long as you promise to do it today?'

'I promise,' Camilla said. 'Don't you think we should tell your mother about the cards for James? She has probably sent him one or two herself and you can mail some more together, in Norway.'

'No!' Suniva grabbed Camilla's arm. 'No. You have to swear you won't tell anyone. Swear!'

'I won't tell anyone,' Camilla said, hands held up in surrender. 'But *you* should, because it's silly to hide things that don't need to be hidden. Everyone in your family loves James. There's no need to have secrets about him.'

'If Ma loved him, she wouldn't have left him behind,' Suniva said, her features set and stubborn. 'And you mustn't tell, because you've promised.

There was intensity in Suniva when she talked about James, and Camilla wondered if her parents understood the true depth of her attachment to him. She did not know if the boy had the same powerful feelings, and she was beginning to regret that an innocent diversion had become a deception. It was too late now to raise the subject with Hannah, but she resolved to do so when she returned to Kenya.

'Cheer up,' she said, prying open Suniva's small fingers and disengaging herself as the porter rang the doorbell and handed over the morning's newspapers. 'I'll go to the first post office I see, as soon as— Oh, God! Oh shit!'

The front page of the *Daily Mirror* carried a photograph of Tom Bartlett kissing her outside Langan's Brasserie.

Romance sizzles between international model and fashion designer, Camilla Broughton-Smith and longtime friend and agent, Tom Bartlett.

She did not read the rubbish that followed the blaring caption, but stuffed the paper behind a cushion on the sofa, biting her lip with dismay.

'That's a picture of you,' Suniva said with glee. 'With Tom kissing you on the lips! I knew he was your boyfriend! Can I have it, to keep?'

'No, you can't,' Camilla snapped. 'And I don't want you to say anything about it to anyone. I'll keep your secret if you keep mine.'

'It's a deal,' Suniva said, and she was smiling.

When they said goodbye at the airport Camilla was filled with a sense of loss and dejection. She had commitments that would keep her in Europe for several weeks. Her new collection of clothes had been well received and she was more than satisfied with the orders pouring in from department stores on both sides of the Atlantic, but she was tired of the sales meetings and the days and nights crammed with interviews, and guest appearances at parties filled with people that she barely knew. The superficial admiration she inspired and the constant intrusion of the press was exhausting. During Hannah's visit she had revelled in the freedom of having cancelled her appointments, but now it was time to throw herself back into the thick of the fashion world again.

She wanted to be gone, to be back in her Nairobi studio, drawing and cutting samples. Her greatest satisfaction lay in working with the women at Langani. They were proud of their skills and they laughed at the idea of the impact made by their handiwork, in cities that were beyond their knowledge or imagination. Camilla had a large pinboard on one wall of the long, airy room, and she updated it constantly with photographs of shows in faraway places. The sight of Langani clothes and accessories worn by pale, long-legged girls with pouting faces and eyelids painted in strange colours made the *bibis* roar with laughter, and they could not understand the small breasts and protruding collarbones that the young women displayed.

'Eh, they are not eating well, those poor girls,' they said. 'They would be no use in a man's bed, all skin and bone like a sick *ngombe*. They must be sent home to their mothers, to fatten them up for a good bride price. What good are they like that?'

Their dark, cheerful faces and their willingness to learn were so different from the people who manufactured Camilla's ready-to-wear collections in Europe and the United States, where even the smallest changes were a matter of negotiation on piecework and extra time and balance sheets.

Above all, she wanted to retain the increasingly faint hope of reviving her love affair with Anthony. In spite of her involvement in his professional life, there had been no indication on his part that he would ever return to the passionate relationship they had once shared. No sign that he now regarded Camilla as anything more than his closest friend and supporter. Hannah's remarks had awakened a deep-seated doubt. It had taken him the best part of three years to recover from his injury. He had chafed at the long, painful sessions of physiotherapy, raged at the slow process of learning to balance and then to walk with crutches and, finally, to use his new leg and learn to drive the safari car that Indar Singh had adapted for him. Although he suffered from bouts of angry depression, he refused to consider medical treatment for his dark moods. He had made Camilla a director of his company. Occasionally she accompanied him if she had convinced the guests to sign up for a safari, or if they were returning clients who had met her on a previous visit. But she did not share Anthony's quarters, and the camp staff shook their heads and wondered when the bwana would come to his senses.

Now that Hannah and Lars were leaving, she longed to return to Nairobi. In her heart she struggled to convince herself that if she wanted him enough, waited long enough, Anthony would come round. He was whole again, and she hoped that it was only a matter of time. She was well aware, however, that almost seven years had gone by since she had returned to Kenya for her father's funeral and stayed on to take care of the man she loved. There were many nights when she lay awake, wrapped in the loneliness and uncertainty of her outwardly glamorous life, and the escalating fear that Anthony Chapman would never again want her for his own.

'We'll see you in Nairobi,' Hannah said, surprised by Camilla's distress. 'London was wonderful, it really was. We had a *lekker* time and you spoiled us rotten. Come home soon.'

'I'll be there as soon as I can.' Camilla was crying openly. 'I love you, Han. I love you all.'

It wasn't until they were in the departure lounge that Lars saw the *Daily Mirror*.

'Camilla might not be so badly off with Tom,' he said, grinning at the headline. 'He is crazy for her, even if she chooses not to acknowledge it.'

'I don't think it would work,' Hannah said. 'She is still in love with Anthony, you know. Like Sarah went on loving Piet, although he didn't notice her for years. She kept hoping, though, and finally he woke up to reality and asked her to marry him. It was only days before he died, but at least she knew that he loved her too.' She moved closer to her husband and tucked her hand under his arm. 'But there's one thing I know for certain.'

'My Hannah. Always so certain,' he said. 'What is it this time?'

'That you are just right for me, that we are always in tune about everything that is important, and I am the luckiest girl alive.'

They were words that she would remember. Words that would come back to haunt her all too soon.

Chapter 3

Kenya, July 1977

It was almost dark when Rabindrah Singh parked his car and unlocked the front door of the house. Once upon a time they had never bothered with keys, unless they were leaving on safari or on an overseas journey. But the better Nairobi suburbs had become frequent targets for robberies, and the old feeling of security was gone, bringing in its place an army of night watchmen and uniformed security guards that patrolled the grounds of those who could afford them.

The garden had taken on the soft hue of evening, and in the distance the knuckles of the Ngong Hills had turned into a mauve silhouette as the sun slid behind a belt of gum trees. Sarah's dusty Land Rover was in the driveway, still loaded with equipment. The lights were on inside the house and there was a fire in the sitting room. He stood for a moment in its orange glow, listening to a Beethoven concerto playing at full volume. A rangy dog appeared, tail wagging as Rabindrah stooped to pat her.

'Hello, Tatu. I see your mistress is home. Sarah? Where are you?'

'In the bath.' The voice was muffled, lost in the swell of the music. 'Get us a drink, will you?'

'Mama Sarah said I should serve dinner early, after her long safari.' The houseboy appeared with a chilled Tusker beer.

'No, Chege. There has been a change. We are going out for dinner.' Rabindrah added a gin and tonic to the tray. 'I'll take this in to Mama Sarah. Chai in the morning as usual, please. And instead of cooking dinner, you can unload the Land Rover and lock everything away in the store. *Asante sana.*'

He swallowed a first draught of beer and then headed for the bathroom, pushing open the door to gaze down on his wife, submerged in a sea of bubbles.

'Hello, you!' Sarah raised herself out of the water far enough for him to see her breasts creamed with froth and the tops of her brown knees. Her hair was wet and sun-streaked from several weeks in the bush, and stood out in a crown of tendrils around her face. She was smiling.

'You look wonderful.' Rabindrah put down the tray and leaned over to kiss her, relieved to see her features so relaxed.

She laughed. 'You should have seen me when I got home. All red dust and sweat. It's taken me a good hour and gallons of water to soak the grime out of my system. I feel almost human now.' She wound her arms around his neck, leaving a damp trail down his shirt. 'Want to join me?'

He stripped off and climbed into the bath, passing her the tumbler. They lay facing one another in the warm, steamy atmosphere, surveying each other over the rims of their glasses. The concerto reached its final crescendo, and Sarah put down her drink and leaned forward, creating a series of small waves that slapped onto the bathroom floor as she kissed him.

'How was Turkana country?' he asked.

'I wish you had been with me.' Sarah sat back, recognising the deliberate move away from intimacy. 'There are plenty of good stories up there. Enough for us to think about a new book.'

'I couldn't have left Nairobi for all that time.'

'A weekend would have been pretty good,' she said, aware that she had highlighted the distance between them.

'I wish I'd had the opportunity, but there was the trip to the Seychelles following the overthrow of Jimmy Mancham, and a piece about independence in Djibouti. And then the feature on Kenyan athletes to file.' He sounded defensive. 'I'm trying to diversify, and I've told Gordon I don't want to write any more about dispossessed Asians.'

'Are you happy with your recent article on that subject?' She picked up the soap, pressing herself against him, sliding her fingers along his back.

'It's good,' Rabindrah said. 'Very good, in fact. It will create plenty of argument over the weekend, and make me unpopular with all sides of the issue – black, brown and white.' He remained determinedly focused on his work. 'I'll probably be in hotter water than this. You know how the politicians like to use Asians as fodder, to distract the *wananchi* from the shortcomings of their leaders. There were things I couldn't say, though.'

'Such as?'

'Such as the methods that some Indian businessmen are using to hide or transfer assets. In ordinary times I would expose them, but right now I can't help feeling some sympathy for them. They are all afraid that what happened in Uganda with Amin could be repeated here, and thousands of Asians could be slung out without warning. So they're using some pretty dodgy methods to hang on to whatever is left of their money, and provide for their families in the future . . .' His voice tailed off.

'What sort of methods?'

'Just a little more than the usual sharp practices, I suppose. Let's talk about it another time.' He reached for his drink. 'By the way, Gordon would like to buy some of your Turkana pictures. He is planning an article on commercial fishing up there. Tell me about your trip.'

'It was extraordinary. I had forgotten how harsh the landscape is. And everything that goes on up there is a total contrast to what is happening in the corridors of power in Nairobi.'

'More like sewers than corridors these days,' Rabindrah said.

'It was like an oven in the day time – more than 100 degrees. The glare gave me a ferocious headache, in spite of my hat and dark glasses. I drank so much water that I thought my teeth would float away, but my throat was still parched and sore.' She took a gulp of her gin and tonic, as if the thirst had stayed with her. 'The dust made my eyes sting, and it was hard to be sure of sharp focus. I thought the cameras might die on me at one point, when the wind whipped up a series of dust devils that got in between my teeth, up my nose and under my nails. And into all the equipment and storage boxes. I'll have to take everything apart tomorrow and clean out the remaining grit.'

'So, explain to me exactly why you wanted me to share this with you.' He was laughing at her. 'I seem to be missing the appeal of the whole thing.'

'Being together comes to mind.' She knew that there was a hint of bitterness in her words and she changed her tone, wanting to draw him back into the world they had once shared. 'There is an awful lot we could write about and photograph up there. The lives and the beauty and strength of the Turkana people. Plus the Leakey discoveries of ever more ancient bones. It's amazing to think that such an arid, unforgiving land is probably the place where mankind was born, millions of years ago. I thought about that at night, listening to the lake and the rattle of the doum palms, and the scratch of sand blowing on my tent. The moon was so round and heavy that it looked as if it might tumble out of the sky and plummet into the lake.'

'I imagine you had to keep your eyes open on the sandflats,' he said.

'I could see the crocs, and even when I couldn't I was horribly aware of them. Thousands of eyes watching, calculating, lying in wait, jaws open to bare their horrible teeth.' Sarah shuddered. 'I can never feel anything but repulsion towards them. The fishermen set out on such fragile rafts every day, and they often stand knee deep in that infested water, with their fishing baskets and only a spear as protection from those rapacious creatures. Even the children play and splash in the shallows. I don't know how more of them don't get eaten.'

'I'll come with you on your next expedition,' Rabindrah said. 'I'd like to go back to that area. Perhaps we could do another camel safari, too.'

'I'd love that. The northern desert is my favourite place.' Sarah's eyes were shining. 'It's wild and challenging up there, and stubbornly unchanged. It gave me a chance to try and clear my head. Get things into a better perspective.' She hurried on, changing the subject, not wishing to dwell on a painful issue. 'I'll be able to show you some of my pictures by tomorrow evening.'

She stopped to sip her drink, wanting to tell him how desperately she had missed him, how much she had thought about the first glorious years of their marriage when they had travelled together in the arid north and worked on their book about nomadic tribes. A time when they had walked through the empty land with the smell of dust in their nostrils, following the herders of scrawny goats and cattle. They had trudged through sand drifts, and crossed dry river beds spotted with scant vegetation that retained a miraculous hold in the rock-strewn landscape. A time when they had slept out under the brightest stars in the universe, watching the moon tremble on the jagged rim of a mountain, making love with infinite passion, rising in the cool of early morning to begin another day filled with a sense of optimism and adventure. A time when everything was perfect. It seemed so long ago.

'Did you see Hannah on her way to Europe?' Sarah backed away from the threat of despondency.

'Yes, they had lunch with me on the day they left. I took them to the airport. They were very excited,' Rabindrah said. 'Except for Suniva, who had thrown a tantrum because James had been left behind.'

'That's a situation they are going to have to address,' Sarah said. 'I've mentioned it to Hannah before. That boy lives in a kind of limbo between the house and the staff quarters, and one day it will create a problem.'

'I have some other, rather surprising news for you,' Rabindrah said. 'But I'm afraid it means that we have to get out of this bath right now. We're going out tonight.'

'Oh, no.' Sarah was dismayed. 'Surely you could have made some excuse. It's our first night together for more than a month. Besides, I'm whacked. Isn't it something we can put off?'

'No. It's Lila. She got engaged while you were away. I thought you would want to see her before the wedding tomorrow.'

'Lila? Getting married tomorrow?' Sarah was astounded.

'Anjit Auntie phoned to know if we would come for the celebration tonight. It's for immediate family.' Rabindrah stepped out of the bath and wrapped himself in a towel. 'I didn't see how we could refuse. Anyway, Lila is one of your closest friends, apart from being my favourite cousin.'

'My God! This is awfully sudden, isn't it? What does Kuldip Auntie say?'

'I meant to phone her, but I've been too busy. You know how it is. I don't have the low-down, and Lila's parents are full of gushy phrases about the great match she has made.'

'You should have contacted Kuldip while I was away,' Sarah said. 'She hasn't been well recently, and she thinks of you as a son. It means a great deal to her when you phone or drop round there.'

She had formed a bond with Rabindrah's aunt and was grateful for her kindness and discreetly-offered advice. Kuldip was the one female member of the Singh family who seemed to understand the cross-cultural currents in which Sarah sometimes felt she might drown.

'Guilty as charged,' Rabindrah said with casual detachment. 'Still, I was surprised I didn't know about the engagement earlier. That Lila didn't tell me herself.'

'Who is the lucky fellow?' Sarah rose dripping from the bath, resentful at having to hurry.

'His name is Harjeet Singh. My mother and Kuldip and Anjit Auntie are all good friends with his family. The parents grew up together in Nairobi. I smell an arrangement by the matriarchal committee. Come on – your fingers and toes are all crinkly from being in the water for so long, and we'll be late.'

'I don't remember that name,' Sarah said. 'Have we ever met him?'

'Apparently Lila has known him since they were children, but he has been living in England for years. His family got in under the net, before the British decided we weren't real citizens, and they didn't want any more of us invading the sceptred isle.'

'How come you can't place him?'

'I don't remember every Sikh I've ever met,' Rabindrah said. 'I left here when I was eighteen, and stayed on in the UK after university, in case you've forgotten. There's no reason I should know him. Do you know everyone in County Sligo?'

'What a ridiculous question.' Her laugh was dismissive. 'That's completely different. I grew up here, not in Ireland. I've never spent more than a few weeks at a time in Sligo. It's simply the place where my parents chose to live after they left Kenya. And I certainly did know most of the European community in Mombasa, when I was a child there. In fact, I still remember the majority of them clearly.'

'Don't get so huffy,' he said, taking a towel and rubbing her back.

'I wish I'd known. I would have tried to come home earlier.' Sarah moved into the bedroom. 'Do you honestly think this is a good thing? For Lila, I mean. I'm not knocking arranged marriages, really I'm not. It's part of your culture, and many of them turn out well. But Lila is so independent-minded, and she loves working with Camilla. Dealing with the sales and the overseas buyers. And she told me a few months ago that she was thinking of opening a boutique of her own. Here in Nairobi.'

'Dreams change. Plans change. She has made a new choice.'

'Mmnn, so it seems. It's just the suddenness of it. Honestly, Rabindrah, have you ever so much as heard her mention anyone called Harjeet? Or any potential suitor? I saw her before I went to Turkana, and his name never came up. Surely she would have said something about getting engaged, if this match was already in the pipeline.'

'From her parents' viewpoint she looks like she's on the shelf. That might have come into the calculations,' Rabindrah said.

'That's ridiculous. She has only just turned twenty-seven,' Sarah said. 'That's no reason to be stampeded into a marriage.'

'It may not have anything to do with it,' Rabindrah said. 'But we'll never know, if we don't get a move on.'

'Yes, I suppose so.' Sarah sighed, as she opened the wardrobe. 'I only hope she likes him.'

Rabindrah wagged his head from side to side and shook a finger at her, imitating Lila's mother in an exaggerated Indian falsetto. 'Oh you know, my dears, he is coming from such a good family, isn't it? And so clever he is. My God, what a lucky girl to catch such a man. And at her age, too. Best quality marriage, isn't it?' He was glad to see Sarah laughing. 'You are right, though. It is a little disturbing.' He buttoned the top of his tunic, and moved towards the door, returning to Hindi mode. 'However, all this chattering is not getting you ready, I am telling you. So come along now, Mrs Singh, you cannot be going out like that, you know!'

In the bedroom, Sarah made up her face and slipped into a green silk dress she had commissioned from her favourite Indian tailor in Bazaar Street. The colour deepened the green of her eyes, and the fabric emphasised her small, neat form. She fastened on a pair of gold earrings that had been a birthday gift from her husband and spun round to face him, seeking approval. Wanting him to really see her.

'Highly beauteous,' he said, grinning at her. 'Let's go and congratulate the bride to be.'

'I'm sorry, but I still can't imagine Lila agreeing to this situation so suddenly.' Sarah closed the car door. 'Maybe when they were growing up she had a crush on him, and she has been secretly hankering after him ever since. There must be something with a hint of romance to it. It's impossible to see her walking into a lifelong partnership in any other circumstances.'

'An arranged marriage isn't always a bad thing, as you've already pointed out,' Rabindrah said. 'Families who know one another well, and understand their children, can be very successful at choosing suitable partners.'

'Oh, come on! I bet there isn't a Sikh man anywhere who would meekly submit to parental choice. Only the girls are pressured into that kind of pact. Things aren't the way they are written down in your holy book. Men and women are definitely *not* equal in your society. They have very carefully defined and separate roles, whatever they might pretend.'

Rabindrah put up a hand in mock defence. 'Don't attack me – I'm not involved in these goings-on. The girls do have a say, anyway. They can refuse a boy if they don't like him.'

'Great. And then they are castigated for putting the family in a bad light. Or left on the shelf until they are desperate enough to accept anyone.'

'Let me remind you that the landed gentry in most of Western Europe is shamelessly engaged in marrying off their sons and daughters to suitable breeding stock, with their coming out seasons and country house weekends, and all that,' Rabindrah said. 'Almost every culture has some kind of formal matchmaking. Hindus, Christians, Jews, Muslims – none of the mothers can resist it. We are just more open about ours.'

'But Western girls can't be forced into arranged marriages,' Sarah said. 'That idea gradually disappeared after the First World War. When women took charge of their own money and careers.'

'We both know Lila. If she didn't want to marry this fellow, no one would be able to force her,' he said, irritated by her criticism. 'Her parents are not despots. You know Gulab and Anjit well – they're gracious and cultured and realistic.'

'I can't think why you're suddenly in favour of arranged marriage,' she said. 'You, of all people – the black sheep who did the unacceptable thing and married an Irish girl. Wrong race, wrong faith, wrong colour. Despite your parents' dire warnings, and Kuldip Auntie's strenuous efforts to procure a more suitable bride.'

'Aren't you fortunate that I had the strength to resist even the most tempting of her offerings, Mrs Singh? That I chose you for the Anand Karaj.' He looked at her fleetingly, taking his eyes off the road for a moment and almost running into a cyclist wobbling along the edge of the crumbling tarmac, with no light on his bicycle.

'But we weren't permitted the Anand Karaj, were we? No Blissful Union ceremony in the holy gurdwara for us. Since I'm not a Sikh.'

'I was happy to be married by your friend Father Bidoli. We've made our own blissful union.'

Sarah's mouth curved up at the corners, and she felt hopeful as they drove across the city in companionable silence. She had almost forgotten her usual sense of dread when they walked into Gulab Singh's family compound.

'Brace yourself,' Rabindrah said, taking her hand. 'This is going to go on for hours. These ceremonies are usually strung out over days or weeks. But on this occasion the engagement and marriage are being rolled into a three-day period, because the groom and his family have to return to England at the weekend. Business commitments, apparently.'

'And Lila will go with him?' Sarah was shocked. 'At the end of the week?'

'Yes. Her union of bliss will commence under the grey skies of Birmingham, with all the joy that has to offer.'

'Birmingham.' Sarah shuddered. 'I got lost once, driving around Birmingham. It looked grim and drab. I thought I'd never escape.'

Gulab Singh's residence was large and sprawling, and surrounded by a high wall. In the garden, coloured lanterns hung in the trees and the smell of cooking drifted in the air, competing with the cloying scent of moonflowers and jasmine. Members of the family stood outside in colourful clumps, or drifted through open doors into the living and dining areas where the heavily ornate furniture had been pushed back against the walls. The women wore embroidered saris or the traditional Punjabi *salwaar kameez*. Most were bedecked with their finest jewellery, fastened around necks, dangling from pierced ears, flashing on arms and wrists and ankles. The majority of the men had chosen long tunics and turbans in festive colours, but there were Western suits here and there. Rabindrah was one of the few without a beard or headdress, but he had bowed to tradition in so far as he was wearing a long tunic and Punjabi trousers that complemented his lean frame.

'Rabindrah! And Sarah too! How good you could both come.'

Anjit Kaur Singh looked resplendent in a new ensemble, her oiled and flower-dressed hair gleaming, gold bangles weighing down her outstretched hands. A triple rope of filigree gold, set with rubies, adorned her plump neck. Family heirlooms, only taken out on special occasions. These were the items she would sew into the linings of her clothes and baggage if the family had to leave Kenya suddenly, Sarah thought. Insurance against an uncertain future.

'I was afraid you would miss our celebration, Sarah. More than a month you have been travelling, isn't it? So long to be away from your husband. Such a shame. When did you reach home?'

'Only this evening. I'm so glad I got here in time.' Sarah pasted a smile on her face, determined to ignore the implied criticism, wanting to remind Anjit that Sikh men had been known to leave their wives in distant countries for years, without ever setting eyes on them. 'This is quite a surprise,' she said. 'I had no idea that Lila—'

'Come and see your grandmother, Rabindrah. She has been asking for you both.' Anjit steered them towards the large chair where the old lady was holding court.

'Better get it over with now.' Rabindrah was aware of Sarah's ill-concealed dismay. 'Don't let the old dragon get under your skin. Remember, it's not just you – she'll be having a wonderful time slicing everybody to pieces.'

'Rabindrah, you are looking so handsome. And your wife has come back to you, my goodness.' Lakhbir Kaur Singh sat in state, receiving the tributes of her family. She had always harboured a fondness for her grandson, with his refined, classical features and British education. A small woman, her delicate appearance masked an iron will, and she had a tongue like a viper. 'Come and sit with me, Sarah. Tell me what you have been doing.' Her eyes gleamed with malice as she patted the seat beside her, waving her grandson away. Rabindrah shrugged and stood to one side, out of the direct line of fire.

'Two minutes and you rescue me,' Sarah muttered. She sat down and turned to his grandmother with as much grace as she could muster. 'What a happy occasion. I expect you know the bridegroom? I'm looking forward to meeting him, and seeing Lila.'

'He will be here shortly, with his parents. Such a good match, isn't it? Harjeet has an excellent job in his father's business. Very prosperous, they are telling me. And they will have a fine house in Birmingham, Anjit says. A good place to bring up a family.'

Lakhbir leaned forward and lowered her tone, and Sarah steadied herself for the inevitable enquiry.

'No other news?' The old lady stared at her in meaningful accusation, and Sarah looked down to avoid the penetration of her beady eyes.

'No. No other news,' she said. 'I have been up in the north for the last few weeks, photographing the Turkana people. It is a harsh place, but inspirational too. I've been thinking that—'

'Well, it will come if it will come.' Lakhbir cut her off and sighed theatrically. 'You should spend more time at home, my dear. All this dashing about, and passing the important days away from your husband is not good for—' She brightened. 'Look, here is Anoop coming to say hello to you. Yes, another happy event. Very soon now. Her second, you know.'

'Oh how uncomfortable it is, all this standing around.' Anoop settled herself in a chair and patted her stomach. She turned to Lakhbir, her voice dropping to a conspiratorial whisper. 'I have been to the gurdwara, as you advised, and I am sure now this one is a boy. My husband will be so proud.' She smiled at Sarah. 'My first was a girl, you know, but girls can be very helpful too. Children are so important, don't you think? Oh, I see Rabindrah over there.' She gave a small wave of greeting. 'We never see him at family gatherings. It is as though he has been snatched away from us.'

Rabindrah was standing in front of them, his smile less than friendly as he took in his wife's wan expression, and Anoop's protruding belly and satisfied air. She had never forgiven him for marrying Sarah, and she lost no opportunity to boast about her family in front of the Irish intruder who had stolen the husband of her choice.

'Anoop, how are you? Sarah, it's time we found the bride-to-be. Excuse me, Grandmother.' He took his wife's hand and moved away.

'I can't abide that girl,' Sarah said. 'And as for your grandmother—'

'Pay no attention to the old bat. She's the same with everyone. And Anoop – well, we all know she was after my body, and she can't stand it that she had to settle for a fat, pasty husband nearly twice her age while you got my lean, vigorous physique. I mean, wouldn't you be jealous?' He was relieved to see her respond to a little teasing, and to watch the strain evaporate from her face.

Gulab Uncle appeared beside them, a tall, jovial man with a noticeable paunch and a loud laugh. He wore a traditional turban but was dressed in a Savile Row suit, and he held a glass of amber liquid in his hand. His greeting was affectionate and he hailed a passing servant and provided Sarah with a soft drink and a selection of sweetmeats. She stood on the periphery, listening as Gulab lamented the state of the nation, and the injustices being heaped upon the Asian community.

'We are not helped by the Government of India, with Nehru referring to us as 'a guest race' in our own country,' he said with indignation. 'And what are we to do, those of us who took out Kenya citizenship, when the policy now is Africanisation. No matter that we are Kenyans born here, with parents who were born here also. It no longer counts that we threw in our lot with the Africans at Independence. I'm telling you, they will find a way of chucking us out if they can, just as Amin did in Uganda.'

Rabindrah had no wish to become embroiled in this kind of conversation, but within minutes he was surrounded by other family members, all eager to discuss the unfair refusal to renew trading licences to Indian businessmen, even though they held Kenyan passports.

'Come into my study, dear friends,' Gulab said. 'I have something interesting I would like to show you.'

Sarah smiled, knowing that the real reason for the invitation was to pour glasses of whisky and other varieties of alcohol that he kept in the cabinet housing the radio and gramophone, along with the substantial collection of records that satisfied his wide taste in music. Drawn away by his uncle, Rabindrah raised a hand in a gesture of encouragement as Anjit Auntie bore down on Sarah and led her away into the main living room.

'And here she is – my beautiful girl, so soon to be married! I thought sometimes it would never happen, with her being so picky and rebellious and all. But we are waiting now for the bridegroom and his family. They are coming any minute.'

Lila sat on a silk cushion on the floor, surrounded by a clutch of admiring relatives and friends. She was dressed in a gold embroidered *salwaar kameez*, her hair fastened into a smooth chignon and decorated with flowers. Most of her slim fingers were ringed, and her arms were decorated with gold bangles. She looked up with huge, kohl-rimmed eyes as Sarah bent to embrace her.

'Congratulations, Lila. I'm so happy for you. I wish you could have brought him for dinner, so we could get to know each other a little. But I hear you are rushing off to England almost immediately. Where is he?'

Sarah sat down cross-legged beside her friend, talking high and fast as she always did when she was unsure of herself. There was a burst of laughter and chatter around her as everyone tried to describe Harjeet Singh, and she was reminded of a flock of starlings – glossy and preening in their iridescent plumage. Lila, however, gazed wordlessly at Sarah, her smile enigmatic. The sound of drums and chanting broke into the moment that hung between them, and everyone rose to greet the bridegroom and his family.

'Here they are, coming now with the wedding veil, the *chunni*,' Anjit Auntie said. 'Oh, you will see how generous they have been with Lila's wedding gifts. Such fine clothes and jewels. And we will have the *mangni* ceremony here at home, because Harjeet's father and mother do not have a residence in Nairobi any more. Only a big mansion in jolly old England, you know.'

In the swirl of colour and sound that followed there were drumbeats, prayers and songs, garlands of flowers bestowed and exchanged, gifts of sweetmeats and saffron, flowers and coconut and dried fruits, and wads of money in fat envelopes. Lila rose to her feet with eyes demurely downcast, to welcome her bridegroom and his parents.

Rabindrah came to offer congratulations, his lips twitching with amusement. His independent-minded cousin had never looked so meek. 'I wonder how long she'll be able to last in this biddable role?' he murmured to Sarah, as they watched the proceedings.

Lila bowed and placed her palms together in a greeting of respect before accepting the perfumed oils, and the velvet boxes containing gold jewellery and precious stones. It was late by the time Harjeet Singh had placed an engagement ring on Lila's finger, and she had reciprocated by offering him a plain gold band. Hours passed, punctuated by chanting and dances, and the decoration of Lila's hands and feet with henna. As the night wore on, the bride's transformation created a breathtakingly exotic stranger from the pages of Eastern legend. It was difficult for Sarah to equate the vision with the carefree girl she knew so well, the modern young woman who favoured jeans and sandals and a cotton shirt, who tied her hair in a casual knot, or let it fall free to blow in the wind.

In a corner beside one of the long windows, Rabindrah made an attempt to free himself from one of Anjit Auntie's lectures.

'What did you expect, when you made such an unsuitable match? A European woman who spends her time alone in the bush, running after wild animals and primitive native tribes. Photographing naked men, even! It is not natural. Ten years of wanderings, when she should be at home taking care of her husband's needs. Starting a family before it is too late! Sarah has not turned out to be the kind of wife you need, Rabindrah.'

Sarah heard her name, but she could not catch the rest of Anjit's words and as she drew nearer Rabindrah strode angrily away from his aunt to join a group of men on the other side of the room. She stepped into the cool of the courtyard, her head spinning from the heated room, the increasingly raucous singing and the constant beating of drums. A violent headache throbbed behind her eyes, and every joint in her body ached. The journey south in the rattling Land Rover had been arduous, although she had stayed overnight at Langani Farm on the way. Now she regretted not having remained there for a second night, to enjoy a quiet dinner with Mike Stead and Eileen, his kindly wife. She could have taken one of the horses out across the plains in the morning, visited the lodge and walked up to Piet's ridge. It would have been infinitely preferable to the family gathering for Lila's engagement, and tomorrow's long wedding ceremony. Her only wish was to leave. Now. Searching through the crowd she spotted Rabindrah deep in discussion with Indar Uncle.

'Sarah, my dear. This is a wonderful occasion, no?' Indar beamed down at her. 'Let me get you some refreshment. How is that Land Rover of yours? I am thinking we should replace it soon. So sad, what happened to your friend Dan Briggs. I was liking that man so much. Only with him would Kuldip and I have spent a week in the bush, my God! And we enjoyed every moment of it, too. How is poor Allie, do you know?'

'Broken up, but extraordinarily brave. I haven't seen her for about two months. Erope has moved to the Mara to work with her, although she will have to obtain an increase in grants if she is to keep him on.'

'Her research with Dan is well known, though, and she has a good reputation. That must be counting for something,' Indar said. 'But it is hard to imagine her without him.'

'It will soon be a year since Dan's death. I've been wondering if we should go down there for a few days. What do you think, Rabindrah? Allie would love to see you.' Sarah turned to her husband and was surprised by his nod of agreement.

'I offered Dan a new vehicle only two months before he was killed.' Indar Uncle sighed. 'He was thinking about it when the brakes failed on that old wreck. If he had made a decision sooner . . . But that is fate and we can not turn back the clock. I am thinking you would be better off with one of the new Toyota Land Cruisers, Sarah, my dear. More comfortable, and I can custom-build the body with extra storage and stronger mounts for your cameras. With a trade discount it would not be so much.'

'That sounds good,' Sarah said. 'I'm impressed with the Land Cruisers

I've seen, and Anthony Chapman has completely switched to using them on safari. Where is Kuldip, by the way?'

'She is not here tonight – not feeling so well. Saving her energy for tomorrow's ceremony at the temple. Maybe you can bring this neglectful husband of yours to visit us. She would love to see you both.'

'I certainly will. And we'll talk about the car,' she said. 'I'm grateful to you for keeping me safe on the road. But right now I have to go home, because I've been travelling since early yesterday morning. Rabindrah, can we steal away?'

'We haven't spoken to Lila's intended,' he said. 'We had better find him and offer our congratulations. Then we can leave.'

Harjeet Singh was standing in the hallway, surrounded by sisters and cousins, laughing as they slapped him on the back and made suggestive remarks about the days to come. He was tall, and had a long, narrow face with a nose that was aquiline, and a full mouth. His eyes were dark and heavy-lidded, but Sarah thought they were too close together. He had the traditional Sikh beard and turban, although he was dressed in a well-cut Western suit.

'Ah, the journalist.' He barely glanced at Rabindrah as introductions were made, and offered Sarah a brief, limp handshake.

'Lila and I have been close friends for many years,' Sarah said. 'I hope we will meet in England one of these days. I'm there fairly often because the books Rabindrah and I write together are published in London.'

Harjeet did not answer but turned away in dismissal, plainly uninterested in further conversation.

'Congratulations,' Sarah called out after him. 'And many happy years for you and Lila.'

He gave no indication that he had heard her, and she shrugged off the slight.

'Rude bugger,' said Rabindrah. 'I hope he isn't always that arrogant. Let's go.'

'What time is the wedding tomorrow?' Sarah closed her eyes and let her head fall back against the seat as they drove away.

'Not until noon.'

'God, I'm beat. I don't know if I can handle two days in a row of snide insinuations from your relatives. It's so utterly heartless.'

'Let's not get onto that subject. Please.' Rabindrah's face was forbidding and he hunched forward, gripping the wheel, driving too fast for the blackness of the night and the random workings of the street lights.

'You know it's true,' she said. 'I dread having to run the gamut of pointed remarks. Your Grandmother, that dreadful Anoop – the whole lot of them. I didn't even have Kuldip Auntie to help me out. What was Anjit saying to you, by the way? I heard my name mentioned.'

'Nothing. She was just asking about our plans generally, now that you are back.'

'Oh, for God's sake,' she said. 'I know what that means. The barren, absentee wife. It's the topic at every family gathering.'

'Sarah, we are not going to discuss that subject now. There's no point. And you were right about going away. I didn't want you to spend all that time alone in Turkana, but earlier this evening I realised that it has been good for you. You seem much better. More—'

'We could try again.' Her voice was soft, but it carried hope.

'It was so painful,' he said. 'We have already suffered too much. And I'm sorry they give you a hard time, but if they knew the whole story it might be better.'

'No, I'll always be the outsider,' she said brokenly. 'Your marriage was a bitter disappointment to them all, and now they feel justified because the woman you chose against their advice can't produce a child. If you'd married a nice Sikh girl this would never have happened. That's the reality behind all the false smiles and the artificial words of welcome. It's too hard, Rabindrah. To keep on taking it, pretending it doesn't hurt. You just don't get it, do you? I'm the one who has to put up with the veiled insults, while you are treated with respect, asked for political advice, admired for your insider knowledge, and whatever else.'

'That's not fair,' he protested, but he knew that she was right. 'In retrospect, though, perhaps we should have told our parents, and maybe Indar and Kuldip who are so fond of you. That would have made them more understanding, more sensitive.'

In the beginning he had ignored the opposition to their marriage, and the shocked disapproval of his family. He was certain that in time they would see what an exceptional person Sarah was. They had both wanted children, but the months stretched into years and then came the mis-carriages. The second one had almost destroyed her, when she had lost the child after four months of pregnancy. Afterwards she had radiated a kind of grief from which Rabindrah felt excluded, while he in turn experienced both helplessness and a sense of personal inadequacy. And he had to admit to frustration and envy each time he saw friends and relatives building young families, and watching their sons and daughters grow.

The years of raised eyebrows and murmurings behind his back were constant reminders that he had done the unacceptable thing, chosen outside of his clan. He had also been unreasonably angry with Sarah and defensive about her criticism of his kind, so that disagreement often escalated into a row followed by hours of hurt silence.

'I can't win here,' he said. 'I feel caught in the middle of a situation where I'm doomed to be disloyal – either to you or to members of my family, no matter what I say.'

'Oh, great! You want to keep all your relatives sweet by remaining silent, when your wife is being insulted. That's just great!' Sarah turned to look out of the window.

At the house she went straight to the bedroom, threw herself down on the bed and lay watching Rabindrah in silence, already regretting her earlier outburst. It was no use being angry with him. She tried to think of something to say, to erase the ugly mood of the journey home.

'So, do you believe this is a traditional arrangement? Because that's how it looked to me.'

'I only know that Lila has made her choice, and she's going to carry it through,' Rabindrah said, putting away his clothes.

'That sounds ominous.' She had picked up something deeper in his comment. 'Everyone I talked to kept blathering on about what a suitable match it is. But there has to be more. I feel it strongly.'

'I spoke to Sanjit.' Rabindrah came to sit down beside her on the bed. 'But only briefly. He is the brother closest to Lila. The match was apparently arranged between the two families, because Gulab and Anjit have serious financial problems. Gulab Uncle is a Kenya citizen, but he has been forced to pay out thousands of shillings in bribes every month to keep his trading licence. The demands for money have grown out of all proportion to what he makes from the sawmill and his other business interests, and he is in imminent danger of losing everything. He applied months ago for residence in the UK, giving the numbers of their original British passports, and using my father as their nearest relative and as a reference. But the application has been refused. Too late, and not a close enough connection for a displaced *jundibhai*.'

'God, how dreadful,' Sarah said. 'Gulab works hard and he employs more than twenty African staff. He pays them reasonably well and they can only suffer if he leaves. Although I suppose some politician has told them they can take over the sawmill themselves, if they get rid of the Indian boss.'

'The point is that Lila will eventually be entitled to a full British passport, because her husband is a British citizen and she herself was born in a British colony.'

'No. The point is that she is being sold off to rescue her family.' Sarah kept her tone flat, not wanting to sound dramatic or to make him angry again.

'I don't see it quite that baldly,' Rabindrah said. 'Gulab feels he is giving his daughter a more secure future and a better life, compared to what is on offer here. The plan is for Harjeet's family to refinance Gulab's holding company in Nairobi, and to become major shareholders. And they have invited two African politicians and a Kikuyu businessman to sit on the board as directors, with no duties and suitably enticing rewards.'

'They wouldn't, by any chance, be the ones collecting the bribes?'

'How did you guess?' Rabindrah's disgust was evident. 'Anyway, the bottom line is that Gulab will keep his licence, and the new company will be able to send money out of the country, ostensibly for investment and expansion purposes. It also means that the family should be able to travel between here and Birmingham on a regular basis, because Manjit Singh, Lila's father-in-law, has his headquarters there. And eventually Gulab hopes to gain British citizenship.'

'Is all this legal?'

'If you have an African businessman or a politician on your side, anything can be called legal these days. Meanwhile, Harjeet is in a position to provide well for Lila. His father has been very successful in the UK. Hard times make hard choices, Sarah. She may be a hell of a lot better off married to a prosperous businessman in England, with her family secure around her, rather than heading for God knows where as a refugee.'

'In a practical sense, you're right.' Sarah sighed, and stood up. 'I just wish she had been in a position to choose a true soul mate. I hope Harjeet will be good to her. I didn't like him much, and you said yourself he was arrogant.'

'We only saw him for less than five minutes, surrounded by a gaggle of people demanding his attention,' Rabindrah said. 'He wasn't very approachable, I agree. But he may be a good bloke. Works hard, by all accounts.'

'He's hardly unique in that,' Sarah pointed out. 'And it's not an excuse for being downright rude. Most of our friends work just as hard as Harjeet.'

'True, the Asians have wound up in an impossible position here, no matter how long or hard they work. Because they have not understood the importance of becoming involved politically in this country. There isn't a single Asian member in the Kenya parliament, for example. No one to stand up for our interests. Plenty of our people took out citizenship, but they never became citizens in the true sense of the word. Most of us have been too busy keeping our heads down and trying to squirrel away sufficient money to get out of here if necessary. Because it's all about Africanisation, these days. If you are a brown or a white Kenyan, you are at a disadvantage. Especially when it comes to business licences and trading permits and so on.'

'It's two o'clock in the morning,' she said wearily. 'I can't listen to any more of this stuff.'

'These are the realities of Lila's situation,' he said quietly. 'And you were the one who brought up the subject. I thought you were concerned for her.'

'I am,' Sarah said, pulling off her clothes and talking over her shoulder as she cleaned her face. 'I'm really sorry. And terribly worried that she is caught up in this web of complications and hypocrisy. But I've been travelling and working for days and weeks, and right now I just want to go to sleep.' She climbed into bed and closed her eyes. 'Anyway, thank God we don't have to show up at the wedding ceremony until around midday.'

Rabindrah went into the bathroom, and closed the door. He was riled by the way she had cut him off, but relieved that there would be no further discussion tonight about the decision Lila had made. He felt a deepening anxiety for his cousin. The idea of such a pragmatic arrangement had affronted Sarah's definition of freedom, and her professed dislike of

Harjeet was undoubtedly linked to her opinion of the match. Still, she was a good judge of character, and she had an unnerving sixth sense when it came to possible disaster looming in the background, unnoticed by others. Rabindrah had to admit that his first impression of the man was not favourable.

Lying beside Sarah he listened to her breathing, and knew she was not asleep. He wanted to reach out and take her in his arms or just touch her, to reassure her. But the space between them in the bed seemed to stretch beyond his ability to cross. He turned over, and closed his eyes.

Chapter 4

Norway, July 1977

They did not stop in Oslo, except to transfer to another flight that would take them north to Trondheim where Jorgen Olsen was waiting for them. He was a tall, big-boned man with rugged features and silver hair, and an ability to project a strength that was immediately comforting. Lars in thirty years, Hannah thought, as he put his arms around her and his grandchildren and greeted his son.

Piet, who had wriggled and complained during most of the plane journey, now became less fractious.

'Come, we will visit Trondheim another day,' Jorgen said to him. 'Now I will take you straight to the farm, where your grandmother is waiting.'

They climbed into the car, with Lars in front, beside his father. Hannah and the children sat in the back with the windows wound all the way down, allowing the sweet scent of summer to drift across their faces, awed by the precipitous mountains that plunged into deep blue water. They drove through forests of dark spruce and pine trees, secret and cool, to emerge into open pastures that were lush and dotted with wooden houses and barns in red and white and yellow, their steep roofs and long windows and flower boxes catching the evening sun. All neat, freshly painted, pristine, picture-perfect.

'I didn't know people could have their houses in such bright colours,' Suniva said. 'Ma, can we have a painted house when we go home?'

'I don't think it would look so good at Langani, after a week or two,' Hannah said, laughing at the idea. 'When the dust has kicked up and blown onto the paint, and the ants have made trails along the outside, and the woodpeckers and hornbills and beetles have tried drilling holes in the wooden walls. I think we will keep our stone house, with the bougainvillea that climbs up the verandah and hides the things we don't need to notice.'

'All the cows have been washed,' Piet said, his eyes wide with amazement. 'Look at them, Suniva. They are not like our *ngombes*, all dusty with mud on their feet. Grandpa, do you wash your cows every day? I think they have been brushed too. Ma, what would Achole say if he saw these cows?'

But Hannah had fallen silent as the car crested a last hill and the Olsen farm came into view. She put her arms around Lars's neck as they reached the place where he was born. The main house was long and narrow and painted white, with a slate roof and gables at either end that were finished with a wooden trim. In front of it was a meadow that ran down to the edge of a fjord, the glassy surface still and calm. Four additional buildings stood close by, one of which was a barn that housed the dairy. Behind the grassy fields a forest reared up, clinging to a rocky hillside whose ancient surface was pitted and cracked with the marks of harsh weather.

'Like Pa's picture books that we have at home,' Piet said.

'Oh look! You have a red house!' Suniva opened the door of the car and leapt out, before Jorgen had put on the handbrake or turned off the ignition. She gazed up at the barn with delight. 'And a big white one. Look, Piet! Look! There is a grey one too, with carving. Look!'

Piet had wandered away and was standing alone, absorbed in the formation of the mountains, and the silver torrent of a waterfall that appeared from a fissure in the rocks high above him, tumbling down to disappear into the woods behind the house.

'Trolls,' he called back to Hannah. 'This is where the trolls live. Up there, hiding in the rocks. I can hear their noise in my head.' He placed his hands over his ears. 'I can hear them all the time.'

'Maybe you will see them, if you look carefully,' Hannah said, walking over to take his hand, but he ignored her and continued to gaze upwards. 'Come on, Piet. Grandma is waiting for us and there is so much to see.'

'What is this one, with the stairs and the verandah hanging in the air?' It was Suniva who asked the question, craning her neck to look at the carved wooden balcony.

'You've changed it,' Lars said, with surprise. 'Put windows in.'

'It is called a *stabbur*,' Jorgen said, in reply to Suniva's question. 'In the old days we kept seed and other things there. Whatever we needed to store for the farm. It is built on stilts, you see, and we used to hang salted meats from the ceiling, so that mice and rats and other greedy animals could not climb up and get at them. If you like it, maybe it can be yours one day.'

'When?' Suniva was admiring the façade and the steep, outside staircase leading to the upper floor. 'When can I have it?'

'Suniva!' Hannah was prevented from remonstrating further by the appearance of Kirsten Olsen.

She emerged from the front door of the farmhouse, smoothing her skirt, looking anxious. But when her son put his arms around her and rocked her gently she nodded and smiled and wiped her eyes, her heart too full to find any words.

'Let's go inside,' Jorgen said, gesturing towards the grey building. 'We will put the luggage away and see how it is, your Norwegian house. I hope you will like what we have done.'

'You've altered it for us?' Lars looked more closely at the old building. 'With a new door and windows.'

'*Ja*.' Jorgen nodded, his smile huge. 'For you and Hannah and the children. We have made the old *stabbur* into a second dwelling. Just for you.'

Inside, the walls and floors were made of wood. They stepped into a space that served as a sitting room, with a pot-bellied iron stove in the centre of the back wall.

'We have a stove at home,' Suniva said, fascinated by the old glazed tiles on the rounded chimney, and the polished metal door. 'Kamau cooks on our stove, but it doesn't look at all like this. Why does it go up to the ceiling?'

'This one is for heating the room in winter,' Lars said. 'You put logs inside and it keeps everyone as warm as toast. The chimney goes all the way up, inside the house. So it heats the rooms above at the same time.'

A sofa and chairs and shelves stacked with books and pottery separated the living room from a kitchen and dining area, and the cupboards had brightly painted doors depicting flowers and birds and animals. The walls were decorated with hand-woven textiles and samplers, and a series of photographs that showed Lars as a child and a teenager, and later as a young man. White curtains fluttered from bedroom windows that overlooked a swathe of green, and the smell and rustle of the trees filled the rooms. The childrens' wooden beds had painted sides and headboards and hand stitched quilts. Pots of geraniums and roses, juniper and birch and fruit trees were mixed with a scattering of wild flowers, and through them a path led to the edge of the cobalt water, where a rowing boat was tied to a wooden jetty. In the distance they could see the herd of cows that were Jorgen's passion. There was a view of the mountains, still carrying a dusting of summer snow, and in the opposite direction the outline of a village was visible.

'It's magnificent, what you have done.' Lars's voice was clogged with emotion. 'You must have worked so hard since the weather turned, to get it ready for us.'

'I had old Nilsen to help me,' Jorgen said, with pride. 'Last year we converted a barn together, for his daughter. He was glad to return the favour. Your mother did the rest – the furniture and the other things you would need.' His smile was shy. 'I did not know what details inside would be important.'

'Look – some of the cows are painted red and white too,' Suniva said, pointing out of the window. 'I must draw pictures of them.'

'There are eight red and white cows,' Jorgen said. 'The others have black and white markings. Each one has a name, and the leading cow has a bell with a sound that you will soon recognise. Good, strong cows that breed well and milk well. Not much trouble at all if you look after them. And Grandma Kirsten has some goats, good for milk and for making cheese. We smoke some meats and fish, too, in that smaller building over there.'

'Can we meet the cows now, and learn their names?' Suniva had followed her grandfather to the window, and now she tugged at the old man's hand.

'Not yet.' Lars put his arm around his mother's thin shoulders. 'Because we are going to the main house where your grandma has prepared supper. And then you are going to bed, because we have travelled a long way, and it is late at night for you. Tomorrow we will meet the cows. Come along, Piet. Piet?'

'What?' Piet turned around to face his father.

'Pay attention,' Lars said in a stronger tone. 'Supper and then bed.'

'Bed? It looks like the middle of the day,' Piet said.

'No bed for me,' Suniva shouted at the top of her voice, whirling around in a circle, taking Piet by the hand. 'There is too much to see. I couldn't go to bed.'

'No bed for me,' Piet echoed, but his face was flushed and he was clearly tired after the journey.

The main house was much larger than the *stabbur*. There were two living rooms, one for everyday use, with its well-worn armchairs and sofa, a scattered collection of newspapers and knitting wool and embroidery threads, books and reading glasses and a television set. The second room was more formal, and Lars explained that it was only used when there were neighbours and other guests to be entertained. The polished floors were scattered with rugs, except for the kitchen which was covered with brightly coloured linoleum. On the walls were framed photographs, many of them in faded sepia tones.

'There are cows standing on a boat! Can I go on the water with the cows?' Piet stared in amazement at the old pictures.

'Before we had big trucks, we took the cattle on rafts across the fjord to the other side, and walked them up into the high pastures. That is where the grazing was best in the summer,' Jorgen said. 'Your great-aunt lived in a little house up there. She would look after the animals until the cold weather came, and then they would be brought down again.'

'I wish we could do that now. Today.' Suniva was enchanted.

'It looks good,' Jorgen said, smiling. 'But it was a long journey, and sometimes dangerous. I'm afraid the lorry is more efficient.'

Kirsten had laid the table with her best dishes, and a cloth and napkins that she had embroidered with cross stitch. They bowed their heads as Jorgen thanked God for the gift of their safe arrival and for the food that his wife had prepared. Steaming plates of salmon were accompanied by home-grown vegetables and flatbread. When the dessert came Lars exclaimed with delight.

'There are no strawberries on earth like these,' he said, as his mother served him a generous helping. 'I have not had them for years. Now, stir some of this cream in with them and you will never find a better taste. Take up your spoon, Hannah, and see how good it is.'

In spite of the long journey from London it proved difficult to persuade the children to go to bed, with the daylight still bright outside. When they were finally tucked in, Hannah and Lars decided to return to the main house for coffee. But Piet became agitated, pressing his hands over his ears, and finally burying his head under the pillow.

'My ears are hurting, Ma,' he said. 'And I can hear the trolls.' He clung to Hannah, begging her to stay with him, ignoring Suniva who reached over and punched him lightly, calling out that he was acting like a baby rather than a nine-year-old.

'You go back to the main house,' Hannah said to Lars. 'I'll wait here until he is settled.'

It was Jorgen who came to look for his daughter-in-law, and he stayed on with the children, starting a night-time ritual of story-telling that would continue for the whole visit. He sat in a rocking chair beside their beds.

'Listen, now,' he said, his voice loud, owing to the increasing deafness that had come over him of late. 'Each night while you are here I am going to tell you a story of the great days of the Viking ships. And the fierce kings and brave warriors who were your ancestors, and who rode the waves to glory.'

Hannah had been apprehensive about joining Lars and his mother after dinner, dreading the forced, stilted conversation, but the time passed pleasantly enough as she helped with the washing up, and tried to learn some new Norwegian phrases and names from Kirsten. The atmosphere was softened by coffee, spiked with shots of a homemade liqueur that Hannah had never tasted before. It made her cough as she swallowed the first mouthful, but soon she was sitting back and enjoying the warm sensation in her stomach.

'Father makes the liqueur himself. It is *heimbrent*, but when it is poured into the coffee we call the mixture *karsk*. We often give it to visitors, because it puts everyone in a good mood very quickly.' Lars was laughing and filling her cup again when Jorgen appeared.

'The children are sleeping,' he said. 'But I think Piet may have another ear infection. Perhaps we should take him to the doctor tomorrow.'

'Ach, that is such a pity,' Hannah said. 'He only just recovered from the last one, and we thought he would be fine where there is no dust or flies or biting *dudus*.'

They sat down together and Lars translated back and forth for Hannah and his mother, telling tales of his childhood escapades until they were all laughing without restraint.

*

On the following morning they visited the family doctor, a longtime friend of Jorgen's, who prescribed antibiotic drops for Piet, and advised that the child should use ear plugs if he was swimming.

'He has a perforation in one eardrum,' Dr Petersen said. 'This is something that can happen after a series of infections, but it often heals itself. You will need to wait for a few weeks to see if that will be the case, and in the meantime the drops will cure the present condition and take away any pain.' He smiled at Hannah and patted the boy on the head. 'A fine young man. I can see why Jorgen is so proud of you and of his grandchildren.'

After two days Hannah began to feel more at ease. Sitting under a summer sky, she shelled peas from Kirsten's vegetable garden and watched her family laughing and splashing in the icy water of the fjord.

'The boy seems much better,' Jorgen said. 'Already the pain is less. We must make sure to keep the ears dry and he will be fine.'

'I hope so,' Hannah said. 'He has had several of these infections lately and I worry about it a great deal.'

'You baby Piet too much,' Lars said as Hannah fussed over their son each time he headed for the fjord. 'He needs toughening up.'

'How can you say such a thing?' She was full of indignation. 'He is susceptible to these problems with his ears. He can't help that.'

'Yes, but he needs to be more independent generally,' Lars said. 'You are over-protective of him, because you see so much of your brother in him, growing again into a young man. But this Piet is our son, Han, and he needs to make his way. Graze his knees, tumble off his bike, swim in the fjord, without anyone running after him.'

'You're a fine one to talk,' she said, resenting his criticism. 'Suniva can get you to do anything she likes, and you are never able to resist her.'

'That's true,' he said, laughing and taking her into his arms. 'Maybe we are both hopeless parents. We can only hope our children will survive that.'

In the light of the summer evenings Suniva and Piet remained outside long after their normal bedtime, displaying a boundless energy. At breakfast time they sat in the kitchen eating bowls of barley porridge with their grandfather, pouring on cream and raisins and thick syrup. Then they set off to visit the dairy, or to fish from Jorgen's boat. Lars took them on long walks through the forests, looking for wild strawberries, chasing butterflies through the grass, and making daisy chains. Suniva sat for hours with the box of paints and crayons that Camilla had given her, making portraits of her grandparents and drawing the cows and the mountains, and the boats on the sparkling water. The beauty of the place stole their hearts, but for Hannah its perfection was also unsettling and there were moments when she longed for the tickle of African dust in her nose, the thin air of a highland morning, the low rasping sound of a leopard in the darkness, and the slight edge of danger that heightened each unpredictable day.

The Olsen farm was hard work for an ageing couple. There were milk cows and two bulls, and a number of calves to be reared. The dairy was housed in the red barn, with the hay stored above it on the second floor. Jorgen took care of the cattle and the milking machines, and he also cleaned the stalls, put the cows out to pasture and arranged the feed. Hannah was awed by the gleaming cleanliness of the dairy and the smooth hum of modern machinery that seemed to function with such fluid efficiency. It was cool inside where the cattle stood, patient and calm, and there was no hint of dust in the air, or red mud splattering the floor. Even the hay had a sweet smell that was different from her African fodder.

'They have better manners than our cows,' Suniva said. 'They're clean and tidy, and they even eat more slowly. There's no noise in here either – no herd boys shouting or whistling or clacking their sticks together, or spitting on the straw like Achole. It's too quiet, Ma.'

The milk was stored in a cooling tank where it was collected every second day by a truck, and transported to the local cooperative. Kirsten kept chickens, and looked after a flock of white goats that she milked for cheese. She also cooked and shopped and cleaned the house without any outside help, and Hannah wondered what she must have thought of the domestic staff and herdsmen and gardeners and night-watchmen employed at Langani. Jorgen grew barley on some of his thirty-five acres, and potatoes and cabbage. He took care of the farm accounts, and he was also responsible for buying and selling the livestock. They rose early each day to attend to the milking process, and to turn the cattle out and collect eggs. When Hannah asked if they ever brought in anyone to assist them, Jorgen shook his head.

'We manage it together, as you are seeing now,' he said. 'If we are bringing in hay for the cows, or harvesting the barley, our neighbours come to give us a hand and we do the same for them. That is the custom around here. But soon we will be a little old for running the farm alone. That is something we have to think about, although it is hard to come to terms with such an idea. To acknowledge that we are not what we were.'

Hannah noticed that her mother-in-law had aged considerably since her last visit to Langani, two years previously. She and Hannah worked companionably in the house and out of doors, taking care of tasks that would have been carried out by the household staff at Langani. Years had passed since Hannah had physically involved herself in domestic chores, and the associations were not happy. She remembered vividly the moment when Jan van der Beer had insisted on abandoning the country of his birth, immediately following Kenya's Independence. Whilst he had left his son to run Langani, Hannah had been obliged to go south with her parents, leaving the home she loved for the run-down bungalow they had been allocated on the Rhodesian tobacco farm owned by Jan's brutal cousin. She had buried her memories of those miserable years, when Jan had been treated like a casual labourer, and Lottie had sought her daughter's help with the cooking and cleaning and laundry, and the delivery of the sewing she was forced to take in to make ends meet. Hannah's love for her father had been slowly extinguished as his consumption of alcohol increased his brooding, and his resentful eyes became dulled and bloodshot and mean with despair.

But now she found that helping Kirsten Olsen was a rewarding experience. Her hands were twisted with arthritis, and she had trouble with her knees that made it painful for her to bend or to walk any distance. Hannah's contribution saved the older woman from housework that caused her pain. Gradually, they both began to enjoy the game of communicating by pointing and demonstrating and repeating words in Norwegian and English. Hannah made beds, hung sheets and towels and clothes out to dry in the fresh air, dusted and polished, and spent time in the kitchen learning to make the dishes that Jorgen liked best, or offering recipes of her own. In the village she carried the shopping basket and was introduced to everyone they met. Kirsten beamed with pleasure and talked animatedly in her slightly querulous, sing-song voice, demonstrating an unexpectedly jolly side to her personality, while Hannah shook hands and smiled endlessly until her cheeks and jaw ached with the effort. One or two family friends and acquaintances spoke English, and asked questions about the dangers of living close to wild beasts and black men with spears. Their interest in Lars's African family and their offers of hospitality created a warm place in Hannah's heart. Her responses, although often limited by language, were filled with genuine gratitude and pleasure. Most of Lars's old school and college friends spoke English, and there were days of laughter and exchanged anecdotes when their families got together for a fishing expedition, or a simple meal of freshly caught trout, or salmon smoked on the farms.

The children swam in the blue water that was too cold for Hannah, and helped to collect eggs from the hens. They tried their hand at milking the goats and making cheese, and Suniva sat on a wooden stool that Jorgen had given her and drew endless pictures, while Piet learned the best times and places to catch a plump fish. The afternoons were long and hot, and it was difficult for them to believe that the sun could be so fierce in a place so distant from the equator. After a few days they were all glowing and tanned, as though they had spent a week on the Indian Ocean. But in spite of the pleasure he found in his many pastimes, Piet was often irritable. He would suddenly leave a game with Suniva to sit alone and read from one of the books that Hannah had bought him in London, paying no attention when they called him in for meals or to join an excursion.

'He doesn't listen to me when I speak to him,' Hannah said. 'He has never behaved like this before. I don't know what to do, Lars.'

'We're on holiday,' Lars said. 'Let's not worry about it for now. You can take a firmer hand when we get home.'

Kirsten shook her head and made a comment to Jorgen in a low voice. But he frowned and signalled to her, in an effort to prevent her airing an opinion.

Although the entire family spent a day in Trondheim, awed by the beauty of the great cathedral where the kings of Norway were crowned, and enchanted by the coloured timber houses and the river, they spent almost all of their time at the farm. Lars was content to devote much of each day to his father, discussing the cattle and the cost and feasibility of further modernising the dairy, strolling through the fields to inspect the barley.

They would take walks, or row along the fjord and fish, or visit neigh-bours that Lars had known since childhood. It was clear to him that the effort of keeping up the farm was an increasing strain on his parents. They no longer picked all the fruit in the orchard for Kirsten's summer jam making, and there were weeds in her flower garden that Hannah discreetly attended to. The management of the property was slowing down, creaking along at the same pace as its ageing proprietors, and it made Lars sad to see their frailty. Occasionally he was overcome by guilt at having stayed away so long, and neglected his parents' needs.

'We will come more often,' he promised his father. 'It is a part of the childrens' lives now and Hannah, too, is happy here.'

Lars's fortieth birthday fell towards the end of their stay and his sister, Ilse, and her family had been invited to come from Copenhagen where they lived. The day was spent in preparation, carrying out the wooden table and chairs from the *stabbur*, along with a blue and white checked cloth, glasses and plates and cutlery. They were placed in the shade of a tree that curved downwards to trail several of its branches in the water. The smell of freshly baked bread and cakes drew the children inside from the meadow, where Suniva had been picking wild flowers to put in a jug for her father's birthday supper. Kirsten handed them bowls of eggs and flour and sugar, and large wooden spoons to mix pancakes.

Both children had been given Norwegian national costumes by their grandparents, and even Suniva did not object to dressing in the white embroidered blouse and apron over a full, dark skirt. Several decorative bands of colour were stitched around the hem, and a bright sash encircled her waist. She stood with unaccustomed patience while Hannah combed out the tangle of her hair, braided it neatly and pinned it up around her head.

'She is a true Norwegian, *ja*,' Jorgen said, when he saw her. 'Looking so much like you and Lars — sturdy and blonde. And the boy, too. Beautiful grandchildren from Africa I have.'

He grunted with satisfaction, and there was such joy and affection in his whole bearing that Hannah pressed his knobbled hand and he put his arm around her, in a silent message of kinship and approval. Then she caught Lars's eye, and they smiled at their secret.

During the morning Jorgen and Lars drove to the nearby village and returned with a basket of fresh shrimp that Kirsten placed in an enormous pot on the stove until they emerged from the bubbling water, pink and succulent.

'My God, they're huge! I've never seen such shrimp,' Hannah said, sucking the sweet juice out of the shell and biting into the flesh. 'Or tasted anything like these. Even the best ones at the coast aren't like this.'

'It's the cold water,' Lars said. 'Summer for me was always about shrimps, and fresh strawberries with pancakes and thick cream and sugar. Mmnnn.' He smacked his lips and peeled another shellfish for Hannah as his mother chased him away, laughing. 'All right – we won't eat all of the dinner in advance,' he said. 'Come on, Han. We need to get ready before the rest of the family arrives.'

'I'm so glad we came,' Hannah said, as they dressed for the evening's events. 'It means so much to your parents to have the children here. You were right, Lars. They should know the part of them that is Norwegian. That is what my mother said, years ago, when Pa objected to me going to school at the convent. She said I should understand the other half of me, the half that is Italian and Catholic. Lottie did not want me to grow up as an Afrikaans girl, boxed in by the unbending attitudes of the Dutch Reformers.'

'I don't remember Jan as a narrow-minded Boer.'

'Pa was determined never to be like that,' Hannah said. 'He knew that many of the older men were hypocrites. They made the members of the Dutch Reform community stick to endless rules that hung over everyone like a black cloud. Pa said they hated to see anyone filled with joy. He never believed in the dour Afrikaners in black hats and coats and stiff backs, who stood so stern and proud in the church. And he discovered, as a teenager, that many of them drank and played cards secretly in the back room of an Indian *duka* in town, and took African women for their pleasure, while forbidding their children to sing or dance or play games on a Sunday. But he also thought Ma's Catholic ideas were too frivolous, and he didn't pay any heed to her beliefs either.'

Lars's slow smile reached his eyes. 'It looks as though you swallowed a good slice of Lottie's more liberal views,' he said.

She shot a questioning look in his direction and saw his amusement, but her face reddened nevertheless. He never referred to her wild behaviour in the days when she had rebelled against being part of the downward spiral in her parents' life. When her beloved pa finally became a bitter and abusive drunk, Hannah had stolen her mother's savings and fled back to Kenya. She had found Lars at Langani, managing the farm with Piet. The big Norwegian had struck her then as a second older brother, ready to rein her in and treat her like a child, in cahoots with the sibling she already had.

'I can't imagine how you and Piet put up with me when I came back from Rhodesia,' she said. 'You already had more than enough to contend with, clearing up the unexpected debts that Pa had left behind, and getting the place solvent again.'

'You weren't so bad,' Lars said. 'I can think of one or two good points. And you needed a little slack to get over the hard knocks.'

At the time, Hannah had not noticed his growing affection for her. Instead she became infatuated with Viktor Szustak, the architect who had helped Piet to draw up the original plans for Langani Lodge. A passionate affair sizzled between them, but then her brother had been snatched from her. Lars had taken charge of Langani after Piet's murder, but when he finally confessed his love for her Hannah rejected him, and he left the farm. The affair with Viktor had ended soon afterwards. He was an inveterate womaniser with no intention of marrying or settling down and he had left her alone and humiliated, unaware that she was pregnant with his child. And then Sarah had contacted Lars and persuaded him to return to the farm.

'Come outside, Han.' His words brought her back to the present. 'The light is beautiful, like you and our children. Let us go out and celebrate how blessed we are.'

'Do you ever think of Viktor? Do you ever feel angry or sad about what I did?'

The words jumped out of her throat, surprising her as much as they did Lars. It was a subject they never discussed, but here in the peace of the blue evening it did not seem to threaten.

'No. I never think of him,' Lars said. 'Suniva is my daughter in every sense but one, and that is irrelevant. We do not need to think about Viktor.'

'I will never, ever forget the day you came back to Langani. The way you took me on, pregnant and stubborn and angry,' she said. 'That is what I remember, more than anything.'

She was about to kiss him when she heard the sound of a car. 'Here's your sister,' she said. 'This is going to be a very special evening. *Lekker,* heh?'

There were embraces between the women, while the men shook hands and slapped one another on the back, and talked about how long it seemed since they had visited Langani. Lars and his sister were totally different from one another in appearance. Ilse was tall and dark-haired, with a dynamic personality and a wide, generous smile that was followed by hearty laughter. Her eyes were brimming with love as she looked her brother up and down, and then put her arms around him.

'You finally brought them,' she said. 'That is so good. Even for me, because it has made Karl take time off and come to the farm. It is more than a year since we were here together, you know.' She turned to Hannah in explanation. 'He is so busy in Copenhagen that we do not often have time for family reunions.'

'Where are your children?' Hannah was surprised at their absence. 'We were looking forward to seeing them. Especially these two.' She nodded towards Suniva and Piet, standing to one side, self-conscious in their Norwegian costumes.

'They have gone to summer camp.' Ilse's expression darkened. 'Their Danish cousins were going, and Karl said it would be good for them.'

'They have been here on several occasions. It's time they had wider horizons.' Karl's lips were pursed in censure and he spread out sausage-like fingers. 'They should not be spending all their holidays with their mother.'

'I can't see what harm there is in that,' Ilse said. 'At their age –'

'They will not learn anything new or useful here. It is better for them to experience a more diverse world,' Karl said with finality, oblivious to the hurt on his wife's face.

'Come,' Jorgen said, linking arms with Ilse. 'Your mother and Hannah have prepared a feast for us, and we will start with some beer, and even French wine that Lars brought all the way from London.' He laughed. 'My son the wine smuggler, *ja.*'

Hannah followed them down to the water's edge, walking beside Karl. She darted a glance at his pink, chubby face and the expensive shirt that was a little tight. In the hot afternoon, his skin was covered in a light film of sweat and he looked flushed and uncomfortable in his city clothes. Even his eyes seemed pink, and he peered out through pale lashes at his rural surroundings. Suspicion and disapproval were evident in his frown and the gesturing of his pudgy hands, as he waved away summer flies and mopped his brow with a handkerchief.

'I didn't expect it to be this beautiful,' Hannah said. 'And the colours here are rich and deep. You must love the contrast to the city, when you come to visit.'

'I am not a country boy, personally,' he said. 'There are many other places more interesting and stimulating to me. But Ilse feels she must come whenever there is a suitable time for her to be away. She is devoted to her parents. Her family obligations.'

'Being here is not an obligation.' Ilse had overheard her husband and stepped back to correct him, her cheeks flushed with anger.

'Call it what you will,' Karl said. 'The old folk are too often on your mind. They have become a drain recently, making you feel guilty.'

Hannah felt certain that her sister-in-law did not see a visit to her parents as an encumbrance of any kind. She had formed a solid friendship with Ilse from the day they met in Kenya. They had both grown up on farms which remained important anchors in their lives, places that defined their ideals of home and security. It was plain, however, that Ilse's relationship with Karl had deteriorated.

For a while they sat by the lake, absorbing the afternoon sunshine. After a time Suniva took out her sketchbook and began a new drawing, while Piet wandered away to watch the fish rise and to try his luck with a rod that Jorgen had bought him on their morning expedition to the village.

'He's so like my brother at the same age,' Hannah said. 'Every living thing fascinates him. Piet used to collect beetles and frogs and small snakes, and he kept a menagerie of strange creatures in his room, feeding them and studying them. It drove Ma mad sometimes, when she opened a drawer to put his socks into it, and found a snake coiled up with a half-eaten mouse, right there in the middle of his clothes.'

'You must miss him still,' Ilse said.

'Every day. But I have been given another Piet, so like him that it often seems he has come back to us.'

'You have a wonderful, spirited daughter, too.' Ilse tilted her head a little, observing Suniva as she sat with her eyes screwed up, calculating the perspective and distance required in her drawing. 'You know, when I think about you and Lars, I feel like a real nobody. So dull.'

'What on earth does that mean?' Hannah was astonished. 'You have a successful husband, three great children, a beautiful house outside Copenhagen with a housekeeper, plus the dogs and cats, and two horses. It's a dream lifestyle.'

'Yes, but it's all very rigid. Shut in. And when I see your children here and at Langani, interested in everything they see, not needing to have amusements organised for them – even the games they play are their own imaginings – well, I wonder if our kids are not too inward-looking. I worry that they are already being herded into a much narrower way of seeing.'

'That's unlikely,' Hannah said reassuringly. 'You and Karl lead a varied life. You travel, you read, you're interested in all kinds of cultural things that don't exist in our children's world, out in the African *bundu*.'

'I suppose so. And maybe Karl is right – summer camp will be good for them. Away from the city. Away from me. He says I cling to them too much. Being on their own will make them more independent and exercise their minds better.' She sounded unsure.

'Children become self-reliant in their own time,' Hannah said. 'Suniva was fiercely independent from the beginning, and full of a mad kind of courage that gets her into all kinds of scrapes. Piet is gentler, less bold, more of a dreamer like my brother was. But he's only nine years old, and he runs around at Langani without being afraid of anything. I think he is doing fine.'

'I loved being at your farm.' Ilse's voice was wistful. 'I hope we can come back again, although it might just be me and the children. Karl has crossed Kenya off his checklist, now that he has seen it. He will move on to other things, but for me Langani was the experience I would most like to repeat. I wouldn't have the courage to live in Africa, though, or to face what you and Lars confront every day.'

'You never went to stay with your uncle when he was coffee farming in Kenya?'

'No.' Ilse smiled. 'That was something special for Lars, an adventure that my teenage brother had – I was totally excluded from those holidays. Anyway, I don't think our parents could have afforded to send two of us to Africa. In fact, I believe Uncle Per always paid for Lars to go to Kenya, and those visits shaped his life. Led him back to you, in the end. Strange, isn't it?'

'Strange and wonderful,' Hannah said. 'I owe your uncle a big debt, and I told him that many times before he left for Australia.'

They took their places at the table where Kirsten had set down bowls of shrimp along the centre, accompanied by loaves of crusty bread warm from the oven, with thick slabs of butter and cheese, and salads from her vegetable garden. Shafts of golden light filtered through the trees, illuminating the pleasure in their faces, turning the table into a hallowed place of friendship and joy.

'Stretch out, put your hands deep into the bowl and take a big fistful of shrimp onto your plate,' Lars said. 'Then the real work starts. But the reward is so good that you will never forget it as long as you live.' He tucked a napkin under his chin and plunged in with relish, scooping up the shrimp and demonstrating to the children how to peel them and to make the most of each morsel.

A sailing boat caught the breeze, tacking in close to the shore so that they could hear the creak of the sail being tightened, and the sound of the waves licking the hull. Hannah sat utterly still, her life taking on a dreamlike quality as she gazed around the table. The murmur of voices that she loved rose and fell and drifted around her, and everything she had ever said or done seemed to have led to the simple harmony of this moment. She closed her eyes and allowed the sensation to take hold of her, drawing the contentment into her deepest self so that she could store it there and return to it at will. Lars had been right to insist on making a real connection with his family, and to bring her to this other world for a short time. She turned to look at him, jubilant and laughing, and when he gazed back at her she felt that he knew everything in her heart.

They raised their glasses to Lars, brought out more food and wine from the house, and shared family stories in the pale, balmy evening. Even Karl softened a little after several shots of *heimbrent* and became a witty and clever raconteur, so that Hannah could see what might have attracted Ilse to him. But she did not think her sister-in-law was happy, and the realisation made her deeply thankful for her own good fortune.

'Now then,' Jorgen said, rising to his feet and reaching out to Piet and

Suniva. 'It is time to teach you a Norwegian dance for happy occasions. And everyone will join in.'

They held hands, Ilse and Lars singing out the old verses, Jorgen hopping like a young hare for all his big limbs and usually slow gait, coaxing every member of the family into the circle so that soon they were all following his movements, making their steps tighter and faster. Even Kirsten's arthritic form seemed to bend and sway, until they all finally collapsed onto the grass, singing the last of the chorus and laughing without a care in the world.

In the morning Hannah awoke to the sound of the children calling to each other outside. Lars was already up and she could hear him in the bathroom. She swung her feet out of bed and went to the window to take in the cool air. It would not stay like this for long. Each day had been hotter than the one before, and she needed to make sure that the children had sunhats and t-shirts for protection. Below her she saw Ilse and Suniva getting into the car and driving away, presumably to run an errand in the village. There was no sign of Piet, but he had taken to having an early breakfast with Jorgen and then setting out with his grandfather on the morning rounds of the farm.

'It seems we're all alone, Lars,' she called out. 'Are we having breakfast here or with your mother?'

He emerged from the bathroom and grabbed her, tumbling her onto the bed.

'Hannah,' he whispered holding the soft weight of her breast in his hand, kissing her throat. 'I love you so much. Han, let's make a baby. Let's make a little Norwegian baby.'

She pulled away to look at him and to put her hands on his face, kissing him and making love to him with a passion that mirrored the first time they had found each other. Afterwards, as they lay holding each other, Hannah smiled to herself, certain that she had conceived a child.

'You're not safe without your children around to protect you,' he said at last, brushing his lips over her sunburned shoulders. 'But you can let down your guard for now, because I am starving beyond words.'

They found Karl at the main house, drinking coffee. 'I have received a call from my office that means I should go back today,' he said. 'Ilse will stay, though. She can follow at the weekend, so she will be home when the children get back from camp.'

Hannah glanced at Lars and saw that he was pleased with the news. His sister was always more relaxed and spontaneous when Karl was not around, and so were his parents.

'I saw Ilse and Suniva going off somewhere in the car,' she said.

'Oh, yes.' Karl's semi-permanent frown appeared. 'She is a persistent child, your daughter.'

'Meaning?' Hannah did not like his tone. It held no hint of teasing or amusement.

'She has been pestering Ilse since yesterday and this morning she wanted to drive to the post office and buy stamps. Insisted it was urgent. A nuisance, really, because I can't leave until they come back.'

'Stamps?' Hannah was puzzled. 'Whatever for? Anyway, I'm sure they won't be long if they know you are anxious to be on your way.'

'She wanted to send some drawings and postcards to her little black friend,' Karl said. 'The orphan you took in.'

'To James?' Hannah was even more surprised.

'A risky idea, trying to bridge the gap between black and white, and the contrast between their primitive society and ours. But I applaud your principles. Where is the boy now?'

'He's at Langani,' Hannah said. 'Doing just fine.'

'Well, at least you didn't bring him over here,' Karl said with a smirk. 'Can you imagine the reaction of the people in this area, if Lars had turned up with some darkie child. That would have set tongues wagging.' His laugh was derisive.

Hannah threw him a look of wordless fury and left the room. She returned to the *stabbur* and made the children's beds and her own, swept the living area and dusted surfaces that were already clean until her anger had subsided. Then she sat down and made coffee that she was drinking when Suniva returned.

'Where have you been?' Hannah said. 'I hear you were badgering Ilse to take you into the village. That's not nice, Suniva. And what did you need from there, anyway?'

'Some stamps.'

'What for? And why right now?'

'Because I've run out, and I wanted to post my drawings and a card to James.'

'I see,' Hannah said. 'Well, you could have bought them next time Grandma was going to the store.'

'No. He'll be waiting. Because I have been sending him cards almost every day, from London and from here. If I hadn't bought more stamps today he would think I've forgotten.'

'Where did you get the stamps and the cards in London?'

'From Camilla. She helped me to choose the best pictures. She said James could share our holiday if I wrote to him every day, and told him about the places we had seen. And then he wouldn't be lonely. So we bought the cards and everything together. And Grandma helped me find some here.'

'I see,' said Hannah, again. 'I hope you thanked Ilse properly for this morning.'

'Of course I did.' Suniva was defensive, but not about Ilse. She was aware that her mother was annoyed. Angry even, although she was trying to hide it. Camilla had told her it was wrong to keep the postcards a secret, but she wanted it to be something that was her own. She stood pouting for a moment, looking into the distance. 'Can I go now?'

'I suggest you see if Grandma Kirsten needs help with anything. If not then maybe we can find your father, when Karl has gone, and take the boat out.'

'Yes!'

Suniva was skipping, smiling, already running out of the room and across the grass before Hannah had time to analyse her own disquiet. But what was there to be anxious about? Suniva had sent cards to James because she missed him. Still, she was disappointed that she had not known about it, and annoyed that Camilla had made it into a kind of secret. She sighed, stood up and went in search of her husband. The one constant in her life, the rock upon which she built her days. Lifting a hand to toss her long braid over her shoulder, she put Suniva and James out of her mind.

Karl was standing beside the car. He shook Lars's hand and gestured to Hannah.

'Suniva! Piet! Come and say goodbye to your Uncle Karl,' Hannah called out.

'Don't worry about the children,' Karl said. 'It's not necessary to interrupt their game, and saying goodbye to me would have little meaning for them.' He turned to Lars. 'I hope you'll consider what I've said to you. Discuss it with your wife.' His voice held a note of concern that Hannah thought uncharacteristic, and she felt a sense of alarm. Then he was gone.

'What were you talking about with Karl?' She looked at Lars and was surprised by his grave expression.

'I don't think . . . No, I can't believe . . .' He trailed off and then changed his mind. 'There's only one way to say this, Han. Karl asked me if Piet could have sustained hearing loss as a result of these ear infections.'

'Hearing loss?'

'He thinks Piet might not be responding to questions, or coming when he's called, because he can't hear us.'

'That's not possible,' Hannah said. 'He doesn't always ignore us. And he's even speaking Norwegian with Jorgen and Kirsten.'

'With Jorgen, *ja*. But Father's voice is loud because he is deaf himself. We've never thought about it, Han, but it is possible. Piet can't be entirely deaf, it's true. But he could have some hearing problems.'

'Have you mentioned this to Jorgen?' Hannah sat down on the wooden bench outside the front door. The sun was pouring down on her, but she felt cold.

'He was there when Karl brought it up,' Lars said. 'And he said that Mother had also noticed it, but he had told her she was being foolish.'

'My God. Oh, my God, our little boy. My Piet.' Her eyes were full of tears. 'How come I didn't notice it myself, Lars? I can't believe it.'

'He has been complaining about noises in his head,' Lars said. 'But I thought he was imagining them – like the trolls he has mentioned.'

'If it is at all likely, then we must get him tested as soon as we arrive home.' Hannah brushed tears away.

'Maybe we should do that now.'

'But then we would have to take him to Trondheim to see a specialist we don't know. Maybe someone who doesn't speak English.'

'Most specialists here speak English,' Lars said. 'But we could start by going back to Dr Petersen. He has known our family for years, and he is a fine, reliable man. He could take another look at Piet's ears.'

'Yes. Let's start here, instead of frightening him by going to see a stranger in a big city. Then, if anything is wrong we can decide what to do and where. It would be better to know if we have really missed the signs. Oh, God, Lars, I hope it isn't so.'

'I hope so too. But if Piet does have a problem, then he must have all the help we can give him. I'll telephone and set up an appointment for tomorrow.' He held out his hand and she rose to her feet. 'Let's find the children and Ilse, and I will take them for a walk, up to the source of the waterfall. Maybe Father is not busy and he will come too.'

'I'll join you,' Hannah said. She did not want to be left alone with Kirsten, now that the subject of Piet's hearing had been raised. There was no point in gloomy surmise. Time and expertise would reveal the truth of the matter.

They set out together, puffing and panting as the track grew steeper and more rocky. Ahead of her, Hannah noticed that Piet clung to his grandfather's hand, but there was nothing in his manner or action to suggest that the boy was unaware of what was being said. She stepped up her pace and caught up with them.

'Don't worry,' Jorgen said gently. 'I will be extra careful with him. We will be prudent all the way up and back, and he will know from me what is right and what is dangerous.'

She smiled tremulously at him and nodded her head, unable to speak. But when they reached the place where the water rushed out of the rocks to fall in a torrent onto the stream below, she wondered whether Piet could hear the sound. And she was too afraid to ask.

In the small surgery, Dr Petersen examined Piet's ears once more, smiling at him, making small jokes in halting English, noting the boy's slow response. Finally he offered his opinion.

'Your son needs to see a specialist,' he said. 'He still has the perforation in one eardrum, and in my view there is hearing loss in both ears, due to a series of infections. Also he has ringing sounds in his head. Tinnitus, it is called. You must keep the ears dry and continue with the antibiotic drops. It is vital that you avoid another infection, and you should have him examined again soon.'

'How soon?' Hannah looked at him with fear-filled eyes. 'Does he need to see someone here? Right away?'

'I think time is too short now, unless you decide to stay on and have him treated here. But that could take several months, and Lars tells me that you still have good doctors in Africa.' Dr Petersen's smile was kind. 'So it is probably best to go home where you will all be in familiar surroundings. Don't worry too much – there are many solutions for such things. For now, the best thing is to keep the child cheerful, and to enjoy the rest of your stay with Jorgen.'

Two days later Ilse left them, full of regret when she sought out Hannah to say goodbye.

'I always feel good here,' she said. 'So much at peace.' She lowered her voice and her hand fastened around Hannah's arm with a sense of desperation. 'The truth is, I don't really want to go home at all. Of course I'm longing to see the children tomorrow, but Karl makes me feel stupid. Inept. He's very clever in his business, and he has a much broader view of the world than I do. We have dinner parties where there are discussions that make me feel provincial and ignorant, even though I try to read all the papers and some of his books. Understand world issues and the stock markets and so on. But I don't think I'm very successful at it.'

'Ilse, you are the warmest wife and mother. I'm sure he knows that, and your friends all know it too. There is nothing more important at the centre of your home than plain, old-fashioned love.'

'I think he is disappointed in me, really,' Ilse said. 'Sometimes I wonder if I would be able to go on if we did not have the children to share. And he is wrong about their being better off at summer camp. They love it here and so do I. It is the place where we can all be light-hearted. Where I can be myself, laugh out loud and sing, and enjoy playing games with them.'

'Karl is a lucky man,' Hannah said. 'You mustn't let anyone make you think otherwise.'

'Thank you,' Ilse said. 'I'm so happy for you and Lars, still crazy about each other. And a little envious too.'

'I'm grateful every day that he chose me,' Hannah said. 'I shouldn't have waited so long to see the other part of his life, but being here together with the children will bring us even closer.'

'So, tell me,' Ilse said, leaning forward, almost whispering. 'What has he decided?'

'Decided?'

'About Father's offer for you to take over the farm.' She stepped back, seeing too late the blank expression on Hannah's face. 'Oh God! You didn't know – I'm sorry, Hannah. I assumed he had told you. That you'd talked about it. But you probably haven't had time.'

'No. We haven't had time.' Hannah could feel the pulse jumping in her throat as her breathing turned shallow with dread.

'You must have noticed how frail they are getting, our parents. Mother especially. And Karl would never live here. So they asked Lars to think about coming back to Norway. Kenya is so uncertain now, for all of you. More dangerous and difficult, and maybe no longer ideal for bringing up and educating the children.' She hesitated. 'Especially if Piet has a problem. So they thought you might like to take over this place. Father wants to give you the farm.'

'I don't think that is a possibility,' Hannah said, fighting every impulse in her body to scream out her shock. 'We would never consider leaving Langani.'

'I knew you would feel like that,' Ilse said. 'And I can understand it perfectly. Please don't mention to Lars that I told you. He has obviously put it aside as not being practical, otherwise he would have talked to you about it. Goodbye, dearest Hannah. Keep in touch, won't you? Your friendship means a lot to me.'

'How could you have discussed it with Jorgen and Kirsten, or imagined us ever living here? And how come even Ilse knew, and I was the only one left out? By all of you!'

'It wasn't like that,' Lars said patiently.

'I always believed you were completely open with me. And now I find you have been talking about rearranging our entire lives behind my back. I suppose Karl was there too, that repulsive, pompous little man. I don't know why Ilse stays with him, I really don't.'

'He wasn't there,' Lars said, his voice sounding less conciliatory. 'Calm down, Hannah. We have—'

'How could we live here, on this tiny farm with your parents?' Panic rose in her, creating a volatile mix with anger. 'It's dark for half the year, for God's sake. What on earth would we do all day? What would I do? I can't believe you talked to them about abandoning Langani. The place where we have always been together.'

'Hannah, you're going completely overboard. Calm down. You're shouting.'

'I don't give a damn if I'm shouting,' she yelled. 'You had no right to keep this from me. No right at all.'

'I haven't given them any indication that we would be willing or able to take over this farm,' Lars said. 'It is a simple hope that they had, that's all. This property has been in my family for generations like Langani has been in yours, and they would love to see it stay that way when they can no longer manage it. They want to give it to us because it seems more secure, from their point of view. And Ilse is not in a position to help them out, as you can see.'

'I don't want to hear any more about this,' Hannah said. 'We have a few days of our holiday left and I will make the best of it for the children. But what I want most of all is to go home.'

'Han, they simply asked me if we would ever consider—'

'Never!' Hannah spat out the word. 'Langani is my birthplace and our childrens' birthplace. My heritage and theirs. I thought we both felt the same way about that, and now I have discovered that you talked about abandoning our home and our country, and you never even thought I should be consulted.'

'That's not true.'

'It is true!' She slammed her fist on the table, wincing at the self-inflicted pain. 'You talked to your parents and your sister about it. But not to me. Not to your wife. Well, I'll tell you something, Lars, in case this subject ever comes up again. Langani is my home and I will never, ever leave it. Not until the day I'm carried out of there, feet first, in a box.'

Chapter 5

'Rabindrah — you're home early.' Sarah looked up from a spread of photographs on her desk. 'What's the news?'

'Nothing special. Unless you count corruption, land grabbing by politicians, funds earmarked for various developments that have mysteriously disappeared, tucked away in private bank accounts by helpful Swiss bankers.'

'Isn't there anything cheerful at all?' She bent over one of the prints, peering through a magnifying glass at some detail that only a perfectionist would have noticed.

'Here's today's paper. The horoscope might be your best bet. Can I get you something?' He kissed her lightly, gestured to the drinks tray and poured himself a whisky and soda.

'I'll have my usual, please.' Sarah gathered up her prints into a pile, and accepted a gin and tonic.

'There was one thing, though. Gordon gave me this.' Rabindrah reached into his briefcase and took out a copy of the *Daily Mirror*.

'Oh Lord!' Sarah stared at the picture of Camilla and Tom. 'I wonder if Anthony has seen this?'

'He's on safari. Won't be back for a while.'

'Perhaps she has finally given up on him and thrown in her lot with Tom.' Sarah crumpled the paper and threw it into the bin. 'And who could blame her?'

'Tom is a good friend. Successful and amusing and clever,' Rabindrah said. 'But I don't think he has ever read a book in his life, whereas she gobbles up two or three a week, no matter what else she's doing. And he isn't comfortable unless he is in the big city, so she would have to leave Kenya and base herself permanently in London. I can't see her doing that.'

'No. This is still home for her,' Sarah said. 'She has spent more time away recently, but I think that is because it hurts when she sees Anthony too often. She is blissfully happy when he takes her out on safari with him, but afterwards it's hard for her to accept that nothing has changed between them.'

'Half of his clients want to go home and brag that the most glamorous girl in the world was in camp with them,' Rabindrah pointed out. 'That's the real reason he asks her to join him in the *bundu*.'

'Oh, I think that's too harsh,' Sarah said. 'Anyway, it's not just Anthony who keeps her coming back here. She thinks of Hannah and me as her only family, and she really does love designing the clothes and accessories at Langani. That side of her work interests her far more than the thousands of factory-made dresses churned out in New York and London, with her name on the label.'

'At least they have made her independently rich,' Rabindrah said. 'So, how was your day?'

'I was on the radio to Allie this morning. She sounded pretty low. Bound to be, really. Next week will be the first anniversary of Dan's death.' She fell silent for a moment. The image of the friend and mentor who had been her first employer was vivid in her mind. 'I hate to think of her alone at such a sad time,' she said. 'I tried to persuade her to come here for a few days. Erope would keep things going for her, but she wouldn't budge. She was adamant.'

'Poor Allie,' he said with compassion. 'Isn't her nephew supposed to be flying out from Scotland to work with her?'

'Hugo. Yes, he is. When, and if, his work permit is approved.' She hesitated. 'I wondered if we could go to the Mara since she won't come up here. Couldn't you take a few days off? Do an article on her cheetah research? I think we should cover the subject. Perhaps we could even turn it into a book. Together.'

'I don't know if I can find the time to –'

'It would be like a fresh start. Full circle, almost.' She stood up and slid her arms around his waist. 'Our first joint assignment was the book on Dan and Allie's elephant project. This new one would be a tribute to Allie's courage, facing up to her loss by starting out on something different. And cheetahs make superb photographic material.'

He disengaged himself and went to stand by the fire.

'We've had a bad year.' She pressed him for an answer. 'A lot of that was my fault and I'm sorry. I couldn't deal with — you know. I think I went a bit mad. I had invested so much hope in that second pregnancy, and when I lost the baby — Well, I couldn't cope. I didn't want to keep brooding over it, but I wasn't able to stop.' She sat down again and dropped her head into her hands. 'I wanted so much to hold our child. But he was dead.'

'He was dead for me, too.'

'I understand, now, how those poor women who steal someone else's baby can be driven to such extremes.' Sarah went on, heedless of the despair in Rabindrah's words, talking almost to herself. 'It's a sort of insanity, and I couldn't escape from my particular version of it. Even though it was unfair, because you were grieving too and I shut you out. I lost sight of the good things in our lives.' She was threatened by tears and swallowed them, knowing how much he dreaded seeing her cry. 'Since it happened, we seem to be living separate existences. We must find our way back to what we had. Working on a new book together could be the opportunity we both need. And we would be doing something for Allie at the same time. Raising interest in her research, getting more financial backing for her. We could donate a percentage of the sales to her project, as we did with the elephant book. Your text, my pictures. That has always been a great combination.' She laughed shakily. 'How could we lose?'

Rabindrah was moved by her honesty. He knew he was equally guilty of allowing the distances to open wider and wider between them, yet he had felt helpless to address the problem. And he understood what this apology had cost her.

'All right,' he said. 'We'll go and visit Allie. See if she would like us to write about her cheetahs. And if she agrees, we'll talk to John Sinclair about a new publishing deal. Maybe even go to London. He should be pleased to see us back in tandem.'

'We could go to London?' She seized on the idea, astonished and pleased. 'When?'

'Next month, perhaps. I haven't taken a holiday since early last year and we both deserve the break. My parents would be glad to see us, and we could visit Lila in her Birmingham palace. And then go over to your family in Sligo. They have been complaining that we haven't paid them a visit for a long time. So, yes. Why not?'

Sarah jumped to her feet and hugged her husband.

'Brilliant! Thank you, thank you! A new book project for us, and a holiday as well? I'll get Allie on the radio right away.'

'Before I change my mind?' He was laughing at her excitement.

'Before Gordon Hedley sends you off on an investigation that takes you away for weeks – that's what!'

'I'm not the only one who goes away for weeks at a time,' he protested, a slight edge in his tone.

Sarah put a finger to his lips. 'No, you're not. But this time we are going together. And we can test drive the new Land Cruiser. Indar Uncle said he would have it ready this week.'

Sarah had taken Indar Singh's advice and bought the vehicle from him at a trade discount. It had been adapted for her photographic needs, with a custom-made metal frame added onto the superstructure to secure and support her cameras as she ploughed across rough terrain.

Four days later they set out at dawn, the car packed to capacity with supplies for the camp, spare parts for the generator which Allie had asked them to bring, and all Sarah's photographic equipment and rolls of film. The sun was already well up when they stopped at the top of the escarpment to gaze over the wide gash of the Rift Valley, stretching into the distance before them on its march down the continent all the way south to Mozambique. They joined heavily laden trucks, and buses overflowing with passengers, luggage and livestock, winding their way slowly down the steep road to the valley floor. When they turned off the tarmac towards Narok the huge open plains spread out before them, dotted for miles with the spiky covering of whistling thorns, and broken by the rearing silhouettes of volcanic cones. Plains game grazed the landscape in the company of the Maasai and their bony cattle. The air was filled with the swirl of dust mixed with sunlight to form a smoking orange haze, punctured here and there by the vivid red of a herdsman's *shuka*, the black curl of an ostrich plume, the sharp stripe of zebra flanks, and stretching up towards the thinner, whiter light, the long paved necks of giraffe.

'There is nothing so glorious as this on all the earth, is there?' Sarah gave a sigh of pure joy. 'No matter how much time I spend in the bush, the spell never loses its potency. To smell the dust and feel the heat, and see all the colours and shapes and textures. We are so lucky to be a part of this life, on this day, in this landscape.' She reached out and closed her hand over his brown fingers on the steering wheel.

'You're deeply philosophical today.' He grinned at her. 'Happy, too.'

'Truly happy. I always feel lighter, freer, away from Nairobi. I wish we could stay out here all the time, but I know you need to be close to your work. For now, though, I have you all to myself.'

They stopped for a picnic under an acacia tree. Sitting in the shade with their backs against its rough trunk they ate their sandwiches and opened the thermos of coffee, watching the distant spirals of a group of vultures circling a predator's kill. A secretary bird stalked importantly across the stubbled ground in front of them, pausing to pick up whatever insects presented themselves in his path. In the lacy crown of the tree, cicadas were busy with their raucous noonday buzz, and a blue and orange lizard lay sunning itself on a nearby rock, eyes closed, breath fanning in and out of its garish gullet. Sarah closed her eyes and listened to the sounds of the bush around her. She had to try and move on with her life, but she recognised there were dreams she would have to abandon, if they were to keep their marriage alive.

'I'm going to live for now,' she said, aloud. 'I made up my mind while I was up in Turkana that I would make a new start. We haven't made love since we lost the baby. But there is so much for us to share, and we'll be all right, won't we?' She needed his understanding. 'Even if we never have a child, we have each other. That's enough, isn't it?'

There was no response and she bent forward to search his face. He was leaning back against the tree, legs stretched out, head drooping. His eyes were closed. Sarah wondered when he had dropped off, and whether he had heard anything she had said. These things were so hard to express, and he hadn't even been listening. But they had been up before dawn, and he had done all the driving so far. He was bound to be tired. There were lines of weariness on his face that she had not noticed before, and he looked vulnerable sitting there in the sun, asleep. His half-empty thermos cup had slid onto the ground, and she watched a green lizard shimmy up to investigate the contents, its bulging eyes swivelling towards her, its tongue flickering out at the dark, sweet liquid. She sat very still beside her husband, not wanting to disturb him, content to be travelling in his company.

At Narok, they stopped at a *duka* and bought cold drinks from the rusting fridge, before starting out along the rough road into the northern Mara, bouncing into potholes concealed by thick layers of dust, trying to maintain a steady pace over the bone-rattling, corrugated surface. The heat raised a series of mirages over the shimmer of tall grass, and the glare was intense. Sarah had taken the wheel, and Rabindrah dozed fitfully. The ground began to rise again, and the bush closed in on them in a series of wooded hills. They crawled upwards on a twisting road, winding through dense trees, until they came at last to the final, open plateau. Standing on the horizon was the blue outline of the Siria escarpment, and the far-away humps of the Ngama Hills. Ahead of them, the golden grasslands rolled away as far as the eye could see. On either side of the Land Cruiser thousands of wildebeest marched along the primeval route of their annual migration, herds of zebra and smaller groups of gazelle on the outer flanks of the slow-moving columns.

Sarah turned off the car engine beside a balanites tree, its cascade of thorny branches bearing small globes of green fruit, limbs stretching over the vehicle to provide the only shade for miles around. She jumped down, stiff from the drive, and stood in its dappled shelter, raising her arms high above her head in a gesture of greeting.

'Wake up, Rabindrah!' she called out, gazing down on the dark mass of migrating herds and the boundless landscape. 'Look at this. The marvel of all those animals, treading a path that goes further back in time than anyone knows, starting out on a journey that many of them will never complete. It makes my spine tingle. Get out the other thermos, will you? I could murder a cup of tea right now.'

She already had her camera in operation when he clambered out of the vehicle and handed her a cup. She took it gratefully. 'What a place! I'm looking forward to spending time here again.'

They stood drinking their tea and sharing a packet of biscuits, surveying the vast bowl spread out before them, dotted with termite mounds on which the topi liked to stand watch over their surroundings. Here and there the branching candelabra of a euphorbia rose out of the yellow grasslands, isolated sentinels of the savannah under whose shadow groups of wildebeest crowded together to escape the pitiless eye of the sun.

'On the home run,' Sarah said, as they started out again.

This time Rabindrah was at the wheel. They followed the band of forest along the course of the Mara River as it scythed through the land, to meander into the Serengeti Plains of neighbouring Tanzania.

Allie had chosen the north-eastern section for her research camp, a place of wooded parkland and open plains. She considered it the best habitat for cheetah because there were fewer lions and hyenas, the most dangerous enemies to stalk her subjects and steal their food. Turning off a narrow track into a stand of umbrella thorns, fig trees and African olives, they came at last to Allie's compound. The camp was made up of a series of tents on a sandy cliff overlooking a bend in the Talek River. A thorn hedge surrounded the small, shady clearing and when Sarah switched off the engine, she and Rabindrah sat still for a moment, listening to the whistle and chat of birds and the snorting of hippo in the water below. At the sound of the car, Allie emerged from the mess tent to welcome them.

'Come and sit down,' she said. 'You must be tired and thirsty. Did you have an early start?'

'Five-thirty.' Sarah hugged her fiercely. 'It's a long haul, and the roads are getting worse and worse. The new car is excellent though, and we have everything you asked for. The place already looks like home, Allie.'

She stepped back to examine her friend, concerned at how thin she had become. Allie Briggs had always been small and wiry, but now Sarah noted how drawn she was. Her khaki trousers and bush shirt looked too large, a canvas belt pulling in overlapping inches of waistband. Her thick hair had been tied back with a scarf, and buried under an old bush hat. It was a size too big for her, and Sarah recognised it as the one Dan had always worn. She remembered Allie chiding her husband, telling him that it was time to get rid of the battered old thing, but he had insisted that it was his best protection from the sun and too comfortable to let go. Sarah had a vision of him, lying where he had been thrown from the Land Rover, his life seeping away into the African earth, and she shivered. He had probably been wearing that hat when he died and now it was Allie's last link to him, the scent and feel of it a continual reminder of his presence.

The section of the mess tent used as a work space still held the long table that Sarah remembered from their base at Buffalo Springs. It was covered in charts, files and maps, and haphazard piles of notebooks. Dan's battered typewriter sat in the centre of the chaos, a lonely page of white paper sticking up crookedly from its carriage like a flag of truce on a battlefield.

A voice hailed her, and Sarah turned to see Erope, her research partner from the days when she had worked on the Briggs's elephant research project up at Buffalo Springs. The tall, graceful Samburu greeted them both with a wide smile and they repaired to the main tent and sat down together, much as they had done in the past at the close of a day's work, to compare notes and observations over a cold beer. Soon they were deep in discussion about Allie's project and objectives, and the problems that had arisen since she had set up her new camp.

'We've had encouragement from park officials, and the Ministry of Wildlife and Tourism for the work we want to do,' Allie said. 'However, they have no funding, in spite of the fees tourists pay to visit the area. I'm afraid most of the revenue is gobbled up by greedy officials in Narok, and that includes some of the Maasai elders.'

'Where are you finding the money to keep the project going?' Sarah asked.

'I still have some of the start-up grant from the African Wildlife Foundation, but that won't last much longer. Dan and I had a small house in the States, and I sold it. I figured I was never likely to go and live there, even if I were to leave Africa one day, which I hope will never happen.'

'You're a fixture, Allie. The work you do here will always be needed,' Rabindrah said.

'Mmnn. Perhaps. Anyway, I do have family with a place outside Glasgow, and a small house on the heavenly island of Lismore. So I could throw myself on the mercy of my brother in my old age and decrepitude, if I wound up really desperate.' She smiled, a little uncertain. 'No seriously, they were so kind, wanting me to go back and stay with them, after . . .' She paused for a second, as if to gather strength to say her husband's name. 'After Dan's accident. And it was lovely, for a few weeks. But I couldn't live there permanently. So the sale of the American house helps to keep me going, although it won't last long if I have to rely on it as my sole means of support. I've put in for grants from the usual foundations and got some positive reaction, but nothing concrete yet. It all takes time.'

'We have a few ideas on that subject which we can talk about while we're here,' Rabindrah said. 'It must be an interesting challenge, studying a new species.'

'Dan's old format works well. I still use his system of identifying individual and family groups, their preferred habitat, and feeding patterns. But now we are dealing with carnivores whose hunting methods and social structures are completely unlike the elephant herds. There are less than one hundred cheetah in the Mara. They can be hard to find, so we are still at the basic stage of counting and measuring the extent of each group's territory. The steady drop in population over the last few years will be one of the main themes of this study. What are the causes – destruction of habitat, poaching, other predators? And moving on from there, what is the most practical form of conservation that can be put into place, to protect them. There is more than enough for Erope and me to deal with.'

'How is your family, Erope?' Sarah asked, remembering her visits to his *manyatta* in Samburu country.

'They are well.' There was no mistaking his pride. 'My boys are going to school now, so they are staying in Buffalo Springs with their mother, and helping her to look after the cattle and goats. It is better for them to be with my clan.'

'And how do you like returning to the world of research?' Rabindrah asked.

'I am glad to be with Allie again,' Erope said, his smile wide. 'I worked with the Game Department for a time, but there is much dishonesty. Too many lazy people, too much corruption. I became tired of it. So when Allie told me she was going to start a new study and she needed an assistant, it was not a difficult choice.'

'This man has been my salvation,' Allie said. 'I could never have put my camp together without his help. And Anthony makes a point of dropping in when he has interesting clients. He is always good company and he also invites Erope and me over for lunch or dinner in his camp, when he's around. A couple of his safari guests have given donations to my project. He's shameless when he wants to extract money out of them, full of charm and enthusiasm that are irresistible. His arrival is always a welcome diversion for Erope and me. One can become a little tired of listening to the hippos and hyenas tuning up every evening.'

'He runs a wonderful camp,' Sarah said. 'And I'm delighted he still steers some of his well-heeled travellers into parting with cash for your cheetahs. Like the elephants were beneficiaries while you were in Buffalo Springs.'

'Tell me about Camilla,' Allie said. 'She has been here with him a couple of times, but otherwise he only mentions her in passing. What's going on there? And what about Hannah and the family? It must have been fun for them to be in London.'

'None of us can figure out the state of play between Anthony and Camilla, but I'm inclined to think she still carries a torch for him although he seems blind to it,' Sarah said. 'There was a picture in the *Daily Mirror* recently, with Tom Bartlett kissing Camilla. I don't know whether Anthony saw it, or whether it would mean anything if he did. Meantime I've spoken to Hannah briefly on the telephone. They had a marvellous time in London and now they are in Norway.'

'It's good for Hannah to be exposed to such a different way of life,' Allie said. 'Change clears the cobwebs out of our brains. Makes us challenge ourselves, whether we like it or not.'

'Has it been hard to begin again from scratch?' It was Sarah who asked the question.

'It was difficult, at the start, but I couldn't have stayed in Buffalo Springs,' Allie said. 'Cheetahs have always been my favourite of the big cats. Lions and leopards are magnificent, but there's something about the cheetah that appeals to me. They have such grace. And a long, fascinating history – they are actually the oldest of all the big cat species, and yet they're gentler. You never hear of cheetah stalking and killing humans. Not like lions and leopards. They've lived alongside mankind very successfully over the centuries.'

'We have friends who keep a couple of tame cheetahs outside of Nairobi. In a huge garden, with a wire enclosure for night-time,' Rabindrah said. 'It's still not something I would care to do, though.'

'Cheetahs were kept as hunting companions at the time of the early Sumerians, and the Pharaohs,' Allie said. 'I often thought that I'd like to study them, but Dan was completely immersed in his elephants.' She stopped.

'Then he must be glad to see you fulfilling that dream.' Sarah stood up, seeing the tightening around Allie's eyes. 'Why don't we go and look for some of your protégées.'

Allie took up the offer with gratitude and they walked out into the sunshine and moved through the camp, delighted to see Ahmed, the cook, whose ability with a primus stove and an oven made from an old kerosene *debbi* had never ceased to astonish Sarah.

'I realised I couldn't do without Ahmed,' Allie said. 'Boiling an egg is a challenge for me, and I'm old enough to know that cooking will never be one of my strengths. I could do with a mechanic, though. If we'd had one at Buffalo Springs, Dan might never have—'

'It was an accident, Allie,' Rabindrah said with quiet insistence. 'Nothing to do with mechanics. A tragic accident that no one could have prevented.'

'I know, I know. In the back of my head I realise it, but there's always that awful sense of "if only". If I'd stopped him going out that day, or gone with him. Or if I'd set out to look for him sooner . . .'

'It was a terrible thing.' Sarah shuddered, thinking of the old vehicle sliding out of control, hurtling down the slope of the *lugga*, imagining Dan's body thrown against the rocks. 'I know how you feel. That's why we came.'

'I reckoned I would be better off alone today, but I'm glad you're here. Thank you.' Allie searched in her pocket for a handkerchief. 'I'm sorry. I'll be all right in a minute. Why don't we take your new car, Sarah? Erope and I have been following a mother with three cubs, and we might get a glimpse of them if we go soon.'

They left the camp in the new Toyota, with Sarah eager to test the camera platform Indar had constructed for her. All around them the long lines of the migration marched in slow procession, winding their way across the savannah, stopping to graze or to wait for their calves to catch them up. Alongside the thousands of wildebeest were groups of plump, glossy zebra, and Thomson's gazelle. In the distance a herd of buffalo snorted and jostled for position near a patch of muddy water. They drove up a gentle incline and came to a halt.

'There,' Erope said.

A grassy hummock rose out of the plain to their left. Sitting on it, enjoying a perfect vantage point from which to track game and watch for enemies, was the sleek, elegant outline of a female cheetah. They edged the car slowly towards her so that she would not be spooked by their presence, and disappear. The evening sun had set her gold, spotted fur into a fiery nimbus, and her long tail flicked idly to and fro as she watched a herd of Thomson's gazelle moving in her direction, unaware of her presence. There was a sudden movement in the thick grass below her, and a cub pounced on the swinging tail. Through her telephoto lens, Sarah could see two more cubs, rolling and jumping over one another in a mock battle.

'This is Lara.' Allie's voice was a light whisper. 'She had five cubs initially, but there's a high mortality rate among litters because the mother often has to leave her young to go hunting. She moves them from one den to another constantly, to keep predators off the scent. But ninety per cent of them don't survive those first weeks.'

'When can they start hunting themselves?' Rabindrah asked.

'They follow their mother from the time they are about six weeks old,' Erope said. 'Watching and learning from everything she does.'

'Lara has been hiding out in that wooded area to the west,' Allie said. 'There's plenty of small game around here, so she hasn't had to travel too far afield in search of food.'

Lara had selected her target for the evening. Her eyes narrowed, she slid down from her lookout, flattened herself, and began to glide on her stomach through the long grass, towards the herd. Her cubs stopped rolling about and sat up, watching intently. A young gazelle had strayed to the edge of the group, oblivious to the imminent danger. Sarah and Rabindrah watched, spellbound, as the cheetah gathered herself for the rush. Suddenly, she burst from her hiding place at full speed, stampeding the herd, singling out her prey, careening across the last distance, jinking and turning on powerful paws with every move the gazelle made to escape. Dust rose in funnels with each twist and swing of her gallop. Legs stretching and bunching in great leaps, her whole body was airborne for seconds at a time. She used her muscular tail for balance as she launched herself at the fleeing victim, landing on its back with a thud, her jaws clamped on its neck. It went down in silent sacrifice, while the remainder of the herd fled, leaping over one another in panic. The cheetah crouched, panting, over her prize, gathering her strength again before lifting the gazelle and dragging it in the direction of the waiting cubs.

'She is at her most vulnerable right now,' Allie said. 'She has used up every bit of *nguvu* in her chase. If a hyena or a lion came after her at this moment, it could attack her and steal her prey. That would mean certain death for the cubs. Many cheetahs are lost to stronger predators, because of competition for food.'

The long, late shadows of the afternoon had mellowed the landscape as

Lara, her chest heaving from the effort, reached the cubs in safety. When Erope drove away the whole family was enjoying the kill, this time undisturbed.

Dinner that night was overshadowed by their shared grief for the loss of Dan. Sarah almost expected to see him leaning over the work table, studying his charts, humming under his breath *'There's a yellow rose in Texas that I am going to see.'* He never got any further than the first line, because he could not remember the rest, and neither could he sing. But it was a sign of contentment and deep interest in whatever he was working on, and she had loved his tuneless song. She could still visualise him, nursing his glass of whisky, seated in the old basket chair in the mess tent at Buffalo Springs, his long legs stretched out, bushy eyebrows moving up and down as he made his point in some discussion. She longed to hear his deep, gravelly voice with its American twang, teasing her, or describing some extraordinary experience from the life he had chosen. She missed his sharp wit and his quiet wisdom.

Allie picked at her food, and put away another vodka. She had not mentioned Dan since she sat down, but it was obvious where her thoughts lay. Finally, Sarah leaned across the table and placed a hand on hers.

'Allie, we came to share the anniversary of Dan's death. And we would like to express what we love and remember about him, if that's all right.'

Allie nodded, pressing her lips together, not trusting herself to speak.

'Dan's loss is tragic,' Sarah said. 'But we can still feel him here, in everything around us. The memories from your life together will always sustain you, and I know that he is sharing this new adventure with you. Revelling in every discovery you make. He left a legacy that can never be destroyed, and he could not have a better memorial than you. Now that you have weathered the first hard year, life will begin to get better. And we are all here to support you.'

'You both welcomed me to Buffalo Springs when I was an ignorant duffer.' Rabindrah's smile brought relief to the table. 'Your elephant research, and the book Sarah agreed to produce with me, changed my life. You and Dan gave me new inspiration, and you gave me my wife. So let us raise a glass to the man we all loved and admired. To Dan.'

'To Dan,' Sarah echoed.

'To my friend and teacher, Dan,' Erope said. 'A great man of the world and of our country. And to Allie who will continue his tradition.'

'You are the very best, you three.' Allie stood up to embrace the Samburu before putting her arms around Sarah and Rabindrah. 'Thank you for the love and loyalty you have shown me. And I can only wish you the happiness we had, Dan and I. It was a unique partnership. I have to hang on to that, and I will.'

It was an emotional speech for Allie, normally succinct and pithy, abrupt in her delivery, except when she was talking about her research. Sarah sat back nursing her drink, remembering the evening when the news of the accident had reached her. Dan had gone out with a new tracker that morning, to show him the territory. When a heavy downpour started, the river rose and the *luggas* filled with fast-flowing water, overturning the old Land Rover and sweeping it away. It was Erope who had found Dan, flung up on the edge of a bank with a broken neck and fractured skull. He had been killed instantly. Further down the watercourse the Land Rover lay submerged with the other man dead inside.

As soon as Rabindrah and Sarah heard the news they left for Samburu. By the time they arrived on the following day, the torrent had soaked into the thirsty soil and nothing of the flood remained. It was as if it had never happened, except for the carpet of feathery grass and small, yellow and purple flowers that covered the ground where the water had passed. A troop of gazelle and impala were making the most of the young shoots.

They buried Dan on a rise of ground, overlooking the wild open country. Erope's clan and other Samburu from nearby *manyattas* arrived, dressed in full warrior's regalia, walking alongside the Land Rover that carried his body, chanting and then leaping in traditional dance to pay tribute to the man they had loved and respected.

In the days following the accident Allie had gone about her usual tasks like an automaton, saying nothing, eating and sleeping little. It was Sarah who had telephoned Allie's brother in Scotland. Three days later Stuart Campbell flew in to Samburu, accompanied by his son Hugo. Rabindrah hitched a ride back to Nairobi with the pilot, leaving Sarah the car. Allie was grateful for her brother's presence, but she could not talk to him. She retired early on the evening of his arrival, although Sarah knew she would not be sleeping.

'I'd like to take her back with me,' Stuart said. 'I know she'd not want to leave Kenya for good but she might benefit from a period away, to help her come to terms with what has happened. And she has a very special regard for Hugo, here.'

'I'll be glad to take care of her in Scotland for as long as she would stay.' Hugo nodded, smiling. 'I don't have to go back to the States until October.'

'I didn't realise you lived in America,' Sarah said.

'I'm finishing my PhD. I'll be there until next summer. After that, I'd love to come back and stay with Allie for a while. I might be able to help with her research, if I could get a work permit.'

Sarah recalled Allie describing Hugo as her favourite nephew, saying that they had always been close. She had liked him at once. He was in his early thirties, an anthropologist with the stereotypical, absent-minded look of an academic. His tousled brown hair stood up in a crest on his head, and Allie remarked that it made him look a bit like a mouse bird. But there was a lot more to him. Although he was sensitive to his aunt's distress he was able to make her smile, and behind the horn-rimmed glasses his eyes were humorous and observant.

'Do you think you could try and persuade her, Sarah, to come back to Scotland for a time?' Hugo asked. 'Because my father hasn't been able to make any impression on her, and we don't think she should be here alone.'

'There's no reason why she shouldn't go,' Sarah said. 'The staff always manage the camp perfectly when she and Dan are away. I'll do my best to talk her into it.'

She would soon have to return to Nairobi herself, and she understood Allie's turmoil only too well. On the following afternoon Sarah drove her out to the grave.

'I think it would be good for you to go to Scotland, Allie. You wouldn't have to be away long and you need your family just now. You may not see them all that often, but they love you.' Sarah sat down on a boulder beside her friend. 'Do you remember how glad I was when my parents suddenly turned up here, after Piet's death? And how you and Dan told me I shouldn't hide away.'

'I suppose I could go for a short while.' Allie leaned against a tree. 'I'm so tired, but I can't sleep. When I close my eyes, I see him lying there in the dark.' Her hands clenched. 'It's stupid, but I feel I'd be abandoning him if I left here. He was my anchor and now I don't know where I belong any more. Although it's not in Scotland or Buffalo Springs. I don't want to carry on working here, but I can't think what else I could do.'

'That's why you need time to rest, and reflect. The staff will manage fine. They've all been with you for years, and they can contact me on the radio if there is a problem.' Sarah took her hands. 'Dan won't be alone – he is with you, wherever you go. In your heart and in your memory, just like Piet was for me. But right now, you need to be with people who care for you. Come on, Allie – what do you say?'

'For a short time, then,' Allie said, her voice ragged with exhaustion. 'I'll go for a while.'

In the end, she was away for a month, and when she came back, she had decided to leave Buffalo Springs and go to the Maasai Mara to study cheetah.

They sat late over dinner, opening a bottle of vintage port, reminiscing and laughing at the more outrageous and eccentric things Dan had done. Erope was the first to leave the group, taking Allie's small, weathered hands in his, speaking softly to her in Samburu before disappearing into the darkness. In the silence that followed, Rabindrah raised the prospect of a new book.

'I've discussed this with Gordon Hedley,' he said. 'He is prepared to give me time away from Nairobi over the next year, to do a series of articles for the paper about the Mara and its various inhabitants, with Sarah's pictures as the real selling point. So we could work together again. I also rang John Sinclair in London and he is interested in another coffee table book, if you are, Allie. On the same basis as last time. You get a percentage of the sales for your research fund.'

'What do you think?' Sarah's expression was keen. She wanted this assignment. Not only for Allie's sake, but for her own. 'It would be great for us all to work together again. I've missed that.'

'You don't have to make your mind up right away, although the next three seconds would do for Sarah, as you can see.' Rabindrah chuckled. 'But you might have other issues you want to consider, or someone else you'd like to discuss this with.'

'I don't need any discussion,' Allie said. 'The only question is when can you start?'

'I brought film with me. Just in case.' Sarah laughed out loud with excitement and pleasure. 'We have a week, to begin with. How does that sound? Can you put up with us so soon?'

'Erope and I will be ready at six tomorrow morning,' Allie said. 'It will be like old times.'

'And Dan will be with us all the way.' Sarah put her arms around Allie's slight frame. 'If we're going out first thing, I think we'd better hit the sack. That was a long journey today, and we could both do with some sleep.'

They walked across to their tent under the immensity of a star-laden sky, the rustle of nocturnal creatures all around them, and the hippos snorting as they made their way from the river to their night-time pastures. Sarah slid out of her clothes, and put her arms around her husband.

'Thank you,' she murmured, leaning her head against his shoulder.

'For what?' He touched her hair, but she could sense his distance.

'For coming here with me. For helping Allie.' She took his hands and placed them on her breasts, whispering into his ear. 'Come to bed, Rabindrah. Let's make love.'

'Isn't it a bit soon?' He drew away from her slightly.

'The doctor told us we could go back to a normal relationship,' she said. 'Ages ago. I'm not ill, you know. I had a miscarriage and I took the loss very badly, but I sorted it out in my mind while I was up in Turkana. Now I want us to go back to what we were. I need you. I want you to love me. No charts, no mucus levels, no temperature checks. Just you and me making love like we used to. It's not too soon for that.' She looked up into his face. 'Or is it that you feel it's too late?'

'Sarah.' He drew her close again. 'Be patient. Let's wait a little more.'

'But why should we?'

'No, listen.' He drew her to the narrow bed and sat down beside her, his words coming out with difficulty. 'I need you to understand how it is with me. For so long, before this miscarriage, I felt as if our lovemaking had been reduced to a scientific exercise that had almost nothing to do with love. All we had was ovulation tables and thermometers, and days and hours. We couldn't be spontaneous. It made me feel that I was only required for seed at optimum impregnation times.'

'Oh, no. No. It was never like that,' Sarah said, horrified by what he was saying.

'Yes, it was.' Rabindrah turned away to look out into the starlight. 'I felt my love for you was not enough. That you no longer cared about me for myself. I've wanted a child as much as you, but I couldn't go through these last months again. Your total devastation was frightening. The weeping, the days and days when you lay in bed, or sat around the house unable to get dressed, or speak, or do anything normal. If this is what trying to have babies is going to do to us . . .' He took her face in his hands. 'I can't live like that again. So we should take it slowly for now. Not rush each other. Enjoy being together and working on this book. I'm too tired tonight, anyway, after the long drive.'

'Of course. I understand. We have all the time in the world.'

She smiled at him, ran her hand across the raven black of his hair, the sharp planes of his face. But a great emptiness had opened inside her. She turned away to pull back the bedclothes and lie down, closing her eyes as she heard him get into the canvas bed opposite. His scent was still in her nostrils, and the abyss between them filled her with yearning and frustration.

They were up at dawn, when Ahmed brought early morning tea and filled the canvas wash basins with hot water, so that they could splash the sleep from their faces.

'This morning we will go to the river first,' Erope announced. 'The wildebeest have been gathering on the banks for two days. I think they will make a crossing although many will be lost to the crocodiles, or drowned. And later we will go to find the cheetahs.'

As the sun rose in a bleached morning sky they passed herds of plains game moving in slow columns, several abreast, towards a wide bend in the Mara River. Erope parked the vehicle on a rise close to the edge of the water where the wildebeest were massing in their thousands, ready to cross the brown and silver swirl, and to clamber up the steep verge on the other side. Zebra trotted back and forth along the sides of the phalanx, and the gazelle stood close by with twitching tails and soft, nervous eyes. Flocks of vultures gathered on the vantage points of the surrounding rocks, hunched in anticipation of a feast, squabbling over the bloated carcasses that were the unlucky remnants of yesterday's attempted odyssey. The sandy verge heaved with wildebeest, occasionally surging forward to the selected jumping off point, then retreating as the leaders baulked at the sight of the fast-flowing current, and the crocodiles half-submerged in the water or basking on the shore. At the rear of the waiting throng more animals continued to arrive, pressing forward, driving the head of the column closer to the edge of the bank. The air was loud with the lowing of the herds, calling to one another, snorting and pushing.

Finally, one wildebeest cow gathered enough courage to launch herself off the promontory into the murky water. It was the signal for chaos as the mass behind followed her, hooves thrashing, bearded heads vanishing below the surface only to appear again in the desperate struggle for survival. The river became a churning, plunging tangle of bodies, striving to stay afloat and to avoid being crushed under the weight of the horde. The current caught them as they leapt over one another in panic, and were pulled downstream into the waiting jaws of the crocodiles, to be dragged, flailing, to their deaths. The more nimble gazelles and sturdy zebras surged ahead to gain the far side. But the stampeding, desperate animals had turned the muddy slope into a steep and treacherous pathway on which many could find no purchase, so that they slid back into the river and disappeared.

As Sarah slotted a new roll of film into her camera a wildebeest calf jumped into the water after its mother, and vanished immediately beneath the choppy waves. With her lens trained on the young animal she saw him resurface, only to be pushed below again by the hooves of the frantic herd.

'This is unbearable,' she said, unable to take her eyes off the heaving frenzy below her, willing the small creature to safety. 'Come on, come on! Keep swimming!'

The twin prongs of his horns reappeared briefly in the moving tide, and Allie, Rabindrah and Erope were now following his progress. The current swept him away from the main body of the herd, giving him a better chance of staying afloat, but creating an even greater danger as a crocodile slithered into the river.

'No! No, look out!' Sarah could not prevent herself from calling out as her shutter clicked and whirred over and over, recording this final battle for survival.

The crocodile's jaws opened, ready to snap down on the legs of its prey, but with one final effort the calf sprang onto a rock and stumbled out of reach. The scaly predator sank back into the water and lay with his malevolent eyes breaking the surface, waiting for another meal to be swept into his open jaws. The calf's flanks were heaving with terror as he began to climb the slippery bank and move away from the river's edge, but this proved to be a new obstacle. The earth slid away under his hooves and he fell back several times, scrambling and sliding, bellowing for his mother. All around him was a seething mass of drenched animals, churning up the ground, jumping over one another, tumbling once more as they tried to reach the grassy plain from which they would continue their marathon journey.

'He's almost on dry ground,' Rabindrah said. 'But how will he survive alone?'

'It's amazing how the mother can identify her calf's cry, even in all this madness and noise,' said Allie. 'If she got across, they will find each other.'

Minutes later, a wildebeest cow appeared at the top of the slope. The calf redoubled his efforts, finally stumbling onto solid terrain to nudge his mother in greeting, before the two were swallowed up in the galloping herd.

'I'm completely exhausted!' Sarah put her camera down, weak with relief. 'I feel as if I swam that crossing myself. My pictures would have been useless without the tripod, because my hands were shaking so much.'

'He has reached the other side,' said Erope. 'But there will be many more dangers to follow. He is weak now, and the lions will be waiting.'

'What pandemonium, when the first animal went into the river,' Rabindrah said, gazing at the carnage below them. 'So many of them have perished, or were trampled by their own. I'm not sure I could watch that again.'

'There will always be casualties,' Allie said. 'But that mass of beasts, all crammed together, does keep the crocs at a distance, besides which they are stuffed to capacity from carrying off the ones that drown in the stampede. Let's move on. The lives of our cheetahs will seem pretty calm after that.'

They found Lara without difficulty, positioning themselves under a tree and sitting on the roof of the vehicle. The cubs made several forays from the undergrowth, to take a look at the stationary giant. Soon they were playing in its shade, wrestling and tumbling, and pouncing on one another, unfazed by the human presence that seemed to offer no threat. Lara kept a watchful eye on them, but she did not try to move them away.

Erope explained how to calculate their age from appearance and behaviour.

'Their coats are dark when they are born, so you cannot distinguish the spots at first. The long yellow-grey fur growing down their backs is called a mantle.'

'It protects them from bad weather,' Allie said. 'It also works as camouflage, when their mother has to leave them alone while they are so young.'

Later in the day they came across a pair of young males, about two years old. These two were still inept in their hunting methods, and it was poignant and funny to see their clumsy efforts at chasing down their prey.

'Their mother has left them, in order to breed again,' Allie explained. 'Up till a month ago, there were two female siblings with them. But once they became sexually mature, other dominant males moved in and chased these two laddies away. Brothers from the same litter remain together for life. The partnership helps them to hunt and defend each other from predators. Eventually they will claim territory from other males and find themselves mates.'

The sun began its fiery descent into the receiving plain, and with notebooks bulging, and several completed rolls of film, Erope turned the Toyota towards the camp. After dinner Rabindrah went to bed early, and Sarah and Allie sat out under the broad flysheet of the mess tent, sharing the night with the denizens of the bush.

'What's up?' Allie asked.

'What do you mean?'

'Come on, Sarah. I know you both so well. No eye contact, no physical contact. Something is amiss.' Sarah made a sound of protest, but Allie pressed on. 'I'm a professional at watching, my girl,' she said. 'You are gazing at your man like a lost puppy when you think his attention is elsewhere. And he's like a coiled spring. Have you had a row?'

'Not a row.' Sarah shook her head. Below them, in the river, the hippos snorted with derision at such a simple explanation. 'That would actually be easier to deal with.' She looked into the darkness, weighing her words. 'Allie, did you and Dan want children?' she said at last. 'I mean, was it that it just didn't happen, or did you decide not to?'

'Ah. I begin to see what this is all about.' Allie swirled the drink in her glass. 'Before I married Dan, he made it quite clear that he didn't want children. He felt that a child would change the whole structure of his life and interfere with his work. I was madly in love with him, and at the time I believed that it wouldn't matter. If I could have Dan, the life we shared would be enough.'

'And was it?'

'By and large, yes. There were enormous obstacles to overcome in getting the elephant research established. We had very little money and it all went straight into our work. But it was exciting, romantic. My parents came to visit, and they were horrified by our living conditions.'

'I remember Dan's story about your tent being knocked down by a passing jumbo,' Sarah said.

'We were living in a pretty flimsy structure where scorpions and snakes often invaded the darker corners, and hyenas or baboons stole our meagre supplies. My father gave me some money which was meant to go towards better quarters, but instead we got ourselves a slightly less beat-up Land Rover to follow the elephants. I can't remember ever being so happy.' She hesitated.

'And then?'

'I got broody. Dan insisted that it couldn't work, and I was afraid if I had a child I would ultimately have to make a choice between our marriage – this amazing partnership we had forged – or a baby that I might find myself bringing up alone. I didn't have that level of courage, or commitment to motherhood. So I chose what I already had.'

'Did you ever regret that decision?'

'Sometimes. My brother Stuart and his wife Maggie have five children. Each time I came back here after a holiday with them, I'd dream of what it would be like to have kids of my own.'

'But you didn't press Dan?'

'No.' Allie shrugged, and took a long swallow of her drink. 'There was one time though. I was in Scotland when the youngsters all got measles. Hugo, who was the youngest, had it worst. You met Hugo, last year, remember?'

Sarah nodded.

'He was only eight, and very, very sick. I sat up with him for several nights, to give Maggie a break. I held him, put calamine on the spots, tried to get him comfortable. And through him I really fell in love with the idea of being a mother, of nurturing a child. I found myself desperately longing for it. When I went back to Dan, we had a terrible row.'

'What happened?'

'He said I had to decide. Once and for all. He insisted that if I stayed with him and spent the rest of my life being resentful and angry, I would destroy everything we had. Make our lives hell. So I would have to give up the idea of a baby. Be gracious about it, or find something or someone else to satisfy my maternal cravings.'

'God! That was some ultimatum. Didn't you think of leaving, of finding someone else?'

Allie smiled. 'Funnily enough, that never occurred to me. He was always the one I wanted to spend the rest of my life with – even if he drove me mad at times.'

'So what did you do to get over it?'

'I suppose I made Hugo into a sort of surrogate son. The measles affected his eyesight, and left him with a weak chest, so he was kept out of school for a time. I used to send him letters and photographs about our research, and we kept in close contact all through his growing up. That's probably what launched him on his choice of career.'

'Why did I never meet him at Buffalo Springs, while I was working with you?' Sarah said.

'I wanted to bring him out during school holidays, but Dan vetoed it. He was adamant that he would not be responsible for a child, even on a temporary basis. I suppose he was afraid it would wreck the balance of our lives. Set me off again. It was his one truly blind spot. So I saw Hugo every time I visited Scotland. Maybe that's why I went. Then he left to study in America and we lost contact for a while. A young man, living an exciting new life. I told myself it was natural. But I was bereft. That was around the time I had my fling with Viktor.'

'I wonder what happened to Viktor,' Sarah said. 'Deported like that, with no warning. Hannah had a lucky escape, don't you think?'

'Totally unsuitable for anything but a brief, steamy affair, Viktor Szustak.' Allie nodded agreement. 'He made no secret of that, though. I had a genuinely compassionate letter from him after Dan died. He was in England somewhere, but I haven't heard from him since.'

'So, you and Dan. You were happy without children? Able to let it go?'

'We don't always get the things we hope for most, Sarah. But you both want children, don't you?'

'Yes. Yes, we do. But it hasn't happened – well no, that's not the whole story. I have been pregnant, Allie. Twice.'

'You were pregnant and never told us?'

'I lost the first one very early. But the second pregnancy lasted almost four months. I felt this incredible connection to the child, like a golden line joining us together. Rabindrah and I were so excited. Still, we'd lost the first baby, so we agreed we would wait till we were the full four months on, and well past the danger period, before telling anyone. Just in case. Then one night I woke up, bleeding and sweating. My lovely golden line had disappeared.' Her voice cracked with grief. 'I knew the baby was dead. All the light went out of my life.'

'Oh, Sarah. I'm so sorry. When was this? Why on earth didn't you tell me?'

'I didn't tell anyone. I couldn't talk about it, even to Rabindrah. I felt cursed. First Piet, and then both my babies. After the second miscarriage, the doctor said the foetus was malformed, that it would never have been viable. Nature's way of erasing a mistake. Such clinical terms for that little person I had longed for.'

'I wish I had known. Been able to help you.'

'It was not that long after Dan died and I felt you had enough grief of your own to contend with. When I came out of the hospital I couldn't function at all. Some days I didn't even get out of bed and I couldn't bear the thought of intimacy. It seemed a mockery of all our hopes. Eventually I accepted this recent photo assignment in Turkana country, but what I was really doing was running away. I was up there for more than a month on my own, and it gave me time to think. Brought me to my senses.'

'And now?'

'Now, I want to start afresh. Accept that having a child may never be an option. Be grateful for Rabindrah and what we have. If his bloody family will leave us alone!'

'What's the problem with – no, you don't need to tell me. You haven't produced the next part of the dynasty. So what does Rabindrah have to say about all this?'

'Not much. He's cagey and hurt. He hasn't – I mean we haven't – been able to . . .' She flushed.

'Men and babies and sex are an unpredictable mix.' Allie got up and went inside to refill their glasses. 'He's taken a bad knock, as a husband and a potential father,' she said, when she returned. 'If *you* felt like a failure, you can bet your bottom dollar he feels just as bad, if not worse. Very hard in his culture. But he does love you.'

'I don't know any more.'

'I'm thinking of your wedding day,' Allie said. 'With the two of you having run away like truant children, laughing and telling Father Bidoli to hurry up and get on with it, before the Singh family posse came after you. Dan and I felt privileged that you asked us to be your witnesses. And doubly so, when we realised we were the only ones allowed to attend. Dan was very protective of you, and he always felt you and Rabindrah were meant to be together.'

'Do you think he was right?'

'Patience is the thing. Difficult, I know. You'll have to win him round again. Half of it, I'm sure, is his fear of causing you more pain. Woo him slowly. Talk to him. Go away somewhere, just the two of you.'

'We are,' Sarah said. 'We're going to London, and then on to my parents in Sligo.'

'Look, you would have to discuss this with Rabindrah first, but here's a suggestion. Before you leave, get in touch with your father. He's a doctor – he'll know someone you can go and see while you're there. I mean a fertility specialist. There's a lot that can be done now.'

'I'd be afraid to bring up the subject with Rabindrah. It has become such a bone of contention.'

'All the more reason to deal with it. Don't bury this. If a specialist advises that you are never going to bear children, then at least you know the truth. You accept it and move on. Or consider adoption. I don't know how the two of you would feel about that.'

'I don't know either, but you're right, Allie. Thank you. I didn't intend to bring all this stuff out, right now, with Dan's anniversary, but . . .'

'I'm glad you did. I wish you'd talked to me before. Did Hannah or Camilla know?'

'Yes, they did. In the first few weeks they tried everything to lift me out of my misery. But I felt frozen, unable to move. I even refused to see the doctor in Nairobi – the sight of him would have been too painful. Too close to what I had lost. And I didn't want to go to Ireland and explain it all to my family. I wouldn't have been able to deal with their sympathy, any more than I could have handled it immediately after Piet died. So I stayed in Nairobi. Poor Rabindrah, I don't know how he coped with me.'

'It's always better to share such things,' Allie said.

'I know.' They sat in silence for a time. Then Sarah stirred. 'What about you, Allie? How are you managing?'

'The cheetah research will keep me focused.'

'But it's lonely, isn't it? I'm thinking of companionship, not just work.'

'Ha!' Allie gave a short laugh. 'I suppose you're wondering what I'll do without sex. Isn't that right?'

'I didn't mean to –' Sarah felt the tide of embarrassment flood her cheeks.

'I don't mind.' Allie laughed. 'I'm touched at your concern for my welfare. Dan was a fabulous man, and I loved him more than I can ever express. I'll never love like that again, or fully share my life with another human being in the same way. But you're right. I like sex, and one day I might want someone. Who knows?'

Sarah stood up. 'Better get some sleep. Goodnight, Allie, and thank you for being such a good friend.'

She opened the tent, pulling the metal zipper quietly and listening for a few minutes to the sound of her husband sleeping. When she had put her clothes away she lay down in the narrow cot, moulding her body to the shape of his back, with her head in the warm curve of his neck and shoulder. Within minutes she was asleep.

Chapter 6

Kenya, July 1977

The first blow hit him in the stomach. James doubled over and fell forwards, winded by the pain and the unexpectedness of the assault. He rolled himself into a ball, arms wrapped around his head as sticks and feet attacked him, aiming for every unprotected part of his body. In spite of his efforts, one of them managed to put a heavy boot into his jaw. He tasted blood on his lip, felt it welling through his fingers as he wound his arms tighter around the top of his head, pressing his hands down over his eyes. There were several of them, all older boys, jeering, shouting, beating, kicking. Urine seeped through his trousers and onto his legs and he was filled with shame. A thin trickle of vomit escaped from his mouth as another blow slammed into his shoulder, rolling him into a more vulnerable position. Blood and mucus ran from his nose, and his face was caked with dust. After a while he could barely breathe. He called out for them to stop, gasping with the effort, but his torturers were not listening so he braced himself to withstand the violence until they tired and went away. He knew no one would find him here.

'Rich boy, give us your money!'

'Give us the money that the white mama has sent you from far away!'

'White boy in a black boy's body!'

'*Mȝungu's* pet! Now they are not here to protect you we will take everything. And if you tell them we will beat you some more.'

They had begun to hurl stones at him when they heard the sound of a vehicle in the distance, and saw the bounce of approaching headlights along the tree line. Suddenly it was over. James lay still on the side of the path, curled tight and shaking, as the Land Rover came to a halt. His sobs turned the pressure on his ribcage into a searing agony, forcing him to take shallow breaths, and to try and prevent himself from crying.

'What is happening here?' David bent down beside the boy, lifting him off the ground, moving him more gently when he screamed out in pain, wiping grit and tears and dust off his face. 'Who has beaten you, James?'

'I don't know.' It was a lie, but fear caught hold of his tongue. James could imagine the results if his attackers were punished. He would never be safe again.

'What happened?' David repeated the question. 'Did you get into a fight? What is this about?'

'I was not fighting.'

'Why would you be beaten up if you were not fighting? Did you say something to offend someone?'

But David already knew the answer. The boy kept to himself, worked hard at school and was rarely involved in any rowdy business in the staff compound, or at the labour lines where the farmhands lived. He was considered to be remote and stand-offish, and he had created envy among his peers who regarded him with suspicion because he spent most of his time with Hannah's children. He had even been on safari to Samburu and Meru and Lake Nakuru, and south to Tsavo National Park and the coast where he had spent summer holidays swimming in the salty ocean.

'All right, James. Get into the car slowly and I'll take you home and clean you up. Esther will be waiting for you. She must be worried that you are not in the compound.'

'Esther is not there.'

'Where is she?' David started the vehicle and drove carefully along the track, seeing James wince at every bump, although he did not make a sound as they skittered along the rutted surface.

'It was her day off yesterday, but she did not come back last night. There is a problem on her *shamba*. She is coming tonight. Or tomorrow maybe.'

David grunted with annoyance. Esther's husband often beat her when she returned home, and regularly drank the proceeds of whatever she grew and sold on their small plot of land. There would be a big *shauri* when Hannah came back and found that the ayah had taken extra time off work, and James had been beaten up in her absence. 'Where did you sleep last night?' he asked.

'In my room. Esther did not come back, so old Wanjui gave me food.' James was mumbling, one hand exploring his swollen face, the words barely audible. He tried to rub a trckle of blood away with his sleeve, but the gesture made him whimper with pain. 'This morning I asked your father for porridge from the kitchen, and then I went to the forest and stayed there.'

'How many times have you been told not to go to the forest alone? After the *shauri* with Suniva, you were told not to go there at all, without Achole, or one of the other *watu*. What if you met a leopard? Or a herd of elephant, or the old *nyati* that gored a man last month?'

'I did not meet them.'

'No. But tonight you have met worse animals than these.' David changed his tone, knowing that there was no point in scolding the boy. What he needed was sympathy. 'We are going to the kitchen in the main house, and my father will give you food and help to clean and bandage your other cuts.'

'Eh! What *meneno* is this?' Kamau's wrinkled face folded into new creases as he looked at James. 'Where have you been, *toto*? What has happened to you now? Esther has been looking everywhere for you.'

'Esther should be ashamed of leaving him. She will be in bad trouble for coming back late,' David said. 'Where is Mwangi?'

'It is his night off,' Kamau said.

'Then help me to get the boy cleaned up, Father. He needs tea with plenty of sugar and some hot food. Maybe you have something left over from Bwana Mike's dinner?'

'He is just finishing his meal,' Kamau said. 'Listen, he is getting up from the table and coming this way. Quick, put James into the pantry and shut the door.'

'That was very good.' Mike Stead appeared, carrying some plates and an empty jug of cream. 'You make the best treacle pudding in the world, old man. I've brought in the dishes, since Mwangi is not here to help you and my memsahib is away tonight. If there is some meat left over you could put it in the dogs' bowls. I'd like coffee beside the fire, please, Kamau.'

'*Ndio*, bwana.' The cook nodded, pleased by Stead's gesture. The bwanas did not usually bother about dirty plates left on the table, no matter who was on duty.

'David.' Mike shook hands with him. 'Checking up on your father, heh? Everything all right up at the lodge? Did they fix the water tank?' He was laughing as he asked the question.

'Yes, sir.' David grinned. 'We have built a fence around it, so that the big bull elephant cannot reach it. I think the guests are disappointed. They took many pictures of him, with his trunk inside the tank, taking all our water.'

'I'll bet they will dine out on that for years,' Mike said. 'I'd like to have seen it myself.'

'They made good pictures,' David said. 'The *ndofu* was too close and we were lucky that he was calm. It is very quiet up there now. There are only two couples staying tonight. I have put Ngare on the night shift, with the *askari*. If there is a problem they can reach me on the radio.'

'Good man. I'll drive up some time tomorrow, probably in the evening. Have a beer with the guests and tell them a few tall stories. Goodnight.' He raised a hand in salute and disappeared into the living room. Moments later David heard the sound of the BBC World Service on the radio.

'Come out, James, and have some food,' he said, opening the pantry door to find his charge huddled in the furthest corner. The boy struggled to get to his feet, and David saw that one of his ankles had swollen up and he was limping.

'Did he fall out of a tree like some young baboon?' Kamau was not about to provide any comfort until he had answers. 'I told you to take him with you to the lodge. To keep him out of mischief.'

'He has been beaten.' David's face was grim as he opened a cupboard and took out the first aid box, selecting iodine and bandages and a roll of strapping. 'As well as the cuts, he has hurt his ankle and some ribs. I hope nothing is broken – there is too much swelling to see. James, you must tell me the names of these boys.'

'I did not see them.' James gave a wail of pain as the iodine bit into his wounds, and David pressed gently on his ribcage. 'I was walking back to the house and they came from behind me, shouting. They thought Mama Hannah had sent me money. But I do not know who they were.'

Kamau threw a sceptical look at the child. He had often heard the *watu* talking about James, and the strange fact that he all but lived in the main house. If Mama Hannah was going to take in a black child, they all asked, why had she not picked one from the house compound or the labour lines? It was a waste to choose an unknown boy from the orphanage in Nyeri, when there were so many deserving candidates on her own doorstep. Bwana Piet had been murdered by a man from an orphanage, and it was hard to believe that his sister had taken a risk with another one of the same. It could only bring bad luck.

Many of the farm workers had asked Esther why the boy from Nyeri had been brought to Langani. But she shook her head and pursed her lips in disapproval, not wanting to admit that she had no idea. Her job was to care for him, along with Suniva and Piet. The *wazungu* did all manner of strange things that could not be explained to normal people, and it was not her place to question their motives. She had a good job, a solid house and food. The rest was not her business.

'Come to my place.' David took James by the hand. 'You can sleep there for tonight.'

Inwardly, he was cursing himself for having left the boy alone so much. After the family departure, James had moped around the house for the first few days. David brought him up to the lodge several times and gave him tasks to do, and Esther kept an eye on him when he was at the house. He spent time in the kitchen helping Kamau and Mwangi, but he was morose and withdrawn. Finally, when the postcards and letters began to arrive he had cheered up somewhat. All seemed well until Esther had left to sort out the problem at her *shamba* that could no doubt have waited.

But the cards that saved James from descending into a pit of abject misery had also brought danger. Word spread that letters were coming almost every day, and rumours began to circulate that they contained money sent by Bwana Lars. The taunts started almost immediately, but James ignored them. His world had been illuminated by a new brightness. Suniva was thinking of him, sending him messages through which he could try to imagine and even share her adventures. He asked Kamau for a large, square biscuit tin that lived on the top shelf in the kitchen and was used to store the fruit cakes that Hannah occasionally made. On the front there was a picture of an English village with white houses and thatched roofs, and fences inside of which were small gardens with many flowers. Everything was clean and orderly, and ladies with bonnets and long dresses and parasols strolled past, on a path that overlooked the sea. James thought it was a fitting casket for his most treasured possessions, and wondered if Suniva now dressed like this. The thought made him smile, but it also made him nervous. He did not want her to change too much. Each precious piece of correspondence was stored inside the box, and he hid it in the back of his wardrobe underneath a spare blanket and his school shoes. When there was no one in Esther's house he took it out and read each card and letter again and again, poring over the pictures and trying to visualise the places that Suniva described.

'You must take this boy to the lodge with you tomorrow. Before he gets into any more trouble.' Kamau ladled stew and potatoes into a bowl, watching with sympathy as James struggled to move his jaw. 'Find him something to do up there. He is hanging around my kitchen half the time, looking gloomy and turning the cream sour. You are my son, David, and I advise you to do this. It is not good for him to be here in the house compound with Esther all the time. It will make more trouble for him with the other boys. I cannot look after him and cook for Bwana Stead as well. And Mwangi does not have time either. We are old men, not *ayahs*, and we are both going to retire to our shambas when Mama Hannah comes back from her holiday. It is time.'

'I don't want to go to the lodge.' James was eating slowly, each movement of his jaw sending arrows of pain through his face. He stopped, his spoon poised in mid-air.

'There is nothing for you to do here, until Piet and Suniva come back,' David said, exasperated. 'Up there you can help out in the kitchen and keep the viewing platform tidy. Study the animals.' He laughed. 'And study the guests too, who are as strange as the creatures they have come to see.'

'No. I will not come.'

'It is not a choice,' David said. 'I am in charge of you now.'

'Someone will take my letters if I am not here. When the post comes from the box,' James said. 'They will be stolen.'

'They won't be stolen,' David said. 'Mwangi receives the letters every day and he will keep what belongs to you, and give it to you each evening.'

He helped James into the Land Rover, noticing the flow of silent tears as the boy hauled himself into the front seat. Then they drove round to the staff compound.

David was enormously proud of his house. The building looked much the same as the one that Esther and James lived in, with its corrugated iron roof and mud and wattle walls coated with white distemper. The entrance was shaded by a narrow verandah furnished with two chairs, a rough table on which a kerosene lantern stood, and a series of plants growing in tins that had once held powdered milk or canned vegetables. David had painted them red and put soil and flowers and ferns into them, watering them carefully and keeping them bright and healthy. Inside, the decorations were very different from the other staff houses. Several of Sarah's wildlife photographs hung on the walls, framed and glossy, along with a portrait she had taken of Kamau and David together. The furniture was newly varnished, and covered in bright cloth from the Indian *duka* in Nanyuki. There was a rug on the floor that had been a gift from Camilla, and curtains made from *kangas* in bold colours were threaded on expanding wire. A small kitchen was set into the back wall, and Hannah had given him pots and pans that she no longer needed, so that he could practise cooking new recipes, although no one in the compound was interested in the dishes he prepared for the *wazungu*. He had a small fridge in which he kept beer and occasional bottles of wine that guests at the lodge had not finished. For the main part, however, the other staff members considered him a loner, with ideas above his station. The pursuits of his childhood friends no longer interested him, and he often compared James's situation to his own.

Over time he had saved his wages and used the generous tips and gifts that clients at the lodge had given him, initially putting the money into improving his reading, and gaining knowledge of the local fauna and flora. Later he had carved lamp stands out of discarded pieces of wood, and made shades from wire and coconut fibre, so that the rooms had a warm glow and there were no naked light bulbs to be seen. Camilla had also given him beaded cloth from the workshop that was not up to the standard she required, and he had asked one of the *bibis* who worked on the sewing machines to make this into cushions. He studied Hannah's old magazines to see what the rich people in Nairobi and Europe did with their houses, and adapted as many of their ideas as he could with his limited means and materials. True, his home had floors made of cement and the walls were rough, but there was no other staff house like it at Langani. Or anywhere in the area.

Once he had brought home a white girl who was staying at the lodge. She had begged to be taken to an African house and he had smuggled her in late at night, hushing her when she became a little drunk and insisted on dancing to music on his record player. The experience was one of dizzying excitement, but he never repeated it, knowing that he would lose his job if

Lars or Hannah found out. In any case, it had been extremely difficult to get the girl back to the lodge before daylight without attracting the attention of the night *askari*. Just before dawn David had parked the Land Rover some distance from the main building and insisted that they walk the rest of the way in silence. She had complained bitterly, stumbling along and clinging to him for fear of an encounter with an elephant or a buffalo. In truth he had been disappointed by her instant willingness to remove her clothes and lie with him. He had thought the conquest would set him apart, but the white girl turned out to be no more of a challenge than any of the young Kikuyu women he knew. For the next two days she tried to accost him, asking him to come to her room or to take her out in the Land Rover alone, but he had refused. All in all she had proved a nuisance and he was relieved when her party left the lodge. Now he had James to look after.

'Take a sheet and blanket out of the cupboard and make a bed for yourself, here on the couch,' he said to James. 'Do not go outside. I will fetch your clothes from Esther's house, so that you can be ready to come to the lodge with me early in the morning. We will stay there for three nights, because I am on duty until the weekend.'

James stood still, his heart jumping. His precious biscuit tin was in Esther's house. Could he trust David to bring it for him, tell him where it was hidden? He took a gulp of air and placed his hands on his ribs to try and dull the pain. It was difficult to speak, to form words, when his jaw produced an agonising spasm each time he opened his mouth.

'My box,' he said, his eyes screwed up in desperation. 'I have a box I keep with the things that are important. Esther does not know it is there. If I tell you where it is, will you bring it?'

'Don't worry,' David said. 'I'll bring it.'

It took Esther several minutes to open the door. She stood blocking the entrance, her feet planted well apart, arms akimbo, expression belligerent.

'Not my fault,' she said immediately. 'There was a big problem on my *shamba*. Some thieves had taken my tools and stolen onions and carrots and maize that were ready to harvest, and then the bus broke down and . . .' Her shoulders slumped and the fight went out of her. 'You will not tell Mama Hannah?'

'It is certainly your fault,' David said. 'And I do not see how it can remain hidden from Hannah. Someone is bound to tell her.'

'But not you?'

'I suppose you know that James has been beaten up, because you were not here to look after him. I've come to get his clothes. He can stay at the lodge and help out while I am on duty. That is how I started out, and it will not do him any harm.'

'You were different,' Esther said. 'You spent your time with your own people, and did not become confused with the question of who you were. Although now it looks as though you are in danger of forgetting this. I have heard what happened, and I am sure James knows who beat him. But he will never tell, because he is frightened they will come after him again. The other boys are jealous, and now there is no one here to keep him from harm, because they went off and left him.'

'If you knew all this, then you should have come back on time,' David said.

'They should have taken him with them.' Esther repeated the words defiantly. 'Like they took him on holiday before, to the coast and on safari.'

'Take him on the plane across the sea? To England?' David stared at her. 'Are you mad, woman?'

'They should make up their minds whether he is the same as their children, or if he is just some poor Kikuyu child that they provide with food and clothes and schooling. Otherwise he will be no one. His life is between two places and he belongs to neither one. This is what the white man has taught since he first came here – to divide us and make us weak. They have taken our land. They have scorned our traditions and put strangers' rules in their place, and now we are neither one thing nor the other.'

'We are an independent nation,' David said. 'We are no longer ruled by anyone but ourselves.'

'Eeh!' Esther spat into the dust. 'And what difference has that made to you or me? Or anyone working on this farm? It means that we carry on in the same way that we always did. Do you remember when the politicians told us, before Uhuru, that we would all have cars and bicycles like the white men? That we would ride free on the buses, and have many acres of land of our own? That is what our leaders said then. Now they are more arrogant than the white men were, and they are cheating us and taking land that does not belong to them or even to their tribes – the best of the land that the *wazungu* returned to us before Independence. One million acres of it. But how many of the million acres did you get? Or me? Or anyone we know?'

'I know families who got ten acres each, and now they are part of a cooperative that grows vegetables and sells them to shops,' David said. 'If you thought everyone would be rich, then you are a fool.'

'I'm no fool,' Esther said. 'Yes, people are selling their few vegetables. But they are selling to the same Indian *dukas* that were always there. Because the *wahindi* are still running the businesses. Paying us too little for what we grow, and charging too much for what we buy. And the new African owners of shops and beer halls are doing the same thing.'

'But we can vote, Esther. It is our country, and we can slowly change all this by our votes.' He sought to make her understand the broader picture.

'We will not change it,' she said. 'We will toil our whole lives just as before. But at least you and me, we know who we are and where we came from. Not like that poor boy who does not know anything. James has no family or clan, and he will never have land of his own to till. What girl will want a man like that, when he is grown? I do not know why Mama Hannah took him in. Going to the orphanage in Nyeri and bringing him back here. I am an old woman of fifty years, and I cannot understand these things that are happening, but—'

'I need some clothes for him,' David interrupted her, afraid that something in his expression might betray his knowledge. 'You sit down and finish your food – I can find everything myself.'

'You will not speak to Mama Hannah about this?'

'No,' said David. 'I will not.'

'Will Esther be in trouble?' James mumbled the question as they set out for the lodge the following morning. He was clutching his biscuit tin and a canvas bag with two pairs of shorts, shirts and socks, and a sweater.

'By the time they get back, we will probably have forgotten the whole thing,' David said. 'Your ribs will be healed and I will make sure no one touches you in the meantime. So Esther will not get into trouble. Unless you wish to say something about all this.'

'No.'

James's voice was so heavy with sadness that David took one hand off the wheel and placed it on his shoulder. He would take care of the boy from now on, until the other children came home. He was the only one who knew James's true origins. Even old Kamau and Mwangi had never been told who he was, although Hannah would trust them both with her life. She was tough, Mama Hannah, but she had courage and a good man to share her farm, and two fine children. Still, David had wondered if she might have lost her mind on the day she took in James, the son of her brother's killer. Now he also wondered whether the boy would bring bad luck and even tragedy to the farm, just as his father had done.

When Simon Githiri had first appeared at Langani, with his fine education and his letter of reference from the mission priests in Nyeri, David had been consumed with jealousy and suspicion. Hannah had given the newcomer the job that David had always hoped for. When the safari lodge first opened. Kamau, too, was angered that Hannah had passed over his son for an unknown. But she had been right. At the time, David had only completed primary school, and was working in the kitchen and the farm store. Although he was too proud to admit it, he knew in his heart that he did not have the skills for the reception desk and the office at the lodge. But he had been right about his feelings for Simon.

He was catapulted back to the present by the sight of a male elephant, ambling across the track a few hundred yards further on.

'Look, James,' he said. 'See how big the tusks are – maybe eighty pounds. This is a *mzee*. Walking alone, old and not wanted by the rest of the herd. Not even a younger bull to keep him company, which is sometimes the case. They can be bad-tempered, these solitary ones, so we will stop here and wait until he has gone into the bush on the other side.'

'I have seen him before,' James said, trying to enunciate the words clearly through his swollen lips. 'See, he has a tear on his right ear. I have seen him with Mama Hannah when we were driving. Going to the ridge.'

'We must not worry Mama Hannah over what happened,' David said, sitting with the vehicle in neutral and the engine idling. 'Because she is a very good person and she has done everything for you. And for me.'

'What did she do for you?' James's eyes were bright with interest.

'First she sent me to school, but she was angry because I was lazy and I did not follow my lessons well. Then she took me into the house, and she and my father taught me how to cook so I could help her at the lodge. Later, she sent me back to a special technical school, to learn better English and maths, and all the other things I needed to take care of the guests. And now she is looking after you in the same way.'

'What happened to my mother and father, that they could not look after me?'

It was the first time that James had asked the question outright. For an instant David had no idea how to answer him, but he knew that he must offer a plausible explanation.

'Your father went to find work in Nairobi, and some bad men robbed and killed him,' he said, finding the lie easy on his tongue and his conscience. 'Then your mother came to Langani, looking for work, but there was no job here. Later, she died of a fever and you were left at the orphanage, so Mama Hannah went there and brought you to live at Langani.'

'Did you meet my mother?'

David hesitated, remembering Wanjiru, hardly more than a child herself when she had brought her baby to the farm looking for help. Her husband, Simon Githiri, had vanished, leaving her in the Kikuyu Reserve with their small son. The child's club foot had created derision and fear within the clan, although the only trace that now remained of his deformity was scarring left by surgery. 'No, I never met her,' he lied.

'So why did Mama Hannah take me from the orphanage?' James was looking straight ahead, his fingers gripping the door handle, his face tense.

'Because she remembered your mother, and she saw that you were a boy with *akili* and a good smile on your face. That was before she found out that you could be disobedient, and that you and Piet and Suniva would not pay attention to Esther, and get into all kinds of trouble.' Laughter was in David's answer. 'So you had better behave yourself from now on, otherwise she might find out that there is nothing in your head at all.'

The elephant had moved away to a safe distance and they continued up the steep hill to the lodge, parking at the back of the building where the staff quarters and the stores were located.

'Put your clothes into my room,' David said. 'And then come to the front desk and we will see if there are any animals at the waterhole.'

He watched as James struggled down from the vehicle and limped away to put his few belongings in a safe place. Standing there in the early morning sun David put his hand up and rubbed the back of his head, something he always did when he was uneasy. He sighed, wondering what would become of this lost, helpless child. There was no time to ponder the question. From his vantage point he saw a vehicle coming up the hill to the lodge, trailing a spiral of dust. Minutes later Anthony Chapman, tanned and lean, stepped out of his safari car.

'David, *habari gani*?' He held out his hand, a smile crinkling his eyes. 'What's going on with everyone away? I hope it's quiet and you don't have too much to deal with. I'm on the way to my camp in the Aberdares with two clients. We thought we might have lunch and even stay the night.'

'Everything is good,' David said, shaking hands. 'And we have rooms if you wish to sleep here. I will set up a table for lunch on the edge of the viewing platform. We met an old elephant on the way up the hill, so he may arrive here soon.' He turned to welcome Anthony's guests, and to lead them into the lodge and through the main sitting room and bar area.

'Jeez, what a place!' Charlie Zimmerman had been on safari with Anthony before, but this was his first visit to Langani. 'I've never seen anything like this. Tell me about it.'

'It was built by a close friend of mine,' Anthony said. 'His family were Boers who trekked up here from South Africa at the turn of the century, and carved Langani Farm out of the wilderness. It was Piet's idea to turn part of the ranch into a game conservation area.'

'Is he here? I'd like to meet the guy who created this.' Zimmerman was deeply impressed.

'He died some years ago,' Anthony said. 'His sister, Hannah Olsen, runs it now, with David here as the manager. But she is away on holiday. I've been a partner in the venture since it started.'

'I've never seen anything so beautiful,' Eve Zimmerman said, gazing up at the lofty expanse of thatched roof, suspended on thick poles and floating over the natural rock formation that made up part of the walls. 'Can we see the rooms?'

They left the main lodge, following David along the path to a circular room that jutted out over the cliff face, with a wide view over the magnificent country below and the shrouded peaks of Mount Kenya on the horizon.

'As you can see, the whole structure follows the natural line of the rugged terrain, using the existing boulders to shape the rooms,' Anthony said. 'Everything you see originated on the farm. Stone that has been polished in the workshops, wood for building materials and furniture that was made here. Even the fabrics are dyed and printed on the property. It is pretty special. And there is a small shop beside the reception desk, with beaded bags and shawls and cushion covers that come from Langani, but owned by Camilla Broughton Smith and Hannah Olsen.'

'Camilla the English model?' Charlie shook his head. 'I'd sure like to meet her. She has to be the most glamorous woman on earth. Is she around?'

'I'm afraid not,' Anthony said, smiling. 'Better luck next time.'

'There isn't any glass in the windows.' Eve Zimmerman stood on the balcony of their cottage and watched a herd of buffalo plodding their way up towards the waterhole. 'How do you know a lion won't jump into your bedroom in the middle of the night? And what happens if it rains?'

David laughed. 'We have night watchmen who patrol the place all the time, so no surprise visitors can make their way into the guest quarters. And at night the pathways are lit, so you may be lucky and see the kudus with their fine horns – they often take the path below this building.' He gestured towards the open window spaces. 'There are canvas blinds that can be rolled down if it rains.'

'I don't think I'll sleep a wink,' Eve said. 'But it will be quite an adventure. Let's stay the night, Charlie.'

Anthony was signing the register at the reception desk, when he felt a light tug on his sleeve.

'James! My God, James! What happened to you?' He bent down to embrace the child and heard the gasp of pain. 'Ribs, eh? Your face is a mess and I see your ankle is all strapped up. Did someone pick a fight with you?' He turned to David. 'What the hell happened to him?'

'Some boys attacked him last night.' David cursed inwardly. Now the incident would have to be reported to Hannah and Lars.

'What boys? Why?'

'Some bullies who are jealous of him,' David said.

'For God's sake man, between you and Esther and the rest of the staff, surely you could have prevented this,' Anthony said angrily. 'Have you found these thugs?'

'James says he does not know who they were.' David was annoyed by the implication that he was somehow to blame, and he knew his explanation sounded weak.

'James is terrified to identify them, is more like it,' Anthony said. 'And now that it has happened, who is to say they won't pick on him again? Hannah is going to be furious about this. I don't think the kid should stay here while she is away.'

'He will be with me from now on,' David said. 'I will look after him myself.'

'It's a pity you didn't think of keeping an eye on him before. He should have been with you all along,' Anthony said brusquely. 'I'll take him with me tomorrow, to prevent any more disasters. Stop in Nanyuki and have Dr Markham look at him, to make sure there's no serious damage. Then he can come to the Aberdares and help out there, and in the camps at Meru and Samburu. I'll drop him off on the way back to Nairobi. By then Lars and Hannah will be home. In the meantime, you'd better make it clear that you will find the boys who have done this and have them punished. And their families too, if there is any repetition.'

'I have warned everybody last night, in the compound and on the labour lines, that he must not be touched again,' David said. 'The problem was Esther, who went away for a day and did not come back in time.'

'All the more reason for you to have taken care of him yourself,' Anthony said.

'I was on duty here at the lodge, and I did not know that she—'

'Well, whatever the reason, he will be better off with me, until Lars and Hannah return.' Anthony cut him off, ignoring his excuses. 'See to it that someone fetches enough clothes from the compound. I will take him with me tomorrow, when we head out.'

'This is James,' he said to the Zimmermans as the luggage was loaded into the vehicle on the following morning. 'He is part of the family here at Langani, but it is school holiday time so I'm taking him to help out in camp as kitchen *toto*. He's a good boy, and he loves the bush. James, say good morning to Mr and Mrs Zimmerman.'

'Good morning.' James held out a brown hand and smiled, large eyes full of anticipation at the journey ahead.

'He's so winning that I might steal him, and take him home with me,'

Eve Zimmerman said. 'But what happened to his face? And why is he all bandaged up and limping?'

'He fell out of a tree, so we're going to stop in Nanyuki for a cup of coffee and a quick visit to the local quack, to make sure nothing is broken. Right. Into the back, James.' Anthony helped him up and closed the door.

Then they were gone, the tyres spitting dust and pebbles and sliding in the soft sand as they made their way down the hill. David was left standing in front of the lodge, angered by Anthony's insinuation of blame, and deeply offended that James, the boy he had taught and protected and watched over, whose secret he had kept faithfully for so many years, had not even said goodbye.

Two weeks later every weed had been pulled up from the garden, the hedges were trimmed to perfection, the furniture and the floors in the house had been polished and the windows washed. Curtains and chair covers and bedspreads had been laundered and pressed and put back with care, and vases of flowers were in every room. The dairy had been hosed down, the stables were swept and cleaned and the horses curried. Kamau had a leg of eland roasting to perfection in the oven, and Mwangi had set the drinks tray with the best glasses from the cabinet where Hannah kept the things she used on special occasions.

When the car appeared on the bend in the driveway they were all waiting, wreathed in smiles as Hannah jumped out, hugging Mwangi and Kamau, pressing David's hands, listening to Achole as he told her about the progress of the new calf. Lars shook hands with them all, while the children ran into the house, shouting with excitement. Minutes later Suniva reappeared on the verandah, her face stormy.

'Where's James? I can't find James.'

'He is not here.' David stepped forward, addressing Hannah and Lars, but unable to look them directly in the eye. 'Anthony was at the lodge with some clients, and he took James away on safari.'

'That was generous of him,' Lars said. 'Quite an adventure for young James.'

'Yes, I suppose so.' Hannah was watching David, sensing there was something wrong with what he was saying. But before she had a chance to consider it further, her attention was diverted by the sounds coming from the house. She ran inside and along the corridor, following the wailing sound, afraid that Suniva might have found a scorpion or a snake in her bedroom. Hannah reached for the door knob and turned it. Then turned it again, until she realised that it was locked. Behind the door she could hear her daughter sobbing, beating her fists against the furniture.

'Suniva! Suniva, open up! Come on, Suniva, open the door at once.'

Lars appeared behind Hannah and gently moved her aside. 'James will be back soon. Suniva?'

But Suniva had pushed a chair against the door, jamming the handle. Then she took refuge inside the dark recess of her wardrobe, closing out the world, refusing to partake in a homecoming that had robbed her of the reunion she had dreamed of for so long.

Chapter 7

London, August 1977

'There's a special smell about London, don't you think?' Sarah was arm in arm with her husband as they threaded their way along the crowded pavement to John Sinclair's office.

'Bad or good?' Rabindrah asked.

'Special,' Sarah said. 'I remember it from my childhood. We would stop over here on our way to Ireland. When Dad was on leave. Such noise and activity after the hot, sleepy atmosphere of Mombasa. Horns blowing and throngs of people, red double-decker buses, and big black taxis with acres of room inside, and clip-down seats facing the wrong way.'

'As a student I couldn't afford taxis,' Rabindrah said. 'I did tuck into eggs and bacon with fat sausages and chips, though. My mother would have had a heart attack if she'd seen me eating those things, while she was busy preparing her vegetarian specialities at home.'

'I loved Lyons Corner House, with the windows all steamed up, and the lights in Piccadilly Circus, and the long escalators. I always wanted to go by Tube, but my parents hated being down in the bowels of the earth. You know that blast of air that comes at you down the tunnel when a train is about to arrive?'

'Disgusting. Made me want to choke.' Rabindrah wrinkled his nose. 'Still does.'

'I love it even now,' Sarah said.

'So many cultural joys. And inspired choices!'

'They are part of the smell and character of London,' she said. 'The aroma of the strange and exotic.'

'Pollution. That's what your nostalgia has conjured up for you.'

'Perhaps. But I love it. Like I love the smell of petrol.'

'Petrol?'

'Mmm. That shiver in the air – the vapour floating around the pump when I'm refilling the fuel tank. I like inhaling it. Weird, isn't it?'

'Good God!' Rabindrah looked at her in mock horror. 'I'm married to a fuel sniffer. Maybe even a latent pyromaniac? I think I'll keep this new discovery private.'

They were laughing as they entered the offices of Sinclair & Miller.

'These are splendid.' John Sinclair stood back from the table on which Sarah had spread out her latest photographs. There were atmospheric shots, capturing the dramatic changes in cloud formation over the immensity of the Mara. She had illustrated the grandeur of the place and its wild inhabitants, and the publisher sucked in his breath as he looked at the extraordinary images of the millions of migrating wildebeest accompanied by their acolyte groups of zebra and gazelle, making the time-honoured march across grasslands and rivers to the pastures in the Serengeti.

'This set here is stunning.' He indicated the series Sarah had taken of Lara hunting down the young Thomson's gazelle.

The frames had been shot in quick succession. First, the animal crouched in the long grass, her dappled coat merging with the yellow and black shadows. A close-up revealed the intensity of her stance and her fixed expression as she focused on her prey. Then the chase, with the sleek body flying over the ground at full speed, the landscape a blur as she covered the distance. And finally, the fatal conflict, as the doe rolled over and she sank her jaws into its neck. Flecks of blood from the kill hung suspended in the air and particles of dust burned bright in the lowering sun around them. The doe's eyes were glazed in death, and in the last frame her graceful body was limp as she was dragged away in the cheetah's powerful grip. An elegiac image of the harshness of life in the wild. Savage and strangely beautiful.

'That's Lara, a particularly adept hunter. And these are her cubs.' Sarah showed the publisher another series of prints.

'How far advanced is the text?' John turned to Rabindrah.

'This is the introduction with general information on the history and origins and the geographical distribution of the cheetah.' Rabindrah handed him a folder. 'There are further chapters covering the flora and fauna of the Mara, and the effect on the cheetah population of predators, both animal and human. I also have a section on the way the animals have had to adapt to their changing surroundings. Later chapters will cover social habits and behaviour, mating, the rearing of young, and hunting techniques. I've put in a detailed index at the back of the document, listing the aspects we intend to incorporate.'

'Fine work. Keep at it,' John said. 'What sort of time span are you looking at for this project?'

'Sarah is going straight back to the Mara when we return to Kenya,' Rabindrah said. 'And I will be commuting on a regular basis. We want to cover all the seasons and the development of Lara's cubs. And Allie is hoping to find a male or group of males. We should be ready for editing and layout this time next year.'

'I'll look forward to putting it together. Good to be working with you again. And give my regards to Allie.'

The phone was ringing when Sarah put the key in the lock and she ran to pick up the receiver, already a little breathless from the three flights of stairs.

'Sarah? It's me. Lila.'

'Lila! You got my letter then?'

'Yes. I can come to London on Saturday, rather than your trekking all the way to Birmingham. If that fits in with whatever you and Rabindrah have to do.'

'That sounds grand,' Sarah said. 'How is Harjeet? Will he be with you?'

'I doubt it. He is very busy. I'll take the train and then hop into a taxi. I should be there around noon.'

'That's a pity about Harjeet.' Sarah had been curious to meet the man again, and perhaps revise her first impression. At the same time she felt that Lila would have a chance to talk more openly if she was alone. 'How are you? Your letters don't say much about being married and living in England.'

'I'll tell you everything when I see you,' Lila said. 'This isn't an ideal time, and I don't want to block the phone for too long.'

'Right. Saturday, then.' Sarah turned to Rabindrah. 'Did you hear all that?'

'It will be good to see her,' Rabindrah nodded. 'I'll be curious to know how she has settled in to life in Birmingham.'

'With difficulty, I would say.' Sarah yawned. 'She sounds rather strung up. I'm going to put my feet up for half an hour before we have to go to your parents. Isn't it strange – I can trek for miles in the *bundu*, with thorns and spiky grass and rough ground, and never be half as whacked as I am after a few hours on London pavements. I think it must be all the concrete. No give to it. I'm truly grateful for Camilla's flat. It's so airy and quiet up here. I wonder how she's doing in New York?'

'The same as she always does in New York, I should think,' Rabindrah said. 'Partying day and night, and making money on her new line of clothes. Everything she touches seems to turn to gold.'

They arrived at the home of Jasmer and Nand Kaur Singh at seven o'clock. Rabindrah embraced his mother with evident tenderness, and she brought them inside. Jasmer was standing with his back to the fireplace, tall and distinguished in his impeccably tailored suit and Sikh turban.

'Father.' Rabindrah joined his hands together and inclined his head in a respectful salute, more formal than the spontaneous greeting he had shared with his mother.

Sarah received a warm handshake. Jasmer did not indulge in sentimental gestures, but he was clearly glad to see them both, and he enquired with genuine interest about the new book. Father and son were soon deep in a discussion on political developments in Kenya, and it was obvious that Jasmer had read all the articles Rabindrah had written in recent months. After a few minutes Rabindrah's sisters arrived with their families, and Sarah was surrounded by the children. They grouped themselves around her, dark eyes full of shining expectation, pestering her to recount the latest stories of her adventures in the African bush. It was a place they had heard about from their Kenyan-born parents and relatives, although most of them had never been there. She had an admiring audience, calling out questions, pushing and giggling and reaching out to tug at her arm, hanging on to her every word.

'Children, give Sarah Auntie a little space!' Rabindrah's sister, Pavith, came to the rescue. 'Look, she hasn't even had time for refreshments. You should be taking care of our guest, not persecuting her with your questions. Go and get her a drink, for goodness' sake, and some of the snacks from the tray. And see if there is anything you can do to help in the kitchen. Off with you.'

'I don't mind, really. They are so enthusiastic and we're having fun,' Sarah said, regretting that the children had been shooed away, leaving her as a focal point for Rabindrah's sisters.

The men had become involved in a conversation about the law on British citizenship, and Sarah found herself with the women. Pavith was warm and sympathetic, and had offered acceptance and friendship from the outset. In contrast Nalin, the older sister, had always been more distant and Sarah suspected that she disapproved of her brother's choice of wife. She was relieved when Nalin disappeared into the kitchen and she was left alone with Pavith, catching up on the events in their lives, while the children came back and forth, trying to outdo each other with offerings of spicy savouries.

'We're hoping to see Lila on Saturday,' Sarah said to her sister-in-law. 'Have you spent much time with her since she came to England? Is she well? Happy?'

'I have only seen her once since she arrived,' Pavith replied. 'She doesn't come to London, although some of Harjeet's relatives live in Wimbledon. He's a cold fish and he doesn't socialise much with our family. We are not important or rich enough to be of interest to him, although he asks Father for free legal advice when it suits him.' She shrugged. 'I think Lila would like to see more of us. Harjeet's father is difficult, and the mother is a little mouse with nothing to say. Not in front of her husband and son, anyway. Lila must be lonely. It's a big change, particularly if you have no immediate family nearby.'

'Maybe we can get together over the weekend while she is here,' Sarah said. 'With you and Mohindrah and the children, too.'

'Good idea.' Pavith called out to her husband. 'Mo! Sarah has an idea for Saturday. Lila is coming from Birmingham, and you have to choose somewhere nice for us to have a family lunch.'

Mohindrah Singh was a plump, jolly man with a good sense of humour. 'With all the children that will be a challenge. Will Harjeet be with her?'

'We don't know yet,' Sarah said.

Mo pursed his full lips. 'It would be more enjoyable if that conceited fellow was occupied elsewhere,' he said. 'He is too full of his own importance. But yes, we will organise something for Sarah and Rabindrah, and our lovely cousin.'

As they discussed possible venues, dinner was announced. Sarah took her place at a table laden with steaming bowls of rice and lentils and a variety of vegetable curries, chutneys and pickles that emerged from Nand Kaur's legendary kitchen. During former visits Sarah had written down the recipes and gone with her mother-in-law to buy the spices used in her cooking. But no matter how hard she tried, the outcome was never the same. She leaned back in her chair, enjoying the flavours and textures of the food, and the interaction around the table.

'I am relieved that you have turned your attention away from political controversies and gone back to the subject of wildlife,' Jasmer said, looking at his son with a smile. 'Too many articles on the treatment of the Asian community will make you unpopular with the government. You could even be expelled from Kenya. Or worse, arrested for fomenting disquiet among members of a minority. A dangerous line to tread.'

'I don't think they can expel me. I'm a born and bred citizen of the country,' Rabindrah rejoined. 'Someone has to speak up about injustice and my reports are balanced, I can assure you. The government could make life difficult, it's true. Put pressure on Gordon to Africanise my job at the paper. However, it's easy to sit on the fence and tell me to change my tune, when you are thousands of miles away, having chosen to be safely ensconced in England.'

'You are suggesting I abandoned my community by coming here?' Jasmer flushed with annoyance. He demanded respect from his children and he did not care for his son's tone. 'Because I left the country to provide better security for my family? Because I have not made any statement, or taken a public stand on the Asian dilemma? How or why would I? I have no interests there any more, and it would not be my place. In fact I could cause a great deal of harm.'

'I'm not suggesting that you sold out.' Rabindrah was privately amused to see that he had ruffled the composed exterior for which his father was famous in court. 'You did the best thing, getting out before the situation became so difficult. There are others who were not so lucky, though. They need someone to highlight their problems, even though they are often self-made. I am a journalist. That is my job. Part of it, anyway. But it's not the only thing I write about.'

He caught Sarah's eye and she gave him a tiny frown of warning, feeling it inappropriate for him to needle his father on a subject that always caused disagreement. She drew the focus away from Kenya with a general question of her own about life in London. The rest of the family responded with relief, talking and arguing animatedly about everything that was happening in Britain, the conversation shifting easily from one topic to another. Sarah felt herself more at home in this gathering than among the Nairobi clan. They seemed more open-minded, less hidebound by Sikh tradition. Perhaps it came from having been obliged to adapt to life in England, and from the fact that they lived in a cosmopolitan city. They were intensely interested in the new book and after the meal, copies of her previous collaborations with Rabindrah were produced from their pride of place on the living room bookshelf.

'Is that how you carry your babies, Sarah Auntie?' Pavith's youngest daughter pointed to a picture of a Samburu woman carrying a child on her back. 'When you go out taking pictures?'

There was a brief silence and a look passed between Pavith and her mother.

'I don't have any children,' Sarah said, conscious of their unspoken pity. 'But if I did, I probably would carry them like that. Then I could trek through the bush and still have two hands free to take photographs.' She raised her fingers as though clicking the shutter button. 'Clever, eh?'

There was general laughter, but for Sarah the light had gone out of the evening. Although she continued to smile and chat she longed to return to Camilla's apartment and close her eyes to the world outside. As they left the party, Nand put her hands on Sarah's shoulders

'You must not let it worry you, my dear. All will happen at the right time, if it is to be.'

Sarah dropped her gaze. She was not sure which was worse, the well-meaning efforts to avoid a difficult subject or Grandmother Lakhbir's overt, caustic remarks. Suddenly, she was tired of them all and she felt a fierce longing to be with her own family in Sligo, where she would be able to talk about the problem without any sense of underlying rebuke. Her father had already set up an appointment with a gynaecologist in Dublin, and Sarah hoped that the specialist would be able to explain, at last, why she had to suffer like this, and whether there was a remedy.

At the flat, she went to the bedroom and prepared for bed, listening to the sound of the television in the sitting room. Rabindrah had chosen to stay up and watch the late news. Sarah turned over and punched the pillow in frustration. She did not want his sympathy either, but she felt deserted all the same.

The phone rang on Saturday morning while they were still in bed.

'It's Lila. I caught an early train. I'm at the station.'

'Come straight here,' Sarah said. 'Are you on your own?'

'Yes. Harjeet has a meeting. He often works on weekends. I'll be there as soon as I can get a taxi.'

Sarah dressed quickly, and went to the corner bakery. When Lila arrived, the kitchen was redolent with the smell of fresh coffee and croissants.

'Rabindrah is showering and shaving,' Sarah said. 'So before he appears, tell me about Harjeet, marriage, where you are living – I want to hear everything. You look beautiful, by the way.'

Lila was dressed in designer clothes, and her black hair was swept back and secured with a pearl comb. Sarah thought she looked glamorous but sad, and too thin. They sat down at the kitchen table and poured coffee.

'I'm fine.' Lila's expression was neutral. 'Harjeet is fine.'

'Fine?' Sarah looked at her closely. 'That's it?'

'You know the situation.' Lila concentrated on her croissant. 'Ours was an arranged marriage. A business deal, really. I didn't love him when I married him, and I knew he didn't love me. But I've known him since we were children, and I believed we could make a good life together. I wasn't expecting the earth to move, Sarah. He's not very –' She stopped to search for the right word. 'Demonstrative,' she said at last. 'It's a family trait. His parents are quite formal. Cold, in fact.'

'Were you close, as children?'

'His father, Manjit, was very hard on him, growing up. He had rules and expectations, and Harjeet had to fulfil them or pay a heavy price. We used to talk about it, as kids. For some reason he said things to me that he couldn't discuss with anyone else, especially the other boys, for fear of being called a sissy. One time there was a crowd of us at my parents' house, and everyone except Harjeet wanted to go swimming at the club. I stayed behind to keep him company. When the others left, he showed me why he hadn't gone – there were big red marks on his legs and his back where he had been beaten. I can't remember what for, but it was a minor transgression. He was about thirteen. I took some salve from my mother's medicine cabinet, and rubbed it on the welts. He made me promise not to tell anyone, and then he kissed me! I had no idea what to do or say, so I ran off, giggling like an idiot.'

'Childhood sweethearts,' Sarah said. 'I had hoped there might be a special thing between you.'

'Well, there isn't,' Lila said flatly. 'We used to spend time together, playing tennis and riding our bikes. But then his family left for England. I hardly saw him from that day on, except when they came back to Kenya on short visits. There was a kind of bond between us, though. That shared secret. The kiss. So when his parents spoke to my family about an arrange-ment, I agreed. We were in a desperate situation financially, and Manjit was offering a way out. I thought marriage with Harjeet would not be so bad.'

'And?'

'It's like I said. It's fine.'

'But you were expecting something deeper, after what you shared as children. Is that it?'

'I had hopes.' Lila shrugged off the question. 'But it is early days, and we don't know each other yet. I suppose I placed too much importance on something he has probably forgotten. Maybe he doesn't want to remember such a time, now that he is a man. He is polite, but distant. He does his duty as a husband, but then he turns his back and goes to sleep.' Her smile was wan. 'There are even days when he sleeps in another room, or doesn't come home at night. Of course, we are still living in his parents' home, which is difficult. It's hard to like Manjit. He is a remote, unbending sort of person. And Harjeet is still afraid of him.'

'What about your mother-in-law?'

'Very traditional,' Lila said. 'She never disagrees with her husband or voices an opinion when he is around. A typical, old-fashioned wife whose place is to serve. We don't have much in common, and it's a strain being cooped up in the house with her for hours at a time. I get dragged out to coffee mornings or afternoon tea with her friends, which is deadly. I hope things will be better when our own place is ready, and we can make a life for just the two of us.' She sat stirring her coffee, her eyes vacant for a time. 'I finally told Harjeet I couldn't stay at home all day and do nothing. Now I have a part-time job in the office. Secretarial work. It gets me out of the house for some of the time. Still, I'm not sure I want to become any more involved in their business.'

'I understand that,' Sarah said. 'Living and working with your husband can be difficult. Although it was wonderful when Rabindrah and I were doing books together.'

'At least it makes me feel less claustrophobic,' Lila said. 'I was never one for endless talk of cooking and the best way to clean this and that, and Harjeet's mother is very house-proud. Of course, if I was pregnant everything would be different. Then I would be the golden girl in the family's eyes, with some prestige of my own.' She stopped. 'I'm sorry. This is a bad subject for you.'

'My lack of children is not a taboo subject. It's something I have to deal with and try to accept.' Sarah sighed. 'Anyway, I'm seeing a specialist in Ireland. Next week.'

'Well, at least you and Rabindrah have each other.'

'Oh Lila!' Sarah gazed at her in sympathy. 'I'm sure Harjeet will come to love you. When you move into your own place and he can escape from his father.'

'I don't know when that might be.' Lila shook her head. 'They work together every day, and eventually Harjeet is expected to take over the business.'

'What do they actually do?' Sarah realised she had never enquired before.

'It's an import and export set-up. They buy and sell all kinds of commodities. Not only in the UK, but in Europe and Africa and the Far East. Harjeet is in the office at all hours, and he travels, too. In the beginning I asked if I could go with him occasionally, but he said that would not be possible.' She hesitated, lit a cigarette and blew out a long stream of smoke, measuring her next words. 'Sometimes I worry about it all. About how dangerous it is.'

'Dangerous?' Sarah was puzzled.

'Oh, I'm being foolish. Probably imagining things.' Lila's response was hasty. 'When Harjeet goes back to Kenya with Manjit I become anxious, because I know he doesn't like working there. He doesn't say anything about it, though, so I can't raise the subject. But I've seen things that – anyway, he won't let me go with him, even though I would love to see my parents. They haven't been able to visit me here, either. Manjit promised they would, after we were married, but I suppose it's too soon and visas are complicated.'

The discussion was shelved when Rabindrah appeared and they lingered over breakfast, talking about family and friends in Nairobi. But when she spoke about her parents and her brothers and how desperately she missed them, Lila's tears spilled over and Rabindrah tried to comfort her.

'Tell me about Camilla.' She opened a crocodile-skin handbag with a gold chain and took out a handkerchief. 'I'd love to have seen her when she was in London during July and August, but I know how busy she gets. I always dreamed of running a boutique for her one day. Even here. I'd so love to have something really challenging to do. A project of my own.'

'Would Harjeet set you up in Birmingham?' Rabindrah asked. 'Selling Camilla's fashion accessories and clothes?'

'Not much potential for that kind of thing in Birmingham,' Lila said, her tone wry. 'It's hardly the centre of the fashion world. Unless I held small gatherings in private homes, and invited people to buy privately. Like a posh Tupperware party. But I don't have the contacts for that yet, and my mother-in-law's friends wouldn't be much help. Anyway, that's enough moaning.' She made a brave attempt to brighten her mood. 'Did you see the picture of Camilla and Tom Bartlett plastered all over the *Daily Mirror*? I felt badly for her.'

'I don't think she worries about the kind of rubbish they write about her in gossip columns. Anyway she's in New York for three weeks, and then she goes back to Kenya.' Sarah stood up. 'Let's clear this table and go out on the town. We are meeting Pavith and Mo at one o'clock, but in the meantime there are some wonderful exhibitions to look in on. What would you like to see?'

They left the flat to spend the rest of the morning in the Royal Academy, and then made their way to Hyde Park where Rabindrah's sister and her family were waiting for them, with a large picnic hamper.

'This was Mo's idea,' Pavith said. 'Much better to be in a place where the children can run around. We're lucky it's such a beautiful day.'

They sprawled on two rugs spread out on the grass, enjoying the late summer sunshine. Sarah felt a sense of family that she rarely experienced with her other Indian relatives, and by the end of the afternoon Lila was her old vivacious self.

'Can you stay overnight?' Rabindrah asked his cousin, as they made their way back to Camilla's flat.

'I promised I'd take the six o'clock train,' Lila said with regret. 'Harjeet's auntie – his father's sister – is coming for dinner, and they will expect me to be there. She is not someone who would take kindly to my absence, and neither would Manjit. It was good to see you both – and Pavith, and Mo. I hope they will come to Birmingham one day, and meantime I must try to get away more often. Thank you for a lovely day.' She lowered her voice as she embraced Sarah. 'I hope it goes well with the specialist in Dublin,' she murmured, and then turned to her cousin. 'Give my love to everyone at home, Rabindrah. Tell them how much I miss them all.' With a final wave she climbed into a taxi, and through the window Sarah could see her, valiantly smiling through her tears as she drove away.

'Poor Lila is having a tough time adjusting,' Rabindrah said, as he and Sarah lay in bed that night.

'Yes. It's been hard for her.' Sarah repeated what she had learned. But for some reason she left out Lila's sense of some hidden danger in her husband's business. It seemed to have been a private and perhaps unfounded feeling, and she did not want to make her friend sound foolish. 'I think she would be happy to fall in love with Harjeet, if he gave her any encouragement. What an idiot, to waste such an opportunity! You know who he reminds me of?'

'Who?'

'Anthony. With Camilla.'

'I don't think Harjeet runs after other women, does he? That has always been part of Anthony's problem. As well as finding it impossible to make a commitment.'

'He did ask Camilla to marry him once,' Sarah said in his defence. 'She was on the brink of accepting, but then she thought he had had a fling with some American woman, so she came back to London. She would never have returned to Nairobi at all, if George hadn't died in the crash.'

'She has had her share of misfortunes,' Rabindrah said. 'I hope her long years of waiting for Anthony don't prove to be a waste.'

'He was and is amazingly blind,' Sarah said. 'Just as Harjeet seems unable to use his eyes and ears, and realise what a stunning wife he has acquired.'

'Perhaps he will come round,' Rabindrah said. 'Living in someone else's house, always at someone else's table, beholden to their rules – none of that will do much for romance. The sooner they get their own place the better. But you're right. How could he not be won over by a girl as beautiful and as warm as Lila?'

'How can you lie here beside me, and not be won over by someone who loves you so much?' Sarah said softly.

He leaned over her and kissed her on the lips, and she put her arms around him, hoping that this would be the time for the barriers to fall, willing their old, easy intimacy to grow into new passion. His caress was tender, and she pressed closer, offering herself, moving her hands down his body, showing him her need. But he drew away abruptly.

'I can't,' he said in a low voice. 'I seem to have lost the power.' He sat up, and swung his legs out from the covers. Sarah propped herself up, trailing her fingers down his back, wanting to comfort him.

'What is it, Rabindrah? Can't you tell me what is troubling you? We were always able to talk to one another in the past.'

He was silent, sitting on the side of the bed, his head in his hands. 'I'm having a problem getting an erection,' he said, finally. 'I want to make love to you, Sarah. Really, I do. But my body goes slack at the wrong moment. It's something I have no control over.'

She slid out of the bed, and knelt beside him, taking his hands from his face and looking into his eyes. 'It happens,' she said. 'You lost as much as I did over the past year. When we are calm and happy again, it will all come right. I'm sure of it. So you are not to worry about anything. Lie down again, and let's just hold each other till we sleep.'

In the half light they listened to the hum of late-night London traffic, their arms around one another. It was never completely dark here, Sarah thought. Not like the blackness of an African night. The street lamps left a residue of orange across the city skyline, glowing dully, obliterating the shimmer of distant stars. The sound of revellers drifted up from the pavement below, laughter and good-natured shouts, and the click-clack of high heels on the way home from a restaurant or night club. She lay beside Rabindrah and vowed to restore him, somehow, to the vital lover he had once been. The specialist in Dublin might have some advice, and a solution. And she wondered if Lila would ever find a place in the cold world of Harjeet Singh.

Chapter 8

Ireland, September 1977

Raphael was waiting for them at Dublin Airport. He was as rumpled as ever, his thinning hair blown about by the stiff wind that had caused a bumpy landing. Sarah ran to her father as soon as she spotted him in the crowd, hovering around the arrivals gate. She held on to him tightly, breathing in the familiar smell of pipe tobacco from his old tweed jacket, relieved to find that he had not changed. In her world, where everything seemed to be shifting and unsure, he was one of the constants, a lighthouse shining out a safe passage.

'Dad! Oh Dad, I am so happy to see you. It's been so long . . .'

'Too long.' Raphael smiled at Rabindrah over the top of her head.

'And Mum? I can't wait to see her.'

'She is in great form. Looking forward to your arrival. Now if we can just track down the car . . .'

It took him a long time to figure out where exactly he had parked. They were all laughing as they finally shared his triumph of discovery and piled the baggage into the boot.

'You are impossible, Dad.' Sarah looked at him with devoted amusement. 'He does it every single time,' she said to Rabindrah. 'Forgets which row – sometimes which level.'

'But I always pick a landmark,' Raphael protested. 'So as to be sure I can remember exactly where I parked in relation to the terminal. I'm convinced some imp moves all the cars about, once you lock up and go away. That's the only explanation. It's a conspiracy. Like the disappearance of single socks in the washing machine, that your mother is always complaining about. Ha! There it is. Not where I left it at all. I'm sure of that.'

'All right. It's a wicked conspiracy.' Sarah was laughing as her father drove out onto the main road. 'So, where are we going first?'

'Straight into town,' he said. 'I thought it would be best to get your session with Stephen Devanny over right away. Then we head for Sligo, and you'll see him again in a week or so for the results of whatever tests he arranges. He's the best in the country, and very booked up. We trained in the Mater together and he's doing me a favour today, slotting you in before his usual afternoon appointments. We'll be just in time.'

Sarah was deeply apprehensive about the consultation, aware that what she might learn could destroy the threads of hope to which she still clung. If the prognosis was bad, how would Rabindrah feel, and what would it do to their marriage? She only half listened to the conversation between her father and her husband as they threaded their way through the city traffic. They were discussing the violence in Northern Ireland, and its overspill into bomb attacks in the South and on the British mainland.

'Despite winning the Nobel Peace Prize last year, the northern peace process seems to have stalled again,' Raphael said. 'Now, with the protests by IRA prisoners in the Maze Prison, the situation is becoming even worse. You wouldn't believe the number of splinter organisations on both sides of the struggle, most of them more than willing to murder a member of an opposing group.'

'It's the kind of brutality people associate with Third World countries, but in fact this type of violence is all over Europe,' Rabindrah said. 'I'm thinking of ETA in Spain and the Baader Meinhof Group in Germany, to name just two.'

'No one seems safe any more, from these barbaric political activists who purport to be waging war in my name and yours. Peace and harmony always appear to be blood-spattered around the edges these days.' Raphael had slowed to a snail's pace. 'How are the Olsens, by the way? Did they enjoy their time in Europe?'

'We saw them just before we left. They had a wonderful holiday, although Piet has had a series of ear infections that might have caused hearing damage,' Rabindrah said.

'I hope they know that he should see a specialist right away.' Raphael was frowning. 'There are some very good fellows in Nairobi that I've known for years, if they want a recommendation. Delay could cause permanent loss.'

'Hannah is taking him to a specialist this week,' Sarah said, looking at her watch, unable to think about her friends in her anxiety to get to the consulting rooms. 'Dad? Aren't we running late?'

'It's all right. We're here.' Raphael turned into a leafy square bordered by tall, red brick Georgian terraces. 'This is it. And a car is pulling out right in front of the building. Hah! What luck!'

The waiting room was full and Sarah wondered how long they would have to sit there. She lifted a magazine to stare unseeingly at the photographs, fretting as the minutes crawled by. But it was not long before the receptionist called them through.

Stephen Devanny was a big, bluff man with a kindly face. Raphael greeted him briefly, then turned to the door.

'I have a couple of messages to do,' he said. 'I'll meet you at the Shelbourne Hotel, say around four? Will that be time enough, Stephen?'

'Should be about right. I've arranged for Sarah to go over to Holles Street Hospital for an ultrasound and blood tests, but that won't take too long.'

Raphael left, and Sarah and Rabindrah sat down opposite the doctor. He smiled encouragingly as he started to make notes.

'Now, I'll need to make notes on your history first,' he said. 'So let's go back to the onset of your periods, Sarah, and start from there.'

She found it easy enough to talk about her growing up, and even the early years of her marriage, but as they moved on to the first miscarriage, a welling up of grief made the story increasingly difficult to tell. When she came to the second tragedy, her voice broke, and Rabindrah had to answer for her after a while. She gripped his hand tightly, her fingers digging into his palm.

'I did not realise that you had miscarried. And I know this is hard.' Stephen Devanny was genuinely sympathetic. 'I'm sorry to make you go through it all over again, but we do need the maximum amount of information if we're to get to the root of the problem. So tell me exactly how the bleeding began, the second time. Was there any pain beforehand? Vomiting?'

Sarah stared out the window, digging down into the bitterness of loss. 'I have to approach this like a scientist,' she said to herself. 'Recite the medical facts. Look only at the physical signs. Not think of my children dying inside me.' She took a deep breath, and began to recount the details, her voice flat, concentrating hard so as not to leave anything out, describing all that had happened including her devastation at the loss of the second baby. When she had finished, there was silence in the room.

'Thank you, my dear,' Dr Devanny said. 'That was very comprehensive and very brave. Now I'd like to examine you, and then I'll send you over to the hospital for your scan and the blood tests. And Rabindrah?'

'Yes?'

'I think it would be as well for you to have a sperm count at the same time. So you will be asked to go through that while Sarah's ultrasound is being carried out.'

'Is that really necessary?' Rabindrah was taken by surprise.

'It's best to explore every possibility although the choice is, of course, entirely yours. Now, let's get your examination over and done with, Sarah.'

She undressed behind a screen and lay down with her eyes shut, willing herself to remain calm during the process. The specialist emerged smiling, presumably for reassurance. But the cheery expression irritated Rabindrah and made him uncomfortable. When Sarah had dressed and returned to her chair, Dr Devanny folded his hands in front of him.

'I can't find anything obviously amiss in my examination, but the ultrasound will show the uterus and the surrounding area more clearly,' he said. 'So I'd like you to head off for your sperm and blood tests now. Within a few days I will have all the results and we will go on from there.' He stood up and held out his hand. 'I can assure you that we will do everything possible to arrive at a solution that will allow you to become parents. We'll make another appointment for you with my secretary. It shouldn't take more than a week to get the analyses back. Is that all right?'

'Yes, thank you.' Sarah's voice was barely above a whisper. She had found the questioning and the probing of the physical examination invasive and distressing, and she longed for a warm, soothing bath and a period of privacy to regain her equilibrium.

'And remember that you have had two pregnancies. Not successful, obviously, but it does mean you are able to conceive naturally, and that is a good sign. So don't be worrying now. Here are the forms you will need to sign for your tests. I'll see you both again, soon.'

Sarah's tests at the hospital seemed straightforward compared to what she had already endured, but when the moment came for Rabindrah to produce a sample of sperm she felt his embarrassment as he took the container and vanished into a cubicle.

'There are some magazines in there that might help,' the nurse said, making his discomfort even more acute.

They met again in the main reception area, neither one able to look directly at the other or to speak of their experiences and what they might mean. It was a relief to reach the Shelbourne Hotel where Raphael was sitting in the large, comfortable lounge. He took a quick look at his daughter's pinched face, and ordered afternoon tea with sandwiches, and toasted scones and jam.

'Bad, was it?' he said.

'Going over everything from the beginning was hard. But she was very brave.' Rabindrah rested a hand on the nape of his wife's neck, and she leaned against him on the sofa, overcome by exhaustion and close to tears. But when the tea came she was surprised to find how hungry she was. They talked deliberately of light-hearted things, and shortly afterwards they set out on the road to the west.

It was late by the time they reached the house at Grange. The sky had faded to a yellow glow after a spectacular sunset, and shadows stretched along the gravel drive as they turned in the gates. The front door stood open and welcoming. Two rough collies rushed out, barking and wagging their plumed tails at the sound of the engine. Betty Mackay followed, her face alight with joy as Sarah jumped out of the car and rushed into her open arms. Minutes later Rabindrah was enfolded in the same warm embrace, and they went into the sitting room where several logs had been set in the enormous grate.

'I lit the fire for you thin-blooded Africans,' Betty said. 'Though it's been so warm these past weeks that the rest of us will want to put on our swimming togs! Now, what about a drink? I have a nice casserole in the oven, if that's all right?' She stood back to look at Sarah, her eyes glistening. 'It's wonderful to have you home again, darling girl. And looking great, the pair of you.'

'Tell us about Tim,' Sarah said. 'Was there anywhere more distant and primitive that he could have chosen?'

'New Guinea is not for the faint-hearted,' Raphael said. 'It is a constant challenge, and tomorrow we will show you his letters and photographs. The people are not easy to deal with. Communication is difficult with more than a hundred tribal languages. And there are few roads in that steep, wild terrain. So Tim is learning to fly, and he loves that.'

'From Sligo to Madang,' Betty said. 'Almost without a backward glance. It's hard to believe sometimes that our children are grown and more than half way across the planet.'

They sat talking about all that had happened since they had been together last, until Rabindrah went upstairs to freshen up, leaving Sarah alone with her parents. She stood up, swallowed hard and began.

'There's something you don't know,' she said. 'I didn't tell you this before, because Rabindrah and I didn't feel that we could discuss it with his family, and so we decided to keep it to ourselves. I think we were wrong, but it was – Well, anyway, the thing is that I have been pregnant.' She heard Betty's gasp of surprise and hurried on. 'Twice. But I miscarried, and then I had a kind of breakdown earlier this year. After the second one . . .'

'Oh my poor child,' Betty said, rising from the armchair and coming to put her arms around Sarah. 'You should have told us. It might have helped, you know. Just to talk about it with the people who love you best.'

'I know that.' Sarah was contrite. 'Only I didn't think it fair to Rabindrah to keep it from his family and not from you.'

'I see why you might not have wanted to tell them. You've hinted before that there was a lot of pressure on you because you hadn't produced a child, which is mainly what a woman is good for in their culture,' Betty said.

'That's not entirely true.' Sarah was defensive. 'They were disappointed for Rabindrah. And a miscarriage often brands a wife as a failure, or someone who brings bad luck to the family.'

'But we are not like them,' Betty said. 'We would have understood, Sarah. You should have had enough confidence in us to know that.'

'It wasn't about confidence,' Sarah said. 'Surely you can understand that –'

'No, I can't really,' Betty said. 'Your father and I are very sad to hear this.'

'Betty, my dear.' Raphael frowned at his wife. 'What is important is that these two young people have lived through these tragedies with great courage. And now we are in a position to help them, and maybe to find a solution to the problem. That is the only thing we need to think about in these circumstances.'

Betty opened her mouth to make a further comment, but she was prevented from doing so by the arrival of Rabindrah, with a package of gifts they had brought from Nairobi and London. When the meal was ready, Betty led them to the dining room, where she had put out the best silver and glassware. The mahogany table shone in the reflection of candlelight, and linen napkins stood in mitred elegance, tucked into Irish crystal goblets. Sarah took Rabindrah's hand, moved by her mother's loving preparations for the homecoming. After dinner they returned to the fire with the dogs settling on the hearthrug beside them.

'You must be tired after all your travels. And the visit to Stephen Devanny.' Betty stroked her daughter's hair. 'Don't worry, my dear. He's the best in his field, Raphael says. When will you have to go back and see him again?'

'Late next week.' Rabindrah realised that Sarah could not cope with any more questions. 'He was very kind and I'm sure his advice will be sound.' He stood up. 'I think we should probably retire. As you say, we've had a long day. Thank you Betty, for your welcome dinner — you know how I love good, traditional Irish fare. And you, Raphael, for all the fetching and carrying. Sarah?'

'Yes, I'll hit the hay too.' She rose and embraced her parents. 'I'm wiped out. I'll see you all tomorrow.'

Dawn brought a soft light that filtered through the curtained windows. Rising quietly so as not to wake her husband, Sarah crept downstairs and outside, calling softly to the dogs to accompany her. It was a cool morning, with only the whistle and rustlings of the birds to disturb the silence. Mist curling over the hedges had blocked out the view of the sea beyond the lawn, but it looked as if it would be a beautiful day. The rising sun would soon clear the air and open up the vista of Sligo Bay and Ben Bulben's stately silhouette. Strolling down to the stables, she stood at each half door, murmuring to the horses inside, laying her cheek against their velvety muzzles, loving their scent and the aroma of hay and grain from their warm breath. Tomorrow she would ride out onto Streedagh Beach and across the dunes to Mullaghmore, if the time of the tides was right. Maybe Rabindrah would come with her.

She walked back to the house and found her father in the kitchen, making coffee.

'You're up early.' He kissed her. 'Did you sleep all right?'

'Like a log. But I wanted to take a look around. It all looks wonderfully unchanged.'

'Well, you know, old dinosaurs like us don't change much, and we like our surroundings to stay the same. There's consolation in familiarity and humdrum, when you get to our age.'

'What's all this talk of old? You're the youngest old dinosaur I've ever met,' Sarah said with a laugh. 'That smells good.' She indicated the percolator, bubbling comfortably on the counter. 'Is Mum still asleep?'

'Yes. I like my early morning start, and she likes her lie-in. That hasn't changed either. Toast?'

'Yes, please. Lots of it, with Mum's homemade marmalade.' She poured two steaming mugs of coffee and they sat companionably at the table, eating breakfast as they had done year after year through her African childhood.

When Rabindrah appeared he was full of energy and completely refreshed. He and Sarah decided to climb Ben Bulben during the morning. It was a steep ascent, scrambling along boggy turf tracks and over granite rocks, but the views from its flat top were spectacular, south across the county, west along the shining expanse of Sligo Bay, out to the Atlantic, and north to the blue spine of the Donegal mountains. The wind buffeted them as they climbed, tearing at their hair and their anoraks when they reached the summit. On the horizon, a bank of rain cloud was rising, black across the silvered water, the sun behind it sending streaks of light down into the sea. On the slopes below them, sheep grazed in slow-moving dots of white against the vivid green of cropped grass, their bleating echoing across the mountain. From the flatlands further down came the calmer lowing of cattle. They could see the house from their vantage point, its slate roof and gracious Georgian windows in clear focus before the coming storm.

'Don't you often feel too far away from your parents?' Rabindrah looked down at the country spread out before him. 'You are much closer to them than I am to my family, and you haven't been able to spend much time with them since they left Kenya.' The words were whipped from his lips by the wind, and Sarah had to strain to hear what he was saying.

'I love visiting them, but I couldn't see myself staying here for more than a few weeks.' She raised her voice to compete with the elements. 'The wet and the cold would drive me mad, for a start. And the west gets more rain than any other part of Ireland, which is saying a lot! Besides, this was never my home, except for a few months before I went out to work for Allie and Dan in Buffalo Springs. Ireland is my parents' life since Dad retired, but Kenya will always be my soul's resting place. Why are you asking?'

'If things began to go badly wrong in Kenya, I wonder what we would do,' Rabindrah said. 'None of us knows what might happen in the future. Africanisation may take our jobs away. And if we weren't able to work, how could we stay? I think we should keep that in the backs of our minds. This country is stable – well, this part of it, anyway – and it is yours. You have the right to earn your living here. No one can stop you.'

'What on earth are you talking about?' Sarah was dumbfounded. 'You love Kenya as much as I do – we are committed to the country. It's our home. You are a citizen, born in Nairobi as were your parents. And although I've managed to keep my Irish passport, I have citizenship too. We couldn't be turfed out. I don't see how you could possibly lose your job.'

'That depends on what I write about,' he said. 'Gordon might be put in a position one day where both of us would be without jobs.'

'Even if that happened we have our book projects,' Sarah said. 'And you could do more freelancing for overseas newspapers. Do you know something you're not telling me?'

'Not really. But you heard what the family said, in London. They are deeply concerned that all non-Africans, and particularly us Asians, are going to find it increasingly difficult to remain there and make a living. Look how badly it has affected Gulab and Anjit. What would have happened to them, if Lila had not been able to secure their future? And it could still blow up in their faces, if their African business partners turn out to be crooks.'

'It wouldn't surprise me at all if they were crooks. But we are not dependent on trading licences like they are. We don't run a business,' Sarah said. 'You're a journalist. I'm a wildlife photographer and a conservationist. There will always be work for us. The problem is that Asians are finding it hard to obtain business permits and trading licences. It's natural that they have become pessimistic. But we're not in those kind of circumstances at all. Jomo Kenyatta, for all his faults, has been happy to keep on anyone who makes a contribution to the country. Strongly encouraged it, in fact.'

'He won't last forever,' Rabindrah said. 'He's already fading, and surrounded by vultures jostling for power.'

A gust of wind almost toppled them, and with it came the first eddy of rain.

'Come on!' Sarah shouted into the swirl of the downpour. 'We'd better get off this mountain before we're blown away.'

She grabbed Rabindrah's hand, and they scrambled and slid down the steep slopes, the rain hurling fat drops after them to speed their descent. By the time they reached the car, they were drenched to the skin, and all further discussion about the future was lost in the race to get home, change out of their saturated clothing, and curl up in front of Betty's open fire.

The week flew by, and Sarah was almost able to forget the impending test results. There were family and friends to visit. She and Rabindrah rode out in the mornings when the weather was fine enough, and they walked the dogs in the hills, or down the long beach where the seals came to sun themselves. Raphael took them sailing in his skiff, out in the bay among a school of dolphins. Sarah lay across the deck, her camera clicking, capturing the light and motion and the sleek backs and powerful tailfins of their marine companions. Their smiling faces and bright intelligent eyes reached across the divide between man and animal to share with her the secrets of the sea. She took a series of shots as Rabindrah leaned over the prow, whooping like a schoolboy with each somersault of the playful creatures diving and surging around the boat. When they turned for home at last, their guard of honour swam beside them to the mouth of the harbour before swinging away towards the open sea, puffing out farewell jets of water into the evening air.

Later, sitting on the steps of the terrace, watching the sun sink into the water, she leaned against Rabindrah.

'Now that's the kind of thing that could tempt me into staying for a while,' she said. 'The sheer exuberance of those creatures. Literally jumping for joy, so totally at home with what and where they are. It was a privilege to share the bay with them today.'

'You can drive Betty's car up to Dublin the day after tomorrow, if you like.' Raphael opened a beer that he handed to his son-in-law. 'In fact, why don't you stay overnight and take in a theatre or a concert or something? It's a pity to trek all that way and have to come back in the one day.'

'Thanks, Raphael. I appreciate it.' Rabindrah hesitated, unaccustomed to sharing his innermost concerns. 'Sarah told you about the miscarriages? We never told my family. She didn't think she could face the questions of my tribe.'

'I'm sure your family would be more understanding if they knew the truth. You might at least think of mentioning it to your mother. I know Sarah is fond of her, and they get on well.'

'Yes. I suppose we should have done that in the first place. But Sarah didn't want their pity or their interference. She was too fragile, especially the second time.'

'A woman who loses two babies *always* needs family support to cope with the aftermath,' Raphael said. 'No matter what she might think. We can only pray that if she gets pregnant again she'll finally go to full term, and have a healthy child. But if the worst happened, and she miscarried . . .'

'I don't know if we should take that risk,' Rabindrah said.

Raphael looked at him keenly. 'What does Sarah say about that?' he asked.

'She's agreed to wait. Not to try again till we know if there's a likelihood of losing another child.'

Rabindrah knew the words were not true. Sarah was willing to risk everything. It was he who was afraid. Afraid of losing the woman who was life and breath to him. Afraid of the crippling depression and despair that had driven her away the last time, so that he had begun to believe she would never return.

'Well, all I can say is that my daughter is a stubborn young woman.' Raphael drained his beer. 'If she's set her heart on this, she won't give up, no matter what the consequences may be.'

The drive to Dublin was a staccato of hurried conversation punctuated by silences. Time dragged in the waiting room. When she eventually heard the doctor's voice in the corridor, Sarah's heart began to hammer under her ribs. In the carpeted room she watched as Stephen Devanny cleared his throat and rustled through case notes and test results. He looked up and smiled the calm smile that was beginning to infuriate them both.

'Well now,' he said. 'It's as I thought. Nothing showed up on Sarah's scan or the ultrasound. A slight narrowing of one of the fallopian tubes, but not so significant that it would prevent ovulation. No, that's not the problem at all.' He turned to another of the printed reports in the file. 'In fact the difficulty is with you, Rabindrah. Your sperm count is abnormally low. I would say this is the reason why conception has been difficult. And when it did occur, unfortunately the egg was fertilised by a defective sperm, so the foetus could not develop.'

Rabindrah stared at Devanny in shock, hardly able to take in what he had heard. 'You are saying this is my fault?'

'Nobody is at fault, Rabindrah. Let me make that clear. There are plenty of men with your condition, and it does not appear to be related to diet, physique, general state of health or sexual appetite. It is, sadly, an area of medicine which is seriously under-researched. In fact we don't even know exactly what a normal sperm count should be, but the lowest figure you should have would be in the region of ten million motile sperm per millilitre. Yours is significantly below that. However, I can tell you that many men with a quarter of that percentage have succeeded in fathering a child. Because in the end, it only takes one sperm to fertilise an egg. Although you have been a long time trying, and both fertilisations have failed ultimately, that will not necessarily prevent success in the future.'

Rabindrah sat utterly still, stunned. Sarah put out a consoling hand, but he flinched at her touch.

'Is there any way of increasing the sperm count, Dr Devanny?' she asked, after the silence had stretched beyond endurable.

'I'm afraid not.' The doctor shook his head regretfully. 'There is no effective treatment as yet. The best way to deal with a low sperm count at present is to increase the fertility potential in the female partner. There is an effective drug on the market that you could try, Sarah, but it does have some side effects. For example, it increases the likelihood of multiple births, which carries a whole other set of risks. I can put you on a course of that treatment, if you would like. And there is also a process called intrauterine insemination.'

'Like they do with cows?' Sarah shuddered. 'It all seems so clinical, somehow. I don't know that I could . . .' Rabindrah had not contributed anything further to the conversation, and she glanced at him, disturbed by his silence.

'I'll give you some literature on this medicine I mentioned, and on the intrauterine process,' Dr Devanny said, gathering together his notes. 'You can take them away to read them at your leisure and discuss the options, before you make any decisions. Raphael will be able to explain the details. And you can contact me again whenever you wish. I'm here to help in any way I can.'

'We're going back to Kenya next week.' Sarah's face was bleak. 'I'll take the information anyway, and discuss it with my father. Thank you.'

'I'm sorry I couldn't offer a more positive or instant solution.' The specialist rose, shook hands with Sarah and gave her copies of the medical reports and the information leaflets. Rabindrah followed her from the room without a word.

In the street, the life of the city swept by in the crowds and the traffic, untouched by their personal tragedy. Sarah reached for Rabindrah's hand and this time he allowed her to take it, but he did not return the pressure of her fingers. He walked quickly, his face set, and she had to hurry to keep pace with him. They turned into Stephen's Green, and followed the paved edge of an ornamental lake where ducks congregated in large numbers, barging and quacking and squabbling noisily over crusts of bread offered by passers-by. There was a bench set in a quiet area of the gardens, surrounded by a hedge, and he sank down, staring at the ground. Sarah sat beside him, searching for the right words to say, but finding nothing.

'All this time,' he said. 'All this time, it never occurred to me that I was the one with the problem. I suppose I considered conception – carrying a child – that was your part of the marriage. I never thought . . . God, Sarah, my family were blaming you, and all the time it was me. My fault.'

'No one is to *blame*. It's a condition you have no control over.' She shook his sleeve, making him turn to face her. 'We could still be lucky. He did stress that. And even if we never have that particular blessing, we'll find other ways of fulfilment.'

'If you had married someone else –'

'Stop, Rabindrah!' She took his face in her hands, and kissed him, trying to dilute the effect of the day's harsh truth. 'I wouldn't ever want to be married to anyone else. I love you. I chose you. I'll never regret that for one minute.'

They sat close for a while, not speaking. 'We should go back to the hotel,' he said, eventually. 'The play starts at eight and we need time to get ready.'

'Of course.' She hesitated. 'Dad will probably ring. Would you rather I didn't say anything?'

Rabindrah had a clear recollection of his conversation with her father. 'No,' he said. 'Tell him the truth. Tell Betty, too.'

'They don't all need to know. If you'd rather . . .'

'Oh, for God's sake, just be honest. I'm not going to hide behind your skirts because I hear something I don't like.'

She was taken aback by his vehemence, and he was immediately contrite.

'I'm sorry. Look, when we get to the hotel, I'm going to stop at the bar and have a drink. You ring your family and explain.'

She nodded, and when he had gone into the bar, she went upstairs to their room and dialled the number for Sligo.

'That's hopeful news,' Raphael said. 'You're only thirty-two years old and you still have time on your side. There is still a reasonable chance, Sarah. A number of my patients have become pregnant in similar circumstances, even without the help of these new drugs.'

His words did little to comfort her, however, and she hung up and sat on the bed, feeling forlorn and alone. Then she thought of Rabindrah and the blow that had shattered him, and she straightened her shoulders and began to prepare for the evening they had planned.

The play was good, and for a time it took their minds off the day's unexpected turn of events. But afterwards they lay awake through most of the night, each feigning sleep, unable to offer one another the comfort they both so badly needed.

They returned to Grange the following day, saying little on the journey. It was raining heavily when they arrived, and Rabindrah thought that the weather accurately reflected the mood of their homecoming. No one was willing to raise the subject of Dr Devanny's report or its implications, but when dinner was over Raphael looked at his daughter and son-in-law, and decided to break the dam of silence.

'Rabindrah and I will take our coffee in my study,' he said. 'Is that all right with you girls?'

The men left the table, Raphael carrying the decanter of whiskey, and the door closed behind them. Sarah felt her knees go weak, and she had to lean on the back of a chair to steady herself.

'Sit down, darling.' Her mother held her as she began to cry, and she sank onto the seat Betty had pulled out for her.

'It's so unfair, Mum. We both wanted children so much and I did all the right things, but nothing worked. And I've been blaming myself all along, wondering if it was a punishment for something.'

'Oh Sarah, love, how could that be?'

'I don't know. Rabindrah's family have been hard to take. And now it turns out it wasn't anything to do with me.' She wiped her eyes. 'In a weird, horrible way, I was glad when Stephen Devanny told us. For myself. Because people have made assumptions that were all wrong, and now I've been vindicated. And then I felt guilty, because Rabindrah is crushed. He can't even look at me, or touch me. I know he feels bad for me, as well as for himself, but I can't get near him to comfort him. To tell him it's all right.'

'Men aren't supposed to give way to their emotions that easily,' Betty said. 'And that may be even more the case with Indian men. It's surely harder for them to deal with such things. They feel they have to put a brave face on it. Be strong. A husband is expected to let his wife cry on his shoulder, but he is more inclined to do his crying alone.'

'I don't mind if he cries. I wish he would. I know you didn't want me to marry him, Mum, but he's a wonderful man. I love him and I know he loves me too, in spite of the hard times we've had with all this.' For a moment Sarah thought of telling her mother that Rabindrah was no longer able to make love to her, but it was too difficult; humiliating somehow. And she felt it would be disloyal to her husband.

'I was wrong about him in the beginning,' Betty said. 'He is a good man and you make a grand couple. To find out that he may never be able to father his own child is a terrible blow to his self-esteem. And his first reactions may well be disbelief, anger, resentment, and then guilt at depriving you of the joy of motherhood. I would say he's very confused right now, and the last thing he wants is to appear weak as well. So you will have to find a way to console him that still allows him to believe he is strong. And you must have patience.'

'I'm not so hot on patience.' Sarah gave a watery sniff.

'Nonsense,' Betty spoke briskly, 'You spend half your life studying wild animals. You must have the same patience as you have in your work, following your elephants or cheetahs in the bush. And when Rabindrah gets into bed beside you, hold him if he is ready to be held, but keep your distance if he is not. He needs space to swing his arms, if only to punch the wall. Go on, off with you!' She shooed her daughter away from the stack of dinner plates. 'I'm doing the washing up. You have another job entirely.'

Sarah stopped at the head of the stairs. She could hear Betty humming softly as she moved around the kitchen, and beyond her the low murmur of voices came from behind the closed door of the study. She wondered what kind of things her father might be saying to Rabindrah to ease his pain. He was a Sikh, a man of the warrior caste. This news had cut him to the core of his being, and she was no longer sure that comforting words and a loving embrace could heal the blow he had received. A blow that she feared might destroy her husband and her marriage.

Chapter 9

Kenya, September 1977

Sarah crouched in the tall grass, her lens trained on the young cheetahs. It was mid-morning with the sun high over the plain, insects buzzing lazily and the heat building like a pressure cooker. She had been following the three brothers over the past few days, recording their habits, their hunting methods, and the way they marked out their territory. Sometimes she rode with both Allie and Erope, but today she was alone with her Samburu colleague and friend. The years since they had worked together on elephant research shrank away to nothing as they picked up their old routine. Allie had reluctantly stayed in camp to tackle her accounts, waving them off with resignation as she returned to the pile of bills and receipts and tax forms.

Now Sarah wiped a trickle of sweat from her face, and settled herself more securely. The cheetah siblings worked well together, stalking as a team, running down their prey in a concerted action, sharing their food and spending time grooming each other. They were a sleek, healthy looking trio. Erope had told her they were about twenty months old. One of the group was clearly the leader, and Allie had named him Ajax because of his superior strength and size. He always instigated the hunt, the other two falling in with his strategy for a kill. Whenever they passed trees, bushes, or termite mounds, he would stop and spray a jet of pungent scent markers to proclaim ownership over the territory, and the other two followed his example.

'They are like twins, those two,' Allie had said when she first showed them to Sarah. 'I've called them Castor and Pollux. At first I could only tell them apart by the fact that the black rings on the end of Castor's tail are wider, and there's a bigger area of white on the tip.'

Ajax was a courageous animal, ready to take on all comers in defence of his brothers. He was easily identifiable from a nick in one ear, a legacy of some previous stand-off with another cheetah, or perhaps a confrontation with a lion. He was resting for the time being, but ever on the alert. His brothers lay close to him, replete after an early morning feast of young warthog. The three animals had demolished the carcass with urgent tearing and chewing, their eyes watchful for the first of the scavengers to be alerted by circling vultures. They had finished most of the meal before several hyenas hunched out of the bush, and the first vultures landed nearby, ready to profit from what was left behind. Grabbing a last morsel, the three cats moved away into the shade, and left the marauders to their squabbling over the little that remained.

As Sarah climbed back into the vehicle, Erope stopped and pointed towards a rise in the ground. Silhouetted against the skyline, she saw a solitary cheetah.

'Is it a female?' Sarah asked, as she trained her binoculars on the visitor.

'Too big,' Erope answered. 'And females do not have a ruff on the neck. He is older than the other three. This one is about two years old and I have seen him before. He had a sister, but she has left him to search for a mate, so he must hunt alone. He smells the others, from their scent markers, and he knows he cannot cross their boundaries. Still, he does not move too far away.'

'He's hungry.' On closer inspection she could see that the animal was not in good condition. He was scrawny, and his coat looked dry. 'Maybe not as good a hunter as the others.'

Erope nodded. 'Now his sister has left him, she will not return. Females can cross every territory when they are in season and looking for a mate, but the male must claim his own area, and fight to preserve it. This one is nervous because he is alone.'

Sarah studied the cheetah, wondering if he would risk coming any nearer. But he made no attempt to approach. Over the next few days she saw him often, hovering on the horizon, watching, waiting. Several times, when he came too close, Ajax stared down the intruder, but inevitably after an hour or two he would return. His hunting skills seemed poor and he made a number of bad choices, trying to bring down antelope that were too big for him to handle alone. Several kicks from flying hooves resulted in a bloodied head, before his potential victim escaped. When Sarah saw him gazing at the three brothers as they gorged on a kill, she felt sorry for him.

'What will become of him?' she asked Allie, later in the day.

'Nature does not support the weak in this kind of environment,' Allie said. 'You saw that in the north with the elephants. If this animal can't learn to make it on his own, he will soon be dead. It's the natural way of keeping the species strong and viable, sad though it may seem. The talented hunters, the fiercest fighters – their genes are the ones needed for the next generation.'

'I would like to see this one survive,' Sarah said. 'He's thin, but he's a beautiful specimen. Big, and with lovely markings. He's not getting enough food, though, and cheetahs don't eat carrion, do they?'

'No. Only fresh meat. They won't store a kill, or touch an old carcass. They won't even go back to one of their own kills, after another predator has snatched some of it. Much of what they catch is stolen from them. There is one advantage, however, in this day and age – it's more difficult for poachers to nab them, because they won't come to dead bait.'

'Well, I hope he can get his act together,' Sarah said. 'I'm going to concentrate on him over the next week or two, if that's all right with you. If he watches Ajax and the twins hunting, he might learn a thing or two and bring down dinner on his own.'

'Sarah, you never change!' Allie was laughing. 'Always on the side of the underdog. Or whatever poor creature is out there battling for life against the odds. But you had better get back to accepting nature's failures. Cheetahs have a high mortality rate, despite their speed and agility. You'll see a lot of them die, I'm afraid. What about giving your new friend a name?'

'Irial,' Sarah answered promptly. 'It's an Irish name, meaning 'lost one'. I think that suits him.'

'Hmmn. I hope he survives, then. For your sake.' Allie stood up and stretched. 'I'm for bed.' She lit a paraffin lamp and trimmed the wick. 'When is Rabindrah coming back?'

'He might be able to make it next week, for a few days.'

Sarah's tone was neutral, and Allie sat down again, looking at her with sympathy.

'Still dealing with the outcome of those tests?'

'Damn it, Allie,' Sarah sighed with frustration. 'I understand that it's a blow, but we have to accept the life we have, and be grateful for it.'

'I'm glad you have come to realise that,' Allie said.

'It's not as though he can never father a child,' Sarah said, stung by her friend's down-to-earth comment. 'The specialist was at pains to point out that if we had conceived twice, we could do it again. Things are not as impossible as we had feared. And I started on this fertility drug even though . . .'

'What?'

'It makes me rather wound up. I have terrible mood swings that I try to hide. I'm pretty sure it is the medicine, because I have only felt like that since I started taking it. The doctor in Dublin warned me about possible side effects. However, I'm willing to put up with that.'

'You had a bad time emotionally earlier in the year,' Allie reminded her.

'True. But I've been feeling pretty calm and well-balanced since I came back from Lake Turkana,' Sarah said.

'Well, I hope the side effects of this medicine won't hurt you. What about Rabindrah?'

'He has shut down inside. He doesn't want to discuss the issue. I wonder how long it will take for him to – to . . .' Sarah rose without finishing the sentence, and took up her lantern. 'Anyway, it's no good going round and round. As Mum said, I have to give him time. Meanwhile, I'll concentrate on Irial, and take the best photos I can. It's wonderful being back with you and Erope. Goodnight, Allie.'

'Goodnight. Keep strong, kiddo. And hopeful. It will work out. I'll come with you tomorrow, and inspect your new protégé.'

Allie watched until the reflected glow of the lantern shone out from the side of Sarah's tent. She wondered if she should say anything to Rabindrah on his next visit. Remind him how much his wife loved him, regardless of their chances as parents. But he would probably be offended if he thought that Sarah had discussed such intimate problems with anyone else. It was a minefield. With a sigh, she set off for her own sleeping quarters, calling out as she went, 'All finished, Ahmed. Chai at six, please.'

They spent the next morning looking for the three brothers, but there was no sign of them, or of Irial. Late in the afternoon they came upon a pack of hyenas gorging themselves on a Thomson's gazelle. In a dense outcrop of bushes nearby they could just make out the form of a cheetah, his body camouflaged by the vegetation. It was Erope who spotted him.

'It is the lone one,' he said quietly. 'He must have made the kill, and been driven from it by these *fisi*.'

'I hope he managed to eat some of it before they arrived,' Sarah said.

Vultures had also joined the throng around the carcass, and pitched battles broke out between the birds and hyenas as they jostled for strips of the red, glistening meat. Irial sat in his hiding place, watching his hard-earned meal being gobbled up.

'How frustrating,' Sarah said, pity in her voice. 'And yet he just sits there. Patient. Accepting.'

'If he was not alone, he might try to defend his kill,' Erope answered. 'But a cheetah could not survive a battle with several hyenas. A bite on the leg from the jaws of a *fisi* could be fatal. He would not be able to run, or hunt, and then he would starve. So he must let it go.'

'He'll probably hunt again when he's rested,' Allie said. 'He seems to have brought down a sizeable Tommie, though. Looks like Irial is finally learning.'

'I wonder where the other three have got to.' Sarah scanned the horizon through her binoculars. 'Is Irial hunting here because it's outside their territory?'

'Possibly, but it's not the best choice he could have made,' Allie said. 'There are more lions around here, and hyena. He'll have a tougher job keeping anything he brings down.'

They went in search of Lara and her cubs but this evening they, too, had disappeared from view. At sundown, they drove into camp, covered in dust and ready for cold drinks and hot showers. Ahmed hurried out to meet them.

'There is a radio message,' he told Allie. 'From the Bwana Hugo. He will arrive in Nairobi during the weekend.'

'Great news!' Allie was delighted. 'I've been half-expecting him since he got his doctorate, but I wasn't sure that he would actually make it.' She saw that Sarah had caught the loneliness in her voice, and her tone became brisk and practical. 'Better get the spare tent ready, Ahmed. And I must find someone to meet him, and see if I can book a seat on a plane into Keekorok. I wonder how long he'll be able to stay.'

'I'm sure Rabindrah would collect Hugo from the airport and run him out to Wilson when there's a plane coming down. In the meantime he could stay at our house. I might even be able to talk my absentee husband into joining us again. Let's get on the radio.'

Rabindrah and Hugo arrived a week later. Sarah greeted her husband with unabashed delight.

'I've missed you,' she said. 'We have new discoveries for you to write up.'

'Well, Dr Campbell.' Allie was smiling at her pale, lanky nephew. 'I suppose we should all bow and touch our forelocks! You look as though you could do with some sunshine and fresh air.'

'I'm the product of glorious Scottish weather,' Hugo said, laughing as he kissed his aunt. 'It's terrific to be here. Good to see you again, Sarah. Your husband has been a great host. He showed me some of your photographs for the new book. I hope I can help Allie, and take care of some donkey work for you both. Contribute something to the final result.'

Sarah held out a hand in welcome, and they gathered the bags and piled them into the Toyota.

'I showed Hugo the maps we've been working from,' Rabindrah said, as they climbed into the vehicle. 'The drive will help him to get his bearings.'

Sarah had started the car when several zebras wandered onto the airstrip. The plane was at the end of the dirt runway, engines revving for take-off.

'Better get rid of these fat fellows in their pyjamas,' she said, driving towards the herd and forcing them to break into a fast trot, and to wheel away from the strip. They were all laughing as they set off for the camp, Hugo and Allie in the back seat, standing in the open roof hatch as she explained the terrain and the best places to find the animals they were following. They saw a family of ostrich, large numbers of wildebeest, gazelle and impala, several topi and Maasai giraffe. A herd of buffalo lowered their heads belligerently as they passed by. But there were no big cats.

'It's too hot right now,' Allie said. 'Let's go back to camp. You can stow your things and have lunch. We'll head out in the afternoon, in pursuit of cheetahs.'

'I saw Indar and Kuldip yesterday,' Rabindrah said, as he and Sarah walked to their tent. 'And Indar wants to know how the car is doing, now that you have put it to work.'

'The bars he rigged are excellent, and the ledges and shelves inside the vehicle. It's the best car I've ever had,' Sarah said. She sat down on the camp bed and pulled off her safari boots, replacing them with open sandals. 'How is Kuldip? I'm glad you went to visit her.'

'She says she's fine, but she has lost a lot of weight and she is always tired. Dr Patel has told them it's nothing serious – a female malaise that will pass if she takes plenty of rest and some Ayurvedic potions he has given her. But I think poor Dr Patel is too old now. He doesn't keep up with the latest research. I suggested they get a second opinion, but you know how they are about medical matters.'

'I'll visit Kuldip as soon as I get back,' Sarah said. 'Bully her. It doesn't sound like a minor ailment to me. She's been unwell for a long time.'

'I have your prints here.' He produced a large folder from his bag. 'Including the pictures from Ireland. The ones with the dolphins are wonderful.'

He sat down beside her and they sifted through the photographs of the trip to Sligo. Sarah smiled fondly as she looked at a close-up portrait of her father, standing in the rose dusk of evening on the terrace of the old house. He was looking into the sun, smiling and contented, eyes squinting a little in the strong light that shone directly on his kindly face. The next series of prints had been taken on their boat ride in Donegal Bay and she laughed with pleasure at the memory of it. One picture, especially, took her fancy. Rabindrah was leaning over the prow, his hands almost touching a leaping dolphin as it rose out of the bow wave in an arc, its bright eyes and wide, smiling mouth giving it an expression of humorous complicity. 'Wow! That is good, though I say it myself.'

Rabindrah was very close to her, but when she turned to kiss him he stood up quickly. 'We should go to the mess tent,' he said. 'I am starving, all of a sudden.'

Over a cold beer in the shade of the flysheet, they looked at the latest cheetah prints and Allie read the draft of several new chapters that Rabindrah had brought, making changes here and there. At the lunch table Erope summarised their most recent observations, and they discussed the cheetah brothers and the arrival of Irial.

'Have a nap, if you like,' Allie said, when the meal was over. 'It would be absolutely stifling out on the plain right now. We should break Dr Campbell in gently. He won't be much help if he passes out from heat stroke on his first day.'

'Don't interfere with your timetable on my account,' Hugo said. 'I was working in much worse conditions in South America, when I was doing my research fellowship. I'm extremely resilient, I'll have you know. Not just a pretty face.'

'It's better to wait a couple of hours,' Rabindrah said, rising to his feet. 'I'll do the corrections in the text right now, Allie, while they are still fresh in my mind.'

He settled himself at the long table in the back of the mess tent. Allie sat opposite, hammering away on Dan's ancient typewriter, swearing under her breath at every error she made.

Sarah and Hugo found canvas chairs in the shade of a large fig tree, where they could listen to the call of the birds and the noisy whirr of crickets, and the pod of hippo snorting below them.

'How long will you be able to stay?' Sarah asked.

'I've been offered two university posts. One is in the United States. The other is in Edinburgh. A more prestigious appointment, but accompanied by cold, wet weather. Fortunately, I don't have to make up my mind right away. I'm not returning to work until next September, and I've spent the last two years working flat out on this doctorate. Being out in the field with Allie is all I want to think about for the moment.'

'It's a different field, though. I gather you have been studying a tribe in the Amazon.'

'It's a matter of using my scientific training in a different way,' Hugo said. 'If it works for Allie I would like to stay until next summer. That might also provide an opportunity for me to investigate some of the Maasai customs. It's a topic that intrigues me, and one day I might come back and do some serious research into the subject.'

He took off his glasses and rubbed them with a large handkerchief taken from the pocket of his well-worn safari jacket. Without the spectacles, his face became younger and more vulnerable looking, Sarah thought. His hair was still standing up in an untidy crest, as it had been the last time she had seen him in Samburu. When he spoke, or when something engaged his interest, his head would tilt to one side like a bird, and his gaze was as bright and sharp as Sarah remembered. For all his apparent vagueness, she guessed that he did not miss much. There were laughter lines around his eyes and the corners of his mouth. A man at ease with himself, and with the world in general.

'Will you be going back to Nairobi when Rabindrah leaves?' he asked.

For a second she wondered if Rabindrah had made some comment on the amount of time she spent away from home, but she rejected the thought. While his family might make that sort of remark, he would be unlikely to discuss their domestic arrangements with a virtual stranger. She wondered if she was becoming paranoid.

'I divide my time between here and home,' she said, not responding directly to his question. 'It's the only way to keep continuity in the pictures. But when I am in Nairobi, I'm always on tenterhooks, in case something dramatic happens while I'm away.'

'I'm familiar with your books, of course,' Hugo said. 'And your cheetah pictures are impressive.'

'Luckily Lara and her cubs are comparatively easy to find and photograph, but the males are trickier and more cautious. Last week we found Irial after he had lost his hard-earned dinner, but unfortunately we missed the moment when the hyenas moved in to seize his prey. I'd like to have been there, to see if he put up any resistance, but you need to be in the right spot from first light to sundown to get everything, and that's impossible.'

'I imagine that long vigils are the only way to capture a whole cycle on film?'

'That's it. Hours and hours of sitting in the cold mist of early morning, or boiling heat or afternoon rain, waiting for them to start playing, or mating or hunting. Although the presence of the car sometimes distracts a potential victim and makes it unaware of the cheetah closing in.'

'So you become an unwitting decoy,' Hugo said.

'Yes. And occasionally we do some trekking on foot, in order to find a place where they aren't aware of us, while we have an unobscured view. It means carting cameras and tape recorders and notebooks through the bush in the heat, trying to creep along without making noise, staying down-wind, looking for a vantage point. Not very comfortable, but when you are there for the moment of drama, and the light is right – well! There is nothing like the feeling that brings, regardless of conditions.' Sarah stood up. 'I'd better clean and load my cameras now, and after that we can get moving. Erope and Allie will be leaving soon. I expect you will go with them. Rabindrah?' She called over her shoulder. 'Ready to roll?'

'Give me ten minutes,' he said, without looking up. 'I am almost finished with these corrections.'

They set out to explore the territory, with Rabindrah at the wheel. Lara and her cubs were easy to find and they sat observing the family for a time before driving across the plain to rendezvous with Allie. The shadows of early evening were lengthening when they found her, parked near a rocky outcrop which ran along the base of Rhino Ridge. Erope leaned out of the window, speaking softly, as they came to a halt beside him.

'We have found two of the brothers,' he said. 'But Ajax is not with them, and they are uneasy. We have been waiting since four o'clock to see if the big one would return, but he has not come.'

'Would they normally go in separate directions?' Hugo asked the question.

'Sometimes. He might have picked up the scent of a female in season, and decided to try his luck,' Allie said. 'Still, if they were separated during a hunt they should be back together by sundown.'

'They are waiting for him,' Erope said. 'A little time ago, they went up to the top of the rocks there and called to him, but he did not respond. There is blood on the flank of the one called Castor. It is possible they were defending a kill from other predators, and Ajax was chased away in a different direction. Or he is hurt and could not follow them.'

The two young males were lying up in dense vegetation, and without Erope's legendary eyesight Sarah knew that none of them would have seen the well-camouflaged animals.

'I can see the gash on Castor's flank.' Allie trained the binoculars on her subjects. 'Looks like he's taken a swipe from a lion. What do you say, Erope?'

'It is the mark of a lion's claw rather than a bite. When he got up earlier, he was limping. Pollux does not seem to be hurt.'

'Have you seen any sign of a kill?' Sarah asked.

Erope shook his head. 'It could be anywhere. Maybe you could stay here, Allie, in case Ajax returns. I will go in Sarah's car to try and find the place. If he has been mauled, he will not have gone far.'

'I'll stay with you, Allie,' Hugo said.

'Good. Rabindrah, you go with Sarah and follow up this story.'

'I'll drive, if you like,' Rabindrah said. 'Then you'll have your hands free for the camera, Sarah, and Erope can concentrate on tracking.'

They started slowly along the edge of the ridge, Erope leaning out to scan the ground as they drove, searching for signs of the direction the cheetahs had come from. Sarah had a strong premonition that she tried in vain to disregard. If Ajax had taken on a lion in order to defend his kill or his brothers, the chances of survival would be slim. She imagined him mortally wounded, torn to shreds, his glorious dappled coat ripped asunder, his flesh reduced to fodder for scavengers.

'We will go the other way,' Erope said, after a few minutes. 'I see nothing here.'

Rabindrah turned in a wide arc, passing Allie and Hugo and signalling their new route in the direction of Olare Orok, a small tributary of the Talek River. Emerging from a canopy of trees, Sarah spotted the tell-tale circle of vultures, a dark curl against the evening sky. Rabindrah struck out across the plain and as they drew nearer the remains of a full grown wildebeest became visible. The carcass was surrounded by a pride of lions, with the inevitable hyenas and an enterprising jackal coursing the perimeter. A large male, resplendent with his black mane, had already gorged himself and was dozing close by. The lions had obviously taken possession of the kill some hours before. The cubs, always designated to wait until the males and adult females had had their fill, were feeding.

'That's a big wildebeest to bring down – even with three cheetahs working together,' Sarah said. 'This may not be the right kill.' Hope flared. 'I don't see any sign of Ajax.'

Erope was scanning the horizon. 'The other two ran away towards Rhino Ridge.' He was pointing behind him. 'If Ajax followed them, we should have seen his spoor, or his carcass.'

'He could have tried to reach their favourite place, near our camp,' Sarah said.

'Too far.' Erope was definite. 'If he is hurt he will look for cover nearby. He was lucky the kill was so big, because the lions would only chase him for long enough to drive him away. He must try to get far from the hyenas, though. Soon they will have their turn and then they will follow the scent of his blood. We will go back towards the river.'

Moving slowly across the yellowed grassland, Erope suddenly put up a hand and Rabindrah stopped the car. The Samburu jumped down, and squatted over an area where some creature had been lying on the ground. Sarah trained her lens on the depressed circle of earth, seeing with dread the tell-tale signs of blood, spattered across the flattened stalks of grass.

'Do you think it's him?' she asked, her voice tight.

'It is a cheetah.' Erope straightened, and followed the track. 'You can see the marks of his pads. Here. And here. Look, the blood has dried. From the colour, and the way that the grass lies, it is some hours since he was here.'

They set off again, stopping every few minutes to check the trail, working their way along the edge of the riverine forest. Giant figs and fever trees spread their boughs over the water, where kingfishers dived in blue and orange iridescent flashes, and monkeys chattered. A *kopje* loomed above the river and once again Erope signalled them to stop. There were streaks of blood at the base, and they got out of the car and began to climb cautiously upwards. Near the top they discovered Ajax, lying out on the bare rock. Several large gashes marked his flank, and one deep score had opened his chest. His long, rough tongue protruded from his mouth, and blood bubbled on his open jaw. The beautiful amber eyes were dimmed with approaching death, and ants and beetles were already busy foraging at the entrance to his wounds.

'Isn't there anything we could do to help him?' Sarah saw the breath heaving from his body in short gasps and began to move towards the stricken animal.

'It is too late. You know this.' Erope put a restraining hand on her arm.

'But he is suffering so dreadfully. What about the first aid box in the car? Rabindrah, there would be painkillers in it.'

'This is a wild animal, near to death.' Erope's voice was stern. 'He is still dangerous. You can do nothing for him now, Sarah. He has come to this high place to die.'

The words resonated in her head, bringing images of another ridge, another death. Desperate, she shook off the Samburu's hand and crawled slowly across the rock towards the dying cheetah, heedless of Rabindrah's frantic protests. Tears slid down her face as she reached out a tentative hand.

'Sarah – come back, for God's sake. Sarah!' Rabindrah called out in panic, and Erope made a soft grunt of disapproval. But their reactions went unheeded.

'I know we can't save you,' Sarah said, as her hand came into contact with the spotted fur. She could feel the quivering of his muscles under her fingers, like a silent string orchestra, vibrating through his body in this last battle. He did not flinch at her touch or try to attack her as she began to stroke him. 'I won't let some stinking *fisi* tear you apart while you are still alive. I will stay with you. I can at least do that.'

The cheetah did not move. Only his shallow, laboured breathing stirred the air around him as Sarah inched closer to kneel beside him, talking softly, stroking him, willing him a quiet passing. The rock was rough under her knees, and she could feel grit and small stones digging into her flesh, but she did not alter her position. She spoke to the dying animal of his beauty and his grace and her admiration for him, and of green grass and sunlight and freedom from pain. Her eyes were blurred, and she did not know how long she knelt there at her vigil. At last she became aware of Erope's hand on her shoulder, and saw that death had stolen over the cheetah. The quivering had stopped. His once-glowing eyes had dulled and he lay stiff, the blood congealed around his mouth and on his matted coat.

Erope and Rabindrah helped her to her feet, and she made her way down the rocky incline in the pale mauve evening.

'What about Ajax?' she asked, grief overwhelming her as they left the *kopje*.

'We must leave him in the place he has chosen,' Erope said.

Sarah could not argue. There was nothing more she could do. Scavengers would come and devour the body, but that was the natural way. It was the best way, now that he was dead. She knew she should take some pictures for the record, but she could not bear to go back and look on the ruin of such a magnificent creature.

'I know this is unprofessional,' she said, climbing into the Land Cruiser and rummaging in her basket for tissues. 'It's just that I've been so close to him these last weeks, and he was such a stunning specimen. Oh shit! Life can be such shit! We had better let Allie and Hugo know. Let's go.'

When they reached the other vehicle, it was Erope who described what they had seen as Sarah sat in the car, dazed and silent.

'Back to camp. Now.' Those were Allie's only words.

'What about the injury to Castor?' Rabindrah asked. 'Will he be all right?'

'It doesn't look deep,' Allie said. 'We'll drive out in the morning and check up on him. If the wound looks infected, I'm afraid there's not much we can do. He will have to cope on his own, if he can.'

When they reached the camp Sarah went straight to her tent, and Ahmed brought hot water for a shower. Afterwards she crawled into bed and lay curled up, unable to erase her last image of Ajax. Even when she closed her eyes he was there, stretched in death against the unyielding rock and the soft translucence of the evening sky. He must have made an extraordinary effort, with such terrible injuries, to reach the top of the outcrop. Instinctively on watch to the end. Maybe waiting and hoping that his brothers might find him. She wondered if they would ever know what had happened to him. Rabindrah came and stayed with her for a while, before moving outside to sit under the flysheet until he thought she had fallen asleep.

'How is she doing?' Allie asked, when he returned to the mess tent.

'She has gone to bed,' Rabindrah said. 'It's probably better for her to sleep.'

'She seemed horribly upset,' Hugo said, as they ate dinner beside the campfire.

'I know one is not supposed to get emotionally involved in this line of work, but she always identifies closely with whatever she is studying, be it animals or people.' Rabindrah said in her defence. 'It's what makes her such an outstanding photographer.'

That's true,' Allie said. 'She is part artist and part scientist. It's a rare gift. And sometimes a liability, I suppose.'

'But what a gift,' Hugo said. 'I've never seen anything like her photographs.'

'I told Hugo that it was one of the reasons Dan took her on.' Allie smiled, recalling the young girl she had first met in Buffalo Springs, hope and enthusiasm blazing in her eyes as she took the prints out of her portfolio. 'She had no research experience in the field at that time, but he recognised her ability to understand and to observe in the clarity of her pictures.'

'It was highly dangerous, what she did on the rock,' Rabindrah said, unable to banish the image of his wife and the dying cheetah. 'Crazy. A

166

wild animal, in pain and fear. If he had been stronger, he could have attacked her.'

'I do not think so,' Erope said, summing it up in his mind. 'She has a special feeling at such times, and I believe the cheetah knew she was not a threat.'

'It must have been an extraordinary thing to witness.' Hugo was shaking his head. 'Foolhardy, but gloriously brave.'

'Yes. She is both of those things,' Allie said, rising from the table. 'Goodnight, then. We will see tomorrow how the other two are managing on their own. Let's leave around six.'

'I'll type up my notes,' Rabindrah said. 'Until the lamp runs out of fuel.'

Erope raised a hand and walked away, vanishing into the blackness as Hugo unfolded his gangling frame and set out for his sleeping quarters. All around him he could hear the sounds of Africa. Hyenas yipped and cackled, hippos honked and splashed and puffed in the river, and from an immeasurable distance the deep, grunting sound of a lion drifted across the plains on the night wind. He carried a small torch, flashing it in an arc occasionally to avoid an unexpected encounter with a nocturnal predator. Shining the narrow beam away from the river he was surprised to see Sarah, wrapped in a thick sweater and a blanket, sitting on a chair outside her tent. He hesitated, unsure as to whether he should speak to her, or leave her to her solitary reflections.

'Hello,' she said softly. 'Everyone else abandoned you and gone to bed? I suppose Rabindrah is banging away at his notes.'

'That's right.' He paused, not knowing whether to say goodnight and continue on his way.

'Come and join me, if you're not too whacked,' Sarah said. 'It's wonderful sitting here at night, listening to all the activity around us. So vibrant and alive, and at the same time invisible.'

They sat side by side on canvas chairs, comfortable with one another's company. It was Sarah who broke their silence. In the kind anonymity of darkness an urgent need rose in her, driving her to communicate with someone she sensed as a kindred soul.

'I got a bit carried away this afternoon,' she said.

'From what I hear, it was understandable,' Hugo said, and then cursed himself. He did not want her to think she had been the subject of a discussion in her absence. 'And you were—'

167

'Utterly unscientific.' Sarah cut him off, not wishing for a statement of sympathy. 'You see, I'm pretty emotional right now, because of some medicine I'm taking. So it's hard to keep my feelings tamped down. I was never much good at hiding them anyway.'

He did not make any comment, and now she could not stop herself from continuing, from trying to articulate what she felt and why, without danger of familiarity or pre-judgement on the part of her listener. She wanted to express her feelings to this stranger that she felt she knew, with his quiet aura of empathy.

'My fiancé was murdered twelve years ago, and he died on the rocks like that,' she said. 'And I wish he hadn't been all alone in his pain and suffering. That I could have been there to touch him, and offer him some comfort at the end. When I found Rabindrah it seemed like a miracle that I could love again. But we haven't been able to have children, and that became an obsession with me. I miscarried twice, you see, and then I went a little mad for a while. Now we can't seem to get back to where we once were.'

She had begun to cry as her confidences spilled out into the blue-black night, but she was determined to rid herself of the memories that had surged through her earlier in the day.

'The thing is, I've begun to feel angry,' she said. 'And resentful. For years I thought it was my fault. Everyone did. But it's not my fault, or anyone's. So I'm here with Allie, because I love and admire her, and I love my work. And I'm also here because I don't know whether my husband wants me any more, or whether our marriage can continue at all. In fact, I'm beginning to believe that I should accept those things and move on.' She stopped to wipe the tears from her face with the back of her hand.

Hugo leaned back in his chair and waited, absorbing her sadness. It was several minutes before she spoke again and her voice was tired and dispirited.

'I'm also here because I can't keep trying and trying,' she said. 'And maybe I don't want Rabindrah any more either. Over the last while our life together has been cruel and hard. So perhaps we are not meant to be, after all.'

For a long time Hugo did not move or attempt to offer a gesture of sympathy. He felt it would be out of place, although he had a strong desire to console her. Then Sarah laughed out loud, a hollow sound edged with desolation.

'I don't know why I've told you all this,' she said. 'But I'm glad I did, and I'm grateful to you for listening.'

'I'm glad you did, too,' Hugo said. 'I'm honoured by your trust.'

'Goodnight, then.' She emerged from her swaddling of blankets and sweaters and stood up, so that he noticed again how small she was.

'Goodnight, Sarah,' he said, rising to his feet. He flicked the button on his torch and walked away towards his tent. It seemed a million miles away, and he knew he must not look back.

Chapter 10

Kenya, September 1977

Anthony Chapman strolled into the Long Bar of the New Stanley Hotel and ordered a cold Tusker. It was lunchtime and the place was buzzing with Nairobi gossip and discussions about business, politics and corruption.

'How are things, old chap?' Jeff Danielson was his usual, bleary-eyed self, but jovial. 'Safari business holding up well?'

'It is for me,' Anthony said. 'I flew in from Samburu an hour ago. Repeat clients. I have new ones coming in early next week, so I'm busy. All well on your *shamba*?'

'Can't complain. It's many a long year since we've seen coffee prices so good.' Jeff ordered another beer, although the one he was working on was still half full. 'Last year's shortfall in Brazil has been a bonus for us. So much so that Mitzi and I have decided to go and see our boy in Australia, and meet the grandchildren. Never thought we'd be able to do it, but looks like this is the time.'

'Good news,' Anthony said, impressed that Jeff had persuaded his dreary, pessimistic wife to contemplate such a thing, even in the best of times.

'Ah. The great white hunter and conservation expert is in town.' The voice was grating, the man fleshy and loud, his belly bulging out of khaki trousers, straining the buttons of his safari jacket.

'Hello, Max.'

Anthony made no effort to mask his dislike. Max Cramer was the owner of a cheap package tour company with a reputation for dangerous drivers and poorly maintained vehicles. They had had several run-ins over the fact that Max's guides were known for harassing game, crowding in too close and disturbing the animals, driving off the official tracks in the parks and damaging vegetation, chasing the herds to obtain more exciting photos for their clients. The list of offences was endless, but in spite of complaints from many other safari firms Max made no real effort to castigate his drivers. He was said to be untouchable as a result of heavy bribes to park officials and Nairobi politicians, and the astute placement of a high-ranking politician on his board of directors.

'Having a little trouble with the old love life?' Max could barely contain his delight.

'Are you?' Anthony deflected the question.

'Not me, mate.' Max chuckled. 'Didn't you see your posh girlfriend plastered all over the *Daily Mirror* a while ago. In a clinch with her so-called agent. I thought all the men in that business were a bunch of faggots?'

'Whoa! Steady on, man.' Danielson lurched sideways and put out a placating hand. 'You don't want to believe everything you see in the papers. Least of all in a rag like that.'

Anthony turned his back on Cramer, his mouth hard, a cold rage rising in him. It was difficult to restrain himself from directing a swift fist into the man's sweaty corpulence. He lifted his glass, but the beer tasted sour in his mouth and he put it back down on the bar, making an attempt to engage one or two people in small talk. He had no right to be angry. The state of his relationship with Camilla was something that he pushed into the back of his mind each time it came up, and he had no idea what she might have said or done to precipitate Cramer's malicious comment. Leaving was not an option, however. He had arranged to meet Johnson Kiberu for lunch. The government minister was a good man, tough and incorruptible, with the canny ability to back down from an impasse and find an alternative way to resolve a problem. He was also the chairman of the Wildlife Conservation Committee and he had worked closely with George Broughton-Smith, Camilla's father. After George's death, Kiberu had suggested that Anthony take his place on the committee.

'I'm flattered, Johnson,' Anthony had said. 'Honoured, actually. But I can't take on any extra responsibility, until I have finished with hospitals and rehabilitation. In addition, I don't want to become embroiled in the politics of the job. I haven't the patience or the instinct for getting things past tricky officials. That was George's genius – the combination of his diplomatic experience and his ability to use rough tactics at the right moment. I'd rather stay on as an adviser to the committee and contribute to projects where I have special knowledge of local conditions.'

'But you might think it over?' Johnson was not willing to concede defeat.

'I couldn't take on that role without giving up most of my safaris,' Anthony said. 'Right now I'm concentrating on getting fit enough to be back in the parks and reserves with my clients. I can't take too much of Nairobi. My place is out there in the *bundu* with the wildlife we are trying to save. It's as essential to me as breathing.'

During his long recovery, however, he and Kiberu had worked together to resolve some of the greatest problems in the management of the national parks, but it was a slow and frustrating task. Today, they had arranged to meet at twelve-thirty, and although Kiberu was always late Anthony downed the rest of his beer and escaped from the Long Bar, aware of the ribald comments that followed him.

'Anthony, hope you got back in time to snatch your girl from that poncer in London. Shows us all we can't be out in the *bundu* for too long.'

'*Pole*, old man. Better keep a closer eye on her from now on. Bunch of flowers should do the trick. Hah hah!'

The comments and chuckles infuriated him as he strode away. The lounge upstairs was mobbed, and he cursed himself for not remembering that Friday was the day when locals and tourists swarmed into the main dining room, to demolish the smorgasbord that was a speciality of the New Stanley Hotel. Many a deal had been struck over Friday lunch, and washed down with beer and schnapps. And there were always people involved in an illicit affair, lingering over coffee and aquavit before wandering away unsteadily to an afternoon assignation, unaware that by now the whole town knew about them. He scanned the room in search of Kiberu and was relieved to see him, already installed in a comfortable chair with a gin and tonic in front of him.

'Johnson, good to see you.' Anthony sat down and ordered a drink. 'What's going on?'

'I have been waiting for you to return. There is something urgent that we need to deal with.' Johnson lowered his tone. 'I have not discussed this issue with anyone else. It is a delicate matter with big players involved.'

'Let's hear it.'

'There is a particular group of smugglers who have become extremely powerful. In the last six months they have paid poachers to kill dozens of rhino, and thousands of elephant in Tsavo and up in the north. They've got away with several tons of ivory and plenty of rhino horn, to say nothing of kudu and buffalo heads, bongo, leopard pelts and other game trophies.'

'Sounds all too familiar.' Anthony sat back in his chair, waiting. Johnson would not have set up this meeting to bemoan the state of the war against poaching.

'Not only are these people dealing in horn and ivory and pelts, but they are also exporting live animals for sale to private buyers.'

'Ah yes,' Anthony said. 'The ladies who want a pet leopard on their white leather sofas in the Hamptons, or a chimpanzee at the dining table. I've had many requests like that.'

'But this time I have a lead,' Johnson said. 'I know where the next cargo is being consolidated and held, before being shipped overseas.'

'So you're going to confiscate it?'

'I don't want to do that right away. I have been trying to find out from my source when the next load is going to be exported. If I know the date, there is a chance of catching the boss of this organisation red-handed. Then I will make a public example of him. Put him and his *rafikis* in jail for a long, long time. It would be a huge feather in our caps.'

'No doubt about that.'

'The government anti-poaching programme is a laughing stock,' Kiberu said. 'There is not enough money to keep the units operational. More than half of the vehicles are lying idle with no money for spare parts. In some areas the petrol supply is being syphoned off and sold by local officials. Morale is bad. The wardens and rangers are lazy, and worse still, corrupt. Poachers bribe them with amounts that are more than three times their salaries, and give them guns too. We can't compete, and there are powerful people in Nairobi who turn a blind eye to all the rules.'

'I'm pretty sure we could name several of them.' Anthony's laugh was contemptuous. 'It's no secret that there are ministers in on every deal involving the shooting and selling of animals.'

'That is part of the reason I do not favour the ban on legal hunting,' Johnson said. 'Most professional hunters had integrity, and they reported and tracked poachers better than any unit we had. It was in their interest to do so. Now, without them, killing in the parks has become far easier for an increasing number of armed bandits. The latest estimate is that we are losing about one thousand elephants every month to poachers, and the figure is rising.'

'Yes, I've heard the numbers and seen the carcasses. There are plenty of big shots in the government making money on exporting ivory and horn and other trophies. What can I do to help?' Anthony could not see his role in Johnson's plan.

'According to my sources, there is a big cargo about to be shipped from a go-down in Mombasa. The building belongs to a trading company owned by Asians, but they are fronted by a Kikuyu businessman and two leading politicians, all pocketing their share. In turn the Kenya company is owned by a consortium registered in Liechenstein.'

'Sounds well organised, smells like rotting *nyama*.'

'Yes. But this time I think I can catch them with the goods. With independent witnesses on the scene. Preferably people who have nothing to do with the government or the National Parks. People who are not afraid to spill the beans in court. And someone from the press who can be tipped off and will be there, when this shipment is loaded onto a boat for export.'

'You're organising a sting.' Anthony smiled.

'This outfit has a respectable bank account in Nairobi, but nothing compared to what they must be salting away elsewhere,' Johnson continued. 'I hear from my informant that the big boss from out of town will be in Mombasa for the next shipment. It's a large one, and I think there are millions of dollars involved.'

'Is your source willing to give evidence that would nail them down? Can't he give you a definite date for this little export venture?'

'My source is afraid for his life. If he is discovered passing information, or if any leads can be traced back to him . . .' Johnson made a slashing movement across the base of his neck. 'And I can't trust anyone in my office not to leak this.'

'I'm still not sure how I can help you.'

'Rabindrah Singh is a good friend of yours,' Johnson said. 'I would like him to investigate and publish this story, under his name. I can supply him with statistics, accounts of incidents for which I could not find witnesses courageous enough to give evidence, or when the small fry involved disappeared. I also have the names of the politicians involved in this case.

Most other journalists would be scared of losing their jobs if they pointed the finger at Africans with influence. But Singh is fearless, and he would not hesitate to expose powerful people. Even key players in the Asian community.'

'Jesus Christ, Johnson! Shopping his own people is a delicate matter.' Anthony was doubtful. 'They have their faults, the Indian businessmen, but the government is putting the squeeze on them unfairly. Africanising their jobs and refusing to renew their trading licences, even though they are citizens of this country. And their African replacements are even more greedy, in many cases. Anyway, that's another subject. Have you discussed this operation with Rabindrah?'

'I thought you might do that, since he and Sarah are close friends of yours, and internationally known for their books on conservation.' Johnson raised his eyebows. 'If he is willing to cooperate, we could meet and talk it over.'

'A story like this would put him in a tricky situation, personally.'

'Do you know any other journalist who could be trusted to investigate and expose these people? Who would not be afraid of the outcome? And Gordon Hedley is the kind of editor who would publish this, even if he thought he would be thrown out of his job as a result.'

Anthony made no response for a time. It was true that Rabindrah had criticised the Asian community in some of his writing, but there was an underlying sympathy for their plight, even in the hardest hitting articles. Still, there was no question as to his integrity, and he and Sarah shared a rabid hatred of poachers.

'I'll see what I can do,' he said at last. 'They've just come back from Europe. I think they are both in the Mara with Allie Briggs. Give me a few days and I'll get back to you.'

They moved in to join the crowd at the smorgasbord table, and spent the next hour discussing ideas on the conservation agenda, and the best methods of obtaining sufficient funding for future projects. Anthony refused the powerful schnapps offered with the coffee, and left Kiberu to enjoy his liqueur alone.

Outside on the street he greeted a few friends in the Thorn Tree Café, before climbing into his safari vehicle. He headed for his office and the time-consuming task of going through the letters and bills that had accumulated in his absence. With Camilla away in Europe there would be more than the usual pile of correspondence. She often helped his African secretary, Rose, and translated French and Italian enquiries into English so that they could be answered. But at least the accounts would be under control. Since Duncan Harper had joined them, that burden had been lifted off Anthony's shoulders.

During the two years that followed the accident Camilla had watched him run his office as he struggled through pain-filled days of physical therapy, tried to cope with several temporary prostheses, and finally learned to use the permanent fitting for the red, chafing stump that remained of his leg.

'You are dealing with huge personal adjustments,' she said at the end of a particularly harrowing day. 'Pushing yourself too hard. Your business is growing and now you are out on safari again, in addition to keeping control of the office and the stores and vehicles. Plus your accounts and tax returns. You need an office manager, Anthony. Someone who is a chartered accountant might be good. It's no use employing a couple of bookkeepers, and then going through the figures every time you are back in town, staying up until God knows when to verify each tiny detail yourself.'

'Not my best suit,' he admitted. 'But it's the only way to keep control of everything.'

'There isn't another company owner or director in Nairobi that spends this much time immersed in the small print of his business,' Camilla said. 'Of course you must direct and oversee the operation of the company as a whole. But your most important role is to take people on safari, create an unforgettable experience, show them the magnificent adventure of the African bush. If I had to do all my own accounting, here or in London and New York, I'd be a wreck. And I wouldn't be able to concentrate on what I'm really good at.'

Some months later she had found Duncan Harper. He was a sad-faced little man, precise and unassuming, with good references from a big accounting firm in Leeds. His marriage had broken down, he said, and he needed a new start far away from the vitriol of the divorce. Camilla had pressed for him to be taken on. Four years later Anthony had come to rely on him and to feel that his company accounts and administration were in good hands. He was grateful for the hours that he could devote to other tasks, and with Camilla's international connections producing a seemingly inexhaustible list of clients, he had begun to brood less about his disability. Now he could do almost everything that he had been able to accomplish before the crash. But the loss of his leg had taken a high toll, and he knew that Camilla had suffered when it came to the change in their personal relationship.

She had arrived from London the day after the helicopter crash, to attend her father's funeral. At the hospital Anthony had driven her away from his bedside, not wanting to see or feel her pity. Afterwards he had lain there alone, tormented by the horror of the amputation and by the agony of phantom pain. He had tried to save her father's life and failed. In the days and nights that followed, he raged at the futile effort that had cost him a limb and robbed him of the self-confidence he had always taken for granted.

But Camilla had persisted. After the funeral she had stayed on in Nairobi, visiting Anthony every day, sitting beside him, or in the nearby waiting room when he closed his eyes and would not speak because the fury or the pain had become insupportable. His mother and one of his sisters had flown out from England, but neither had been of much help. Daphne Chapman had lost her husband in a hunting accident years before, and had left the country at once. It was clear that she hated being back in Kenya, where another ugly event might now claim the life of her only son. She sat in his room, dabbing at her eyes with a handkerchief and trying to persuade Anthony to turn his back on Kenya. His sister spent most of her time at the Muthaiga Club, unable to face the sight of her maimed sibling and the implications of his disability. After two weeks, when his life was no longer in danger and he had made it plain that he would not leave the country, both women had departed. It was a relief for all of them.

When the time came, Camilla had brought him home, organised the nurse who came to help him every day, driven him into town for physio-therapy, travelled to London with him to consult specialists. She had installed handrails in the house to help him get around, and rearranged the furniture so that he could navigate more easily with his crutches. Outside, in the shade of the verandah, she set up a desk and chairs, and a chaise longue where he could look out over the lawn. It was a quiet place to read and to take care of office paperwork, or to sit with his binoculars and observe the habits of sunbirds and starlings in all their glossy brilliance, and scarlet-winged turacos as they hopped through the trees in search of berries. Camilla watched, unflinching, each time the raw stump of his leg was unbandaged and freshly dressed, and learned to take care of the task herself. Whenever despair engulfed him she urged him on with a determined but compassionate single-mindedness as he tried to achieve balance, helping him up when he fell, cursing and screaming with frustration, humiliated and close to madness.

Sometimes he had longed to wake up from a drugged sleep and find that she had gone, that her calm perfection was no longer there to torture him. But Camilla never wavered. When she thought he did not need her she worked on new ideas for the workshop at Langani, or for Saul Greenberg who manufactured and produced her lines of clothing in London and New York. After a while she invited Sarah and Rabindrah for dinner and was glad to see Anthony animated and laughing during the evening. When he had learned to use his new leg and was steady on his feet, Sarah brought him to Indar Singh who designed a special safari vehicle for him with modified pedals. Soon afterwards he drove Camilla up-country to spend a few days at Langani. She was always there when he needed something, seldom intrusive, never flustered or reproachful when he retreated into a world of futile resentment. As time moved on he began to feel an unreasonable hatred for her serenity and patience.

A year had gone by when she came into his bedroom one night and lay down beside him. But when she began to caress him he rolled away from her, so that she would not see his tearful self-pity. He was unable to touch her, or allow her to ease the searing wound in his psyche. She had become someone else – had turned herself into his mother and his nurse, his therapist and secretary and his mentor. He could no longer visualise a return to their former passion, or think of making love to her with his mutilated body over which he had so little control.

'I love you,' she had whispered.

But he did not answer. He was a cripple. The strong, careless symmetry of his physique had been ruined. He was convinced she was there out of pity, out of guilt that he had been hideously maimed for her father's sake. Anthony knew that she would never admit to these feelings, and he was determined not to allow either of them to be trapped in the consequences of his trauma. On that one night she had lain down beside him for more than an hour. When she realised that he was awake and rigid with anxiety she had slipped away, leaving him to wait for the first shaft of light to cast a grey shadow on another wretched day. Over the next few weeks Camilla had slept in the guest room or at the small flat she kept near State House. She began to model again, shuttling between Kenya, Europe and New York, and Anthony was unable to cross the void he had created between them.

After a while he had needed a woman, and easily found a candidate at one of the nightclubs popular with tourists in town. He had gone back to the French girl's hotel room and had sex with her, not needing to do more than display a greedy urgency that made her giggle. He took her without even removing his clothes or giving anything of himself except his own fast release. She had begun to strip off her remaining underwear, smiling and beckoning him to join her on the bed for more sustained pleasures, when he left. He did not even see the surprise and anger on her face as he closed the door and walked away down the corridor. It became an easy habit. Sometimes he seduced one of his safari guests, always being careful, waiting until the night before departure when his action could never be questioned or repeated.

At last, Camilla had returned from one of her visits to New York and over dinner she asked him the direct question he had dreaded.

'Do you still love me, Anthony? I need to know.'

'Have you found someone else?' He hardened himself for her reply.

'It's more than two years since the accident,' she said, avoiding any direct response to his question. 'You have been extraordinarily courageous, and I know that has taken up all your energy and concentration. But there is more to living, my darling. You know that I want to give you much, much more.'

Anthony could not meet her gaze. He was afraid to think about what he would do if she walked out of his life. She was his anchor, the one who had urged him on each time he had come close to total annihilation. She had coped with his troughs of depression and drinking bouts and incoherent rages, his occasional disappearances when he had driven off without explanation into the wilderness, and not returned for days.

'I can't offer you anything beyond what we have now,' he said. 'I'm a different man. I have a disability that no woman should have to deal with on a permanent basis. And I can't be responsible for someone else's life, when I'm not in control of my own. I'm grateful for everything you are and have been, but it would be wrong to pretend that things could ever go back to the way they were before. Those days are gone, Camilla. That is the truth.'

He heard her small gasp of pain, saw her hands trembling as she lifted her glass of wine from the table. Then she bent her head so that the shimmer of her hair hid her face. Her voice was breaking when she spoke again.

'At least you're honest. I have to thank you for that.' Lipstick flared on her dinner napkin as she touched her mouth and rose to leave the table. 'I'm going to bed now. It's a monster trip from New York, and I'm exhausted. Besides, there's nothing more to say.'

When he rose in the morning she was gone. The wardrobe in the guest room was empty and all her belongings had vanished with her. Joshua made no comment, but padded around the house with an expression of dark misery that spoke louder than any question or hint of accusation. Anthony made an attempt at an explanation that neither of them believed, and the subject was never mentioned again. But he longed for the sound of her footsteps, the light timbre of her voice, the inspiration of her laughter. He missed the jars of cosmetics in the bathroom, the scent of her perfume, her handwriting on the shopping list in the kitchen. Her car in the garage. She had planted banks of dahlias and roses and cannas in the garden, and now they turned bright faces to him in accusation. He thought briefly of telephoning her and asking her to come back, but he could not bring himself to do it. Several days later he went out on an extended safari. She was in London when he returned and they did not meet again for several months. Inevitably he ran into her one day at the Thorn Tree Café.

'Could we have dinner,' he asked, with some embarrassment. 'I'd like to —'

'Yes. Of course we could,' she said, smiling with dazzling effect. 'I'm free most evenings next week.'

'Tonight,' he said. 'What about tonight, at Muthaiga?'

She was at her most ravishing when they met in the lounge, her lovely body wrapped in a blue dress that matched her eyes. When he had put away his first drink and ordered dinner, he spoke fast and straight.

'I'm terribly sorry I disappointed you,' he said. 'But I thought it was better to—'

'It was,' she said. 'Tell me how things are going. I had dinner with two sets of mutual friends in New York last week. The Elkins and the Cohens. They loved their time with you. I expect you have their confirmation by now, for another safari in December.'

'I have.' Anthony leaned forward. 'And I'd like to propose something to you.' He chided himself immediately for the unfortunate choice of words. 'After everything you've done.'

'I haven't done anything much,' she answered, longing for him to say he loved her, to ask her to return to the cottage. Knowing that he would not.

'You've been largely responsible for the increase in my safari bookings,' he said. 'And for making my camps into something exceptional that no one else can offer. So I'd like you to become a full partner in the company. I want to give you half the shares.'

For a moment she did not answer, but he watched as small beads of perspiration appeared on her forehead and upper lip.

'What a novel idea,' she said with irony. 'A way of writing off any feeling of debt you might have, when there shouldn't be one. It's a generous offer, but if I accept it will alter my role in the company. Give it an official aspect, and maybe added responsibilities that I'm not sure I want. Or need.'

'I'm not asking you to spend more time on my business.' He was taken aback by her reaction. 'But you've put so much effort into keeping me going, through all the ups and downs, and without any kind of reward or compensation. Insisting on Duncan was one of your best ideas, even though you had to force me into hiring him. I want to show you how grateful I am, Camilla, by making you a real part of the company. The entire office and camp staff owe you as much as I do, and they have a deep respect for you. It's a case of making it official.'

'I'll let you know in the next few days,' she said, her tone abrupt. 'Let's finish our dinner before it gets cold. And since this has turned into a business meeting, maybe you can write it off against your taxes.'

Anthony heard the rebuke in her voice and knew that he had offended her, but the idea that he had done something wrong made him defensive. He moved the conversation on to generalities, but the remainder of the evening became a strained encounter and they were both glad when it was over.

'Perhaps you'll let me know what you have decided over the weekend,' he said, as he opened the door of her car for her. 'I'm going on safari again on Wednesday, and if you are agreeable I would like to finalise the paperwork before I leave.'

When she had driven away he felt uneasy, irritated by the notion that he had caused an upset by offering her half of all he had. His leg ached, his head was throbbing from the wine, and he was tired and dispirited. The prospect of going home to an empty house was not appealing. He turned off one of the main city roundabouts and drove up a hill to park outside the Panafric Hotel, jiggling his car keys as he made his way to the bar.

'Large Glenlivet, please, George,' he said to the barman. 'No ice. A little water in a separate jug. *Asante sana.*'

Seated on the bar stool he looked around the room and saw the girl immediately. He had forgotten how sensational she was, how powerful her sexuality. She was sitting close to a man twice her age, and an American judging by his clothes. Her scarlet-tipped fingers were curled round his arm and she was laughing, her mouth wide and luscious, her head tilted on the swan-like neck that was encircled by a collar fashioned from glass beads and heavy silver. Anthony knew she had spotted him, and seen his glance slide away. He finished his drink in one swallow and was paying the bill when she came to stand beside him.

'Two more glasses of champagne,' she said to George, her voice as husky as he remembered. She was wearing a red dress, cut very low, clinging to her breasts and hips and her long legs. Her black hair was plaited in dozens of braids and finished with silver beads that stroked her shoulders when she moved her head. 'How are you, Anthony?'

'Doing well, thank you. You seem to be in fine form too, in your chosen occupation. Excuse me, Zahra, but I was just leaving, actually. *Salaams.*' His disdain and condemnation were evident.

'What did you think I would do, when your girlfriend threw me out?' Her voice was a low, angry growl as she spat out the words. 'Did you think I would sink back into the gutter she fished me out of? Or did you think I would just curl up and disappear, because she caught me with my arms around your neck, the bitch?'

'She taught you all the tricks of the fashion trade,' he said. 'Gave you fine clothes and money, and brought people from London to photograph you. Created an opportunity you would never have dreamed of.'

'And she took it away in an instant, because she thought you were going to fuck me,' Zahra said. 'Do you know what I went through after that? How I grovelled and fought and picked the pockets and wallets of my pathetic clients? Hid in dingy rooms waiting to be caught by the police, or the pimp of some other girl on the same beat. Got knocked around like before. You smug bastard! How dare you look down on me. You were as hot as I was that night, and you ruined me. Couldn't she see that you are like every other man, whose brains are mainly in his cock? It was your fault more than mine, and you never gave it a second thought or wondered what might happen to me.'

She picked up the two flutes of champagne, and threw him a glance full of venom before moving away. When she crossed the room and bent to put the glasses down on the table, he could see the man ogling the dark curve of her breasts with frantic impatience. He ignored the drinks she had brought, murmured something in her ear, and then they were gone.

'Is she here often?' Anthony ordered another whisky. 'I thought ladies of the night were not allowed to ply their trade in this hotel.'

'She works at the casino. Sometimes she comes back here with a guest who has won plenty of money, but he has to be a high-roller. And she knows the bosses of the hotel. Yes, she knows them very well.' George laughed. 'She never makes trouble,' he said. 'Never gets drunk or loud, keeps her men quiet and well-behaved. Not like some. She's class. No *shauris* with Zahra, and no one crosses her either.'

Out in the bush for the next three weeks, Anthony thought of her constantly. She was right. He had wanted her on the night of Camilla's fashion gala almost seven years ago, and he had encouraged her to flirt with him. Then Camilla had found them in the corridor, the Somali girl's arms draped around him as he drew her close to kiss her. At the time he had considered it a harmless flirtation. Something that happened for a brief moment when Camilla had forgotten him, surrounded as she was by celebrities and fashionable friends from London who were clearly amused by her affair with a mere safari guide. Anthony was convinced that the whole storm would settle down in a matter of days. When Zahra had appeared at his house on the following morning he had turned her away without hesitation, and never thought about her again. But Camilla had left him anyway, and gone back to London.

He swallowed his drink, feeling guilty now, although there was really no need for that. Zahra had been a common prostitute and a part-time waitress living in a Nairobi slum when Camilla found her. Now she was a high-class call girl. Exotic, beautiful, and evidently successful. It would only be a matter of time before she persuaded some besotted client to marry her and take her out of the trade. Out of the country. He had seen it many times before. Still, he could not expel her from his mind. When the safari was over he returned to Nairobi and went looking for her at the casino.

'She is not working tonight,' one of the female croupiers told him, sullen and annoyed that he was not interested in her own obvious charms.

'When will she be back?'

'It's not my business to keep watch over her,' the girl said, pouting and making eyes at him. 'Right now she's not working. That's all. You want to play or not?'

'Not tonight. Thanks.' He made for the exit, glancing round the room as he went. At the roulette table furthest away there was a figure with his back to Anthony. There was something vaguely familiar about him, and he was setting down thousands of dollars' worth of chips onto his chosen numbers. The clatter and spin of the game brought silence as the gamblers waited for chance to play its role. When the ball had settled there was a sigh of sympathy and pleasure at his loss. The man stood up and headed for the cashier, pulling his wallet out of his pocket, willing to purchase more chips and try his luck again. Anthony was surprised to see that the loser was Duncan Harper. He turned away and made for the nearest exit. Better not to be stuck with polite commiseration, when it was someone he knew. Worse still, a man who worked for him. Recognition could put him in a position where he might have to refuse a request for a loan, and the result would be embarrassing. He felt an acute sense of relief as the door closed behind him, and he was standing alone in the cold night air.

He returned the next night and found Zahra at the blackjack table, her sultry appearance exuding sexual allure. She did not acknowledge him when he sat down to play. It was not long before he lost an amount that brought him to his senses, and he left the game and went to the bar where he could watch her from a distance.

'I came to apologise,' he said, following her when her time at the table was up.

'Leave me alone.' She hurled a contemptuous look in his direction and walked quickly towards a private exit.

'I have to see you,' he said, planting himself between her and the door.

'You can't afford it,' she said, her tone hostile. 'What's the matter with you, anyway? Is Camilla away? Do you want to try something different — something black? Is that it?'

'I lost my leg in an accident.' He blurted out the pent-up words that he had never articulated plainly before. 'Several years ago. It almost destroyed me. We're not together any more, Camilla and I. Please.'

'You're the same as anyone else. One hundred dollars for an hour, five hundred to spend the whole night. Cash in advance, as soon as we get outside.' Zahra eyed him coolly, smiling with satisfaction at how shocked he was. Outside in the car park she stood waiting as he took out the money, and then she counted the notes and put them into her handbag, snapping it shut with businesslike finality. 'Where do you want to go?'

He drove her to a hotel where he was not known. In the bedroom he unbuckled his belt, unfastened his trousers and sat back in an armchair as she took off her clothes and displayed her sinewy body and the long satin limbs. She leaned over the chair to offer breasts with plum-coloured nipples that he wanted to touch and to kiss, more than he had ever wanted anything in his life.

'Sit on me,' he said, reaching his arms around her waist. 'Slide onto my lap and take me inside you.'

'Get up,' she said, disengaging herself and backing away from him. 'Get up out of the chair and I will take your clothes off, and we will make love on the bed.'

'Zahra,' he said. 'For God's sake —'

She ignored his protests, pulling him up and removing his jacket and shirt, sliding her hands around to his back, stroking and smoothing and rubbing her breasts against him, kissing him with soft lips, licking his ears and his neck and chest, biting him, moving her hands over every part of him, whispering to him so that he did not register the moment when she helped him onto the bed and took off all his clothing. When it was over he wept unashamedly and she held his head in her hands and kissed his mouth and began to sing to him, something soft in her native tongue that sounded like a lullaby. He felt at peace for the first time in a long while, and he was still holding her in his arms as he closed his eyes and sank into sleep.

185

For ten days, as he awaited his next safari clients, he saw her every day and when he was not with her he could think of nothing else. After the first two nights, she allowed him to come to her modest but spotlessly clean apartment in the city centre. Their love-making became a drug, a part of his existence that he could not do without, a compulsion. On his last evening in Nairobi he waited until her shift at the casino was finished and then took her back to his cottage in Karen. It was still dark when he woke and looked at the bedside clock. Five in the morning. He sat up and looked at her in his bed. And thought of Joshua.

'Wake up,' he said, shaking her. 'Zahra, wake up. I'm leaving this morning and you have to get out of here before Joshua comes in with the tea. Look, I'll call a taxi and—'

'My God, you are some stinking piece of white shit,' she said, instantly awake and resentful. 'Do you ever think about anyone but yourself? What the hell does it matter if your bloody houseboy sees me here?'

'What?' Her reaction was like a bucket of cold water thrown over the still smoking memories of the night.

'Get dressed,' she said with contempt. 'You can drive me into the city right now. And don't ever come looking for me again, or I'll make sure all of Nairobi knows about this.'

'You surely didn't think – look here, you said yourself it was like any other transaction.' He felt cheap as he said the words, because she had been tender and sensitive, and he knew that she had somehow given him back a part of his manhood that had been missing. That he would always be grateful to her.

She did not bother to reply but went into the bathroom to shower and dress. While the door was closed he opened the locked drawer of his desk, took out a thousand dollars and slipped it into her handbag. They drove in hostile silence into town. She would not allow him to take her to her apartment, and when she had stepped out of his car on Kenyatta Avenue she leaned through his window and repeated her message.

'Never, ever again,' she said. And then she turned her back and walked away so that he would not see the sad humiliation in her eyes.

The episode taught him a lesson, and from then onwards Anthony returned to the simple pastime of casual sex with strangers in Kenya, and brief liaisons on overseas marketing trips. There was a wealthy married woman in New York whom he saw once a year, knowing it was a safe arrangement that suited both of them. When he thought of Zahra he felt he had narrowly avoided involvement in something with messy repercussions, and he never went near the casino again. Once he saw her in a nightclub with another patron, but he did not acknowledge her. He had enough problems to deal with, without recklessly creating more.

Camilla had remained supportive as time passed, appearing and disappearing as and when her own schedule allowed it. She seemed to be leading a successful life that kept her shuttling between Nairobi and Langani Farm and the fashion capitals of the world, where she still reigned supreme as a model and designer and an international socialite. Sometimes Anthony wondered if she also had occasional affairs, but he always shied away from any conversation or gossip that might reveal the details of her private life. All in all, he had things pretty well under control.

Until today.

After parting company with Johnson Kiberu he drove to his office. In the reception area he received a couple of sideways glances and smiles, and he was not sure whether he was imagining a sly amusement behind them. He closed his door and began to look through the stack of mail and memos on his desk. It was halfway down the pile of papers among the press clippings, and Anthony wondered who had put it there. He stared at the photograph of Camilla and Tom Bartlett, and in one searing moment he understood how inward-looking he had been. He had not allowed himself to believe that she could love him, that she could still think of him as a whole man, that she would be willing to trust him with her life. And now it was probably too late.

Except that Tom Bartlett was an idiot. A prancing, posing nonentity whose part in her life Anthony had always considered superficial. He had come out to Kenya a couple of times. Listening to them talk about clothes and handbags and lipsticks and photographers, Anthony had always wondered how these trivial items could be of interest to a real man. Or of any importance at all, except from the viewpoint of making obscene amounts of money out of millions of vain and foolish women. And men, too, these days. Bartlett had a reputation as a good agent, although Camilla never allowed anyone to make important decisions without her full agreement. In all probability Tom could be summed up as a clever conman with his smart one-liners, delivered in a sharp Cockney accent and accompanied by a jaunty insolence. Useful when sorting out Camilla's contracts and schedules. Still, they had been close for years, and she used only kind words to describe him whenever his name came up.

All his friends must have read the piece in the *Daily Mirror*, and Anthony only hoped that Joshua and the camp staff had not seen it. He could not afford to lose the respect of his *watu*. Having re-read the headline and looked at the photograph again, Anthony crumpled the picture and threw it away. Then he changed his mind, retrieved and smoothed it out again, and put the page into his briefcase.

He checked in with Duncan Harper and with his secretary Rose, before making his way to the go-down to look over the equipment for the next safari, and finalise the staff roster. But as he ran his eye down pages of lists and figures, the only thing he could see clearly was the photograph of Camilla and Tom. He could not rid himself of the idea that the caption might be true. She had waited so long, only to face rejection at every turn. Could she have given up, decided to throw her life away on Bartlett because he had been her unflagging support and confidant for years? The more he thought about it, the more probable it seemed. Returning to the main office, Anthony shut himself away. From deep inside him a terrible explosion of regret burst into his consciousness, making him lightheaded, confused, disoriented. Seething with rage. Mad with jealousy and fear. How lacking in courage he had been, allowing Camilla to keep his business going during his long, rocky recovery, taking her for granted as she introduced new safari clients and devised the changes and improvements that had brought him wealth and recognition.

It took him an hour to decide on a course of action. Finally, he lifted the telephone and began to make his calls. The last one was to Rabindrah.

'Are you willing to take part in this investigation that Johnson is setting up?' Anthony asked, after he had explained the situation. 'It may put you in a dangerous position. Apparently there are people in very high places involved, including an Asian businessman. And God knows what might happen to Gordon Hedley if you manage to collect enough evidence and he agrees to publish something incriminating about a group of powerful Africans on the take. There could be dire consequences for both of you.'

'I'm a journalist and a conservationist,' Rabindrah said, needled by the suggestion that he might refuse any involvement for personal reasons. 'I will never hesitate to write the truth, to denounce people who are abusing the law, especially those who are supposed to be making it. It might be best not to mention this to Sarah, though, until we see whether there is a story to break. She has been through so much lately. Tell Kiberu I will get a seat on the morning plane from Keekorok tomorrow. I presume he has some background material for me to start on.'

When he had finished all the calls on his list, Anthony opened his drawer and took out a flask of whisky. He tipped back his head, swallowed hard and then returned to the telephone. Far away he could hear the ringing sound, and for a long moment no one answered. Then he heard her voice, cool and businesslike.

'Hello?'

'It's Anthony.' He had to stop and clear his throat. 'How are you, Camilla?' He had not telephoned her since something had needed clarification in the office weeks ago. The call would be out of the blue, and he was aware that he sounded strained.

'Are you all right? You're not ill, are you? Is everything going smoothly?'

'Everything is fine.' He realised that she had caught a different note in his voice. 'I'm phoning to find out when you are coming back.'

'I'm staying on for another three weeks,' she said. 'I've been invited to appear on a rather good television panel game, but I will be back for Hannah's birthday. I'll have to spend a couple of days in Nairobi, and then I'll head for Langani.'

'The thing is, I'm planning a special celebration for her and I thought we could all go to the coast for a few days.'

'Are you sure Lars and Hannah would leave the farm again, so soon?' Camilla was doubtful. 'I thought their priority was to spend time in Nairobi getting Piet sorted out.'

'Lars says it's a terrific idea. After all the worry they could do with a short break, and the hearing specialist wants to wait a little while before making a decision on Piet's treatment. Sarah and Rabindrah can be there too.'

'That sounds good. I'll come back a little earlier. Where, at the coast?'

'I'll let you know when you get here. Just one other thing,' he said, feeling ridiculous, knowing she would find his request out of character. 'I thought we could do something rather glamorous. Perhaps 1930s-style clothes and so on. Since Hannah is hitting the three-three mark.'

'Hannah? Glamorous Thirties?' She laughed. 'It doesn't sound like her at all. Or you, in fact. But I'm willing to play the game. I'll bring something for us girls to wear. It's not the kind of thing you can pick up in a *duka* in Narok or Nanyuki. Will you be around if I give you my date of arrival?'

'Possibly,' he said. 'I have another safari before you get here, and it will depend on where the clients want to spend the last few days of their safari.'

'Oh. Fine, then.'

'*Salaams*, Camilla.' He was smiling a little. She had sounded disappointed by his vague answer. 'See you soon.'

It took a further hour before Anthony was satisfied that everything he had to arrange was in place, and then he went home and got extremely drunk.

Chapter 11

Kenya, September 1977

A squall of rain during the night left the grasslands shimmering, with wisps of steam rising into the air as the sun laid its hot breath over the damp, red earth. Tender shoots had sprung up instantly across the plains, greening the savannah, offering their bounty to the grazing animals. Allie and Erope decided to return to the rock where Ajax had died, to see whether the body was still there. The other three left camp together, hoping to locate the two remaining cheetahs. Sarah was businesslike and professional as they discussed the possible behaviour patterns of the survivors, and she gave no indication of the grief that had been manifest the night before.

'It is a testing time for these two learning to hunt without their leader,' she said as she fixed her camera to its support. 'Especially since one of them is injured, and that gash on Castor's leg could go septic. That would be crucial to their survival.'

The going was slow, with the black cotton soil sucking at the tyres, forcing them to slide off the track on several occasions. Finally, Hugo and Rabindrah were obliged to wedge several logs under the vehicle and push from the back. Sarah revved the engine and the wheels spun, looking for purchase, spraying the two men with mud so that they climbed back into the Land Cruiser covered with their own dark spots. It took them more than an hour to reach the site where they had left the surviving brothers. Both were there, pacing back and forth in front of the dense bushes where they had lain up during the night, frequently springing up onto a nearby rock and letting out a series of sharp, loud yips that echoed around the scree as they searched for their missing sibling.

'They are calling Ajax,' Sarah explained to Hugo, as she raised her binoculars. 'A cheetah can't roar like a lion. Its voice box is not designed for that. These two are pretty desperate. They have always relied on Ajax to lead them. Luckily, the wound on Castor's flank doesn't seem to be infected, though.'

'When will they hunt again?' Hugo asked.

'They would normally be looking for prey right now,' she answered. 'They must be waiting for Ajax.'

Half an hour later the two animals moved up the rocks to a vantage point overlooking the plain. They stayed there most of the day, rising only to call out, and to search the moving herds of game on the grassland below for signs of their brother. Around midday they walked out onto the veldt and made two unsuccessful attempts to chase down a gazelle and then a warthog, but Castor was having trouble putting his foot to the ground. Shortly afterwards they were back on the rock once again.

'It doesn't look too good,' Sarah said, explaining the situation to Allie and Erope when they arrived. 'I know we are not supposed to intervene, but a shot of antibiotics would help. It would be terrible if we lost a second one.'

'The cheetah would have to be tranquillised and transported to Narok, in order for the vet to treat him,' Allie said. 'That would mean more trauma for him, and even greater harassment for Pollux who would be left alone. I think we should wait. These animals sometimes go several days without making a kill. But I agree that they are waiting for Ajax, poor creatures.'

Sarah hesitated before she asked the question that had been burning into her brain all morning. 'Did you find him?'

'No.' Allie looked at her with sympathy. 'Even the bloodstains had been washed away by last night's rain. It's as if he was never there.'

Sarah could not decide if she was relieved. Some other creature had benefited from the remains, and the cycle of life in the bush went on as it had always done. She found herself hoping it had been a leopard, and not a hyena, that had taken him away.

'Let's go and search for Lara,' Allie said. 'We can come back here later to see if there is any change in these two.'

At sundown, as the two cars headed back to camp, Allie spotted Irial moving towards Rhino Ridge, looking around carefully before stopping to spray as he went.

'He's getting bolder,' she remarked. 'He's in the brothers' territory now. Perhaps he has seen that the dominant male has gone, and the others have done nothing all day to protect their range. The scents of their passing have started to fade, especially after that downpour. So Irial may be extending his area of operations.'

'Would he try to drive the two remaining brothers off their patch?' Hugo was intrigued. 'Challenge them, the way lions do when a pride is invaded?'

'Cheetahs are not that bloodthirsty,' Allie said. 'They will fight if they have to, but in general they don't seek out confrontation, unless there is rivalry for a female. In circumstances like this where the two residents are young and inexperienced, a new contender might move in and take over.'

'Would they ever accept one another? Join forces?' Sarah squinted through her lens. 'That would be so much better for all three, wouldn't it?'

'Highly unlikely,' Allie said. 'Unless they are different litters from the same mother.'

They watched Irial for some time, observing his progress along the ridge and down onto the scrubland. In the fast approaching dusk, he crept along like a ghost, his spots appearing to move and meld with the shadows. Far across the plain a lion roared and coughed his message to a mate. The lone cheetah paused, turned towards the undergrowth, and vanished.

It took the brothers several days before they were able to make a successful kill. Finally, driven by extreme hunger, they launched a risky attack on a full grown impala which lashed out with sharp hooves, almost impaling Pollux on its lyre-shaped horns, before springing away across the plain. During the afternoon they managed, at last, to bring down a young Thomson's gazelle. Considering their long fast there was not a great deal of meat but Sarah was relieved that they had managed to find some food, since the situation had become critical. Back at camp they sat around the fire, discussing their observations and writing the day's reports.

'What if Irial does decide to challenge the other two, and they try to see him off?' Sarah said. 'It would be terrible if they ended up destroying each other. Oh, no. I really don't want to think about it.'

'I see Ahmed has hot water in the showers,' Allie said. 'See you for a drink when we're all cleaned up.'

Inside the mess tent the radio crackled into life, and Rabindrah went to answer it. He spoke into the receiver for several minutes, and when he made his way to the sleeping tent he was shaking his head in resignation.

'Gordon Hedley,' he said, in the first of a misguided series of lies designed to keep Sarah from worry, now that she was so happily immersed in her work. 'He tried to contact me earlier. I'm needed back in Nairobi urgently to cover a breaking story.'

'Can't he use someone else?' Her protest held a trace of anger. 'We have something really unusual going on here.'

'Seems not. I'll get back as soon as I can, but this sounds important. I'll try and leave on the morning plane from Keekorok.'

'I'll drop you,' Allie said, when she heard the news. 'Erope, you can drive and we'll go on to the *duka* at Lolgorien for a few supplies.' She turned to Rabindrah and put a hand on his arm. 'It is a shame you have to leave right now but we'll keep you posted. Hugo will write up everything, until you come back.'

After dinner Rabindrah left the small group sitting out in the starlight, and went to put his belongings into a canvas bag. When he turned to pick up a shirt he was surprised to see that Sarah had come quietly into the tent and was sitting on her bed, weeping.

'What is it?' He sat down beside her, dismayed at the sight of more tears. 'I won't be away for long, and you know there's nothing I can do. We need the money from my newspaper job, until the book is published. Please don't cry.'

'We don't need the money that badly,' she said. 'And it's the right time of the month. Ovulation. I want us to try again. Here, away from everything in Nairobi. I've been taking my medication, and—'

'Sarah!' His face was grim. 'I thought that discovering the reason for our not having children would remove this fixation from your mind. Specially when it turns out it's not your problem at all. It's mine.'

'You heard what Stephen Devanny said. Being on this drug could do it.'

'This treatment has sent you completely overboard.' His voice rose in anger and frustration. 'Your moods are up and down like the big dipper in a fairground. You're sliding back to the way you were when you lost the last baby, Sarah, and it's dangerous.'

'No, I'm not. I only want to—'

'Besides, no matter how fertile you become it won't alter the fact that I'm not likely to make you pregnant. That's the bottom line.'

'You have. You did. Make me pregnant. Twice.'

'And they died.' It was a brutal statement and he closed his eyes for a moment. 'Our children died because my sperm made them malformed. Any others could be the same. They might all die before birth, these babies you want to make. Or we could succeed, only to find the child was handicapped. You are a very strong person, but I don't think I could deal with that. I'm being honest with you.'

'I don't believe a specialist would have put me on this medicine and advised us to keep trying, if he thought it would only produce dead or deformed babies!'

'He said we should be patient.' He was very angry now, and he turned his back to her.

'Yes. Yes, he did. But we don't have to be bloody well celibate.' Sarah hit back, his attitude confounding her. 'There's always some excuse, Rabindrah. I need you, but you are on another planet. Steering away from everything we used to share. You don't kiss me or caress me, or even talk to me any more. You don't even look at me straight. I don't really know whether you love me or hate me.' Her voice was shaking. 'In fact, I wonder if you are repelled by me. You never offer even the smallest expression of love or tenderness any more, in case it might lead to something else.'

'Sshhh, Sarah. Sshhh. You're going off the deep end again.' He grasped her hands, trying to soothe her, to get her to lower her voice which was rising to a wail. 'Of course I love you—'

'Don't humour me, as if I was a fractious child.' She snatched her hands away. 'I'm your wife, although I don't feel like a wife any more. And now you're going away, and I can't bear it!'

'You could come back with me,' he said.

'No, I bloody couldn't and you know it! This is a crucial time with the cheetahs, and I need to record whatever happens. I understand that you want to go back to your other work, and I suppose I have to accept that. But I don't have to like it. You could at least grasp that. I've turned into a walking tap, I know, but I'm not going to stop the fertility treatment, whatever it does to my equilibrium. Because I believe it's worth anything to try again, Rabindrah. It's not only about making a baby. It's about wanting to touch you, and love you, and have you make love to me. Why is that so unreasonable?'

'It's not. Of course it's not.'

Rabindrah held her, waiting for her tears to stop. Then he undressed her and lay down beside her, his mouth finding hers, moving down to her breasts, her belly. Their lovemaking was slow and strong until he entered her and suddenly his erection softened, went flaccid. He began to move more urgently against her, but the moment was gone and he turned his back to her. She could feel his shame, and she did not know what she could say or do.

'It doesn't matter,' she whispered. 'We've been away from each other for too long, and you've had so much to deal with. It will come back. Just hold me.'

He did not move, and though she caressed him he neither spoke nor responded. Eventually, when he thought she had fallen asleep he slipped into his own bed and lay on his back, eyes open in the darkness, staring at the roof of the tent.

In the morning he put his bag in Allie's Land Rover, and held Sarah briefly.

'I'm sorry,' he said into her ear. 'About last night. Maybe in Nairobi, or when I can get back here things will be better. We'll talk then.'

'I'll miss you,' she said, her face buried in his shoulder. 'Try to call on the radio this evening. And make sure you see Kuldip Auntie. Tell her I'll visit her as soon as I get back to Nairobi.' She could not stop the words, although she knew that he was impatient to be on his way. 'If you meet up with Anthony, let him know all about the cheetahs. I think he has a safari in the Mara soon, and Allie always loves to see him. Oh, and find out when Camilla gets back.'

'Time to go,' Allie said, as Erope started the engine. 'Keep that nephew of mine on his toes, Sarah. We should be back around five.'

Sarah watched the car disappear in its trail of dust, and a great loneliness washed over her. But she was determined not to give in to another bout of weeping. She straightened her shoulders, took a deep breath, and turned to Hugo.

'We'll check on the brothers first,' she said. 'Then try to find Irial. If we can't locate any of them, we'll drop in on Lara and her cubs.'

Castor and Pollux were no longer in their favoured place, and Sarah hoped this was a good sign. She got out of the car and scrambled onto higher ground. Hugo followed, and they stood looking over the plain and the outline of the outcrop where they had found Ajax. Sarah's heart contracted, the sharp, sticky odour of congealed blood and the feel of the cheetah's rich coat strong in her memory. She shivered.

'Are you all right?' Hugo was concerned.

'Fine. Just distancing myself from . . .'

'From the death of your cheetah.'

'He didn't belong to anyone, but I must admit that I felt a special bond with him. Somehow, after all these years, I can never get used to the suddenness with which death brushes against you in this country – how quickly and savagely life can be snatched away.'

Hugo pushed his hands deep in his pockets, and looked down at his feet. Sarah wondered if her outpouring on the previous night had embarrassed him. Although she had no regrets she did not wish to go down that route again. She returned to the topic of the cheetahs.

'I would have thought if one of them was going to die it would have been Irial,' she said. 'Never Ajax. But that's the bush.' She braced herself. 'We should search for the brothers between here and the river.'

They meandered in and out of a series of dried-out *luggas*, making their way across a savannah dotted with topi and wildebeest. In the forest a troop of baboons screeched and swung in the boughs of the trees. The adults stared down at the slow-moving vehicle below them, scratching their heads, old men's faces solemn and curious. Their young scampered higher into the topmost branches, leaping at each other and swinging wildly over the open roof of the car. There was a crashing, cracking noise up ahead, and a family of elephants emerged from the thick vegetation, uprooting young trees with casual force as they passed, eating the leaves and tender stems.

'Stop, Hugo.' Sarah reached for her camera, and stood up on the seat to get a better shot.

In a matter of a few minutes, the great creatures had melted away into rough scrubland, the bushes closing around them as if they had never been there. Except for one young bull who stayed behind to examine the car. Feeling the need to exhibit his importance, he took up an aggressive stance, ears flapping, trunk raised in the air, a trumpeting show of strength. He made a few short rushes towards the vehicle. When he turned to look for acknowledgement from his family and realised they were no longer there he rushed away in search of his mother, trunk outstretched and tail up, calling frantically for her as he went. Sarah was chuckling as she put down her camera.

'There is something endearing about a small elephant from the rear.' Hugo was laughing too. 'The enormous ears, and the wrinkly legs, not quite co-ordinated, and that ridiculous tail.'

They drove on at a leisurely pace, stopping to admire two waterbuck standing on the edge of a clearing, their long velvety ears and thick fur translucent in the morning sunshine. The grasslands were teeming with gazelle and impala, many with young in tow.

'This is a good place to hunt,' Sarah said. 'We might find the duo now.'

'I thought by this time they would have found shelter, from the fierce heat.'

'Not always. Lions and hyenas are generally not out and about, or they are already sated on an early morning kill of their own.' Sarah stopped the vehicle on a rise and swept the plain with the binoculars. 'The herds are less alert, more sluggish in their reactions. This is a strategic time for cheetahs to hunt. And there they are! Look!' She pointed ahead to where there was movement in the long stalks of red oat grass. 'They've ear-marked a small gazelle.'

Hugo followed the line of her finger and saw their prey, drifting perilously close to hidden danger. Mesmerised, he watched as the two cats exploded without warning out of the grass, stampeding the herd, and springing on their victim. It was all over in seconds. By the time Sarah had brought the vehicle closer, the cheetahs had already eaten most of the flesh from the carcass. Both animals were watchful, stopping in between mouthfuls to look around, their muzzles bright red with blood.

'It's astonishing how fast they can strip off the meat,' Hugo said.

'Necessity,' Sarah answered, scanning the horizon. 'They have to be quick if they want to keep it, and that's rather a small meal for the two of them. No sign of Irial, though.'

She glanced at Hugo and saw that he was making a pencil sketch of the cheetahs in his notebook. There was an economy of line in the drawing, but he had invested the animals with movement and life, portraying their edgy stance as they fed.

'Those are good,' she said, taking a closer look.

'I love to draw.' He flushed at her compliment. 'I've been doodling for as long as I can remember. It was Allie who encouraged me to take it more seriously. As a child, I used to send her my best drawings, and she hounded my parents to pay for private lessons. At one time I had dreams of becoming a full-time artist, but as a teenager I was gradually drawn into the world of scientific study, so I decided to keep my drawing and painting for pleasure.'

'What would you say to our using some of your sketches for this new book?' Sarah leafed through his drawings with interest. 'They could make great chapter headings, for example.'

'Really?' Hugo's surprise was engaging.

'I'd have to ask Rabindrah. And John Sinclair, of course.'

'I'd be pleased to contribute if they are considered good enough. For Allie.' He hesitated, then plunged with uncharacteristic recklessness. 'And for you.'

They moved off in search of Irial. He was lying on a termite mound, panting heavily while a herd of impala grazed some distance away.

'See how fast he is breathing?' Sarah said. 'I'd say he has been on a chase. After one that got away.'

'Do you want to stay with him, then?'

'I think so. He seems to be building up to a confrontation with the brothers, but the fact that they have eaten will give them an advantage if he tries a challenge.'

They spent another hour waiting, but Irial did not move. The extreme heat in the cab of the Toyota built up, and as the minutes went by they found themselves talking more about their lives, and the paths that had led them to this place in Africa. Sarah had decided to move to a shadier spot when the cheetah rose, stretched his long, lean body to its full extent, and gave a mighty yawn. Then, with a quick look around, he trotted off in the direction of the river, stopping at every tree and mound of earth to sniff out and examine the scents left by other animals, and to deposit faeces and his own pungent spray.

'Each tree or bush or rock is a veritable noticeboard of information. He can smell precisely which animals have passed,' Sarah explained. 'The scent of the brothers is already familiar, and if there is a female around he will know whether she's in season, and which way she went.'

She watched Irial through her binoculars until he was almost out of sight, and then started the car. They followed at a distance that would not threaten or distract him and he led them unerringly to the place where Castor and Pollux were already engaged in stalking a herd of zebra that had congregated in a natural depression with a little water. Several foals moved through the grass, close to their mothers. The cheetahs were poised slightly above the shallow bowl, with a panoramic view of the whole herd. Hugo joined Sarah as she stood up carefully to get a better camera angle from the roof.

Irial was also watching from a vantage point of his own. He lay flat, tail flicking with anticipation, golden eyes trained unblinkingly on the hunt. A young zebra, diverted by something in the dense grass, trotted away from the shelter of its mother's flank. It was the signal for the brothers to make their move. One raced to separate the foal from its companions while the other placed himself between the victim and its mother. The herd galloped away, panicked by the smell of the cats, the screams of the mother and the clouds of dust rising around them. With a last powerful spring, Castor landed on the zebra's rump while Pollux swung sharply to swipe at the forelegs. The victim sank onto the trampled earth and they used their dew claws to disembowel it and began to feed.

'It's always so brutal,' Hugo said, with horrified fascination. 'I can't help wanting the zebra to escape and yet I know the cheetahs must eat. How do you get used to all this killing and blood?'

'I don't,' Sarah said. 'As you have already seen.'

'It's certainly different from studying tribal customs in South America.' Hugo adjusted his glasses. 'I did find an enormous snake in my hammock once, and we seemed to be under attack from every insect in the Amazon, but I didn't encounter this much gore on such a regular basis.'

'It's certainly a change from studying elephants,' Sarah said. 'They don't prey on other animals, but they are targets of other predators. Mainly poachers, which is distressing in the extreme.' She turned to look for Irial, and froze. 'Hugo, look! Watch Irial!'

The lone cheetah had started down the edge of the bowl, crawling on his belly in the direction of the two brothers and their kill. Sarah held her breath, not sure if she could bear to see these three tearing each other apart in a fight over supremacy and food. Irial approached, halting every few minutes to check whether he had been observed, but the brothers continued to feed, their concentration focused on the meat. Sarah waited for the outsider to make his rush and scatter his rivals from their kill. But he stopped again. Then he did something wholly unexpected, sitting upright so that the other two could see him. Hugo looked at Sarah but she shook her head and shrugged, unable to understand what was happening. Castor and Pollux had become aware of the trespasser and now they, too, sat up straight and stared back at him.

'Oh, God. Please don't let them fight.' Sarah gripped Hugo's arm and began to pray under her breath.

Castor's tail flicked ominously, but he did not move. Pollux crouched down, waiting perhaps for a signal from his brother. Then Irial was within a few feet of them and they faced each other for several tense moments. Everything around them seemed to be motionless and all other sound had died, except for the breathing of the three cats which she was convinced she could hear. Suddenly abandoning the stand-off, Castor returned to the dead zebra, followed by his brother. Then Irial slid down beside them to bury his muzzle in the fresh, glistening haunch of the foal, and the three cheetahs continued to feed as though they had always been part of the same sibling group.

'Amazing! Unreal,' Sarah said, over and over again. She stopped filming, hugged Hugo in delight and then returned to her lens, the shutter clicking furiously as she sought to capture every aspect of the astonishing event. 'And we have been fortunate enough to see it. What a pity Rabindrah missed this, and Allie too.'

They stood together in the open hatch, watching as the three cheetahs demolished the carcass and moved into the shade of the grey, furrowed trunk and silvery leaves of a leleshwa bush.

'Look at them grooming each other.' Sarah was jubilant. 'They are a family now. Irial has company, and the others have a replacement for their brother. They are going to be all right, Hugo.'

When they drove into the camp Sarah leapt from the car and raced over to recount the day's extraordinary events, her eyes shining with excitement. Allie listened in near disbelief, and even Erope declared himself astonished as they repaired to the mess tent to celebrate.

'We'll take a look in the morning,' Allie said, lifting her chilled beer in a toast. 'If they are still together, it will make for an exceptional report on behaviour patterns. And maybe some new funding. I must say, the best part of this profession is the way that animals never cease to surprise you. Good work, both of you.'

'Can I try Rabindrah on the radio?' Sarah thought of him, alone in Nairobi, researching an article that could never have the significance of the event she had witnessed.

'Pity he wasn't here,' Allie said. 'Go ahead and tell him what he missed.'

There was no reply from the house in Nairobi, however, and Sarah found that she did not paticularly mind. It would have been difficult to describe the day's events without seeming to chide him for not being with her.

'Hugo's notes and observations are precise,' Allie said, as Sarah returned to her chair beside the fire. 'You two make a good team. You're on exactly the same wavelength.'

'You're right,' Sarah said.

She turned to smile at Hugo, but he did not meet her eyes. Instead he rose to his feet, knocking over the remains of his wine, and with an inaudible remark he stumbled out into the darkness.

Chapter 12

Kenya, September 1977

There was no sign of Anthony when the aircraft from London landed on a clear morning. Camilla chided herself for having indulged in yet another fantasy as she allowed the airline staff to escort her to the VIP lounge and locate her baggage. The journey had seemed longer than usual, and she had been unable to sleep or even to listen to the music on the headphones. Outside the customs area she saw Sammy, Anthony's senior safari driver. His round face was beaming.

'Anthony has asked me to drive you to Wilson Airport,' he said. 'The plane is waiting to take you to Lamu. He is already there, at the Peponi Hotel.'

'Lamu? How lovely.' She smiled at him. 'But I have *kazi mingi* waiting for me. I need two days in Nairobi and Langani. So if you wouldn't mind driving me home instead, that would be wonderful.'

'*Hapana.*' Sammy assumed a solemn expression, respectful but stubborn. 'I must take you to Wilson Airport,' he repeated. 'The plane is waiting.'

'I'm too tired to discuss this, Sammy,' she said. 'And too busy. I'll telephone Bwana Anthony when I get home, and tell him I will come down in time for Hannah's birthday.'

'He said you must come today,' Sammy said.

'This is ridiculous.' Camilla was annoyed and disbelieving. 'I will fly down on the day of the birthday. But first I must go to Langani. Maybe I will travel with the Olsens.'

'Anthony has arranged everything already,' Sammy insisted. 'The plane is waiting.' Beyond that he would say no more, standing beside her with an air of unyielding determination.

'Give me some change.' Camilla was too weary to pursue the

argument. 'I need to go back into the terminal and make a phone call.' Inside the arrivals hall she found a telephone and dialled Langani where Mwangi answered the telephone.

'Mama Hannah is not here right now,' he said in answer to her enquiry. 'Bwana Lars is out too.'

'I am planning to drive up to Langani late this afternoon,' Camilla said. 'I have some things to deliver to the workshop. Do you know what time Mama Hannah will be back at the house?'

There was hesitation before Mwangi spoke again. '*Hapana*. But I think she will not be here soon.'

She said goodbye, hung up and then dialled the Singh house. There was no answer and she stood beside the telephone, pondering her next move. A wave of fatigue caught her and she thought of the rush of appointments she had crammed into her last few days in London. Perhaps it was not essential to drive up to the farm immediately.

'Compromise, Sammy.' She threw her hands up in the air, only half laughing. 'If you take me home so I can collect some clothes for the coast, I'll go to Lamu. I will have to phone Wilson Airport though, and tell them I'll be late taking off.'

Anthony was waiting at the airstrip on Manda Island, tanned and fit. His hair had more ginger lights in it, and he had collected a galaxy of new freckles from the sun. Laughter lit his eyes, and his lean, grinning face was more relaxed than she had seen it in years.

'*Karibuni*,' he said, kissing her cheek. He stole a glance at her, serene and beautiful. It took less than a minute for him to discover that her calm exterior was a disguise.

'I love Lamu as you well know, but I don't like being summoned,' she said. 'I'm not some lowly member of your staff that has to drop everything and come running when you call. I was planning to go up to Langani, and Hannah's birthday isn't for another two days. What on earth were you thinking?'

'I was thinking you might need a break after London,' he said. 'You always try to do too much into the last few days. Take the bags and put them on the *mashua*, Ali, please.'

She climbed into the low, wooden boat and sat in the bow as the outboard engine roared into action. For the next fifteen minutes it was

204

impossible to speak as they sped across the channel towards Lamu, and turned along the coast past the town and the main jetty with its dhows at anchor, heading towards the village of Shela.

For Camilla the island had always been a place of happy childhood memories where her parents had taken her to visit Henri Bernier, one of their closest friends. In those days they had driven north from Mombasa, crossing creeks on hand-pulled ferries, bouncing along rutted dirt roads before leaving the car on the mainland and stepping into a small dhow for the last part of the journey to Shela. The Bernier house had been a traditional Swahili residence built around a courtyard filled with rampant bougainvillea, hibiscus and frangipani trees. Inside there were polished floors with a scattering of Persian rugs, and elaborately carved island furniture. At high tide the sea lapped against the walls, and below her bedroom was a wide, silver beach. Fishermen came and went in their boats, and dhows under sail arrived from destinations near and far. Women shrouded in black *bui buis* walked the beach with their children, and donkeys with matchstick legs carried saddlebags full of sand and coral blocks for building. Camilla had never been lonely in Lamu, although she was often alone. After a while the village children lost their shyness and came to swim with her in front of the house. They taught her how to run with their hoops, through the narrow paths between tall, thatched houses. She liked to listen to the call to prayer from the mosque, and to hear the slap of sandals as the faithful made their way past the house to worship.

Local people would stop and greet the little girl on mornings when she set out to walk to Lamu town. Flat-topped acacia trees spread a lacy shade across the footpath that bordered the ocean. Passing traffic included the owners of *dukas* who sometimes walked, but were more often astride small, sturdy donkeys, with the rider's feet almost touching the ground. Men wearing colourful *kikois*, or white robes and round, embroidered hats, sat on stone benches along the sea front. Resting at anchor were dhows bound for the Persian Gulf, unloading food and *debbis* of paraffin, dry goods, chickens and goats, bags of rice and flour and bolts of cloth. Squatting in the shade of a local boat under construction, Camilla learned to admire the curve of each hull and prow as judged by the boat-builder's expert eye. She liked to watch as the planks were coaxed gently into place with a skill handed down through countless generations. Fruit sellers in the market square called out to the *mʒungu toto*, offering mangos dripping with juice and paw-paws sprinkled with lime, or fat, sugary bananas. At her favourite stall she always stopped and handed over a portion of her pocket money for a green coconut, with the top sliced off by the sharp blade of a panga. Tipping her head back she gulped down the sweet water, allowing it to run down her chin onto her cotton dress. Then the vendor would offer a spoon chiselled from the husk, and she used it to scrape out the soft, sweet lining of the green fruit. Camilla was always in trouble on days when her mother decided to join her. On these occasions Marina Broughton-Smith wore a large straw hat and a long, filmy dress or skirt that covered her unblemished skin, in the same way as the women of Lamu hid themselves beneath their black *bui buis* for different reasons. 'George darling, look at that child,' Marina would say, about Camilla, in the soft, breathless voice that managed to sound disparaging. 'Her clothes are covered in some sticky mess, and her face and hands are filthy. God knows what fly-ridden food she has been eating. I hope she won't catch some dreadful disease and spoil our holiday.'

But Camilla was never ill, and Henri was skilled in the art of directing Marina's attention to some exotic plant or artefact. Out of the corner of her eye Camilla could see him choosing ingredients for dinner, explaining his choices to her beautiful mother, while the houseboy stowed everything in a spacious *kikapu*. Then they would continue through the narrow alley-ways, where he pointed out the symbols on the ancient carved doors with their brass studs, or recommend the purchase of some Arab silver in one of the old shops, and Marina would smile and forget about her irritating daughter. The visit to town usually ended on the verandah at Petley's Hotel overlooking the waterfront, or with one of Henri's friends who offered tea in small glasses, or juice from freshly squeezed local oranges. Her parents sipped gin and tonics with wedges of lime, and ate spicy seafood fritters.

In retrospect, Camilla realised that Lamu was the place where Marina had almost always been happy. In the old Swahili house, there were no long silences or acrimonious conversations between her parents. No doors slammed as her father took refuge in his study and her mother isolated herself in her bedroom, ensuring that everyone in the house could hear her discreet but audible sobbing. Life, as Camilla knew it in Nairobi, under-went a miraculous transformation in Lamu. The days became as soft as the ocean breezes that blew the great dhows to and from faraway ports, and childhood became a reality.

In the evening she sat on a low stool at Henri's feet, leaning against him as he turned up the pressure lamp to read to her. His leatherbound books told the story of the island and its varied inhabitants down through the centuries. At night she slept in a room where a paraffin lamp lit the waves that danced beneath her window. Camilla closed her eyes then, and listened to the music of the sea, praying to God and to Allah that she could stay here and never, ever return to the cold, angry mansion her parents inhabited in Nairobi.

During her years in London, as she rose to stardom in the world of fashion, Henri's health had deteriorated and he had sold the house at Shela and gone to live in Mombasa. At first, Camilla decided never to go back there. But the property had become the Peponi Hotel, owned and run by Danish friends who had kept its peace and integrity intact, and she had enjoyed her infrequent visits.

Her mood softened as she crossed the shining body of water. The smell of the sea, and the slow, seductive air began to seep into her mind and body. When she took off her sandals and waded ashore she saw Hannah first, waiting on the hotel terrace. Her loud laughter reminded Camilla of the way she had erupted into the same ribald sound at school, before covering her mouth as one of the nuns reprimanded her for the unladylike noise. Sarah was hugging her and smiling when Rabindrah and Lars appeared, followed by Suniva and Piet. And James.

'So this is where you were all hiding when I phoned your houses this morning. But why the secrecy? And don't you feel guilty at having turned Mwangi into a barefaced liar?'

'It's my birthday weekend,' Hannah said. 'And Anthony insisted on organising it so that you wouldn't know we were waiting for you. Now that you've arrived we can really start to celebrate.'

They stood on the terrace above the beach, friends reunited and easy in one another's company. As children they had come from the most diverse backgrounds, but had grown to love one another through their differences, and to share a passion and respect for the untamed splendour of their chosen country. A land that had taken away, with heedless savagery, both people and possessions that they treasured. A place where one day there might be no trace of their passing across its dusty plains, or through its verdant highlands. But they loved it still.

'I'm astonished by your elaborate planning,' Camilla said, as Anthony accompanied her to her room. 'It seems a little out of character, although I'm certainly not complaining.'

'I thought it would be an ideal place for Hannah's birthday, and I know you haven't been here for some time,' he said. 'As for Sarah, she has always been a fish in human disguise since her Mombasa childhood. There are only so many elephants and cheetahs she can take, before she starts to pine for the sea.'

'Such imagination and generosity of spirit,' she said lightly, looking around the room, taking in the carved four-poster bed, the old copper trays and lanterns, and the bowl of frangipani blossoms. 'You are a master of surprises, it seems.'

'And there may be more,' he said. 'In the meantime, lunch is ready.'

'He insisted that we should be somewhere special for my birthday,' Hannah said, as they lay in the blue balm of the afternoon sea. 'That it had been too long since we had done something together. Although we did have a quarrel recently. I was pissed off with him for taking James away from the farm, while we were in Norway.'

'Why did he do that?' Camila asked.

'After we left, James was beaten up by some boys from the labour lines. So Anthony decided to let him help out in camp, in order to keep him out of trouble until we came home.'

'Sounds sensible to me,' Camilla said.

'I didn't think it was the right way to deal with the problem,' Hannah said. 'We spoke to him on the phone from Norway, but he didn't tell us what had happened. Or ask our opinion on what should be done.'

'He didn't want to spoil your holiday,' Sarah said.

'He's a dictator at heart.' Camilla's comment was tempered by a smile.

'Well, it upset David.' Hannah would not be easily mollified. 'Anthony suggested that he was partly to blame for what happened, although he certainly wasn't. So David, and even old Kamau, are still angry over the whole thing. And Suniva threw a vile tantrum when she got home and found James wasn't there. You might have told me about the postcards, by the way.'

'I assumed Suniva would tell you.' Camilla felt like a coward for blaming the child.

'You must admit it was a good idea to take James away,' Sarah said. 'David's nose may be temporarily out of joint, but that will pass.'

'I suppose. But Suniva's letters and postcards turned out to be part of the problem,' Hannah said. 'A rumour started flying round that I was sending money to James, and the other farm boys got jealous. And ugly.'

'Oh dear. The road to hell and all that.' Camilla raised a languid hand from the water. 'I'm sorry, Han.'

'No, I'm sorry.' Hannah was suddenly ashamed. 'I don't know why I brought it up. We had the best time with you in London, and we will never forget a minute of it. Never. And we loved our holiday in Norway, although it was overshadowed by Piet's problem.'

'Explain what the specialist has said.' Sarah felt her heart go out to the little boy.

'He has a ruptured eardrum on one side that may close up on its own. More importantly both ears have been affected by the string of infections that have bugged him over the last year or so,' Hannah said. 'We had no idea such things could cause a build-up of damage inside the structure of the ear, but Dr Enright's tests showed that Piet has lost more than sixty per cent of his hearing. I can't forgive myself for not having understood sooner why he had become so withdrawn. He has had a series of antibiotic injections and he is taking tablets to prevent any new infections. There are earplugs in both ears to prevent any risk of an ear infection, because it's impossible to keep him out of the sea.'

'So what happens next?' Camilla looked at the boy, happily filling a bucket with water and wetting the sand he was using to build a fortress.

'We need to wait a few weeks before making a final decision about surgery,' Hannah said. 'It is still possible that the hearing will return in the perforated ear. If not . . .' Her voice caught in her throat and she plunged under the water for a moment.

'Prayers,' Camilla said. 'We had better get onto one of your candle-lighting programmes, Sarah.'

'I'm not sure how effective they are,' Sarah said. 'I seem to have had my line cut for quite a while.'

'Anyhow, I'm optimistic.' Hannah resurfaced, composed once more. 'Some of the damage might reverse itself, and the surgery has a good

209

chance of success. Meantime we've had several sessions with a teacher for the deaf who gave us plenty of advice about how to deal with everyday issues and keep his spirits up. It's not easy, but we are learning. Suniva has taken it in her stride. She makes sure he doesn't miss anything, by poking him in the ribs when he hasn't heard us. And James drags him into everything they are saying and doing. The three of them have already invented a communications system all their own, and they are learning sign language and making it fun, pulling faces and laughing with Piet, and so.' She sighed. 'With all this going on, and the farm so dry with the rains having failed, I'm not sure what we are doing here at all.'

'It's great to see James here.' Sarah was looking at the children, laughing and splashing each other in the warm sea.

'He has always come with us on holidays to the coast, and on safari.' Hannah's tone was prickly. 'I don't know why everyone keeps battering me over the head with questions about James. Look at him, fooling around as usual with the other two. Having fun. What the hell else am I supposed to do for him?'

'You've given him a life and a family who loves him, and those are the most precious gifts anyone can have,' Sarah said, in an attempt to soothe. 'The three of them are having a great time. And so are we.'

'When Anthony first suggested coming down here I said no. We have just spent a huge chunk of our savings on our trip to Europe,' Hannah said. 'It was Lars who insisted it would be good for us all, after the worry of discovering Piet's problems.'

'I had no hesitation,' Sarah said. 'I love being in the *bundu*, but I'll always be a child of the Indian Ocean. Rabindrah was keen too, and that was a pleasant surprise. I've hardly seen him of late.'

'What does that mean?' Camilla detected a note of despondency. 'Are things not going well with the new book?'

'He's having a hard time adjusting to the news from the specialist in Ireland,' Sarah said.

'Yes, that must be difficult for him.' Camilla swam closer to Sarah, splashing her with affection. 'But at least you know that you can have a child. You said on the phone that the specialist had suggested fertility drugs.'

'I'm taking them,' Sarah said. 'But you need sex as well, and that's in short supply.'

'Ach, maybe it's good that we are all here.' Hannah was surprised by the bitterness in the statement. 'It might cheer Lars up. It's been tough between us, too, since this business with Piet. And we had a terrible row in his parents' house. Behind my back, they suggested that we sell up at Langani and take over their farm in squeaky clean Norway.'

'I can't imagine Lars going for that, and I'm sure they didn't mean to upset you,' Sarah said.

'You're right, but I was furious that they had discussed it with Lars and Ilse, when I wasn't there to comment. That was a passion cooler, I can tell you.'

'Good God! I'm really out of date here,' Camilla said. 'Any more news I should hear?'

'I have some other news,' Hannah said. 'I'm pregnant.'

'Pregnant *and* passion cooler? They don't strike me as being part of the same equation,' Camilla said, laughing. 'That's marvellous, Han. Really terrific.'

'I'm so happy for you and Lars,' Sarah said, her smile valiant. 'It will be great for the other three, a new member of the family.'

'It was in Norway.' Hannah was conscious of the effect of her news on Sarah. 'Before we had our quarrel. Maybe having another child born in Kenya will convince Lars that we belong here. I don't know – I've been avoiding the subject.'

'If any place can work its magic on Lars, it will be Lamu,' Camilla said. 'And the same goes for Rabindrah. Whatever we are doing here.'

'We are here on Anthony's orders,' Sarah said. 'To loll around in the sea and forget our cares. I haven't been here for years and I love the fact that it's still the same. No cars, the same buildings with thatched roofs and the donkeys and goats and cats all wandering around the sandy alleyways. It's heaven.'

'I hate to say this.' Camilla said it anyway. 'But in my experience Anthony never does things without a reason, and it's usually something that will work out to his advantage. I thought the idea of a 1930s party and the glamorous clothes was very odd.'

'What's this? What glamorous clothes?' Sarah said.

'He didn't tell you?' Camilla said. 'Just as well I brought dresses for us all. It was quite a challenge, though, to select something that would look movie-style glamorous and still be wearable in this climate.'

'What on earth are you talking about? I don't know anything about this,' Hannah said.

'Me neither,' Sarah was astonished.

'I knew he was up to something,' Camilla said with a mixture of triumph and disgust. 'I'll bet he has some filthy rich clients flying in here tomorrow, and he wants us all here to impress them. As though we are on a Happy Valley movie set.'

'He's not that calculating,' Sarah said, ignoring Camilla's obvious disbelief. 'He does seem distracted, though. And wound up. We haven't seen much of him. He spent all day yesterday in Lamu town, or on the telephone in the office.'

'I think we should tell him it's too hot for dressing up in that fancy gear,' Camilla said. '*Kikois* and coastal clothes would be much better for your birthday, Hannah. You're elected to pick a moment tomorrow and tell him, since it's your celebration.'

'Why am I always given the best assignments?' Hannah made a face and laughed. 'I'll do it, though, because I don't think I can fit into whatever you brought from London.' She turned her head towards Camilla. 'Has he said anything about the photo of you and Tom? He must have seen it, or at least heard about it. We haven't dared to mention it.'

'He hasn't said anything to me about anything,' Camilla said, frowning. 'Still, I'm thrilled about the birthday party, Han, even if he has other guests up his sleeve. I just hope there isn't anyone from the press. Do you remember how angry I was when he flew me up to his camp in Shaba, and I found some writer from the travel section of the *New York Times*. I was on parade day and night.'

'He's never done anything like this before,' Hannah said. 'It's not his style.'

'That's not true.' Sarah floated on her back, eyes closed. Remembering. 'He set up a camp for us on your twenty-first birthday, Han. In Samburu. Piet was with us.' She did not remind them that Piet had had eyes only for Camilla at the time. 'That's when I first met Allie and Dan, and landed myself a job. But it was Anthony who organised the safari.'

'That was in another life,' Camilla said. 'Long ago, when we were young and naive and optimistic.'

'But do you think he saw the *Daily Mirror*?' Hannah rose out of the sea and wrung the salt water from her yellow hair. 'He was away on safari when it came out, but you can buy that rag on every news stand in Nairobi and someone must have brought it to his attention.'

'I saw it, and several people mentioned it to Rabindrah and me,' Sarah said.

'Oh, for God's sake,' Camilla snapped. 'What if he did see it? It didn't mean anything, and what business is it of his, anyway?'

'I'm glad to hear that, at long last,' Hannah said, with satisfaction. 'It's what I told you in London. You do too much for Anthony, and you don't ask for anything in return. And Tom is crazy about you, even though you choose to ignore it. So maybe it does mean something, from Tom's point of view especially.'

'When I came back here for Daddy's funeral it was you and Sarah who insisted I should stay on, if I cared about Anthony,' Camilla said. 'So I've stayed. Built myself a life here, although I had settled down perfectly well with Edward, and promised him I would never come back to Kenya or see Anthony again. My life in London was stable and organised.'

'You never really loved Edward.' Sarah was definite. 'He was dependable and secure. But too old and too dedicated to his work. In those days you never really wanted anyone except Anthony, even when he let you down.'

'Well, I'm managing perfectly well without him now, so times have changed,' Camilla said.

'But he's never far away,' Sarah said.

'Where *is* Anthony, by the way?' Hannah spread a towel on the beach and lay down in the sun. 'Might he join us for a swim?'

'He is on the verandah of our room.' Sarah gestured upwards. 'Talking to Rabindrah about some story he is working on. In fact, I wonder if that is why my husband is here at all. He has been so immersed in research lately, that I have barely seen him in the Mara. I don't even know what the topic is, although Anthony seems to be in on it, somehow.'

'Of course that's not the reason Rabindrah is here,' Camilla said. 'As for Anthony, he won't swim if there's anyone else around. He would have to take the leg off and have someone help him into the water. He can't bring himself to do it, even in front of us.'

'I can understand that,' Sarah said. 'It would be tough for him to go hobbling and supported into the sea, with the stump of his leg bared to the world.'

'I think it would be good for his morale,' Camilla said. 'But I've never been able to persuade him. Well, I'm for a short session with my book, followed by a long siesta. I didn't sleep much on the plane and it's catching up with me fast. What's the programme for this evening?'

'I suppose we'll meet in the bar around seven,' Hannah said. 'A siesta sounds like a good idea. I'll ask one of the staff to keep an eye on the children, although they hate the idea of supervision at this age. Just look at them – they are growing by the minute, especially James. I had to buy them all new clothes and shoes last week and it won't be long before I have to do it again. I don't see any sign of Lars, so I suspect he is already prone somewhere, snoozing off the beer and wine.'

They spent the following morning in Lamu town. Below the piers, dhows and smaller fishing boats were tied up, and traders haggled over the rows of slim, sturdy *bariti* poles for sale. Prized for construction, they were used as a base on which to lay smooth plaster for the walls, and to support the thickly woven *makuti* thatch that ensured a dry covering for every traditional house. In the cool, dark shops, Indian and Swahili traders offered sacks of spices from the east, bags of maize meal and sugar, candles and paraffin oil and sweet drinks in brown glass bottles. Housewives bargained with the shopkeepers for yards of printed *kitenge* fabric and jewellery to wear under their long robes, eyes flashing with the challenge of the exchange. There was henna for painting on the hands and feet of young girls promised in wedlock, along with sweet-smelling soaps and oils and perfumes, beaded and plastic sandals, pots and pans, dried fish and rice in woven sacks that would eventually be used as boat sails once the contents had been stored or eaten.

'Hot. I'm far too hot,' Hannah said, as they emerged onto the waterfront and made their way to Petley's Hotel in search of cold drinks.

'My parents always loved this funny old place,' Camilla said. 'And they were able to order a drink here which was a relief for Marina who couldn't survive for too long without a gin and tonic.'

'Couldn't she have one delivered on demand, at Shela?' Sarah asked.

'Henri Bernier used to read to me each evening at Shela.' Camilla was smiling. 'Stories about the history of the area. I treasured those hours as my own special time with him. Years later I discovered that during those moments George and Marina were sitting on the balcony of their room, sipping gin or Scotch that they had brought in their luggage at Henri's suggestion. He had converted to Islam, and alcohol was a pleasure officially forbidden within a Muslim household. So they drank private cocktails before dinner, and Petley's was their watering hole during the daytime.'

For the remainder of the day they enjoyed playing games with the children on the beach, their cares vanishing in the soft coastal air and the gentle pull of the outgoing tide. In the evening they walked along the sea road to dine with Anthony's old friend and mentor, Bunny Allen, who had been a professional hunter since the 1920s. His house was on the beach, a sprawl of whitewashed walls shaded by lofty thatch and an open terrace framed by a riot of bougainvillea. His career as a hunter had made him as famous as the European royalty and American movie stars who went on safari with him. The dinner conversation abounded with tales of wild romance, shooting adventures and descriptions of maulings by lions and leopards and charging buffalo. He was rumoured to have been the lover of Ava Gardner and Grace Kelly, and the bush pilot and author Beryl Markham. He refused to confirm the identities of the many celebrated beauties he had apparently seduced, although he enjoyed his reputation and did not deny any tales of his romantic entanglements. It was past midnight when they walked back along the beach to Peponi.

'*Lala salama*,' Anthony said, as his guests made their way across the moonlit lawn. For a while he stood on the edge of the sea, looking out across the dark swell of the ocean and offering an unaccustomed prayer for love that he did not deserve.

On the following evening they assembled on the terrace, above the swell and murmur of the tide. The men were wearing cotton shirts over the traditional *kikois* wrapped around their waists. Sarah and Hannah had selected kaftans embroidered at Langani, and Hannah had put up her hair in a French roll into which she had fastened sprigs of bougainvillea. Camilla appeared last, with her impeccable sense of timing. She had chosen a length of blue and turquoise *kitenge* cloth and wound it round her body, fastening it over one shoulder. There was a wide belt of beaten Arab silver around her waist, and she wore a silver choker and a bracelet decorated with shells.

'Oh, look at Camilla! Like a princess out of the sea,' Suniva said, and the children gathered round to inspect and admire her.

There was a magnum of champagne on a table in the garden, and Anthony offered Camilla the first glass. He was grinning, but Camilla sensed something in him, an edgy intensity that crept towards her, making her wish she had not come. There was no part of him that she did not know, no flicker in his eye or twitch of his mouth that she did not recognise, no suffering that she had not experienced with him. And his charged energy made her apprehensive.

'Happy days, everyone,' he said, raising his glass.

Rabindrah was sitting on the coral wall, making no move to join the conversation or the toast.

'Twelve years,' Hannah said softly. 'Tomorrow will be twelve years since my big birthday at Anthony's camp in Samburu. It seems so long ago. So much has happened, and we have all faced loss and tragedy. But in spite of it all the three of us, Sarah and Camilla and me, have kept the pledge we made at Langani, with Piet as our witness. When we all cut our hands and mixed our blood, to make us sisters.'

'We made the vow again, on the beach at Watamu. Remember? It was New Year's Eve. The last one before Independence,' Sarah said. 'Before we were all sent away.'

'You were with us that night, Anthony.' Hannah reached for his hand. 'Everything was so uncertain, with people not knowing whether to leave the country, or stay on and have enough faith to become citizens. We were all young enough to be sure that we would stay, even though we were made to spend some time away. And we were right. This is where we still belong. This is home.' She saw Lars shift in his chair, knew that he understood the underlying message in her words. 'So I think we should make our promise again tonight. Because we have stuck together for almost fifteen years since that first time, and I hope we always will.'

They clasped hands, each one saying the words they had first repeated at Langani Farm when they were schoolgirls. The children stood on the edge of the circle, wide-eyed and silent, recognising the solemnity of the moment as the words were repeated once more.

'We promise never to forget, always to stay true to our friendship, always to be there for our sisters.'

'I have a promise of my own to make, this evening.'

Everyone turned to look at Anthony, standing a little apart, moonlight picking out the gold flecks in his eyes, highlighting the aquiline nose and the lean planes of his face. His expression was unusually grave, his body poised like an antelope. Waiting, testing the air. Then he spoke again.

'I promise to love and to honour, to cherish and to comfort and be true to Camilla Broughton-Smith, for richer or poorer, in sickness or in health, in sadness and in joy, for better or for worse, and to bestow upon her, for ever, my heart's deepest devotion. For as long as we both shall live.' He moved closer to her. 'Will you marry me, Camilla? I know I don't deserve you, but will you?'

Camilla stared at him, fearing that all reality had deserted her, that the night sky and its wild scattering of stars were leading her along a path that could only prove to be another mirage. She hesitated, not knowing whether she could erase the tattered leftovers of hope, or whether this might turn out to be another illusion. The sea air felt cold on her face and she remained motionless for several moments, until the apprehension she had felt all day left her to be replaced by an ecstatic singing in her heart.

'Yes, Anthony,' she said. 'I will marry you and love you as long as we both shall live.'

Chapter 13

Kenya, September 1977

Sarah lay back in her chair, her body smothered with sun lotion that had left oily fingermarks on the pages of her book. The juice on the table beside her was the kind she remembered from childhood, squeezed from the small, green oranges that grew along the coast and were as sweet as the sea air. Beyond the coral wall she could see the seductive glitter of the Indian Ocean, a flash of blue visible through the rampant spill of bougainvillea and yellow alamanda. A large dhow passed by under sail, heading out to sea, following the centuries-old trade route to the Middle East and India. Behind the hotel, she heard the call to midday prayers at the mosque. When she realised that the wedding would be on the island, she had thought of Allie.

'There is a charter plane coming in this afternoon.' Anthony's grin was broad and knowing, the flecks dancing in his eyes. 'Allie will be on board with a few chums from Nairobi and places further afield.'

'Which chums? Who else is coming?'

Sarah had been burning with curiosity and she called out the news to Hannah and Lars who were splashing in the sea, their laughter echoing in the wind. But in spite of pressure from them all, Anthony refused to disclose the names of any other guests, and finally they gave up their efforts.

Just before noon he appeared, his long stride relaxed and confident. 'Looks like you found a good spot there, under the frangipani tree.' He sat down beside her.

'It's heaven,' Sarah said. 'I must say that you took a huge chance organising all this, and keeping it a secret. Now I understand the need for glamorous dresses, which seemed incomprehensible.'

'I knew it didn't sound like me.' Anthony sounded bashful. 'I'm surprised Camilla didn't smell a rat and grill me.'

'Oh, you know how she always jumps at an opportunity to get Hannah and me properly dressed up,' Sarah said. 'But what if she had said "no"?'

'Then I would have got my just deserts, I suppose.' He threw his head back and laughed, but when he looked at her his expression had become sombre. 'The truth is, it might have finished me off, had she refused me. No. It would have been the end of me, in fact.'

'So you gambled and won, and we are all thrilled,' Sarah said. 'I have to give you credit for your optimism. Pretty brave.'

'I wasn't feeling brave last night, with all of you standing there. I tried all day not to imagine what would happen if . . .' He stopped.

'Well, the outcome is everything you hoped for, and a wedding in Lamu is a dream,' Sarah said. 'Rabindrah has been working flat out in Nairobi lately, and I'm astonished that he has taken any time off. Hugo has more or less taken over the text of the cheetah book. He has become a co-author at this stage, although he denies it because he's kind and modest.'

'Where is Rabindrah?'

'I'm surprised you need to ask.' She could not suppress her resentment. 'Holed up in our room, surrounded by files and pieces of paper. Working on something so sensitive that I can't be trusted to read it.' Her feeling of annoyance made her sit up suddenly, and she knocked over her orange juice and swore softly. 'You've had several long discussions, the two of you. I suppose you must know what he is writing about?'

'The world of investigative journalism is a foreign place, as far as I'm concerned.' Anthony looked out to sea.

'That's not a direct answer.' She recognised the evasion. 'It's just as well I brought a good book to keep me company. Here we are in the middle of a living heritage, with the beach and the ocean a few steps away, and he hasn't even noticed them. Or me. You need to watch out for that kind of married bliss, Anthony.' Her voice sounded sour, even to her own ears.

'He must be working on something important.' He had always admired her stoicism and her sense of balance, and he had never heard her sound so disheartened. For the first time he realised that she had become profoundly sad. 'It's probably something Gordon has asked him not to discuss.'

'How come you are so sure of that, and I'm not?' She took off her sunglasses so that she could see him more clearly, read his eyes. 'I've never been out of the loop before, when it comes to sensitive issues.'

'I'm sure you're not out of the loop,' he said, his smile apologetic, his gaze directed away from her and she realised he was embarrassed by the suggestion that he knew something about Rabindrah's current assignment. 'I'm sorry I said—'

'It's all right, Anthony,' she said, cutting him off and getting up from her chair. 'I'm going to find a *kanga* to wrap around me for lunch.' She put a hand on his arm. 'It's wonderful to be here and it's the happiest occasion for all of us. That's what is important.'

In the bedroom Rabindrah was poring over a handwritten list in a grubby exercise book. He put it into a file and glanced up at her, checking his watch. 'Oh God, it can't be nearly one. I'm sorry, Sarah. I meant to come out for a swim and a walk on the beach, but I just got caught up in all this.'

'You don't notice the time when you're busy.' She padded barefoot across the polished floor, her feet cooled by its smooth, dark surface. 'Are you coming for a beer?'

'I need to fit in a little more work before the fun starts in earnest. A Tusker would put me to sleep for the afternoon. I'll join you in a few minutes though, and have something non-alcoholic.'

She looked at him for a long moment, making no spoken comment, wondering whether the man she had married had gone forever. Or whether the spark had finally died, put out by her obsessive need for a child. Wondering if she really cared any more. Gradually, as she stood there, beads of perspiration began to form on her forehead, and a familiar sensation rose inside her, a presentiment so strong that she could taste it. Her head started to spin and in her mind she could see smoke, hear strange sounds, smell fear. She sat down in a chair, gripping the wooden arms, trying to control the deep sense of foreboding that had crept up through her body as though she had absorbed it from the ground itself.

'Sarah? Are you all right?'

She watched as Rabindrah moved towards her, out of focus, his head looming larger and larger so that his body was all wrong, distorted, like something she had once seen in a fairground mirror.

'I must have been in the sun for too long.' Her voice was faint. 'Could you get me a glass of water, please?'

'Here you are.' He poured from a flask beside the bed. 'Do you think you need a doctor?'

'No. I'm all right now, thanks.' She leaned her head against the cushions for a while, and then smiled. 'It's gone. I'm perfectly fine.'

'Maybe you should lie down for a while,' he said, holding out his hand.

'I said I'm fine.' For some reason she did not want him to touch her. 'I'll see you in the bar. But don't be too long, or you'll hold up lunch.'

Lars and Anthony were already ensconced on the terrace, and Hannah was struggling with children and beach towels.

'When do we start the birthday celebrations, and where is the bride-to-be?' Sarah asked, catching Piet and drying him down.

'Birthday party is tonight,' Anthony said. 'And Camilla has taken a boat to Bunny Allen's house to drop off everything you girls will need to get ready for the wedding ceremony. She'll be back any minute, because she wants to be ready for the guests when they fly in this afternoon.'

Camilla arrived moments later, the pale oval of her face shaded by a straw hat. She had continued into town from the Allen house and walked back to Shela along the sea front. Although the air was humid and the temperature had soared, the heat seemed to have had no effect on her. She looked cool and composed as she sat on a bar stool, swinging slender legs, her eyes never leaving Anthony. Now and again he put his hand lightly on her bare arm, as if to reassure himself that she was there. They ate lunch in the cool dining room, lingering over coffee and talking of the ceremony that would take place on the following afternoon.

'Lars, you might want to come with me on the boat to Manda. Meet the plane.' Anthony stood up first, draining his coffee cup and picking up an old straw hat. 'I'm sure the girls have things to do that don't require our assistance.'

'Siesta.' Hannah and Sarah said the word in unison and left the table in search of a peaceful interlude.

It was almost two hours later when Hannah heard the boats skimming their way towards Shela. She and Sarah had spent part of the afternoon trying on the dresses that Camilla had brought from London, laughing at Anthony's clumsy but successful attempt to disguise the fact that the clothes were for a wedding. Afterwards Hannah lay on the four-poster bed, reluctant to leave the dim room and the whirring of the fan. The children were next door, unusually quiet, presumably asleep in the afternoon heat. They had been up since dawn, and she had insisted that they take a rest if they wanted to join the birthday dinner. Reluctantly, she pushed her feet into sandals, wanting to be there when Anthony's guests arrived. Moments later James and Suniva appeared, followed by Piet, still rubbing the sleep from his eyes but sensing excitement.

'Do you know who is coming, or how many?' Sarah had asked Camilla earlier. 'I mean, it's odd not to have had any warning, or a chance to put people on the guest list for your own wedding.'

'I only know it's a very small number, and he promised I wouldn't be disappointed,' Camilla said. 'He did let me in on the identity of one guest, though, and based on that I think he has done pretty well.'

'Whose name did he mention? And why that particular one?' Hannah was consumed with curiosity.

'Was it poor old Tom, I wonder?' Sarah felt sorry for him.

'I'm sworn to secrecy.' Camilla was enjoying her ability to tantalise, and she could not be persuaded to offer even a small clue.

They stood together as the boat drew nearer. Sarah waved at Allie and Hugo, clearly visible in the bow as the craft drew nearer. It was impossible to see the other passengers who had chosen to sit under a tarpaulin, in order to escape the sun and spray of the crossing. The tide was in, and small, choppy waves beat against the hull as the engine slowed and then sputtered to a halt below the landing steps and the terrace. There was laughter as Tom Bartlett rose to his feet and wobbled uncertainly.

'Blimey! That's more planes and boats than I've ever been in, over a twenty-four hour period. I'd only have done it for you, darling.' He threw his arms around Camilla in a sweaty embrace. 'You're breaking my bloody heart. You know that. I cried all the way from London, but I had to be here. In case you change your mind and need a replacement bridegroom.'

Sarah had greeted Allie and Hugo, and now she stared speechless as Lila stepped out of the boat in their wake.

'I didn't even know, until the last minute, that I would be in the country.' Lila hugged her friend. 'Harjeet is spending a few days in Nairobi on business, and he finally agreed that I could come and visit my parents. There was no reply from your number, so I rang Anthony and he said you were all coming here for Hannah's birthday. And now I hear it is a wedding, too.'

Hannah's high-pitched scream made them all turn around. She had rushed down the steps and into the water, her *kanga* floating around her like a gaudy flower.

'Ma! Oh Ma, please tell me it isn't a dream.' She reached out her arms, laughing and crying, babbling incoherently as Lottie stepped down into the blue sea and was instantly surrounded by her grandchildren, clamouring for her attention, calling out her name, pulling at her wet trousers.

'You did this for me.' Hannah looked at Anthony, flinging her arms around his neck. 'For all of us, I know, but especially for me. And I'll never, ever forget.'

'It's your birthday gift, Han.'

'Did you know?' Hannah looked at her husband, dazed.

'Not until I saw them coming off the plane,' he said. 'And here is Mario, at last.'

'Mario.' Hannah's voice was choked as she put her arms around Lottie's husband. 'She has brought you to Kenya, after all this time. Ach, it's too much to take in.'

'Lottie, darling Lottie.' Camilla's eyes were starred with tears. 'My friend, and my mother too, all through our school days and our happy times at Langani. Anthony told me last night that you were coming, and I could hardly contain myself today. I had to get away from here this morning, because I was afraid I wouldn't be able to keep the secret if I stayed.'

Hugo had taken off his bush shirt and plunged into the ocean with the children, while the remainder of the party arranged themselves around the bar or on the terrace.

'Good God, here is my little cousin!' Rabindrah strode across the grass, all smiles. 'Have you really abandoned the delights of Birmingham for this?'

'I can't believe it myself.' Lila looked around her, inhaling the ocean air, touching the waxy blossoms of the frangipani tree, listening to the rattle of the palms as she gazed up at the cloudless blue of an African sky. 'I bet it's raining in "jolly old", and they're all sitting in front of the telly watching *Emmerdale Farm*.'

'I think that's enough drama for the time being,' Anthony said. 'Let's move into the shade and get the bags ashore.'

As the boat was unloaded, Sarah moved away from the excitement to study Lottie from a distance. They had last seen one another on holiday with Lars and Hannah and the children on the coast south of Mombasa. But on that occasion Lottie had flown out from Siena alone, and she had been evasive when asked why Mario could not have accompanied her. Today, the old lines of grief and suffering were gone from her face, and the laughter that Sarah had once believed to be permanently extinguished shone in her dark eyes. Violence had taken the lives of her son and her husband, and almost destroyed her. After Jan van de Beer's death she had taken refuge with her brother Sergio, in South Africa. Eventually she married Mario Campezi and went to live in Italy. But she had confided to Sarah at their last meeting that she did not think she would ever return to Langani. Her old home remained so full of painful memories that she had been unable to imagine passing through the rooms, or walking on the land that had exacted such dreadful sacrifice.

'You are Sarah. I've seen Lottie's photographs of you, and of course I know the books you have done with your husband.' Mario was a tall, olive-skinned man, his black hair streaked with grey. His features were somewhat stern, but he had a smile that suggested kindness and sympathy. When he spoke, his voice was deep and full of the music of his country. 'Lottie told me that she has always looked on you and Camilla as her own daughters. And that is Rabindrah, over there?'

Rabindrah was standing beside Lila, laughing and animated as though he did not have a care in the world. It was a face Sarah had not seen in a long time, and she was ashamed of the jealousy that flared in her. She forced a smile and beckoned him. A moment later he was standing beside Mario, exchanging the first revelations and opinions on the path to friendship.

It was not long before all the travellers took to their rooms, to chase away jet-lag and the results of Peponi's famous cocktail, a harmless-seeming but lethal mixture of gin and fresh lime, laced with cane sugar and Angostura bitters, and a token splash of soda. Sarah picked up her book and made her way across the lawn. As she neared her room she was surprised to hear Anthony, deep in yet another discussion with Rabindrah. She stood outside the door, uncertain as to whether she should join them. But the sting of exclusion made her turn away, and she was relieved to see Lila settling herself on a chaise in the shade.

'How long can you stay?' Sarah sat down beside her.

'Another week, I think. It depends on Harjeet and how long it takes to complete whatever deal he is organising.'

'Your parents must have been thrilled to see you.'

'Father took it in his stride,' Lila said. 'He seems very busy and preoccupied, but Mother was over the moon. It was as though I had been away for twenty years, and she wasn't all that happy about giving me up for the weekend. Indar Uncle and Kuldip were also pleased that I had come. She is not well, Sarah, and Indar is worried. But at least she has agreed to go to a new doctor with more up-to-date ideas. So we will see. They hope you will be back in Nairobi before too long – Kuldip is so fond of you. They both are.'

'I'll drop in on them as soon as I can. When I am next in the city to sort out photos and other things. Tell me about your new house.' Sarah did not want to ask a direct question about Lila's husband, any more than she wanted to answer one about her own.

'Oh, we have finally moved in, and it is comfortable. "Top-quality living, you know. No expense spared, I am telling you." ' Lila wagged her head from side to side in a Hindi manner, but the joke did not reach her eyes. 'Truthfully, it's cold. Like my husband. I wasn't allowed to choose the house or the furniture, any more than I was able to choose him. But at least we have privacy. A place of our own that may improve things, if I am patient.' She changed the subject, not wanting her English life to elbow its way into the tropical afternoon. 'What about you? Have you been in the Mara most of the time? Allie's nephew seems like a good person. We sat next to each other on the plane from Nairobi.'

'He works well with her. With all of us,' Sarah said.

'Harjeet and I were on the same flight as Tom Bartlett, coming from London. Do you think he could help me find something to do in the fashion world?'

'You'll have time to ask him,' Sarah said, although she wondered what Lila could accomplish in Birmingham. 'You'll have to choose your moment, though. He professes to be nursing a broken heart, now stewing in alcohol.'

'And what about Rabindrah? It's hard for a man to accept that—'

'It's not half as bloody hard as it has been for me.' Sarah did not bother to contain her long-buried resentment. 'Now that we know I'm not the primary cause of our childless marriage, he is behaving as if it's the end of the world.'

'I'm sorry,' Lila said, aware that she had judged the situation superficially. 'It never occurred to me that you weren't completely happy, in spite of not having children.'

'You know, I'd rather not talk about it,' Sarah said. 'Because I am really happy right now. No clouds hanging over us. Camilla is daring to be madly, openly in love again, and God knows she's waited long enough to deserve this.'

She closed her eyes, holding onto the images of small dhows bobbing in the gentle waves and donkeys trotting along the white sand. When she awoke Lila was gone and she returned to her room. It was empty, and she lay down on the bed and prayed for her heart to be reconciled with her losses and to celebrate the joys of her friends. When her husband returned and lay down quietly beside her, she did not feel his hand reach out and cover her fingers as she slept.

A wafer moon lay on its back above the dark sea when they gathered once more. Hugo sat with the children, encouraging Suniva to show him the pictures she had painted during the day and offering his own sketchbook for inspection. Sarah wandered across the lawn to join them, waving a vaguely dismissive hand in the air when asked about Rabindrah's whereabouts.

'He has been scribbling away most of the afternoon.' Her tone was carefully nonchalant. 'He'll be here in a minute.'

On this night of her birthday, Hannah seemed to have put aside any differences with Lars. They sat together on the wall, holding hands, focused on one another, looking up as Lottie came to join them.

'I have something to ask you both,' Lottie said. 'I'd like to stay on for a while. For a month, maybe. And go with you to Langani.'

'Oh, Ma.' Hannah was unable to continue.

'Sarah has had more courage than me. She never stopped going to the farm.' Lottie did not look at her daughter, but at Mario. 'I've been back to Kenya twice because I had to see my grandchildren, but I wasn't ready for Langani. It is Mario who has given me the strength for what I should have done long ago. He has made me understand that this was the moment when I must go back.'

The evening passed in a gentle haze, and after dinner they sat out under the stars and strolled along the beach, reluctant to bid farewell to the joy of the day. It was almost midnight when they finally began to drift away to bed.

'Happy birthday, my brave and wonderful daughter,' Lottie said, one hand smoothing the flaxen hair in a gesture reminiscent of childhood. 'We have so much to say to one another over the coming weeks, but tonight I need only tell you that I love you. Goodnight, darling. And sweet dreams.'

On their wedding day, as the small dhow dropped its sails and Camilla stepped onto the sand, her beauty made Anthony want to weep. He could not imagine how he had failed to see, for so long, the exquisite planes of her face, the perfection of her winged eyebrows, the mouth that was sensuous and sweet, the long, straight back and the soft nape of her neck. He stared in wonder at her, wanting to reach out and place his arms around her in a gesture that would keep her beside him for eternity. He could not know that an hour ago she had been frozen with last-minute nerves, that it was Sarah who had raided Bunny Allen's fridge and opened a bottle of champagne in an effort to steady them all. The dress lay on the bed, waiting for Camilla to finish with her make-up. But her hands were trembling as she stood in front of the mirror, unable to move or speak. Hannah stepped forward first, wrapping strong arms around her friend, using the tone she employed to soothe her children when they were afraid. Sarah picked up the hairbrush and began to make long, calming strokes, before threading the first flowers into the shining veil of blonde hair. Minutes passed as Camilla took a series of deep breaths, eyes closed, long fingers pressed together at the tips as she tried to bring her crazily fluctuating emotions under control. At last she sighed and held out her arms, and Hannah slipped the gown over her head, smoothing it down so that it clung to her body. It had been made at Langani and was ready for a London boutique, until Camilla had decided that it would be perfect for Hannah's birthday celebration. The beaded hem swirled around her ankles as she moved back to the mirror, to fasten on the Italian Renaissance necklace that had been her parents' gift for her twenty-first birthday. Then she smiled.

'I'm ready,' she said. 'I'm ready for the life I had almost given up believing in. Or hoping that it would ever happen. I'm so, so ready for this life.'

Now she stood on the beach in the blessing of early evening light. Her bouquet of tropical flowers had been picked at dawn and kept in the fridge, and the children scattered baskets of fresh petals onto the sand in front of her as she began to walk towards Anthony. Sarah and Hannah moved with her, in pale, filmy gowns that drifted in the soft air. They were followed by Suniva in a voile dress and a small crown of frangipani flowers, and Piet and James in white shorts and shirts with sprigs of bougainvillea in the button holes. All around them the people of Shela village had gathered to watch as the small procession made its way up the beach.

'Bloody breathtaking is all I can say.' Tom Bartlett leaned across to whisper the words to Sarah, making no attempt to disguise teary eyes as he gazed, trancelike, at Camilla. 'He's a lucky bastard, and if he doesn't look after her, I'll bloody kill him.'

Lars stepped forward to lead the bride to the bower of palm fronds and tropical flowers that had been woven into a canopy for the wedding service. Sarah glanced around to try and catch Rabindrah's eye and was surprised to see him talking to the barman who had come down onto the beach, with a note in his hand. But her attention was immediately drawn away, as the boat carrying the district commissioner and the local Anglican priest arrived to perform the civil ceremony and the marriage blessing. Even when she saw her husband running up the steps and into the hotel, she could only remain at Camilla's side as they took their places and the formalities began.

Camilla's eyes, deepened by the reflection of the ocean, were fixed on Anthony as he took her hand. His voice was choked as he repeated the words that would make them man and wife. But Camilla was steady and unhesitating, and she reached up to touch his cheek as he spoke, squeezing his fingers when he stumbled, overcome, on one of the responses.

'Wasn't that the most beautiful ceremony you have ever seen?' Lila came to stand beside Sarah when the ceremony was over. 'And where is Rabindrah, by the way?'

'I don't know.' Sarah looked around, puzzled. 'I saw him talking to the barman earlier, and then the service started. He must be in our room, I suppose. I'll go and find him.'

She set out across the lawn, her steps light. Camilla's joy would spill over onto them all, she thought. Even Rabindrah could not fail to experience the sense of happiness they all shared on this perfect evening. She opened the door of the bedroom, but it was empty. Frowning, she made her way back to the bar.

'There is a message for you, madam.' The barman handed her a small piece of paper.

'A message?' Sarah looked down at the offering, her heart plummeting.

'From Mr Singh. He has left in the boat that brought the DC and the padre.'

'What?' She looked at him blankly for a moment, rocked by rage and disappointment. Her stomach cramped as she opened the note.

Sarah,

I have been called away to cover an urgent development in the story I have been researching. I'm so sorry, but I cannot delay or pass this on to anyone else. It is very sensitive and important, and as you know it has taken me weeks of background work and investigation. I'll be back as quickly as possible, hopefully tomorrow. Hate to miss this happy event. Please enjoy it to the full.

Rabindrah.

Her friends passed her on the way into dinner, holding out an arm, offering to escort her. But she could only stand rooted to the spot, looking out to sea where the wake of her husband's departure had long faded into the swell. Finally she made her way to the table and seated herself between Hugo and Lars.

'Champagne,' she said in a brittle voice. 'Gallons of it. I must be at least two glasses behind.'

Later she sat on the terrace in the moonlight, talking to Lottie and Mario, determined to display her happiness for Camilla and Anthony, whilst trying to contain her wrath at not knowing her husband's where-abouts or the reason for his disappearance. When the dancing started she flung herself into it, laughing and slightly unsteady as she accepted another drink and allowed first Tom, and then Hugo, to swing her in mad, dizzying circles around the floor. She had no idea what time it was when she fell into bed, the floor and ceiling reeling around her as she groaned and reached out an arm towards Rabindrah, only to remember that she was alone.

Far along the beach, in the shelter of the dunes, Camilla undressed her
husband with gentle fingers, as he leaned on her, acquiescent and silent.
Finally she led him to the water's edge, unfastening his lower leg and
laying it on a towel. Then she placed his arm around her shoulders and
brought him with her into the buoyant, infinite kindness of the sea.

Chapter 14

Kenya, September 1977

On arrival at Mombasa, Rabindrah was met by a policeman who handed him a set of keys and pointed at a nondescript station wagon in the airport car park. There was an envelope on the driver's seat and he opened it to find a single written line with an address and a time. He sat for a while, looking at the neatly folded paper, feeling as though he had been projected into a bad thriller, and wondering if he was hallucinating. Finally he put the key into the ignition and headed for town, winding down the windows to let in the scent of coconut fires being kindled for evening meals and the sound of talk and laughter coming from the small shops and stalls along the roadside. By the time he arrived in the Old Port, he had overcome his sense of the surreal and was looking forward to whatever events might unfold during the night ahead.

He was early for his strange assignation, so he took the narrow path down to the water's edge and stood on the sand, enjoying the smell of seaweed in the air. The massive bulk of Fort Jesus reared up above him, silent, impervious to the changes wrought in its shadow for more than three hundred years. The battle-scarred walls, punctuated by the snouts of black cannons, had repelled Turkish invaders and withstood more than three centuries of wars and skirmishes as Arabs, Turks, Omanis and European powers fought for control of the valuable trade routes to India and along the African coast. Dhows rode the gentle swell of deeper water, and a fisherman laid out his nets on the small beach. It was a peaceful scene and looking around him it was difficult for Rabindrah to fully consider the implications of what he was about to do, and the possible consequences in terms of his personal life and his career.

Over the past few weeks he had pored over records of the illegal trade in ivory and animal trophies. He knew from Johnson Kiberu that the vessel he would be watching that night was bound for Antwerp. Unlicensed exports were often shipped to the European ports of former colonial nations and Belgium was a favoured destination, along with France and Germany. From there the cargo would make its way to the lucrative markets of the Far East where the ivory was then carved and polished. Rhino horn, increasingly rare, was made into dagger handles prized in the Yemen, or ground into powder to be used for medicinal purposes and as a so-called aphrodisiac in China and Korea. A large proportion of the Hong Kong trade subsequently found its way into the United States.

It had been hard to obtain reliable estimates of illegal exports. Because of their clandestine nature, these shipments only appeared in official trade statistics after they had passed through several intermediate countries. Despite the hunting ban in Kenya, the ivory trade was remarkably resilient. As soon as one channel was blocked, another would open up. The absence of effective controls over shipments in and out of the country, coupled with unbridled corruption, had made Mombasa an ideal base from which merchants could dispose of smuggled goods with relative ease.

Rabindrah was aware that numerous governments and international conservation agencies were trying to impose more vigilant policing and stringent regulations on exports. But they had a long way to go in reducing consumer demand for game trophies. Kiberu believed that a worldwide ban on trading ivory and rhino horn would be the only way to achieve adequate protection, and that both species should be placed on an international danger list. Heavier ivory had become harder to obtain as the older elephants were decimated by indiscriminate killing, and sizeable tusks were now rare. It was a sign of how serious the problem had become. Since his return from the Mara, Rabindrah had travelled to several national parks and had seen for himself the bloody, rotting carcasses, tusks and horns hacked away, with poachers often leaving the animals to die in horrible agony. It was abundantly clear that animals were being slaughtered in huge numbers through bribery of officials at every level, and he agreed with Kiberu that the situation was desperate. But yesterday, in Lamu, he had expressed some reservations to Anthony.

'Poaching is barbaric, and it's only possible because of greed in high places,' Rabindrah said. 'I have to admire Kiberu for what he is trying to do, but exposing high-stakes players is going to be a dangerous goal that may cost him his job. Even threaten his life.'

'I gather you still haven't told Sarah what you are investigating.' Anthony could hear the disquiet underlining Rabindrah's remarks.

'No. If this was a general article about poaching in Kenya, I would have said something to her. But poaching and smuggling make for extreme violence, and this assignment is like taking on the Mafia in their own backyard. These Somali bandits are heavily armed, murderous thugs, and the people who deal with them will do anything to protect their own backs and continue to rake in money. I'm soon going to be in a rather dangerous position myself, whatever the outcome. And the fact that there are Asians involved is bound to make me a pariah in some places. Particularly if any of them are jailed or deported as a result of my investigation.'

'But you are still committed to it?'

'I certainly am.' Rabindrah squinted down at a page of neatly written figures, and then rubbed his eyes. 'I hope we will catch a few local crooks, but you can bet that the real fat cats will still end up with splendid mansions and bank accounts in Europe or the Far East. Completely untouchable.'

'That may well turn out to be the case, yes,' Anthony said.

'I suppose we are right to trust Kiberu.' Rabindrah tapped a pen on the table beside him. 'To assume he is on the level himself and not on some personal, anti-Asian witch hunt. Or even on the take.'

'Good God, man!' Anthony was shocked. 'Johnson is completely genuine. He has declared an all-out war on poachers, and he is taking a big risk in exposing his political peers who are up to their necks in this. Look here, if there are Asians involved, it's a measure of his trust in your integrity that he has asked you to expose them. And if they are wrongly accused, then who better than you to defend them?'

'That's why I'm going ahead.' Rabindrah was already regretting his comments on the Minister. 'But it has me rattled.'

'Maybe you should say something to Sarah, before this goes any further?'

'No.' Rabindrah had been emphatic. 'I've never kept anything from her before, but on this occasion the less she knows right now, the better. Kiberu was right to emphasise the closed nature of the information he has given me.'

Remembering the words he had spoken only twenty-four hours earlier, Rabindrah sat down on a bench and smoked several cigarettes before retracing his steps to enter the Old Town. A nagging sense of doubt had begun to make him question his decision. Sarah would be extremely angry at his sudden disappearance. And worried too. Not that he had been given any last-minute opportunity to explain, before leaving the wedding ceremony. There had been no time to draw her aside and embark on explanations, and he had not wanted to make his departure conspicuous. After a terse telephone conversation with Kiberu he had simply followed the minister's orders and taken the DC's boat to Manda Airport where a charter plane was waiting. Still, it was not too late to phone Sarah, to try and reassure her in some way. Passing a line of old houses whose carved wooden balconies hung out over the narrow streets, he looked around for a telephone box. But the only one available was out of order, its receiver dangling in the cabin, the coin box forced open and covered in scratched messages of love and lust.

The address he had been given turned out to be a run-down café, and he ducked to avoid hitting his head on the lintel of the doorway as he entered the small room. There were five tables with rickety, mismatched chairs, marooned like crumbling outcrops on a cement floor that had once been red. The plaster on the walls was peeling, and a ceiling fan rotated wheezily, its shaft wobbling so that it looked as if it might tumble from its housing at any moment, onto the patrons below. One elderly man was sitting at the bar and the African proprietor was a portly man in a tatty *kanzu*, with a beaded muslim cap on his head. Swahili music crackled from a radio behind the counter, and an ancient fridge hummed in the background.

'*Salaam.*' Rabindrah seated himself at the table nearest to the door, well away from the fan. He ordered a cold beer which came without a glass. Flies buzzed around the dim room, and there was a strong smell of fish and hot cornmeal emanating from a small kitchen, visible behind the bar. Within minutes a man walked in from the street, and glanced around. Thin and furtive-looking, his gaze settled on Rabindrah and he hesitated before speaking.

'Mr Singh?'

'Yes. Can I get you a beer?'

'I will have coffee. I am Yussuf.'

Nothing more was said until the proprietor had produced a glass of thick Arab coffee, and retired to his place behind the counter. Yussuf ladled two spoons of sugar into the black liquid before he spoke. His anxiety was evident and his eyes darted around the room as though to assure himself that there were no hidden eavesdroppers. Rabindrah studied him in silence, noting the lined and pitted face, the shabby clothes. It had taken considerable persuasion before Johnson Kiberu's informant had agreed to meet him and to pass on details of the time and date on which the next consignment of illegal trophies would be shipped from Mombasa. Yussuf worked as a night watchman in the go-down from which the cargo would be loaded, but he was terrified of his employers and of his own fate if he was discovered leaking information.

Rabindrah had no illusions as to what might happen if he himself was caught nosing around the warehouse, or on the ship if he could get on board. He saw that the watchman's hands were shaking as he lifted his glass of coffee and was relieved that he had not been able to telephone Sarah. If he managed to get a story for the paper and put a group of poachers and traders behind bars, then she would forgive his disappearance. He did not want to consider the alternatives.

'You have information about a shipment?'

Yussuf nodded. 'It will be tonight,' he answered. 'Late. They only bring the ivory and the skins when the rest of the cargo is on board, and the ship is ready to leave.'

'Will they load from the lorry straight onto the ship?'

'No. They drive the truck into the warehouse, and hide the goods in packing cases. Then they cover them with other things for export. The boss checks every crate before it is loaded on board, and before he pays out the *baksheesh* to the captain. He does not trust anyone.'

'Then you must get me inside the go-down, Yussuf. Before they come.'

'It is not possible.' The man added more sugar to his coffee and stirred frantically, refusing to meet Rabindrah's gaze. 'If they find out, they will kill me!'

'I need to see it for myself,' Rabindrah insisted. 'That is what I have been told by Mr Kiberu.' If his informant was about to back out, maybe the use of the minister's name would be leverage.

Yussuf's eyes widened. Whatever fear he had of his employers, he was obviously just as terrified of Kiberu. Rabindrah wondered what particular threat or promise had resulted in the man's uneasy compliance thus far.

'I must get into the warehouse,' he repeated. 'I will hide in there before the boss comes, wait till everybody has gone, and then leave. No one will know.' He took out his wallet and selected a fat wad of notes. 'I will pay you half now, and the rest as soon as I have the information that Mr Kiberu wants. If what you have told him is true.'

Yussuf gazed at the money, and his fingers twitched on the spoon he was holding. He licked his lips, glanced around to ensure that no one was watching him, and then put out his hand.

'You will pay me the rest tonight. *Inshallah.*'

'Agreed.' Rabindrah slid the notes across the table, and they disappeared within a second.

'Now, you must tell me everything you know about this operation,' Rabindrah said. 'How often do they make these deliveries? Do they come regularly? Who brings the goods?'

'We do not know when the lorry will come, until one or two days before,' Yussuf answered. 'But it is always a ship from Belgium. When that vessel ties up in Kilindini Harbour and takes on its other cargo, then I know the lorry will come. As soon as the ivory and the horns and skins are on board, the ship leaves with the pilot boat at first light.'

'Who comes with the lorry? Is it always the same men?'

'The same driver. And they have Somali guards. With guns. Also, they bring porters from up-country. They do not use the regular men from the docks.'

'And the boss man?'

'He arrives in his own car,' Yussuf said. 'Separate.'

'Who is he? Can you tell me his name?'

The watchman was breathing hard as he shook his head. He either could not or would not reveal the man's identity.

'He never says his name. I never ask. Better not to know. He is an Indian man. Rich. Big car, smart clothes, gold watch. He comes with two bodyguards. Very bad men, those guards.' Yussuf shuddered. 'They also have guns and sharp knives. They would slit your throat in a second. I have seen . . .' His hands began to shake so badly that he was forced to put down his coffee. He raised a hand across his forehead and upper lip, mortally afraid, wiping away an outbreak of sweat. 'I do not know any names. I only open the go-down when the lorry comes, and I lock it again when they are gone.'

'Does the boss come alone?'

'Sometimes there is another man with him. Younger. I do not look at them. They speak in their own language. They do not talk to me. Only give me my money. It is better like this. I do not want to know who they are.' He looked at Rabindrah directly for the first time, and his voice was hoarse with fear. 'You must not let them see you. If they catch you inside, they will kill you. And me too, because they will know I let you in!'

'They won't see me. You have nothing to fear. Can you take me there now?'

'Not now. I will meet you on the pier. There is a small shed behind Warehouse 13. You will be there at nine o'clock, when it is dark and all the other cargo has been loaded. I will come for you when there is no one around.'

They parted company a few minutes later, Yussuf slipping away into the darkening evening. Rabindrah drove towards Kilindini and checked into a run-down hotel near the entrance to the docks.

In the shabby room, he dressed in a soiled, loose-fitting tunic and baggy pants. Taking a tin of shoe polish and a plastic bag of soil from his pocket he smeared some of each onto his face, and wound a Muslim-style turban around his head. Satisfied with his grubby appearance, he sat down and checked the camera he had brought with him, borrowed from Sarah's equipment bag. She would not be happy when she discovered it was missing, but it was small and had a powerful zoom lens and special film that she used to take night pictures of wildlife. It would be ideal for this particular assignment. He slid it into the pocket of his trousers with his notebook and a torch, and slipped out into the street where people were milling about the doors of local bars, and loud music spilled out into the night. The smell of spicy curry made him hungry, and he wished he had had time for a meal. It was going to be a long night. No one looked at him as he started the car and drove away. Following Yussuf's instructions, he left the vehicle further down the quay and worked his way on foot to Warehouse 13, where he settled down in the shadow of a corrugated iron shed.

Time crawled and Rabindrah peered at his watch in the dim light, and tried to ease himself into a more comfortable position amongst the wooden crates on the wharf. Almost ten o'clock and still no sign of Yussuf. The high whine of a mosquito's dive sang in his ear and he slapped at his neck, cursing quietly. He was being eaten alive. Every limb ached from crouching in the narrow space between the stacked containers, but it was the only place where he could retain a good view of the Belgian vessel at the dock, and still remain out of the sight of anyone on deck or on the quay. There had been a fair amount of activity earlier on when the loading lights beamed down on the rusted sides of the ship, and derricks swung back and forth. The clatter of chains and the groaning, sputtering sound of the lifting gear filled the night. African porters hauled great burlap loads into wide-meshed nets, and attached them to the crane hooks, sweating and straining and shouting as the cargo was hoisted from the ground and lowered through the open hatchway, to be stacked in the cavern of the hold.

Now everything was quiet, and the dock seemed deserted. Night shadows had taken possession of the ship and the wharf, scattered pools of light puddled the rough concrete surface of the quayside, gleaming on oily reflections in the harbour water, and on the ink-black hawsers that bound the vessel to the shore. There was a pervading odour of tar and hemp from the ropes that lay coiled like giant snakes beside the gangplank, and a sharp metallic smell of leaded paint and rust. On the foredeck, a solitary figure tossed his cigarette butt in a showery arc to land in the sea below. He stood there for a moment, leaning out over the rails and whistling tunelessly, his gaze fixed on the rows of crates below. For a moment Rabindrah thought he had been seen, or that his own shadow had cast its shape onto the pier. But the sailor moved away across the deck and vanished, leaving only a low buzz of insects as they danced around the lights.

Rabindrah glanced down at his watch once more, apprehensive, wondering whether his contact had deliberately set him up, or given him false information. If the man had decided not to appear and no additional cargo was delivered to the warehouse tonight, his departure from Lamu would have been a total waste, with nothing to show for hours of discomfort. Not to mention the problems he would encounter when he saw Sarah again. A large cockroach ran over his foot and he shuddered and shifted his position again. He was now convinced that the whole operation had been aborted and the wretched watchman had taken the money and made a run for it. Then he felt a hand on his shoulder, and froze. Turning, he saw Yussuf standing behind him. He had heard nothing – the man had moved with great stealth. Rabindrah was about to speak, but the watchman shook his head in warning. He moved away, keeping close to the shed, beckoning Rabindrah to follow.

The go-down was in darkness. Yussuf turned the keys in the massive padlocks, and pulled away the chain. Then he pushed the steel doors apart by a small margin, disappearing through the opening with Rabindrah close behind him. The building resembled a vast cavern, laden to the roof with rows of pallets stacked with wooden packing cases. There was a strong, musty smell of hessian, timber, oil and dust. The towering rows of crates, lined up against the walls of the shed, gave the warehouse a sinister quality in the darkness. As though they were waiting to topple down at any moment on the unwary intruder. Inside the doors a space had been left clear, wide enough to turn a lorry. On the ground, several packing cases stood open, waiting to receive their contraband. They were stamped with export numbers, logos, and the initials of an export firm. A forklift truck stood in the far corner, with nets and hooks laid out to receive the goods for loading onto the ship.

'I was beginning to think you would not come,' Rabindrah said, his voice low as he moved around the space and shone his torch onto the crates and photographed the company names that appeared on the sides of the containers. Several dozen boxes, already sealed, stood on the ground near the door. Presumably bona fide cargo which would surround the illegal merchandise, once it was in the ship's hold.

'There were people here. From the ship. It was not safe earlier.' Yussuf stood watching him, ill at ease. 'You must find a place where you will not be seen. They will come soon.'

Rabindrah scouted around the warehouse, and chose a vantage point in deep shadow where a tall container had been placed between two stacks of crates. From the top of the container he would have a clear view of the door and the area around it, and the lens would be more than adequate for good pictures. Nobody would have reason to look up in this particular direction, unless the sound of the camera alerted them. He would time the shutter action with the noise of loading and unloading. Yussuf returned to the entrance and stared back into the gloom to ensure that Rabindrah was not visible. After a minute he signalled that he was satisfied. Then he went out, pulling the door across behind him, and Rabindrah was left alone. It took a few moments for his eyes to become accustomed to the darkness. He could hear the scurry of rats across the dirt floor, light scratchings and an occasional squeak. A gecko hung upside down above him, supported by the sticky pads on his feet, lunging every now and then at an unwary insect in a series of speedy forays that were followed by the flap and crunch of the victim being disposed of satisfactorily.

Time passed. There was silence outside, and Rabindrah began to feel sleepy. It had been a long day, with the most difficult and dangerous part still to come. His eyes closed for what seemed like a few seconds and then snapped into wakefulness. The chug of a diesel engine grew louder together with the sound of grinding gears from a heavily laden vehicle. It came to a stop outside, and he heard men moving about. Then the clunk of the padlock being released. The sliding doors were pulled back to their full width in a protesting shriek of metal, and the lorry reversed into the shed. Rabindrah shrank into the gloom, flattening himself along the top of the container. He had not considered how vulnerable he might be in the glare of headlights. He felt weak with relief when the angle of the lights hit an area well away from his hiding place although the lorry was relatively near, so that he could see its contents as they were unloaded.

Yussuf pulled a switch at the door, and two arc lights sprang to life, setting the scene into sharp relief. He glanced nervously towards the container before looking quickly away. Rabindrah felt reasonably confident that he could not be seen from below, with the tower of crates on either side of him creating deep shadow. He pressed himself a few feet further into the darkness, camera primed, and waited.

There were eight men below him. Three of them were Somali, tall and hard-faced, dressed in turbans and loose robes and carrying high-powered rifles, fingers on the triggers, alert and unsmiling. The rest were African porters who moved to the rear of the vehicle and waited. Another set of headlights beamed onto the dockside before turning into the warehouse. Four men climbed out of the grey Mercedes, but Rabindrah could not get a good look at them because they had parked on the far side of the lorry which was blocking his view. He cursed his luck, silently. But within minutes they had walked around to a spot where he was looking down onto the tops of their heads and he cursed again. They were wearing Sikh-style turbans. Not only Asians, but of his own community. One man was heavy-set and obviously making the decisions. The boss. The other, taller and leaner, said very little, simply directing the porters and following orders. Two more Somalis stood beside them – presumably the personal bodyguards that Yussuf especially feared. There was a short discussion in Swahili between the boss and the guards and then the Sikhs moved aside, talking in low voices. Rabindrah strained to hear the Urdu conversation, but it was difficult at this distance to catch the words. He leaned forward a little in an effort to make out what they were saying, wishing they would move further into his line of vision so that he could get them on film. The porters worked quickly, efficient and silent as they loosened the ties of the tarpaulin that covered the back of the truck. There was no chatter or whistling or the occasional shouts and snatches of song that he had heard earlier from the regular dockside workers. Finally, the tail gate of the truck was lowered with a clang, and the canvas covers were pushed aside.

Rabindrah drew in his breath when he saw what was inside. Elephant tusks from at least fifty animals were stacked on top of each other, some mature and several feet in length, others quite small so that they must have been hacked off a calf no more than three years old. The wanton destruction of so many magnificent creatures, to satisfy the greed of some foreign collector half way round the world, filled him with disgust. He could see in his mind's eye the great mound of a dead matriarch and her calf, mutilated and left to rot in the bush while the family group touched them gently with their trunks, pushing with their feet in a vain attempt to raise their fallen companions. Often they would try to cover the dead with earth and foliage. Elephants were the only animals, Sarah had told him, who made this homage to their dead. Beneath the ivory were stacks of skins – leopard, lion and zebra, colobus monkey, and a forest of horns from rhino, buffalo and kudu. It was an enormous haul. The porters hoisted the ivories from the truck, and laid them on the ground to be checked before they were placed in the open crates. Rabindrah used the noise of their work to start shooting his pictures.

The two Asians moved forward into the light, still facing away from him as he trained his lens, ready for the moment when one of them would turn around. The younger man was holding a clipboard with a sheaf of papers attached. At last he walked around the elephant tusks that had been laid out on the ground, examining them for size, checking them against his list, and as he did so Rabindrah got a clear view of his features for the first time. The shock almost caused him to drop the camera as he saw Harjeet Singh framed in his viewfinder, his narrow face with its heavy eyelids caught in the telephoto lens as though he was inches away. There was no mistaking Lila's husband. And the older man with him, the boss, was his father. Rabindrah looked at the man Lila had married in order to rescue her family. With rage and loathing he thought of his cousin, sent into exile, forced to leave her family and friends to become a hostage to greed and evil.

Without thinking, he pressed the shutter, three, four times in quick succession, and the whir and click echoed into a sudden lull of silence. Harjeet turned his head to identify the sound, looking directly into the lens. Rabindrah moved back involuntarily, and the torch that had been wedged at his feet dislodged and rolled with a clatter down onto the floor of the shed. There was a shout from one of the guards, as he raised his rifle and fired. The bullet ricocheted off the crate beside Rabindrah's head and he ducked further back, cursing, sweating with fear, trying to work his way deep into the pile of packing cases and out of the line of fire.

Three Somalis moved towards the stack, while down on the floor, one of the guards seized Yussuf and dragged him to where Harjeet's father was standing. Rabindrah could hear his voice, laced with menace, demanding in Swahili that the watchman tell him who had been allowed into the warehouse. Yussuf dropped to the ground, grovelling, frantic, denying any knowledge of an intruder. The bodyguard raised his rifle, the muzzle against the watchman's temple, and the unfortunate man lifted his hands in supplication, weeping and begging for mercy. Rabindrah made up his mind. Stowing the camera inside his clothing he stood up, waving his arms.

'Stop!' he shouted. 'Please sirs, do not be shooting. I am coming down.'

Harjeet glanced at his father, then jerked his head to the Somali to hold his fire as Rabindrah emerged from the shadows and climbed down. The guards had lined up, all pointing their weapons at him and there was a double click of a breech being loaded, making him wonder if he would be struck down before he even reached the ground. In the seconds when he had understood that the watchman was about to be executed, Rabindrah had not been able to think of any other plan, except to distract the two men and buy a little time. The loose clothes and his dirty, sweating face and ragged turban made him look like a labourer. He had only met Harjeet once, briefly, when they were surrounded by a crowd of relations, and he did not think he would be remembered. There was no reason why the man should associate him with his journalist cousin.

'Who are you? How did you get in here?' Harjeet was the first to speak. His father was examining Rabindrah as he descended from the container.

'Amin Dhala, sirs. I am waiting for your illustrious persons, so that I can ask you for a job.' He glanced from Harjeet to his father, and flashed an ingratiating smile. 'I am hard-working man, sirs. I can do many things –'

'How did you know we would be here? Did he tell you?' Harjeet aimed a kick at Yussuf who lay paralysed with fear, his forehead pressed to the ground.

'I am not knowing him, sir. And likewise this man is not knowing me. I am hearing about your very fine enterprise from a man on the ship. So I wait. This man on the ship, he is knowing you will come tonight. So when porter who works in the day goes outside for smoking, I am coming inside and hiding.' He wagged his finger at the prone figure of the watchman. 'I am not needing him to help me.'

As soon as his feet touched the floor, a guard grabbed Rabindrah and dragged him towards the two Sikhs, jabbering incoherently, trying to gain seconds as he measured the distance to the door of the go-down. It would be madness to try to make a run for it but he could not fathom any other way to escape. Then his eyes caught a glint of metal that caused his heart to leap into his throat. The keys were still in the ignition of the Mercedes, and the driver's door was open. The guard nearest to him was watching his employer, his mouth slightly open as he followed the unexpected turn of events. Rabindrah lunged at him, taking him off balance and grabbing his rifle. His fingers closed on the trigger and he fired in all directions as he leapt for the door of the car. Slamming into the driver's seat he gunned the engine, and drove straight at another Somali who threw himself out of the way. Shouting at Yussuf to get in, he slewed the car in a rally turn, catching a third Somali with the back bumper. The man fell with a thud, but one of the other bandits was up and firing through the windscreen. Rabindrah ducked an explosion of flying glass and felt a stabbing sensation in his shoulder. The tyres began to hiss as more bullets punctured the rubber and thudded into the bonnet, hitting the radiator. Yussuf was trying to rise, eyes wide with terror, but he was too slow.

'Kill them! Kill them both!' It was Manjit Singh who shouted the order.

The Somali nearest to the watchman swung his arm, and his panga whistled downwards, almost severing the watchman's head from his body. Everything seemed to go into slow motion for Rabindrah. Yussuf, his hands clutching his neck, toppled sideways, a scarlet fountain gushing from the wound. It hit Harjeet, spewing over his face and shoulders. He swerved instinctively and fell against his father causing the older man to crash against the car. Rabindrah accelerated and more shots rang out as a police jeep full of armed *askaris* careened through the entrance of the warehouse. For several minutes a gun battle waged across the floor of the shed, and Rabindrah crouched down behind the steering wheel of the car until all the remaining Somalis had been silenced and their bodies lay on the ground, arms flung sideways, weapons scattered across the warehouse. Two *askaris* lay dead or wounded beside them.

In the eerie stillness that followed Rabindrah saw, through the haze and stench of cordite that thickened the air, the still form of the watchman, his head at a grotesque angle to his crumpled body, blood still pooling over the cement floor around him. Dimly, and with the crackle of rifle fire echoing in his ears, Rabindrah watched Harjeet trying to crawl away, sobbing and wiping himself ineffectually with a handkerchief, in an attempt to clean the murdered watchman's blood from his face. His father lay on his side, groaning, his leg twisted in an unnatural pose. Rabindrah staggered from the Mercedes, dimly aware of the growing pain in his shoulder and the blood seeping down his sleeve. Ignoring it, he grabbed Lila's husband by the lapels of his jacket, hauling him to his feet. Revulsion and rage at the barbarity of the execution filled him as he shook Harjeet, shouting out in frustration.

'You filthy shit! You bloody little prick! You are a fucking disgrace to your family and your whole community. And I'll see to it that you are put away for years!'

'Who are you? The police?' Harjeet was staring at him, fearful and uncomprehending.

'I'm your wife's cousin. I'm investigating this stinking trade, and look at what has come crawling out from under the stones. I hope you rot in jail for a long time. A bloody century wouldn't be enough!' He pushed Harjeet away from him in disgust.

'You are the reporter. Rabindrah.' Harjeet smiled suddenly, his eyes glowing with malice. 'You think we will go down on your evidence? That you will be a hero?' He took a step forward, his face within inches of Rabindrah's. 'Well, consider this, you fucking stool pigeon, you licker of black backsides. If you are so fond of your little cousin, you had better ask yourself what her involvement in this business might be!'

'Lila would never be part of any criminal activity.' Rabindrah was conscious of a police inspector stepping across the bodies, bending to inspect an injured colleague before taking out his notebook and moving on.

'Don't fool yourself, man.' Harjeet's face had been transformed into a triumphant sneer. 'Lila has been very useful to us and her father has been only too glad to share in the profits of our business. His scruples have never prevented him holding ivory for us. Very convenient to have family up-country, with plenty of storage away from the prying eyes of the law. If you submit evidence against my father and me, Lila's family will suffer the same fate as us. And that poor old fool, Gulab, will not thank you.'

The police inspector and two *askaris* had drawn closer, and Harjeet was taken into custody.

'Mr Rabindrah Singh?' The inspector held out his hand in greeting. 'We have a car outside that will take you straight to the hospital. I see you have been shot.'

'Shot?' Rabindrah glanced at his arm, but his gaze returned involuntarily to Yussuf's corpse. 'The watchman,' he said. 'I am sure Minister Kiberu will want to know what happened to him.' The horror of what he had witnessed threatened to overcome him, and he had to sit down on one of the crates, waiting for the nausea and dizziness to pass.

'Sir? We will take you to the hospital now.'

'I must fly back to Nairobi first thing in the morning.' Rabindrah had not taken in the inspector's words. 'To deliver my report direct to Minister Kiberu. I need a telephone to talk to him now.'

'Yes, sir.' The policeman's expression was unreadable. 'I will contact him myself in a few minutes. But first you must go to the hospital.'

Rabindrah had begun to feel as though he was slowly leaving his body, drifting away from the bloody scene that surrounded him. Until Harjeet

Singh, handcuffed and following his father's stretcher, passed him. The sneering smile was still faintly visible.

'Remember,' he said.

At the hospital Rabindrah was swabbed, stitched, bathed and placed in a private room with a policeman outside the door. But his mind was in turmoil as he tried to work out a way to protect Lila and her family. Of course Harjeet could have been lying, in order to extricate himself and his father from a lengthy prison sentence. Except that the basic premise of the story rang true. He struggled to take Sarah's camera out of the pile of clothing that had been put away in a cupboard. His breathing was ragged and the pain in his shoulder made him groan out loud, as he stumbled back to his bed and slid it under the thin mattress cover where he would be aware of its knobbly shape pressing into his spine. His action made him feel faintly ridiculous, as though he was still trapped in the realm of a bad thriller. But he feared that somehow the photographic evidence might disappear if he could not physically guard it himself, feel it beneath his body. He was sweating and nauseous when he rang the bell.

'I need to make a phone call,' he said to the nurse as her image swam before him. 'I have to talk to my wife. And I think I'm going to be ill.'

'My goodness, you are as pale as ashes, Mr Singh.' The girl opened a small cabinet and took out a bowl in time for Rabindrah to vomit into it. 'You must rest now. You are suffering from shock and the pain of the bullet wound. The doctor left instructions to give you a sedative, so I'm going to give you an injection now. We will contact your wife first thing in the morning. It is very late, you know.'

'No. I have to tell her. I need to . . .'

He did not remember anything else until the hot, yellow light of morning prised his eyes open and he awoke to throbbing pain. He pushed himself into a sitting position, grunting with the effort, and rang for the nurse. This time she helped him to put through a call to Lamu. He tried to remain calm and logical as he heard Sarah's voice on the line.

'Where on earth are you? I've been worried sick, racking my brains to think where you could have gone, or why you left the wedding like that. Anthony thought you might be in Mombasa covering a story, so I phoned Gordon but he didn't know anything about it. What is this all about?

What the hell is happening, Rabindrah?'

She listened to his explanations in silence, but he left out any description of Yussuf's barbaric end, his own injury and Harjeet's threats and he knew his story sounded incomplete and unconvincing. Finally, he told her that he had been shot.

'It's only a graze,' he said. 'A superficial wound.'

'A superficial bullet wound? What do you mean, superficial? Oh God! You could be dead, Rabindrah! Are you all right? Are you telling me everything?'

'I've been stitched up and I'm fine.'

'But why were you there? Why did it have to be you? I mean, Johnson Kiberu must have known there was a family link with Harjeet. Look, I'll join you in Mombasa. When are you getting out of the hospital? How badly hurt are you, really?'

Her questions, fuelled by anxiety for his safety, tore down the line and cut through his feeble attempts to pacify her, building further resentment between them as he tried to play down the seriousness of what had happened. But she knew him too well. Knew he was holding back. In his own mind he began to wonder whether Kiberu had set him up. And whether Anthony, too, had been aware that Lila's husband was involved. Had they excluded him from their knowledge, so that he would not be tempted to tamper with any of the facts? 'You know, we cannot rely on these wily Indians or tell where their loyalties lie.' He could almost hear Kiberu saying the words. So much for trust and integrity.

'We could travel back to Nairobi together, and take Lila with us,' Sarah said. 'I'm sure she doesn't know what has happened. She's not even up yet.'

'No, don't come here. Or to Nairobi. You were going to Langani with Hannah and Lottie and I think you should still do that. I'm about to be discharged, but I have to spend the next couple of days turning in a report for Kiberu. And the paper. Is Anthony there?'

'He left early this morning with Camilla. They've gone north to spend their honeymoon in Shaba, where his *watu* have set up a camp.'

'You have to get Lila out of the country. As soon as possible. What about Tom Bartlett? When is he leaving for London?'

'Tonight. He is sharing a charter to Nairobi with Allie and Hugo this afternoon, and picking up the London flight tonight,' Sarah said. 'But Lila will want to say goodbye to her family. They are going to be shocked when they learn about this. Oh God! I'm just beginning to realise what a terrible position she is in.' She thought again. 'Surely it would be better if she stayed here with her parents?'

'No, Sarah. She must not go near the house. It's vital that she leaves before she is rounded up as a witness, or even an accomplice. You've got to persuade her to fly out tonight. I'll speak to Gulab and Anjit. They will understand why it is safer for her to go. You must break the news to Lila now, as soon as you hang up, and try to get her a place on that charter. I'll catch up with you at Langani.'

'When?'

'I don't know,' he said, concealing a plan that was forming in his mind, knowing he must not be tempted to explain it. 'As soon as I can.'

'Don't you have any idea when that will be? And don't you need to see a doctor in Nairobi before you go to work?'

'No. I'm in good shape, and this is going to make major copy.' He knew he was digging himself a deeper pit.

'Wonderful.' Her voice was cold and he felt the hurt of her exclusion. 'I see now what your priorities are. I'll find Lila and do the best I can for her. Goodbye, then.'

'Sarah—'

'I can see that I'm of no importance at this moment. I'll wait to hear from you later. Goodbye.'

Rabindrah leaned back against his pillows, waiting for the nurse to respond to the bell. He was weary and sick at heart, and the grazes on his cheek from the shattered windscreen of Manjit's car throbbed angrily. Bolts of pain shot down his arm and across his chest each time he moved. He wished that Sarah was there, that she could let him rest his head on her breast and fall asleep in her arms. But she was angry and upset and far away, unaware that he had almost been executed. That an innocent man had had his head hacked off because he, Rabindrah, had made a thoughtless mistake. He wanted to lift the telephone again and tell her all this, but he could not. Because he was afraid he would break down and then he would not be able to set out for Nairobi, to find Gulab and see what could be done to protect him. And because time was running out for Lila.

When the nurse pushed the door open, he had managed to struggle into

248

his filthy clothes from the night before. Against her objections he insisted on discharging himself. A taxi took him back to the hotel and waited while he changed into his own shirt and trousers. Then he drove to the airport.

Chapter 15

Kenya, September 1977

Immediately after take-off, Rabindrah swallowed two codeine tablets and tried to find a comfortable position. Eventually he drifted into an uneasy sleep, punctuated by flashes of horror. The scene in the go-down replayed itself endlessly, with Yussuf's life blood pumping out in a red, viscous fountain from the stump of his neck as he toppled to the ground. Rabindrah saw himself at the wheel of the car, with the face of the Somali executioner leering in through the windscreen. He tried to shout out, but his vocal chords felt as if they had been shredded, leaving him defenceless and impotent in the face of danger. At last, the drone of the plane's engine seeped through the nightmare, and he woke to find the aircraft making its descent into Kenyatta Airport.

'Take me to Wilson aerodrome,' he said to the first driver in the taxi line.

As they hurtled through the late morning traffic he wondered whether Gulab had heard about the arrests. He had not wanted to explain by telephone the dreadful events he had witnessed, and his own role in them. His stomach heaved at the realisation that his family was embroiled in such a detestable business, and that he had been trapped into bringing them to justice. At Wilson he picked up his own car, wincing each time he changed gear or turned the wheel. When he reached Gulab's residence he knocked on the front door, and a houseboy opened it.

'Is Bwana Gulab here? Let him know I'm here – it's urgent.'

But Gulab had heard voices and appeared in the hallway, taking in his nephew's shadowed, unshaven face, the sling holding his left arm in place, and the grim expression.

'Rabindrah! My God, you are looking terrible. What is the matter? Have you had an accident? I thought you were in Lamu at the wedding. With Lila. Let me call Anjit and we will have some tea.'

'Don't call anyone.'

Rabindrah's tone struck a chord of alarm in his uncle. He led the way to his study and closed the door behind them.

'This must be something important, to justify such an unexpected visit.' Gulab's laugh was nervous.

Rabindrah felt his control snap. He was bone tired and his injury was burning deep in his shoulder and across his chest. It was possible that the police could be on their way here to start enquiries, or even to make an arrest. He strode forward and, using his good arm, pushed Gulab down onto a chair.

'Tell me you are not involved in handling ivory and other illegal goods for Manjit Singh. Tell me!'

Gulab's face turned ashen and he gripped the arms of the chair and tried to stand up, turning away from his nephew. Refusing to meet his eye. It was all the admission Rabindrah needed, and he forced his uncle back into the chair with a ferocity that shocked them both. There was a sound behind them and both men turned to see Anjit in the doorway.

'Rabindrah? What are you doing here? Gulab, you look as though you have seen a ghost. Is something wrong? Is Lila . . . ?'

'She is all right.' Gulab's head was bowed, his words feeble.

'So what has happened?' Anjit turned to face Rabindrah. 'Why have you come here?'

'It's a matter that I have to sort out with Gulab.'

'No. There is something else.' She sat down. 'You had better tell me what it is.'

'He is asking about Manjit and Harjeet. About their business.' Gulab's words were barely audible. 'He knows what they are doing.'

'Oh God! I knew you should never have agreed to work for them, husband. I told you—'

'Stop! Leave the room now. Please. Go and take care of your household, and we will talk later. Leave, Anjit.'

'Does this affect Lila? Has something happened that would put her in a bad position?' She looked at them wildly. 'Tell me, for God's sake! I am her mother!'

'We will discuss this later,' Gulab said, taking her arm and ushering her to the door. 'Do not worry about Lila. She will not come to any harm.'

Anjit flung a look of apprehension at Rabindrah, hesitated for a moment and then left them alone in a highly charged silence that had a loudness of its own.

'So she knows about this.' Rabindrah had a moment of despair.

'No, no. She is not involved in any way,' Gulab said defensively.

'How could you allow yourself to get embroiled in this vile business, Uncle?' Rabindrah's contempt was obvious. 'Did you not understand that you would be putting your whole family in the most dangerous position? Are you really so greedy and so stupid that no one else matters – not your wife or your sons, or the daughter you sold off for your own security?'

'How did you discover all this?' Gulab clutched the side of the desk in panic.

'I was asked to investigate a poaching ring. For a government minister, and for the paper. There is a big crackdown on illegal trafficking since the hunting ban, and the Wildlife Ministry has been watching the go-down in Mombasa. You know the place, Gulab. I was there last night, on a tip-off. And so were your bloody in-laws – Manjit Singh and Harjeet, with their gun-toting Somali goons and a load of ivory and other illegal trophies.'

'But you are not going to write about them in the paper, are you? Think what it could do to us all!'

'It's a little late to be worrying about that,' Rabindrah said, sickened by his uncle's whining tone. 'The police raided the Mombasa warehouse last night.'

'Manjit Singh is a clever man.' Gulab was following another train of thought, trying to remain hopeful. 'He will find a way out. They will not be able to prove he has done anything wrong.'

'They are in jail, Gulab. They will both be there for a very long time.'

'In jail? Did you do this? Turn them in? Were you responsible? My God, they are your own community, your own family Rabindrah!'

'Have you any idea what kind of people they are, Uncle? Last night they tried to shoot me. They executed their night watchman. Cut off his head with a panga, right in front of me. On Manjit's orders.' Rabindrah shuddered, nauseated by the memory. 'I would be dead if the police hadn't been on the spot, waiting to raid the place and arrest them.'

Gulab buried his head in his hands. 'Can you help them?' he whispered.

'Why would I want to?' Rabindrah's words emerged in a snarl.

'They are family now. Harjeet is––'

'Not family I wish to acknowledge. They deserve to rot in prison, and

I would personally throw away the key. Harjeet threatened me last night, before the police took him away. He told me that you and your family were involved in the business. Up to your necks. He said that if he went down, he would bring you all with him. You, Anjit and your children. Even Lila, his own wife. That's the kind of *shenzi* bastard to whom you sold off your daughter. So you had better tell me the whole truth. How long have you been doing this? How deeply are you involved?'

'I hold goods for them. Nothing more. Ivory, skins, rhino horn –' Gulab stared down at the desk.

'Where?'

'At my sawmill near Nanyuki. When the ship comes I send my lorries to Mombasa with the goods.' He heard Rabindrah's hiss of rage, and his voice broke. 'That is all I am doing. I had no part in the poaching, the killing. I have not hurt anyone. I am swearing to you. Only I stored for them. I had to! It was a part of the deal.'

'How could you make such a deal?' Rabindrah leaned over his uncle, cradling his arm to ease the searing pain of movement.

'You do not understand how bad things were!' Gulab was sweating profusely, wringing his hands in anxiety. 'We always lived well. I admit that. I like luxury. I like to spoil my children, give to my wife every comfort. Good saris and jewels so she has her place in the community. I have worked hard all my life, to earn the money I made. But since Independence, I have had to pay bribes, larger every month. To African partners who did nothing, but always wanted a bigger share of the takings. To government officials to keep my trading licence. I was going bankrupt. My sawmill, my hardware store, everything I have spent my life building – it was all going to be lost. My God, man! We had no money left, and nowhere to go if the business folded. Nowhere !'

'Could you not have got help from the family? From Indar? Or is he also part of this trafficking scheme?' Rabindrah held his breath, afraid of the answer.

'No. He is not so badly affected in his business. Half the government vehicles are maintained by him. They need his skills, the spare parts for their engines. But I was afraid, Rabindrah. And ashamed. How would I provide for my family? Where could we go, with nothing to live on? There was no money to marry my daughter, or find good wives for my sons. These politicians are taking away our livelihood and we cannot go to England with Kenya passports. So what is left? India? I have been there one time only and I could not wait to get out! We do not belong there, in those crowded, filthy cities.'

Rabindrah spun away to look out the window into the well-tended garden, shocked by Gulab's desperation and cowardice, appalled that he himself had not seen how the policy of Africanisation was destroying his own family.

'Then Manjit Singh came here on one of his business trips.' Gulab stopped to mop the perspiration from his face. 'He found out what a bad situation I was in. So he offered to put me on the board of a company he owned. With three African shareholders – two of them are politicians, he was telling me. The company would pay the bribes, and Manjit said he would give me a large sum of cash every month, in return for a storage place at the sawmill. No questions asked. Whenever he gave the order, one of my lorries would be sent to Mombasa with his goods from my store. All he wanted was for me to be there when goods were coming and going, and to keep the place securely locked at all times, with an *askari* outside. He would organise everything else.'

'But you knew what type of goods they were.' Rabindrah looked down at the figure of his uncle slumped over the desk, all trace of his bluff cheerfulness gone. 'You must have known that they were smuggling. Paying poachers.'

'Yes. I knew it.' The man was broken. 'At first I was refusing. It was too dangerous, I told him. I did not want to be mixed up in any illegal business. I had enough problems. But then he said Harjeet would take Lila as a wife. She would have a fine home in the UK, and after they were married, he would arrange passports and entry visas for my family.' Gulab looked up at his nephew in despair. 'What was I to do, Rabindrah? I was on the verge of bankruptcy. I had no dowry to offer my daughter and she was getting older. Already a less attractive proposition, you know.'

'A commodity. A piece of meat to be traded, like an old *ngombe*. That is how you thought of your daughter.' Rabindrah moved away to prevent himself from striking his uncle.

'No, I was thinking that this would be a good marriage for Lila,' Gulab said. 'Security for Anjit and the family. A way out of here. I could not pass up such an offer.'

'Did your sons know what was going on? Or Anjit?' Rabindrah

dreaded the answer. 'If they were also involved, it will be impossible to extricate them.'

'Only Anjit.' Gulab raised his head. 'She disagreed with me, but I forbade her to speak about the subject. Even to me. My sons and Lila – they knew nothing. Nothing at all. Manjit said if I told anyone there would be no deal.' He was unable to prevent himself from weeping.

'Tell me the rest,' Rabindrah said brutally. 'There's no use snivelling now.'

'I took Manjit to the sawmill at Nanyuki and he chose one of the buildings outside the main compound. A storage shed where we used to have a manager sleeping . I had the doors reinforced, put special locks on and a weighing platform. I told Arjan, my son who runs the sawmill, that it would be for my personal use from now on, and he never asked any questions. After all, he only runs the place for me.' His effort at a smile turned into a grimace. 'I think he suspected I was taking an African *bibi* there sometimes, because he laughed and said if I wanted to go there when no one was working it was no business of his. I let him go on believing that.'

It was a small relief, Rabindrah thought. Unless Manjit Singh or his son had already been questioned and had implicated Gulab in their criminal dealings. But Rabindrah did not think so, otherwise the police would have come calling earlier in the morning, and his uncle would be under arrest.

'There is ivory there now. And skins.' Gulab delivered the next blow. 'Coming only yesterday, too late to be on the boat this time.'

'Bloody hell, Uncle! Is there no end to this?'

'I am begging you to help me, Rabindrah. For the family. Please! Is there something you can do? Could you not speak to this politician who has sent you to investigate?' Gulab's voice was a piteous quaver. 'Does Lila know about all this? What will happen to her now?'

'Lila is leaving for England tonight.'

'Back to Harjeet's family? No, no! They will not be taking her now. She must come home to her mother.'

'She can't stay in Kenya. It is too dangerous for her. The police might accuse her of being an accessory and arrest her.'

'But we must see her before she leaves, her mother and I.'

'Out of the question. She will be flying from Lamu straight into Kenyatta Airport, and leaving with a friend of Camilla's. He will organise somewhere for her to stay when she gets to London.'

'You must talk to this minister, about Harjeet and his father. See what can be done.'

'Definitely not. Johnson Kiberu cannot be bribed and he is determined to follow up this case.' Rabindrah was repelled by his uncle's endless wheedling. 'He has plenty of evidence, including the cargo seized by the police last night. It's everything he needed. And he is right.'

'Then I am finished. We are all finished.' Gulab hunched over in his chair, sobbing openly.

'Not if you are the only one who knows how this business was set up. Get up, man. You will have to come with me right now, if you want to try and salvage something of your family.' Rabindrah saw hesitation. 'Do not waste time, Gulab. Tell Anjit you are going to the office – you mustn't be found here if the police come to call. We have to move fast. Go!'

When his uncle had left the room, Rabindrah lifted the phone, and called the operator.

'I need to make a radio call to Anthony Chapman's radio frequency – to his camp at Shaba.'

'Rabindrah!' Anthony's voice was cheerful. 'It's wonderful up here. We saw a magnificent leopard on the way from the airstrip this morning. My wife and I.' He laughed. 'You never told me it would be this good. I hope you're going to tell me why you did a runner from the wedding, old chap. That was a bit strange.'

Rabindrah felt animosity rising to the surface. This man, who was supposed to be his friend, had possibly betrayed him. And there he was, lying back in his luxurious tented camp with his new wife, without a thought for what might have caused such a sudden disappearance.

'You set me up, Anthony,' he said angrily. 'You and your powerful chum. You knew who was going to be in that warehouse, and you let me walk into the trap. What did you think I would do, if you had warned me? Help them to escape? Was that it?'

'What warehouse? Who would escape? What the hell is all this, Rabindrah?' Anthony sounded puzzled. Then disbelieving. His tone was cool when he continued. 'I assume you are talking about the poaching investigation, but as you well know I have no knowledge of any progress being made. None at all. That is between you and Johnson.'

'I don't want to talk about this on an open radio channel,' Rabindrah said. 'Could you leave the camp and phone me at home?'

'It's miles from here to any telephone, with no guarantee that it will be working,' Anthony said. 'And it seems to have slipped your mind that this is the first day of my honeymoon. Where are you? Is it really that urgent?'

'I'm in Nairobi. Kiberu organised a sting last night. It's vital that I explain it to you, but not on the radio.'

'This had better be good,' Anthony said. 'I'll phone you in a couple of hours.'

'Your report and the photographs will clinch the case,' Johnson Kiberu said on the telephone. 'We thought we had watertight evidence before, but so far these people have wriggled out of every attempt to indict them. Like Mafia gangsters in America or Sicily. Hah, hah! I will order the Inspector in Mombasa to let them stew in the prison and the hospital for a few days, with no way to communicate with each other or anyone else. It is to our advantage to keep them apart.'

'I'll be in your office later this afternoon,' Rabindrah said. 'I assume I can also give the story to Gordon?'

'Yes, yes. It will be ideal to have the details in tomorrow's paper. You have done a fine job, my friend. It shows that we can all work together, when it comes to something important. This is the true spirit of *Harambee*! I will see you later.'

There was a click on the line and then silence. Rabindrah sat back. His first problem was to find a safe place for Gulab. He made one more call to his own house, and told Chege that he should go out and shop for the coming week.

'I am coming back tonight,' Rabindrah said. 'And Mama Sarah will be home in a day or two. So you had better get everything you need for the kitchen and the store. Go to the *duka*, please, Chege, and stock up on the usual list, on my account. Don't forget to leave the chit on my desk. You can take the evening off because I will not be home until late so I won't need dinner. *Asante*.' He opened the study door and called for Anjit who came at once, her plump face creased with concern.

'What is it? Where is Gulab?'

'Gulab and I are going out for a while,' Rabindrah said to the frightened woman. 'I will leave my car in your garage and drive with him. If anyone comes here, you do not know where he has gone.'

'But where are you taking him?'

'To a business meeting. That's all you need to know.'

Anjit was weeping on the doorstep as they drove away, heading straight for the house at Langata.

There was no one there except for the dog who growled at Gulab and attached herself to Rabindrah like a limpet. The house felt cold and empty, and for a moment he was tempted to telephone Sarah. But he knew that she would question him about his uncle and aunt, their reaction to Harjeet's arrest, and the fact that they would not be able to see Lila before she left the country. In addition, she would surely sense that something else was afoot, and ask him again about joining her at Langani. Rabindrah sighed and headed straight into Sarah's darkroom to develop the photographs from the previous evening, making copies for Johnson Kiberu and a proof sheet that Gordon could use for selection purposes. Then he placed the roll of film in its black plastic container, buried it in a small tin of tea leaves and put it in his briefcase. It took him a further hour to type up his report for the minister and to write a second version for the paper. Half way through his final draft, the telephone rang.

'What on earth is going on down there?' Anthony sounded terse.

'Kiberu sent me to a go-down in Mombasa last night, to wait for a lorryload of ivory and skins to be exported. The bosses were Asians, as suspected. But they turned out to be Lila's husband and her father-in-law, as you may have known from the start.'

'Christ, Rabindrah, I had no clue as to who they were.' There was outrage in Anthony's tone. 'How could you think that?

'Well, your friend Kiberu must have known there was a connection. I was shot in the shoulder, by the way, while one less fortunate poor bastard got his head sliced off. By the time it was over there must have been half a dozen dead bodies lying around, and Lila's husband and father-in-law were both arrested.'

'Jesus, I can hardly grasp this. How bad is the injury? Have you seen a doctor?' Anthony was aghast.

'I'm operational and your chum Kiberu has had all his dreams come true. Poachers, smugglers, crooked politicians, a money trail and an Indian journalist grassing on his own family. Very neat. But there is more.' Rabindrah broke into Anthony's attempted response. 'I need help urgently. I want you to drive south for the night and give me a hand. You got me into this mess and you owe me one now.'

'As I understand it, two crooks and some bandits are dead or under arrest, and they will no doubt grass on the local politicians on the make. It looks like you did a brilliant job. Where do I fit into all this?'

'Look, I'll be delighted if Manjit Singh and his son spend an eternity in prison. But I've discovered that Lila's father is also involved. He could be arrested any moment, as an accessory. Worse, he has more tusks, and I don't know what else, hidden at his sawmill near Nanyuki.'

'What?' Anthony groaned in disbelief. 'God, what a bloody mess. What will happen to poor Lila now?'

'Sarah is trying to arrange for her to fly to London tonight. With Tom.'

'And where does that leave you?'

'Family and friends in my own community will say I betrayed them. I expected that, and I can live with it, but I don't want to see Gulab go to prison. He was duped into his involvement through stupidity and desperation, and if his sawmill is searched that will be the end of him.'

'No doubt about that,' Anthony said, with no hint of sympathy.

'They won't stop there, though. The government will use him as an excuse to search and seize property from his relatives, including Indar who knows nothing about this. They will find ways to rescind all their trading licences. Some of the family could be deported, or conditions will become impossible and they will be unable to stay and make a living.'

'You're talking about a fait accompli, Rabindrah. I don't see what you can do for Gulab at this stage. Except to hope that his daughter gets out of the country.'

'I want you to meet me in Nanyuki this evening. We have to help him get rid of everything stored at the sawmill, and I don't know how or where we can dispose of it. I've no idea whether I could bury the stuff somewhere out in the *bundu*, and if so where. But it has to go. Tonight.'

'How can you be sure the police aren't up there already?'

'I can't. But I think Manjit and his son will not give anything away yet. Because they are hoping I will suppress some of the evidence for Lila's sake. Lie about what I saw, about their involvement. Maybe say they were hostages of the Somali goons that were their bodyguards. I don't know. But there is a chance for Gulab.'

'It sounds like a long shot.' Anthony was sceptical. 'And you are sticking your neck way, way out. Taking a huge risk for your uncle, who should have known better.'

'I'm taking a risk for Lila. Are you with me, Anthony? Can I count on you, man?'

Rabindrah lit a cigarette and waited for a response, glancing up as Gulab came into the study.

'It seems to me that you are on some kind of self-destruct mission – in terms of your personal safety and your career,' Anthony said. 'It's mad and dangerous, what you are proposing. I'll meet you in Nanyuki. In the car park of the Sportsman's Arms, around seven.'

'We are leaving now,' Rabindrah said to his uncle who had stopped pacing the room and was helping himself to a large whisky. 'But I don't want you to be seen in town with me, so I'm going to drop you off at the museum. You can stroll around while I go to see Kiberu and Gordon Hedley.'

'The museum? Why would I go to the museum?'

'Because no one would ever think of looking for you there. It's a public place and you will not be noticed if you walk about like any other visitor. I will be back for you as soon as I can.'

He went first to the newspaper offices. Gordon Hedley ordered coffee, and closed the door immediately.

'You're bloody lucky to be alive,' he said after listening to Rabindrah's account of the previous night's events. 'What a haul. What a story! Are we authorised to run it?'

'Absolutely. Tomorrow's paper.' Rabindrah opened his attaché case and handed over his article with the proof sheet and the brightly painted tin. 'Film is in here. I suggest you keep it well concealed. And you had better use the dark room with someone you can trust entirely. This is dynamite.'

'I'll guard it with my life. Where are you going now? What about a drink later on, to celebrate? Maybe Sarah could join us. She must be very proud of you.'

'She's going to Langani today. I'm going to lie low this evening, and let this shoulder settle down. It's giving me gyp. But thanks, anyway.'

Unusually, he was not kept waiting when he arrived at the Ministry of Wildlife. Johnson Kiberu was seated at his desk, looking sleek and satisfied.

'A very successful operation,' he said, rising to shake hands with Rabindrah, waving him to a seat in front of his large desk as he rifled through the sheaf of photographs. 'This is better than anything I had hoped for. You have been extremely courageous. I heard you were injured.'

'It's nothing major. But Yussuf was not so fortunate.'

'Yussuf?' Kiberu looked blank.

'Your informant. The night watchman. He was decapitated by one of the poachers. I had promised him money, but I don't know how it can reach his family, unless . . . .' Rabindrah left the sentence hanging.

'Ah, yes.' Johnson Kiberu gave a great sigh. 'Most unfortunate, poor fellow. These Somalis are dangerous men. I will see to it that the family is compensated.' He looked at Rabindrah, and back at the photographs. 'I have spoken to the chief inspector in Mombasa. They will not question either of the men until tomorrow, or even the day after. The younger one is in solitary confinement. He has asked to see his father, but he has been given to understand that Manjit Singh is in a hospital cell and is not permitted any visitors. He must be wondering whether he will have to take the whole rap himself. Does Hedley have everything he needs?'

'Yes. He will run the story in the morning.'

'I will make an official statement on television tomorrow afternoon,' Johnson said. 'Do you have the negatives of these photographs in some safe place?'

'Yes, I do.'

'Very good.' Johnson smiled expansively. 'There will be an arraignment, of course, and a court case at which you will be the chief witness.'

There was a short silence as Rabindrah weighed his words before bringing up his relationship to Harjeet and Manjit Singh.

'I know the two prisoners, slightly,' he said. 'There is a marriage connection.'

'You mean that you are related?'

'Not directly.' Rabindrah could not gauge whether the minister's surprise was genuine. 'Harjeet Singh, the younger man, is married to one of my cousins. I have only met him once, during the marriage formalities. His family lives in England, so I never came across them before or since. Until last night.'

'That must have been something of a shock.' Johnson Kiberu closed the file, his expression giving nothing away.

'Harjeet Singh's wife knew nothing about his criminal side,' Rabindrah said. 'I'm more than happy to see both father and son put away for a very long time. But I certainly would not like my cousin to suffer.'

'I cannot see why she should be implicated, if she is in the UK,' Johnson said.

'Lila is on holiday here in Kenya. A guest at Anthony and Camilla's wedding, actually.' Rabindrah paused before deciding to take the risk. 'She is leaving tonight for London.'

'Ah. Then we must make sure that she departs without incident.' There was no trace of hesitation on Kiberu's part. 'By the way, the Mzee is very happy about this. He has said he would like to meet you himself, once these people have been locked away. But of course, it will depend on his health. He does not have many audiences now. I will let you know about the date.'

'The President?' Rabindrah was astonished.

'He is pleased to know that we are all working together, to eradicate this terrible trade. You have made a substantial contribution to the fight. All that remains is for the police to obtain a signed statement from you, to be used with the photographic evidence. The Inspector in Mombasa was expecting to take care of this, but you had left the hospital when he arrived with the papers. So we should arrange it for this evening, either here or at your house. Then all formalities will be in order, and the courts can set a date for the trial.' Kiberu lifted the telephone.

'I really would like to see Sarah this evening,' Rabindrah said. 'I left Lamu yesterday without any explanation, and she knows that I was injured last night. So I have some explaining to do.' He smiled and shrugged. 'Wives are more difficult than police when it comes to explanations, and I am already in hot water.'

'Tomorrow, then.' Kiberu chuckled at the vagaries of women on which he considered himself an expert. 'I can understand that Sarah would like you to herself tonight.' He stood up and held out his hand. 'I will ask Chief Inspector Ochieng to telephone you first thing in the morning. And we will meet again soon.'

There was little conversation during the drive to Nanyuki. The route was congested, with a stream of buses and lorries belching exhaust fumes, laden far beyond capacity with sacks and crates and a variety of human cargo squeezed into every available inch. The sides of the tarmac had crumbled and the road fell away into the ditch in many places, so that Rabindrah found it impossible to avoid the frequent craters whose sharp edges reduced tyres to shreds in no time. The flicker of charcoal fires and the smell of grilling meat made him realise that he had not eaten anything all day. His shoulder had begun to telegraph messages of searing pain, and every movement of his hands and arms on the steering wheel made the sensation more acute.

'I need to stop for a few minutes,' he said to Gulab. 'I'm going to buy beer and *nyama choma*.

He pulled off the road and stopped at a brightly painted stall to order grilled meat and corn cobs. The beer was cold and Rabindrah washed down two painkillers, glancing at his watch to calculate how long it would be before they took effect. Gulab leaned on the car, morose and weary. After a few minutes he took his food and threw it into a discarded oil drum that served as a rubbish bin. There were several Kikuyu men around the grill, drunk on millet beer and Tuskers, laughing loudly and jostling each other, making sly remarks to Rabindrah.

'Eh, *Wahindi*! What are you doing here with us? Why are you not at home making money from your own *dukas*? Making us poor with your high prices.'

Rabindrah smiled and shrugged, but one of the men was more aggressive than the rest and moved forward, deliberately pushing against Rabindrah so that the Tusker was knocked out of his hand into the dirt. No one noticed the saloon car coming up behind them, slowing down, leaving the main road, approaching the knot of drinkers. The back window was rolled down and Rabindrah saw the gunman take aim at him. He threw himself down as the shot rang out, and the small crowd scattered as the bullet ricocheted off the kiosk. Before he could scramble to his feet, the vehicle turned with a screech of tyres and sped away in the direction of Nairobi. Chaos erupted, shouts rang out, and people rushed into the road, pointing and picking up stones to throw after the fast moving tail lights of the departing car. Gulab cowered on the ground, shaking and moaning until Rabindrah took his arm.

'Get in,' he said between gritted teeth. 'We have to leave. Hurry.'

They swerved out onto the road, narrowly avoiding a swaying lorry, and raced towards Nanyuki.

'Was it for me?' Gulab was trembling, his fingers wound tightly together.

'I doubt it,' Rabindrah said. 'The papers are full of these random shootings. Maybe it was an attempted robbery, but there were too many people around the shop. If they had wanted to shoot you, Uncle, they had a perfect target. But these days it is best to get away from scenes like that.'

Rabindrah drove fast but as they neared Nanyuki it began to rain, slowing his progress. At the Sportsman's Arms, he saw Anthony's vehicle parked in an area with no security lights.

'Stay in the car,' he said to his uncle. 'I'll tell you when you need to move, or to do something. In the meantime, keep out of sight.'

'Camilla has been on the radio to Lamu.' Anthony's expression was watchful. 'Lila is confirmed on tonight's plane with Tom. She can stay in Camilla's flat for as long as she likes. So, unless something unexpected happens, your cousin should be boarding the plane in the next hour or so.'

'Gulab is in the car,' Rabindrah said. 'The sawmill is six miles away. You know this area well, so I thought—'

'We'll take my vehicle.' Anthony interrupted any further comment. 'Better suited for the track up to the sawmill. With this downpour it will be muddy. It's been bloody cold sitting here, waiting for you. Thank God I had a little hooch, and a couple of sandwiches.'

He tipped his head back and drained a silver hip flask, as Rabindrah beckoned his uncle and opened the back door of the Land Cruiser. They left immediately, heading out of town toward the section of forest where the mill was located. Gulab gave directions and within fifteen minutes they saw the main entrance to the compound in front of them.

'Take the side road,' he said. 'To the shed at the far west of the fence. There is a watchman, but he is paid by Manjit and he never asks questions.'

They drove along the rutted surface of the track until the building came into sight. It was standing in a wide clearing, and was made of wood with a corrugated iron roof. The double doors at the front were fortified with heavy bolts and padlocks, and the small, grime-covered windows were barred and gave no hint of what was stored inside. A thin African, dressed in an old army greatcoat and carrying a rifle, emerged from behind the shed. Gulab indicated to his nephew and Anthony that they should remain in the dark interior of the safari car. Rabindrah watched from the front passenger seat, fearful of another massacre as the man fingered the trigger of his weapon.

'Your boss has been arrested.' Gulab was talking urgently. 'And you will be next, if they find you in this place when they come to search. You must help me open the shed and then leave. Go back to your *shamba*. Otherwise they will put you in prison for a very long time.'

The man's eyes glittered with fear. He dropped the gun and helped Gulab to release the locks and open the doors. Rabindrah left the vehicle and felt his gorge rise as he saw the contents of the interior. A pile of elephant tusks, rhino, buffalo and kudu horn, and dozens of leopard skins were stacked against the sides of the shed, mute witness to the wanton destruction of their victims, gunned down or snared with loops of steel, dying in agony. Many of the trophies were still spattered with blood, and shreds of dried skin and muscle hung like fringes from the pelts. On one side of the shed were two lorries, both new and fitted with sturdy tyres.

'Christ Almighty!' Anthony had joined them. 'I can't believe he has all this, in addtion to the cargo in Mombasa.'

'Apparently this has been brought in since the last truckload left a few days ago,' Rabindrah said. 'It's a big operation. Wholesale bloody slaughter.'

'What to do now?' Gulab was leaning against the door as Anthony swung a powerful flashlight, illuminating every corner of the building.

'We need to load all this into your lorries,' Anthony said. 'Get this fellow to help us. It's going to be difficult to lift these tusks. Thank God there aren't too many of them. Come on. *Haraka*.'

They worked in silence, panting with exertion. Rabindrah could only lift the lighter skins – the remaining trophies were too much for his wounded shoulder. Glancing at Gulab, he wondered if the effort might precipitate a heart attack. His uncle's face had turned purple and sweat poured down his cheeks, darkening his shirt and jacket as he strained and hauled. The ivory was bulky and awkward and they had to wrestle it onto the truckbed.

'Where are you taking this?' Gulab wanted to know. 'How will I get my lorries back, when you have disposed of all these things?'

'Pay off the *askari* and get rid of him,' Anthony said over his shoulder. He could not bring himself to look at either Rabindrah or his uncle.

Gulab produced a stack of notes from his bush jacket and held them out.

The watchman did not require any further encouragement. Within seconds he had put down his rifle and melted into the shadows of the forest.

'I should explain to you what has happened,' Gulab began. 'I am in a most unfortunate position, you see. Because—'

'I don't want to know anything about your position,' Anthony said. 'I'm not here to help you. I'm here because I'm a friend of Rabindrah and after tonight I never want to lay eyes on you again. Now let's get on and do this. I have to be back in Shaba in the morning.'

'What did you tell Camilla?' Rabindrah wondered if Anthony had been any more open with his wife than he himself had been with Sarah.

'She knows what went on in Mombasa, and that you and I are getting Lila's father out of a jam. That's all.' Anthony turned his attention to Gulab. 'Mr Singh, I'd like you to sit in my vehicle and wait. Don't move or do anything until I tell you.' Anthony motioned Rabindrah aside and lowered his voice. 'I need help with the jerry cans in the back of my car.' He strode back to the Land Cruiser and opened the back door. 'We need to get all these *debbis* out and the tusks will have to be soaked individually. I've brought enough varieties of fuel and other highly flammable liquids to burn down half the country. It's not easy to burn ivory down to ash. In fact, I'm not even sure that it's possible, but we'll give it our best try. When that's done I'll reverse down the track. We'll have to get the hell out of here as quickly as possible or we may be blown up ourselves.'

'What are you doing?' Gulab twisted round in his seat. 'What is in these *debbis*?'

'Stay where you are,' Rabindrah said. 'And don't speak. Your job is to keep a lookout, in case anyone comes.'

For the next fifteen minutes they lugged the cans from the safari car into the shed, laying them along the wooden walls of the building. As they worked, Rabindrah realised the simplicity of Anthony's plan, but he said nothing as he fetched and carried in silence, ignoring his uncle's repeated questions and trying to overcome the increasing agony in his injured shoulder and chest. Finally, when every trophy on the trucks had been soaked, Anthony pulled up the green tarpaulins and tied them down. Then he walked back to his car.

'Mr Singh, give me the keys of your lorries and your shed.'

Gulab stared at him in confusion. 'What, you are not going to drive the trucks out now? You are going to leave all the evidence there? But suppose the police are coming to inspect the place – what then?'

'Do as he says,' Rabindrah ordered.

'But who will be driving my lorries? And where?' Gulab had still not understood.

'The trucks are not going anywhere,' Anthony said. 'Keys, Mr Singh. Please?'

'What?' There was a note of panic in Gulab's voice, as realisation finally dawned on him. 'Sir, you are not going to burn my lorries? And all the goods – very valuable things. Oh my God!'

'You are a bloody criminal.' Anthony moved closer, his tone menacing. 'If your partners bring up your name you will soon be joining them in jail. As a Kenyan, and a conservationist, I would be delighted to see that happen. But your daughter and nephew are friends of mine, and for that reason alone I am going to try and destroy the evidence that has been left in your shed. You have thirty seconds to hand over your keys, or you are out of my vehicle, and I am leaving you here to fend for yourself.'

'But the trucks – they are new and most costly. I will be losing thousands. My associates will be very angry. I thought you would take the lorries out. Drive them away, put them somewhere safe until we can—'

'Let's get this straight, Mr Singh,' Anthony interrupted. 'No one is going to profit from this haul. Ivory and horn need extremely high temperatures to burn completely. We need the fuel in the tanks of the trucks, as well as everything I brought, to burn this place and its contents to ashes. As quickly as possible. So what is it to be?'

'Do it, Uncle,' Rabindrah said. 'Manjit Singh and his son will certainly try to implicate you. This is the only way.' He held out his hand.

With trembling fingers, Gulab dropped the keys of the shed and the two lorries into his nephew's open palm. Then he sat with his head buried in his hands.

Anthony switched on his lights and backed down the track. On the muddy road the vehicle slid against the banks, hitting a tree with the bumper and smashing the left tail light. He parked and walked back to the shed with Rabindrah. His heart had begun to jump as they opened the last cans of fuel and sprinkled petrol across the floor and up the sides of the walls, soaking the cabs and engines of the lorries and finishing with the tarpaulins. The smell was overpowering in the confined space and

Anthony's memory triggered an alarm as he set a fuse, running a length of fuel-soaked rope from one of the lorry cabs out to the edge of the clearing.

His memory was filled with the smell of the fire that had cost him his leg, and George Broughton-Smith his life. He could hear the crackle, feel the smoke choking him, bringing him back to the day that he had tried to pull Camilla's father from the ruins of the helicopter. For a moment he felt a terrible pain running down his leg and he grasped his knee in a desperate effort to preserve the limb that was burning and then bleeding as part of the aircraft fell like a guillotine across him. He made an involuntary sound of anguish as he reached down and realised there was nothing to feel except the unyielding material of his false limb.

'Come on.' Rabindrah was dragging him away from the place where he stood rooted to the ground. 'Come with me, man. Time to go.'

When they reached the car he pushed Anthony into the driver's seat. 'Start up the engine,' he said. 'I'll go back and light the fuse.'

Gulab's voice rose from the back seat in a wail of protest. 'This is my timber and my lorries! My livelihood! You cannot be going to burn it all. I will be ruined. Completely ruined . . .'

'Shut up, you miserable, fucking crook,' Rabindrah was screaming. 'You should be on your knees to this man. Now stay quiet and don't say another word, or I will personally lock you in the bloody shed with your trucks and let you take the punishment you deserve!'

Without waiting for a response, he ran back up the path, falling in the mud, swearing in pain as his shoulder hit the earth, and then righting himself and charging on until he reached the shed. He threw the keys of the trucks inside, closed and locked the doors, and lit the frayed end of the rope. Even on the soggy ground it ignited quickly. For a moment he waited, wanting to make sure that the flames ran into the warehouse. Then he heard the thrumming, booming sound of the fire taking hold, and he raced back to leap into the seat beside Anthony as they drove away, skidding and churning and squelching on their journey down the dark, muddy road. Around them, nocturnal animals frightened by the sound and the smell of the fire, were already on the move.

'At least the deep part of the forest is wet,' Rabindrah said. 'What burns on the edges will grow again. And this is far enough away from the town that they will not be able to save anything in the shed, by the time the fire brigade gets here.' There was no immediate response and Rabindrah reached out a hand and placed it on Anthony's arm. 'Anthony?'

'Yes?'

'Thank you. I can't begin to say – Look, I'm sorry.'

'This is no place for a chat,' Anthony said. 'We need to get out of here without turning over.'

They were halfway to the main road when they heard the first explosion and saw the flames shooting up into the air, lighting the night sky in a lurid orange glow. Gulab was weeping openly as the car bumped and rocked. When they reached the outskirts of Nanyuki another enormous belch of fire erupted into the night sky. People had come out of their houses and were standing on the side of the road looking up the hill into the blazing forest. When Anthony drove into the car park of the Sportsman's Arms a fire engine roared past, its siren howling as it raced towards the conflagration.

They parted company without a word, and went their separate ways.

Chapter 16

Kenya, September 1977

Lottie closed her eyes and prayed for fortitude as the car rounded the curve of the driveway to reveal the first glimpse of her former home. Then she clasped Mario's hand and looked. The house was framed by acacia trees and flowering shrubs, its stone façade bathed in sunlight. Several feet above ground the verandah, furnished with sofas and wicker chairs, offered shade from the hot, invasive light of the afternoon. In front of the house, the lawn was bordered by a series of flowerbeds that she had mapped out during the first years of her marriage. The riot of colours made her catch her breath as she saw how faithfully Hannah had continued to preserve the zinnias and dahlias, the fuchsias and roses and red hot pokers, and the banks of African periwinkles. Sunbirds flew between the rainbow palette of blossoms and the cooing of doves floated in the blue air, emphasising the tranquillity of the place. Its beauty seemed utterly calm and peaceful, with the old house growing out of the earth as though it had always been there. There was no indication of the sacrifice that it had exacted for its preservation.

The dogs rushed out as Lottie stepped from the car, barking with excitement, running around the family, clamouring for attention. The staff had lined up on the steps of the verandah. Kamau and Mwangi were the first to come forward although they had retired as planned soon after Hannah's return from Norway. Tears made runnels down their wrinkled faces as they bent over her outstretched hands, murmuring traditional words of welcome, their smiles reflecting approval of the new bwana that she had found to take care of her. Last time she had come here it was to bring Jan van der Beer's ashes back to the farm and scatter them in the river. She had believed then, that it would be her final visit to Langani. But now she glanced at Mario, acknowledging with gratitude his encouragement and quiet insistence that she make the journey back into the past.

As Lottie entered the house a small sound between a gasp and a sob escaped her lips. In the sitting room Sarah stood aside, and Hannah hovered as her mother admired new sofa covers, ran her fingers over familiar objects, lingered in front of family portraits that Sarah had taken over the years. Jan's favourite chair still stood beside the fire, a colobus pelt spread across the back. Paintings of African wildlife and landscapes hung on the whitewashed walls, and photographs crowded the mantel-piece. Mwangi had overseen the placing of flowers on occasional tables and on the sideboard, arranged in the way that Lottie had taught him when she had been a new bride and he had started work in the house as a shy, awkward boy from the labour lines. Piet and Suniva tugged at her arm, urging her to come and see their bedrooms, to admire the possessions they treasured most and the pictures they had chosen or painted for their walls. James stood uncertainly on the edge of the excitement, and Lottie drew him into her surrounding circle as they toured the house where she had lived for most of her married life. The home where her children had grown up, and where her grandchildren had now taken their places.

'Tea on the verandah?' Hannah was waiting when they had seen it all.

'Yes. That would be lovely.' Lottie sat down and looked out at the mountain, its peak hidden under layers of white cloud. Kamau, back in the kitchen for this momentous day of Lottie's return, brought tea and a lemon cake he had made to celebrate her miraculous return.

'Would you like to come with Lars and me after this? To the dairy and the stables and to drive round the farm?' Hannah asked.

'We'll come!' Suniva was on her feet immediately, taking James by the arm, jostling Piet into joining the expedition. 'Going to the dairy with Pa,' she said, standing directly in front of him, using the pitch and tone she had developed for her brother, satisfied when he nodded and smiled.

'I'll wait until tomorrow,' Lottie said. 'Then Mario and I will come and explore every corner. Slowly, so we don't miss a thing. You go ahead. We'll see you all later.'

'Sarah? You probably want to stay near the phone,' Hannah said. 'Rabindrah is bound to be on the line any minute.'

'Maybe.' Sarah did not trust herself to comment further. 'In any case, I have a good book I didn't finish in Lamu.'

'Piet is such a valiant boy,' Lottie said, when they had all gone. 'It's remarkable how the other two communicate with him, and don't allow him to feel left out. But at the same time they make no special allowances or give him any quarter. It's an intuitive thing, and it's very special.'

'He is adapting well,' Sarah said. 'He can already lipread, and his biggest problem is when he can't see the person talking to him. But it's sad to know that he can't hear a bird sing, or a lion roaring out on the plains.'

'Hannah has told me that he is falling behind in school,' Lottie said.

'Why is that?' Sarah frowned. 'There is nothing wrong with his brain.'

'Absolutely not,' Lottie said. 'The reason is exactly what you have just described – if the teacher is writing on the blackboard with his back turned, Piet misses a great deal of what is going on. It has made him very unsure of himself, and Hannah spends hours every evening going over all his lessons to help him keep up.'

'Poor Han. She certainly has her hands full right now, with all Piet's requirements and being pregnant,' Sarah said.

'At least Suniva and James keep each other occupied.'

'That's true.' Sarah nodded. 'They are so close that Hannah is uneasy about it.'

'I can't see why,' Lottie said. 'James seems to be a bright, well-mannered boy with an endearing personality.'

'He's great, and he works hard at school,' Sarah said. 'In fact, he usually brings home better marks than Piet, or even Suniva.'

'I sometimes wonder if Hannah and Lars should have adopted him. Or at least taken him into the house as a full member of the family. I don't really care for this strange arrangement where he sleeps in the staff compound at night.'

'I think Hannah would have found that impossible in the beginning.' Sarah stopped to reflect on the dark days after Piet's death. 'It was a heroic gesture on her part, bringing James here at all. But it's true that he doesn't really belong anywhere, and Han has become defensive about the subject.'

'How many people know his story?'

'David is the only staff member who is aware of James's origins. He was with Lars and me when we first tracked down Simon Githiri's family in the Kikuyu Reserve. The day we first saw James with his mother.'

'What does Lars think about all this?' Lottie said. 'He is always so balanced.'

'Lars feels that James has a secure home, a good education and plenty of love, and that is enough.'

'He certainly seems content,' Lottie said.

'He is. Or was, until he was beaten up.' Sarah was frowning. 'Lately I feel his situation is a ticking timebomb. I'm surprised he hasn't begun to ask questions about his parents. Where he came from and where he belongs.'

'Sometimes children know intuitively how to avoid questions with answers they might not like. And Lars is right, in a general sense. Many African children are brought up by people other than their parents. On the family *shamba* with a grandmother, for example. Poverty, disease, death — there are all sorts of reasons. He has been given a great opportunity, that boy.'

'Yes,' Sarah said. 'The only difference is that he has crossed the lines between races and clans and cultures, even by today's standards. James will soon understand that, because it will be forced upon him.'

'Perhaps.' Lottie was saddened by the complexity of the situation, and the unintended consequences of her daughter's act of forgiveness. 'We can never change the fact that James is Simon Githiri's son, and none of us will ever manage to put his origins entirely out of our heads. I only hope he never discovers that.'

'It's all over now, Lottie,' Sarah said. 'There is no reason why James should learn the truth.'

'Lars told me about the offer his parents made, and the rift it caused.' Lottie changed the subject.

'I can't imagine Lars ever giving up Langani to go and farm in Norway,' Sarah said. 'He has put his heart and soul into this place for so many years, and he knows Hannah would never leave.'

'This country challenges you at every step, knocks you sideways when you least expect it, sucks every ounce of energy and commitment out of you.' Lottie looked out at the garden she had created, and the wild plains beyond the neatly clipped hedge. 'It demands so much. Demands everything! And if you are not careful you can end up a dried-out, empty husk, a slave to the land, without ever knowing what has happened to you.'

'There are gifts here too, Lottie.' Sarah smiled. 'Created by you and Janni, and his parents and grandparents before him. And I have never found anything as inspiring as an African morning, with all its magnificence spread out before you. There is no better way to start a day. I hope you and Mario will come to the Mara before you go back.'

'I would love that.' Lottie was delighted. 'He has been on safari in South Africa, but that isn't the same thing at all. Anyway, I'll leave you to your book, although Rabindrah will probably ring soon and then your literary pleasures will be forgotten.'

She touched Sarah's cheek with affection and made her way to the bedroom where she sat down in an armchair beside the window. Mario was unpacking clothes and taking out the gifts they had brought for the staff. In the distance she could see the clear outline of the ridge. The place she had never dared to visit since the day that Piet's funeral pyre had been lit, and the last physical remains of her son had ascended into the bleached-out sky. The past that she had ignored for so long suddenly slipped into focus, and Lottie knew that she was ready to yield to its memories.

'Darling, I'm going up to the ridge,' she said. 'I would like to do that now, at the beginning. I'll ask Sarah to take me, in memory of the love we shared for Piet. I'll be fine – please don't worry.' Mario held her briefly, tilting her face upwards and kissing her with tenderness. She was glad when he did not offer to accompany her, and she put her arms tight around him before picking up a sweater and leaving the room.

Sarah had seated herself in one of the wicker armchairs on the verandah with a book in her hands, but she seemed to be staring out at the lawn, almost trancelike. The sound of Lottie's footsteps made her look round.

'No news yet?'

'Nothing,' Sarah said, her voice flat.

'I'm sorry, my dear.'

'I've been so frightened all day, especially since I arrived here and there was no message for me. Only silence. I've tried not to think about it, but I keep remembering the evening when Piet didn't call on the radio, and we finally went to the lodge and the ridge where he had died.'

'Oh, my dear, I'm sure Rabindrah hasn't come to any serious harm, otherwise you would have heard something.'

'I don't know, Lottie.' Sarah twisted her hands. 'I don't understand why he couldn't have told me about this investigation. I know it was dangerous, but I would have backed him all the way. I've always fought for wildlife conservation, made it my career. It's one of the issues we have always agreed on. This has made me realise how the whole texture of our marriage has frayed. How disconnected we have become.'

'There will be a reason for what has happened today, and I don't believe it will be about any lack of trust,' Lottie said, dismayed by the defeat in Sarah's voice.

'Rabindrah and I have weathered all kinds of issues together, but recently I feel I don't know him at all. I still haven't a clue where he went after the phone call this morning, and I can't accept that he has had no chance to telephone me since then. This is something he has never done before. I just can't fathom it.'

'Sarah, the most important thing is that you love each other, and when you see Rabindrah, as I'm sure you will any moment, you have to remember it's the only thing that really matters.'

'I used to think that, but so many obstacles have got in our way.' Sarah's words were heavy. 'Now I don't know whether we can ever get back to where we were. Or whether I have the courage to go on trying, when Rabindrah seems to have given up.'

'I was thinking of going up to Piet's ridge,' Lottie said tentatively. 'Would you come with me, Sarah? Although you might miss Rabindrah if he telephones.'

'I'll come.' Sarah jumped up. Perhaps this was the place where she might find some comfort and allay her fears. 'I'll go and get the car keys.'

They left at once, not making much conversation as Lottie gazed out at the golden ripple of the wheat in the wind and the mantle of trees that coiled along the banks of the river. Herds of plains game looked up as the vehicle passed them and then returned to their grazing. At the foot of the track leading up to the ridge she hesitated, her resolve weakening, now that the moment of decision had come.

'I know about the cairn, about the tree Lars planted and the stones you collected – how beautiful you have all made it. When I brought Janni's ashes to Langani, Hannah wanted me to come up here with her, but I could not go near the place where my son had died so horribly. Where I could no longer hold on to the picture of him young and laughing and alive.'

'I have come to look on it as a place of peace,' Sarah said. 'But if this still doesn't feel right, we can go back. That's fine with me, and I'm sure it's fine with Piet too.'

'No.' Lottie braced herself. 'I have to do this now. It is time.'

At the top of the path she made a strangled sound as she approached the memorial to her son. Then she knelt down and closed her eyes, touching the white rocks in a caress, her lips moving in prayer. The wind sighed in the branches of the tortillis tree as Lottie took a small gold cross and chain from her pocket. She bent down and lifted one of the stones, laid the crucifix gently in the soil underneath, and then covered the place again.

'It was the cross my mother gave him, when he was christened,' she said. 'I kept it with me because it was something he always carried in his pocket. But it should be here, not locked away in a drawer thousands of miles from where his spirit rests.'

She rose to her feet and moved to the edge of the steep promontory, looking down over the plains and the wheatfields and the house where she had loved and lived for so many years. This was the place that Jan van der Beer had fought for during the years of the Mau Mau Emergency, when the Kikuyu tribe had risen up in their bloody effort to take back the land the white man had stolen from them. The place that had slowly turned a loving husband and father into a haunted, drunken being, filled with self-loathing and remorse. She turned away from the edge, and sat down on the boulder where Piet had dreamed of taking over his heritage. Her grandchildren's heritage. She had loved it once, never contemplated a day when she would have to leave its wild glory.

'My son is gone, Sarah, but for the first time I feel he really is at peace,' she said eventually, lifting her face to the rosy sky. 'I think I can release him at last.'

'We have all had to let go, Lottie, and to forgive. In order to live again.'

'You understood that long ago, my dear. I'm only getting there now. Thanks to Mario.'

Sarah sat down beside her. 'I'm so glad you found him.'

'I never imagined I could have an affair with a stranger.' Lottie's gaze was directed into the past. 'But Piet was dead, and Janni was drinking heavily, and life in Rhodesia was intolerable. Five perfect days were all we had, while I was on holiday with my brother in Johannesburg.'

'And then you went back to Janni.'

'He was still my husband, no matter what he had become,' Lottie said.

'A man who had lived in hell from the day Piet died. I couldn't walk away and leave him alone with his demons.'

'Poor Janni. He never forgave himself.'

'Would you ever forgive yourself if your child died as a direct result of something you had done?' Lottie's words were harsh. 'Oh yes, it was in the days of the Mau Mau, and everyone tracking the gangs up in the forests was a little crazy. You cannot fight and kill other men without changing the core of yourself. All wars are the same in that respect. Janni sought to redress the tragedy of his brother who had been murdered purely because he was a white landowner. But on the way he lost himself, and when Piet died Janni knew at once that it was an act of revenge. That he was responsible for the death of his own son.'

'How do you feel about Janni now? Today.' Sarah wondered if she had any right to pose the question.

'I feel pity. But I also feel contempt for what he did, and for what he became. I have never been able to forgive him. It is only to you that I can admit that, Sarah, knowing how you loved Piet and yet you went to the jail where his murderer was dying, and you forgave him. On that day when you gave Simon Githiri absolution, you ended the whole cycle of grief and terror.'

'It was Hannah who ended it, by bringing James here. Although it hasn't ended for you,' Sarah said.

'Up to now, I could not see myself ever finding peace of mind or happiness here.'

'You went back to Johannesburg instead, and fell in love with Mario, all over again?'

'Love? I no longer knew what the word meant.' Lottie shook her head. 'After a time, Mario persuaded me to go to Italy with him, although I felt nothing at all for him. In reality, I was simply afraid to be alone.'

'What changed?'

'He had lost his wife and daughter some years before. In a car accident. And finally I grew ashamed of my self-indulgent grief, and the way I accepted all that he offered and gave nothing in return. I woke up to the fact that he deserved to start a new life, without me. I was too damaged.'

'You left him?' Sarah was astonished.

'I tried, but he begged me not to go. He said I was the only bright thing in his world, and he would wait for me to love him again. I was ashamed of having taken so much from him, only to run away and leave him with his own sadness and loss. So I decided to stay.' Lottie was drained by the memories that had poured from her after so long, and she sat in silence for a time before continuing. 'Although it may sound strange, love grew out of that resolve. Once I found the courage to let him touch the part of myself that I had shut down so tightly.'

Sarah sat back, thinking of her own turmoil after Piet's death, and the slow, halting acceptance that love could come to her again. But now her marriage, her second chance, seemed to be on the brink of disintegration. Did it really come down to such a simple decision, in the end? To see it through, no matter what. Should she wait for love to reignite, or stand up and walk away from all the pain and recriminations that had wormed their way into her feelings for Rabindrah?

'You made the right choice, Lottie,' she said, with a hint of envy.

'We have found a rare happiness. But it was not until now that I could face Langani. I know Hannah must have been hurt by that. It's probably why she has never come to stay with us in Italy, although I have spent holidays with them all at the coast.'

'She thought Mario did not want you to reopen your old life.'

'Oh no! He has always said I must come back. Lay the ghosts. When Anthony telephoned about Hannah's birthday, it was Mario who insisted that we accept.' Lottie kissed Sarah's cheek. 'Thank you for coming here with me this evening. For helping me to reach the turning point.' She paused for a moment. 'I'm going to ask Piet now to help you, and I know that he will. The love you had for each other will never die, Sarah, and I know he is listening to both of us. Here together for the first time. Take heart, my dear. You will find a way back to Rabindrah. And if Lars and Hannah remain at Langani and hand it down to their children, then maybe Janni, too, will rest in peace.'

'I like that idea,' Sarah said.

They sat close together, listening to the liquid song of an oriole, watching in silence as a pair of dikdik came into the clearing, teetering on pin-like legs, large, black-veined ears twitching as they nibbled at a small bush close to Piet's cairn. They looked up occasionally with huge, dark eyes to assess any potential danger from their audience, but the air was filled with tranquillity and they made no attempt to skitter away. The heat was beginning to fade with the sinking sun, and when the delicate animals moved on Lottie unfastened the sweater from around her shoulders and slipped her arms into the sleeves.

'I'm sure there is a good reason for Rabindrah's actions,' she said, knowing that Sarah was still thinking about the whereabouts of her husband, perhaps feeling guilty about being away from the telephone for so long. 'Investigating this story took huge courage. He must have known last night would be dangerous, and that is probably why he said nothing to you. Let's go back and see if there is any message. He may even be there, waiting.'

'I felt ill this morning, when he told me what had happened. He was shot, for God's sake! He could have been killed. But then he disappeared again and now I feel bloody furious. And hurt. He shouldn't have left me in the dark.'

'Men almost always get those things wrong.' Lottie stood up. 'He will have a whole series of problems to face as a result of this investigation. His family are likely to have very mixed feelings about what he has done, and there must be a risk of Lila being stopped, when she tries to board the plane tonight.'

'Oh, God. I hadn't even thought of that,' Sarah said, as they began to scramble back down the track. 'It's going to be hard for her to leave without seeing her parents.'

They had reached the base of the ridge when Sarah put a finger to her lips and they came to an immediate halt. In front of them a small, thickset animal with a grey mantel and short, black legs was clambering down from a tree, keeping his hold on the trunk with powerful claws.

'A ratel! How wonderful! It's rare to find one,' Lottie whispered in delight. 'There must be bees up there.'

'I love them, too,' Sarah said. 'They are the most ferocious, short-tempered little buggers. I've seen them attack much larger animals, and claw the honey out of hives. Even the bees can't sting them through those thick layers of fur and fat. I heard a honey bird earlier, so this fellow must have been following it straight to the honeycomb.'

'Let's hope he doesn't try and scare us off with that terrible smell,' Lottie said. 'It is a thousand times worse than anything a skunk can put out.'

'You know, it was Piet who first showed me one, and told me that ratel is the Afrikaans name for a badger,' Sarah recalled. 'And now one suddenly appears in our path! Look, he's not even running away, which is what they usually do. He's just watching us. I think Piet has been listening to us, Lottie. In fact I know he has, and it makes me feel good again.'

There was no sign of Rabindrah when they arrived back at the house, nor had he left any message. Lars poured a drink for Sarah, and sat her down beside the fire. It was not long before the children appeared to distract her, but she grew more anxious as the evening wore on. Although she tried to bury her unease she was increasingly haunted by memories of the night when Piet had gone missing, and she had found his ruined body on the bloodsoaked soil.

It was after eleven, and Lottie and Mario had retired when headlights swept the driveway and the verandah walls.

'It must be Rabindrah!' Hannah stood by the door as Lars went outside with the dogs.

It was raining heavily and he stood on the steps of the house, waiting to identify the passengers in the car. Sarah followed more slowly, trying to control the boiling confusion of relief and anger. Her heart was hammering, closing her throat, as she saw Rabindrah get out of a car she did not recognise. But before she had a chance to form any words, or decide what approach to take, Gulab Singh emerged from the driver's side to join them.

'Relieved to see you, my friend.' It was Lars who spoke first, his manner a little too hearty. 'We were getting pretty worried about you, especially poor Sarah here. Come out of the rain and tell us what's been going on.'

'Gulab is on his way to Nairobi.' Rabindrah shook Lars by the hand but directed his answer to Sarah. 'He needs to get back tonight but I wanted to stop on the way and explain what has been happening.'

'Where on earth have you been since this morning?' Sarah took in the cuts and bruises on her husband's face, the dark circles under his eyes and the sling supporting his arm. Both men were pale with cold and exhaustion as they stood before her in their mud-stained clothes. 'Have you any idea what I've been through today, worrying about you? Look at you! Your arm in a sling, your face all cut! What have you been doing since you got out of hospital in Mombasa? Couldn't you have phoned me?'

'Have you heard anything about Lila?' Gulab broke into the stream of questions. 'Did she get away?'

'The plane should have boarded by now.' Sarah spoke more gently, acknowledging the man's concern for his daughter. 'What are you doing here, Gulab?'

'Sarah, there have been complications.' Rabindrah looked at her but did not elaborate, and an uncomfortable silence ensued.

'Let's go into the sitting room,' Hannah suggested. 'It's chilly out here.'

'I must be leaving right away.' Gulab followed Hannah inside. 'Perhaps it would be possible to phone my wife first? She does not know where I am and she might—'

'She might be worried sick.' Sarah flung an angry glance in his direction. 'Just like me.'

'How about a drink?' Lars made his way to the sideboard and took out glasses. 'You both look as though you might need one.'

'What complications are you talking about?' Sarah touched Rabindrah's damaged shoulder. 'Tell me what the doctors have said, and how much damage the bullet did. After that, we can get down to other explanations.'

'I'd love a whisky.' Rabindrah winced as he eased himself into a chair. 'More important for Gulab is the call to Nairobi. We can talk later, about what has happened.'

'The telephone is in the hall, Mr Singh,' Hannah said, but her tone was cool. 'Lars and I have an early start in the morning, so we are going to turn in and leave you to it. I think Sarah is right. Explanations are needed. Glad you're safe, Rabindrah. Goodnight.'

There was silence as Gulab spoke to his wife, his words stumbling over each other as he tried to assure her that he would be home soon. He was apologetic and flustered when he hung up.

'The police have come to see Anjit, but she has told them nothing,' he said to Rabindrah. 'So I will be going now, and I will see you in Nairobi.'

'I'm coming with you, Gulab,' Rabindrah said. 'I have to go back tonight. I'm sorry, Sarah, but it's essential for me to be in Nairobi early in the morning.'

'I'll drive you and we can talk on the way.' She put out a tentative hand to touch his cheek, alarmed by his pallor. 'You look terrible, Rabindrah. If you wait a few minutes, I'll get my stuff, and put it in my car. Gulab, you go on ahead of us. I'm sure Anjit will be waiting up for you.'

Rabindrah felt his anxiety rising. The carnage and violence of the last twenty-four hours might not be over. Although the shooting incident at the roadside stall could have been a repercussion, he did not think he had been followed out of Nairobi. Either way, it would be easy for one of Manjit's associates to find out where he lived, however, and he could not risk Sarah being caught in the crossfire if an attempt was going to be made on his life. She would be safer at Langani.

'I think you should stay here. It's late and it will take a long time to get to Nairobi, driving in this rain.' Rabindrah turned to his uncle. 'We need a few minutes, if you don't mind.'

'I will be waiting in the car,' Gulab said. 'Please thank your friends for the use of the telephone.' He left the house, disappearing into the downpour.

'I could do with a couple of aspirins, if you have any.' Rabindrah moved his arm to a position where the strain was least. His face was pinched from pain and sleep deprivation.

Sarah poured him a second drink and brought tablets from the first aid box in the kitchen. Tension crackled in the air as she stood looking down at him.

'I want to come home with you,' she said. 'You need me to look after you.'

Rabindrah wondered how much he could tell her without frightening her unnecessarily. He knew she would never let him leave with Gulab if she thought he was in danger. Somehow, he had to persuade her to remain at Langani. The only possible thing was to tell her half the story, leaving out any suggestion that he might be at serious risk.

'There are things I have to finish in Nairobi, Sarah. First thing tomorrow I have to give my official statement to the police. After that, there is more copy to turn in to Gordon. Plus another briefing with Johnson Kiberu before his television press conference in the afternoon.'

'I don't see why that would prevent me from driving you to Nairobi,' Sarah said. 'You look like you might pass out any minute.'

'I won't. Gulab will drive and I'll probably fall asleep.'

'But I still want to know where you have been all day, and why Gulab is with you.' She was determined not to back down, and to return to the city with him. 'I think you should explain that right now, before we start out. Because I have a very bad feeling about all this.'

'Harjeet Singh told me last night, just before he was arrested, that Lila's whole family was involved in his illegal export business.'

'That is why Gulab is with you?'

He nodded and then gave her the details straight, watching the horror mount in her eyes as he described the worst moments of his life.

'I flew to Nairobi this morning, to see Gulab. To find out if it was true. For Lila's sake.' He looked at her, waiting for a sympathetic comment.

But Sarah remained silent, forcing him to continue unprompted. It took him some time to explain what he had discovered and the subsequent actions he had taken at the sawmill, but he did not mention the shooting incident on the road to Nanyuki.

'Let me get this right,' she said when his story ended. 'You brought Anthony down from Shaba. From his honeymoon. And then you were both crazy enough to go to the sawmill, where all these slaughtered remains were hidden?' She could not credit what he had told her, or feel any compassion for Gulab's plight. 'You put yourself and Anthony in mortal danger, just to keep that cowardly bastard from going to jail?'

'He is Lila's father,' Rabindrah said. 'He was forced into business with Manjit. He is a victim.'

'Oh no he's not. Gulab sold his daughter to keep himself in business. Lila is the victim here. And as your wife I have been in a panic all day, waiting for news of you. A phone call. Anything. While you were busy destroying evidence of poaching and smuggling, to save your relatives from prosecution.'

'Would you really want to see Gulab in jail? And maybe Lila?'

'What you have just done could have landed you in jail,' she said. 'Where would that have left me? It seems your uncle was a more important consideration than anything that might have happened to your own wife. Does our future not mean anything to you? Have you forgotten that my whole working life has been spent on wildlife conservation? Did you ever think about the risk for Anthony, who sits on a conservation committee with Johnson Kiberu. And can you not see that Gulab never considered anyone in his family, least of all you, when he agreed to sell his daughter to a crook who deals with poachers and death?'

'It was Anthony who dragged me into this whole thing.' Rabindrah aired his earlier suspicions, desperate to make some kind of defence, knowing full well that he was insulting a man who had proved to be a loyal friend. 'For all I know, he was aware that I would be putting the finger on my own relatives. Maybe he didn't tell me, in case I couldn't be trusted to go through with it.'

'You are sick. I won't listen to any more of this,' Sarah said, clapping her hands over her ears. 'Anthony would never have done that to you, but the irony of the whole thing is that he would have been right. You compromised your integrity tonight. In fact, you ended up no better than your uncle.'

'That is not true.' He was enraged by her lack of understanding. 'You are overlooking the fact that I have exposed people in a major poaching ring. Nailed them solid, and almost lost my life doing it. The story is going to be all over the papers tomorrow. Kiberu will be making a statement on television in the afternoon, using my photographs and my report. The foreign papers will certainly pick it up, which will be important for conservation in Kenya and internationally. I'm not proud of what I did at the sawmill. What I saw there sickened me, but I had to do it. Not for Gulab, but for the whole family who would have suffered if Harjeet had told the police about the contents of that store.'

'Is Indar involved in this too?' Sarah's eyes were blazing.

'No. Sarah, I didn't talk to you today because I didn't want to involve you in any of this. And until I've given my statement to the police and I have Kiberu's assurance that the whole thing is over, I think you should stay here, where you are safe.'

'Fine. I'll do exactly that.' Her words were cold. 'Since you have a grateful relative conveniently waiting out there to drive you to Nairobi.'

'Sarah . . .' He rose with difficulty. 'I know I should have told you about this investigation from the beginning and—'

'Yes, you should. Did you not realise that I would be ill with anxiety when you disappeared in the middle of the bloody wedding? And then vanished a second time, after telling me about a raid in Mombasa in which you were shot? I have been imagining you all day, attacked and bleeding. In need of help. I was terrified. What an idiot I was!' Her face was a portrait of hurt and betrayal.

'I'm sorry,' he said. 'I misjudged the situation and I am so, so sorry. But some good will come out of it. You will see. The wildlife of this country will be better protected in the parks and—'

'Did you consider, for even a moment, the risk of bringing that despicable man here, to a private wildlife sanctuary? Someone who is actively involved in poaching, who might be followed by the police?'

'We haven't been followed,' Rabindrah said wearily, although he was not sure of the truth of his statement.

'Or did you stop to ask yourself whether his presence might implicate Lars and Hannah in some way? Give some dicey politician a way of getting at them? Obviously not, but maybe you will, on your way back to Nairobi.'

'I'll come back tomorrow. I realise I've handled this very badly.'

'I'm going to the Mara tomorrow,' she said, making the decision as the words left her mouth. 'You clearly don't want me around while you sort out your family affairs and advance your career. In fact, you have rejected my every offer of help. I don't think we should see each other for a while, Rabindrah. Our lives have drifted much further apart than I had realised. There isn't anything else we can say to each other right now.'

'Please, Sarah! Don't judge me just on what has happened with Gulab.' He took her arm and pulled her towards him, longing to tell her the whole truth. That he was afraid for his own life, and more importantly for hers. 'Not everything is as black or white as you make out. At least give me some credit for what I did in Mombasa. Gordon is more than satisfied with that, and Kiberu says the President wants to see me. To thank me. So I have achieved something. And we still have the cheetah book to work on, with Allie.'

'You should leave now.' She pulled away from him. 'For Hannah's sake. And I can't think how we can work together with Allie after this.'

'Why?' he asked. 'Dammit, Sarah, I'm not a monster. When you calm down, maybe we can talk about this. Rationally.'

She did not reply. Instead she flung open the door to the verandah and stood watching the car until the diminishing wink of its tail lights disappeared into the night.

Chapter 17

Kenya, September 1977

On the way south from Langani Gulab had offered to drive, but his shaking hands and panicky mutterings made it unlikely that he would be able to concentrate, or to detect signs that they were being followed. Rabindrah took the wheel, and he had wanted to shout at his uncle as the older man snored in the passenger seat, or to make him somehow suffer the consequences of his cowardice. But it would have achieved nothing.

A hint of dawn had crept into the sky when they reached Nairobi. There was no visible police presence outside Gulab's house, and Rabindrah picked up his car and left immediately, beyond exhaustion and unable to face the prospect of talking to Anjit or answering her questions. Sarah's fury burned like salt in the open sore that the last two days had made of his emotions. His insistence that she stay at Langani while he went back to Nairobi had hurt her deeply, but he felt that she should have tried to understand his motives before denouncing him. He knew he had handled things badly, but he could not see what other path had been open to him.

He turned towards home, thinking that he might crawl into bed without even bothering to eat, although he was famished. More than anything he longed to sleep, and he struggled to keep alert during the last, interminable moments in the car. His eyes were gritty, his head throbbed and his shoulder was an unrelenting source of pain. He felt feverish. Shadows leapt out at him from the roadside, forming strange shapes in the head-lights as though someone was about to hurl themselves in front of his wheels, and he found himself swerving involuntarily to avoid imaginary obstacles. The rain had stopped and he opened the windows and drummed with his fist on the dashboard in an effort to keep himself awake. Relief swept over him as he turned, at last, into his own driveway.

As soon as he switched off the engine he saw that the front door was ajar, although there were no lights on inside the house. Keeping an eye on the darkened opening, he took out a heavy torch that he kept in the glove box. He wondered where the dog could be. Tatu was always there to greet him, tail wagging, wet nose pressing into the palm of his hand. He went up the steps onto the verandah, holding the torch as a possible weapon, ready to defend himself as best he could. The house waited, silent. He moved around the door, and stood pressed against the wall in the hallway, listening, clutching the flashlight. Nothing stirred. Reaching out cautiously, he pushed the light switch to find that he was still in darkness. He crept along the passage, moving stealthily towards the telephone table and lifting the receiver. There was no dial tone. Peering at the back of the phone, he realised that the line had been cut near the connection point. The dog had not barked, or come to meet him, and he risked calling out softly.

'Tatu?' He gave a low whistle, but there was no response and he turned on the torch and shone the powerful beam into the sitting room.

The place looked as though a hurricane had passed through it. Tables were overturned, Sarah's papers and photographs and his own files littered the room, pages scattered where they had been thrown. Drawers had been opened and their contents hurled out. With a profound sense of dread, because he knew what the invaders had been looking for, he went to Sarah's darkroom. This too had been ransacked, with developing materials thrown off the shelves and folders of photographs rifled.

Moving faster, he made his way along the corridor, beaming the light into the empty rooms on either side. He did not believe there was anyone still in the house, and he called for Chege but there was no answer from the staff quarters. The dog was lying in the kitchen beside the back door, a greenish froth around her jaws, her mouth pulled back in a rictus of agony. The remains of a half-chewed piece of beef lay on the floor beside her. Above the sink, the glass in the window had been smashed, leaving a jagged opening. This must be where they had broken in, tossing the poisoned meat to Tatu and waiting until she had eaten it. Then the panels of the door had been splintered and the lock jemmied open, giving the raiders access to the house.

Rabindrah knelt on the ground, swearing and crying at the same time, cradling the dog in his arms. She was stiff and cold and he thought she must have been dead for a number of hours. He lifted her, ignoring the agonising jolt in his shoulder, and carried her to her basket to lay her gently on her old blanket. Then he took out his handkerchief and wiped away the froth from her soft muzzle, peppered with grey hairs. Tatu had been his birthday gift to Sarah seven years ago, and from her first weeks as a puppy she had gnawed her way through shoes and furniture and into their hearts. He stared down at the dead dog, wishing for some way to turn back the clock, to revisit a happier time.

A larger worry loomed in his consciousness. Where was Chege? Had he also been attacked and injured? He lurched to his feet, took up the torch again and walked out to the staff quarters. The small building stood under the trees at the back of the garden, and the door was ajar. He hesitated, listening, but there was no sound from within. He switched on the torch, afraid that there would be another body inside. But the place was empty and there was no sign of a struggle. Chege had known that he did not have to prepare dinner, but he would not have stayed out all night. Rabindrah retraced his steps to the main house. His skin was burning, although he was shivering at the same time. As he reached the kitchen his knees began to give way. The ground lurched under his feet, the room swirled in dark eddies around him, and he felt bile rising in his throat. He found himself muttering Sarah's name as he sank down onto the floor, waiting for the spinning to stop. He should get up, go for help, find somewhere to phone in a report to the police. Something. But his body refused to acknowledge the signals from his brain. He closed his eyes to a red tide.

An urgent voice, calling his name repeatedly, brought him back to consciousness. Someone was shaking him, and pain lanced through his injured arm. There was the sound of feet crunching on broken glass as he groaned and opened his eyes. The muscles in his neck and shoulders protested as he raised his head and tried to move his stiff limbs. He concentrated on the voice, squinting in order to focus as the face swam into his vision. Gordon Hedley was crouched in front of him, trying to rouse him. Behind him, a police officer and an *askari* were examining the broken window and bright sunlight poured in through the kitchen door. It must be late. The police moved outside, into the garden, and Rabindrah wearily lifted a hand to wipe his face, aware that spittle had escaped from the side of his mouth as he slept, and run down his chin.

'Good God, man!' Gordon sat back on his hunkers. 'For a moment there I thought you were dead!'

'I thought so, too.' Rabindrah tried to straighten his cramped legs and made an involuntary sound as a fierce pain tore through his shoulder. 'I don't know how long I've been here, and every inch of me seems to have seized up.'

'Here, let me help you up.' Gordon offered a hand. 'Chief Inspector Ochieng is outside, looking at footprints and so on. I'm sorry about your dog.'

Rabindrah glanced at Tatu, lying stiff and cold in her basket. Already she seemed to have shrunk in death, her once glossy coat dull. 'They poisoned her,' he said, unable to prevent the tremor in his voice. 'Bloody shits! Sarah will be devastated.' He shook his head to try and clear it. 'Is there any sign of Chege? I hope he hasn't been hurt or worse.'

'There's nobody here,' Gordon said. 'The police are trying to track him down. He was last seen shopping for you, at the *duka* down the road.'

'It's not like him to disappear.' Rabindrah gave a brief description to one of the policemen who confirmed that Chege was still missing. Then he turned back to Gordon. 'This might sound trivial, but I need something to eat, or I may pass out again.'

'Toast and coffee coming up,' Gordon said. 'And while the kettle is boiling, I'll tell Ochieng and his sidekick that you will be ready for him in about twenty minutes.'

After breakfast they walked into the living room and Rabindrah sat down while Gordon poured him a measure of whisky. 'Drink this to keep you going,' he said. 'You'll need a doctor later this morning. But in the meantime tell me, before the plods come in, what the hell happened since I saw you yesterday?'

Rabindrah hesitated before answering, aware there would be gaps in his story that even Gordon should not know. He started at the beginning, leaving out nothing except the visit to Gulab's house and sawmill.

'After I left you and Kiberu yesterday, I decided to drive up to Langani,' he said. 'And on the way I'm pretty sure someone tried to take a pot shot at me when I stopped on the roadside for something to eat.'

'Christ! Could you identify him?'

'The car was going fast, and it was dusk. I'm not even sure it was me they were after,' Rabindrah said. 'There have been a number of attacks like this on the roads lately, and I might have been in the wrong place at the wrong time. Anyway, when I arrived at Langani, Sarah and I had a row. After my disappearance from Lamu she was furious that I had left the hospital in Mombasa yesterday, without telling her where I was going. I got a real stinger.'

'Serves you bloody right. You should have kept her up to date, and you should also have told me you were coming home. You could have got yourself killed. I'm not surprised she was mad.'

'You can save the lecture – I've had it in spades already,' Rabindrah said. 'What brought you here, anyway?'

'We had an attempted robbery at the paper. Around midnight.' Gordon offered a cigarette and saw Rabindrah wince as he reached out to take it. 'A fellow came in, dressed in a messenger's uniform. He had a package of documents addressed to me, with a government stamp and an urgent notice on it. He was told to drop it on the desk in my office. It was quiet – only half a dozen people around, most of them on the machines. Half an hour later someone went to the photo lab, and found this fellow in there. There was a punch-up and he made a run for it, but he had turned over the whole place. Files and negatives everywhere. No prizes for guessing what he was after. He'd probably have ransacked my office next, if he hadn't been discovered. But your photos had already been printed, and the type had been set. In fact the machines were running it, while he was in the building. Here is this morning's paper. Johnson Kiberu has a press conference scheduled for this afternoon. He looks like the cat that swallowed the cream, and he deserves to be pleased with himself. As do you.'

'What about my film?' Rabindrah was reading his report as he asked the question.

'I took the developed roll home with me last night. It's in my safe, along with your original report. So our visitor didn't get anything, but he certainly made a mess of the place. When you didn't come in this morning and your phone was dead, I called my friend Ochieng who was expecting to hear from you, and we came straight out here.'

'I owe you one,' Rabindrah said, and then described his arrival at the house. 'Chege must have been here last night, when these fellows turned up. I hope he's all right. Why don't you call in the inspector and get the statement over with.'

The next two hours were tedious as the chief inspector wrote down both Rabindrah and Gordon's full names and addresses and then proceeded to take detailed statements from them both, starting with the raid in Mombasa.

'But you did not call the police when you first arrived here,' he said, when Rabindrah had answered all his enquiries. 'That is strange, Mr Singh. Especially when you had already been involved in another incident in Mombasa.'

'My line had been cut,' Rabindrah said with impatience. 'And I was in no state to think rationally. I was injured and I passed out. I didn't come around again until Mr Hedley arrived here with you.' He passed his hand over his eyes, weary beyond endurance.

'I think Mr Singh needs medical attention right away,' Gordon said to Ochieng. 'We seem to have covered everything now. If you have any more questions you can contact us again, later in the day.'

'Let me know when you locate Chege,' Rabindrah said. 'He's a good man and I want to know, the minute you find him.'

The doctor's examination confirmed an infection surrounding the bullet wound, and the need for a strong antibiotic and rest.

'I'd go home, now, and go to bed for a day or two,' Dr Mitchell said.

Rabindrah nodded and left the surgery, stopping to pick up the medicine and then heading for Gordon's office.

'Do you think the burglaries were arranged by Manjit Singh?' Rabindrah wondered bleakly who else among his family or friends could possibly be targets if that was the case.

'I don't think so.' Gordon shook his head. 'He is in jail, and what you have on them is already in the public domain. That part of your report was rolling off the presses by the time the raids took place. It would have been too late to stop it going out. But his African business partners, well that is a different matter. Some of the other material you dug up, and the information you got from Johnson Kiberu, is explosive stuff. He is going after everyone in this consortium, which will finish off at least two high-up chaps in the government. I've had calls from several of the Mzee's closest cronies this morning, anxious to weigh in on the issue. Although for all I know they are up to their necks in similar schemes. These attempted robberies look more like suppression of evidence by the fellows who are company directors on Manjit Singh's board.'

'I need to see Kiberu today,' Rabindrah said. 'We should get together with him to decide what is to be published next.'

'Your position is precarious now, Rabindrah. These goons could decide to shut you up altogether. It might be wise for you to lay low for a few days.'

Rabindrah thought again of the shots fired at the roadside stall. Gordon was right. The raid on the house was a sinister development. What if Sarah had been at home, when they arrived? His limbs felt cold as ice in the morning sunshine.

'I can't let them intimidate me,' he said. 'If Kiberu has the balls to expose them, then I'm with him to the end. But Sarah is another matter. They might go after her.'

'How long will she be at Langani?'

'She is leaving for the Mara today.'

'That may be the best place for her,' Gordon said. 'I doubt if anyone would try getting at her down there. But you may find it wise to leave the country for a week or so. Let the dust settle. In the meantime, you're bunking with us. Maureen is organising the guest quarters for you, and she is all ready to play nurse.' He put up a hand as Rabindrah started to protest. 'I insist. I've been on to Kiberu and he has organised a police guard at my house for the moment. You'll be better working from there, until this is over. I think we should go back to your place now, and pick up whatever you need for the next few days.'

They found Chege in the house, slowly clearing up the shambles surrounding him. There was a large swelling and several cuts on his head and arms. It was clear that he had taken a beating.

'Chege. Thank God you are all right, man. You need to see a doctor right away.' Rabindrah said. 'Leave the clean-up for another time. Do you know who attacked you?'

'I did not see these men. They came in the night,' Chege said. 'Very late. Several of them. I heard glass breaking and Tatu making noise, and I came from my bed. Then I saw the dog. Eeeh! They had killed her! Mama Sarah will be very sad.'

'Can you tell us anything about them?'

'I did not see the faces — only shadows.' Chege put his hand up to his head. 'They beat me. They said they would kill me. I was very afraid. One had a *kiboko*, and he struck me on the head. I fell down. When I woke again it was the day time and they had left me in a ditch on the Langata road. People thought I was drunk when I called out, but a man stopped and helped me to come home. The police were here and the inspector said they would leave an *askari* at night for the rest of the week.'

'I'll take you to the hospital,' Rabindrah said. 'And give you money for a taxi to bring you back. You don't look as though anything is broken, but you will need some *dawa* for all those cuts and bruises. If there is anything else you remember, then you must phone Bwana Hedley. Here is his number. But don't talk to anyone else.'

'I did not see,' Chege shook his head sadly. 'Too dark. Too quick. I am sorry. I will go with you to the hospital, but first we should bury the dog.'

There were two *askaris* already deployed outside Gordon Hedley's house when they arrived. Rabindrah glanced around at the heavy shrubbery that screened the property from the road, and from its neighbours. It would be difficult to prevent anyone who was really determined to get in. Maureen Hedley seemed calm, however, and she welcomed him with affection, brushing aside his apologies.

'This isn't the first time we have had to beef up our security,' she said. 'Now, Gordon says you need to phone Langani, so I'll leave you to it. Here's the phone. But when you have spoken to Sarah you must go to bed for a while. It's just as well she can't see you. You look as though you have been on the razzle for days. Just like my husband, in fact.'

Rabindrah smiled at her as she left the room, closing the door behind her. His stomach churned as he lifted the receiver and dialled, dreading the news he would have to convey. And if Sarah had already left for the Mara would she be safe, alone on the long drive? It would certainly be better for her to hear about Tatu when she had Allie around to comfort her. He hoped that Gordon was right in his feeling that she would be safer in the game park. But he would have to warn Allie. Just in case.

When Hannah answered his phone call, she was decidedly cool. 'Sarah left first thing this morning. She was pretty upset.'

'I have more bad news, I'm afraid,' Rabindrah said. 'There's been a robbery at home. I discovered it when I got back. The thieves poisoned Tatu in order to get into the house. I found her dead. That's going to make it even harder, when I talk to Sarah. This thing just gets worse and worse!'

'Oh God, Rabindrah! I'm so sorry. I know how much you both loved that dog. What was taken?'

'Nothing of value – they were looking for film and documents on this case I've been working on.'

'I read the paper this morning, and I have to congratulate you.' Hannah heard the misery in Rabindrah's voice and felt for him. 'That's quite a coup and it took guts, but I think you should have kept Sarah in the picture.'

'You're right. It was a stupid mistake. And I apologise for arriving so late last night with my uncle. I shouldn't have imposed on you, but I had to see Sarah.'

'Are you in danger over this?'

'Let's say I may be a target for certain politicians involved in the poaching and smuggling. That was the main reason I didn't want Sarah back in Nairobi. With good reason, as it turns out. There are people who would like to get their hands on the rest of the information I have, before it comes to light.'

'I don't know what to say.' Hannah was shocked. 'Only, be careful. And make your peace with Sarah. She is very upset, it's true, but only because of her anxiety about you, and the fact that you've been holding back on the truth. I do have one piece of good news, though. Lila phoned from London about half an hour ago. She is safely installed in Camilla's flat.'

'Thanks, Hannah. That is a big consolation,' Rabindrah said. 'I'll talk to Sarah later.'

'Keep in touch,' Hannah said. 'And good luck.'

Rabindrah stood in the shower for a long time, holding the hose and sluicing the fatigue and misery from his body. Feeling a little better, he sat down at a table and opened the draft of his next report, but after a time the letters waved and shifted in front of him, forcing him to stagger to the bed and lie down. Sleep claimed him instantly, and it was late afternoon when Maureen knocked on his door.

'Gordon is home,' she said. 'He sold your story on. It will be all over the London papers tomorrow, and Kiberu is about to make his statement on television. This is big, big news.'

'This is more shit around the fan than I've seen for years,' Gordon said.

'And the second part of your report will run tomorrow. That will put away two major crooks. Ministers Eliud Muruthi and Walter Ndegwa were handcuffed and frogmarched out of their government offices an hour ago. Both have links to Manjit Singh's companies operating in the Far East. I've brought new documents that were delivered to me about an hour ago, but Kiberu says we need more evidence on the third fellow you've been after. Moses Gacharu has extra powerful connections. I don't think the Mzee or his cronies will meddle in his affairs, unless there is a watertight case against him. This is going to be a very murky pond to fish in.'

'I'll need about an hour to finish tomorrow's piece,' Rabindrah said. 'Look, here's the press conference starting.'

They sat in front of the television, watching as flash bulbs popped and Johnson Kiberu made his speech, citing the arrest of Manjit and Harjeet Singh, naming the two African politicians, and detailing the amount of illegal game trophies and the ivory uncovered in the Mombasa go-down. There would be more disclosures to come within the next few days, he said, and no mercy would be shown in handing down sentences.

'Looks good,' Rabindrah said. 'I'll go and finish tomorrow's piece now, and maybe I can—'

'I have some other news for you,' Gordon interrupted. 'You are leaving for another assignment, early in the morning.'

'No. No, I want to keep my hand in on this. I can't drop it, now that I've come this far,' said Rabindrah.

'Out of the country for a while, is an order from your editor's office.' Gordon would brook no argument. 'There is going to be a massive mopping-up operation now. I will keep you advised and you can send me your comments by phone or telex to be edited and printed as usual. I've arranged for you to go to the Seychelles. To follow up on the consequences of Albert René's coup in June. Then on to Mauritius and Reunion. An economic and political report on Indian Ocean Islands, with the emphasis on tourism.'

'That's not news, Gordon!' Rabindrah protested. 'I'm onto the biggest case we've written up for a long time. You can't send me on a detour to the seaside.'

'I've discussed this with Kiberu and the chief of police,' Gordon said. 'There are reasons for you to duck out of sight. Another attempt on your life would be one too many. Third time lucky and all that. I'm not planning on losing the best member of my staff. You need to think of Sarah, too. Maybe she would like to join you in the Seychelles while you are there. The endemic wildlife of the islands would be a good distraction for her. I want you both safe, as skilled professionals, and very close friends.'

'Thank you.' Rabindrah offered no further argument, moved by the kindness in Gordon's rough tone.

'I'll bring you back if something extraordinary happens,' Gordon said. 'Now, let's get tomorrow's story out of the way, after which you should try Sarah on the radio. She must be in camp by now and I'm sure she has reached the stage where she will be happy to talk to you. No more secrets, though.'

'No more secrets,' Rabindrah said, as he sat down at the typewriter, smiling.

Chapter 18

Kenya, October 1977

Sarah arrived in the Mara, tired and dusty, to find Hugo sitting in the shade of the mess tent with his notebook and typewriter.

'Welcome back.' He smiled and stood up, pushing a hand through his unruly hair. He was sunburnt after his days at the coast, with a scattering of new freckles on his face and arms.

'My goodness,' she said. 'You are barely recognisable from the person who arrived here a few weeks ago, looking like a—'

'A pasty academic, with milk-white skin and no hope of surviving in the bush.'

'That's about it,' she said, lifted by the sound of her own laughter. 'Anyhow, you certainly look good now. Oh! You've turned scarlet. I always thought I was the only person in the world to go that fierce shade of red.'

'It's another thing we have in common, then,' he said, embarrassed by both the compliment and her observation. 'Allie and Erope are out looking for Lara and the cubs. When we heard the news on the radio, we thought you were going to be in Nairobi for a few days. Looks like Rabindrah uncovered a major poaching operation. What a coup, or a scoop, as they call it. You must be proud of him. Where is he now?'

'I saw him at Langani last night. On his way back to Nairobi.'

'Sit down and I'll get you a cold drink. Or tea, if you are really thirsty.'

'I'll go and stow my stuff first.'

Sarah escaped to her tent. She could not face the prospect of talking about her husband, and when she had put her belongings away she sat on her bed, staring out at the river. It was a relief to be back in camp, with only animals to think about. Everything else was too raw. She would take her pictures, lose herself in her work. She had done it before, up in

297

Turkana. After the baby. Her mind skittered away from another painful subject. She gathered up her cameras and notebooks and returned to the mess tent.

'Ahmed is rustling up tea,' Hugo said. 'You probably want to save Rabindrah's heroic exploits for later, when you can tell us all at the same time.'

'Good idea. So, tell me what has been going on while I was away.'

'Allie and Erope have found a new female with two cubs, much younger than Lara's,' Hugo said. 'Not far away, although the mother has been moving her young frequently. She's not as good a hunter as Lara, so she has to leave them for longer when she goes out looking for food.'

'I'd love to see her. Has she got a name yet?' Sarah asked.

'Isis,' Hugo said with a grin. 'Because of her smouldering black eyeliner.' He tidied his papers into a neat pile, and picked up his notebooks. 'Shall we go in your car? The other one is a real bone-rattler.'

Sarah breathed in the smell of dust and hot scrubland and listened to the insects and birds, and a kind of serenity enveloped her. Nobody needed to know how bad it had all become in her other world.

'There is something about it that gets to you, isn't there?' Hugo said. 'Makes you feel better, no matter what is going on. I haven't been here that long, but I understand it already.'

'Is it that obvious?' Sarah heard the concern in his comment.

'Only to very perspicacious people,' he said. 'And those kind are extremely discreet. Can I help at all?'

'I can't talk about this. I'm sorry.' She could not break down now. She would not.

'I'm not looking for information,' Hugo assured her. 'I only want to remind you that you are with friends who care about you deeply. That's all. No prying.'

'Thanks.' It was all she felt able to say.

'Look – there is Isis, at the edge of that thicket. Isn't she a beautiful specimen?'

Sarah had her camera at the ready as Hugo approached slowly.

'She's less relaxed than the others, so I won't go any closer,' he said, stopping some distance away. 'Allie and Erope have obviously gone on to look at something else. I can see the tyre marks where they turned.'

They sat watching the cheetah. She was smaller and leaner than Lara, and her two cubs were almost invisible in the dappled honey of the long grass. She looked up at the car as it came to a halt, watchful, her tail flicking slightly to betray her uneasiness, the golden eyes ringed with their black Egyptian-style outlines, gazing with regal disdain straight into the camera. The cubs stirred, their tiny heads and paws pressing and nuzzling against her as they suckled, the mantles of grey-white fur acting as a perfect camouflage.

'Did she only have two, or has she lost some of her litter?' Sarah kept her voice low.

'Allie thinks she might have had more, but we have only seen these ones. Others could have died or been taken by predators. She's very young. Erope thinks this could be her first litter.'

Sarah stood up carefully to get a better view from the open roof space. The click of the shutter made the animal flinch and flatten her ears against her elegant head, but she did not move away.

'Wonderful. Come on, Isis. Let's have your best profile.'

As if she understood, the cheetah turned to look away into the distance, more at ease now with her human visitors, as Sarah took several more shots.

'She's purring.' Sarah gazed through her lens with delight.

The cubs had finished feeding and they began a game of tag with their mother's tail, jumping and tumbling and worrying the ringed end. Isis cleaned them with her rough tongue, turning them over with her paw, grooming every inch of their bodies as the camera shutter continued to click. Then she set out across the plain, leaving her young curled up in the deep shade, out of sight and sleeping.

As they made notes and took more photographs, Hugo talked with enthusiasm of life in the Mara and his pleasure at contributing to Allie's work. He asked Sarah no questions about herself and she offered no information, but she felt a great weight lifting from her as she looked out over the baked grassland and watched the animals going about the age-old business of searching for food and water. When the sun had disappeared below the horizon Isis returned, and they were glad to see traces of blood on her muzzle, and the bulge of a full belly. As she disappeared into the thicket they started the car and drove back to camp.

Allie and Erope were already in the mess tent and they sat together in the cool of the evening.

'What's the news from Rabindrah?' Allie asked, but after Sarah's stilted description of his experiences she dropped the subject and they drifted away to enjoy the benefit of hot showers and the pleasure of freshly laundered, dust-free clothes. They were finishing dinner when the radio gasped into life. Sarah stood up as soon as she heard Rabindrah's voice on the line.

'I can't talk to him now,' she said, flushing under Allie's questioning gaze. 'Tell him I'm fine, but I've gone to bed. We'll talk tomorrow.' Without further comment, she walked out into the darkness in the direction of her tent.

'What's going on, Rabindrah?' Allie asked, when she had delivered Sarah's message. 'She's been very quiet all evening, and she bolted as soon as she heard your voice.'

Rabindrah kept his explanations short, but he felt obliged to tell Allie of the attempted shooting on the previous evening, and to describe the robbery in Nairobi, the attack on Chege and Tatu's death.

'This is awful news,' Allie said. 'Sarah ought to hear this from you direct. Are you all right? What about security?'

'I'm fine. Gordon is sending me to the Seychelles tomorrow, to interview President René on the way things have been affected by his coup in June. Kiberu wants me out of the limelight in Nairobi for a few days.' He tried for a moment to lighten his tone. 'I'm beginning to feel like a hitman who has been sent off to cool his heels after a high profile hatchet job. Sarah's safety is my main worry, though. Please don't let her go off anywhere alone. Maybe you could alert the local park officials — tell them there may be poachers in the area and they should be extra vigilant. And perhaps she could drive with Erope for the next few days. He would spot anything unusual within miles. I'm sorry, Allie. I've made a mess of things all round.'

'You've been extremely courageous, at grave danger to yourself,' Allie said. 'I admire you for it, but I think I would have been furious if Dan had taken on something like this without telling me.'

'I know, I know. I got that completely wrong. But you can tell Sarah that I've spoken to Lila, who is safely ensconced in Camilla's London flat. Tom is finding her something to do, so she should be fine for the moment. That is one good thing, at least. And I'm staying with Gordon and Maureen for tonight.'

'I'll pass on that news,' Allie said. 'And I'm sure she'll come round. By tomorrow she will be counting the hours until you get back. How long will you be away?'

'I'm not sure. A week or so,' Rabindrah said. 'I'm doing a series of interviews about the coup. Reasons for it, what effect it has had on tourism, and the economy generally. The flight leaves tomorrow, around midday. She might like to join me for a few days. It's not far, in terms of flying.'

'Sounds like an ideal break after all this. I'll get her to call in the morning, although I don't relish the idea of telling her about the raid on your house, and the dog. Thank God neither one of you was there when those thugs turned up. Be careful, Rabindrah.'

Allie replaced the receiver and turned around to see that she was alone. She sat down beside the fire to reflect, before picking up the whisky bottle and two glasses and walking down to Sarah's tent.

'*Hodi!* Can I come in?'

'Of course.' Sarah pulled back the flap and came out to sit with Allie under the flysheet. She raised her eyebrows as Allie poured a stiff measure for each of them.

'This looks serious,' she said, her voice shaky, her smile too fixed. 'What did Rabindrah have to say?'

Allie repeated the news she had heard as Sarah gulped down her whisky.

'He knows that as far as you are concerned he is a first class pillock – although he didn't say so in quite those words,' Allie said. 'He's desperately sorry, and you must admit that he had reason to be worried about you. Your house boy was badly beaten up, and your dog poisoned. Thank God you weren't in the house when they came.'

'It's not that simple,' Sarah said. 'There are things I can't tell you about this situation. Things that have shown me how much Rabindrah has changed. Beyond recognition, in fact.'

'I know his secrecy has hurt you, but that's the way men are,' Allie said. 'Thinking that they are protecting their loved ones by not telling them what's going on, and driving them crazy instead. But more serious is the continuing threat to Rabindrah's life, while he is working on this case. His courage has put him in great danger.'

'You don't understand!' Sarah jumped up. 'This is not just about Rabindrah and his anti-poaching, anti-corruption crusade. I can't explain the whole story, Allie, but he did something that compromised us both, and our closest friends too. He put everything important at risk to protect someone who didn't deserve it, and I'm not sure I can get past that. Ever.'

'Someone powerful, implicated in the poaching? Is that it?'

'I can't tell you.' Sarah shook her head in misery.

'Sarah, you should know that someone tried to shoot him.'

'Yes. In the go-down. I know about that.'

'And again, yesterday. It must have been on the way to Langani. Did he not tell you?'

'No.' A chill ran through Sarah as she realised that there were facets of the story she did not yet know, because she had not waited to hear them. 'He didn't say much about himself at all.'

'Your man has taken on some powerful and ruthless people in this investigation,' Allie said. 'And the fact that Lila's in-laws are involved makes things worse for him. Whatever he did to make you angry needs to be discussed, not suppressed. I don't deal in scaremongering, but he is still a target, just as Dan was for the poachers in the north. They would have killed him if they had found the right opportunity. Or even me. What if you send Rabindrah away with no word of love or forgiveness, and the worst happens?' Allie stood up. 'Get on the radio early tomorrow, before he leaves for the Seychelles. He is staying at the Hedleys'.'

Sarah nodded, without speaking.

'All right, kiddo. I'll hit the sack and we'll drive out together in the morning. *Chai* at five-thirty. Goodnight.'

The next day dawned, overcast, with the threat of a storm. Sarah made several attempts to contact the Hedley household, but due to the weather conditions the connection proved difficult. She drank another cup of tea and tried again but this time the radio faded completely, as the first clap of thunder rolled over the camp.

'We will try later in the morning,' Erope said. 'When the storm has passed. Right now it is almost overhead. I do not think we will be able to drive very far.'

Rabindrah would probably have left for the airport by then, but there was nothing Sarah could do. She was not sure what she wanted to say to him anyway. With a mental shrug she climbed into the Land Cruiser and headed out.

Heavy banks of cloud had gathered above the plains, to roll in black masses over the parched grassland. The air felt charged with static as the morning progressed, and the sky was split with great forks of lightning that speared the earth and sent cracks of thunder echoing across the darkening landscape. In the distance they saw a lone tree take a direct hit from a bolt of lightning, exploding in a shower of sparks as the first downpour began. There was no sign of any cheetah. Scrambling to close the roof hatch they turned and headed for the camp, hardly able to hear themselves shouting over the noise of the thunderclaps and the rain drumming on the roof. Within seconds the ground under the tyres had turned into a quagmire, and they skidded across the rutted track, the windscreen wipers battling in vain to clear a few seconds of visibility in the deluge.

Sarah wrestled with the wheel as the car careened over the wet ground, sometimes fording small, fast flowing rivers where there had only been dry gullies moments before, or getting bogged down in mud holes that had formed out of the baked, cracked earth. Twice she left Allie at the wheel and jumped out with Hugo and Erope to search for sticks and branches to set under the wheels, pushing until the muddy ground gave up its prisoner. By the time they arrived back at the camp, they were filthy and exhausted.

Things were not looking good there either. The river was rising fast, and Ahmed was concerned for the tents and the supplies. They decided to move all the equipment further away from the water. Everything seemed to be awash. Remembering a similar flash flood in Samburu years before, Allie and Sarah put the research notes and maps into wooden boxes and covered them with tarpaulins to protect them from the ravages of the storm. By four o'clock, the river had risen close to the top of its banks and the brown water roared past, with logs and debris of all kinds spinning and churning in the torrent. They began to fear that the camp might be washed away. The radio was still out of action, and they were discussing whether it might be best to abandon the camp and shelter in the vehicles away from the rising water, when the rain suddenly ceased. In the lull that followed, only the rush of the muddy river could be heard. Far away the grumble of the storm rolled off towards the Serengeti, sending out desultory flashes of sheet lightning across the slowly clearing sky. In the remaining hours of daylight they worked together, reorganising and drying out the camp where everything from papers and books to bedding and firewood had absorbed the damp, or become downright waterlogged.

As darkness approached they sat down at last, and a red, angry sun forced its head through the banks of remaining cloud, before sinking into the sodden earth. Sarah wondered where her husband was now, and whether he was thinking of her as he sat in some plush hotel in the Seychelles. Probably not. He was on a story and all else was secondary. She knew that he was genuinely contrite for not having told her about his investigation, but she was also sure that he had no regrets over his role in saving Gulab from ruin. Mulling it over, she found that she still could not accept or condone what he had done. His disregard for the law, the danger into which he had put them both by going to the sawmill, his protection of Gulab and his selfishness in involving Anthony were beyond her understanding. Worse was the loss of his own integrity. She put him out of her mind, poured herself a drink and sat down beside Hugo and Allie to immerse herself in the world whose rules she understood.

Chapter 19

The maximum security prison at Shimo la Tewa stood close to some of Mombasa's more luxurious beach hotels, but it was not a five-star establishment. In colonial times the local jail had been known as the '*Kingi Georgi Hoteli*' by the inmates. But there had been less prisoners then, the food rations were adequate, and sanitation had been properly maintained. Now, although it had an imposing entrance with large, high gates and an electrified security fence, the inside of the compound consisted of concrete cell blocks with crumbling plaster walls and corrugated iron roofs. The cells were overcrowded, the heat and humidity stultifying, and the place was infested with cockroaches and other vermin. The latrines stank of raw sewage. Open drains ran through the yards. They had been built to avoid flooding during the monsoon rains, but they were blocked up with rubbish. Stagnant water had accumulated, creating a breeding ground for mosquitoes and making the place into a certain source of malaria.

Food was in short supply, especially for remand prisoners who did not have jobs in the prison workshops, or in the grounds. Corrupt officials confiscated most of the meat allowances, and even *posho* rations were meagre. Those with families nearby were allowed to receive extra food if their relatives could afford to bring it and to bribe the guards to let it in. Without outside assistance, inmates had to survive on the portions that came from the prison kitchens.

Harjeet Singh was hungry. His belly growled constantly and his skin was a mass of bites from vermin and mosquitoes. Washing facilities were minimal. He had no clean clothes. His suit had been taken from him when he was remanded to the prison, and he had been given grimy overalls which smelled of stale sweat. His turban was infested with lice, and he longed to cut his hair and shave off his beard, casting ancient tradition out with the rest of the privileges he had lost. Since their arrest he had not seen or spoken to anyone except the guards.

His greatest concern was his father. Manjit Singh had been kept in the prison hospital for the first three days, but since his transfer to the cell that he shared with Harjeet, his health had deteriorated. He was unable to walk. The limb was encased in plaster, the foot had swelled and he was running a fever. Throughout the day and night he alternatively burned with a high temperature, or shivered under a rough blanket that had been grudgingly provided after several requests. A phial of unidentifiable tablets had been given to him but for the most part he was unable to keep them down. In between the bouts of rigors and sweating he babbled incoherently, or lay silent and drained on the narrow bed. Harjeet was convinced that his father was suffering from malaria and perhaps an infection in the broken leg. There was scant medical attention, in spite of their calls for a doctor's visit or a return to the hospital unit.

As far as Harjeet could make out, there were few Asian inmates, and he thought they would have been a soft target for the long-term Africans serving sentences for violent crimes. Not that the warders were much better. They looked on their captives with deep hostility, needing no excuse to strike out or shout and demand bribes for any small, additional rations. They were allowed outside for short periods when the rest of the inmates had been locked away. But Manjit could not move without support, and his son had to half carry him into the exercise yard, and lay him down on the ground in the shade of a scraggy pawpaw tree.

In the beginning, Manjit railed against the authorities, threatening legal action and interventions from powerful friends, demanding to see a lawyer, insisting that his family be allowed to visit him in the jail. All appeals met with a blanket refusal, and protest brought only abuse and the withdrawal of rations. They had no contact with the outside world, and as the days went by he grew weaker and less vociferous. For the past two nights, he had lain staring at the wall, tears of defeat trickling down his face into his unkempt beard. It horrified Harjeet to see his father, of whom he had always been deeply afraid, reduced to a mere shell, lying on a hard flock mattress, muttering to himself and weeping like a woman. As an only son he had lived his life in the terror of this man's shadow, but now the idea of not having that tyranny to hide behind was much, much worse.

After a week the bout of malaria passed, but it was clear that Manjit's leg was infected. Above the plaster cast, the skin was discoloured, and his foot looked tight and increasingly swollen. When anyone touched it, he shouted with pain, and the smell of rotting flesh had begun to permeate the cell.

'My father's leg is very bad. We need to see the doctor,' Harjeet said, when a guard arrived with the tin plates of gruel which constituted their breakfast.

The warder stooped over the stricken man, wrinkling his nose in disgust at the smell that rose from the encased leg.

'I do not think the doctor is coming today,' he said, straightening and preparing to leave. Suddenly, Manjit Singh's arm shot out and, with a last surge of strength, he grabbed the man by his collar, pulling himself up until their faces were level.

'I have had a message sent to my good friend and colleague Mr Moses Gacharu, telling him how you are treating me here. He is close to the President, and it will be bad for you, very bad, if the Mzee discovers how we are being treated. Keeping us locked away with no lawyer is illegal.' His eyes were glazed with madness and pain. The effect on the warder was electric, and he backed away in alarm, as Manjit continued. 'I want to see the governor. I want to be transferred back to the hospital or I will see to it, personally, that you are sent to the prison service in Isiolo, and that you never get back. I can do this. So get me the governor, or you will be sorry.'

He let go of the man's collar and fell back onto the mattress, his eyes never leaving the guard's face. The warder wiped beads of sweat from his forehead, and left the cell quickly. Manjit's breath was coming in shallow gasps as he called his son.

'Harjeet. Listen carefully to what I am telling you. When the governor comes, I will explain that Eliud Muruthi is my business partner, and Walter Ndegwa too. You know that before we left England I had arranged a meeting with Gacharu, to pay his share and finalise the next shipment. He will be coming soon. To get us out of here. To collect his money. I will tell the Governor that Gacharu will certainly have him fired, if we do not receive proper treatment.'

'You cannot threaten him, Father. He will have us beaten, or even killed.'

'No. It is more likely that he will be frightened. These powerful fellows could have him put away. And we will have our own insurance, as soon as I see Gacharu.'

'Insurance? What are you saying?'

'There is evidence of all the money transfers I have made to Muruthi and Ndegwa, into their foreign bank accounts. And notes of all my meetings and the dates on which cash was given to Gacharu. Photographs too, which I took with a small camera whenever I could. I have kept careful records, in case anything like this ever happened, but our fine partners have no idea that these papers exist. That is our insurance. Only your name does not appear on any documents, as a party to these transactions. They will not be able to prove anything against you.'

'Where? Where is this evidence?' Harjeet felt hope and panic rising in equal measure.

'The records are at home. In my personal safe.'

Harjeet balled his fists in frustration. 'What use are they over there?' he hissed. 'We are in a stinking jail in Mombasa. How can we get access to files in England? We cannot even send a message to the family in Nairobi. None of them has contacted us since that little turd turned us in. They are frightened that they will also come under suspicion, so they have abandoned us.'

'I do not believe that. They would not leave us to rot in jail,' Manjit said. 'It is the authorities that have blocked them. But your wife, Harjeet. She can get the records and hand them over to that bastard. To the journalist.'

'To him? It is because of him that we are here. He will not do anything that might help us.' Harjeet had not told his father about the threats made to Rabindrah.

'He is a reporter, Harjeet. It's the biggest story that will ever appear in his name. He will want to publish these documents and have Muruthi and his friends put away.'

'You are going to expose these men?'

'I can use these records as a bargaining chip against my own sentence. And you will be given a light term because they cannot prove anything against you, except that you were in the warehouse.' Manjit fell back against the wall and mopped his forehead with a filthy rag. 'Maybe they will even deport us. Let us go in exchange for the evidence. This Rabindrah must sell the whole story.'

'What are you talking about, Father? The papers have already run it, and more details will only help to keep us in jail. Along with these *nugus* who are part of our company. Did you not tell me that one of these fellows is close to President Kenyatta? Related even. Surely he is the best man to get us out of here.' Harjeet gazed at his father, wondering if the man was hallucinating. His words made no sense.

'Lila must give all my files to her cousin.' Manjit ignored his son's fearful pleas. 'Let him know that we have more information on the Somalis, and where they bury the tusks before they bring them to us for payment. We can use this information to help us. The Kenya Government will be glad to get their hands on this, and deport us quietly. They do not want a scandal that brings down any more politicians, or affects diplomatic relations and aid money coming into the country. And they would not want the journalist to report the conditions in which we are being held. We must get out of here, Harjeet. I cannot stay incarcerated in this place. It will kill me, and your mother too. Our entire family will be ruined. It would be better to be dead. We must – aaarrgh!' Manjit tried to move his position, and cried out involuntarily. From outside they could hear the sound of heavy steps approaching.

'Get a message to your wife.' Manjit gripped his son's arm. 'You will find a way. Bribe one of the guards. Demand that she be brought to visit you, Harjeet. Promise him money. If something happens to me, do not let them think you know anything. Use the journalist. He is very fond of his cousin. He will want to keep Lila and her family safe. You will see.'

The door of the cell was unlocked, and a large man in uniform entered with the guard, and two orderlies carrying a stretcher. He glanced down at Manjit with what passed for a smile, but there was no warmth in his expression. Harjeet was reminded of a hyena circling its fallen victim.

'Mr Singh. I am the Deputy Governor of Shimo la Tewa. The Governor is not here today, so your request was brought to me. I have just spoken on the phone to Mr Gacharu. We are now moving you back to the prison hospital.'

Harjeet stood up to accompany them, but the official stopped him.

'You will remain here,' he said.

'I must stay with him until the doctor comes. I am begging you, sir. My father's leg is bad.'

'The doctor is waiting. He will be seen straight away.'

'You said the doctor was not coming in today.' Harjeet stared accusingly at the guard. The man looked at him, a smirk on his wide lips.

'He made a mistake.' The deputy governor nodded to the orderlies. 'Bring him.'

Two men lifted Manjit onto the stretcher, ignoring his shouts of pain as they carried him away. The cell door clanged shut behind them and Harjeet was left alone, and in mortal fear. He had no great affection for his father. In fact, the idea of love had been beaten out of him from early childhood, mocked as a weakness that only women indulged in. Over the years he had been bludgeoned into obedience and a sort of dependency that had left him incapable of functioning without Manjit's orders. He would have gone insane during the past week without Manjit Singh's wild, angry eyes on him, daring him to fall apart, although the older man was fast disintegrating. Harjeet could not envisage how he would survive alone in this terrible place. His eyes filled with tears of self-pity and an image of his wife filled his mind, her long hair framing the delicate face, her great dark eyes gazing at him with a childlike hope that had gradually dimmed since the first days of their marriage.

'Lila, Lila. Help me,' he muttered. 'I will be a true husband, if you can get me out of here.'

He banged on the door of the cell, off and on throughout the morning, shouting for attention. But no one came. The day wore on endlessly, the silence broken only by the distant cries of other prisoners, and the scratchings of rats and cockroaches that scurried across the floor. A bowl of watery stew was brought in at midday, but the warder would not answer any of his questions. Night fell, and the heat abated a little, but now the mosquitoes were out in force, diving and whining around his ears until he thought he would go mad. Hours passed in a kind of delirium and he did not know what time it was when the guard finally returned, except that it was dark. Without a word he fastened shackles on Harjeet's wrists and ankles, and indicated that he should leave the cell.

Harjeet shuffled along the floodlit pathways, wondering where he was being taken. They came at last to a brightly lit building, and Harjeet realised it was the hospital. A polite orderly in a white uniform met him at the door, raising his hopes as he was brought down a corridor to the far end of the building. They passed two rooms of occupied beds, but there was no sign of Manjit Singh and he assumed his father was too ill for a general ward. The room into which he was directed was dimly lit, and a young African doctor greeted him, his expression grave.

'I am very sorry, Mr Singh. We did what we could, but . . .'

'What do you mean?' Harjeet stared at him, uncomprehendingly. 'What has happened to my father?'

'There was a problem. While we were waiting for an ambulance to bring him to the Coast General Hospital for amputation.'

'Amputation?' Harjeet felt a prickle of horror. 'Why would he need an amputation?'

'It was the only solution. Gangrene had set in. Soon it would have travelled all through his body.'

'Gangrene? But we asked for a doctor days ago. He should have been treated at once. Then it would not have been necessary to take off the leg. Is the operation over? Is he conscious? You must take me to see him.'

'I am afraid you have not understood, Mr Singh. Your father has died from septic poisoning.'

'Dead? He is dead?' Harjeet's voice rose to a bellow. 'Dead because you did not treat him in time? You are telling me that through your negligence he has died from gangrene?'

Harjeet felt the room tilt as waves of nausea engulfed him. He collapsed into a chair, holding his head between shackled hands.

'I am sorry. It happened very fast,' the doctor said. 'Nobody expected it.'

'I must see him.' Harjeet struggled to his feet, chafing against the chains that bound him. 'You must take me to him now. I have a right to see my father.' His voice rose again and an additional warder appeared from the corridor.

The doctor inclined his head, and opened the door into an adjoining room. Neon lights shone from the ceiling, bathing the area in a harsh, white light. Manjit Singh lay on a metal bed, the plaster cast removed from the leg which had swelled to a blue-black appendage, the toes sticking out incongruously from the end of the bulbous foot, the stench of the diseased limb hanging like a miasma over the room. In contrast, his face was deathly pale, the eyes still stared at the ceiling and his fingers remained clenched on the mattress.

Harjeet let out a howl of dismay as he rushed towards the bed and attempted to lift his father into his arms. But he was restrained by the orderlies, and the guard who had reappeared. Shouting his protests he was taken from the room and away from the wards, his words echoing their desolate sound, bouncing off the walls of the long corridor.

'Murderers! You have killed him! Killed him!'

He was placed in a windowless room in another wing of the prison, and left there for a number of hours that he could not estimate. There was no furniture. One dim bulb in an iron cage was attached to the ceiling. He sat on the floor, his mind replaying the gruesome sight that he had witnessed. Harjeet could imagine his father, thrashing and screaming in vain. But they had allowed him to die, and he himself could be next. He might be left here in this cell indefinitely, without food or water. Forgotten.

Fear coursed through Harjeet's body, and he felt his bowels loosening. There was no toilet or pan in the room, and he was aware of the vile stench from his overalls, but he was past caring. Despair overcame him, and he began to weep uncontrollably, rocking himself back and forth, banging his head against the wall of the cell until he reached a trance-like state of hysteria. He had no idea how much time had passed when the door opened. A man in a well-tailored suit was standing there, accompanied by two policemen in uniform. He took out a handkerchief, and held it delicately across his nose.

'I want to see a lawyer.' Harjeet looked at him with dull eyes. 'I know my rights. And I want Mr Eliud Muruthi to be informed about this. And Minister Ndegwa. What has happened here is beyond the law, and there will be trouble when it is made public. I am a British citizen. I want to see the British High Commissioner. I want a lawyer.'

'Mr Singh, I am Johnson Kiberu. I understand your father has died. My condolences. You are to be transferred to another prison. As for the men you have mentioned, I would advise you not to ask for them again. They have been arrested. They are being held in Nairobi, and I understand they are your associates.'

'What?' Had this Kiberu found alternative evidence? Harjeet's sense of terror rose. 'What time is it? What day?'

'It is Sunday morning. Your father's body has been prepared for cremation. That is what you would prefer, I believe. The local Sikh community has kindly agreed to take care of the formalities, since you are leaving Mombasa. These *askaris* will take you to the bathroom and see that you have clean clothes.'

'Leave Mombasa? Where am I going? I need to be at my father's cremation. To light the pyre.'

'I'm afraid that will not be possible, since you are in prison. You will now be transferred to a secure unit in Nairobi to await trial,' Kiberu said. 'Please go with the guards.'

Harjeet allowed himself to be led to a bathroom, and stripped. The shackles were removed and he was permitted to have a shower, the first wash since his incarceration in this hellish place. He scrubbed and tore at his skin until it was raw, and poured disinfectant and soap over his infested scalp so that the stinging sensation brought involuntary tears to his eyes. A clean prison overall was given to him, but he was obliged to throw away his lice-ridden turban and tie his hair into a knot. Then he was handcuffed once more and taken to the governor's office where Johnson Kiberu was waiting.

'This case is now under my ministry's jurisdiction,' Kiberu said. 'I will be supervising the proceedings personally from today.'

Moments later Harjeet was bundled into the back of a black car with tinted windows and a uniformed chauffeur. The gates of the prison opened slowly, and the car slid through, followed by an escort of armed police. They turned in convoy onto the main road and headed for the airport. A small plane was waiting on the airstrip and the prisoner was strapped into the back seat. When Johnson Kiberu had boarded, the aircraft took off and the ground fell away below them. Harjeet was still not sure about this politician's motives, or the reason for a transfer to Nairobi. Dazed and frightened, he tried to figure out whether he was a colleague of Muruthi or Ndegwa. Or Moses Gacharu. Or perhaps he was another player who wanted his share of the spoils and needed to suppress any possible evidence. They were all the same in the end. Corrupt, waiting for their chance to make money and stash it away, outside the country. This one looked sophisticated, spoke like a well-educated fellow and was wearing expensive clothes. A pinprick of hope pierced the chaos in his mind as someone passed him a mug of tea and a packet in which he found sandwiches.

Johnson Kiberu leaned back in his seat and closed his eyes, pleased with the outcome of his little coup. He had been monitoring events in Shimo la Tewa since the two Singhs had been placed in isolation to await trial, but he was infuriated by the fact that the older man had been allowed to die. It was already too late when an informer had telephoned earlier, from the prison hospital. A nursing orderly. The *wahindi* with the bad leg was back in the hospital wing, very sick. Johnson had flown to Mombasa immediately, his arrival at the jail taking everyone by surprise, his anger turning the prison officials into cowering flunkies as he raged at the fact that their treatment of the dead man could be considered illegal, and might result in the case being dismissed.

Johnson suspected that Harjeet was merely an errand boy. A weakling under the thumb of his father. Would the older man have trusted his son enough to give him full access to his business records? He might not have had a choice, although there could be other relatives in England who were privy to his business dealings. Certainly Gulab Singh was just a pawn, although his position was not clear and he was being watched. And then there was Rabindrah. Where had he gone after his return from Mombasa? Johnson had tried to contact him at his office and at home, but without success. Perhaps it was time to talk to Gulab Singh about the fire at the sawmill. A conflagration caused by many gallons of flammable material, and no witnesses. Meanwhile he would put Harjeet in a safe place and let him stew, although he would have to allow him a telephone call and a lawyer. He did not want the case to be thrown out of court for incorrect procedures. With a satisfied sigh, Johnson Kiberu gave himself up to sleep.

Gulab heard the wailing as soon as it started. He jumped from his bed and ran down the stairs to find Anjit, kneeling on the ground, clutching the phone.

'What is it? Are you ill? What has happened? Stop your shrieking, woman, and speak to me!'

Anjit let go of the telephone so that it dangled above the carpet. Still sobbing, she allowed her husband to help her up and then she gave him the news that made his blood run cold.

'It was Harjeet. He has been transferred to Nairobi. Manjit has died in the prison in Mombasa. Harjeet wants you to find him a lawyer. He is telling you to be very careful, Gulab.'

'This cannot be true!' Gulab's anxiety burgeoned into panic. 'Where is Harjeet now? Can we see him?'

'Visitors are refused. Only lawyer is allowed.' She burst into a fresh storm of sobbing. 'Gulab, husband, I am thinking what may happen to us. If we are safe or not.'

Gulab returned to his room and dressed quickly. Then he took a small holdall from the wardrobe, threw some clothes into it and went down to his study. He closed the door, and leant against it, his breath coming fast. He could not believe that Manjit was dead. That man could wriggle out of any situation. He would simply oil the machinery of graft, and engineer his release and that of his son. Anjit had urged her husband to contact their lawyer after the arrests and to push for a visit to the prison, but a letter asking for visitation rights had brought no response. And now this! Had Manjit died of natural causes, or had he been disposed of by his partners? Gulab took out a handkerchief, and mopped at his forehead.

The police had been here once, to question him about the fire at the sawmill. He believed he had dealt with that successfully. No one had seen him near Nanyuki, and Anjit had confirmed that he had been at home with her that evening. But the ivory and other goods had been destroyed, and Manjit's business partners would be angry at the loss of such valuable assets. These African shareholders must have guessed the reason behind the fire at the mill. He might even have to persuade them that he had saved them from suspicion, even if they had lost money. So far, no one had contacted him, but perhaps they were the politicians who had been imprisoned.

He tried to recall if he had ever seen any of these shadowy characters. The *WaBenzi*, they were called, because they were rich and powerful and travelled in the latest Mercedes Benz models, while their relatives and constituents struggled to find enough food and water to survive. Gulab was aware that there were top people in the government who had been behind many of Manjit's deals, but he had never known their identities, nor did he wish to. Now he wondered whether one of these men thought that he, Gulab, could identify him. Could that have been the reason behind the shooting at the food stall, on the way to Nanyuki? What if some murderous thug had already been following him, and that bullet had been meant for him? His fear erupted in an agonised groan. He had to leave Nairobi. If he went away, disappeared, maybe they would leave his family alone.

Staring out of the window he found it impossible to reason, as terror shredded his thought processes. Would his enemies expect him to make a

315

run for it? Were they watching the borders? Entry into England was out of the question on his so-called British passport, and Uganda was no longer a place for anyone of Asian origin. He had relatives in Tanzania, near Arusha. Distant cousins. Would he put them at risk if he went there? Tanzania was the best option, but he could not use the main route from Nairobi to Arusha since the borders between the two countries had been closed.

His hands shaking, Gulab took out a road map and studied it. He might be able to reach Tanzania without potential road blocks if he travelled via Magadi. It was not an enormous distance – three hours or so to Lake Magadi, then west to the shores of Lake Natron, which straddled the border. There would be little traffic on that route, and anyone who was looking for him would not expect him to go that way. He was sure he would be able to bribe his way across at that point, if he was stopped. Everybody in this country had their price. Once safely into Tanzania, he could drive to Arusha without alerting anyone to his presence.

He put the map into his briefcase. Then he opened his safe, took out a wad of dollars in cash that Manjit had given him, to pay the poachers bringing trophies to the sawmill. Wrapping the money in a turban he opened his holdall and pushed it into the bottom of the bag. Then he called his wife into the study.

'Anjit, I have to go away for a few days,' he said, dreading her reaction. It would have been easier to simply disappear, but he needed her to cover for him as long as possible. He had to put as much distance as he could between himself and Nairobi before anyone realised he was gone. When his wife began to wail again, he put a hand over her mouth to silence her, then spoke urgently.

'Be quiet, woman. I will only be away for a short time, and one of our sons can come and stay with you until I return. Yes, Arjan can come down from Nanyuki. Once I have gone you will telephone him, and tell him to come here. I must leave at once.'

'Where are you going? And why?' She pushed his hand away, refusing to display her traditional respect for his decisions. 'This is all Rabindrah's doing. With his ambition and his unsuitable wife he has betrayed the whole family.'

'No, you are wrong. Rabindrah has done his best to help us.' Gulab did not want his nephew to take the blame for a mess that was not of his making. 'He went with me to the sawmill and set fire to the illegal ivory and other goods that I was storing there. That is where we went the night after Manjit was arrested.'

'Gulab! I do not understand! Why would you be doing these things?'

'You know very well where our extra money has come from.' Gulab sighed with exasperation. 'It is only since Lila married that we have been able to live normally again. Pay our bills, continue as before and take money from Manjit for the services I gave him. For the shed and the lorries. That was the price I paid for Lila's future. Rabindrah did not betray us, he tried to protect us. It is only because of him that we are safe from the police. There is no proof now that I was involved with Manjit and his smuggling. But his partners . . .'

Anjit gazed at her husband with horror. 'What will happen to us, husband? Will they arrest us, or kill us all?'

'Some high-up government officials are involved in this. I think it is the ones who have been put in jail. They know Manjit used my sawmill to hide his ivory, but if I am gone there is no reason for them to make trouble for you or the rest of our family. You will stay here and act normally. If anyone comes around looking for me, Arjan can tell them I am away for a few days on business.'

'But what if you do not come back? What if something happens to you?' Fresh tears welled. 'I must be able to speak to someone, husband!'

'Anjit, you can trust no one. Not even our sons. I will contact you when I arrive where I am going. And in a little while you will join me.'

'Where? Where are you going to, Gulab?'

'It is better you do not know.' She would not be able to withstand any interrogation and he realised that he could not tell her the truth. 'I will be quite safe, I promise you. But if anything should go wrong . . .' He paused as she clutched his sleeve. 'If something should happen to me, go to Indar. And Rabindrah. They will help you. I must leave now.'

It was difficult to know whether or not he had been followed. Traffic in the city was heavy and he could not keep watch all the time, but he was unable to identify any one vehicle keeping up with his progress. He did not drive fast, aware that he must not draw attention to himself. The last thing he needed was to be stopped by some officious policeman. Once outside the city limits, however, he speeded up and headed for the Magadi turnoff. The road brought him to the edge of the Rift Valley, leaving the cooler air of the uplands behind and plunging in tight corkscrew turns down the steep cliff onto the plains below. He did not notice the spectacular views that opened out in front of him. There were plenty of reminders of unwary motorists having come to grief on this route. The remains of numerous upturned lorries and wrecked cars lay at the bottom of the escarpment, silent witnesses to a momentary lapse of concentration.

The land turned from green to brown as he reached the plains. Heat shimmered over white rocks that shelved upwards, and the landscape sizzled like some alien planet from another galaxy. In the distance the thrusting mass of Ol Donyo Nyokie rose into the sky, and the road wound its way through cones of dormant volcanoes. Three and a half hours later, parched with thirst and sweating profusely, Gulab made the first stop on his journey. Lake Magadi was an alkaline lake surrounded by volcanic hills, with the Nguruman Escarpment rising up on its western flank, covered in green forests from which fresh river water soaked down into the thirsty land below. High temperatures accelerated the evaporation of the salted volcanic water, turning the surface of the lake into a vista of white soda blocks. The lake itself, crusted with salt crystals and soda ash, glowed in the suffocating heat. The Magadi Soda Company operated a business transporting ash to Mombasa, where it was then shipped out to factories and used to make glass, detergents, toothpaste, dyes, and even sherbet for lollipops. Flamingo, heron, pelican and spoonbill flocked to the lake's sulphurous bounty, staining the landscape a deep pink around its shores.

The place reeked of sulphur and Gulab choked as he rolled down the window. The dusty air swirled around him like a furnace, searing his lungs each time he took a breath. He pulled up outside a *duka* in the small town that had grown up around the lake and went into the welcome dimness of the shop. Ordering a sandwich and a bottle of Coca Cola, he sat on a stool at the counter, wondering if he had done the right thing in choosing this tortuous route. The remoteness of his surroundings made him uneasy. He seemed to be the only human abroad. The heat was unbearable and he was tempted to stop for an hour or so and rest, but he could not imagine any place that would be cool enough to allow sleep. In addition he wanted to reach Lake Natron and cross into Tanzania as soon as possible. He was also concerned about a lorry that had been behind him since he had come down onto the plains. It had not tried to overtake and was probably travelling to Magadi quite legitimately. There was, after all, nowhere else to go on this road.

He bought several bottles of water and left the shop, coming out into the boiling afternoon, blinded for a few seconds as he fumbled for his sunglasses. Checking for any sight of the lorry as he left the town, he was relieved to see that there was no other vehicle on the road. His spirits rose with each mile he put between himself and Nairobi and he tried turning on the radio, but there was only static so he hummed a tune. He did not want to think of Anjit and his children, particularly Lila whom he had so shamefully betrayed. They were better off without him for the present. He began to ascend a rocky escarpment where the road surface was rough, and he had to grip the steering wheel more tightly as he negotiated the sharp bends. As he approached a particularly steep rising curve, the ground falling away on his right into the white glare of the lake, a rock suddenly bounced onto the bonnet of the car and hit the windscreen, making starred, jagged lines across his vision. He swerved, jammed on the brakes, and rounded the corner to see the lorry facing him, taking up the whole road. It began to accelerate, heading straight for him. Wrestling with the steering wheel, his mouth open in a scream, he felt the impact as his car was lifted into the air. Then he was turning and tumbling over and down the cliff edge, the disc of the sun revolving outside his window, glass shards flying at him. He heard a bang, and a roar of orange flame. Then nothing.

Chapter 20

Kenya, October 1977

'Sarah! I couldn't reach you before I left.' Rabindrah could hear the crackle on the line. 'I tried, but your radio had packed up. I gather there was a storm in the area. How are things in the Mara? How are you?'

'Fine. I'm at Narok. I didn't think I would be able to get you from the camp. How long will you be there?'

'I've interviewed President René and other members of the new government. Also businessmen and people involved in the tourist industry. I'm sorry you didn't come for a few days. The bird life and the marine parks are magnificent. I thought a week here would be too long, but I've been bowled over by the beauty of the place, in spite of murky political issues. I'm planning to move on to Mauritius tomorrow, unless you can take a break and join me here. The endemic wildlife is extraordinary, and the flora too.' He looked at the sea, glittering blue in the soft air, the glassy horizon broken by the outline of Silhouette Island in the distance. 'It would be a good place for us to talk. Coup or no coup, Seychelles is a sort of paradise.'

'Rabindrah, I have some bad news,' she broke in. 'I've been trying to get hold of you since yesterday.'

'What is it? Are you all right?'

'It's Gulab,' she said. 'He has been killed in a car crash. I'm so sorry.'

'A crash? Where? How did it happen?'

'He was only found two days ago. He skidded off the road and down an escarpment between Magadi and Lake Natron. Rabindrah?'

'Magadi and Natron?' He was aware that he had stupidly repeated her words. 'What on earth was he doing there?'

'No one seems to know. It was Indar who contacted me with the news and you should ring him after this. He is very upset. I had to phone

Gordon to find out where you were staying and then the phone wasn't working too well in Narok, so it has taken me a while to get hold of you.'

'When is the cremation?'

'Today.' She paused and her tone changed, increasing the distance between them. 'Anjit has told me it will not be necessary for me to attend. I suppose it's hardly surprising. And there's more. Manjit Singh has also died in the prison. I gather he had a gangrene infection.'

'Manjit is dead too?' Rabindrah tried to absorb what she had told him. 'Where is Harjeet?'

'Still in jail, but he has been moved to Nairobi.'

'I'll try and make the plane tomorrow,' he said. 'I suppose Gordon knows about all this?'

'Oh yes. And Kiberu, too.' Her laugh was hard, charged with fear. 'He must be keeping a body count by now. I think you are probably better off sticking to your island tour.'

'No, I'll try to get back tomorrow. Meantime, I think you should stay in the Mara.'

'Is it really true what Allie told me? That someone tried to shoot you?' There was a note of hysteria in the question. 'That Tatu was poisoned and our house was raided?'

'Sarah, Sarah.' He groaned, knowing he would now have to tell her the real dangers to which they were exposed. 'You might not be safe in Nairobi. It's possible that Gulab did not have an accident.'

'What on earth are you trying to say now?'

'I think someone tried to shoot at either Gulab or me on the day we went to the sawmill, although I can't be sure. And I don't know what he was doing driving near Magadi, but it would be easy in that remote area for someone to run him off the road with nobody around to see it.'

'That's horrible. I can't believe such a thing. In fact, I don't know what to believe any more. It all seems totally unreal.'

'It's not unreal at all, I'm afraid, and we cannot take any chances. There are high-profile politicians and businessmen mixed up in all this. They may fear that Manjit and Harjeet have evidence that could put them away. They might have been afraid of Gulab, too. Who knows how many people were aware of what he was hiding at the sawmill? And Kiberu has warned me that I am still at risk. That's why I didn't talk to you about the raid and the investigation in the first place. And that is why Gordon has sent me here.' The line began to hiss and fade before he could hear her reply. 'Sarah!' He was shouting into the receiver. 'Stay in the Mara, please. Sarah? Can you hear me?'

But the line was dead. He spent the next hour telephoning Indar and then Anjit Singh whose reactions to his sympathetic words were decidedly cool. There was nothing to be done but to wait for the first flight to Nairobi. In the afternoon he lay in the shade of a palm tree, watching people dozing in the tropical sun or strolling on the white beach, unaware that there was a life unravelling a few feet away from them. He tried to recall when he had last felt completely at ease, carefree and happy, but any trace of lightness seemed to have escaped him a long, long time ago.

When he stepped off the plane in Nairobi, he was surprised to find a policeman at his side.

'Please come with me, sir. I will take your passport and clear you through immigration.'

'I don't need to give anyone my passport,' Rabindrah said, uneasily. 'I'll go straight to immigration myself.'

'Mr Kiberu is waiting in the VIP lounge, sir. With Mr Hedley.' The policeman was deferential, but his impatience was barely concealed. 'Please also give me your baggage receipts, so that I can find your luggage.'

In the lounge Kiberu stood up and held out his hand. 'Welcome back. I hope you found time to enjoy the islands.'

'I wasn't expecting a welcome home committee,' Rabindrah said.

'I'm sorry about your uncle,' Gordon said. 'Sarah told me she spoke to you on the phone. She's waiting for you at home.'

'I hoped she would be in the Mara,' Rabindrah said.

'There is a police guard on your place,' Gordon said. 'She insisted on coming back. But before you leave for the house, there are a couple of things that Johnson wants to discuss with you.'

The minister gestured for them to sit down and a waiter appeared with coffee and biscuits. When they were alone once more he settled his rotund form into a chair and pressed his fingers into a steeple.

'You have already been told that Manjit Singh is dead.'

'Yes. Sarah told me that,' Rabindrah said.

'He died of gangrene. Apparently.'

'Apparently?' Rabindrah pinched the bridge of his nose, hoping to ease the pressure of a headache, shrinking from any further suggestions of violent consequences within his family.

'I believe it was a case of neglect. Our investigations have also led us to think that your uncle's death was not an accident.' Kiberu watched Rabindrah closely. 'It is possible that he was also involved with Manjit Singh, and that he was the target of other partners still at large. That is why we find his death suspicious in these circumstances.' He held up a hand as Rabindrah was about to speak. 'It is unnecessary to defend him. The police have stated that his car was probably pushed off the road. And you, too, are still at personal risk.'

'I thought you had rounded up all those involved in this investigation. If they are in jail along with Harjeet, and his father is dead, then why would I be at risk? And what can I do about it, anyway? I knew from the start that this story would put me in a dangerous position, personally. But surely that is over now. At least until they come to trial.'

'Ah. That is the problem,' Kiberu said. 'There is one of the company directors whom we have not yet been able to arrest. Moses Gacharu has been more clever in hiding his funds. I am certain that Manjit Singh kept records of his financial dealings with his African partners, but in order to prove their involvement I need those papers. Harjeet is afraid for his life, and with good reason. The man will not talk. Not even to a lawyer. He is terrified that he, too, will be murdered if he says a single word to anyone. Except you.'

'Why me?' Rabindrah felt himself being sucked further down into the quagmire of his own making. 'From Harjeet's point of view I must be the reason for all his present misfortunes.'

'He says he has information that may help us, but he will only disclose it to you.' The minister raised questioning eyebrows, but Rabindrah made no comment. 'Perhaps you would visit him in the prison. Otherwise, as I am sure you are aware, other members of your family may be in jeopardy, and I may not be able to protect them. He is willing to talk to you under one condition.'

'A condition?' Rabindrah had heard the subtle implication that resembled a threat.

'If he tells you what he knows, he wants a guarantee that his wife's family and his own will not be further investigated. He insists that none of them knew anything about poaching or illegal exports.'

'I'm inclined to believe that,' Rabindrah said.

'Then you are more naive than I had supposed,' Kiberu said smoothly. 'I would find it hard to accept, for example, that Gulab Singh was an innocent bystander. The fire at his sawmill was immediately after the seizure of the cargo in Mombasa, and was certainly a case of arson, according to the police. Perhaps he was hiding more goods in that shed. And we have no way of knowing whether any of Harjeet's British relatives are connected with this operation. You must realise that there are some prominent names who would like to prevent the whole investigation from spreading further. We need solid evidence to convict the main players with long sentences. One or two are in the President's office, and even related to him. Although the Mzee, of course, is completely unaware of their criminal activity.'

'Are you able or willing to give the guarantee that Harjeet Singh is asking for?' Rabindrah's mouth was flooded with bitterness as he asked the question. His entire life had been turned upside down, he was in personal danger, and yet the principles for which he had risked his life and damaged his marriage had already come down to deals and protection for the corrupt and the powerful.

'Yes, I am in a position to obtain the guarantee if I so wish.'

'Why don't you tell Harjeet this yourself?' Rabindrah's disgust was growing.

'For some reason, he does not trust me.' Kiberu's smile was slightly menacing. 'So, if you are agreeable, I will take you to the prison now and see that you are escorted home afterwards.'

'Do you have an opinion on this, Gordon?' Rabindrah turned to his friend.

'I don't see another way of bringing this thing to a close. We have an agreement that the paper will be the first to receive and print all the evidence there is, and we will be given information before any other source, as the case proceeds.' Gordon shrugged. 'If Muruthi and Ndegwa are convicted, along with Gacharu and others that Johnson has been investigating, it will frighten off the smaller fry. And the President has agreed to talks about better protection of elephant and rhino, and a larger budget for anti-poaching units in the National Parks and game reserves.'

'Let's go,' Rabindrah said wearily, although he was not sure he could function coherently for much longer.

The interview room in the jail was painted green and lit with fluorescent lights, making Harjeet Singh's unhealthy pallor more noticeable. Dressed in a prison jumpsuit, he had been given a turban and allowed personal toiletries, pens and paper. His eyes were sunken in his thin face and he sat at a wooden table with his head bent. When the door opened he looked up with an air of sullen defeat.

'I want to speak to you in private,' he said to Rabindrah. 'Not with him here.'

'Mr Kiberu is here as my witness. That's the way it goes. Now let's hear what you have to offer.'

In all Rabindrah spent two hours with the man, and left with a sense of utter contempt for Harjeet as he wept and grovelled, and swore an oath that neither his mother, his brothers nor his wife had any idea about the nature of Manjit Singh's business dealings, many of which were legitimate and used as a cover for the vast sums of money made from the smuggling of animal trophies.

'My father kept detailed records.' He directed a nauseating smile at Rabindrah, now that there was a chance of redemption. 'They are in a safe in Birmingham. I am the only one with the combination and I will give it to you, if I am promised a light sentence and then deported back to the UK. My name is not on any of the records, as I was not active in my father's company except as a bookkeeper. The only other connection is my presence in the warehouse on that night, but I had no idea what was going to take place there. All I want to do is to go home and take care of my wife and my mother. I would like you to send these letters to them.'

'You are scum,' Rabindrah said, putting the envelopes in his pocket. 'And I advise you never to try and see my cousin again, or you will have to answer to me. You have ruined Lila's family and I am sure you are directly responsible for Gulab's death. Don't ever forget that, because if you do I will be there to remind you.'

'I want the best lawyer in Nairobi here tomorrow morning,' Harjeet said, his tone becoming bolder. 'And a special guard while I am in prison. And, of course, a written guarantee that—'

'There will be no written guarantee,' Kiberu said. 'You will have to take my word for the fact that you will receive a light sentence and be deported immediately afterwards. We don't need vermin like you in

325

Kenya. Now you will give Rabindrah the code of the safe and its whereabouts. Let us not waste any more time.'

Half an hour later Rabindrah nodded to the policeman on duty in his driveway and walked up the steps of his house to stand face to face with Sarah.

'I've just come from seeing Harjeet in the prison,' he said as he dropped into an armchair. 'Johnson Kiberu was with me, and he has asked me to fly to London tomorrow, in order to collect written evidence that will convict his crooked peers. They are in Manjit's personal safe in Birmingham, and Johnson doesn't trust anyone else to obtain or deliver it.'

'There must be someone,' she said.

'No. I'm the only one with full knowledge of the facts, and Harjeet refused to disclose the whereabouts of his father's safe or the combination to anyone but me. I have to go.' He hesitated before stretching out a tentative hand. 'Gordon has asked me to interview James Mancham, the deposed president of the Seychelles, who is still in London. As a cover. That could be fun. Please come with me, Sarah. To talk. To let me make amends. We could go on to Ireland afterwards, if you like. I will always be deeply ashamed that I put you in any position where you are not completely safe, and where you lost confidence in me. There is nothing I will not do to try and make up for this, and to earn your forgiveness. Nothing.'

She did not answer, but when he moved closer to touch her cheek she flinched. 'What about your family?' she asked. 'Are you still obliged to do more for them?'

'I hope that I can get these papers, so that Lila and Anjit will no longer be under any threat. And then it will all be over.'

'I have to go back to the Mara tomorrow,' she said. 'I owe you an apology for my earlier reaction. What you did in Mombasa was hugely brave, especially if it results in putting away major criminals and preventing others from slaughtering animals. And people. In the case of Gulab, I can understand why you felt you had to help him, although I can never agree with the way you went about it. But the real problem between us is deeper than those issues, because it is a question of trust. Or the lack of it. If you thought I should be kept in ignorance about something that might take away your life, and mine too, then you do not know me at all.

And that is frightening. We were always partners, in good times and bad. In love and loss, as well as in our work. But lately that has not been the case. Not since my second miscarriage and the tests you had in Ireland. Not from the beginning of this investigation which you concealed from me, although Anthony and Johnson Kiberu knew what you were looking into, and you must have been aware that it would put us both at risk. I think you should have warned me about that. I also think that burning the ivory at the sawmill was madness. Both you and Anthony could have been seen, and might still be ruined if anyone ever discovers what you did there.'

'It was a gut reaction. A series of bad judgements. And wrong in part, but . . .'

'We have somehow been catapulted into a world of international criminals, where people we know are bribed, murdered and pushed off cliffs. Where men have their heads sliced off, and attempts have been made on your life. I don't think I can inhabit that kind of world, not even for your sake, and especially from a position of total ignorance. In fact, I need to get away from that kind of existence as soon as possible.'

'Once I get these documents, the whole thing will be over.'

'Maybe. Well, I wish you success in sorting things out for Lila, and I hope you will be able to do that safely.' Her voice was shaking. 'Meantime, you seem to have forgotten our commitment to Allie and to John Sinclair. It's something that still means a great deal to me, though, and I have work to do. A contract to fulfil. There is a deadline that is no longer important to you, but I intend to do my best to keep to it.'

'I'll come to the Mara as soon as I get back from England.' Rabindrah was pleading for a sign of softening in her attitude.

'That's something we will discuss when you return,' Sarah said. 'When and if you have finished with this investigation. Although the project has advanced a great deal since you were last in camp, and Hugo has more or less taken over the writing.'

'I can catch up very quickly on the book,' he said, suppressing his anger. But he knew that it was futile to continue. This was not the time for compromise or healing. 'Have you spoken to Anjit again?'

'No. As I said, she asked me not to come to the cremation. Although Gulab told her how you tried to help him. She is grateful, but she doesn't want to see you. None of your family wants to see either one of us, and that is the truth.'

'I'm going to pack,' he said, realising that there was nothing else left to say as the door of her darkroom closed and she shut him out of her life.

London greeted Rabindrah with lashing rain and faces that reflected the grey skies and the drab winter's day. It was his mother who opened the door when he rang the bell, her face filled with astonishment, but his explanations brought incredulity and sadness to both his parents.

'To think that Gulab could have been so foolish,' Jasmer said. 'It is hard to believe. And what will become of poor Anjit now, and Lila?'

'I need to see Lila as soon as possible,' Rabindrah said. 'I will have to tell her all this, and it won't be easy.' However, a series of telephone calls to Camilla's flat yielded no response and Rabindrah decided to go to Knightsbridge in the hopes of finding his cousin.

'Perhaps I should come with you,' Jasmer suggested, and they set out together in the car. 'She may need legal advice somewhere along the line, and I will be happy to provide it. She is working for the agent fellow, you know. The one who represents Sarah's glamorous friend. She told your mother on the telephone.'

'That's good news,' Rabindrah said. 'The start of an independent future for her. She must not wind up at the beck and call of Harjeet, ever again.'

'A weak man,' Jasmer said. 'But if, as you say, he is released and returns to England, she might take up with him again. After all, she is his wife. Things could be hard for her as a single woman.'

'She wouldn't think of going back to him.' Rabindrah was appalled. 'He's a crook. A younger version of his father.'

'I agree with you,' Jasmer said as he parked the car. 'But women do strange things, and I would guess that the family still has plenty of money from the legitimate businesses in which they are involved. Lila may need that. At any rate, I will help her as much as I can.'

'Get her a divorce,' Rabindrah said. 'And a fat settlement. That's the kind of help she needs.'

He rang the bell at the main entrance to the building, and stood in the shelter of the canopy as the porter shuffled towards them, peering through the etched glass into the wet.

'Kevin, how are you?' Rabindrah held out his hand. 'This is my father Jasmer Singh.'

'Mr Singh. Delighted to see you, sir.' He was smiling. 'Miss Broughton-

Smith, or rather Mrs Chapman, didn't tell me to expect you. Will you be staying here? I have the extra keys.'

'No. My trip was a last-minute decision. Actually I'm looking for my cousin, Lila.'

'Not here any more, she's not,' Kevin said. 'Moved out last weekend. Very sudden it was, with Mr Bartlett coming to help her with her luggage.'

'So where is she?'

'I'm afraid I've no idea. I understand she found a place of her own. Closer to work, she said. Lovely girl. Very considerate. I hope she's settled in comfortably. You'll have to ring Mr Bartlett in the morning and see if he knows where she is.'

'I will,' Rabindrah said. 'Sorry to have disturbed you on such a wretched evening.'

Two telephones were ringing and Tom looked up from his desk which was piled with papers and photographs. He regarded Rabindrah with amazement.

'What on earth are you doing here? Is Sarah with you? Is Camilla all right? And what the fuck is going on in Nairobi? Poor Lila has turned into a wreck, what with the news of her father's accident, and the hysterical mother on the phone, day and night.'

'I've come to explain. Help her straighten things out,' Rabindrah said.

'Well, I'm glad someone is finally here to throw some light on recent events. Make yourselves comfortable in the conference room,' Tom said, pressing a button on the intercom and summoning Lila. 'I'll send in coffee. And a stiff drink, when and if you need one.'

'Tom has been so kind,' Lila said, wiping away tears. 'He stayed with me at Camilla's place for a couple of days, to help me settle in. And now he has given me a job and helped me find a little flat near here. So I have a chance to make a fresh start. When I got the news about Father, I don't know what I would have done without him.'

'I'm glad you have found your feet, little cousin,' Rabindrah said.

'But why was Father on that road? And can you explain why Mother told me not to contact Harjeet's family, because it might be dangerous? Not that I want to see any of them, ever again. But what is going on? For God's sake, explain to me what has happened.'

She listened as Rabindrah told her the full story, her gaze unwavering.

When he had finished talking she clung to him, all her fear tumbling out in a cascade of words and questions still unanswered.

'Lila, there is something we have to do together.' Rabindrah smoothed back her hair. 'We have to go to Birmingham, to see your mother-in-law.'

'No! No, I won't go there,' she cried out. 'You can't ask me to go back to that house.'

'We must do this, Lila. It is the only thing that will keep your mother and the rest of your family from being investigated and harassed, and losing everything they have left.'

She looked at him for a long moment and then began to laugh hysterically. 'You want me to save my family? Why the hell would I want to do that? My parents sold me, Rabindrah. Father must have known Manjit Singh was a criminal when they made the deal. I did what they asked because I loved them, and I was afraid for them. But I don't know how I feel about them now, except that maybe I hate them. Yes – I do hate them!' She stood up and hammered her fists against his chest. 'I'm not going back to my family, do you understand? Not in Birmingham or Nairobi. And if Harjeet stays in jail for the rest of his life, that will suit me just fine. The rest is already over.'

'Lila, this whole thing can never be over until all Manjit's partners are convicted and put away.'

'There will be plenty more crooks to replace them,' she said with revulsion. 'Kenya has become a sink hole of corruption, and my own family were in it up to their necks. It will never get better, no matter what we do.'

'You must come with me to Birmingham.' Rabindrah grabbed her hands. 'I put Sarah and myself in danger the moment I agreed to take on this investigation. If I can't supply the records that Manjit has kept in his safe all through the years, I could lose my life and Sarah would be at risk. That is the truth. The bottom line.'

Her breath was shallow as she attempted to sift the full meaning of his words, aware that once again she would have to put aside her own desires for the sake of the family.

'I'll give you Sajjan's phone number and address,' she said at last. 'You can set up a time to visit her. On your own.'

But Manjit's widow was adamant that she would not see Rabindrah. After almost an hour on the line, during which she railed against him, accused him of treachery, wept endlessly and hung up twice, it was clear that he would make no progress with her.

'Give me the bloody telephone,' Lila said at last. 'I'll speak to her myself.'

A further round of explanations, questions and pleading ensued before Sajjan agreed to the visit. But she was insistent that Lila must accompany Rabindrah.

'We had better go right now,' Lila said in a flat voice. 'Before she changes her mind, or is forced to do so by family pressure at that end. But I'm only going there for you and for Sarah. After that I will not have any further contact with the rest of my family. Never.'

It was after midnight when Rabindrah sank onto his hotel bed and telephoned Johnson Kiberu.

'I'm aware that it's three in the morning in Nairobi, but I thought you would want to know that I have the papers,' he said. 'What should I do with them now?'

'Have them copied and put both sets into a safe deposit box,' Johnson said. 'I will be out of the country for the next two weeks, attending an international wildlife conference in Holland and an aid meeting in Sweden. After that I will come to London and take personal delivery of them. It would not be wise for you to be in Nairobi with these documents in your possession. Hedley says he can spare you until I get back.'

Rabindrah silently cursed his editor, realising that the time difference would make it necessary to delay his call to Gordon until the morning. For the remainder of the night he fell into a broken sleep, tossing and muttering until the first grey light came sneaking through the curtains.

'I need to get home,' he said angrily, when Gordon answered his early morning call. 'I've had enough of my life being taken over by Kiberu and his demands.'

'You still have the pleasure of an interview with Jimmy Mancham,' Gordon said. 'Former King of the Coconut Kingdom, playboy poet, charismatic statesman. And there are a few other Seychellois exiles in London who might have some interesting comments on the new government. It won't do you any harm to be a city boy for a few days. Go and see a show or two, eat well, keep an eye on your pretty cousin. You can afford it, old chap. The paper will pay your expenses, and your bank account is overflowing with the rewards of this scandal. Take a little time off, wind down, buy Sarah an extravagant present.'

Recognising defeat Rabindrah hung up and sat back in his chair. When he had showered and ordered breakfast he decided that he might as well take Gordon's advice and enjoy being stuck in London. A few days of enforced relaxation would hardly be a penance. Camilla and Anthony would be arriving soon, and he could make amends for fleeing the wedding and interrupting their honeymoon. He looked at the theatre page in the *Evening Standard*, rang Lila, and booked tickets for a musical.

'It's going to be all right from now on,' he said to her. 'Another few days and things will be back to normal.'

Chapter 21

Kenya, November 1977

It was early in the morning and they were still in bed when Achole, the chief herdsman, came up to the house, to announce that there was no water in the dairy.

'Someone has cut the main pipe again.' Hannah guessed the source of the problem immediately, as she turned on a tap in the bathroom to hear the gasping, sputtering sound that confirmed her words. 'It's probably a result of the problem with the *watu* who cut through the fence and brought their cattle in on the south side. They were at our trough yesterday, filling *debbis* and buckets and letting their scrawny *ngombes* and goats in to drink.'

'You didn't tell me that last night,' Lars said, frowning.

'You were late coming back from the rugby at the Club, and I was tired.' Hannah wrapped her dressing gown across the swell of her stomach. 'It's hard keeping up with everything. There was a problem at the lodge. The big freezer wasn't working, and no one noticed because we haven't had any guests for several days. I had to throw out all the fish and the meat I put in for the people arriving today. And then Achole came and told me about the break in the fence and the people helping themselves to the water. So I sent two of our rangers down there to chase them away.'

'Poor devils,' Lars said. 'Their livestock are skin and bone. You can hardly blame them for trying to get at any source of water they can reach.'

'If we turn a blind eye to one group we will be inundated,' Hannah said. 'Everyone will get the idea that they can come along with pliers or a good old panga, and hack their way through our fences. The whole area will become a dust bowl, never mind the question of water. We have barely enough for ourselves. Both the dams are low. We can't let people break in and make off with what is left of our supply. Look how thin our own cattle are.'

He knew she was right, but it was a tough rule to enforce during a drought. Beyond the Langani fence, herds of livestock had been gathering for weeks around a small dam, built by the local council some years before. Cattle and goats milled in a screen of dust, their constant passage and growing numbers creating runnels of erosion in the parched soil. Fights had broken out over the inadequate water supply and the press of people and animals, all demanding access. Last week there had been a stampede at a similar water trough nearby. The incident had begun as a sleek Mercedes rolled slowly through the squalor of a small village and came to a halt. A well-tailored, overfed politician had climbed out to gain followers by making a few florid, empty promises. But in less than five minutes he was scrambling back into the air-conditioned cocoon of his car and driving away, followed by angry shouts and a hail of stones. Further north the land had become a cracked surface where even the goats could find little to nibble on, and cattle lay dead on the withered plains.

'I'll go and check the pipeline.' Lars had dressed hurriedly while she was speaking.

'What about breakfast?'

'Fruit from the kitchen, and some toast. You can send sandwiches and a thermos of coffee if I'm not back by noon. We need to discuss the patrols when I get back. Several animals were killed last week by people wanting food, and now this. We have to change the route that the rangers have been taking. Make their schedules less predictable. Maybe we should even take on a couple more.'

'We can't afford that,' Hannah said. 'It would mean getting another vehicle as well, and you want to replace the old harvester.'

Lars pushed his hat back and wiped away the sweat off his face.

'This part of the fence is secure now, Achole,' he said to the herdsman. 'But I want you to stay here until the night patrol arrives. Keep the rest of the food and coffee with you, and do not allow anyone to turn on the water for this trough. If the cement does not harden, the pipes will not be safe.'

'No one will come now,' Achole said. 'It is too soon after the fence was cut, and they will know we are watching. In a few days they will try to get in again, to steal water from another area. And they will kill more gazelle and zebra and eland, for the *nyama*.'

'We will change the patrols tonight, and maybe take on more rangers. I'm going to drive round the rest of the fences now,' Lars said. 'But it is difficult to stop people from walking down through the forest to reach the dams.'

He glanced at the sky as he stood up to leave. A few clouds had gathered, low and sullen, casting their shadows over the gasping land, but there was no smell of rain in the air. Last night there had been a faint growl of thunder and the sudden illumination of sheet lightning, pale and distant. Hannah had nudged him into a half-wakefulness and they had lain still for a time, listening for the sound of the first drops on the roof. Nothing had come of their hopes, and when he sighed and reached out to pull her closer she had turned away, silent and dejected.

As Lars drove away from the fence Achole raised his hand in a salute, but a few yards behind him there was a movement in the trees and the glint of sunlight on beads. Lars slowed the vehicle to peer through the dust that fogged his driving mirror. Three men had emerged from the cover of the surrounding bush, each carrying containers in which they could take away water. They moved cautiously across the hard ground, and stopped beside Achole.

Relatives or *rafikis*, no doubt. For a moment he considered a confrontation but a sense of weariness descended on him. He felt a deep sympathy for the herders whose starving cattle stood patiently on the other side of the boundary, skin stretched across the prominence of jutting ribs, large, moist eyes dulled by lack of food or water. He was disappointed by Achole's blatant dishonesty but reluctant to fire a man who had been a good worker for many years. There must be another solution, something he and Hannah could figure out together, a sharing of resources that would offer temporary relief until the rains came.

Back at the house he found Lottie in the garden, reading under the shade of a flame tree, with a pair of binoculars beside her.

'It's so peaceful,' she said. 'And I'm deeply grateful that Mario brought me back. I only wish he had been able to stay away from his business commitments for a little longer. But hotels are particularly demanding.'

'He will be back, though,' Lars said. 'Now that he has a taste of it. Africa always brings you back.'

'That's true, even when it's an odd, reluctant kind of continuity.' Lottie looked around her. 'I love these ferns and shrubs that Hannah has put in over the years. They have brought birds I haven't seen or heard in the garden before. I sent her off to rest, by the way, and told her I would pick up the children from school. And I've been in the kitchen with Godfrey, making a lemon sponge. It's still strange without Kamau, but I think this young man is going to make a very good cook, with a little help and patience.'

'I'm glad you were here when we arranged the farewell *ngoma* for Kamau and Mwangi,' Lars said. 'Your presence was symbolic, after all the years they were with you. A good omen and a wonderful thing for them both.'

'For me, too,' Lottie said.

'Hannah could not imagine being without them, but you have seen her through the worst of the changeover.'

'David made a fine choice when he picked Godfrey out of all the people who wanted the cook's job.' Lottie smiled. 'He says Kamau likes sitting around on his shamba, ordering his wives about. That he had become very tired lately. Mwangi, too, although neither one of them ever said so.'

'Thirty-six years is a long time,' Lars said. 'It is only in the last few days that Hannah has come to accept that she really can manage without them. Her idea of having a housemaid as well as a new boy has worked out well.'

'She will need them both when the baby is born,' Lottie said. 'Did you manage to secure the fence with Achole?'

He nodded. 'It's like putting a finger in the dyke, though,' he said. 'It's only a temporary measure, and unless we get some rain we may have an incident that will be bad for everyone involved. Still, Hannah is right. We can't allow thousands of local cattle and goats onto the property, or have our water stolen. It's tough.'

'It always was,' Lottie said.

'I used to think one day we could get it right, here at Langani,' Lars said. 'I believed we could do things that would make the unnecessary suffering and the poverty go away. But lately, I'm beginning to realise that it's a cycle we will probably never change, and I'm finding that difficult to accept.' He smiled his slow smile. 'Maybe I'm getting old, eh Lottie?'

She paused before responding, knowing she was treading on delicate ground. 'Do you think your visit to Norway has changed your attitude about the harshness of this country? Made you think differently about Langani?'

'You mean my parents' offer of their farm.' Lars sighed. 'I'm worried about the old folk and how they can carry on, but it's not a place for Hannah and me. Our lives are here, as she has always said. But . . .'

Lottie waited, aware that he was sorting words in his mind, trying to make a statement that was completely honest.

'Since we came back, she has never mentioned Norway at all. She doesn't talk about our holiday or remind the children of the good times they had with their grandparents, and how much love they were given. It's as though the subject is forbidden. As though the time we spent there didn't exist. And while Suniva and Piet originated here, in our African home, I cannot mention the fact that I'm glad this new child was conceived in Norway. In the land I came from. I can't tell her I'm proud of that, and it makes me sad. Even angry.'

He wanted to tell Lottie about the letter, too. About his father's visit to the cardiologist and the tests to come, but he could not bring himself to divulge the news he had not even mentioned to Hannah.

'Dear Lars, you are the best of men,' Lottie said. 'When Piet died it was you who came all the way to Rhodesia to break the news to us. And you knew, didn't you? You knew Janni walked into that hail of gunfire, because he could not contemplate going on.' He did not answer but she persisted, determined that all must be laid bare between them. 'His brute of a cousin, Kobus, told me afterwards that Jan must have gone crazy. That he stood up as though he wanted to make himself a target, and let the rebels shoot him. You knew that, didn't you?'

'Yes, I knew.'

Lars could recall every detail of the bitter night when he had told Jan van der Beer that his son was dead. Janni had left the house almost immediately, a ruined man, his soul rotting away, destroyed by seeds of hatred sown years before, as he fought and killed for control of his family's land and heritage. Hours later there had been the sound of the truck bringing his bullet-ridden form back to the dilapidated house on his cousin's tobacco farm. It was Lars who had found the letter in the dead man's jacket as he took care of the body. A love letter. God knows where he had found it or when, but Jan van der Beer had taken the sheets of paper that Lottie's lover had written, and placed them in the pocket nearest to his heart. Then he had deliberately walked into a hail of gunfire, in order to set her free. Glancing at the first line of Mario's fatal letter, Lars had burned the pages and never mentioned them to anyone. Nor would he do so now.

'You are the foundation of this family,' Lottie said. 'The bedrock on which we all rest and build our lives, including me, although I am in Italy with Mario. Because I know that my daughter and the children are safe in your care.'

'I don't know whether Hannah believes that any more.' Lars's voice was sombre. 'Lately I wonder if she notices me at all, except as someone reliable who can run her farm.'

'Langani belongs to both of you,' Lottie said firmly. 'I don't want to make excuses for her, but with the drought and the dairy and the lodge, and her part in Camilla's workshop, plus the extra attention that Piet needs and being pregnant again, I'm not sure Hannah can think straight at all right now.'

'Piet needs all the help he can get,' Lars agreed. 'But even before this problem with his hearing he has always been . . .' He was reluctant to finish the sentence, articulate the thought in his mind.

'Hannah's obsession,' Lottie said, gently. 'Because he is the living image of the other Piet. He looks the same, speaks in the same voice. His character is identical, and the same dreams are forming in his eyes. A re-incarnation, if there is such a thing. Sometimes I have to drag my own gaze away from him, because it seems that all the years have disappeared and I am back once again with my little boy. My own son.'

'So we remain mired in the past,' he said. 'No matter how hard we try to escape from it.'

'All our years and the memories they leave, whether good or bad, make up our history,' Lottie said. 'If we do not remember the stories of our past and who we are, then we will never know where we are going, or why we are doing what we do now.'

'Lunch is ready!' Hannah's appearance on the verandah brought an end to the conversation. 'I feel full of energy after a couple of hours' sleep. And starving, too. Thanks, Ma. Did you sort out the *shauri* with the water, Lars? I'd like you to come to the lodge with me after lunch. We can make sure the guests are happy, and wait for Anthony and Camilla to show up, all glowing from their honeymoon.'

'Yes, to both questions.' He smiled, but there was a heaviness in his tone that was not noticed by his wife.

'I'm sorry Sarah won't be with us tonight,' Lottie said as they made their way into the dining room. 'The time we spent with her in Allie's camp was glorious – Mario had never seen anything like it. I've been hoping she would come back before I leave next week, but it seems unlikely.'

'She has immersed herself once more in the lives of the cheetahs,' Lars said. 'She is safer, there, however, as things stand.'

'It's what she always does when she runs into a problem. Disappears into the *bundu*. I wouldn't be surprised if none of us sees her for months, although I've asked her to come and spend Christmas here with Rabindrah, if he is around.' Hannah did not sound optimistic. 'Right now, he is still in England, and things between them seem to have gone from bad to worse.'

'It must have been extremely hard on him to have to expose his relatives,' Lottie said. 'Does she not admire his integrity and the way he stuck to his principles?'

'Ach, Ma, who knows? But I hope Sarah will find a way through this soon, because Rabindrah sure as hell needs her now.'

'And what about Johnson Kiberu? Is he really all that he seems?'

'He is exceptional,' Hannah said. 'A politician not lured by money or power. His dedication to this country and to conservation is marvellous to see. He isn't afraid of anyone, and his actions are impartial for the most part. He has even made a couple of unpopular decisions in our favour, for example. Put us in a position where we received our share of conservation funding, even though we are described by his opposition as *wazungus* taking money from real Kenyans.'

'You *are* a real Kenyan,' Lottie said.

'Yes, but today's politicians like to portray us as rich white people with all the best land, so they can blame us for the problems of the *wananchi*. We are easy targets, Ma. An ideal way to disguise their own shortcomings and their greed.'

'What great changes ordinary people expected after Independence, when the white man no longer held the reins of power.' Lottie reflected on the euphoria of the time amongst black Kenyans. 'Only to be sold out by their own kind.'

'Corruption is endemic these days,' Hannah said with a mixture of anger and resignation. 'It is hard to get anything important done, unless you do it yourself without being noticed or asking for help. Or you pull strings in the right places, if you know how. We keep trying, and we succeed enough of the time. Anyway, I'm going up to the lodge with Lars, so I won't be able to help Piet with his homework this evening, but—'

'I'll do his lessons with him,' Lottie said. 'Go with your wonderful husband, and drive up there slowly, so that you can enjoy the beauty you work so hard to maintain. Don't worry about the children. I'll see you up at the lodge later on. With the honeymooners.'

The main room of the lodge was lit by great brass lanterns and flaring torches, and above them the great thatched roof soared into the African sky. Beyond the natural curve of the walls the orchestra of nocturnal sounds had begun, with the scuttle of tiny geckos, the screech of a hyrax, the snapping of a branch as an elephant or a buffalo forged its way through the surrounding bush. Hyenas yipped in the distance and a shy bushbuck stood at the edge of the woodland, motionless and alert, aware of the danger that was an intrinsic part of its life.

Anthony and Camilla sat close together, hands touching lightly, their happiness unmistakable. After a time Hannah introduced them to the other guests, and the room echoed with exclamations of surprise and laughter as the conversation moved from the fashion world of Paris, New York and London, to tales of life on the farm and in the bush. During dinner David lavished attention on them all, but his coolness towards Anthony was evident. Although Hannah had never hinted that any responsibility or blame should be attached to him, it was clear that he still resented Anthony's reprimand after the attack on James, and the fact that the boy had been taken out of his care. It created a small flaw in an otherwise perfect evening.

Wrapped in sweaters and rugs they sat on the viewing platform after dinner, a little apart from the small group of safari guests. Below them, a herd of elephants had arrived at the waterhole, their grey shapes emerging in ghostlike silence from the trees. The children were on their best behaviour, knowing that noise and boisterous games were forbidden. They crouched on the edge of the terrace, Suniva cupping her hands around Piet's ear as she drew his attention to the buffalo who appeared, snorting and shaking his heavy boss, planting his mud-splattered bulk on stocky legs at the water's edge, taking up a central position with characteristic belligerence. James sat beside Anthony, admiration shining on his face. His hero had married Camilla who had been responsible for the precious letters and cards from thousands of miles away, and now he loved her too.

'I'm studying hard,' James said with pride. 'I have come first in all my tests this week. Except art, because Suniva is the best at drawing and painting. And Piet is good at biology. One day I am going to be like you and Sarah, learning about the way the animals live, and how we can take care of them here.'

'Good plan,' Anthony said. 'Would you like to come and help me in camp for a week or so, during your Christmas holidays? That will teach you a great deal more, and earn you some pocket money, too.' He laughed at James's instant agreement and then turned to Suniva. 'Let's see your sketchbook, kid.'

Suniva showed portraits of her family, and of the men and women who worked on the farm, as well as pastels and watercolours of animals standing in the filigreed shade of an acacia tree at noon, or leaping through the air across the bleached grass of the plains.

Lottie went to stand at the edge of the platform, remembering the love with which her son had built the lodge. The place where he was first attacked on the night of his death. Above her the dome of the sky had turned black and the stars that pierced its immensity were jagged and sharp. She shivered, and felt Camilla's hand on her shoulder.

'Such boundless beauty,' Camilla said. 'It's easy to romanticise it, but there is always the knowledge of danger in the African night. In what lies behind the shadows where the stars don't shine their light. That is a large part of what keeps us in its thrall.'

'Do you ever wonder, on nights like this, if you are walking in borrowed light?' Lottie had not meant to ask such a question, particularly of this young woman who had chosen to make her life here, when the riches of the whole world lay at her feet. 'Do you feel this is a place that can never really be ours, no matter how long we stay or how much we care for it?'

'No, I don't feel that,' Camilla said, glancing back at Anthony. Her face was lit with an expression of love that made Lottie turn away from such an intense communication. 'Like Sarah and Hannah, I didn't want to leave here after school, and the success I found in other places never meant much to me. All I really longed for was to come back. To be brave enough to share a life with Anthony. It took me a long time to achieve that, but finally we are together. And we both believe that this is where we should be.'

'I felt that way when I married Janni, all those years ago in Johannesburg.' Lottie was smiling as she remembered her stocky Afrikaans husband carrying her across Langani's simple threshold, and setting her down in a room that was almost bare of furniture. 'He brought me back here from Johannesburg. His Italian bride. His family totally disapproved of his choice. A little like Rabindrah and Sarah.'

'Do you miss the farm?' Camilla was curious.

'I've been away too long now,' Lottie said. 'Found another life so blessed that I cannot help comparing its gentleness to the random mixture of glory and heartbreak I experienced here. But this is Hannah's home, and yours, and Sarah's too. The vital thing is that you believe in it.'

'Grandma? Look at the rhino! And we saw the kudu earlier on! Did you like my drawings?' Suniva was tugging at Lottie's sleeve. 'What about my picture of the warthogs we were laughing at yesterday, with their tails up in the air?'

'I did, and they are wonderful.' Lottie took her hand. 'I think it's time for bed, darling. You have to go to school tomorrow. Why don't you round up Piet and James, and I'll take you all home.'

'She has real talent,' Camilla said as Suniva went to collect the other children. 'A sense of movement and colour and line that is a true gift.'

'Yes.' Lottie laughed. 'Something – maybe the only thing – she inherited from her father. He could bring anything to life with a pen and a sheet of paper, but he didn't give her anything else of himself that is recognisable.' She did not notice the child stopping in her tracks, frowning and unsettled for a moment, before she moved on to where James was listening to another of Anthony's bush stories.

'I hope there will be good news for Piet when he goes back to the specialist,' Camilla said. 'I gather the next visit will be about whether to operate or not. Hannah feels there hasn't been any improvement in his hearing.'

'She is right,' Lottie said. 'But there are so many things they can do these days, including grafting patches onto perforations, and fitting people with new types of hearing aids.'

'I hear he is doing better at school, now that the teachers are aware of his problem.' Anthony came to join them. 'And he has a strong will, like his sister.'

'I think Suniva sometimes feels left out, though,' Lottie said. 'With Piet's extra tuition and a new baby on the way.'

'She is an independent young lady, and very protective of Piet,' Lars said. 'Full of curiosity, too. And the special bond between her and James will keep her going.'

They were interrupted by Hannah, accompanied by the children. 'Are you sure you want to take them home, Ma? I can drive them myself, if you want to stay on for a while.'

'No, my dear. I'm quite tired myself, and happy to go back to the house. Camilla, I'll look forward to seeing you in the morning. Anthony, you are a lucky, lucky man.'

'That's what I tell him, too. At every opportunity.' Camilla was laughing as they said goodnight and settled back into their chairs to talk of the days of their lives already shared, and the promise of the bright times that lay ahead.

It did not take Lottie long to see the children to bed, although she felt a sense of disquiet as James left the main house to join Esther in her quarters. The fire had been kept alight in the sitting room and she sat down and opened the book she was reading. Josephine, the new housemaid, brought her a pot of tea and she settled down in the chair that had once been her favourite, during the early days of her marriage. She did not hear the low whistle, or the sound of Suniva's window opening to let in the cold highland air. And James.

They sat together, James in the small armchair and Suniva perched on the edge of her bed, wrapped in her dressing gown. It was a nightly ritual that had begun some weeks before, when Suniva was castigated at school for turning in late homework on several consecutive days. Hannah had been tired and pressed for time as she helped Piet through his lessons, rushed to the lodge where one of the guests had been taken ill, and returned to the house to find a note from Suniva's form mistress.

'Supper in your room for the rest of the week,' Hannah said, fatigue making her more strict than she needed to be. 'So that you can concentrate on your homework properly, instead of playing games with Piet and James. You are perfectly capable of writing a good essay, and Mrs Gilliat says your maths mistakes are pure carelessness.'

'I always do my homework with James.' Suniva was defiant, but her lip trembled and tears were close.

'That doesn't seem to be bringing good results.' Hannah stood her ground. 'For the moment you will work on your own when you come home from school. In your room. And your father is going to hear about this as soon as he comes in this evening. You have to pull your weight, Suniva. There are more than enough obstacles in our way right now, without your adding another worry to the list.'

On that first night of confinement Suniva had sat at her desk, brooding and miserable, her supper untouched on the tray. She was aware that her mother was in the study with Piet, making sure he had not missed anything vital in the day's lessons. As she picked up her pen to attack her English grammar exercises she heard a whistle and a light tapping on the window. Drawing the curtain aside she peered out into the darkness and then gave a small cry of surprise, as James crept from underneath the jasmine bush and climbed into the room. They had completed her assignments together and then huddled cross-legged on the rug, whispering and giggling over the day's events. Within a week her report card had improved to Hannah's satisfaction and the evening routine returned to normal. But the secret visits continued, deepening the bond between Suniva and James.

'Do you remember the promise?' Suniva had grasped his arm one night as he was about to leave her room. 'The one that Ma and Sarah and Camilla made when they were at school? We heard them say it again in Lamu on Ma's birthday, and we should make one, too.' She stood up and faced him, her expression earnest. 'James Karuri, I promise always to be your true friend and to love you forever. Say it.'

He took her fingers and held them tight in his dark hands. 'Suniva Olsen, I promise always to be your true friend and to love you forever.' He spoke the words solemnly and then leaned forward to plant an awkward kiss on her cheek.

She gasped with surprise, and shut her eyes tight. It was the first time a boy had ever kissed her and she could not think of anything to say or do. But she knew that no words were necessary, and when she opened her eyes again he was gone. More than a month had passed since that night, and he had never kissed her again, but Suniva knew that their promise would never die.

In the workshop, the women crowded around Camilla and Anthony, clapping and singing a marriage song in their thin, high voices, illustrating the words with raucous laughter and unmistakable gestures.

'You must stay at home now, Mama Camilla, to grow fat and make children,' they said, giggling behind their hands and pinching her slim arms. 'Eh! What bride price did your husband pay for so little flesh? You must eat more and become strong for when the time comes!'

'I wish you weren't leaving so soon,' Hannah said as they walked back to the house.

'We only have three days in Nairobi before we leave for New York and London,' Camilla said. 'Actually, I don't want to go anywhere, but I have to finalise the designs for next season's clothes with Saul Greenberg. And Anthony has his annual sales trip, although this time we will do it together. I never realised I could be so content and complete. It is a miracle, what has happened for me at last. I hope we will always be as happy as you and Lars.'

'I hope so too.' Hannah forced out every ounce of gladness she could muster into her reply. 'How about talking to Sarah before you leave here?'

'Yes. Can we get her on the radio? She must find a way through this impasse with Rabindrah, and do it soon.'

'I can't figure it out,' Hannah said. 'She was so angry with him on the night he turned up here with his uncle. Although he had been heroic in Mombasa.'

'There was a reason but you have to promise me you will never repeat it.' Camilla waited until Hannah had nodded agreement, before speaking again. 'No one knows this, but Gulab was holding dozens of elephant tusks and other illegal stuff at his sawmill near Nanyuki, and Rabindrah arranged for him to get rid of it.'

'What? How? And how on earth do *you* know?'

'Because Anthony helped to burn the place down and destroy it all,' Camilla said.

'What a bombshell! I can't believe it.' Hannah was gaping in astonishment. 'You can't have been thrilled to have Anthony burning ivory in Nanyuki while you spent the night alone in Shaba. When did this happen? Oh, no! It must have been the day you arrived there.'

Camilla's honeymoon had not started as expected. Sammy had been waiting on the airstrip at Shaba, his smile as wide as an ocean.

'Mama Chapman,' he said. '*Karibu*.'

'You are the first one to call me that,' Camilla was delighted. 'I will be Mama Chapman for the rest of my life, and I will love it.'

'What in the world have you got in here?' Anthony lifted the smaller of Camilla's two bags and groaned. 'It's a wonder the aircraft took off with this on board.'

'Books,' she said, smiling. 'You know I never go anywhere without books.'

'You won't have time to read them.' He was laughing as he kissed her, touching the pale, vulnerable spot on the nape of her neck where she had piled up her hair, and then standing back to devour her with his eyes.

Minutes later the plane had vanished into the empty glare of the sky. They climbed into the Land Cruiser and drove slowly, passing through a moonscape of dry plains scattered with lava rocks. The earth was parched and split. In the distance, the outline of Shaba's volcanic mountain rose in a purple cone, and a whisper of breeze stirred the heavy leaves of the doum palms scattered across the flatter areas of land. They stopped to allow several reticulated giraffe to lope slowly and gracefully across the sandy track in front of them, and Camilla could hear the sound of weaver birds above the river when Anthony braked and stopped the car.

'Leopard,' he said, pointing upwards. 'In the tree on the left.'

Camilla stood up to look out of the roof hatch, moving slowly so that she would not disturb the magnificent creature. He lay draped along a branch, nonchalant and untroubled, with his long tail and front paws hanging downwards, motionless.

'Look at that stomach, bulging out at the edges.' Anthony handed her the binoculars and chuckled. 'He must have killed recently and dragged his prize up into the branches.'

'There's a gazelle in the fork of the tree,' Camilla said, adjusting the focus. 'And the leopard is looking right at me, with those magnificent green eyes. I can see each individual whisker, and his pink nose. God, such perfection. But there is something totally predatory about him. His power emanates from every beautiful inch, and it's impossible to ignore.'

They sat beneath the tree for a time, watching the leopard yawn and then close his eyes. A flock of vultures was hunched and waiting nearby, their scraggy necks stretched out in anticipation as they squabbled and cackled on the ground, as if the bleached dome of the sky was too hot for any attempt at flight.

'They are hoping something will drop down on them.' Camilla shuddered. 'I shouldn't begrudge them their food, but they give me the creeps.'

'Let's move on,' Anthony said. 'Our reception committee is waiting for us up the road, and we mustn't disappoint them by being late.'

The honeymoon camp had been set up on a bluff above the Uaso Nyiro River and their arrival was greeted with applause from the staff as they gathered around to shake Anthony's hand, and offer Camilla the gift of a bracelet, made from Somali silver and blue glass beads.

'We'll have lunch, and a siesta,' Anthony said. 'And then we'll go and look for some game.'

He led her to the mess tent and as they sat down her hair brushed his face, making him want her fiercely. She caught the desire in him and offered a smile. On the opposite bank a herd of Grevy's zebra had come down to drink. Camilla had always liked their distinguishing narrow stripes and white stomachs, and their large, rounded ears.

'They are definitely more handsome than other zebras,' she said. 'Maybe it's because they are taller, and they don't look like they are wearing football jerseys or pyjamas that are several sizes too tight.'

But there had been no time for Anthony to make a comment of his own, as the radio telephone squawked into action and hijacked the first day of their married life.

'I'll come to Nanyuki with you,' Camilla said at once. 'I can do some of the driving.'

'No, darling, it's totally unnecessary.' He held her lightly and stroked her hair.

'I won't be able to relax until you are back,' she said. 'It would be better if I could stay at the Safari Club. Wait for you there. We could both spend the night, and come back here in the morning.'

'No. We've only just arrived, and the camp is all set up. It would be pointless to drag you down to Nanyuki.' He was adamant, and an hour later he was gone, leaving her to spend the afternoon on a game drive with Sammy. It was late at night when the radio call finally came through, its whirr and crackle distorting Anthony's voice. Her hands were shaking as she grasped the receiver.

'Everything has been taken care of, darling. Can't talk now, but I'll tell you all in the morning. I'm at the Safari Club – they kindly found me a room and something to eat. See you for breakfast, around eight.'

The camp staff had retired except for Leleruk, the night watchman, who stood on the edge of the river, leaning on his spear and looking out into the starlight beyond the camp fire. Camilla poured herself a brandy and stood up to walk to the sleeping tent. The Samburu was instantly at her side, his white teeth gleaming in the darkness as he took the lantern from her, walking through the camp a few feet ahead of her and shining his torch round in wide circles.

'Mama safe here tonight. No elephant or buffalo walking in the camp while Leleruk is guarding you,' he said proudly, waiting as she unzipped the tent.

No husband either, Camilla thought, as she set the lamp down on the bedside table. She looked down at the bed, sheets and pillows pristine and waiting. And empty.

She had woken at dawn. On the opposite bank of the river a herd of elephant arrived to drink and bathe, pushing the smaller calves gently into the water and teaching them how to splash and roll in the muddy shallows. A crocodile watched from a nearby vantage point, but the smallest calf was surrounded by adults and he closed his reptilian eyes and waited for an easier opportunity.

When she had looked down at her watch for the tenth time she took it off, resolving not to think about where Anthony might be and how long it would take him to get to the camp. She had endured his comings and goings for years, but now everything had changed and she suddenly wanted him constantly in her sight, beside her, close enough so that she could see the flecks in his eyes, the laugh lines on his face when he smiled. She would have to find a way to mask this new urgency to some degree, even if she could not control it. And she must remain outwardly independent. He would not be happy if she allowed this clinging feeling to rule her emotions or to influence their lives. Minutes later she heard the sound of the Land Cruiser and jumped to her feet, filled with unstoppable joy. Resolution was thrown to the winds as she ran through the camp and flung herself into his arms.

'I'm starving,' he said, grinning down at her. 'I could smell the bacon frying from half a mile down the road. It's astonishing that the place isn't surrounded by ravenous lions. Francis, porridge and eggs and sausages. With toast and coffee, please. We'll leave last night's adventures for a private discussion later on. By the way, have I told you this morning that I adore you, Mrs Chapman?'

They had lingered over breakfast, feeding the starlings around their feet, watching each other with stolen glances as the staff smiled their own private smiles. In spite of the rising heat, the air felt soft around them as they sat in a puddle of shadow, holding hands and laughing at the antics of the vervet monkeys and a herd of elephant on the other side of the river.

'Look at the tiny one in the centre,' Camilla said. 'Tucked in between the mother's huge legs, having such fun spraying water with its little trunk.'

'Can't be more than a month old,' Anthony said. 'Do you want babies, Camilla?' He laughed at the surprise on her face. 'I want lots of blond *totos* running around our house, darling. Let's makes lots of babies, starting now.'

After their lovemaking they lay in the rumpled sheets, not talking, unwilling to bring the business of the outside world into the perfection of their private space, sighing a little with the heat as the arid savannah beyond the camp surrendered itself to the white hot sun.

There had been no further interruptions during the weeks of their honeymoon.

'Thank God nothing went wrong at the sawmill.' Camilla came back to the present, and placed an arm around Hannah's shoulders. 'We're never going to mention this again. I only wanted you to understand why Sarah was so upset.'

'I do understand it now. What about Lila?'

'A bargaining chip for her father. She didn't know anything about his deal with her new in-laws.'

'So much for the joys of arranged marriage,' Hannah said. 'Where is she going to stay when you get to London?'

'She has moved into a place of her own. Tom took her on as his secretary and assistant. His office was always a frightful mess, and Lila is organised and methodical, and good with figures.' Camilla laughed. 'He told me he had helped her to furnish her pad, and apparently he takes her out to dinner sometimes. So who knows what may come of that?'

'Oh my.' Hannah was chuckling as she considered the possibilities. 'I always said Tom was fickle and fast. I love it!'

'I don't know where it is going, if anywhere,' Camilla said. 'But worse things could happen.'

As they reached the house they were met by Lars, his face grey with strain.

'Pa has had a heart attack,' he said. 'I had a phone call a few minutes ago. He's in the hospital, having an operation. They don't know whether he will make it, Han. Mother is with him, and Ilse is on her way there.'

'Lars.' Hannah put her arms around him. 'What a terrible shock. Poor Kirsten – she must be frantic with worry. What can we do?'

'Wait. We can only wait and hope. It will be three or four hours before we know anything.'

'We'll stay on,' Anthony said. 'Until you have some news. Darling, we can leave sometime tomorrow, in case there is some way we can help while Lars works out the best thing to do. What do you say?'

'Absolutely,' Camilla said. 'Of course we'll stay.'

In the background, Lottie stood grave and silent, her eyes full of compassion as Lars led Hannah into the study.

'I knew there was a problem,' he said. 'I had a letter from him recently. He had had some tests and things didn't look so good.'

'You never mentioned that.' Hannah looked at him, taken aback. 'Why on earth didn't you say something?'

'You never asked about them,' Lars said. 'Since we got home you've barely mentioned my parents, except to make sure the children wrote their thank-you letters. I didn't think you were interested in hearing about them.'

'That's ridiculous,' Hannah was defensive, recognising that he was right. 'Of course I'm interested in them. Of course I care. I just didn't want to . . .'

'To remember their offer, made in all innocence and with generosity,' he said. 'An offer I refused at once, even though I knew how disappointed they would be. But you chose to turn it into a reason for shutting them out of our lives, and our children's lives.'

'Lars, I'm sorry.' She sat down, slumping sideways in the chair. 'I'm terribly sorry. I've been stupid and selfish about two good, kind people. Ach, I was so afraid you would be tempted to make us leave here, and I shouldn't have been.' She reached up her arms and drew him down to her. 'It will be all right,' she said. 'Jorgen is a strong man, fit for his age. He'll make it through. I'm sure he will. And then we can bring them here for a holiday, or we'll go back to Norway with the children. No matter what it takes. Come, let's go into the sitting room and wait with everyone else. It will help to pass the time.'

Late in the afternoon the sound of the telephone made Lars rush into the hall. For a moment or two he stood there without speaking, holding the receiver in his hand, looking into its blackness. Kirsten came onto the line but could only weep incoherently. Finally, it was Ilse who made the request.

'He has come through,' she said. 'But he will be in intensive care for a few days, and there is serious damage to the heart. I'm not sure what this means for the future, or how long that might be. I think you should come. Be with Mother for a little while. I can stay a week, but maybe you could take over from me afterwards. Drive her to the hospital, help out with the farm until Father gets home and makes some arrangements with the neighbours.'

'I will be there as soon as I can,' Lars said. 'Before the end of the week.'

The children returned from school to hear the news, Suniva sobbing into her mother's lap, while Piet gazed at his father in tearful silence.

'Do you want to come for a walk with me?' Camilla asked the children. 'We can go somewhere lovely and think about your grandpa and the wonderful times you had together. And we will pick some flowers for him and say a special prayer to help him get strong again.'

'Yes,' said Suniva. 'But first I want to give Pa something that will help him, too.'

She ran out of the sitting room and returned moments later with a sketch book that Camilla had given her in London. Opening the cover she flicked through the pages until she came to the drawing she had made of Jorgen, sitting at the kitchen table with his pipe in a clay bowl beside him.

'It's for you,' she said, hugging Lars. 'Later we can sit down together, and you can draw you own picture of him. And Pa, I know that you have given me everything you ever could.'

'Thank you,' he said gravely, surprised by the strangeness of her words, making a supreme effort to hide his distress. 'But you know I can't draw, because I've always used my hands for other things like tractors and fixing fences. So this will be even more important because it is so true to him, and I know how much he liked it.'

'You just don't remember how to draw,' she said, smiling. 'Probably because you haven't had time to practise for so long. So this picture of Grandpa Jorgen is to remind you.'

'Ilse wants me to come for a week or so,' Lars said to Hannah later, as they tried to decide what to do. 'To be with them. I should have paid more attention before. Spoken to him on the telephone more often. Tried to work something out. But I didn't want to upset you.'

'You can't blame yourself for not knowing,' Hannah said. 'And I don't like your suggestion that I am somehow responsible for your not going to see Jorgen.'

'I'm not saying that at all.' Lars placed his hands flat on his desk, shoulders hunched. 'Hannah, please let us not have a disagreement right now. It is only important to arrange things so I can leave. And I am thinking you should come with me. Just for a few days.'

She stared at him, dismayed. 'We can't both leave the farm again, and the children. Besides, Piet is due to see the specialist in Nairobi next Thursday. This is an important time for him.'

'We could delay that,' he said, trying to persuade her gently, realising how she feared for their son. 'Maybe Lottie would stay on until we get back. For a week or so. We could also ask Sarah if she would come and help with the children.'

'No, Lars.' Hannah bit her lip, then shook her head. 'I don't think—'

'I wonder if I am of any importance to you any more,' he said, his eyes bright with sudden anger. 'My father may be dying, and I am asking you as my wife to come with me to Norway. To try and help my mother, and maybe to say goodbye to him for the last time. And all you can think of are reasons why you cannot or will not go.'

'No,' she said. 'No, it's not like that at all. You are the most important person in my life. I love you Lars, more than anyone on earth.

But I'm pregnant, and it's such a long way, and I'm worried about Piet.'

'I'm going out for a while,' he said, picking up the paperweight on his desk and quickly replacing it, to avoid his desire to hurl it against the wall and shock her into his reality. 'I need some time alone.'

He walked past her and left the room without looking back. From the window Hannah saw him striding towards the garage, and then there was the sound of the car starting up. She returned to the living room and sat down with her head in her hands.

'He needs to be on his own for a bit,' she said to Lottie, the words muffled. 'He wants me to go to Norway with him, Ma, but I can't delay Piet's visit to the specialist. It's not reasonable.'

'I think you should go with him,' Lottie said. 'I'll stay here with the children, and Mike Stead will help with anything urgent on the farm, like before. Lars needs you, my dear, and a decision on Piet's operation can be put back for a week or so. If it is necessary at all.'

'Where are the children?' Hannah raised her head. 'I should be with them. They must be very sad.'

'Piet went for a walk with Camilla. James and Suniva are somewhere with Anthony,' Lottie said. 'And when Lars comes back, you should tell him that you will go with him. That is vital, Hannah, and you must understand it.'

Hannah stood up. 'No, I'm not going, Ma. I'm staying here with the children, and taking Piet to the specialist. That is the most important thing. In any case, we can't afford for both of us to go to Norway. We've just had two holidays, and we have problems with the drought, and all kinds of *watu* cutting the fences and trying to move in with their livestock. People are stealing our water, breaking the pipes, killing our game for *nyama*. I need to be here. If things get any worse in Norway, then I'll have to think again. But for the moment I'm staying here. And that is final.'

'I think this forest house you have built is wonderful, but it's not very safe.' Anthony stood back and surveyed the small structure. 'You see – that's leopard spoor.' He pointed at the pug mark in the loamy earth. 'And it's not long since he was here. This is a big male, and there are plenty of buffalo and elephant crashing around too.'

'It's our own special place,' Suniva said. 'We collected all the sticks and leaves and tied them together ourselves, with creeper. It's dry inside, even when it rains.'

'We always make a fire so that the big animals will not come close,' James said. 'Like you do in your camp. Old Juma taught us that a long time ago, before he retired. When we were *totos*.'

'Hannah is not happy when you disappear into the forest,' Anthony said. 'And it's wrong to make her worry about you.'

'She is frightened of the forest, because it's where the man hid,' Suniva said. 'After he killed Uncle Piet. That's why she never comes here.'

'Well, it may be all right to spend time here in the daytime,' Anthony said. 'But never in the early morning, or when evening comes.'

'Pa has taught us the ways of the animals. How to listen and to know what the trees and the birds and the wind are saying,' Suniva said with assurance. 'He comes sometimes, to make sure that the house is still strong. We don't want anyone else.'

'Some boys from the labour lines followed me here once, and later they came back and pulled the place down.' James thumped his fist against a nearby tree trunk, his eyes darkening. 'Achole went after them with a big *rungu*, and then they were scared so they never came back. We built it again and made it better. And if they ever come back I will fight them.'

'I imagine you're talking about the same boys who beat you up.' Anthony turned to James. 'You should ignore them. They are bullies and there are plenty of them around, everywhere. I used to get teased at school, and some of the older chaps tried to pick fights with me. I hated it. They called me names because I was skinny and I had ginger hair and long legs with knobbly knees. And I was no good at rugby.'

'But they did not say you had no father and mother.' James stared down at the ground and poked a stick into the soil. 'They did not mock you because you had no clan or family of your own.'

'No. They didn't do that.' Anthony put his hand on the boy's shoulder. 'But most of those tough-looking boys don't have good lives, although they are with their clans. Their fathers or older brothers often beat them. They also have a hard time working on the *shambas* and keeping the goats when they are not at school. Often there is no one at home to help them with their homework, so they don't do well in class. I think many of the boys who try to make trouble for you are jealous, because Mama Hannah and Lars take such good care of you.'

354

'David says my father is dead. And my mother too. He says Mama Hannah picked me out of the orphanage because I had a good smile and *akili*. Did you know that?'

'I certainly did,' Anthony laughed and chucked the boy under the chin. 'And she was right.'

'Where did Ma find James?' Suniva's eyes were bright with curiosity. 'Which orphanage?'

'You have to ask her that question.' Anthony had no idea what Hannah's official version of the story might be, or what David had already said.

'Did you ever meet my father or my mother?' James's question was hopeful.

'I didn't. But I'm sure they were good people and they tried their best to make sure you would be safe.' Anthony's heart twisted in sympathy. It was difficult to know how he could quell the doubts that had finally come to the surface of James's consciousness.

'How did they die, my parents?' The enquiry came out of desperation. 'Did it hurt them when they died? Do you think they went to heaven?'

'I don't know how they died, or why,' Anthony said. 'But I can promise you they would be very proud if they could see you now. And if there is a place called heaven, then they will be watching you with happiness, knowing that you have found a good place to live your life.'

'I hope I will always live here, at Langani,' James said. 'Because I have no other place. That is what Suniva says, too. That we must live here for ever and ever.'

'And we will.' Suniva took his hand. 'As long as we wish for it, that is what will happen.'

'Then all you need to do is wish hard enough,' Anthony said. 'That applies to most things in life. Now, let's go and see if Lars has any more news from Norway. And we will all make a wish that Grandpa Jorgen will soon be well again.'

Chapter 22

London, November 1977

'Toast of the bloody town.' Tom Bartlett put his feet up on his desk and lit a cigar. 'Conquerers of the world's glossies and tabloids. The great white hunter and his society beauty. I've never seen so many magazine articles and pictures and what all. Thank God you're going home. I'm totally exhausted.'

'And much, much richer, as our accountant has just informed us.' Camilla laughed and patted his cheek. 'You are a dear, clever boy. I still can't believe you got me the designer of the year thing. And the order from Bergdorf Goodman that will make Saul Greenberg richer than both of us put together. I'll never forget his face when we signed the contract in New York. His eyes were glued to the paper, and he didn't budge from the table until he was sure the ink was totally dry.'

'In all his martini-driven fantasies he never dreamed he would make anything but cheap frocks for office girls,' Tom said.

'I'd like to remind you that some of those were mine,' Camilla said. 'It was a lucky day for both of us when you persuaded me to team up with him. We've made pots of money on those little dresses with my name on the label.'

'They were for the mass market,' Tom said. 'Now he's reached the top. He's into Bergdorf's, thanks to your classy new designs. If he goes any higher he'll have a permanent nose bleed.'

'He sees himself at all the posh parties in New York from now on, with the most glamorous women wearing our gowns. Dear old Saul. I'm glad for him.'

'I wish you would change your mind and do the Cartier pictures,' Tom said.

'No,' she said. 'And don't bother to tell me I'm getting too long in the tooth for another chance later on. You threaten me with that every time I come here. It's time to go home Tom. Besides, you've just said you're tired of me being here.'

She stood up, tall and leggy and slender, her blue eyes shining, her face more lovely than ever. He had never believed she would actually marry Anthony and take the greatest chance of her life.

'What about London and New York and Paris, and the circles you move in there,' he had asked her in Lamu, on the night before her wedding. 'Can you really abandon all that permanently, and bury yourself in the middle of nowhere.'

'This isn't the middle of nowhere,' she had said, making a sweeping gesture over the scented garden and the moonlit sea. 'I'll still divide my time between Kenya and London or New York. I'm still going to work, but as of now, this is the centre of my world.'

'OK, Lamu is spectacular. But life in Nairobi ain't exactly glamorous. An out-of-date film at some smelly cinema, followed by a hunk of eland washed down with a bottle of indifferent wine, and some old man in a long coat with a panga outside your house, in case someone tries to rob or kill you. It's not quite what you're used to, darling.' He had been openly sceptical. 'What about all those nights at West End theatre openings? What about arriving at the Tate and the Royal Academy and the opera, in a limousine as the star guest? How about the tables specially reserved for you in the best restaurants in London and New York?' He leaned close, his face within inches of her own.

'What rubbish you talk,' she said, pushing him away. 'Those are things I will look forward to when I come to Europe. I never wanted to be in the centre of what you are describing. It happened by accident, and I'm grateful for the success I've had. But I don't want to live the rest of my life playing a role that was imposed on me because I'm good-looking. I'd much rather go to an event because I want to, rather than because I'm paid to be part of it.'

'You'll miss it,' Tom had insisted. 'You're starry-eyed now, but reality will set in when you have spent six months in dusty old Karen, swatting mosquitoes and warding off all kinds of creepy crawlies, with the lawn dried up from drought, and the electricity and the phone on the blink half the time.'

'Oh for heaven's sake, Tom.' She burst out laughing. 'We might have to find a better house, eventually, or even build one. That would be fun. Anyway, I never wanted to live in a Grade 1 listed building, or a penthouse on Park Avenue, where the walls of my residence dictate who I am and what I'm expected to be.'

'Mark my words, darling,' Tom had said, wagging his finger at her. 'You won't be able to change that drastically, without paying a heavy price. Your fantasy world will soon start to evaporate.'

Now he had to admit, grudgingly, that she was thriving. Marriage suited her, but there was something different in the way she looked today. She was glowing, incandescent almost, and there was a softness about her that he had never seen before.

'Let's have lunch,' he said, and was disappointed when she shook her head.

'No. I have a date with Anthony. Just the two of us. But we can do dinner. We're both free tonight – no cocktail parties, interviews, client meetings.'

'Three's a crowd,' he said, his mouth curling downwards. 'And I can't compete with your jungle boy.'

'From what I've seen, you have other things on your mind. Lila is definitely smitten. But you must be careful, Tom. She is not some London dollybird you can play with. She has been through a bad experience and she's vulnerable and scared. I know you have looked after her well. But don't play with her emotions.'

'Since her smart-arse cousin arrived she has spent more time with him than she has with me,' Tom said.

'Like me, Rabindrah is more than ready to get back to Nairobi,' Camilla said, reaching for her coat and handbag. 'The *Daily Telegraph* has commissioned him to do a couple of articles about the rights of Commonwealth citizens to enter Britain. When that is finished he'll be off, leaving you a clear field. And his father is sorting out Lila's legal problems so she can eventually get a divorce.'

'He'll be off when his boss in Nairobi thinks it's safe for him to go home,' Tom said. 'By the way, I thought I'd take Lila to your cottage in the Cotswolds next weekend. That might be a charming little diversion.'

'You can use it any time,' she said. 'I had forgotten how quaint it is, and how beautifully Mother decorated it. I loved taking Anthony down there. So tell me, is this one of your passing fancies, or have you really fallen for her?'

'You are in far too much of a hurry to discuss the complexities of my love life,' he said, still sulky over her refusal of lunch. 'Off you go, then.'

'Let me know if you change your mind about dinner,' she said, leaning over to kiss his cheek. 'We could invite Lila and Rabindrah too, if you like.'

'Sounds like a bloody circus,' he said, refusing to be mollified. 'I'll let you know later.'

She left his office, running down the steep stairs, her heart beating with impatience as she searched for a taxi. It was raw in the street and she pulled the collar of her fur coat close to her face, and snuggled deep into its warmth. She had chosen a quiet table at the Connaught for lunch, and was pleased to see that Anthony had not yet arrived.

'Welcome back, madam.' The maître d'hôtel appeared as soon as she stood in the entrance to the dining room. 'I have your table for two in the corner. Can I get you something to drink while you are waiting?'

'Champagne,' she said, bestowing her most dazzling smile on him. 'It's a celebration.'

She saw Anthony minutes later, crossing the room to join her, and to learn the secret she had kept from him until today. Since this morning's confirmation in the Harley Street consulting room she had rehearsed the words a thousand times, memorising her announcement and then revising it, so that she would be able to convey the full meaning of the miracle they had created together. She looked up at him, melting with the joy of seeing him, anticipating his reaction, already feeling the presence of their child inside her.

'Sweetheart.' Anthony sat down beside her and pulled his chair closer. His face was grave, and she studied him with disquiet.

'Is something the matter? Is your leg bothering you?'

He did not answer immediately. Instead he waited until the champagne had been poured and then lifted his glass. 'To survival,' he said.

'Survival?'

'Darling, I have been on the phone to Nairobi. Practically all morning. Something has happened while we were away. I'm going to tell it to you straight. Duncan Harper has cleaned out our bank accounts and disappeared. Left the country, probably. The police are looking for him, but I'm sure it's too late.'

'What?' Time stood still as she stared at him in disbelief. 'Duncan? But he's so solid, so reliable. He's meticulous to the point of driving you into a frenzy. He can't have done that. There must be some mistake.'

'There's no mistake,' he said grimly. 'He didn't show up for work on Monday, and everyone in the office assumed he was sick. But he didn't appear yesterday either, when the cheques had to be signed for salaries and wages, and food and beverage supplies for the camps, and all the usual bills. Rose phoned his house but there was no reply. Finally she went round there, thinking he might be really ill, or that he had been attacked and robbed.' His fingers gripped the edge of the table, knuckles white with tension on the tanned fingers. 'He was gone. The wardrobes were empty. Nothing personal left behind. The houseboy said he had been paid early – just before the weekend – and Duncan had told him he was going away for a few days. But the landlord phoned our office this morning and said he hadn't received the rent for December.'

'What are you going to do?' The day had been so full of promise, but now she could only will herself to remain in her chair as her stomach roiled and nausea rose, and the joy of the occasion withered. 'What can we do?'

'I've made reservations on tonight's flight,' he said. 'It's a few days earlier than planned, but we have to leave now.'

'We'll need money in Nairobi,' she said, taking refuge in practicalities. 'I'd better arrange a transfer from my account here.'

'You're right,' he said, running his hand through his hair, unable to look at her directly, aware that his resolve to protect her, to take care of her always, had already been destroyed. Instead, he was going to be reliant on her for an enormous sum of money, and she would still have to be their anchor, the one who would continue to keep his life on track, just as before.

'I'm afraid you will have to wire some funds, to keep the office going until we can sort this out. Can you arrange enough to pay salaries for last month, and the next three or four months of the season? Plus supplies and booking fees, and vehicle maintenance for all the safaris booked from December to April? Enough to keep us afloat until we can work out what to do.'

'Of course I can. Tom and I have to take care of the usual outgoings here, for manufacturing and distributing the clothes and accessories,' she said, recognising his humiliation. 'And advertising costs, plus Tom's fees. But I can certainly send a sum that will tide us over.'

'Christ, this is going to be really tough,' he said. 'Duncan fucking Harper had access to both our local and overseas company accounts. I made him a signatory almost two years ago, and he has taken just about everything. If I could find him I would beat the hell out of the puny little shit, and throw him to the crocs. I could tell from Rose's voice that the staff are scared of losing their jobs, and I have to reassure them that they will be paid. We can't afford to lose any of the office or camping team, just as the season is about to start.'

'They'll stay,' Camilla said. 'Most of them have been with you for years. Once they get their salaries they'll be fine.'

'There is one good thing that has come out of this.' He tried to smile. 'We can't afford to use any outside guides for the moment, so you and I will have to take the clients out together, once we get an office manager sorted out. Think of all the mornings we will wake up to the sounds of the bush, and watch the moon rise over the Mara, or the Chyulu Hills.'

'I'm thinking,' she said, glad that he did not notice the catch in her throat.

'I've set up a meeting with the bank tomorrow morning, as soon as we arrive in Nairobi. We'll have to see what they can come up with in terms of credit, until we get straightened out again. It's you and me, Camilla. I never dreamed that anything like this could happen, but we can weather this.'

'Yes,' she said, her voice sounding all wrong in her own ears as she repeated the words. She took a measured breath in an attempt to steady herself. 'Together we can do anything.'

'Why the champagne, by the way?' He looked at her and raised his glass, not waiting for an answer. 'Anyway, we may as well enjoy it, because we will be drinking it very sparingly from now on.'

'I wanted to celebrate every blissful day that we have been married,' she said, smiling through her pain as their perfect future evaporated into the grey afteroon. 'And all the days to come.'

'I adore you,' he said, smiling at last. 'I love you first and last and beyond all else, and I'll make this up to you. What has happened is catastrophic, but we will survive it and everything else that comes our way. Now let's order. I need food and I need to make love to you, and we're going to find time for both, before we fly out tonight.'

'I can't leave this evening,' Camilla said. 'I need to see the bank and make arrangements for regular wire transfers over the next few months. Tie up a few things I discussed with Tom this morning.' She bit her lip. 'This is all my fault, you know. I was the one who found Duncan and insisted that you take him on.'

'Of course it's not your fault,' he said.

'Yes, it is. I should have checked him out more carefully. But he was so efficient from the beginning and I trusted him. I didn't follow up on his references. Not even the accounting firm where he had worked before he left for Kenya.' She was determined not to cry, but her eyes were brimming. 'I'm so sorry. So very sorry.'

'Darling, this man ran our company perfectly, from the day he walked in the door. Neither one of us could ever have guessed he would turn out to be a crook. The annual audits brought up nothing but the smallest queries. Careless handling of petty cash by the *watu*, and the usual pilfering at the go-down. When Rose called this morning I was sure she had everything wrong. It was only after I rang Jonathan Chalmers at the bank that I realised it was all too true.'

'But what on earth would have made Duncan do this, out of the blue?' She grappled for calm as she waited for some kind of explanation.

'There is one thing,' he said, thoughtfully. 'An odd little incident. I never thought about it at the time, but now I wonder if it has some significance. I saw Duncan one night in the casino. He had lost a big sum of money, but he went to the cashier to buy more chips. He was obviously making a night of it.'

'You were in the casino?' She was surprised. 'And you think he could be a big gambler?'

'It's possible,' Anthony said. 'Can you remember the name of the company he worked for here, before he came out to Kenya?'

Camilla frowned, trying to recall the details. 'His last job in the UK was with a big firm in Leeds. The reference was glowing. Signed by the managing director who said Duncan was leaving for personal reasons, and the company regretted his departure. All the usual stuff when someone valuable moves on. If you remember, he told us he had split up with his wife and wanted to get as far away as he could.'

'Well, there isn't anything we can do until tomorrow,' he said. 'So let's enjoy our celebration. Two months and a lifetime more to go, with each moment better than the last. Are you sure you can't fly out with me tonight?'

'I'll be with you as soon as I can,' she said, forcing herself to swallow a mouthful of fish that tasted like ashes. 'But this afternoon you should go straight back to the flat and start packing, while I drop in at the bank and start things rolling. You'll have to phone the airline and cancel my flight.'

'Oh, God.' His face was etched with strain. 'I haven't really come to grips with this, and suddenly it seems pretty bad.'

'We are going to be fine.' She adopted a practical tone to steady herself, keeping her voice level. 'And we'll find a new office manager. Maybe someone we know who has worked in one of the major accounting firms in Nairobi, and would like a change. It will take time to straighten it all out, but we will do it. And then we can spend our time out on safari together. That will be wonderful.'

'What are you doing back here? You look as if you've been struck by lightning,' Tom said. 'What happened to your lovebird lunch? Have you had a fight?'

His manner changed instantly when Camilla told him the news and asked to use his conference room to make some telephone calls.

'Anything I can do,' he said. 'I'm sorry, darling. Life's a bitch sometimes, but at least it's only money. Things could be so much worse. Shit, don't cry. I can't bear to see you cry, Camilla. Here – drink some coffee. I'm going to lace it with a slug of brandy, because you look as though you might pass out on me.' He sat down beside her, watching as she tried to control her trembling hands and began to write a list. 'If you need me just buzz. Do you want Lila to come in and help you?'

'No. I can't face anyone right now. Would you tell her that dinner is off? In fact, could you ring Rabindrah too, and tell him the whole, sorry tale,' she said. 'Oh, and I need the number of a company in Leeds, if you could find that for me. Here's the name. Thanks, Tom.'

The receptionist of the chartered accounting firm was puzzled when Camilla asked for Jeff Baggott, the managing director.

'We don't have anyone called Baggott here,' she said. 'The head of our company is Lloyd Macartney. No, he's not someone new. He's been here for ten years.'

She was reluctant to put Camilla through, but after some persuasion Macartney finally took the call. He was cautious at first, but his attitude softened as he listened to her story and recognised her name.

'I remember Harper,' he said. 'We had to let him go. Personal problems. And yes, you're right. He had gambling debts that led to him losing his wife and his house. Then the bank pulled the rug on his overdraft, and he was finished. He must have written the reference himself, using our company letterhead and a false name for the referee. I suppose he took a chance that no one would check him out from so far away.'

'He was right.' She pounded her fist against her forehead. 'And I'm paying the price for my carelessness. Thank you for your help.'

Her visit to the bank was brief, although the manager who had taken care of her account for many years was alarmed by the size of the transfer she requested. Her last call left her weeping at the long, polished table, her head down on her arms, her body convulsed with sobs as she said goodbye to her most precious dream.

Anthony made love to her with more tenderness than she had ever known, his hands cupped around her face as he kissed her, his eyes devouring every detail of her.

'Just remember we will be together again in a few days,' he said a little later when he had packed and was ready to go. 'Nothing else matters.'

He was horribly wrong but she nodded, speechless, afraid she might form the words she did not want him to hear. Instead she flung herself into his arms one last time before he lifted his suitcase and she heard his steps fade on the stairs.

She looked down into the square and saw him walk towards the waiting taxi, his figure vanishing in the blur of rain.

'Rabindrah?' She had hesitated before dialling his number, but she did not have the courage to return to the flat alone, and she felt that she could trust him.

'Camilla, where the hell have you been? I'm so relieved to hear from you. Tom told me what had happened with Duncan Harper in Nairobi. I've been trying to get hold of you for two days, phoning you at home and at Tom's office. I even came round to the flat yesterday. Are you all right? Have you heard from Anthony?'

'I spoke to him yesterday, and again this morning. He's sorting things out, but it's a mess that will take time. Look, I wonder if you would collect me from – well, here's the address. It's a clinic. I need to get back to my flat. Could you come for me, Rabindrah? I don't want to take a taxi on my own.'

'Are you ill? This problem with Harper must have come as a terrible shock.' Perhaps it had all been too much for her. She sounded as though she was on the edge of a breakdown.

'Just come,' she said, her voice breaking. 'And don't tell anyone you've spoken to me. Please.'

'I'm on my way,' he said. 'I'm with Father, working on evidence for Lila's divorce case. But I'll be with you in about twenty minutes.'

'I have to follow up on a story,' he said to Jasmer, ignoring the lift of the eyebrows and the frown that followed. 'You'd better tell Mother I might not be in for dinner this evening. I'll be back as soon as I can.'

Camilla was waiting in the reception area, her face deathly pale, her eyes hidden beneath large sunglasses that made the daylight as dark as her own inner space. They drove in silence to Knightsbridge. Wordlessly, she walked up the stairs to the flat, pausing twice on the long flight. In the sitting room she sat down and tried to suppress the memory of her love-making with Anthony before he had left her to her choice. She gave a small groan and bent forwards.

'What——?' Rabindrah did not have time to finish the question.

'I've had an abortion,' she said, her voice dull.

'Oh, no. Oh, God.' He placed his hand over his eyes, appalled by the bald announcement. 'Camilla, I don't know what – Oh, my God. Have you told Anthony? Is he all right with this, on top of everything else?'

'He didn't know I was pregnant. I was going to tell him at lunch the other day, but then he . . .' Her words were flat, matter of fact. 'He needs me now, full time between the office and the safaris. And I've told Tom that I'll take on a couple of big European advertising campaigns in the spring. To make the extra money we need. I wouldn't have been able to do any of those things if I was pregnant.'

'But shouldn't you have –? This is a terrible thing. My God, your first child and . . .'

'Don't judge me, Rabindrah. I did what I had to do. And you can never tell anyone. No one at all. Not ever. Promise me that you will never tell.'

He nodded his assent, his heart sinking as he took in the news. 'You have my word,' he said. 'I'm so sorry.'

They sat in silence on the sofa but after a time she began to shiver, her body trembling and then shaking as her teeth began to chatter. He wrapped his arms around her and tried to soothe her.

'Come and lie down,' he said. 'I'll help you into bed, and find a hot water bottle and some extra blankets. Should I call your doctor?'

'No. He gave me some sedatives. They're in my bag.' The words were barely audible, but when he handed her the tablet and a glass of water she could no longer speak through the tears that were choking her.

He led her into the bedroom and then went to boil the kettle and fill the water bottle as she undressed. When he returned she was lying on the bed wrapped in Anthony's dressing gown, her face turned into the pillow where the scent of him still lingered. The trembling had stopped and she was dry-eyed.

'Thank you,' she said. 'Thank you so much for bringing me here. I didn't want to come into the place alone, you see. But now I'll just take the pill and sleep. And you won't tell anyone you've seen me, will you?'

'No, I won't. But Tom will want to know where you've been. I rang him yesterday, when I couldn't find you. He thought you might have gone to your cottage in the country, but he said there was no reply when he rang there.'

'I spoke to him this morning,' she said. 'Told him I was down there, but I didn't want to talk to anyone until I had sorted things out in my head. You must go now, Rabindrah. I'm fine and I'll be asleep soon. I'm planning to leave for Nairobi early next week, but we can have lunch or dinner before I go.'

He hesitated but Camilla waved him away, a half smile on her lips, seemingly calm. She heard the door close quietly and got up, unable to find any comfort in the idea of lying in bed. Instead she sat in the chair by the window, staring into the oncoming darkness, listening to the wind and the sound of bare, spidery branches tapping on the glass. She felt increasingly cold as her mind turned into a black vortex of grief. Her body was very still, hands limp on the arms of the chair, trancelike, until she felt the warm seeping of blood that represented the last remains of her child. In the bathroom she glanced at her face but looked away at once, unable to bear the agony reflected in her eyes. Somewhere in the distance she heard a terrible sound that she did not recognise, and then Rabindrah was beside her, holding her in a firm grip, talking through a wall of sound that she now knew to be her own despair.

'Camilla, I'm here. I hadn't reached the door onto the street before I knew I must stay with you. Come back into the sitting room. You won't be on your own. I'll make us some tea, and I promise you won't be alone again until you are ready. Look, you haven't taken your tablet. You must swallow it now, while I'm watching. It will help, Camilla. You need it.'

Her expression was blank, but she obeyed him and then allowed him to settle her on the sofa. From the kitchen he kept up a steady flow of words, his voice low and quiet. They drank their tea slowly, until the sedative took effect and she lay down on the couch and finally slept. Rabindrah placed a rug over her and sat in an armchair, dozing on and off, watching the rhythm of her breathing, thinking about what she had done. A child. She had been carrying a child, the new life that he and Sarah had always longed for, had struggled to create, until their efforts had perhaps destroyed their marriage. But Camilla had chosen to terminate her first pregnancy. Made a ruthless choice, seemingly without hesitation, for the sake of her husband. He shuddered. Was that the basic difference in their two marriages, Rabindrah wondered. The fact that for Camilla it would always be Anthony who came first, whereas – His line of thought was interrupted by the insistent sound of the telephone.

'Don't answer it.' Camilla stirred on the sofa and opened her eyes. 'I can't talk to anyone. Not yet.' She sat up and placed her feet carefully on the floor, as if uncertain of her balance. Then she stood up and moved around the room, turning on table lamps and lighting the fire, so that the room became warm and comforting. 'What time is it?'

'Almost ten,' he said. 'But the rain has stopped and the wind has let up a little. At one point I thought those branches were going to come through the window. When did you last have something to eat? Are you hungry?'

'I shouldn't have involved you in this,' she said. 'You of all people, when you have been through so much with Sarah and I have chosen not to keep my baby. I've been very selfish and I'm sorry, but I knew I could trust you and that you would try to understand.' He made no reply and she hurried away from the subject. 'Yes, I'm hungry. I couldn't eat anything in the clinic, and now I'm very hungry.'

'I'll go and get us a ruby,' he said. 'From the Indian place round the corner.'

'If you wait a minute I'll come with you,' she said. 'A good curry sounds perfect.'

'It's cold out there.' Rabindrah put a restraining hand on her shoulder. 'I think you should stay by the fire.'

'It's cold in here,' she said, placing her hand on her heart. 'I'm coming with you. It's a statement, not a discussion.'

They chose chicken masala and rice and bhajis and took them back to the flat, eating as though they had been without food for days, following up with more tea, and then returned to the large sofa.

'A brandy,' she said. 'I think I need that. Will you stay here tonight, Rabindrah?' This time she did not look at him, afraid of refusal. 'I know it's a lot to ask but I'm not sure I can be alone.'

'Of course I'll stay,' he said. 'You can wake me if you need anything, or if you feel bad.'

'I do feel bad,' she said in a low voice. 'Bad to the core. And after what I've done, I wonder if I could ever be a real mother. Maybe I'm like Marina. She was never a mother and I just existed without her. Until the last months of her life when she made an effort to build a bridge between us. It was a valiant try, but it came too late and it was more for herself than it was for me.'

'You'll be a wonderful mother one day,' he said gently.

'I don't know.' Her voice was so quiet that Rabindrah had to lean forward in order to hear her. 'I adored my father, you know, but when I discovered that he was a lover of men rather than women, I dropped him. And I never found my way back to the unconditional love I thought I had for him. So perhaps I deserved to be an orphan, and maybe I'll wind up childless as a punishment for what I have just done.' She raised her face, willing him to acknowledge her most private admissions. 'I did it for Anthony. And I will guard him and all that he needs, unconditionally and in every way, no matter what it takes. So, if there is a God, I hope he will forgive me for loving my husband so much.'

'I think you should go to bed now.' Rabindrah took her hand, seeing the fear in her eyes. 'Don't worry. I'll leave the bedroom door open, so I'll know if you need me. Call me if you have a bad dream, or you feel any pain.'

She buried her head in his shoulder. 'Thank you,' she said. 'I'll never forget this. Never.'

When she had shut herself into the bathroom he wondered if he should telephone his parents and say that he would not be back for the night. But it was past midnight. They would be in bed by now, and he could not think of any brief explanation that would sound plausible. He decided to ring in the morning, and to invent some tale about an interview with a subject who insisted on spinning out his story over an all-night drinking session.

The winter's day was cold and clear, and the grey drizzle had vanished, leaving the dark arms of the trees reaching into a glassy sky. Rabindrah looked in on Camilla and found that she was still asleep, her body so still that he bent down in order to feel her breath on his face. When he had showered and dressed he let himself out of the flat and went to the French bakery on the corner. Sarah had loved the mornings when he had woken up first and brought her freshly baked croissants. He felt a sadness that hurt him more than any physical pain as he returned with his package, and began to prepare coffee.

The suddenness of Camilla's appearance made him jump as her fingers brushed his sleeve. Her face was very pale and she had dressed in warm trousers and a sweater.

'I've just spoken to the doctor and I need to go to the clinic,' she said. 'I'm bleeding heavily. He says it's probably the passing of normal clots, but he wants to check up on me.'

'Sit by the window,' Rabindrah said. 'I'll get a taxi on Brompton Road, but don't come down until you see me in the Square. It's very cold out there.'

They spent three hours at the clinic, but Camilla was finally released with stern instructions that she must remain in bed, or at least off her feet, for the next forty-eight hours. And then there would be another appointment. The doctor could not say when he thought it would be safe to travel. On the way back to Knightsbridge she tried to persuade Rabindrah that she would be fine on her own. But his eyes took in her ghostlike appearance, and he knew that he would stay.

'You have to tell him,' he said, when she lifted the telephone to dial Nairobi.

But she shook her head, making a warning gesture as Anthony came onto the line and described his day. The police had not found Duncan, but the evidence was all too clear when the bank handed over records of recent withdrawals. A few days before his disappearance the bank manager, Jonathan Chalmers, had taken him aside and questioned the unusual amounts of cash and money transfers being arranged. Suppliers were anxious, Duncan had explained. There were so many problems with forgeries and bouncing cheques that he had negotiated considerable discounts for cash payments. Other transactions included large sums wired to overseas accounts, ostensibly for new camping equipment for the coming season. Harper had produced a telex message that had apparently come from Anthony in the United States, authorising the payments. The money had been sent to a company in Italy. He had probably used it to pay his casino debts, Chalmers suggested to Anthony, embarrassed and apologetic.

'We have new overdraft facilities, Camilla, and the funds you wired have arrived,' Anthony said. 'I'm still trying to sort out a stack of unpaid bills, but I'll soon have a handle on how we can manage the season. Now tell me your news, darling. Most importantly, tell me when you will be here. It's as though half of me is missing. This independent old bushman is no good without you anymore.'

'I'll be there soon,' Camilla said. 'There are a couple of fashion shoots I have agreed to do in April and May when our safari season is over, and the contracts need to be signed. I won't delay a moment longer than necessary.' She listened for a minute or two longer and smiled. 'I love you too,' she said then, and put down the receiver.

'You should have told him,' Rabindrah said. 'I made that mistake with Sarah, and I'm still paying for it.'

'No. He has enough to think about. It's done and there is no going back. What purpose would it serve to cause him the same pain I am feeling? He would be angry that I made the decision by myself, and humiliated that I did it because he was in trouble. No, I will never tell him, and neither will you. Let's make ourselves a resolution not to discuss this anymore. Because it's over and I'm going to be all right now, with all that you have done to see me through, and the medicine they gave me this morning. My cleaning lady will be here tomorrow, so she can shop and look after things. We'll have a cup of tea and then you should go back to your parents' place. Aren't you planning to leave for Nairobi in a couple of days?'

'Yes. According to Gordon, things are quiet. As much as they can be. Of course, I'll be at some risk for quite a while, but there are new scandals and other issues on the table in Nairobi, and my story is out of the papers for the moment.' His smile was tentative, hopeful. 'I think Sarah will be in Nairobi.'

'Good. It's time you kissed and made up,' she said. 'I know she was upset about what you did for your uncle, but the poor man is dead. I'm sure she will be ready to look at it differently now.'

'I don't know,' he said, his shoulders sagging as his own troubles reared up in the forefront of his mind. 'I would do anything to get back to the place where we started. Or somewhere near to it.'

'I'm all for that.' Camilla kissed his cheek. 'Here's to the place where we started. Drink up, darling Rabindrah. It's time for you to go.'

He made the call from a phone box on Brompton Road. Outside the rain had started again and the slanting, slashing force of it hammered on the glass panes, combining with the rumble of the traffic to make hearing a challenge.

'Sarah? I'm glad you are back in Nairobi because I'm planning to leave London tomorrow on the night flight. Will you meet me? I think the plane gets in around eight.'

'Yes. Of course. Where are you? It sounds noisy.'

'With my parents. Catching up over the last couple days. The articles for the *Daily Telegraph* are finished, and I've been helping Father to sort things out for Lila. We went to Birmingham to see the mother-in-law again. It was dismal. My parents send their salaams. As usual.'

'So when did you get back from Birmingham?' She sounded strained.

'Late yesterday,' he said. 'Terrible place. I was glad to be out of there, with the weeping widow and all the questions about Harjeet.'

'I can imagine,' she said, her tone changing. 'Did your mother happen to tell you I rang yesterday afternoon and last night? That I talked to her for some time.'

'Yes, yes. I mean, no. I was very late. She probably forgot.'

'I suppose she also forgot to tell you that Kuldip Auntie has had major surgery for cancer, and is still in intensive care?'

'Kuldip Auntie? In hospital?' His astonishment gave him away.

'That's right. As you would know if you had been at home, or even spoken to your parents, over the last two days. But you haven't. I rang again this morning and your mother told me she hadn't seen you since the day before yesterday. That you told Jasmer you wouldn't be home for dinner that night, and then you just vanished. Again. I phoned Lila but she didn't know where you were either, which is strange if you were in

Birmingham or somewhere doing things for her. And there was no answer from Camilla's flat, so that was no help either.'

'Sarah—'

'Why are you lying to me Rabindrah? Where have you been this time, and why are you bloody well lying again?'

'Sarah, calm down. It's nothing. Nothing. I was following a story and—'

'I won't damn well calm down! Being unable to trust anything you say is not "nothing"! In my book it's called lies and deceit. If that is all you can now bring to our marriage then we have precisely "nothing" left. You made me a promise, before you left for London, that there would be no more secrecy. But now you're surrounded by it, all over again. I don't know what you are involved in this time, but it clearly excludes me. I'm still the discarded wife who doesn't rate the courtesy of truth. And all you can tell me is to calm down, you condescending, arrogant bastard!'

'I'm not involved in any investigation!' Rabindrah was shouting now. 'I couldn't tell my parents where I was. I couldn't tell anyone. It was a private matter. Nothing to do with them, or with us!'

'What private matter? Why can't you tell me?'

'Because I gave my word!'

'Obviously to someone who rates higher than I do.'

'My God, Sarah! I don't want to keep anything from you, but believe me this is something she can't—'

'She? Who is "she" Rabindrah? Is it Lila? Tell me. I can't take any more deceit. All the fear, the police around our house, people being killed, the feeling of always being under some unknown threat.' She was sobbing. 'I can't bear it, and you've left me here to live with it all, while you are thousands of miles away having disappeared yet again.'

'Oh God! God!' He pounded the wall of the telephone box. 'I've been with Camilla.'

'Camilla? You're with Anthony and Camilla?' Sarah was incredulous, her laughter high-pitched and out of control. 'What is so secret about that?'

'Anthony is in Nairobi,' Rabindrah said. 'Duncan Harper has run off with all the company funds and Anthony left to try and sort things out. But Camilla was pregnant, and there has been a crisis.'

'She had a miscarriage? Oh, I am so, so sorry. Oh, poor Camilla. I know how it is. We know how that is. Anthony must be devastated, with all this coming at the same time. I'll phone him. Maybe go round there or invite him to dinner. Try to cheer him up. Can I speak to Camilla? Are you with her now? Let me have a word with her.'

'No. No, Sarah. Listen to me.' Rabindrah made a decision, knowing that his marriage was hanging by a thread, throwing away any idea of keeping his promise to Camilla. 'You can't say anything to Anthony. She had to . . . She couldn't have the baby. Not now. She decided it was impossible in the circumstances. And afterwards I was the only one she could turn to. But Anthony doesn't know.'

'I don't understand.' There was a protracted silence and then her voice changed. 'Wait. Are you telling me she had an abortion?' As the truth dawned on her, Sarah felt as though she was plummeting off a precipice, tumbling down, down, her heart turning over in a sick feeling of disbelief. She did not want to hear what Rabindrah was saying. A life. A tiny life that was Camilla's child. Anthony's child. The kind of life that she herself had yearned for, struggled for, wept over when it was lost: a life that should have been treasured, protected, welcomed. And Camilla had destroyed it. There could be no reason to justify such an action. There could never be reason enough for that.

Thousands of miles away Rabindrah heard her cry of despair. 'Sarah? Sarah, listen to me. Let me explain it. Sarah!'

He shouted her name repeatedly across the miles of ocean and land that divided them, but she did not answer although she had not hung up. Finally, he became aware of the impatient knocking on the window of the telephone box. He replaced the heavy, black receiver, nodded to the angry woman who had been standing outside in the rain, and walked away into the cold, wet afternoon.

Chapter 23

Kenya, November 1977

Sarah dropped the receiver and fled to the bathroom. Behind her she could hear Rabindrah's disembodied voice shouting through the phone into the empty hall. She closed the door to block out his words and stood in front of the mirror, her jaw clenched tight, her fists curled, fingers digging into the palms. The world had tilted out of place. Love, as she knew it, had been hurled recklessly into the ether. A pitiless God had taken away Piet, her first love. And then her babies. Her husband had betrayed her. And now Camilla had aborted her baby, snuffed out the life within her and consigned it to the waste of a hospital incinerator. And Rabindrah, who knew what it was to long for a child, had been a party to it. How could he have condoned Camilla's actions, when even Anthony had not been consulted on the brutal decision? She no longer knew her husband, any more than she knew the woman who had been her friend since childhood. They had become strangers. Monstrous, murdering strangers.

She turned on the cold tap and splashed water onto her face, slapping at her skin as all her Catholic beliefs and upbringing rose to the surface. She imagined she could hear the lost child crying out, as she had heard the fading sounds of her own miscarried infants, for days after they were gone. Pressing her face into the towel, she relived those moments and then buried them, along with the image of her husband and her friend.

In the darkroom she turned on the light and began sorting through the latest series of pictures she had shot in the Mara, forcing herself back into the harmony of the wild, to a place that offered an orderly life. It was after midnight when she put the best prints into her portfolio, gathered up her cameras, and locked the front door. As she drove away, the sound of the telephone's engaged signal was still sending its high-pitched whine echoing through the empty house.

She had no recollection of the journey, driving through the night, not thinking, functioning in a mist that allowed her to steer, change gears, dip and dim the headlights, and cover the miles. Her only intent was to get to the Mara, to watch the animals she had been studying and recording. Nothing more. There was nothing more.

It was six in the morning when she drove into Allie's camp, bone weary, her eyes red-rimmed and gritty. Ahmed was bringing *chai* to Allie's tent, and he greeted her with surprise. Sarah gave him a vague smile, and moved on towards her own quarters without saying anything. All she wanted was to lie down and sleep for an hour or two, before going out into the healing wilderness.

'*Hodi*. Tea and toast seemed like a possibility.' Allie appeared minutes later, balancing a tray. 'I thought you were staying in Nairobi for the African Wildlife Federation thing tomorrow. To present our case for more funding, and wait for Rabindrah.' She put down the tray and turned. 'Sarah? My God! What has happened to you?'

Sarah sat up, her face cold as stone. 'I forgot about the meeting. I'm sorry, Allie, but I couldn't stay in Nairobi. I had to get back here. My marriage is over, and this is the only place I want to be.'

'You look like someone on the edge of a breakdown. I know you went through pure hell after your last miscarriage, and that things haven't been right between you and Rabindrah for a while.' Allie sat down and poured tea. 'Maybe you should go back to Ireland for a while, to your family.'

'No. I can't go there.'

'You know, it was you who persuaded me to go to Scotland after Dan died. To step back, and look at things from a different perspective. And I have to say this plainly, because you are very dear to me.' Allie put her hands on Sarah's shoulders and looked at her squarely. 'You are in bad shape, my dear, and you need to take stock of what is happening in your life. Learn to live with what you have been given, and to recognise happiness, even when it comes in a form outside your preconceptions.'

Sarah shifted away, unable to meet Allie's gaze. She could not bring herself to tell the truth, and she resented the implication that she was giving in to self-pity.

'It's not that simple.'

'Simple? Of course not. But you have been overwrought and angry for a long time. It's particularly noticeable to people who love you, and it is also the wedge that will drive them away. You can't go on punishing yourself and Rabindrah, and everyone in your immediate circle, for the fact that you don't have a family. You told me before that the fertility medication was playing havoc with your emotions. So it might be worth stopping this treatment you're on, before you allow it to derail your life. Only you can make that decision, but it is a suggestion. You have to find another focus, Sarah. Or leave. Leave your marriage, leave the country, leave whatever is making you so unhappy. Because you cannot go on as you are.'

'I'm not in a state because of the medicine. I've stopped taking it. You can't use it all the time, and anyway Rabindrah and I are not – well, anyhow, I can only say I'm sorry.'

'It's OK, kid, as Dan used to say. It will all work out, if you take time to think. I suggest you have a shower, sleep for a while and then go and look for the cheetahs. I will have to leave for Nairobi sometime today. To do the presentation at the AWF meeting.' She shook her head as Sarah began to protest. 'I want you to stay here and take a long look at your situation.' She gave Sarah a gentle shake. 'Eat, sleep and think. I'd better get going.'

'You can use our house if you like,' Sarah said, trying to make up for her thoughtlessness. 'Chege is there, and Rabindrah should be back from London soon. I'm sorry, Allie. I know you hate these presentations, and I've really screwed this up.'

'It's fine. Time I did a bit of my own begging. Thanks for the offer of a bed, but I'll stay in a house belonging to friends who are at the coast. You might remember it.' She laughed. 'That was where Dan fixed you those lethal martinis years ago. You got comically drunk, as I recall. And Rabindrah, whom you barely knew, had to drive you back to Anthony's place where you were staying.'

'That does seem like a very long time ago,' Sarah said, forcing a smile. 'By the way, I brought some new photos down. They're in my folder over there. You might like to look them over before you leave.'

'I will.' Allie took the pictures and ducked out into the bright morning, talking over her shoulder. 'I'll be away for a few days. Till the end of the week, anyway. You can continue with Hugo. The usual routine. And think about what I've said.'

Sarah sat on the bed, her body jangling with exhaustion. When she heard the water sloshing into the shower bucket outside, she went to wash away the grime of the journey and then returned to her tent. She slept deeply and did not hear Allie leaving the camp in a cloud of dust and farewells.

It was mid-afternoon when she finally woke up, dressed, and walked out into the heat. In the mess tent Hugo stood up to greet her, making no comment on her unexpected return. She took a cold beer from the fridge, and accepted a plate of salad, realising that she was ravenously hungry and that she had hardly eaten since the day before. As Hugo filled her in on the cheetahs she listened in silence, already calmed by the routine of camp life.

'I feel Isis is comfortable with me now,' he said, giving his glasses a wipe, and pushing them up on his nose again. 'Look, here are some sketches of the cubs from yesterday. What do you think?'

Sarah laughed at the drawings. He had portrayed the small cats chasing one another through the long grass, pouncing on their mother as she dozed in the shade, or lying in the protection of her sleek body, sated with milk, their tummies bulging.

'Shall we go and find them?' Hugo put his notes and sketches away in a series of neatly titled folders.

'I'm ready.' Sarah had noticed, soon after his arrival, that while his appearance was always rumpled and untidy Hugo's work was meticulous, with notes and drawings filed away in perfect order. He had even taken to tidying Allie's papers as he went along. 'Where is Erope, by the way? Maybe he will want to come with us.'

'He went with Allie.'

'To Nairobi?' She was taken aback.

'Um, well, she thought she might need his help with the presentation.' Hugo looked embarrassed. 'They will share the driving, and the chores she needs to do.'

Sarah turned away, a flush climbing her neck and flooding her cheeks. It was her fault that Allie had had to rush off, without any preparation. And she hated speaking in public. Erope would be a help to her. He was articulate, knowledgeable and had great presence.

'I feel badly about skipping the fund meeting, but I had to get back here.' Although she had slept, she still felt as though she had been through a mangle, and she was relieved when he asked no questions. 'We can take my car. I'll put the cameras in place, and you drive.'

The landscape had softened to a gold patina, with umber shadows springing out in elongated forms from the trees and animals that dotted the plains. Hugo had commandeered an old bush hat left behind by some safari guide, and he wore it low over his forehead, shielding his freckled face from the sun. He had clip-on sunshades over his glasses, and the hair on his forearms and hands had turned to a blond pelt in the afternoon light. Like Piet's, Sarah remembered, catching her breath.

'Sorry. Was it the pothole I hit?' Hugo heard the little gasp.

'No. It was something I remembered. Nothing to do with your driving.'

'At least I'm not in Allie's class,' he said. 'I have to admit to constant terror when she gets behind the wheel. I don't know how she has survived this long without serious injury. I didn't ask if you would prefer to drive?'

'No. I had enough of that last night.' She stared out the window.

'Sarah, if you want to talk . . . You know you can trust me.'

'I have a problem I can't discuss. It's nothing to do with trust. I can't talk about it. What's important is just being here.'

'Food for the broken soul,' he said, looking at her pinched face. 'I understand. Now, this is where Isis was yesterday.'

They reached a rise in the land and stopped beneath a balanites tree. Ahmed had put a large thermos and a packet of sandwiches in the picnic basket, and they drank tea as they sat looking out over the plains. A light wind had sprung up and a herd of impala grazed among ripples of swaying grass, as though they were moving through a yellow sea.

'No sign of Isis.' Sarah had the binoculars. 'There's plenty of food for her, but the younger animals are in the centre of the group. See? She may have decided not to take them on.'

They drove down towards the herd, following a grassy track that levelled out on the plain below. Across the other side of the flatland was a rocky mound covered in thick vegetation, ideal as a lookout and a place to hide the cubs.

'It's a pity we don't have Erope,' Hugo said, squinting into the lowering sun as they drove towards the rocks. 'He always knows where to look.'

'Yes,' Sarah agreed. 'It's an innate part of him, that ability to track. He started very young, looking after the family livestock in the *bundu*. The herders are usually small boys and they have to know how to read what is around them, and to recognise danger, or they don't survive. But Erope has a special gift. He taught me so much when we worked together on the elephants. It's great that he and Allie make such a perfect team.'

'They certainly do!' Hugo exploded with laughter, causing Sarah to turn towards him puzzled.

'What's so funny? What is that supposed to mean?' she said.

'Well, you know . . .' His face was scarlet and he took off his hat to run his fingers through his hair.

'What do I know?'

'Look, I thought you . . . That it was obvious. Since you and Allie are so close. Anyway . . .' Hugo's smile broadened, and his eyes were full of mischief.

Sarah stared at him, open-mouthed.

'Oh, come on, Sarah,' he said, still grinning. 'You must have seen it. Lately, they nearly always share the drives, go out earlier or come in later, sit over the camp fire long after everyone has gone to bed. Don't look so shocked. It's good for Allie. You probably have nearly all the material you need for this book. Soon you will go back to life in Nairobi and a new subject or another lecture tour. And I will have to return to the academic world. Allie will be lonely then. It can be pretty isolated in this camp, month in month out.'

'Good God! I never thought of Allie and Erope. Not like that. He has a wife and several *totos* in Buffalo Springs.'

'We're not talking about marriage, for goodness sake. This relationship . . . well, I think it suits them both.'

'But he's much younger than her, and so different. He will always be a tribesman, despite the Western veneer.'

'I'd say that appeals to her unconventional soul. Anyway, age and background have nothing to do with it, when attraction is running strong . . .' Hugo trailed off, gripping the steering wheel hard. 'Allie is very pragmatic,' he went on, after a brief silence. 'They enjoy each other, but she is not the kind to become besotted with him, like a wee teenage girl, and pine away if and when it comes to an end. They respect each other. They've been friends and colleagues for a long time. Why not lovers? Good luck to them – that's what I say.'

Sarah started to laugh, throwing her head back, enjoying the astonishment and the warmth she felt for Allie. 'No wonder she didn't want to stay in my house in Nairobi,' she said. 'Just as well. Can you imagine if Rabindrah had arrived and found them in bed? And Chege wouldn't be able to contain himself. He'd have it all over the city in a flash.'

'Do you mind?' Hugo examined her closely.

'No, I don't.' Sarah felt a small shiver for a second, as she closed out the image of Dan that rose unbidden to her mind. Dan was gone. Like Piet. And Rabindrah, now cut off from her, impossibly tainted by her sense of repulsion. Why should Allie not find solace in her long-time friend?

'You're right,' she said. 'Erope is a good partner for her, in every sense. They have a common purpose in their love of the country and its wild inhabitants. And now in taking care of each other.' She was still smiling, her eyes closed, and inside she felt a deep yearning for the time when she and Rabindrah had shared a passion like that, lying out under the stars, making love in the African night. But that was gone. All gone.

Hugo stopped and turned off the engine, and she opened her eyes. They were near the rocky mound, but the ground was pitted with holes and covered with low scrubby bushes that concealed scattered boulders.

'Let's see if we can pick up any tracks,' Sarah said.

They climbed out of the vehicle and squatted down, looking for signs, but there was nothing to point the way towards the cheetah and her family.

'Maybe you should drive now.' Hugo handed over the keys. 'This is going to get pretty rough, and I don't want to be the one who overturns your posh Land Cruiser with all its special fittings.'

They drove slowly round the base of the hill until Hugo grabbed her shoulder in warning. Ahead of them there was a flash of movement, followed by the growl and screech of a cat, fighting for its life. Blood smears and a trail of flattened grass led into the bushes, and Sarah recognised the telltale signs of a kill having been dragged towards the thicket. In the shadows she could make out the carcass of a large male impala. Isis was crouched nearby, not eating, and the reason was instantly apparent. Her success in bringing down her prey had exacted a heavy penalty. In the struggle, she had been gored by the victim's sharp horns, and there was a deep gash across her chest.

'It must have taken an astonishing effort on her part to drag the carcass this far,' Sarah said, looking at the cheetah with dismay. 'The cubs should be here somewhere. Oh, God. This is bad.'

The smell of blood had brought two hyenas onto the scene. The cheetah was under attack from both sides and too weak to defend herself as they lunged forward, snapping at her.

'Why doesn't she try to get away?' Hugo said. 'Come on, Isis, move! Move!'

In the thicket behind her, the cubs flattened themselves against the rock, frozen with fear. Isis was the only thing between them and the two hulking predators who made a concerted rush on her again. She swiped at one with her claws but she could not deal with both of them and Hugo put his hands in front of his eyes as she was flung into the air by the second hyena. As she landed, the animal seized her by the throat. There was a sickening crunch and she fell, limp, onto the ground. The first attacker loped past her and snatched up one of the cubs, shaking it in massive jaws like a rag doll. A terrified mewling echoed out across the space between the car and the battleground,

'No! No! No!' With a roar of fury, Sarah gunned the engine and drove straight at the two hyenas, her foot jammed down on the accelerator, the horn blaring.

'Christ, Sarah, what are you doing! You're crazy!' Hugo was shouting at her. 'You'll turn us over. Smash up the engine!'

He braced himself, screwing his eyes shut as the wall of rocks loomed up in front of the windscreen. The hyenas turned at the sound of the car bearing down on them. The first one was clipped on the leg, and it fled, limping, into the bush, while the other was tossed over the bonnet to land with a thud behind them. The vehicle hit a boulder. Sarah heard the screech of a thorn bush against the grille on the front of the car as it careened to one side at a sharp angle and stopped abruptly, an ominous hissing sound coming from the engine.

'What the blazes was that about?' Hugo's voice was shaking with anger. An egg-shaped bump was rising on his forehead, where he had collided with the windscreen, and he bent down to scrabble for his glasses.

Sarah paid no attention to him. Instead, she jumped from the Land Cruiser and ran towards Isis. The cheetah's neck had been broken and her killer was also dead, from the impact of the car. Beside them, the sad remains of the male cub lay disembowelled on the grass. Sarah touched it briefly and then started searching, moving towards the dense thicket. Behind her, Hugo staggered from the car, calling to her.

'Sarah! For God's sake, there could be anything in there! Come back, you idiot!'

She continued to ignore him and crouched on the ground, murmuring softly. When she stood up again he saw that she was holding the other cub in her arms. Smeared with blood, it was staring wide-eyed, ears flattened against its head, terrified, trembling, too traumatised to attempt an escape. Sarah seemed totally calm, oblivious to the accident and the dead animals.

'We'll take this one back to camp,' she said.

'You know the brief. We can observe but we can't interfere. Nature must take its course.'

'I am not letting another creature die,' she said defiantly. 'There is too much death. Too many people who don't care about preserving life. I won't abandon this cub. So you'd better help me, Hugo, because we are in the middle of nowhere, with three carcasses around us, and there are going to be a lot more predators joining us soon. It looks like I've punctured the radiator, but somehow we have to leave this place as fast as we can. Even if we don't get very far.'

She took a sweater from the back seat and wrapped it around the cheetah, emptying her camera bag, and placing the cub inside. Then she got into the driver's seat, and started the engine. Steam plumed upwards as she shifted the gear into reverse and shouted at Hugo.

'Push! Hard as you can!'

With a groaning sound the car backed up, almost toppling, then miraculously righting itself. Sarah jumped out and opened the bonnet.

'I was right,' she said. 'There's a hole in the front of the radiator. It's leaking.'

'We'll have to wait for it to cool before we can fix it,' Hugo said. 'I don't want third-degree burns, as well as a bump the size of a boulder on my face. Look in the picnic basket. There should be some tinfoil from the sandwiches. Rather unusual tool, but I'm pretty sure it will do.'

They waited, edgy and impatient, until there was no further sign of steam. Then Hugo opened the cap, folded the foil and pushed it firmly into the hole, flattening the edges against the outside of the radiator. Then he poured in the water from the canteen that Sarah always carried. The light was failing and they could hear the cackle of hyenas not far off, and the distant sound of a lion. A pitiful mewl and twitter came from inside the car as the cub called out for its mother and sibling.

'Have to have a pee,' Hugo said, peering into the engine. 'Look away, for decency's sake.'

'What? Can't you wait until we've put some distance between us and the creatures moving in to mop up?'

'I'm topping up the radiator,' he said. 'I'm the most inventive mechanic you'll ever come across.'

'You drive,' Sarah said, still laughing as he completed his task.

'Right. We'll take it slowly and try to keep the needle from moving upwards. You'd better pray we make it to the river, so we can fill the radiator again. Or at least that we are well away from here, before the engine conks out.'

They set off into the gathering dusk, crawling along, watching the temperature gauge climb up the scale. As they moved away from the rocks, the hunched shape of another hyena appeared in silhouette on top of the hill. Minutes later came the grunt of a lion, closer now, and the sharp bark of a jackal. Hugo increased the speed a little and they bounced away over the grassland until they came to the river. Then they followed the winding banks, stopping twice for water before they reached the camp.

Ahmed came running as they drove in, concerned over their late return. Mama Allie had been on the radio, he said. She would call later, to make sure they were back safely. Hot water was waiting in the shower tents and dinner was ready. As Sarah emerged from the car, his eyes widened. During the final part of the journey the cheetah cub had climbed, shivering, out of the bag and into the shelter of her arms. It was trembling at the unaccustomed light and noise and there was a deep bite mark on its hind leg, but otherwise it seemed unharmed.

'Dinner a little later, Ahmed. A *fisi* has killed its mother.' Sarah examined the cub. 'It's a female. I need hot water and the medicine kit, to clean this wound. A *fisi* bite is dangerous.' She turned to Hugo. 'We need warm milk mixed with water. We can use a dropper from one of the medicine bottles, although it will take a long time to feed her that way. I'm sure she won't be able to lap yet.'

Ahmed stared at Hugo's forehead, clicked his tongue sympathetically, and went to find what she wanted.

383

'How are you going to explain this to Allie, when she calls?' Hugo asked with some amusement.

'That will be your problem,' Sarah said, unable to meet his eye. 'I have to deal with this gash or the cub will die. It may already be infected.'

In the mess tent she opened the medicine kit and took out sterile dressings. Ahmed reappeared, with a basin of hot water and together they placed the cub on a clean towel under the light. It stirred and mewed, twisting in distress as Sarah cut the matted fur away from the wound, and cleaned it. Hugo watched as she dealt with the tiny animal, holding down the squirming patient while she stitched its leg. The cook was plainly delighted with the unexpected drama, exclaiming in admiration as Hugo gave a graphic description of the battle that had taken place.

'Eeehh! Mama Sarah has done a brave thing,' he said. 'And this small *duma* is a good omen. It will get better and bring good luck to the camp.'

'He can try that theory out on Allie,' Hugo said under his breath. 'Before she breaks our necks and sends us off to join Isis.'

'The cub may not survive,' Sarah said. 'We don't know if we will be able to feed her, or whether this wound will become infected.'

It was Hugo who took the radio call while Sarah was trying to get some warmed milk into the cheetah's mouth. It spat and struggled, spraying liquid all over her clothes, before swallowing a small amount and curling up in the crook of her arm. Soon it had fallen into an exhausted sleep.

'What did you tell Allie?'

'Not a thing.' He was laughing. 'We didn't need her on the warpath tonight, and we don't want to spoil her fun in Nairobi by introducing an aggravating subject. Do we?'

'Of course not,' Sarah agreed, grinning.

'I said we were late because the radiator had given us some trouble. Which is true. I just left out a few salient details. What about a drink? I could do with a large whisky.'

'Good thinking.' Sarah looked at her accomplice, registering how bruised and battered he was. 'I'm sorry for nearly killing you when I rammed those brutes. You're going to have a massive shiner tomorrow, I'm afraid. Maybe I should put some ice on that bump. Does it hurt?'

'Not really. And I'm sorry for yelling at you.' He took a large gulp of Scotch and felt the welcome heat in his throat. 'It was in pure, unadulterated terror. I thought you were going to drive straight into the rock face.'

'I probably would have, if the smaller boulder and the thorn tree hadn't got in the way.'

'Let's shower and eat,' Hugo said. 'And treat ourselves to a bottle of wine. Celebrate our survival.'

After dinner, Sarah gathered her sweater around the sleeping cub, and stood up carefully. 'I'll keep this little creature with me tonight. Can you bring my cameras, and the lamps?'

They said goodnight to Ahmed and made their way to Sarah's tent where Hugo emptied out a basket of film and lined the makeshift bed with a towel before placing the cheetah inside. It did not stir. Perhaps it would not wake ever again, Sarah thought. Now that the crisis was over, reaction was setting in. Looking down at the tiny, helpless form, she was swamped by the events of the afternoon and realised how crazy her action had been. Irresponsible. She had put Hugo's life at risk, as well as her own. And for what? The poor little cub would probably not survive, from infection or shock. Was there no respite from the chain of violence and death? She had returned to the Mara to find the peace she craved, only to experience more destruction. Images flashed across her mind with strobe intensity, and she pressed her hands against her eyes to try and make them stop. Isis being flung into the air, the crack of her breaking neck, the cub in the hyena's jaws. Hugo's voice was coming from far away.

'Sarah? You need to lie down.'

She curled up with her back to him and buried her face in the pillow as all the events of the past year rose over her like a towering wave, threatening to crush her with the force of remembering. Her life had been smashed to pieces once again, and she was being sucked away into a sink hole of emptiness. Then Hugo's arms were round her.

'Talk to me, Sarah. Tell me everything.'

Through the night, she spilled out the wreckage of her life, keeping nothing back, finding an unbelievable release in forming the words that expressed all her rage and disillusionment, her confusion and guilt. Hugo held her, stroked her hair, warmed the part of her that had given up on life and hope. He lay beside her on the narrow camp bed, kissed her tear-streaked face and murmured words of comfort, until at last she slept.

When dawn broke and birdsong filled the tent she woke to find him watching her. Their lips met with a tenderness that turned to urgency and passion. She closed her eyes, feeling the deep pleasure of his caress, letting his hands move over her body in long, light strokes. Their first love-making was sweet and unhurried, a delight of discovery. It had been so long since she had felt such freedom and she clung to him, breathless, shaken by the power of the experience. As they lay together afterwards she studied his face, vulnerable without his glasses, ran her fingers through his unruly hair and touched the bruise on his forehead. She had been right about the shiner – both eyes were ringed with purple.

'You look like a panda.' Her laughter was soft. 'I'm so sorry I did that to you.'

There was a slight noise from the floor, and she leaned over and peeped into the basket. The cub was sitting up, examining its surroundings. It gazed back at her, eyes bright, and chirred softly.

'She's made it, Hugo. I think she's going to be all right. We must organise some milk. You'd better get dressed. Ahmed will be turning up any minute with the *chai*, and you'll need to be decent.'

She pulled on her clothes and knelt on the floor, lifting the cub from the basket, smiling as the animal sniffed tentatively at her hand, and nuzzled her face. Hugo dressed and passed her, running his fingers across the nape of her neck. Outside, she heard Ahmed approaching the tent with the morning tea.

'*Karibu*, Ahmed,' she called to him. 'Come in and see what our good work has done.'

'Eeeh! *Duma kidogo ananawiri*. I go for milk.' He rushed off, whistling cheerfully.

'We should try and get some goat's milk,' Sarah said as they fed the cheetah with some difficulty. 'It would be easier to digest. There's a *manyatta* not far from here. We can take the old jeep and buy a milking goat. They'll ask an outrageous price, but it will be worth it. And we must drive to Narok and talk to the warden. There is a good mechanic in his *boma* who might come and fix the radiator. I'd hate to have to order a new one.' She thought of having to contact Indar Uncle and groaned inwardly. But Hugo was chuckling.

'What? What's so funny now?'

'You are,' he said. 'Last night, you drove into a bloody great rock to save a tiny animal, after which you helped me patch a radiator to prevent us from being eaten, and then you turned into a vet, put away dinner and a great deal of wine, and finally collapsed into a dark hole, so that I feared you might not survive the night. And here you are in the morning, looking glorious, making plans for the day as usual. You are extraordinary.'

'You saved me last night, Hugo.' She kissed the palm of his hand. 'I had reached the lowest point in my life, and you brought me out of it. So let's make the most of what we have been given.'

They put the cheetah into the basket and entrusted her to Ahmed while they went in search of supplies. The cook's face creased with pleasure as he took over his new charge.

'You must think of a name for her,' Sarah said.

'We will call her Hiba,' Ahmed said, with great solemnity.

'Perfect.' Sarah was delighted.

'What does it mean?' Hugo asked.

'It means a present – a gift of love.' Sarah touched his hand.

They smiled at each other as they raided Allie's store for sugar, tea, and maize meal to barter with the Maasai, in exchange for a goat to wet-nurse their baby. Narok was their first stop and they parked in front of the Indian-owned *duka* in search of feeding bottles and teats.

'Very lucky, you are, Mrs Singh,' said the owner. 'My wife was bringing these things from Nairobi only last week for Maasai child with sick mother. Not usually in stock.'

'Thank God Allie isn't telepathic,' Hugo said as they drove away. 'Of all the things she has had on her shopping lists over the years, baby bottles would never have entered her mind.'

'She wasn't allowed to think of feeding babies,' Sarah said. 'You are her surrogate son, the child she never had because she loved Dan so much.'

'Is that true?' Hugo was profoundly moved. 'She always seemed to me the free-spirited adventurer who didn't want links or ties. I felt lucky that she stayed in touch with me. Wrote to me about her life. I hoped each year that she would ask me to come to Buffalo Springs, but she never did.'

'She never could,' Sarah said. 'You know that I loved and admired Dan, but he had a blind spot about children, and he didn't want any in his life or in his camp. He ruled. What he said was what Allie did. No – that sounds slavish, which is wrong. It's what she wanted to do.'

'Thank you for telling me this,' Hugo said. 'I was sick, you know, when I was a kid. And I think my parents were always disappointed that I turned out to be a sort of weakling, with poor eyesight and bouts of asthma, and no interest in fishing the freezing lochs and rivers of Scotland. Allie's insight into another world was my escape. But I was always sad that I could never share it, because I thought she didn't love me quite enough, either.'

'She loved you the best,' Sarah said, with laughter dancng in her eyes. 'And that is why *you* are going to tell her what I did was right.'

The warden was not in his office, but they left a message and continued on to the *manyatta* where Sarah negotiated for an hour, sweating in the heat, her face and hair buzzing with flies as she bargained with the elders. It was Hugo who pushed the bleating, protesting goat into the back seat of the vehicle.

They spent the next morning recording the movements of Lara and her family, and returned to camp at noon to find that the warden had come to inspect the cub.

'She's very young,' he said. 'It will take work and luck for her to survive. This is an open area. She will be vulnerable to predators. It might be better to bring her to the animal orphanage in Nairobi.'

'She belongs here, in the Mara,' Sarah said. 'We can take care of her between us, and eventually she can be released back into her own habitat. It's a perfect opportunity to study the development of such a young animal and to try to rehabilitate her when she is old enough.'

'What does Allie have to say about all this?' The warden was curious. He knew she had strict rules and had always admired her unbending sense of discipline.

'She's in Nairobi till the end of the week,' Hugo said, avoiding Sarah's gaze and smiling confidently at the warden. 'But she sees it as a great opportunity for research. Not something she would want to pass up.'

'Well, I will be interested to watch the progress.' The warden accepted a cold beer and an offer of lunch. 'She looks healthy right now and you did a good job on her leg.'

Hiba's wound healed well, and she was soon moving about with only a slight limp. Ahmed took over the milking of the goat, and kept it in his quarters at night for safety. Allie called a day later to say that that she had confirmation of further funding, and that the first part of her study was to be published in a scientific paper. Erope had also addressed the AWF meeting, explaining the details illustrated by Sarah's photographs, and his own ideas of the delicate balance between the wildlife and the Maasai inhabitants of the region.

'I think that's what clinched it,' Allie said, brimming with enthusiasm about the outcome of the meeting, and what they would be able to do with the extra money. 'How are things at your end? What about the Land Cruiser?'

She had never been at ease on the telephone. Her words formed staccato questions with not much opportunity for a reply. Sarah was vague, unwilling to broach the thorny question of the cheetah cub over the line.

'The radiator is banjaxed,' she said. 'The warden's mechanic can patch it, so it will function until I am next in Nairobi. In the meantime we are using the old jeep which is holding up quite well. When will you be back?' She felt a tightening in her throat and realised that she did not want Allie to come home just yet.

'Oh . . .' Allie hesitated. 'I thought I might stay on for a few days. Maybe go down to Tsavo and see how they are managing the elephant problem. Would you mind?'

'Sounds like a great idea.' Sarah caught Hugo's eye and put a finger to his mouth as he began to chuckle again. 'We'll see you next week.'

The days passed in a haze of joy for Sarah. She spent every second with Hugo, out in the bush, watching the other cheetahs, or lying close in the tent at night. They had a tacit understanding that they would not think or talk about the future. Only the present was important, a kiss, a caress, a look, making love under the shade of an acacia tree in the wilderness, laughing like teenagers about the cramped conditions in the back of the jeep or the narrow camp bed, exploring one another with tenderness, surrendering to passion, whispering in the dark. She revelled in an airy, light-hearted freedom that she had not felt for a long time. There were no constraints, no thoughts of fertility, only the expression of desire and a fulfilment that left her deeply satisfied. He understood her, seemed to anticipate her needs and answer them with sensitivity. She felt as though her feet had stopped touching the ground, and she was flying. They laughed about nothing and about everything, rejoiced in the beauty of their surroundings, touched each other with reverence and delight. The rest of the world drifted away into some other dimension.

Allie and Erope arrived late on a Monday evening. Sarah ran to greet them, throwing her arms around an astonished Allie.

'Whoa! Steady on.' Allie disentangled herself. 'Are you all right?'

'Never better.'

Sarah's green eyes were shining and her skin glowed. She looked bright and healthy and joyful, and Allie sighed with relief. The broken waif, ashen-faced, distraught and on the edge of collapse had disappeared and a complete transformation seemed to have taken place. She turned to her nephew who was hovering in the background, and greeted him with affection, remarking on his bruises with concern.

'Oh, it's nothing to how I looked last week,' he said. 'I'm fine now.'

Sarah was congratulating Erope on his part in the presentation when Ahmed appeared, holding the cub. Allie stopped dead.

'What the hell is this?'

Sarah began talking very fast, explaining the circumstances. 'It was my decision, Allie. I had to save her. And I'm not sorry, although I know you have reservations about—'

'Damn right I do!' Allie's face was stern. 'You know the basis on which we work here. We are scientists, observers. This is not a rescue centre. How are we supposed to take care of this animal?'

'Hiba. Her name is Hiba. She has survived against incredible odds. Look at her Allie! I couldn't let the hyena kill her too.'

'Sentimental flight of fancy,' Allie said firmly. 'You read things into animal behaviour for which there is no scientific basis. I'm really disappointed in you, Sarah.'

'I don't agree with you there,' Hugo said. 'I know we are not supposed to intervene, but we did. The warden has seen her, too, and he is interested in how she will fare. She's feeding well, from the milking goat we bought from the Maasai.'

'You did what?' Allie had noticed Hugo's spirited defence and its implications were not lost on her. But she was sidetracked by the goat. 'We now have a bloody goat in camp?'

'We had to have milk she could digest.' Sarah was gazing at her, all the brightness draining from her face. 'Ahmed is happy to milk the goat.'

Ahmed began to speak, but Allie put up her hand.

'And what happens when she has to be weaned? We can't feed her domestic animals – otherwise she'll end up raiding all the Maasai *bomas* whenever she wants dinner. Had you considered that? If she's to be returned to the wild, which is what I presume you had in mind, Sarah, someone will have to teach her to hunt. And until she can bring down her own prey, there is the problem of fresh game meat for her.'

'I know that.' Sarah was dejected. 'I admit that my first thought was to save the cub. But then I realised what a great project she could be. Part of our research. And we can do it, between us. I mean, look at the Adamsons with their lions. And Joy has raised a cheetah. Erope?'

'We could learn much from this,' the Samburu said to Allie. 'Sometimes fate puts a thing in your path, and then you must take it. Let this Hiba stay. Who knows how much extra support you will get for your work, if people see how you saved an animal from the jaws of death.'

He took the cub and put it in Allie's hands. It had just finished a bottle of milk and chirped sleepily.

'All right, she stays. For now.' Allie's expression softened. 'But I am not operating an animal orphanage here. This is the only creature we will ever keep, and if it proves too problematic we'll have to think of an alternative. Ahmed, get me a large vodka, please. I've obviously gone off my head. Along with everyone else in this place. And sit down, for Chrissake. All of you.'

Sarah caught Hugo's eye with an expression that reminded Allie of the way she had looked on her wedding day. She had been holding Rabindrah's hand then, and smiling the same luminous smile. Oh no, she thought. Sarah and Hugo. What the bloody hell will happen now?

In the following days, Allie watched her nephew and Sarah and worried about them. They were unable to hide their feelings, a look, a touch giving them away at every turn. She said nothing, however. After all, who was she to dispense advice about love and romance? She was pretty certain Hugo had guessed her relationship with Erope, and she wondered if Sarah knew too. But that was different. She was a free woman, and Erope's marital status within his tribe did not preclude his taking another mate. He was young and strong and virile, and they enjoyed one another. They had a bond which had progressed over time into a satisfying sexual fulfilment.

Hugo and Sarah were another matter. Sarah's marriage was in difficulty, perhaps over, but there were issues that would have to be addressed before she could find real happiness or peace with someone else. And Hugo was not a philanderer who would be satisfied with a casual affair. He, too, could end up badly hurt. In the meantime, they continued to follow the cheetahs in the wild and to take care of Hiba. Erope watched, and shrugged when Allie looked at him questioningly.

'Soon she must decide,' he said. 'Sarah will not live two lives.'

The time for a decision came sooner than expected.

'Mr Rabindrah has been on the radio,' Ahmed said, as Allie returned from her day's observations. 'He wanted to talk to Mama Sarah, but I said she was out. He will come in two days with Bwana Anthony who is moving his camp here.'

When Sarah and Hugo drove in, Allie took her aside. 'Sarah . . .'

'What is it?' Sarah saw the concern in Allie's face.

'Rabindrah called. He is coming to the Mara with Anthony, and he wants to see you.'

Sarah stood very still. The beautiful cocoon in which she had been wrapped was unravelling. She had known it would, sometime. Just not so soon.

'I can't talk to him,' she said, all lightness stripped away from her.

'You'll have to, eventually, although this is not the best place,' Allie said. She waited, but Sarah said nothing more. 'When you decide, let me know what you plan to do,' she said, and left.

She saw Hugo walk to Sarah's tent after his shower, and they did not join her for their usual sundowner. Erope arrived and they sat together in silence, looking into the fire. At dinner no one mentioned Rabindrah's call. Afterwards, Allie picked up the cub, and her basket.

'I'm going to have an early night,' she said. 'I'll take Hiba with me. Give you a break from your baby-sitting duties.'

Sarah left a few minutes later and the two men sat for a time, each absorbed in his own thoughts. Then Erope stood up.

'My friend, every moment stays with us,' he said. 'We must always make a light for the dark days.'

In the small, perfect world of her tent Sarah leaned against Hugo.

'I love you,' he said. 'It's not the best time to say it, but maybe it's the only time I can. I want to make you happy and I believe I can do that. Devote my whole life to it. But you have to believe it too. I know you need time and that's all right. I can wait.'

She put her finger on his lips, to silence him.

'I do need time,' she whispered. 'To decide what I have to do. But for tonight I want you to hold me. Love me. Let me love you, in whatever way I am able. I feel as if I'm crippled and struggling for balance. Tonight, I need you to take me as I am, because you are the most loving of men.'

He kissed and undressed her and laid her down on the bed. When he began to caress her she pressed against him, wrapping her legs around him, murmuring his name over and over again. Through the night they held one another, made love, slept, woke and touched until desire brought them together again.

When dawn came she was asleep, her hair tousled, her lips bruised with his kisses. He leaned down, and she opened her eyes.

'I have to go away,' she said.

'I know.' He brushed a lock of hair from her face. 'Where to?'

'Somewhere I can think things out. I need to do that, before I speak to Rabindrah.'

'I meant what I said. Everything. I'll wait for you. I'm a patient man and I love you.'

Her eyes filled with tears. 'Hugo,' she said. 'Dearest Hugo.'

'No. Don't cry. And we are not going to say goodbye. I'm going out with Erope now. And when you're ready, when you've decided, you will tell me. If you want me, I'll come and get you, wherever you are.'

He stood up, dressed quickly and kissed her one last time. Then he was gone.

Sarah walked over to the mess tent where Allie was having breakfast, the cheetah in her lap.

'I'm going to leave, Allie. I know it's as sudden as my last arrival, and I hope it won't cause too many logistical problems. But I have to work things out, like you said. I thought I could do that here, but as you can see, it hasn't happened quite that way. I'm going to head for Langani. Do you want me to take her?' She gestured at the cheetah. 'She could easily be raised there.'

'No. She has arrived here, and this is where she will stay,' Allie said. 'Rabindrah will call again, you know.'

'Yes. Tell him I have to figure out what I really want from life, and I have to do it alone. But I'd rather he didn't know where I've gone.' She tickled the cub. 'I'm sorry for landing her on you, Allie.'

'It's all right. We'll take care of her until you come back. You will come back?'

'In a while. When I can behave like a rational scientist again.'

'Do you want breakfast?'

'No, just a thermos of coffee. I'll hit the road. Could you call Hannah on the radio and let her know I'm coming? And Allie?'

'Yes?'

'Thank you. For everything. I wish things had worked out the way we'd . . .' She was unable to complete the sentence, unsure as to what she wanted to say.

'Life is strange like that. Take care of yourself, Sarah. Stay in touch.'

As she drove out of the compound, she could see Allie standing under a tree, holding the little cheetah in her arms. There was no sign of Hugo.

Chapter 24

Kenya, November 1977

She drove too fast, wanting to put as much mileage between herself and the Mara as possible, in case she weakened and changed her mind. Hugo was in her thoughts, his scent in her nostrils, the feel of his arms around her and the memory of his lovemaking still in her blood. He was strong, steady, calm. She would be safe with him. He understood her. He made her laugh. Perhaps she should turn around now, go back, tell Rabindrah it was over. She had found someone who loved her above all else, who would always cherish her and put her first. She was tired of being tossed around, of never knowing what was coming next. But she could not wait for Rabindrah in Allie's camp, end her marriage in the place where she had given herself to Hugo. That would be too cruel. She kept driving, halting on the side of the road long enough to buy petrol and a packet of biscuits, and drink her coffee.

Hannah came out to meet her, followed by a rush of dogs.

'You look so well when you are pregnant,' Sarah said.

'I'm glad you've come,' Hannah said. 'Now we can catch up on everybody's news. We haven't had a chance to talk since the wedding. It'll be *lekker*!'

'Everybody?'

'Camilla arrived last night. She's with the *bibis* in the workshop at the moment, but she'll be back soon.'

'I thought Camilla was in London.'

'She came back last week. I suppose you know about the dreadful thing that happened?'

'What dreadful thing?' Sarah turned away. Had Hannah also condoned the abortion? Was she to be the only one floundering in the quicksands of grief and outrage.

'Duncan Harper ran off with all the company money. Camilla has had to bring in every penny she owns to keep Anthony going. She did several photo shoots before she left, to earn some extra money. And now she has to get as much clothing out into the local market as possible. She is even selling her cottage in England, although she hopes to hang on to the flat. She looks exhausted. Convinced that it's her fault for taking Duncan on in the first place.'

'Is she going on to Anthony's camp in the Mara?' Sarah cleared her throat with difficulty.

'I don't know. She needs to be in the office for a while, once she leaves the farm. But we will have a couple of days together. Great, hey?'

'Does she know I'm here?'

'No. I thought I'd keep it as a surprise. Sarah? Is there something wrong? And what is happening between you and Rabindrah?'

Obviously Hannah knew nothing about the abortion. A darkness was spreading through Sarah's head. She could not sit here, making small talk. She would have to leave, before Camilla came back from the workshop.

'I'm not feeling terribly well,' she said. 'I think I'll go on to Nairobi.'

'You can't start out again today. Go and lie down. I'll send tea with Josephine. You'll feel better when you've had a rest.'

Sarah stood at the window of the bedroom, looking out at Piet's ridge. She had thought she might go up there to reflect, to ask for the wisdom she needed. Now she just wanted to run. It was all she seemed able to do these days.

There was a knock and she turned to see Camilla framed in the doorway. Her face was drawn and gaunt, and her eyes had sunk into their sockets. She stared at Sarah, her body stiff and challenging.

'Sarah, we've both been through so much.' Her voice cracked and Sarah's first instinct was to offer comfort. Then she thought of the dead child, and the role Rabindrah had played in the conspiracy and she shook her head, holding out a hand in protest, keeping a distance between them.

'Why aren't you in the Mara?' Camilla said. 'Rabindrah is going there with Anthony tomorrow. To see you. He loves you, Sarah. You have to remember that. It's not right, the way you're treating him.'

'How can you tell me what is right?' Sarah was ice cold. Only isolated words that Camilla said were filtering through. 'How could you? How could you take your child's life, and make my husband a party to it?'

'He wasn't a party to it.' Camilla swayed and reached out to steady herself on a chair. 'He knew nothing about it until I asked him to bring me back from the clinic. When it was over. I couldn't bear to be alone.'

Sarah put her hands over her ears. 'I can't listen to this. I don't want to know.'

'Don't do that!' Camilla said, determined to be heard. 'Rabindrah didn't judge me. He tried to understand. He stayed with me through the darkest time of my life, as he has stayed with you. How dare you appoint yourself as my judge. Do you know what I went through over the years, waiting for Anthony? Have you any idea how it was? All those lonely nights in London and Paris and New York, with roomfuls of strangers ogling me, pawing me, seeing and wanting only the glamour. While you had a husband who loved you, day and night, through all your misfortunes. When did you last laugh out loud with him, dance with him, look at him and think he was beautiful? You're driven by anger these days, Sarah. It's corroding the person you were, eating into your marriage and your friendships. Poisoning you. You need to think about what you and Rabindrah had together, and be thankful for it.'

Sarah had put her few belongings back into her travel bag, and now she tried to push past Camilla who stood blocking the door.

'Do you think I didn't suffer torment over my baby?' she said quietly. 'That I'm not suffering now? Well, damn you, anyway. You're great at spouting high-minded principles and so-called Christian values. But where is your compassion? Rabindrah has far more of it than you, and you're punishing him for it. I love Anthony. Beyond anyone and anything. After all this time we are finally together, and I would give my life for him. Any life. But you have become completely self-absorbed. Oblivious to your husband and to everyone else around you. Obsessed with not having children. The Sarah we all loved has gone, and you have to find her again. You must.'

Sarah picked up her bag and left the room, with Camilla's words ricocheting in the corridor behind her, tearing into her, ripping away the caul of protection she had fashioned around herself. She could not stomach any further revelations.

'Go on, run away if you like. It's what I used to do until you stopped me, Sarah. But you are a coward.' Camilla's words echoed in the distance.

'You always set great store by promises and friendship, but they no longer mean anything to you. Sarah!'

As Sarah left the house, both of her friends came running out onto the front steps and called to her, but she did not stop. Sometime later she found herself on Piet's ridge. In the stillness, Camilla's words came back to her. Clear and complete as though she was hearing them for the first time, the truth in them burning like acid, still too hard to accept. Who was she, indeed, to stand in judgement on anyone? She had made a solemn promise to Rabindrah, to love and cherish him for the rest of their lives. No matter what. Now she recognised that she was equally guilty of betrayal. He had tried to make her understand what he had done for his uncle. Then for Camilla. And she had not listened to him, or to anyone. Instead she had flung herself into an affair with Hugo, not caring who might be hurt, when or if it ended.

'How did I turn into someone so lacking in understanding and tolerance,' she said to Piet. 'Someone who can't see into the hearts of the people I love. Who can't see at all.'

She thought of Rabindrah, leaving for the Mara tomorrow. Wanting her still, in spite of what she had become. If she went back to him, she would leave a trail of devastation in her wake.

'Tell me what to do, Piet,' she said, sinking down onto her heels beside the cairn. 'Please tell me how I can put things right.'

But the only sound she could hear was the wind, whipping the branches of the surrounding trees, threatening rain. It was getting late and she rose to her feet, stiff and sore and still undecided on a course of action. The stones of the cairn glowed in the yellow light of an impending storm. She waited for some sort of sign but the place remained silent. As though even Piet had turned his back on her.

She thought of going back to the farm. Of facing her friends and trying to make amends. But that was impossible. Camilla had not told Hannah about the abortion, so what could she say to explain her behaviour? How could she cross the minefield of the terrible things they had said to one another? Sick at heart, she touched the mound with her fingers and walked away down the path to the car.

Rabindrah's steps were slow and weary as he put his key in the lock, and opened the front door. In the sitting room he switched on a table lamp and sat down in an armchair. The fire was set and Chege had laid the table for a solitary dinner.

Everywhere around him there were Sarah's belongings. Papers, photographs, her sweater on the back of a chair, scribbled reminders that she wrote to herself. Even the smell of her perfume lingered in the air. The room was full of her, making its emptiness more pronounced. She was gone. He had lost her for good this time. Through his own stupid pride, and neglect. He had refused to fully acknowledge her suffering over the years, left her alone when she needed him, excluded her from the most important decision of his career and caused outrage over his involvement with Gulab. Worst of all, she believed that he had played a willing part in Camilla's heartbreaking decision.

Allie had told him on the radio that Sarah had gone, unable to face confrontation of any kind, desperately in need of time and space for herself. The best thing he could do was to wait. Now he sat in the empty house, surrounded by the dregs of a life. He heard the front door open and for a moment he wondered about his security and whether the *askari* was still outside. Standing up, he walked into the hall and saw her silhouette in the doorway.

'Sarah?'

She did not speak as they faced one another across the broken pieces of their marriage.

'Sarah, I love you. I haven't expressed it well lately, but I promise you, I'll never let you down again. Don't leave me. Let me show you what you are to me, please.'

She did not speak as she moved past him into the sitting room, creating a distance between them.

'We failed each other, Rabindrah,' she said. 'We got lost. Went about things the wrong way.' Her throat hurt as she tried to assemble the right words. 'I don't know if we can start afresh, but maybe we could try. Only we have to do it slowly.'

He nodded, sensing the loosening of tension between them but not wanting to say or do anything that might break the delicate wire on which they were balanced.

'I'm sorry about Gulab,' he said. 'I didn't—'

'He's gone, poor man. And you have ensured that Lila is safe. I understand how important that is.'

'And Camilla –'

'I feel sorry for Anthony with all his problems,' Sarah said. 'I still cannot accept what she did, but I know you had no part in her decision and in the end she is the one who will always have to live with it. For now, all we can hope to do is sort out our own future. That should keep us pretty occupied, don't you think?'

Before he could answer her, she went to the kitchen, divided the meal that Chege had prepared, and re-set the table. They sat down together, their conversation punctuated by interruptions and silences and an awareness of the uncertain landscape before them. After dinner they listened to a Prokofiev violin concerto, and then made their way to the bedroom. Like a newly-wed he allowed her private time to undress in the bathroom. Lying in bed, she listened to the familiar, mundane sound of him brushing his teeth, swirling mouthwash, splashing his face. When he came to join her he took her hand and they lay in silence, together but carefully apart, until they fell asleep.

'We've been invited to dinner with Gordon and Maureen,' he said, a week later. 'In a new Italian place. What do you think?'

At the Hedleys' table she drank her wine and watched her husband, seeing him as if for the first time. He was in a spirited political discussion with his host, and she felt again the excitement she had experienced in the beginning of their relationship as she listened to his deep laugh, saw the way he moved his hands, how his eyes glowed with passion for his subject. How he could laugh at himself as well. On the way home, a current hummed between them and she stole glances at him and then looked away. At the house, she went in to tidy her desk while he parked the car. He came in quietly, and stood watching her for a moment.

'Would you like a night cap?' he asked.

She looked up and pushed her notes aside, her eyes fixed on his face, her mouth soft. 'No,' she said. Her voice was slightly breathless and she flushed and glanced away. 'I'd rather you kissed me. It's been a long time.'

He lifted her out of the chair and wrapped her in a tight embrace, almost afraid he would wake up and find he was dreaming. They slid together to their knees, touching, kissing, pulling off their clothes and murmuring familiar endearments as they rediscovered one another. He wanted her above all else, wanted to reach into the core of her and show her the force of his love. And then for a second, he was afraid. As he moved away from her she reached out, digging her fingers into his back, whispering her need. Fiercely, she drew him into her, taking his head in her hands, kissing his mouth and smiling when she heard his cry of triumph.

In the shower they stood close together, laughing and splashing one another, and then went to the bedroom to make love once more, this time slowly and tenderly until he fell asleep in her arms. She lay in his embrace, and with deep sadness closed away the memory of the other nights. The sweetness of another lover whom she knew she would never forget. But this was her place, here with Rabindrah. The place that she must once again learn to call home.

Chapter 25

Kenya, December 1977

Hannah bulldozed her way into the chaotic press of traffic, her hands clammy on the steering wheel as she snaked through a gap between an overloaded bus and a safari vehicle, competing to enter the main thoroughfare of Kenyatta Avenue. Bicycles swerved in front of her, and pedestrians made suicidal forays between cars and lorries that poured out exhaust fumes, and threatened to topple into the crowds as they rounded corners or changed lanes without warning.

Once she had escaped the noonday glare, the hospital was an oasis of calm. She passed through the waiting area where people were standing patiently against the walls, or sitting on the steps outside, because there were not enough chairs and benches. Within ten minutes she had been ushered into the specialist's consulting room where Dr Enright completed his examination of Piet. He was precise and straightforward in his assessment.

'I'm afraid the perforation has not healed, as we had hoped,' he said. 'But you must already know that, because Piet's hearing has not improved during the waiting time. In addition, he has a condition in both ears that is called cholesteatoma which is a result of poor functioning of the Eustachian Tube, as well as frequent infections in the middle ear. What happens is that the infections cause skin to become tough and form a sac that gradually increases in size. Over time cholesteatoma can damage or destroy the delicate bone structure in the middle ear and lead to deafness.'

Deafness. It was the first time she had heard the bald confirmation of Piet's problem and Hannah straightened herself in her chair and tried to look directly at the specialist, wanting to prevent her fear from being transmitted to her child.

'What happens now? What will you be able to do for him?' Her hands were shaking and she clasped them tightly in her lap and smiled at Piet, blissfully unaware of the sentence that had been handed down to him.

'Surgery is the only option,' said Dr Enright. 'Piet has already had antibiotics and special cleaning of the relevant part of his ears. But today's tests show that an operation is the only way to try and improve his hearing level and prevent further damage, so we should go ahead with the surgery. We can schedule him for Wednesday of next week.'

'That's in five days.' Hannah thought of her son in an operating theatre, lying unconscious under the bright lamps, steel instruments probing and cutting and stitching. She turned her head away from Piet, no longer able to mask her fear. If only Lars was with her. 'My husband is in Norway,' she said. 'I would rather wait until he comes back. He will be returning the week before Christmas and I would like him to be here, if the delay doesn't make a difference to Piet's condition.'

'That is perfectly understandable,' Dr Enright said. 'It will mean putting off the operation until late January or early February, however. I will be away on holiday after next week, and then I'm flying to London for a medical conference. Unless you would like to consult another specialist.'

'No,' Hannah said. She had chosen Enright after making careful enquiries, and his track record and kindly manner had impressed her. 'We wouldn't want to do that. I think I had better telephone Lars, if I can get through, and let you know this afternoon what we have decided about the time.' She shook his hand and nodded to Piet to do the same.

'Am I going back to the hospital today, to mend my ears?' he asked as they returned to the car.

'No, darling, we are going to do your operation after Pa comes home.'

The boy had put his hands over his ears, his face screwed up in distress. Hannah bent down and tipped his face up so that he could see her lips.

'Can you hear the horrible noises?' she asked him gently.

He nodded, his face a picture of misery.

'They will be gone soon, darling,' Hannah said. 'For now you can think about the new kite we bought this morning, until the sounds go away. We'll try it out in Sarah's garden this afternoon.'

'I wish Grandma Lottie was still here,' Piet said. 'I wish she hadn't gone home to Italy. Why does everyone have to go away? Are you going away, like Pa and Grandma Lottie? When is Pa coming home?'

'Pa will be home next week.' She ruffled his blond head. 'And I'm not going anywhere. I'm a stay at home ma. Don't forget that Sarah will be back tonight, too. With all kinds of stories about the cheetahs. Now, stop dragging your feet. It's lunchtime and I'm hungry.'

After lunch she had a cool shower to rid herself of the city's dust and then she lay down on the bed, her body as heavy as the surrounding air. There would be a thunderstorm this afternoon and she hoped that Sarah and Rabindrah would not get caught on the road out of the Mara, where they could be bogged down for hours. In a state of half-wakefulness she thought of Lars in a series of multiplying images. Lars dancing with her, playing rugby, looking at her over the rim of his beer tankard with a promise in his eyes. Lars laughing as she tumbled into the river while retrieving a fishing fly caught on a log, Lars cursing and cajoling the tractor into action, Lars beside her in their bed. Lars inside her. She felt ashamed of the selfish resentment she had displayed when he left for Norway, and she longed for his return. They would love each other like before, all disagreements forgotten, as they settled on a date that would bring back Piet's hearing. And make the necessary preparations for the new baby. When he was well enough, Jorgen would come to Langani with Kirsten, to see the child that had been conceived in Norway. She resolved to write them a letter that would reach them soon after Lars had left, and bring some comfort.

Outside the window she could hear the children playing in the garden, but it was mainly Suniva and James who were calling to each other while Piet's responses were infrequent. Hannah pushed herself up with reluctance, wanting to ensure that no one was left out of their game. She had barely grasped the rules when the first, fat raindrops began to fall and they ran across the lawn and into the house, giggling and jostling as she towelled their hair and searched for dry clothes. Chege brought tea and they were deep into a game of Monopoly when she heard the sound of the Land Cruiser. Leaving the children, Hannah went outside to help unload the vehicle.

'You made it before the rain really set in.' She took the picnic box from the back seat.

'Only because my wife drives like a lunatic. Great to see you, Hannah,' Rabindrah said. 'Let's hear your news. But on the verandah, or we'll be drenched.'

'Did Lottie get away without any delays? How did it go with Dr Enright?' Sarah's questions came tumbling out as she ran for shelter.

'Lottie is fine. She rang from Italy,' Hannah said. 'As for Piet, surgery is the only option. It sounds difficult, and he may need more than one operation. Afterwards they have to move him very carefully, and prevent any coughing or straining that could create pressure in the middle ear. It's hard to keep a boy of his age still, even for five minutes, but I suppose I'll be able to manage.' She was close to tears. 'Oh, Sarah, I'm so tired, and we've been through so much lately that I seem to have lost my bearings altogether. Lost my mind. I'm on the edge and I'm scared. I can't cope with Piet's operation, and being pregnant, and Suniva and James, and everything at the farm, without Lars.'

'Of course you must wait until Lars comes home, to go through with this surgery,' Sarah said.

'That is what I would like, but it means a delay, because Dr Enright is going away. Although he doesn't seem to think the existing damage will increase significantly before he gets back. We'll have to be very careful to avoid post-operation infections afterwards, so it might be best to stay in Nairobi over that period. In case something else goes wrong.'

'You can both stay here, whenever it's necessary and for as long as you like,' Sarah said. 'Sit down, Han, while I give Rabindrah a hand, and then we'll talk some more.'

'How is everything in the Mara?' Hannah watched as Rabindrah and Chege made repeated dashes into the rain to bring in stacks of notebooks, a typewriter and aluminium cases filled with rolls of film.

'Allie is doing fine,' Rabindrah said. 'Maybe you girls could rustle up tea. I'll need something hot after this.'

'It's still strange not to have Tatu run out and welcome us,' Sarah said. 'That wagging tail and the way she wiggled and slobbered over us when we made a fuss of her. I really miss my dog although I suppose it's just as well she's not here. We've been away so much lately, in the Mara and on a trip to Amboseli to see the mountain in all its glory.'

'How is the little cheetah?' Hannah asked. 'Are there any photographs that the children could see?'

'I have masses of pictures, and Allie is besotted with Hiba,' Sarah said. 'Despite her initial protestations.'

'She must miss Hugo now that you and Rabindrah have come back to

Nairobi,' Hannah said, as she waited for the kettle. 'I can't understand why he took off so suddenly. It was very odd, when he had become such an important part of the team, with his beautiful drawings and so.'

'It wasn't odd at all,' Sarah said crisply, but she could feel the tell-tale flush rise from her throat to flood her cheeks. 'He went to Scotland for his father's birthday. Besides, she has Erope for company.'

'Yes but he's a Samburu.' Hannah saw the flash of humour in Sarah's eyes and mistook it for something else. 'Ach, come on, Sarah. We were all brought up differently, and even you and Camilla and me come from diverse backgrounds, although we have white skins. What matters is that we try to get along. But I'm not hypocritical enough to pretend we are exactly the same, black, white or brown, just because that is what we are told to say these days. It's more important to be realistic about the differences between us, and try to respect them.'

'Mmnn. I've been trying to live along those lines for a number of years,' Sarah said. 'In case you hadn't noticed.'

'What I meant about Allie, is that she and Hugo come from the same family and place. They have university degrees, they read the same books and like the same kind of music and they share all kinds of other interests. Erope can't make up for that. And it's patronising for you to laugh at my ideas about a multi-racial society. They are much more honest and practical than the speeches that diplomats and politicians are spewing out these days.'

'Yes, they are indeed.'

'So, what I'm saying is that it must be lonely for Allie without her nephew. Even though she has had Erope with her for years. I imagine you found it strange without Hugo, too.'

'We managed perfectly well,' Sarah said.

'Why are you blushing? You've turned absolutely scarlet.' Hannah stared at her and then burst out laughing. 'Ach, what a *domkopf* am I,' she said. 'He fell for you, didn't he? I bet that's why he skipped off while you were there. So that Rabindrah wouldn't guess. I noticed him eyeing you in Lamu.'

'What a load of nonsense,' Sarah said. 'Hugo and I are good friends, and Allie is the reason he came here. Anyway he is coming back and then he will be with her until next summer. Before he returns to Scotland for his university teaching post.'

'Just good friends.' Hannah's smile broadened. 'That's what film stars say, when the rumours are getting hot. Anyway, it's good for the ego to have an admirer every now and again. Hey, Rabindrah! You look like a drowned rat.'

'And you look well,' he said. 'Even though you have been dealing with everything at Langani on your own. How long can you stay?'

'I was thinking of leaving in the morning,' Hannah said. 'I'll be back next week, to deliver clothes and bags to some of the Nairobi boutiques, and to meet Lars. I'm grateful to you for letting us stay here. It was fun being with Lottie before she left, and the children have had a great time. I'm sure you and Sarah would like the place to yourselves now, and I need to get back to the farm. With Camilla constantly out in the *bundu*, or stuck in the office in Nairobi, there is only me to keep the workshop going. Did you see them in the Mara at all?'

'No.' Sarah's expression was neutral. 'There wasn't time.'

She left the room abruptly and Hannah wondered yet again what had caused such a rift between her two dearest friends. It seemed there was always someone on Sarah's blacklist these days. Still, at least it wasn't Rabindrah any more. She looked at him with raised eyebrows and he gave a small shrug, but did not offer any explanation.

'I saw Anthony and Camilla,' he said in a low voice. 'They're fine and they had happy clients with them. But I didn't mention it to Sarah, and I'd rather you didn't either. By the way, I'm getting her a dog for Christmas. It's a surprise, so don't say anything about that.'

'Don't worry, my lips are sealed,' Hannah said, laughing. 'And I'm sure whatever it is with Camilla will blow over in time.'

Hannah woke up early in the morning and lay still, as a beam of sunlight found its way into the cool depth of the bedroom, and a Hadada Ibis called out a raucous greeting from the lawn. Then she heard another noise that made her sit up and reach for her dressing gown, fearing that Piet was ill. She padded along the hall to the bedroom he was sharing with James, but they were still asleep and she realised that the sound was coming from the bathroom that Sarah and Rabindrah used. The door was slightly ajar and Hannah pushed it open and looked in.

'Ach, Sarah! What's wrong? Have you been vomiting all night? I hope it wasn't any of the food I bought.'

Sarah was sitting on the floor. She raised her head from the toilet bowl, her face ashen, her hair plastered to a clammy forehead. 'I don't know what's the matter with me,' she said. 'I must have picked up some bug in the Mara, because I've been like this, on and off, for about three weeks.' She stood up shakily. 'I hope it's not an amoeba or bilharzia. Maybe I should have a blood test. Anyway, it's over now, and I'm going to get some tea. Do you want to join me?' She splashed her face and ran a comb through her hair. 'Shit, I look like a ghost. Better shape up before Rabindrah wakes up.'

They made their way to the kitchen and when the tea was made they sat at the table with a tin of biscuits.

'Sarah?' There was a slight hesitation as Hannah wondered whether she should broach a subject that had always been sensitive. 'Are you – I mean, could you be . . .' She plunged. 'Do you think you might be pregnant?'

'What?' Sarah had her cup half way to her lips, and she put it back on the saucer with a clatter.

'Are you still on those drugs? Could this be morning sickness?'

'No. No, I don't want to think about that. I can't go down that road,' Sarah said, her face portraying a mixture of confusion and fear and some other emotion that Hannah could not define.

'But you have thought about it, in the back of your mind. Haven't you? Does Rabindrah know you've been throwing up like this?'

'No. When I wake up feeling sick I go out to the long drop tent. No one hears me out there.'

'You should have a test.' Hannah reached out but Sarah withdrew her hands from the table and buried them in her lap. 'Don't be scared, Sarah. I'll come with you. Let's ring and make an appointment for this morning, and we'll go together. Before I leave for Langani.'

'It can't be that,' Sarah whispered. 'Oh, God. You don't understand. It's impossible, the whole thing. I can't be pregnant. It would be . . .'

'It's not impossible at all,' Hannah said. 'Go and have your bath or shower, and after breakfast we'll pay a little visit to your doctor. Come on, Sarah, you need to be sure, one way or the other.'

'Sure?' Her voice sounded slightly hysterical. 'One way or the other? You don't know what you're talking about.'

'I know. There's no such thing as sure, after all you have been through,' Hannah said, oblivious to the underlying issue. 'But you must find out if you are pregnant. You can ring the surgery at eight, and we'll take off as soon as we can after that. I'll phone tomorrow to see if you have the results.'

'You can't tell Rabindrah.' Sarah's eyes were wild. 'Swear to me that you won't tell him.'

'My lips are so sealed that you wouldn't believe it.' Hannah was smiling as she repeated the words for the second time, and headed for her bedroom.

Sarah stood in the doorway of the church, almost afraid to go inside. She had turned her back on the merciless, avenging God who had taken her children, punished her for sins that she could not identify or even recall. And now the faith she had abandoned had dealt her a wild card that she did not know how to play. She felt the nausea rising again, and her entire system went into spasm. Clutching her stomach, she moved to a pew in front of the Madonna holding her infant. Candles flickered, a smell of incense lingered in the air, and the light fell in rainbow shafts from the stained glass windows onto the mosaic floor. She sat in the cool and quiet, unable to pray. What was she going to do? Part of her was singing out her gratitude for the blessing she had received, while another, darker voice warned of the danger this baby presented. For a moment she had an inkling of the torture that Camilla had endured, although she still could not accept the solution. She would carry this child. It was the gift above all gifts for which she had waited so long. And yet, it might bring about the destruction of her marriage. How could she tell Rabindrah about the life growing within her, see the joy and the exhilaration in his eyes, and know that the child might not be his? What would it do to him if he discovered that she had conceived with Hugo in the space of a few short days of passion, after all their years of failure?

For there was no way of knowing for certain whose child it was. She had questioned her doctor about calculating the time of conception, and listened intently to his reply. The words had been intended to comfort a terrified mother who had lost two babies already, and was having trouble believing that she was pregnant again.

'It's early days, Sarah,' he had said. 'I can't put an exact date on conception, but the test is positive. However, with your history, we will have to monitor you very closely. You seem to be in excellent health, and the nausea is a good sign – plenty of the right hormones in your system. I don't see any cause for worry, but you must take it easy. No long safaris out in the bush for the moment. I will want to see you regularly.' He smiled his encouragement. 'Relax, my dear. Enjoy this, every moment of it. And congratulations to you and Rabindrah.'

Should she tell Rabindrah about Hugo? No. No, she could never disclose her affair. Even if he forgave her infidelity they would not be able to endure nine months together, wondering whose child she was bringing into the world. She couldn't tell anyone. Not her husband, her parents, not Hannah. If there had been anyone she might have confided in, it would have been Camilla. She realised that now. But it was out of the question, after what had been said during their confrontation. And in the light of her dilemma, Camilla's choice seemed even more horrifying than before. No. This would have to be her own burden. All she could do now was pray. For the safety of her child, and the salvation of her marriage. Sarah closed her eyes and tried to remember the words of the prayers she had always known, but Hugo's face appeared before her. She forced the image away, her stomach knotting again. Placing a protective hand on her belly, she vowed to nurture this tiny life, no matter what the consequences might be. She stood up, walked over to the statue of the Madonna, and lit a candle.

'Help us,' she whispered. It was the only prayer that her lips could form.

Rabindrah was seated in front of his typewriter when Sarah arrived home. For two days he had been editing sections of the manuscript that Allie had not deemed sufficiently accurate. She stood in the doorway, gazing at his lean form and aquiline nose.

'I think this is fine now.' He looked up and raised a hand in greeting. 'Maybe we should go back to the camp for a few days and let Allie check it out for the last time, before we send the whole thing to London? What do you think? By the way, Hannah rang from Langani to talk to you. She said she would ring back later. And this afternoon I wondered if we could—'

'I'm pregnant.'

She heard him draw in his breath, saw his skin pale as the news percolated. Then the slow rising of hope and apprehension reached his eyes, and his smile turned into a half sob as he stood up. When he put his arms around her and kissed her forehead she began to weep.

'It's wonderful,' he said softly. 'I am the happiest man alive, and you are going to be fine. This time it will be all right. I know it, and you needn't be afraid.'

Sarah leaned against him, speechless, unable to contain the overpowering joy and the swirling currents of guilt and defiance. She was going to have a baby. She had been given another chance. By whom or through what exact circumstances she did not know. But there was a chance.

Chapter 26

Kenya, December 1977

When Camilla's plane landed in the Mara, she watched her husband's long, striding walk as he crossed the airstrip and felt an unbearable rawness, a sense of guilt and repentance that she could not share. A splinter of deception had punctured the perfect bond between them, and it continued to fester in her mind. In the heat of the afternoon, when the Metcalfs had retired for a siesta, Anthony reached out for her.

'I've wanted you every moment,' he said, his eyes hungry. 'I want you now.'

But she could not offer the lovemaking that he longed for. No sexual relations for six weeks, the doctor had said. Just to be on the safe side. Something she could not explain to Anthony.

'Are you angry, Camilla?' He was puzzled and disappointed by her reticence. 'Is this because I've failed you? I know it's taken everything you owned to keep us afloat. But it will come back to you, and I plan to work until I drop to make you financially secure again.'

'Of course I'm not angry, darling,' she said. 'I'm simply tired from running around in London, fitting in extra work and television and interviews. Nairobi was rushed, too, because there was so much to go over with Evelyn. She will run the office very well, with her reputation and all her years of accounting experience in African Wildlife Lodges. But I've been up until after midnight almost every night, going over the papers again, making sure there aren't any more nasty surprises, and following up on any clients that look undecided.'

'I did all that before you came back,' Anthony said. 'I don't know why you would want to go over it all again, unless you feel I wasn't thorough enough.'

'Of course you were,' she said. 'It's only that — Oh, it's no use trying to explain. The work at Langani took patience and concentration. The *bibis* are always willing, but I had to teach them how to cut and sew anything new. I need a little time, to get back on my feet and feel normal again. Hold me, darling, please. And then I'll be safe and loved and not ashamed of the things I've got so terribly wrong.'

'It wasn't your fault,' he said. 'Duncan planned this cleverly, making his getaway at an ideal moment when we weren't here. You mustn't brood, Camilla. We are not going to live with regret hanging over us, clouding our future. This time next year we will have made a full recovery, what with the busy safari schedule and your posh designer clothes coming out in America.'

They did not make love during the week she spent in the Mara, and he became increasingly perplexed and then sullen. Whilst he kept up his usual façade of professional charm, there was friction during their private moments.

'Have you changed your mind about me? About us?' Doubt had begun to plague him. 'I suppose your friend Tom has been crowing with delight at my troubles. Reminding you that you should never have left the good life for the dark continent and my primitive talents.'

'He has been wonderful,' she said, defensively. 'Not only did he offer to defer his fees for the time being, but he also bought my cottage in Burford.'

'Oh, Christ,' he said. 'I'm sorry, Camilla. I know you were fond of that place.'

'Actually, I don't know why I kept it so long,' she said. 'I suppose it was because my mother felt comfortable there during the last weeks of her life. At peace with herself and with Daddy, after all the years of bitterness between them. But I've hardly used it since. In fact, Tom has been down there far more often than I have, bringing a string of girlfriends, the latest one being Lila. It is rather romantic, as you said yourself, but I can't think when we would use it.' There was umistakable sadness in her voice.

He did not press her again and she felt increasingly apart from him, haunted by the memory of the abortion and her quarrel with Sarah. She knew, now, what it was to lose a child and it seemed tragic that she could not share her loss with the one person who had experienced the same agony.

It was Anthony who suggested a visit to Allie's camp.

413

'I don't think I'll join you,' Camilla said. 'I want to work with Francis on something new on the dinner menu. A dessert he hasn't done before.'

'But you haven't seen Allie since our wedding,' Anthony said, irritated by her response. 'She will be hurt if she finds out you were here and didn't drop in on her.'

'I ran into Sarah at Langani and we had an argument. I'd rather not see her for the time being, and I imagine she feels the same.'

'That girl has had a run-in with everyone over the last few months.' Anthony was exasperated. 'Maybe she will calm down now, get a grip, since things seem to be back on track with Rabindrah. Sometimes I wonder where the original Sarah went, with her generosity and insight. Anyway, she has gone back to Nairobi. It's just Allie and Hugo in camp right now. And Erope.'

The Metcalfs were enchanted by the opportunity of seeing and holding the young cheetah, and meeting Allie whose research they had read about in Sarah's books on elephants and the northern tribes of Kenya. Camilla sat at the edge of the admiring circle, watching Hiba chase her tail and climb into Gina Metcalf's lap to be fed from her bottle. She felt frayed and isolated in the midst of the conversation and laughter, and she longed for a time alone with Anthony. To erase the images, the sounds and smells of the clinic, the bright light hanging over her in the theatre as she closed her eyes, counted to ten, and gave up her child.

The last days of their safari were spent at Lake Nakuru, driving out across the salt flats to admire more than a million pink and scarlet flamingo feeding on the algae in the shallow water, and to study the variety of bird and animal life along the lake shores.

'I think my favourites are the squadrons of pelicans, flying over us and bobbing in the water,' Gina Metcalf said. 'I didn't need to see that fat python, though. I'm not convinced that it won't visit us in our tent, Anthony, no matter what you say. I love this campsite, by the way, with the long stretches of grass and the spread of the thorn trees between the tents. So spacious. It's like having a whole world of your own.'

It was not a python that turned out to be the climax of their safari, however. On the following night they were woken by the terrified barking of zebra and the noise of pounding hooves close to the tents. Moments later came the bone-chilling sound of a lion, roaring at close quarters. Anthony fastened on his limb, dressed in haste and vanished into the darkness with a flashlight as Camilla peered out of the tent that she had zipped up to chest height, although she had no idea what protection this could afford her.

'What's happening?' Chuck Metcalf called out from the guest tent. 'Are we under attack?'

'Sounds like a lion kill.' Camilla had snatched up a shirt and trousers. 'Pull on some clothes. Anthony has gone for the car.'

They were all waiting when Anthony returned in his vehicle and motioned for them to get in. Leleruk was already standing in the back, shining a powerful lamp into the darkness. Within minutes they saw the lion, on the edge of a small *lugga* a few hundred yards from the camp. He was crouched over a zebra, grunting and tugging at its innards, stopping occasionally to call out the news of his kill. In the distance they could hear the frantic shrieks of the herd, and the whup whup of hyenas as they gathered to share in the pickings. Anthony edged forward, not wanting to chase the victor from his meal. The lion had no fear of them, however, and as they drew nearer he rose and swung around to face them brazenly, swinging his long tail, licking bloodied jaws and standing his ground, marking the earth with several swipes of one huge paw.

'He's warning us not to come any further,' Anthony said quietly. 'And he's not going to move away, this old *simba*. He knows who is boss here, and we'll have to keep an eye on him for the next day or so. I'm sure he will still be around tomorrow, so we'll back off now. Leleruk can build up an extra fire at the end of the tents, just in case our friend decides to takes a walk.'

'I will do it,' Leleruk said. 'And if he is coming any nearer, I have my spear. I would be proud to kill him.'

'I hope that won't be necessary,' Camilla said, unsure about the laughter that had erupted from the watchman. The slim spear suddenly looked fragile as a weapon of defence.

'No killing inside a National Park. Not even to beef up your honour and impress the women.' Anthony was grinning. 'Bad luck, Leleruk.'

The lion roared intermittently for the remainder of the night, preventing anyone in the camp from sleep. At daybreak he was resting in the shade of an acacia tree. He had eaten a large portion of his kill and his stomach was distended. His golden eyes were half closed in a battle-scarred face and he sat motionless and regal, panting lightly and watching the vehicle.

'I'll never use the word "magnificent" to describe anything else, ever again,' Gina said. 'Looking at him now, I don't care how many sleepless nights he causes us. Even the hyenas haven't dared come too close, although he is alone.'

'We're going to fetch three of the *watu* and come back with a second vehicle and some rope,' Anthony said. 'This old fellow's larder is a little too near to our tents.'

'What can you do about that?' Camilla asked.

'Move his lunch,' Anthony said, laughing at her alarm. 'We can't have him as a close neighbour. You are going to drive this vehicle, while Musioka, Karanja and I take the supply truck with the big winch. Team-work, Mama Chapman. *Harambee!*'

In camp, excitement and wide smiles greeted the plan. The tent staff took out binoculars and climbed into the acacia trees for a good view. Half an hour later Anthony drove the truck back to the lion and his kill. In the Land Cruiser the Metcalfs sat in the back seat, windows rolled halfway up, with Camilla at the wheel. She was nervous but determined that no one should guess, and she kept her hands steady by holding tight to the steering wheel as she listened to Anthony's instructions. Flies buzzed around the vehicle and thorny bushes scraped the side of the car, setting her teeth on edge.

'A little closer. Round to the left of him. Away from the kill.' Anthony called out commands from a position on the other side of the rotting zebra. 'Musioka, you start making a big *matata* now. Bang on the roof with your stick. You too, Leleruk. Rev up the engine to distract the lion, Camilla. Go on – louder. Get him up on his feet, but be ready to reverse as fast as you can, if he looks as though he might spring.'

The noise of banging drummed through her head, and sweat trickled down her back and formed on her forehead and above her lip. The lion glowered at them and opened his mouth wide, displaying a pink tongue and powerful incisors. His tawny eyes were angry and a low growl made her draw in her breath and shiver in the already stifling heat of the morning. More terrifying was the sight of Musioka on the back of the truck, coiling several yards of rope into a neat circle on the flatbed and then leaning far out over the chassis to hurl it into the air. Camilla held her breath as the lasso landed neatly around the half-eaten carcass and the lion leapt to his feet, snarling and tossing his maned head. He took a few steps forward and crouched as though ready to spring, but then changed his mind and turned to bound away into a thicket. Weak with fright and relief she watched as Musioka slowly winched the kill closer to the truck.

'Drive directly behind me,' Anthony called out to Camilla. 'The back of the truck is unprotected, and he could come for us from anywhere in the bush.'

He set off slowly, not wanting to lose their hold on the sad, bouncing remains of the zebra as they dragged it along the rutted surface of the track. When they had covered a distance that he thought sufficient, Anthony turned into the shade of a tree and climbed down from the truck, bending to unfasten the rope. Camilla opened the door of the Land Cruiser to join him, but he waved her back.

'Stay in the vehicle, all of you' he said. 'He can still appear out of nowhere.'

But there was no sign of the lion, and Anthony told his men to bring the truck back to camp.

'Let's hope the old boy comes to claim the rest of his meal before the scavengers get too much of it. And that he stays over here, from now on. Move over, darling and I'll drive now. Leleruk — you can go back with the other two.' He climbed into the vehicle with Camilla and the Metcalfs and for a moment there was an awestruck silence.

'Holy smoke,' Gina said as they drove away in search of other game. 'I'm not sure what we could be looking for after that. It was amazing to watch his kill being moved, but it's kind of disappointing to think we won't see the old guy again. Camilla, you were fearless. If I'd been behind the wheel I would have frozen with terror when he got up onto his feet.'

It was late afternoon when they returned to camp. Gina sat down at the fire.

'I'll join you in a few minutes,' Camilla said. 'I'm going to freshen up.'

'I'm for a cocktail first,' Chuck said, and his wife nodded agreement. He reappeared a few minutes later with drinks for them all.

'Chuck, sit down, right now.' Anthony was leaning against a tree, motionless, looking down the length of the campsite, his voice low and urgent. 'Sit down, and don't move an inch.'

'What?' Chuck kept walking towards his wife.

'Sit bloody down, man. And don't make any sound or movement.' Anthony pushed him firmly into a canvas chair. 'The lion is in camp. He's probably thirsty after having eaten so well, and he's using this clearing as the fastest way to the river.'

At the end of the clearing the old *simba* had appeared, strolling across the grass with huge, ambling paws.

'Anthony, sir! Mama Camilla is in the shower. Musioka brought water a few minutes ago.' Sammy called out the information from where he was standing with the rest of the staff, beside the safari car.

'Jesus!' Anthony's face paled.

The lion was moving towards the furthest tent. The tent from which Camilla might emerge at any moment, if she was not in the shower already. Anthony prayed that she would not come out of either one. The great cat stopped and looked around, his tail twitching as he decided on the best route to the water. After a brief hesitation he padded forward again, heading for the gap between the sleeping tent and the shower. In one swift movement Anthony made a rush for the car and turned the key in the ignition. He put the vehicle into gear and revved the engine. The lion stopped again, uncertain as to the meaning of the noise. Anthony made one long blast on the horn and started down the clearing at full speed.

Camilla stood in the shower under the bucket of hot water, inhaling its smoky scent, humming a song. When she heard the car and the unusual sound of the horn she opened the flap of the small enclosure and looked out. The lion was standing a few yards away from her, his eyes unblinking in the dusk.

'Oh, God!' She retreated behind the flimsy canvas, peering through a small gap, grasping a towel and wrapping it around her. Her breath had turned into the same shallow, panting sound that the lion had made earlier in the day. 'Don't punish me, dear God. Don't let me die here. Not now. Oh, please, I can't die now.'

The vehicle raced down the campsite, setting a course between the shower tent and the lion, and she saw that the passenger door had been flung open.

'I'm going to turn hard left with the door open,' Anthony shouted. 'Run for the car, Camilla. Run.'

Camilla took a deep breath, feeling the acrid fire of terror in her throat.

Clutching the towel around her she rushed out of the shower tent as the vehicle careered towards her, lights full on, horn blaring. She flung herself into the car, landing in a heap of twisted limbs as Anthony passed the lion and turned again, forcing it to back away towards the direction from which it had come.

'That should deter any further visits during the cocktail hour,' he said, as Camilla struggled to a sitting position, fastening the towel as best she could, shock waves still reverberating in her head, the adrenalin rush slowing to a trickle. 'Let's find you some clothes and then we'll be ready for the strongest drink I've ever needed.'

'What about the lion?' she asked, a seed of doubt sprouting when she thought of the hours of darkness that lay ahead.

'We will light a second fire down this end of the site and I'll have Karanja stay up with Leleruk tonight,' he said, seeing the flicker of apprehension in her eyes. 'I promise you we will be quite safe.'

When Samson had poured strong drinks, they lifted their glasses in a moment of silent gratitude before embarking on the post mortem of the events. It was late by the time they had finished dinner, and both the Metcalfs and Camilla were slightly reluctant when it came to walking to their tents, even with three of the camp staff and several lanterns to guide them.

When she had pulled up the zipper Camilla turned and flung herself into Anthony's arms, weeping.

'Hey, what's this? No harm could have come to you, darling. The moment I knew you were in that shower you were safe.' He wrapped his arms around her and drew her down onto the bed, close to him, her head buried in his shoulder. 'Camilla, don't cry. I know it's delayed shock, but I will always keep you safe, darling. Always.'

'We were going to have a baby.' The words came out before she could stop them.

'What? A baby? Why didn't you tell me?' It took him a moment to understand the full meaning of what she had said. 'What do you mean by "were"?'

'I had a miscarriage.' For her own sake she was afraid to tell him the truth, nor could she bring herself to share with him her sorrow and her guilt at what she had done. 'That's why I was delayed in London. That's why I haven't been able to . . .'

'Darling, darling, I'm so sorry.' He held her, knowing that the shock of his financial loss had caused this.

'I've been so desperately sad. So low. And I know now that I never understood how Sarah felt.' She gulped down a sob. 'The doctor said that I can have more children and I hope we will. I hope I deserve that because I don't want to be like Sarah and Rabindrah. I don't want us to—'

'Darling, you know that miscarriages are not rare. It must have been so distressing for you, on your own, but you are going to be fine. And we will have beautiful *totos*, whenever you're ready again. Camilla, I adore you. I want you with me every moment, so I can see you and touch you. Closer. Come closer. My love for you is far beyond anything I ever believed possible, and that is what will make everything we do come right in the end.'

She was so moved by his ardour that she found herself unable to respond with words. Instead she laced her fingers through his and covered him with kisses. She had once told Sarah that happiness was a fleeting thing, not to be trusted or relied upon. But now she felt she had been wrong. It was the first time she had ever allowed herself to believe totally in another human being, and she revelled in her new-found confidence, and in the aching, rushing love she felt for her husband.

All around them the strange music of the African night rose to a crescendo. In the distance Camilla could see the glow of the second campfire beyond their sleeping quarters, the flames causing flickering shapes to dance across the fragile walls of the tent. Beyond the fire Leleruk was standing in the orange light, the beads and metal coils he wore around his neck and wrists and ankles glinting in the darkness. He raised his spear and plunged it firmly into the ground so that it stood trembling beside him, and then he laughed out loud.

When Anthony turned out the lamp he fell asleep instantly, but Camilla lay beside him, listening and waiting. There was no sign of the lion's presence, however, and at last she turned over and curved her body to fit her husband's sleeping form, praying that there would be no threat or danger to this man who loved her beyond all expectation.

Anthony had only two days before his next clients arrived for a Christmas expedition that would take them north to Samburu and Meru and he had decided to stay with the crew, organising the movement of the trucks and tents and equipment, while Camilla flew back to Nairobi with the Metcalfs.

'It's our last night, and we'd sure love you to join us for dinner,' Bob Metcalf said to her. 'Would you mind if we went to the casino? After all that time in the bush with no temptations, I feel like an evening with a cabaret and a flutter at the tables.'

'Your choice,' Camilla said, with a bright smile and a sinking heart. She hated the casino; the food was indifferent and she had no interest in gambling. But the Metcalfs had already booked their next safari, and had recommended friends who would arrive in March and she did not want to offend them.

'Sammy will pick you up at eight, from the Norfolk,' she said. 'I'll meet you there. In the meantime, he will be with you all day, if you want to visit the museum, or do some shopping.'

She left them at the Norfolk Hotel and drove straight to the office where there was a hum of energy and determination, as the staff followed Anthony's lead and pulled together to survive. At home she lay down for an hour and then took a long bath. When she walked into the restaurant at the casino she had hidden any fatigue beneath her make-up. Dinner seemed endless and the cabaret was loud, making her head ache.

'I have an early start in the morning,' she said, as the Metcalfs purchased their chips. 'So I'll say goodbye here, and leave you to Lady Luck.'

'Roulette first,' Gina said. 'Then blackjack, which is Chuck's thing. My dear, we have had the most wonderful experience of our lives, and we cannot thank you both enough. We'll see you next year and maybe before that, in Boston.'

Camilla embraced them, turned away, and came face to face with Zahra.

'What do you want?' The Somali girl spoke with ill-concealed insolence. 'I read in the paper that you married him. He hasn't been here for months, and he didn't come at my invitation. I told him I never wanted to see him again. If he is fooling around somewhere, it's nothing to do with me.'

'You slept with him.' A deathly calm came over Camilla.

'It was months ago. He said you weren't together any more. He was in bad shape. So don't come here making trouble for me.'

'Did you know someone called Duncan Harper?' Camilla eyed the girl.

'Little prick. All the girls here hate him. Cheap. Always whining and asking me to do it for less money. A loser. I hear the bosses are looking for him, but he's gone.'

'You sleep with the clients, then.'

'What of it? Are you going to get me thrown out of this job for what I do when I leave here? Just like you threw me out before, and fucked up my life.'

'Do you know where Duncan Harper went?'

'No.' Zahra's eyes slid away.

'He stole all Anthony's money,' Camilla said. 'Almost bankrupted him. I'm not here to cause trouble for you, Zahra, but I could make it worth your while, if you can tell me more about Duncan Harper.'

'Worth my while? I have a job. I have a life. I can eat and sleep in a comfortable bed. I don't need anything from you.' Her gaze was directed at the tables, skimming the room for a likely prospect later on in the evening.

'Do you remember Tom Bartlett? And my friend Joe Blandford, the photographer?'

'I have to go back to my shift,' Zahra said. 'Don't bother to come here again, or ask any more questions. About anyone. I've had enough shit from your kind.'

'I'll give you a return ticket to London, and arrange for you to be photographed by Joe.' Camilla saw a perfect opportunity to cajole the girl into giving her the information she needed on Harper, and to remove the risk of Anthony running into her again. 'Tom will organise somewhere for you to stay and make up a portfolio for you. Introduce you to some influential people. Nothing may come of it, but I think you could still have a career in modelling. Take two weeks off work and try it. Think of it as a holiday. But first I need to know about Duncan. Anything you can remember.'

'What are you really after?' Zahra's expression was incredulous. 'Is this some trick, or a revenge for my having slept with Anthony? I tell you, he was a mess. Crying like a baby, ashamed of his body, of what happened to his leg. I did it out of pity.'

'Tell me where Duncan went.' Camilla's stomach turned as she tasted the bile of jealousy. 'Tell me, and I promise I'll get you to London.'

'South Africa. He told me he was going to Johannesburg.' Zahra's laugh was full of contempt. 'Offered to take me there and set me up in business with some friend of his. Cheap, lying little shit.'

'What was the name of the friend in Johannesburg?' Camilla grasped her arm, saw the girl wince.

'Neville Bateman,' Zahra said. 'That's the man who was going to set him up. He thought I would be stupid enough to give him a night of free fucking, by promising me I could be a part of his scheme. Can you imagine? A black girl in business with two white men, in a place where you can't even ride in the same bus or eat in the same restaurant. There's only one name for that kind of business. He took me for an idiot. A cheap lay.' Her eyes narrowed. 'I went to his house that night and made him take off his clothes. Then I stood behind him and put my arm tight around his neck so he couldn't move. He was excited. Thought I was going to start by roughing him up a little. I took his balls in my hand and squeezed them until he was screaming at the top of his voice. And I bit him. On his ugly, white, scrawny neck. Deep, so there was plenty of blood. Then I took his keys and his car, and I left.'

'Get a passport,' Camilla said. 'Ring me when you have it. Here's my number. I have a friend in the British High Commission who will give you a visitor's visa. Goodnight.'

In the morning she rose early, made herself a cup of tea and watched the clock until she knew that her lawyer would be in his office. Then she lifted the telephone.

'Duncan Harper is in Johannesburg,' she said. 'This is how you can find him.'

Chapter 27

Kenya, December 1977

'I can't wait to see Lars.' Hannah's voice was happy. 'I think I've fallen in love with him all over again. After all these years of marriage. What about that, heh?'

'Sounds ideal,' Camilla said, thinking of Anthony with a detonation of longing.

'Everything from the workshop is in the back of the car. I'll help you deliver it. And thanks for the bed tonight.'

They spent the day delivering Christmas orders to Nairobi's boutiques and gift shops. It was late in the evening when they finally sat down for a drink on the verandah. Beyond them the garden had been swallowed by the darkness, leaving only the scent of jasmine and the silhouette of the Ngong Hills beneath an extravagant glitter of stars.

'Pregnancy suits me, you know,' Hannah said. 'We hadn't thought of having another baby after Piet. But this feels right.' She glanced sideways at Camilla's small waist and flat stomach. 'Aren't you and Anthony tempted to make a beautiful blond or ginger-haired *toto*? Or have you decided to enjoy being together and on safari for a year or two, without any other responsibilities?'

'No. I hope we won't have to wait too long.' Camilla was tempted to divulge the truth, but a voice in her head warned her to be careful.

'I'm sorry.' Hannah registered the forlorn note in the words. 'I'm sure you want to sort out this whole financial thing first. It must be such a worry and you've been so brave.'

'We'll be fine, if all the safari bookings come in as planned. I'm going back to London and New York in April, for a couple of shoots and a television series that will pay well.'

Hannah sat forward. 'Are you going back to acting?'

'No. I'm on the panel of a talent show. I can't do a play. With rehearsals and run time I would be away too long. Television pays better, anyway. And I hope the new range of clothes in America will go well.' Camilla laughed. 'As Tom kindly pointed out, I'm getting too old for the best fashion shoots and advertising campaigns. He says the African sun has been drawing lines on my face, and soon I won't be able to hide them. So this may be the last glossy magazine cover.'

'What rubbish,' Hannah said. 'You look as unblemished and perfect as ever. He's jealous, that's all.' Her next words came fast. 'Have you heard from Sarah?'

'Not a word.' Camilla crossed her arms, hugging her private regrets.

'She's pregnant,' Hannah said.

'What?' Camilla straightened. 'That is wonderful. When is the baby due?' Her delight was genuine, but she felt a profound sadness that she had not heard the miraculous news directly from Sarah.

'Sometime in August,' Hannah said. 'She only found out a week ago. I was hoping this would make her come around. Contact you.'

'It hasn't,' Camilla said, acknowledging that there were some wounds that might never heal. 'I'm thrilled for her. I only hope and pray that this time nothing will go wrong.'

'Rabindrah is like a mother hen, and she is spending most of her time at home. She feels fine and they are coming to Langani for Christmas. You'll be in Samburu with Anthony, won't you? Maybe she will talk to you on the radio, when we call up on Christmas Day or for New Year. I don't know what you two rowed about. It can't have been a matter of life and death.'

But it had been a matter of life and death, and Camilla knew that Sarah would not call at Christmas. Perhaps she would never call again.

The children had made homecoming gifts and Lars opened each package slowly, enjoying the mounting excitement as they stood around him waiting for signs of pleasure and approval. Suniva had painted a portrait of him, and James had made the frame. Piet's present was a leopard he had carved, with eyes made out of stones from the river. They sat up looking at photographs taken in Norway, listening to his account of Jorgen's gradual recovery, and laughing as Lars described a day's skiing with old friends when his rusty manoeuvres resulted in numerous falls. Finally he had decided to retire to the bar for coffee and brandy, rather than trying to remain upright on the steeper slopes that his companions frequented. When the children had reluctantly gone to bed, Hannah leaned her head against his shoulder.

'I'm sorry I wasn't with you, to help you care for Jorgen and Kirsten,' she said. 'I missed you every day. And I looked inside myself and recognised the worst part of me. The stubborn, shortsighted part that I hope you won't see again. Soon Piet will be able to hear, and we will have the baby. A new beginning for all of us.'

He put his hand on her elbow to propel her gently to the bedroom. She fell asleep quickly, grateful for the comfort of his body, never noticing that he remained wide awake until the dawn crept into the room and another scorching day began.

Christmas came and went, with Rabindrah and Sarah arriving full of laughter and hope, and loaded with gifts for everyone. On the anniversary of Piet's death they made their annual pilgrimage to the cairn, and stood on the ridge looking out over the land. As they turned to leave Sarah remained behind for a few moments, sitting on the white stones and talking to her first love, whispering her secret, aware that he knew everything she had ever suffered and that he would understand. When she rose to her feet she found Rabindrah waiting, and he took her arm to lead her down the stony path to safety.

It was not until the end of January that Hannah noticed the change in Lars. He spent long periods of time alone in the wheat fields, or driving round the farm. His visits to the group of huts that made up the labour lines became more frequent, and he ordered building materials and fresh whitewash to create more showers and toilets. In Hannah's small clinic he installed new benches and an area where the *totos* could play in a clean, thatched area with woven matting on the floor, instead of rolling around in the accustomed red dirt under the blazing sun. Late in the evening he would sit at his desk making notes and paying bills, but sometimes she would find him staring out of the window and when she spoke his name he did not seem to hear her.

'I think we should improve the school,' he said one evening, as they stood on the verandah in the darkening blue of the sky, watching the mountain peak become a black finger pointing at the emerging stars. A snatch of music escaped from the closed door of the sitting room where Nderi was lighting the fire. 'And I want to put a new roof on it and try to find a second teacher. Maybe one of the young volunteers that come out from Europe for a few months at a time. I've been thinking about an education centre where older children from other areas could come and learn about the wildlife we are trying to protect.'

'Where would we find the money for all that?' Hannah asked. 'The anti-poaching patrols are costing us more than the grants we get from the AWF and the government. And Piet goes to Nairobi next week. It's expensive staying in the city, even with Sarah or Camilla. The hospital bills and medicines will make a big hole in our bank account. Our insurance doesn't cover everything, Lars. We can't afford to think about anything else for the moment.' She tucked her hand into his. 'What is the matter? You seem out of sorts. Depressed. Is there something I don't know? Something you are keeping from me?'

'No, Han. Everything is fine. These are thoughts for the future. Things we should do one day, to make our property a better place for the people around us. They have so little, and I'd like to do more for them.'

'Langani has a kindergarten school and a clinic,' Hannah said. 'Our workers are well-paid and Camilla provides additional jobs for women. The conservation area protects the game on our land and we employ rangers for the patrols. That is as much as we can do, for now. We can't take care of the whole country, and all its problems. This is Africa and we have to accept the best and worst of it. We don't live in a socialist country with a small population and plenty of money.'

He knew she was right but although he tried to be more cheerful, his general mood remained sombre. He had returned from Norway with an urgent desire to be home, to be close to Hannah and the children, and the new baby who would soon become part of their world. But a recent letter from his mother had created a sense of unease as he read of Jorgen's frequent bouts of fatigue and the amount of medication he now relied upon. Increasingly Lars found himself torn between his need to be with his wife and children, and his guilt at having left his parents to struggle unaided through the harsh darkness of winter. In addition his absence had brought into sharper focus the hardships in the nearby *shambas* and villages, and the suffering of the less fortunate owners of small, parched plots on Langani's boundaries.

Looking around the house with its spacious rooms, its rugs and cushions, the deep, comfortable furniture and modern plumbing, he experienced a new sense of dismay at the shortages of food and water outside his private oasis. Labour conditions at Langani were far better than on most farms, and he knew that much of the abject poverty surrounding him was the result of corruption or a refusal by the local tribespeople to change their traditions, and to reduce the number of their livestock and adapt to modern methods of agriculture. Aid money continued to arrive from the Western world, but large percentages were deposited into the private accounts of wealthy politicians and business-men, while the rest of the nation begged for assistance, and the rains failed those with only a few acres on which they hoped to grow food. There was little he could do, but the knowledge frustrated him. Once upon a time he had lived with the certainty that he and Hannah would one day be able to hand on a more prosperous farm to their children, with better conditions for the people who worked on their land. Now he was no longer sure, and there were days when he was barely able to go out and face the harsh conditions and the poverty that were beginning to make him feel defeated.

'Sarah should be here before dark.' Hannah was busy organising fresh bed linen and towels. 'She thought it would be good to settle in for a few days before we leave with Piet. And Rabindrah will join her for the weekend. I'm going to find Suniva, to help with flowers.'

'She'll be a reluctant helper,' Lars said, laughing. 'Although she might put a few stalks in a bowl, since they are for Sarah.'

Hannah heard the whispering as she reached her daughter's bedroom. Then a giggle, quickly suppressed.

'Show me. Please.' It was James's voice, urgent.

'Sshhh.' The giggle again. 'OK. But let's do another kiss first. On my lips, like you see in films. Like Ma and Pa. Then you can see under my shirt.'

Hannah grasped the knob but the door was locked and she jiggled the handle and pounded with her fist. 'Suniva! James! What the hell is going on?' Suniva flung open the door and stood on the threshold, defiant.

'Get out of this room, James, and go to the compound.' Hannah was incensed. 'Lars will speak to you later. Suniva you will stay here, until I tell you otherwise.'

Hannah watched as James slunk past her and speeded up along the corridor, making for the kitchen and the staff entrance to the house. Then she shut her daughter in and returned to the office.

'What is all the fuss about? I saw James going past here like a rocket.'

Lars listened to her angry explanation, tilting his chair out and back so that Hannah feared the legs might give way underneath him. When he laughed and pulled her towards him she was infuriated.

'They have to be separated,' she said. 'This is a nightmare. I never thought – What are you laughing at? Can't you see how terrible this is?'

'They are innocent children, Han. Playing games. Discovering who they are. We all tried it. In corners at school, in cupboards, or behind hedges and walls. Anywhere at all.'

'No. It can't be with him, no matter how innocent they are. James is thirteen years old. This cannot go on for a minute longer.'

'They are inseparable,' he said. 'They always have been. Just talk to Suniva calmly and quietly, and I will explain to James that kissing and asking girls to take their clothes off is disrespectful, and not allowed. We shouldn't turn this into a major incident. You just need to lay down some rules.'

'No. They are together all the time, and whatever we say will make no difference. They are too close. Too bound up in each other. They have to be separated, Lars. We should send Suniva to boarding school.'

'That's ridiculous and unnecessary,' he said. 'You are overreacting, Han. You told me a few days ago we need to be careful with money.'

'She is going to boarding school,' Hannah said. 'And you had better deal with James. Right now.'

'Where is Suniva?' Sarah sat down by the fire with a soft drink in her hand. She had decided to drive up and spend three days at the farm, while Rabindrah was covering a story that kept him chasing people for interviews both day and night. 'I haven't seen her this evening. Or James. Are they out on some adventure?'

Hannah looked away. It was Lars who explained why the children had been sent to their rooms until the morning, and that Nderi would bring a tray of supper into Suniva, in her solitary confinement.

'Oh, Lord,' Sarah said, trying to hide a smile, knowing that Hannah would not take kindly to laughter. 'I remember the first crush I had. It was while we were on holiday in Ireland. I was about eleven, and a boy kissed me on top of a haystack. I had no idea what to do, so I fled inside, but I kept hoping he would find me and do it again. He didn't, though. He was probably just as scared as I was.'

'Well, they are not scared. I have decided to phone the convent in Msongari tomorrow. They might have a place for Suniva next term. If so, I'll see them when we take Piet down for his operation.'

'I can't imagine Suniva in a boarding school,' Sarah said. 'She would feel so confined, so boxed in. Aren't you—'

'You're going to tell me I'm overreacting,' Hannah said angrily. 'Well, I'm not. It's time Suniva stopped running around like a wild thing. She is going to school in Nairobi, and that's it. Besides, I'm going to be dealing with Piet's operation and recovery, with a new baby on my hands and all the usual demands around here.'

'We must be careful that Suniva doesn't feel excluded, with your attention always focused on other things,' Lars said. 'She's not as strong and independent as you think.'

'How are you feeling, Sarah?' Hannah changed the subject.

'Absolutely great. I've stopped throwing up for the moment. Dr Roberts says I'm doing fine but there will be no more bouncing up and down to the Mara, for the time being. We have enough material anyway, so I have plenty to do at home.'

Hannah went to bed first. 'I'm not sleeping so well now,' she said. 'Too big to be comfortable. If I stay up any longer I'll be useless in the morning.'

'She is wrong about Suniva and James,' Lars said when he was alone with Sarah. 'Maybe tomorrow you can persuade her that she doesn't have to be so drastic.'

'I'll try. But once Hannah has an idea, good or bad, it is hard to dissuade her.'

'This is not only about what happened today,' Lars said. 'She has mentioned twice to me how James resembles his father more and more as he grows up. That is what makes her uneasy. In her heart she fears that if he looks like Simon, perhaps he will become like him.'

'I do see the likeness, but the circumstances are completely different. Simon was a product of childhood trauma and his uncle's hatred and brutality. James has had love and security all his life, thanks to you and

Hannah. He is gentle and sweet-natured, like his mother. Hannah has nothing to fear.'

'I know you are right.' He paused. 'I'm so happy for you, Sarah. You look different. Soft, and very beautiful.'

'Thank you,' she said, astonished at the compliment. It was unusual for Lars to put things in such language.

'I'd like to see Camilla pregnant now,' he said, pouring himself a vodka and acknowledging her refusal with a smile. 'Wouldn't it be special if the three of you, always so close, produced children around the same time? I suppose you know that she had a miscarriage? Anthony was very upset, because he thought that his financial disaster might have brought it on. But he told Hannah that the doctor in London saw no reason for Camilla not to become pregnant again.'

The sound of breaking glass made him turn, to find Sarah picking up shards of the tumbler she had knocked over.

'Sorry,' she said, rising from her chair. 'That was clumsy of me. Goodnight, Lars. I'll see you in the morning.'

'Goodnight.' He cursed himself for broaching the subject of miscarriage with Sarah at such a sensitive time. She had probably not been told for that very reason. There were more pressing things on his mind, however, and he sat for a long time, watching the fire die away and thinking of his children and his parents, and of Hannah whom he loved above all else in the world.

It was later than usual when Suniva heard the soft tapping on the window. She scrambled out of bed and lifted the catch so that James could climb into the room.

'I'm sorry,' he said. 'I made trouble for you.'

'They are going to send me away to boarding school. In Nairobi,' Suniva said, tears brimming. 'I went to the sitting room door to listen and I heard Ma saying it.'

'Don't cry,' James said. 'When you come back I will be here, waiting for you. I will always be waiting for you. And we can write letters and send pictures, like before.'

'But we won't be together. In our forest house, reading and talking and swimming in the river. I will be far away, and you will forget those things.'

'I will never forget,' James said. 'I will go to our house every day, after school. And when you miss me you will close your eyes and I will be there, inside your head. I will always be there.'

He leaned forward and kissed her on her cheek and then he was gone, leaving her to curl up in her bed with her eyes squeezed tightly shut as she committed every detail of him to memory.

The morning was bright, with the yolk of the sun already burning the dew off the lawn when David telephoned to say that a rhino with a calf had been spotted below the viewing platform. James had reappeared and, after a talk with Lars, he had made a barely audible apology to Hannah with eyes downcast and head bent between hunched shoulders. She did not comment but piled the three children and Sarah into her Land Rover and drove up to the lodge. They spent the morning watching as the rhino snorted and puffed and then departed, leaving the other creatures of the forest to take their turn to lick the salt and drink at the water hole. Afterwards, James elected to go to a football match with David as the others headed back to the farm. When they reached the house Piet raced inside to find his father and depict the scene.

Lars was standing like a statue beside the telephone. 'He's gone,' he said, bewildered, tears pouring unchecked down his broad cheeks. 'They couldn't do anything more. He had a second, massive heart attack a few minutes ago, and he has gone.'

They gathered around, mourning silently with him, holding his hands. Finally he sat down with Hannah at his feet, her head resting on his knees as he tried to come to terms with his father's death. Silence took over the house, nosing its way into familiar corners, sucking the warmth out of the bright day. The telephone rang intermittently. Arrangements were made for the removal of Jorgen's body, discussions took place with regard to his wish to be buried in the small cemetery close to the farm. Dates were mentioned. James was still at the football match and Esther took the other children for a walk. Sarah retired to her room to leave Lars and Hannah to their private decisions.

'I will have to go for the funeral,' Lars said. 'I know Piet's operation is set for next week, but I'm sure it can be delayed for a short time. Mother needs me to be there. She is completely distraught. I can't leave Ilse to deal with everything. Besides she has just told me that Karl has been having an affair. I must go, Hannah. You know how important it is.'

'More important than your son? More important than your wife?' All her resolutions flew out the window as she looked at him, afraid to be alone again with her deaf son and the baby coming so soon. 'You can't go, Lars.' Her voice rose. 'Please. You mustn't go away again. It's not fair on me. Even Lottie isn't here now.'

'I need some fresh air,' Lars said, turning on his heel, shockwaves still reverberating in his head as he strode out into the afternoon glare. 'We'll talk about this when I can think more clearly.'

He backed out of the garage and drove away, wanting to distance himself as quickly as possible from the house. From Hannah. He was not sure where he was going, but he thought that the river would be somewhere he could work things out. There was a place where the children liked to swim and fish, and he had gone there often with Jorgen during his father's visits to the farm. They had walked upstream from the clear, still pool to an incline with rushing, silver water and rocks where the largest trout hid below the surface, waiting for flies and insects to come their way. He remembered driving Jorgen along the bank, pointing out birds and monkeys, discussing their fishing strategy and the flies they would use, and the possibility of hearing or seeing a leopard.

His eyes were blurred with tears as he turned onto a grassy track, taking the bend too fast so that the car swerved out of control. He wrenched at the wheel and jammed his foot onto the brake as the warning shout came from the trees. And then he saw Piet, kneeling in the emerald grass, holding the fishing rod his grandfather had given him, his back to the oncoming vehicle, the dappled light shining on his golden hair. For an endless moment the child remained still, unaware of the engine noise, not hearing Esther's terrified shrieks of warning or his sister's cries as they rushed towards him. Lars felt the thud of impact as the boy was lifted into the air and hurtled towards the windscreen. Glass cracked and fell around him. The car hit a tree stump and came to a halt. The sun glared down onto his son's bloodied face and arms, highlighting the protruding bones and the lolling head with random cruelty. Esther and Suniva tugged at the doors, screaming as Lars struggled out of the twisted wreckage. He picked up his son with exquisite gentleness, and placed his ear on Piet's chest. Then there was silence.

They were in the sitting room when the farm truck arrived. Sarah saw them first and stifled the sound that rose in her throat as Lars walked into the house, unspeakable agony in his eyes, carrying Piet in his arms, the child's limbs dangling and helpless. It was Hannah who reached him first, as the sound of weeping swelled around her. She gazed in horror at the lacerations on the child's face and the skewed position of his jaw. Whimpering, she reached out and felt the sticky wetness of blood, saw the boy's closed, swollen eyes, the glass embedded in his cheek, the knobs and splinters of bone that had pierced the skin of his legs and arm.

'Oh God!' she screamed, her arms stretched out helplessly towards the small, broken body. 'Oh my God, Lars! What have you done to my son?'

Chapter 28

Kenya, January 1978

For Lars, the hours peeled away in layer upon layer of torture. There was a blackness all around him, pierced by momentary flashes of sight and sound. Hannah, kneeling by their unconscious child, her breath coming in gasps of disbelief. Suniva sitting bolt upright in a chair by the window, trembling and silent. Sarah on the phone, explaining the horror of the circumstances to the family doctor in Nanyuki, to Kirsten and Ilse preparing for the funeral in Norway, and to Lottie. Dr Markham bending over Piet, dressing and bandaging, stemming the bleeding from his neck where a shard of glass had punctured the skin, gently easing bones back into place, trying to stabilise him before he could be moved.

'This will take him as far as Nairobi,' he said at last. 'We can put him on the stretcher now, and get him into the Land Rover. The Flying Doctor Service is on its way and the surgeon in Nairobi has been alerted. Lars, give me a hand here. I'm sorry about your father. He was a fine man and I enjoyed meeting him on his visits.'

But Lars could not grasp the enormity of what had happened. The kindly words only served to increase his horror as Piet was lifted onto the stretcher, his body deathly still, his hair matted with the blood they had not been able to wash away, his eyelids torn and swollen.

'What do you think . . . ?' Hannah twisted her hands, staring through eyes glowing with anguish.

'Whatever I tell you now would only be a guess,' Dr Markham said. 'He has a severe concussion that needs examination urgently, and several broken bones that will have to be reset and put in plaster. His jaw is broken, and the lacerations need stitching. Perhaps by a plastic surgeon, so that he will not be scarred.'

'But is he in pain?' She could barely speak the words that followed. 'Will he live?'

'My dear, he can't feel any pain.' Dr Markham tried to offer a crumb of solace. 'His pulse is strong and that is a good sign. The most important thing now is to get him to Nairobi. I'll take my car to the airstrip and brief the medical team on the plane. They will keep an eye on you, too, since your pregnancy is quite far along and a shock like this can have unexpected results.'

'I'll stay and collect the things you will need in Nairobi,' Sarah said. 'Suniva, you wait with me.'

'Ma, I want to come with you. Please can I come with you?' Suniva grabbed her mother's arm but Hannah disengaged herself, shaking her head, unable to respond or to comfort her daughter. 'Ma, is Piet going to die?'

'Come, Suniva. You and I have to find some of Piet's favourite things,' Sarah said. 'Then we will head for Nairobi. That is the best way we can help, now.'

Hannah, beyond tears and recriminations, winced at every bump and sway of their tortuous journey, her eyes never leaving her son, all her energies willing him to survive. She had not looked at her husband or spoken to him since he had carried Piet into the house. Lars gripped the side of the stretcher, but he could not turn his gaze to his child, could not bear to look on the shattered face and broken limbs and know that he had done this. He stood on the airstrip dazed by the thrumming of the propellers and the smell of hot fuel, watching as Hannah climbed into the cramped cabin space beside the stretcher. There had not been enough room for him on the plane, and only the roar of the engines and a cloud of dust told him they were gone. He stared at the empty sky, glassy-eyed, as Dr Markham spoke to him about holding up, remaining strong. Everything possible would be done to save Piet, the doctor said. Hope and prayer were the best way to fill the time. Lars sagged against the car, his mind trapped in its own private hell. Then he turned the vehicle and drove back to the farm like a madman, roaring out his anguish into the pitiless landscape.

'I've spoken to Lottie again,' Sarah said, as he came into the house, his tread as heavy as an old man. 'She is flying out at the weekend. Meantime, you can all stay with us in Nairobi, until things become clearer.'

436

Lars stared at her blankly, unable to comprehend what she was saying. Then he collapsed into a chair. Suniva took a few hesitant steps towards him and put her hand in his, but he looked at her as if she were a stranger, unable to give or receive solace.

'Lars, you have had two severe shocks,' Sarah said, calling for Nderi and ordering coffee. When it came she stirred in three spoons of sugar and laced it with brandy. 'Try to remember that children have extraordinary powers of recuperation. He will come out of this. I know he will.' Behind her she heard Suniva begin to sob. 'Help me to put everything into the car,' she said, taking the child's hand in the hopes of distracting her, even briefly.

'What about James? He is still at the football match with David.' Suniva's confusion was pitiful as she tried to come to terms with the wave of events that had crashed into their lives and swept them far from any place they knew. 'Can James come with us?'

'He'll be better off here, for the moment.' Sarah hugged the girl. 'I've spoken to David and they will be at the lodge together for the next couple of nights. James loves being there and we can phone him when we have some news. Now, your pa has finished his coffee, so let's start out for Nairobi.'

'Mrs Olsen, I am Mr Harries. Your son's surgeon.' The tall, grey-haired man had a firm handshake and his manner was open and direct. 'Piet has a number of fractures, including his collarbone and the left femur, one ankle and his right arm. The arm and leg will require the insertion of plates. In addition there are severe lacerations on his face and neck, and other parts of his body. Dr Markham managed to stem the bleeding on these wounds, and I believe I can stitch them in a way that will leave minimal scarring. His jaw is broken, and will have to be rewired so that the structural bones and muscles of the face can be restored to their original position, and held together until they heal. But I'm afraid his head and face have taken the main impact of the accident.'

'Is he conscious? Can I talk to him?' Hannah's tear-stained face was pitiful.

'I don't believe in glossing over things that may be long-term issues, Mrs Olsen, and I think you are the kind of person who would prefer to know the facts as they are.' His eyes were kind as he sat down beside her, looking directly into her stricken face. 'He has now been thoroughly examined and we have the X-rays needed to indicate the necessary procedures. Your son is in a coma at this time. He has a fractured skull, and what is called subdural hematoma. This is a name for internal bleeding which causes pressure on the brain. We are preparing him for surgery now, and the first thing we have to do is to drill into the skull to remove the blood and relieve the pressure, in order to try and avoid brain damage.'

'Is his brain-damaged now?' Hannah's face drained of colour.

'I'm afraid we have no way of knowing.' There was a pause before the surgeon spoke again. 'The release of the pressure on the brain is not a long process, but the remainder of the surgery will take some time. He'll be in theatre for several hours.' His expression was sombre. 'We will do our best to get him through this, but while you are waiting it might be wise to go and rest somewhere. We can telephone you as soon as he is out of the theatre.'

'I'd rather stay here. Where I feel close to him.'

'I can understand that. I'll see if there is an empty private room that you can use. One of the staff will provide you with tea or coffee and something to eat, and I'll report back to you as soon as Piet is in the recovery room.'

'Thank you.' The effort of saying the words made Hannah want to vomit and she put her head down, to stem the nausea that had risen into the back of her mouth.

'Your husband is on his way, I gather? Good. The reception staff will let him know where to find you, as soon as he gets here. I'm sure you will be glad of his support. Is there someone you would like to contact in the meantime to keep you company?'

'Yes. Thank you. I would like to phone my friend Camilla Chapman, although she may be out on safari.'

'I'll get one of the nurses to show you where the telephone is, and I will be back to talk to you as soon as I can.' He put his hand on her shoulder in a gesture of compassion, and then she heard the door of the waiting room close quietly. When she raised her head she was alone.

'Mrs Olsen, would you like to come with me and I'll show you the telephone booth. And we are preparing a room you can use while you wait for your son to come out of surgery.' A young nurse had appeared, uniform pressed, hair tucked beneath the starched cap. She gave a smile of encouragement. 'When you have made your call, I will be in the nurses' station down the hall and I'll organise some refreshments for you.'

In the small cabin Hannah sat on a stool and dialled Camilla's number, but there was no reply. In the room assigned to her she drank some tea and sat, rigid, in an armchair. At first she tried to pray but no words or phrases came to mind, and after a while a fierce anger grew in her at the thought of the silent, avenging deity who might take her boy. She had lost her adored brother and then he had reappeared in the form of her son, perfect, unharmed, unblemished. Only to be struck down once more. She wept until there were no more tears left within, and then dozed until her head jerked upwards to thrust her back into the nightmare of reality.

Two hours later she heard footsteps and looked up, steeling herself for the surgeon's assessment. But it was Lars who appeared in the doorway. He stood there, motionless, and she lowered her eyes, unable to deal with his agony or reach out her hand to offer a sign of mutual suffering or reassurance. He opened his mouth to speak, but no sound emerged and he sat down in a chair on the other side of the room and waited, silence thickening the air, until he wanted to reach out and smash everything within his grasp. She did not notice the cuts and bruises on his own face and arms, nor did she ask about Suniva. The pressure in the room had become unbearable by the time Mr Harries opened the door, still wearing his surgical gown and cap.

'Mr Olsen, I'm glad you are here,' he said. 'Your son is now in the recovery room and we will soon be transferring him to the intensive care unit, where he will be monitored until we can gauge his condition.'

'What about the skull fracture and the bleeding?' Hannah could not control her shaking limbs.

'We were able to drain the blood and relieve the pressure. We do not yet know, however, whether any lasting damage has taken place.'

'Brain damage?' Lars stood up, his large hands opening in helpless entreaty.

'That is a possibility, as I explained to your wife.' The surgeon realised that the unfortunate father was unaware of the full extent of his child's injuries. He wondered how he himself would be able to cope with having accidentally caused such an appalling situation, and made a note to choose a moment when he could tactfully suggest a few sessions with a psychiatrist, to help the man through what had happened and the possible aftermath. His sympathy grew as he outlined, once more, the potential complications that lay in wait for the child.

As the litany continued Lars wanted to put his hands over his ears and blot out the surgeon's voice. Each word was a spear that increased his torment, another accusation to make against himself. If Piet survived at all, he might never move or see or smile again. He had destroyed his son. And his own father was already dead. Had he been in Norway during Jorgen's last days, none of this would have happened. He would have had a chance to express the love and gratitude he had felt for the old man, said the words that could only pass between father and son. Words that he might never be able to share with Piet. He sat down, his eyes closed, and wished he had been the one who had died.

Hannah stood apart, her eyes puffy and bloodshot, her blank face masking the turmoil inside. Finally, she spoke to the surgeon. 'My son is deaf. Did you know that? He was due for surgery here, in this hospital. Next week.'

'I'm aware of that, Mrs Olsen,' Mr Harries said. 'But there's nothing we can do to address his hearing at the moment. I will send a nurse to advise you, as soon as you can see Piet. He will have numerous tubes and dressings and plaster casts on his body, but these are nothing to be alarmed about. I must warn you, however, that we have no idea as to when he may regain consciousness.'

'Do you mean hours? Days?' Lars shook his head as if trying to rid himself of the nightmarish implication he had detected in the surgeon's statement.

'That is something I cannot tell you at this time.'

'I don't understand,' Hannah said, wiping clammy palms on her trousers. 'You drilled holes in his skull, wired his jaw, set his bones. Surely there will be a time when the anaesthetic wears off and he will come round.'

'Mrs Olsen, your son is in a coma,' Mr Harries said. 'He cannot feel anything – has not felt anything since the accident, and we do not know when he will regain consciousness. We can only wait patiently and hope that he will recover. But there is no way of knowing how long that might take. I am so very sorry.'

As the first days crawled by Hannah refused to leave Piet's bedside, in spite of the advice of the doctors. The child remained unconscious, tubes delivering medicine and nutrition to his shattered frame. His limbs were encased in plaster casts, his head partially bandaged, his eyes and nose puffy and blackened with bruises so that he was unrecognisable. He lay inert, apart from an occasional fluttering of his eyelids. Each time Lars went into the intensive care unit, the agony of what he had done made him physically ill, and he could not stay for more than a few minutes. Instead, he wandered the corridors, or sat outside in the grounds, not talking to anyone. Hannah paid little heed to his coming or going as she sat beside the child, stroking his fingers, speaking softly to him about the familiar things of his short life, singing the lullabies he had known during his infancy.

Sarah and Rabindrah were constant visitors, both offering to stay with Piet for several hours so that Hannah could go to the house and rest. In spite of their entreaties, however, she refused to leave his side. During the day they visited the hospital, and took Suniva to the Nairobi Museum or the National Park or the Animal Orphanage. James arrived by bus from Nanyuki and stayed for the weekend, spending most of his time with Piet, talking to him about the games they would play when he had recovered. At the house Sarah showed Suniva how to use one of her cameras, and they set up a training programme for Swala, the new and fast-growing puppy. In the evenings they did their best to make things appear normal for Lars when he came back, watching the television news, discussing their day, eating dinner together. Ilse telephoned to describe Jorgen's funeral and the large number of people who had come to honour him. Even Kirsten tried to offer words of comfort, in spite of her own sorrow. As the end of the week approached, Lars had become so morose that he was unable to manage a conversation with Suniva, although he saw her desperate need for hope and support. Sarah noticed that he drank increasing quantities of alcohol. Sometimes she heard him stagger as he went to bed, and she feared for him in his solitary state of anguish.

'It's too horrible, this suffering,' she said, lying beside Rabindrah in the darkness, staring up at the ceiling. 'I feel so helpless. There don't seem to be any words or actions that will bring him relief. He has always been the strong one, the one everyone depended on. Now that has been taken from him. His father is gone and he blames himself for the accident. And for the fact that he can do nothing for either Piet or Hannah. In fact, she has totally blanked him out.'

441

'I wonder if it wouldn't be better if that poor child died,' Rabindrah said.

'Oh God, no!'

'It may sound shocking, but what if he is permanently brain-damaged? What kind of life can he expect? How on earth will Hannah cope with a new baby, and a severely handicapped child? And how will Lars live with the boy as a daily reminder?'

'I don't know,' she said. 'I've been thinking of saying something to Hannah about comforting Lars, but she is under such pressure that I don't think this is the time. So I just pray. For all of them and the baby that is coming soon.'

Four days after the accident Camilla telephoned the hospital. 'We only heard the news a few minutes ago,' she said. 'The radio hasn't been working well at Shaba, but now we are at Langani with clients. I can come back to Nairobi early and do anything that might help. Anthony will bring James to the next camp over the weekend, and down to Nairobi once the school holidays begin. So don't worry about him. How is Lars bearing up? And Suniva?'

'The only thing we can do is to wait.' Hannah's words were bleak, and she did not answer the question about her husband and daughter, or comment on James. 'They say that if you want something badly enough it will come to you. I hope that's true because I have never wanted anything more than to see Piet open his eyes, and smile at me.'

'We thought you might like to move into our house, if you are going to be in Nairobi for a while,' Camilla said. 'It is closer to the hospital than Sarah and Rabindrah's place, and we would be glad to have someone there, rather than leaving it empty when we are away. We are not going to be around much over the next few weeks, so you would have it mostly to yourselves. I'll let Joshua know. You can ring him any time.'

But whenever anyone tried to encourage Hannah to leave the hospital for a few hours she became angry. Finally, Mr Harries took her aside during his morning round of the wards.

'Mrs Olsen – may I call you Hannah?' He smiled at her, but his manner was grave. 'I know that you do not want to leave your boy for even a moment. But you must realise that exhaustion and stress can severely damage the health of the baby you are carrying, in which case you would

442

not be able to care for either yourself or your children. The ward sister is organising a fold-up bed to be placed in Piet's room for your use. However, I must urge you to share this vigil. There is no way of telling how long he will take to come out of his present state, and you cannot remain at his side, day and night, over an extended period of time. His father, and your friend Mrs Singh, are more than willing to sit with him, and you would be advised immediately in the event of any change. You will endanger your own wellbeing, if you do not take some time away from the hospital. This could be a long process.'

'Define "long process".' Hannah dug her nails into her palms. 'Tell me if it is going to be a month or a year. Tell me something, for God's sake! Something I can go on, or hope for!'

She knew before he shook his head that there was nothing he could say, and she buried her face in her hands. The sound of knocking made her straighten to see Lottie framed in the doorway.

'Darling, darling, darling.' Lottie's arms were around her, and they clung together and wept before turning to touch Piet's hand on the coverlet.

'We will pray for a miracle,' Lottie said, kissing his bruised eyelids. 'If we pray together, as a family, God will hear us. I know he will.'

'I've tried,' Hannah said, wiping her eyes. 'I've tried so hard but the words don't come, Ma. They just don't come.'

'Well, we are going to try again now,' Lottie said. 'Here are Lars and Suniva and Sarah, who will also join us. Then I will stay here while you go back to Sarah's house to sleep, and to care for yourself. Because you must be strong when Piet comes back to us.'

Lars looked at her, his haggard face etched with gratitude, as she indicated that they should all join hands. They made a circle around Piet's bed, following Lottie's words of entreaty, echoing her plea for mercy as she tried to bind them together once more.

'She doesn't see me, hear me, want to know me,' Lars said to Lottie. 'I try to be optimistic for Suniva's sake, because she is frightened. Not only by the sight of Piet, but by the fact that her mother has ceased to notice she exists. I should take her home to Langani. Let her go back to school and live some kind of normal life. I can't stay away from the farm much longer. And I think we should move into Anthony and Camilla's house, because

443

we have already been here for over a week, and Sarah needs rest and privacy too.' He stopped. 'There are days when I don't think I can go on, Lottie. Or whether it's even worth trying. What have I done to deserve a punishment such as this? God only knows what will happen to us all when the baby is born.'

'Perhaps that is what will bring Hannah back into the world,' Lottie said.

She was not convinced by the statement, nor was there any response from Lars until suddenly, he sank to his knees, and began to sob. Lottie knelt beside him as the thin veneer cracked, and he let loose the anguish that had filled him, body and soul, since the day his father had died and he had maimed his son. Suniva came running in from the garden at the sound, and her face blanched.

'Is he dead?' she whispered, staring at her father. 'Pa, is Piet dead?'

'No, darling,' Lottie said gently. 'Your pa has gone through so much and he has been trying too hard to hold in all his sadness. Now he is letting it go.'

'Pa.' Suniva sat down beside them on the floor, and leaned against Lars. 'I know you are full to bursting with sadness, Pa. About Grandpa, and knocking over Piet. But Grandpa knows why you couldn't go for his funeral. And Piet will wake up and get better. He will, because we all prayed together for him. Then Ma will bring him home. We will all be able to go home soon, won't we?' She turned to Lottie.

'That is what we hope for,' Lottie said, her heart close to breaking. Catastrophe had once again torn at the roots of their lives. 'But while we are waiting, you might like to go home with your pa. Back to the farm, and to school. You could come down here at the weekends, to be with Ma, so she won't miss you. What do you think?'

'Yes,' said Suniva. 'I want to go home. I don't think Ma will know we have gone, because she doesn't think about us any more.' She lifted the corner of her shirt and wiped the tears from her father's broad cheeks. 'Let's go and see Piet,' she said. 'And then you can take me home. Do you think James will be waiting?'

Suniva ran through the forest, her heart thudding with excitement. James would be there already. They had signalled to one another as soon as she arrived home and once lunch was over she started out for their hut, her feet barely touching the ground. Feeling as though she was flying she sped across the uneven surface, knotted with tree roots and stones, hardly aware of the branches that grew across the path. Bursting into the clearing, she saw him, crouched over the fire he had started between the hearth stones, blowing on the kindling until the flames began to crackle out of the dry sticks and moss. He looked up and a smile of pure joy broke across his mouth to light his eyes. She hunkered down beside him. There was no need for words as they placed their palms together and looked, mapping each other, knees touching, in silent, intense communion. Leaning forward, their two foreheads met, blonde hair brushing against the mahogany gleam of his skin. And time was a dimension away.

'Is there any change?'

'Nothing.' Suniva's eyes were locked on the only face that could offer her a glimpse of joy. 'I don't know if he will ever wake up.'

'I brought a gourd,' he said. 'We can make a cut in our hands and let the blood drop into it. I have seen the old men on the farm make a request to the God N'gai in this way. And we will ask him to honour our sacrifice, and make Piet well. If you want. If you are not afraid?'

'No. Let's do it now.'

He took out his penknife, and held the blade in the flames. With a swift motion, he sliced into the flesh at the base of his thumb, and then took Suniva's hand in his.

'Ready?'

'Yes.'

The knife slid across her hand, and she held his gaze without flinching. A bright red trickle swelled out of the cut, and he pressed it to his own. As the blood mingled and dripped into the gourd he chanted softly in Kikuyu.

'Please, Great God N'Gai, if you love us, let Piet wake up and be with us again,' Suniva whispered.

She began to hum with James, watching the slow, red drip, feeling the sting of the open wound, looking into the fire, seeing Piet's swollen, battered face in the flames, his eyes still closed. James took the gourd, and emptied the contents into the fire.

'We offer our blood to the Great God N'gai so that he may bring back our brother. For Suniva and me,' he said.

Staring, hypnotised, into the flickering light Suniva saw her brother's face in the heart of the flames, his blue eyes open and smiling into hers, and she toppled backwards in fright.

'What did you see?' James helped her to her feet.

'I'm not sure. I thought I saw Piet's face. I thought he was . . .' She was reluctant to say the words, to put her hopes to the test.

James took some moss and pressed it into the cut on her hand. 'Keep it clean,' he said, holding her palm against his chest as she leaned on him for a moment, her eyes closed.

'I don't want them to send me away to school,' she said. 'With Piet in the hospital and you here, I think I would die.'

'Maybe they won't.' He put his arms around her. 'Maybe Piet will get better now, and then we will all be together again.'

'Yes.' She pressed his hand to her cheek and then turned away. 'Race you home.'

They ran together down the steep path, her feet echoing his steps, her breath on the back of his neck, as the forest vibrated with their passing.

'I've been summoned to court,' Rabindrah said. 'Now that he has the documents from Manjit's safe, Kiberu is confident that he will be able to get convictions all round. With the exception of Moses Gacharu. There wasn't a word about him in any of the records, and he seems to have been paid in cash. There are photos of him receiving money, but they are undated and it would be difficult to use them as watertight proof of anything. But the other two will be tried along with Harjeet, and I'm the main witness. Think how popular that will make me in the Asian community!'

'It doesn't matter,' Sarah said. 'Anjit told Indar Uncle what you did to protect Gulab, although it was foolish of her, and dangerous too. Still, it does mean that the closest members of your family know the full story. I hear Harjeet has an extremely clever lawyer. He'll probably get off with a light sentence. Didn't he make a deal, before he handed over the papers?'

'I don't know whether that will be honoured,' Rabindrah said. 'Nothing was written down, and Kiberu is determined to make an example of all of them, although he is more concerned with nailing his greedy colleagues. It will be interesting to see what happens. By the way, have you heard from Lila recently?'

'Not a word,' Sarah said. 'I hope no news is good news. Your father has probably worked out her divorce settlement by now, and she might also have a sizzling romance going with Tom.'

'I'm not sure I would wish that on her,' Rabindrah said. 'Did you see Hannah today? Any change?'

'I didn't go to the hospital,' Sarah said. 'I was tired.'

'I suppose that means Camilla was there.' He sighed. 'Don't you think it's time you put that issue aside, after all that has happened? Haven't we learned that life can change in the blink of an eye. Can't we be grateful for our blessings, and overlook other peoples' imperfections?'

But she left him without answering, closing herself into the darkroom to print out a series of photographs that Suniva had taken of the puppy. Knowing that Camilla had lied to Anthony, turned her abortion into a miscarriage, had opened the wound all over again in Sarah's mind, but she knew that Rabindrah was right. She was increasingly ashamed of the estrangement and it was stubborn pride that prevented her from lifting the telephone to cross the chasm she had created. Earlier today she had decided to drive to the house in Karen and try to make her peace. Or go to the hospital at a time when both of her childhood friends would be there, in Piet's room, where all former disagreements would seem irrelevant. She had not been able to do it, however, and Rabindrah's comment struck her hard, making her feel like a hypocrite as she touched her rounded belly and thought about the child growing inside her. Perhaps she would be able to find the right opportunity within the next week or so. It would at least take an unnecessary misery out of their lives, and allow them to comfort Hannah together.

'Lars has taken Suniva back to Langani,' Lottie said as she sat beside her grandson. 'Hannah, we need to talk about this. He lost his father and was unable to see him laid to rest. And through an accident that is horrible beyond belief, he harmed his own child. You must find it in you, Hannah, to give him the love and comfort he needs. There has been enough tragedy. Whatever happens to Piet, you must help your husband. Stand by him. Lars has given everything he has, to make you secure and happy. You cannot let him down now.'

'I try to rationalise it,' Hannah said, but the vision of her battered child exploded into her head even as she spoke. 'To tell myself it was an accident, that it could have happened to anyone. But it didn't. It happened to my Piet, to my little boy. And he may never recover. Never wake up again. Tell me you could accept that, go straight back to the way things were. Look at me, Ma, and tell me you could do that.'

'You have to try,' Lottie said, her voice hard. 'No matter what it takes, you have to keep your family together.'

'I don't know how. I'm terrified that Piet will die when I'm not there. That he will be taken from me like he was before. I can't think of anything else.'

'Hannah, the combined effects of this trauma and your pregnancy are making you feel like this. But you have to begin looking at things in another light. Or if you can't, then get help. For yourself and Lars. You must weather this together, because you will not survive it on your own.'

'Leave me alone. Please.' Hannah stood up abruptly, grimacing as she straightened. 'I can't listen to any more.'

She had reached the door when she heard the first sound, a small, soft groan that was followed by the fluttering of his eyelids. And then his eyes opened, blue and unfocused and wide with terror.

'Ma,' he whispered. 'Ma.'

Chapter 29

'It's a miracle,' Camilla said, as she sat beside Lottie in the waiting room. 'There is no other way to describe it.'

'It will take time and a great deal of patience.' Lottie smiled through tears. 'Lars is over the moon. He is on his way down from Langani, although none of us knows what will happen next. Whether there will be any more progress, or when. And Sarah should be here in a few minutes.'

'I'll be back tomorrow, then,' Camilla said, her expression changing.

'What happened between you?' Lottie could not understand what had caused such a rift between her surrogate daughters, who had loved each other since childhood. 'Is this disagreement really worth the destruction of a bond that began so long ago? Can't you put it aside, whatever it is, for Hannah's sake? For all your sakes?'

Camilla took a deep breath, her stomach churning. 'When Duncan Harper almost bankrupted us, I used all my capital and savings to pay the debts and keep our company afloat. I had to go back to modelling, to ensure that we had enough cash flow, and I was lucky enough to do a Cartier shoot that Tom arranged, and some other, smaller jobs.'

'You sold him your cottage.' Lottie's voice was filled with sympathy.

'Yes.' Camilla nodded. 'Then Anthony needed me on safari as a second guide because we couldn't afford to hire anyone from outside. And Hannah and I worked at turning out extra clothes at the workshop. That was the only way we have been able to survive financially. It still is.'

'So where does Sarah come into this?'

'When Duncan disappeared, I had just discovered I was pregnant. I had an abortion.' She described the terrible state in which she had found herself, and Rabindrah's compassionate response to her cry for help. 'Sarah has never forgiven me. I don't think she ever will, and I can't really blame her. I'm not sure I will ever be able to forgive myself either.'

'Oh, my dear girl.' Lottie took her hand. 'I'm so sorry. What did Anthony have to say about it?'

'I told him I had a miscarriage,' Camilla said. 'I didn't want him to know about the terrible thing I had done. He had enough to think about and he would have blamed himself as well as me. Hannah doesn't know any of this. When we get through our financial crisis I can only hope and pray that I will have a baby that I will cherish enough to be forgiven. But perhaps I don't deserve to be a mother after what I did. So now you know.' She kissed Lottie's cheek and stood up. 'I'll see you tomorrow.'

His speech would be slurred, and he would drag his right leg. Perhaps permanently. The question of his hearing would have to be considered later, in the light of other medical requirements. Sign language was an option, but damage to the brain might impair the use of his hands for signing if cognitive ability had also been affected. There would be weeks, probably months, of rehabilitation and it was possible that Piet would never recover full mobility. They should be grateful to have their son back in any kind of promising condition, but it would be unwise to expect too much of him. The pursuit of any academic subjects in the future was questionable.

Lars moved closer to Hannah as they listened to Mr Harries, but she moved away from them both, her eyes hard with determination, undaunted by the long list of complications to be faced. He was awake. He knew her and he had said her name. Piet was alive. She would bring him home and he would heal.

Lottie left for Italy, promising to return during the summer months. Over Hannah's objections Piet was transferred to a small ward with three other children.

'It will help him to engage with others,' Mr Harries said. 'To begin to notice things and try to communicate. There are two other accident victims in the same room who have recently started on physiotherapy, and the nurses are in and out of there all the time. Believe me, it is the best place for your son at this moment. Isolation will not help him.'

In order to be nearer to the hospital, Hannah accepted the offer of Anthony and Camilla's house, while Lars shuttled between Langani and Nairobi. Their relationship remained distant, every attempt at normal conversation tainted by thoughts and feelings they did not dare to express. After a time they confined themselves to the business of the farm and Suniva's progress at school.

'Why isn't Suniva with you?' Hannah had heard the sound of tyres on the gravel and she came out onto the verandah, her hair pulled into a tight knot at the back of her neck, concerned when she saw that her daughter was not in the car.

'She wanted to stay at home. There is a birthday party for one of her schoolfriends at the Club.' Lars stood in the driveway alone, his overnight bag in his hand.

'I went to the convent at Msongari yesterday,' Hannah said. 'She can start as a boarder after Easter, even though it isn't the beginning of the school year. They agreed to take her because of our situation. You'd better come in. It looks like it might rain.'

'Is that a good idea?'

'Rain? I think so. Everything is very dry.' Hannah deliberately misunderstood his question.

'You know I am referring to Suniva,' he said angrily. 'I don't think we should send her away to school right now. There has been too much disruption in her life and she already feels disconnected. Unimportant, compared to everything else.'

'Piet is about to start rehabilitation.' Hannah lowered herself into a chair, heavy and tired. 'He is going to be here for weeks, and you can't manage the farm and take care of all Suniva's needs. I don't want her running wild all over the place at Langani, with James constantly in tow and no one to watch them.'

'I watch them, and so do Esther and David. We all watch over them.'

'She will be better off at Msongari.' Hannah was insistent. 'The nuns were sympathetic. They said we could take her out occasionally. Sarah can collect her on a Sunday for lunch, and she will come home for half-term.'

'She's not going to be happy cooped up in a boarding school, and she is doing fine where she is, keeping up well with her lessons, riding her horse, doing the things she has always done. This is not a good time for change. Besides, James isn't a problem. She needs him, Hannah, and they are just children with the natural curiosity of their age.'

'How would you know?' Hannah countered. 'You're out on the farm all day while they disappear into the forest, or run off who knows where, as soon as they come home from school. Esther can't control them. She never could. At the weekends they are probably together all the time, when Suniva is not here. She is old enough now. Sarah and Camilla were in boarding school at that age. It didn't do them any harm.'

'Don't you plan to come home occasionally? Just for a night or two?'

'I can't leave Piet for that length of time.' Hannah was definite.

'Sarah is here,' Lars said. 'She sees him almost every day. And Camilla visits him when she is in town.'

'She's not in Nairobi often. But, as it happens, she and Anthony are here tonight and we are going out to dinner with them. I'm looking forward to it.'

'In that case I'll drop in on Piet now, before we have to go anywhere,' Lars said. 'I'd like to see how much progress he has made since last week.'

'His speech is poor,' Hannah said. 'He cried endlessly today, because he is still hurting and he can't hear, or make himself understood. They give him tablets for the pain, but they don't want to increase the dosage. That could be harmful in the long run. I took him for a ride in the wheelchair this afternoon to try and cheer him up a little. He is expecting you tomorrow.'

The sound of a car put an end to their conversation, and Lars was relieved when Camilla ran up the steps and put her arms around him. When she stepped back he was surprised by her appearance. She had cut her hair into a short, spiky halo that stood out around her face, and she was too thin. But her eyes were the same cornflower blue, and full of pleasure as she smiled at him.

'We've just been to see Piet,' she said. 'On the way home from the office. They are very accommodating about visits out of hours. And the nurses are sweet with him. Kind and patient.'

'Lars, old chap.' Anthony shook his hand, clapped him on the broad shoulders that carried so much. 'Good to see you. How are you holding up? I'm bringing some clients to Langani next week. I hope you'll join us at the lodge, if you have the time. Han, you look ready to drop. How about some tea, or even a small drink?'

'I'll lie down for an hour,' Hannah said. 'Especially since we are going out for dinner. It's been a long time since I did that, and I want to enjoy it.'

'We are so grateful to you both,' Lars said, when she had left the room.

'It's tough on Hannah, when she insists on spending most of every day at the hospital even when Sarah is there. She is wearing pretty thin but she refuses to take a break. It's no use saying anything to her, though. When it comes to Piet she has tunnel vision. And she has just told me that Suniva is booked into Msongari after Easter.'

'That will be a shock to the system,' Anthony said. 'I remember my first few weeks of being cooped up, following orders day and night, after being out in the *bundu*, on safari with my old man and his trackers and camp staff. I was pretty unhappy for a time, but I got used to it. Suniva will adapt. She is very self-possessed and independent. Young James will miss her, though. Both of his mates gone in one fell swoop. I'll take him out with me during the Easter break. He loves being in camp and he knows how to make himself useful. The clients think he is a great boy, especially the women.'

'I hope you are right about Suniva,' Lars said. 'And thank you again for the use of the house. It has been a godsend, staying here.'

'Stay as long as you like.' Camilla poured him a drink. 'It gives Joshua something to do. I'm leaving for London soon, and then Anthony will be on his own for a while. He'll be glad of the company when he comes home from the next safari.'

They dined in the city centre, and Hannah made an effort to listen to a description of Camilla's new lines of clothing in the United States and to ask about Anthony's safari clients, but after a short time the subject turned to Piet.

'He is having problems talking,' Hannah said. 'We are starting tomorrow with exercises for his limbs, and we also have an appointment with a speech therapist. I want to be there for every session. To encourage him, and to learn how to help him when we go home.'

'You may find he has to work without you some of the time,' Camilla said. 'Therapists often suggest that relatives keep one step removed from the everyday struggle. Besides, you are soon going to have another little person to take care of. Suniva will be great at helping her brother, though. She has always looked out for Piet and it will give her an important role to play. Make her feel less left out.'

'Why does everyone keep harping on about Suniva?' Hannah's face flushed with annoyance. 'I don't think it's fair to bang on about her being marginalised. Piet almost lost his life. He has to be the focus for all of us right now, until he is whole again. And that's it.' She was close to tears as she put down her spoon and pushed her plate aside.

'You're right, Han, and you mustn't be upset.' Camilla's tone was reassuring, as the noise of the restaurant rose to absorb Hannah's shrill response. 'Look, you must be exhausted and we are both pretty tired.' She turned to Anthony. 'Let's ask for the bill and go home. I could do with an early night after the drive down from Samburu. The road is a disgrace, given the amount of money the government gets for maintenance.'

'You can be sure those funds are going into well-maintained Mercedes, rather than the roads they travel on,' Anthony said. 'The *WaBenzi* don't care if they burst a tyre or three – some poor sod will always be press-ganged into coming up with another one.'

'Whatever will become of them?' Camilla asked later, as she slid into bed beside her husband, feeling the spell of him envelop her.

'I adore you,' he whispered. 'I'm besotted with you, and I love it. Come closer, because at this moment I can't think about anyone else but you and me, in our private world. I'm not willing to have guests.'

In the bedroom across the hall Lars was still awake. He had poured himself a large cognac and downed it fast before retiring. The heat of it lay in his stomach, making him hope that it would induce sleep. But it did not prove to be a solution and when he closed his eyes the memory of Piet, whole and beautiful, haunted him, and he did not even hear the whine of the mosquito that circled his head. Beside him Hannah was already asleep, her back turned to him. He thought of the days gone by when he had felt the weight and softness of her breasts in his hands, and she had wrapped her strong legs around him, loving him and trusting in all that he did. She looked the same, her knees bent, hands spread out flat beneath her cheek, her flaxen hair on the pillow. He knew every contour of her, every small movement and twitch of muscle that indicated the dreams in which he no longer figured. They were irreconcilably divided by what he had done to their son. Soon there would be a new child born into their disintegrating family, but Lars doubted that he would ever be a true part of them all again. He thought of his father, and the way they had shaken hands on the day of their last parting. There had been an expression in Jorgen's eyes that Lars had tried not to define, but now he thought it was the knowledge that they would not see each other again. He did not dare to hope that life might one day return to the way it had once been, and he wondered if it was worth living at all.

Nothing could have prepared Hannah for the ordeal that Piet experienced. Each new movement caused him to moan and screw his eyes shut as his mangled limbs were massaged and stretched. At last the day came when he was helped into a standing position, his hands gripping a pair of crutches. Hannah watched, holding her breath, unable to prevent herself from crying out as he fell, screaming out in frustration. The parallel bars seemed an equally impossible goal, and he threw himself onto the floor, sobbing and curling his body into a defensive ball.

'He can't hear what you're saying, for God's sake!' Hannah turned on Judy Canning, the physiotherapist. 'Don't you understand that my son is deaf? Unless you stand in front of him and help him, he doesn't know what you want him to do.'

'Mrs Olsen, this is not a question of hearing. Piet's ability to understand is much slower right now. I have demonstrated what I want him to do, but he doesn't always remember. He isn't able to follow because his brain is damaged, as well as his hearing.'

'Oh God, it's too cruel. It's too much.' Hannah bent to help the child to his feet, but the physiotherapist put a restraining hand on her arm.

'He can get up,' Judy said quietly. 'You must let him do it alone. This is going to be a long, slow process and it is particularly difficult for a boy of this age. Piet may never be able to use his right leg and arm in a normal way. It's fortunate that he has any movement at all. It would be best if you were not here for all these sessions. He must learn to rely on himself. To make his own way, without pity. You have to accept that.'

'I will not accept it,' Hannah said. 'I will make him better. I will do whatever it takes to make him whole. My son will go to school, and run and play and learn, like any other boy. You will see.'

When he had been returned to the ward Hannah left the hospital and went to the public library, immersing herself in every book and pamphlet she could find on brain injuries. Armed with her newfound knowledge she threw herself into his fight. But Piet tired quickly and was easily discouraged. He frequently forgot the most simple instructions and was prone to temper tantrums and brutal headaches.

Against all the doctors' advice, she insisted on bringing him back to Langani.

'Hannah, he isn't ready,' Mr Harries said. 'You can't manage his needs on a farm, miles from any medical help.'

'Rest and quiet, good food, fresh air and exercise. That is what will help him,' she said. 'I am taking him home.'

As they turned off the main road on the day of his return, Piet's eyes were alight with excitement for the first time since he had opened them to live again. The wheatfields shone in the sunlight, stretching away towards the mountain. They stopped to watch herds of zebra and gazelle grazing in the short grass. Above them, a bateleur eagle waltzed and circled in the cloudless sky, and a bright array of birds and monkeys called out a welcome from the canopy of Cape chestnut trees that lined the driveway. Suniva and James raced towards the car, clutching at Piet's hands, pushing and laughing as they saw his crooked smile and heard his garbled words of pleasure. The staff were standing on the steps, reaching out to touch the child, unspoken sympathy in their faces as they saw the extent of his disability. One leg was still in plaster and his facial scars stood out, livid red, against his pallor. The journey had exhausted him, and he wanted only to lie quiet in his bed. Lars carried him straight to his room where Suniva had hung up paper garlands, and pasted her best paintings onto the walls and the furniture.

'You are home, my boy,' Hannah said, helping him into bed. 'Safe and sound. Soon you will be well again because you are back at Langani.' But when Suniva and James crowded around the bedside and Lars pulled up a chair, she sent them away. 'He needs to sleep after that long journey,' she said, shooing husband and children out of the room, barring them all from the private world she had created where no one else belonged.

When she finally decided to rest for an hour, Piet lay staring out at the garden until a shadow crossed the window frame. He struggled to raise himself from the pillows, making jumbled words of welcome as James and Suniva slid into the room to sit beside him on the bed, hushing him with fingers on their lips, making faces, telling him stories in mime, until he was laughing, his eyes bright with the idea that he was part of their triumvirate once more. It became a daily game for them all, sneaking into his room or diving out of the window when they heard footsteps approaching. Their shared secret gave Piet a sense of mischief and conspiracy, an innocent rebellion that drove his determination to be whole again, to run outside with them, to fish and walk in the forest and recapture his normal life.

'What about going to Langani for the weekend?' Sarah put down her book. 'They must have settled in by now, but I can hear from Hannah's voice that it isn't easy. And God only knows how Lars is faring. They could do with a little light relief.'

'It's a bumpy road.' Rabindrah put his hand on her belly. 'We have to look after two of you now.'

'We will. We do.'

He was so tender, so solicitous. Every time he spoke about the baby she felt a surge of elation and panic, but she had resolved to put the outcome from her mind, and to give her growing child only thoughts of joy and welcome. Whatever the outcome, she would deal with it when the time came.

They set out on the following morning, taking it easy, stopping to admire the mountain as the snowy peak reared up out of the cloud base. The road was lined with the glassy green of coffee farms, with long trays of beans drying in the sun. Roadside stalls were piled with pyramids of fruit and vegetables, and women staggered up the narrow red paths that led to their huts, bent down under the piles of firewood fastened by a leather strap to their foreheads.

'Beasts of burden, victims of circumcision, trapped in an endlessly primitive existence, always at the beck and call of their fathers and brothers and husbands.' Sarah put her hands over her eyes for a moment. 'See no evil. Is that what we are supposed to do? Accept the beauty of the place and close our eyes to cruelty and drudgery? Is that a good enough world for our child?'

'It is changing. Slowly.' Rabindrah gestured out of the window. 'There are more schools, more hospitals and roads, more opportunities. But the pressures on arable land, and the sharing of it by man and beast can only become more of an issue. Speaking of land, there is something I'd like to ask you. Something I've been thinking about lately.'

'What's that?'

457

'I was wondering if we should buy a few acres and build a house of our own.'

'Do you really mean that?' She turned to look at him, amazed and delighted. 'Where would we look?'

'Maybe around Gigiri. We could have a big garden to grow fruit and flowers. I'm thinking of a house where our children will wake up to the sound of birds and the sight of beautiful trees. Flame trees and bougainvillea, and the smell of jasmine and roses. And spare bedrooms and bathrooms, and a bigger darkroom for you and a study. A family house. That's what we need now, and we can afford it.'

She stared ahead at the road, speechless, thinking of the baby. How would Rabindrah ever be able to look at her again, or at her child, if he knew what she had done? And what would happen if he discovered the truth? She thrust the thought away.

'Well?'

'I'm . . . I'm overwhelmed,' she said. 'Truly.'

He threw his head back and laughed. 'I've never seen you so nonplussed,' he said. 'I'm glad I can still surprise you. Let's keep the idea to ourselves, until we've found somewhere, and then we'll unleash our plans on our friends.'

By the time Sarah and Rabindrah had been at Langani for twenty-four hours, they realised that the household revolved almost exclusively around Piet's needs. Handrails had been fixed to the walls in most areas of the house. Each morning, after breakfast, Hannah started him on his exercises. A room beside Camilla's workshop had been turned into a space with a table and chair where he worked laboriously, picking up and fitting together a selection of wooden blocks of differing shapes and colours, watching his mother as she pointed at one item or another and mouthed or signed their names. Suniva had painted the objects, all of which had been made in the farm workshop. She rushed to help him at every turn, hoping that her presence in her brother's life would make Hannah change her mind and that she would not be sent away after the school holidays. She had begun to hope that the whole idea had been forgotten. The accident had put everything else aside, and that was one good thing about it, Suniva thought, with a tug of guilt. Both she and James had quickly learned to sign, and their hands moved deftly as they encouraged Piet to try and copy them and understand their meaning. Next door the *bibis* cut bolts of cloth, sewed on beads, sang their tribal songs to the whirring of the sewing machines, and looked in to encourage him.

Hannah had taken on a physiotherapist who arrived each afternoon, to work with Piet. He was a tall Luo from the shores of Lake Victoria who had been trained in the Aga Khan Hospital in Nairobi. His smile was enough to warm the hearts of everyone around him. Patient and gentle, Otieno was unfazed by Piet's failures or rages or periods of despondency, and he derived as much satisfaction from every small sign of improvement as the boy himself. Although Piet's balance was poor and his falls ate into his confidence, he gradually learned to use the bars and then his crutches. He was less steady on these, the drag of the leg more pronounced as he attempted to take a few halting steps.

Hannah had moved a second bed into Piet's bedroom, so that she would be near him if he was distressed during the night. Unaware of the secret visits to his room during the day, she held everyone at arm's length, determined to build up her son's strength. After one session when she had helped him up several times, she stood with her hands in the small of her back, giving way to a spasm of pain. When Lars tried to hold her and rub her back she disengaged herself, making him aware that she could not bear to have him in close proximity. He left the house, and went back to work on the farm, and they did not see him again until shortly before dinner when he telephoned his mother in Norway, and then sat down with Rabindrah to listen to the evening news on the BBC. He sank a large whisky and immediately poured another which he swallowed almost as fast. Sarah sat with the two men, listening to the main headlines of the day, watching as Lars made himself a third drink and worrying about this increasing trend. Norwegians had a reputation for putting away prodigious amounts of alcohol, but Lars had never been a heavy drinker. It made her uneasy and she left the room and went in search of Hannah who was sitting outside on the verandah in the dark.

Sarah noticed that her eyes were shadowed with weariness. 'How are things going? This is taking a heavy toll on you, Han.'

'But he is improving, isn't he?' It was more of an appeal than a question. 'He is so much better off at home.'

'Yes, he is,' Sarah said. 'Only you must try to avoid spreading yourself too thin. What you are doing for Piet is wonderful and it will surely make him strong again.' She made a fast decision and spoke out. 'But Lars needs you too. Have you seen him at all, since this accident?'

'Of course I've seen him.' Hannah was instantly resentful. 'I see him every day.'

'No. You pass him on your way to and from whatever you are doing, but you look right through him. If you really saw him, it might worry you. He's going down, Hannah. I see it, because I've been there myself, not so long ago. He is mourning just like I was, and he is ripped apart by the consequences of this accident. You have locked him out of Piet's recovery. He can't forgive himself for what he has done to his son, and he believes you can't forgive him either. So there is no place to go where he can live with himself. And that's wrong.'

'You know, Sarah, your ideas of right and wrong have become absolutely rigid, and you have taken to making judgements from some place on high that most of us can never reach. I'm doing the best I bloody can. And if that's not good enough for you, then I'm afraid you are going to be disappointed.' Hannah stood up.

'I'm sorry,' Sarah said. 'I was only trying to—'

'I'm more grateful to you and Rabindrah than you will ever know,' Hannah said. 'You have supported me through this whole nightmare, let me stay in your house, spent time with Piet, given everything you could. But you are not entitled to meddle in my relationship with Lars. And since we are on the subject of relationships, I would like to know why you still don't talk to Camilla. She has worked like a maniac to keep Anthony afloat, tearing around between the office and the camps and the workshop here, never complaining, always there for him, always there for me and for Piet. And soon she will be going to London, even though she hates leaving here. She has a strength and a sense of love and loyalty that neither one of us can match. Why can't you let go of whatever it was that caused the quarrel between you? How come she has been designated top of your list of flawed souls?' She stood up with difficulty. 'And while you think about that, I'll see if Piet is asleep and then I'm going to bed, because I'm too tired for dinner and small talk with big, lofty people.'

They all retired early, and it was after midnight when Sarah heard the knock on the bedroom door.

'Hannah? Are you all right? What is it?'

'Is something the matter with Piet? Can we help?' Rabindrah had already put his feet on the floor and was reaching for his dressing gown.

'The baby.' Hannah doubled over. 'The baby is coming. Lars is going to drive me to the hospital in Nanyuki. Keep an eye on Piet and Suniva. And keep your fingers crossed for me, because it's about six weeks too early. Just pray, Sarah.'

The child was born a few hours later. A boy, weighing less than five pounds. Tiny and helpless, yet clinging to life with tenacity. Hannah lay sleepless in the hospital bed, the lights dimmed, the corridors and wards silent around her. Her mind was spinning and her heart felt leaden in her chest as she acknowledged the needs of the frail little creature, come too soon into the world. She could never again think of herself as having created a private sanctuary for her family, a place filled with happiness and security. The world she knew had shifted and vanished, leaving her in chilly isolation.

'I have given our baby a name,' Lars said, as the infant was taken away to be placed in the dome of an incubator. But she did not answer, or seem to care and he had touched her gently on the arm and left her to follow the nurse.

Dressed in a white coat, mask and gloves, he stood watching his newborn son breathing with the help of an oxygen tube. He laid his hands on the Perspex wall of the incubator, yearning to communicate the protective love he felt.

'If you would like to put your hands in through the side here, Mr Olsen, you can hold him.'

The nurse smiled encouragement, and he did as he was told. The baby was perfectly formed but so small that he was afraid to touch the minuscule body, in case it crumbled under the sheer size of his hands. His fingers curled around the head in its tiny gauze cap, and he spoke softly.

'I will name you Jorgen,' he said. 'Your grandfather would have liked that.'

When the baby was brought home from the premature care unit, Hannah found herself on a treadmill that filled every waking moment. Between Piet's daily schedule and her everyday tasks on the farm and at the lodge, she had even less time for Lars or her daughter. It was Camilla who organised Suniva's school uniform, had the name tapes sewn onto her clothes in the workshop, and packed the tin trunk with the list of contents pasted inside the lid. On the day of departure, there were tears in Hannah's eyes, but Suniva could feel the underlying relief in her mother. When she leaned out of the car to wave one last time, Hannah had already left the verandah and returned to Piet's side.

On the steps of the school, Suniva stood in her blue pinafore and white shirt, the sleeves of her blazer drooping over her hands, too large, bought for growing into. Already one of her socks had slid down from knee to ankle, and the blue felt hat framed her woebegone face like a sad halo. Lars kissed his daughter goodbye, unable to look at her directly, or to answer the accusation in her eyes. He knew he had betrayed her, but there was nothing he could do. There were no words he could say to console her as she clung to him, her face buried in his jacket.

'Why do I have to stay here, Pa? Can't I go home with you? I'll be good. I'll help with everything and never get in the way. I promise, Pa, I do.'

'Come along, Suniva.' A bell rang and the nun detached her gently, drawing her inside the door. 'Time to unpack and meet your new class mates. You should leave now, Mr Olsen. She will be fine.'

He went slowly down the steps. At the bottom, he turned back, searching for some word of comfort, a promise that would let her know she was not forgotten. But the space where she had been standing was empty. Brushing a hand across his eyes to clear his vision, he walked back to the car, started the engine and drove away.

Chapter 30

Kenya, April 1978

Suniva opened the door onto the fire escape, and crept down the metal stairs. All was quiet. The nuns were in chapel and most of the pupils were in the common room, so it should be safe to make for the gate. Dodging behind thick clumps of oleander and bougainvillea, she ran down the avenue and within a few minutes she had reached the gates.

It wasn't that she hated the school, but she had to get home. Ma and Pa were not speaking to one another. Not like they used to, leaning against each other, smiling that special smile they had when they thought no one was watching. They hadn't smiled like that for ages. And Piet. Ma spent all her time with him, doing things to make him move: eye exercises, leg exercises, lifting his arms like so, stretching out his legs, wiggling his toes, making his fingers touch his nose. He could stand up on his own now, without falling over, and walk a short distance with his crutches. That was good for him, but he would be missing her secret visits with James. She knew how important they were to him. Ma didn't have time for games and the new baby cried all the time, and Pa looked stern and worried. She knew she could help, but Ma kept shushing her away, and wouldn't look at her straight.

Sometimes she wondered if Ma blamed her for the accident. It was Pa who had run over Piet, but she should have been looking out for him. She dreamed about it often – the metal grille on the front of the engine rearing over her brother, while Pa tried to wrench the car off the track. But the big black tyres were turning too slowly and Pa's face, all scrunched up with fear, filled the windscreen. If she had been faster, she might have shoved Piet out of the way, except that her legs wouldn't move. All she could see through the dust was the front of the car, and Pa's face. She had shouted, and waved her arms, but Piet had stopped to tie a fishing fly on his rod and he wasn't watching her, so the shouting didn't do any good. There was a noise of splintering glass, and a thump, and then everything was quiet. Afterwards came the sound of Pa, crying. She had wanted to tell him not to cry, that it was OK, but it wasn't. Piet was lying in a funny way, his arms thrown out like when he pretended he was flying. Only he wasn't. He was lying on the dirt with blood all over his face. Not moving at all.

After he was brought to hospital the baby came too soon, and nothing was the same any more. Suniva thought Ma would have preferred it if she had been run over, rather than Piet. Ever since he had gone deaf he had had all the attention. She tried not to be jealous but it was hard. And now that Grandpa Jorgen had died, Pa was sad and gloomy too. Why could things not have stayed as they were? She longed to see James. To be in their special place in the forest. When they were together, things did not seem so bad. Here in the big school she had no one she could talk to. If she stayed here, they would forget all about her.

As the weeks of term progressed, Suniva had become silent and withdrawn and her schoolwork began to suffer. She was sullen in class, and her teachers expressed concern at her behaviour. Sister Martha, her head of form, tried to draw her out, but she could not tell the nun what was really troubling her. How could she say things about her family that would make them look bad? Make her feel disloyal. Instead she took refuge in rudeness to avoid having to reveal the true nature of her fears.

James wrote now and again, but in stilted words, knowing that the letters would be scrutinised by the nuns before she was allowed to receive them. She read and re-read them, searching for meanings hidden in the prosaic sentences. The other letters that came from home were mostly from Pa, with maybe a few words of greeting from Ma, scrawled in haste at the bottom.

A thin drizzle was beginning to fall as she left the school grounds and made for the nearest bus stop. Suniva had seen people queuing there when Sarah had collected her for Sunday lunch, and she hoped to find her way to the central bus station and get a seat to Nanyuki. It took much longer to walk the distance than she remembered from travelling in Sarah's car, and she began to fear that she had taken the wrong road. Finally, she reached the place where several buses were taking on passengers. There was a large crowd, jostling for seats, proffering money for fares, shouting at the drivers. The vehicles were painted in many colours, and some had names and slogans on them, but no hint as to their destination.

'Can you tell me which bus goes to the main bus station?' Her voice sounded small and a woman with a sack of rice looked at her and cackled.

'What is a *mzungu toto* doing here?' She turned to the crowd, pointing at Suniva. 'Eehh! Look at this one. Where is her father with his big car?'

All around her people began to laugh and to tug at her school bag and her jacket.

'How many *shillingis* you got, *toto*? Let me see your money.' A tall man sidled up to her, his breath smelling of drink, and she began to feel frightened.

A horn sounded behind her, and she looked around to see a car drawing up, its doors rusty and dented, the painted taxi sign peeling. The driver stopped, engine chugging loudly, dark fumes curling from the exhaust pipe. He wound down the passenger window.

'Hey! Little girl. What you doing here?'

'I want to go to the bus station. To get a bus for Nanyuki.' Suniva stood well back from the car.

'I take you,' he said, eyeing her curiously. A small *mzungu* walking around alone was unusual. Where had she come from?

'No. *Asante sana.*' Suniva was polite. She did not want to get into a stranger's car, even if it was a taxi. And besides, she wasn't sure if she would have enough for the fare. 'Is it far?'

'*Mbale sana.* You get in. I take you.' He opened the door of his car, and stood out onto the road, towering over her. He was a big burly man with ebony black, pock-marked skin and a shaven head. 'Come, come!' He was moving towards her, his hand out.

Suniva stepped back in alarm, but at that moment she felt a jolt and then her canvas bag was gone, with all her money and James's letters.

'That's mine!' Suniva let out a shriek, more furious than scared. 'Give it back! I need my money!'

The crowd began to press in on her, everyone shouting, gesticulating. Then she was dragged by a pair of strong arms, out of the melee, away from the jeering mob.

'You come with me now, little *memsahib*. We get out of here *haraka*. Not good place.'

'They took my money.' Suniva stifled a sob. 'I can't pay.'

'Where you come from?' the driver asked.

But Suniva was not going back to school. 'Could you take me to Langata? My aunt lives there. I can show you the house, and she will pay you when we get there.'

She had no idea whether Sarah would be at home, but she could not think of any other plan. All she longed for was someone who would put their arms around her, and tell her everything would work out. She climbed into the taxi, wiping her nose on her sleeve as tears formed against her will and she began to tremble with relief.

There had been a full alert on since she had first been missed at school. Lars and Hannah had been notified and began making phone calls, but no one had heard from their daughter. She had not contacted Sarah, or Camilla, or even James. Suniva had vanished. The rain settled into a steady torrent, and Lars was already on the way to Nairobi to search for his daughter when the taxi turned into Sarah's driveway, carrying its bedraggled fare.

'What on earth have we got here?' Rabindrah stood on the verandah, peering into the rain as the girl emerged from the car and ran into the shelter of Sarah's arms, wet and shivering, as the driver explained the circumstances.

'I'll telephone Langani,' Rabindrah said. 'Hannah needs to know she is safe. And I'll contact the school.'

Sarah paid the taxi man and added a handsome tip. He could easily have driven away, ignored Suniva's plight, and she might never have been seen again.

'I have a *toto* like this one,' he said. 'Too independent. They need much care, these girls. Better to lock them up, until they get a good husband.' He gave a big belly laugh, and handed Sarah a grubby card with his name and the number of the taxi company. 'Next time she want to go to the bus you tell her to ring me and I will drive her. Save lots of trouble.'

Sarah smiled. 'I don't think she'll be going anywhere for a while. But we won't forget.'

The single red tail light vanished into the rain, trailing exhaust, as Sarah took her charge into the bathroom and filled the tub. Afterwards she dried Suniva like a small child, wrapped her in a dressing gown, and sat her down beside the fire where Chege brought her supper.

'I'm glad you are safe and sound,' Sarah said. 'But I hope you are sorry for the scare you gave us all.'

Exhausted, but still defiant, Suniva admitted that she had done a stupid and dangerous thing. But she would not go back to boarding school, she said. And if they forced her, she would run away again.

When her father pulled in to the house, Suniva tried to look as though she was not bothered by his arrival. But Ma had cried on the phone, and she knew that she had done something very bad. They would never allow her to come home now. Lars stood in the doorway, taking in the stubborn jut of her chin that reminded him so much of Hannah.

'Pa?' Her lip was quivering.

He strode in and lifted her from the chair, holding her in a crushing embrace, trying to control the shakiness in his voice as he looked at the little girl he might have lost. If anything had happened to her, it would have been the end of him too.

'Suniva, your mother and I have been very frightened.' His voice was stern. 'I want you to promise me that you will never, never do that again.'

'Your father is right,' Rabindrah said. 'You were lucky this time, but you could have been badly harmed. And then what would we have done?'

'I wanted to come home, Pa.' All the burdens that had weighed on her heart since she had been sent away poured from her in a deluge. Lars looked at Sarah in consternation. He had not had any inkling of the depth of misery in his daughter. It had seemed to both himself and Hannah, when the call came from the convent, that her action had been wilful and rebellious. But there were deeper issues here.

'We will talk about this in the morning,' he said, when her sobs had died down. 'Now I will tuck you into bed, and there will be no more crying.' He carried her to the bedroom and sat beside her until she was asleep. Then he rejoined Sarah and Rabindrah.

'I don't know what to do,' he said, passing a weary hand across his eyes, accepting a drink. 'If she says she will run away from school again, that is what she will do.' He gave a slight smile. 'She is as stubborn and determined as her mother. It is not that Hannah does not want Suniva at home, but she is stretched beyond her limit.'

Sarah was well aware of the situation at Langani. She looked across at Rabindrah and he nodded.

'We have been talking,' she said. 'And we have a solution to propose.

Why doesn't Suniva stay with us during the term time? I will be in Nairobi for the rest of my pregnancy and we would be happy to have her. I can drive her to school every day, oversee homework, and all that. She could go home at weekends and for half-term. We get on well. She is interested in art, and I had already started teaching her to use a camera. There's the garden and Swala and plenty of things we can do together. It's not the same as being at home, but it's a compromise. What do you say?'

Lars looked at his friends, overwhelmed by their generosity. He could not find the words to thank them, but when he smiled his eyes misted over.

'Good,' Sarah said. 'Let's ring Hannah, and ask her what she thinks of the plan. And if she agrees, we'll phone the convent and work things out with them.'

'We can consult Hannah, *ja*,' said Lars. 'But I have decided. This is the best thing for my Suniva. And this is what we shall do.'

Chapter 31

Kenya, May 1978

As he drove through the gates at Langani, Anthony slowed down and tried to work out how he would present his plan to Lars and Hannah. He was sure it would succeed, but less than certain that they would allow him to try.

When he and Camilla dropped in to the farm before Easter, Lars had greeted them. Although it was only eleven o'clock in the morning his breath betrayed the fact that he had already indulged in a beer or two. Hannah had poured coffee as if in a trance, only half listening to Camilla explaining her schedule in London and New York.

'I'll be back in a couple of weeks,' Anthony had said. 'When I sort out a few things in the office and make sure that all is well with Evelyn. By the way, our lawyer has finally tracked down Duncan Harper, although I can't imagine how he found the bastard. I don't think there is a hope in hell of bringing him back from South Africa, but at least there is the satisfaction of knowing he is being interrogated and he is a frightened man. We have set a debt collector on him and threatened him with all kinds of legal shenanigans.'

Now Camilla had left for London, the camp staff had been sent on leave, and Anthony had decided to spend three weeks at the coast while he waited for her to return. Friends had lent him a house on the beach at Msambweni, a small fishing village south of Mombasa where there were no tourists or hotels and he could snorkel and fish and walk on the sand. He thought he might also fit in a visit to the Shimba Hills where the magnificent Roan antelope could be seen. It was half-term in the schools and time to make good on his promise to take James on an expedition. He had hoped to look after the boy during the Easter holidays, but a last-minute booking had come in for a camel safari on which he could not take an additional traveller. Both James and Suniva had seemed more than happy to be together at Langani, however, and to spend time with Piet as he struggled with his programme of rehabilitation. An experience Anthony remembered all too well. As he rounded the curve in the drive, and the house came into view, he was determined that he would win the case for his experiment.

'Hannah, my dear.' He hugged her with enthusiasm. 'How are things going?'

'Not so bad,' she said. 'The baby has settled down and Josephine has turned into a good ayah. He is feeding well and putting on weight.'

'And Piet?'

'Otieno is doing his best,' she said. 'And I am using every spare hour to work with them. Piet is very difficult, though, with his tantrums and a new trick of simply lying down on the floor and refusing to do anything he is asked. Have you come to collect James?'

'I have, yes. And I'd like to take Piet and Otieno too.'

'What?' She gazed at him, open-mouthed. 'Take them where? I thought you were going down to the coast.'

'I am. We are.' He laughed, trying to coax her into a lighter frame of mind. 'I think it would be marvellous to take Piet down there. Let him do his exercises with Otieno on the lawn and in the sea. Try swimming and snorkelling. Have a change of scene.'

'Oh no,' she said, pressing her hands to her cheeks, fearful and already at the point of refusal. 'It's a kind thought, but I couldn't let him do that. What if——?'

'What if he lived like a normal boy for a while, outside this protective circle you have created? There is no reason why he can't travel to the coast, Hannah. There is a doctor at the little cottage hospital in Msambweni, and an even better one in Diani. The worst thing that can happen to him is that he can fall over in the sand, or stand on a sea urchin. The house is well staffed. He will be perfectly safe.'

'But he couldn't go there without proper supervision,' she said. 'Without——'

'Without you. Isn't that what you are trying to say.' Anthony was gentle as he saw the alarm in her eyes, the fear of separation. 'He can, Hannah. And it's time. Time for Piet, and time for you to take a break and spend time with Suniva when she comes home for half-term. James will have to go back to school next Monday, and I will put him on the plane from Mombasa. But I'd like to keep Piet for longer. Camilla will be with us after the weekend, and she can help him with his blocks and colours.'

'He's right.' Lars had entered the room to stand behind Hannah, unnoticed but listening. Now he came out strongly in favour of Anthony's plan. 'I think it's a fine idea. And if it doesn't work, we will come and collect Piet and Otieno, or they can fly back to Nairobi and we will bring them home from there.'

Hannah fought them both for another half hour and then gave in, drained and defeated. But when they went to Piet's exercise room and put the suggestion to him, he shouted with delight and nodded his head.

'I want to go with James,' he said. 'And Otieno. We all want to go to the sea. Can Suniva come too?'

Anthony heard Hannah's intake of breath, and stepped in quickly. In fact, he felt that James and Piet would be better on their own.

'This is men only,' he said. 'It also means that Suniva will have her ma and pa all to herself for a few days, which is what she will like best of all. Won't she, Hannah?'

Hannah nodded. And in her heart, she resolved to give her daughter the special attention she had missed for so long.

They left the farm on the following day, stopping for a night in Tsavo National Park to stay at a tented camp above the Tana River and to laugh as the elephant sprayed themselves with red dust, and wallowed in muddy pools. After breakfast they continued their journey, crossing the island of Mombasa and taking the ferry to the southern mainland. It was early afternoon when they reached the fishing village of Msambweni.

The house was cool and open to the sea breeze, built in traditional style with a woven *makuti* roof supported by *bariti* poles. There were deep verandahs, and the lawn sloped down to a long, empty stretch of beach. Palm fronds swayed in the wind and a palm-nut vulture soared above the white, powdery sand. Fish darted through clumps of coral beneath the turquoise water, and further out the waves broke along the main reef and the cobalt of the deep ocean. Anthony stood on the verandah, watching the triangular sails appearing on the horizon as the outrigger canoes and fishing boats flew homewards, to anchor in the shallow pools in front of the house. Although Piet was tired after the long journey, he insisted on taking his crutches and hobbling slowly to the shore to watch the fishermen carry their masts and sails through the channel in the reef, and store them until the morning.

'*Jambo, rafiki*. What happened to you?' The fisherman looked at the boy and laughed. 'You get run over by a Kenya bus, eh? Well, you will be better here. No cars, and I will take you out in my *ngalawa* so you can catch some fish.' He pointed at the crutches. 'You won't need those things in the sea. My name is Saidi and I am here every day, so you can tell me when you are ready.'

'My friend is deaf,' James said, relieved that Piet had not understood all the words. 'This is Otieno, who is teaching him how to walk and use his arms and legs again. It is hard for him, because he cannot always hear what he has to do.'

'Then the sea will be good, because it will carry him along.' Saidi smiled. 'You must find a mask and snorkel, and then he can swim in the same silence that he already understands.'

James and Piet shared a room on the ground floor, with large windows overlooking the sea and carved Swahili beds. A mosquito net hung over them at night, like a veil drifting in the soft wind. Otieno slept next door, and Anthony took the master suite upstairs, where he could sit on the roof terrace at night and study the stars. On the first morning they made their way to the beach before breakfast, but Piet stood on the sand, reluctant to let go of his crutches.

'I can't swim,' he mumbled, threatening tears. 'I can't do it.'

'Look at me, Piet.' Anthony pulled the boy close, speaking slowly and gesturing so that Piet could read his lips and understand the illustrations of arms and hands. 'Watch me, now. Because I have only one leg, and if I can swim, then you can too. Otieno, give me a hand here.'

He placed his arm on Otieno's shoulder and removed the lower part of his leg, before moving awkwardly into the water. 'Come on, Piet,' he said, throwing himself backwards into a shallow pool. 'You don't need those hobble-sticks here. Come into the sea.'

They established an immediate routine, starting each day with tea and biscuits on the verandah and then walking down to the beach. At first Piet fell on the soft, undulating sand and insisted on clinging to his crutches. But after two days the gardener arrived with a cane on top of which he had carved a handle, in the shape of a dolphin. Instead of working with wooden squares and cubes to improve his coordination, Otieno collected stones and shells on the beach, and pieces of driftwood, using them to make patterns for Piet to copy. The masks and snorkels and fins that Anthony bought had the children begging to go out to the reef with Saidi. When the time came for James to leave, Anthony telephoned the school and negotiated with difficulty a few extra days away from the classroom. Together the two boys learned the names of the fish and the corals, pronouncing them carefully, repeating the sounds, signalling with their hands. Piet's balance and coordination improved as he gained confidence on the grass and along the beach. On the boat he took a line from Saidi and they pulled in parrot fish and kingfish that were proudly presented to the cook, and prepared for dinner. Buoyant and unafraid in the water, Piet began to kick his legs and move his arms, performing the exercises that he had often abandoned at home. His body grew tanned and fit and his speech, although still slurred, took on the enthusiastic sound of a child eager for new knowledge.

The fishermen came to know and admire the strange little group, shaking their heads in wonder as they watched the one-legged *bwana* and the crippled child with his black friend, and the tall Luo who had come from Lake Victoria all the way to the sea and was staying right inside the *wazungu* house. They brought gifts of fish, and their wives arrived at the back door with woven baskets full of sweet, green oranges, bananas and pawpaws for breakfast, and mangoes that they ate in the garden, allowing the juice to run down their faces and onto their sunburnt bodies.

'Camilla will be here tomorrow,' Anthony said at dinner. 'Otieno, you keep Piet company, while I collect my wife and put James on the plane to Nairobi. But I promise this is only the first time that we will come to Msambweni together. We are the best team going.'

'You have done something exceptional.' Camilla lay on the terrace, looking up through the palm trees at a silver moon.

'I still can't get in and out of the water without Otieno, and I must look like a bloody cripple myself, so I'm not exactly the template of a hero,' he said, overwhelmed by her presence, by the fact that they were together again and she had wanted him instantly, climbing the stairs to their room on arrival, pushing the door closed, falling onto the carved bed and joining herself to him with ardour.

'When do you need to go back?' He had not intended to raise the question, but he had to prepare himself for the time when she would leave him again.

She laughed. 'I've only just got here. But I have some news that might surprise you. The whole New York collection sold out. Saul is ecstatic. So I've made a deal with him.'

He waited in silence, sure that she would now have to spend more time in New York, that he would be obliged to let her go again, that they would not be together during the migration in the Mara, or driving across the flats on the edge of Lake Nakuru as the flamingos rose in a pink cloud around them.

'I sold my shares in the New York company,' she said. 'From now on, I'm a consultant. Paid a fee for each collection I design, but not involved in the sales or the advertising. And no more modelling. Anthony, we're going to be fine by the end of the year. Back where we started, or almost. Except that I won't have to keep shuttling to and fro across the water.'

She did not tell him the entire story. Tom Bartlett had welcomed her in the usual way, filling her flat with champagne and flowers, taking her out to dinner on the first evening in London, filling her in on the gossip and scandals in the fashion industry. But she knew he was holding something back. It was not until she took a taxi to his office that she discovered what it was.

'Where is Lila? Has she taken a day off?'

'She isn't working here any more. She chucked it in,' he said, lighting a cigar with his back to her.

'How extraordinary. Last time I was here it looked as though romance had blossomed between you. Or something like it.' Camilla raised her eyebrows. 'Have you had a lover's tiff?'

'No,' he said. 'She just took off, that's all.'

'Surely she left a message for me,' Camilla said. 'I told her I would be arriving this week. This is really odd, Tom. And what happened with Zahra – is there any interest in her portfolio?'

'I expect Lila will contact you.' Tom was evasive. 'You're supposed to be with Joe Blandford by eleven, you know. Better get going, darling. We can catch up on the gossip and all the rest later. I'll be at your flat around eight?'

Her encounter with Joe Blandford had bordered on hostile.

'Bloody hell, Camilla! Why the fuck did you cut off your hair?' He stood close to her, looking at her through his most powerful lens, turning on lights. 'Your skin looks dry as paper and you've sprouted freckles. You're supposed to be a pale, shimmering snow queen to do justice to this jewellery thing. Instead you've turned up looking like a Californian beach babe.'

'Thank you, darling,' she smiled through his stinging remarks. 'I love you too. And I have several marvellous wigs in my bag.' But she was offended by his comments and completely unprepared for what followed.

'A right mess Tom has made with that Indian girl,' Joe said. 'She was organising a shoot for me and she just walked out of his office. Left me juggling magazine editors and models and producers on a job she was supposed to have sorted. And Black Beauty, having caused all this upset, never turned up for her session with me. Because Tom had taken her somewhere and was bonking her blind. The whole bloody thing cost me a fortune. I hope you're not going to send over any more potential talent like that.'

'Back up a moment,' Camilla said. 'Explain this to me again.'

'Tom was hot for the Indian girl. Lila.' Joe was speaking slowly and with exaggerated patience. 'And then you sent sex on long, black legs from Nairobi and poof! It was all over in a flash and Lovely Lila ran off, licking her wounds and leaving me in the shit. Is that plain enough for you? Can you get some of this pale, shiny stuff onto your face and chest now, so we can see if it's possible to photograph you at all?'

Camilla had telephoned Jasmer Singh after the session, but he had no idea where Lila was.

'I have been worried about her,' he said. 'I have her divorce papers and a request for alimony that she has to sign. But I can't locate her.'

Half an hour later the doorbell rang and Camilla opened it, expecting Tom.

'I made a fool of myself.' Lila perched on the edge of the sofa, holding a glass of wine, twitchy as a bird about to take flight. 'I stupidly fell for Tom, you see, and—'

'I've heard it all,' Camilla said, explaining how and why Zahra had arrived in London. 'I'm sorry. This is partly my doing. My one thought was to get her out of Nairobi, in case she would ever get her hooks into Anthony again. It never occurred to me that she could hurt you.'

'Tom is like a slavering dog around her,' Lila said bitterly. 'After the first few days I couldn't watch it, so I left. He phoned me a couple of times. Said I was behaving like a child, and I should come back to work. But I couldn't face seeing that bitch. It was too humiliating.'

'So your heart isn't exactly broken,' Camilla said.

'I thought it was, but it was mainly my ego that took the hit. I'm fine. Over it.' Lila's words belied her forlorn appearance.

'I'm sure you can find another job,' Camilla said. 'I think Joe Blandford would take you on, in the booking office he shares with two other photographers, even though he is pissed off with you right now. If not, I can put you in touch with other people in the business. Don't worry, Lila. Jasmer has your divorce papers ready to sign. You'll be free soon, with any number of choices in front of you.'

'I'm going to Birmingham tomorrow.'

'What on earth for?' Camilla was astonished.

'Harjeet's mother is in a state of utter misery. Many of her so-called friends have cut her off, and the two daughters are useless. One is married to a businessman in Leeds and he has forbidden any contact. The other one sits at home and cries all day.'

'Lila, I don't think you should get involved. Wait until your divorce settlement is finalised and you have some security. Don't go back there now.'

'Sajjan isn't a bad person, Camilla. I can't just leave her there, ashamed and suffering.'

'Have you told Jasmer you are going to see her? No, I thought not. You mustn't do this Lila. Not right now.'

'I have to try and help her through this,' Lila said. 'She was kind to me, you know. And she has admitted that she knew Harjeet was being beaten, until shortly before our marriage. Manjit used to beat her too, but she was too frightened to do anything about it. If she had challenged him, she would have been thrown out, penniless and with nowhere to go.'

'You can't make up for all that happened in that dreadful family,' Camilla said. 'They used you as a bargaining chip in exchange for Gulab's assistance. Now they want you to prop them up while Harjeet is in jail.

Stay away from them, Lila. Move in here tomorrow, and put all that behind you.'

'We have a very strong sense of family, us Sikhs,' Lila said. 'It's bred into us. Instilled in the psyche from the moment we take our first breath. I don't know how long I'll be in Birmingham, but I'll keep in touch. And thanks for your offer of the flat. I may yet take you up on it.'

When Tom arrived later in the evening, there had been a terse exchange before Camilla agreed to join him for dinner.

'I warned you about hurting Lila,' she said, fuming at his lack of decency. 'That Somali girl is an opportunist. Be careful. There is only one thing she really wants from you – money. And she is using the oldest and the simplest way to get it. You're a big boy now and you can look out for yourself, but I don't want to catch even a glimpse of her while I'm here. Or ever again. So please make sure we don't run into each other.'

'You sent her here to protect yourself,' he said. 'Anyway, what's it to you, who I'm sleeping with?'

'It's not a question of who you are sleeping with,' she said, disgusted by his attitude. 'I'm just disillusioned by your complete lack of sensitivity. Actually, I'm disillusioned with everything I've seen since I got here. You have been a good friend and a terrific agent through the years, Tom. But I've had enough of the fashion business. This has been my last shoot. I'm happy with my freckles and tanned skin, and the beginning of crow's feet, and my life with Anthony. I can make enough money in designing now, and that is what I plan to do.' She raised her glass to him. 'Thank you, darling. For everything. I'll always remember the good times. But this is the end of the road.'

She had left for New York three days later, sold out to Saul, and with a light heart boarded the aircraft for Nairobi.

As she walked the beach in the morning, Camilla knew she had made the right decision. A week passed and she spoke to Hannah on the telephone each day, describing Piet's progress, the way the light of childhood had returned to his eyes as he worked with Anthony and Otieno, sailed with Saidi, and swam in the sea.

'I'm coming down to collect him,' Hannah said, as Anthony prepared to return to Nairobi for his first safari into the migration. 'I'll fly to

Mombasa with the baby, if you can send someone to the airport to collect me.'

'I'll be there myself,' Anthony said. 'What about Lars? I'm sure he could do with a weekend at the coast.'

There was a long hesitation before Hannah answered. 'I hadn't thought of it,' she said. 'He probably can't get away, but I'll ask him.'

They were greeted by Piet, standing in the driveway with his dolphin cane, upright and confident, his radiant smile taking all attention away from the scars on his sunburnt face. Hannah handed the baby over to Josephine and hugged her boy, laughing and crying at the same time, stroking his hair, following him onto the verandah where he had laid out his collection of shells, while Lars stood and watched, a prayer of thanks forming in his mind.

When Piet and the baby had gone to bed, Hannah sat on the lawn beneath an almond tree, feeling the caress of the sea air and the tranquillity that crept into her body and soul. For the first time since the accident she was encouraged, and when Lars brought her a drink and settled himself beside her, she turned to smile at him.

'Perhaps they will be all right now.' Camilla watched them from the terrace above, her arms around Anthony. 'Maybe the horror has begun to fade, and they will be able to find their way again.'

'They will,' said Anthony. 'I know it.'

Returning to Langani, Hannah felt revitalised and full of optimism. The rains had come, transforming the farm into a carpet of soft green, and her garden was filled with ferns and flowering shrubs that had burst overnight into a rainbow of new leaf and blossom. Lars restocked the dam with trout, and beyond their fences the desperate herders drifted away to take advantage of new pastures created by the rainfall. Otieno came twice a week, but for the remainder of the time Hannah felt that she could manage Piet's timetable of physical training and speech therapy.

After a month, however, she began to feel the same fatigue that had dogged her before the visit to Msambweni and Piet's enthusiasm faded, making him irritable and unpredictable. On one occasion he hurled a series of wooden cubes at the baby, missing the crib by inches. It was then that the idea came to her.

'We should look for a place at the coast,' she said to Lars.

'You mean rent something in August and take all the children down there? Maybe we can find a house at Msambweni, now that we know the fishermen and Piet did so well there.' He looked up from his desk, pleased with the idea.

'No. That's not what I mean,' she said, slowly. 'I was thinking that we should buy a house of our own. On the beach at Msambweni or Diani, or even on the north coast. A place where we could spend more time. Piet isn't going to be able to go back to school for a while, and I think he would be better off doing his lessons and his exercises by the sea.'

'But what about the farm? And the lodge?'

'We could take Mike Stead on full time,' Hannah said. 'David has been running the lodge for several years now, so all we would need to do there is to bring in a qualified assistant if I'm not around all the time. Anyway, that is something we would have to discuss with Anthony, since he is an equal partner.'

'Han, we couldn't afford to buy a house at the coast. It's a fine idea, but it would cost too much money. Funds we don't have right now.'

'We could find the money,' she said. 'You know we could.'

'I think you are fantasising.' Lars made a weary gesture. 'Rent a house for July and August, by all means. And Christmas too, if you like. But that is all we can think about.'

'You could sell the farm in Norway,' she said, the words sounding bald and shocking.

He pushed back his chair and stood towering over her. 'My mother lives on the farm,' he said. 'It is her home. It has been her home for more than forty years. It is left to Ilse and me, with the provision that she can stay there for the rest of her life, if she wishes.'

'Kirsten must be lonely, now that your father has gone,' Hannah said. 'She could go and live with Ilse. They have a flat attached to their house. They built it for just that purpose. If you told her why you needed the money, I'm sure Kirsten would agree to move out. Neither you nor Ilse want to keep it, so it could be sold and your share would give us what we need for Piet.'

'My mother loves that place.' Lars was incredulous, white with rage. 'Her friends are all around her, and the neighbours help her when she needs it. It is the home she knows. She would hate to live in the city with

Karl and Ilse. In any case, I do not think they will stay together much longer. It is shameful, Hannah, to think of doing such a thing. You must have finally lost your mind. I could never think of treating my mother in that way.'

'Piet is more important than Kirsten now,' she said. 'He is young, and he could remain damaged for the rest of his life. We have seen for ourselves that he would be better off if we divided our time between here and the coast.'

Her comment pierced his heart and he remained there for a moment as he registered the savagery of her assault. He wanted to say something but he was unable to find any words that might make an impression on her. Nor could he describe his sense of loss, the certainty that he was no longer of any use to the people he had always loved. He saw now that she would always blame him for their crippled son. Shame flooded him, searing his mind and body, and when he turned to leave the room he could barely lift his feet, so heavy was the burden that he carried. He was alone in the world. What he had done could never be forgiven or forgotten because the pain he had caused was too great. And he was tired. Tired of seeing the sadness he had caused, tired of trying to make amends.

He lurched down the hall, heading for the locked cupboard outside the dining room. Hannah had placed a mirror with a frame of Arab silver on the opposite wall, and he caught a glimpse of himself as he passed. A man whose hopes and dreams had gone, a man who had destroyed his own family, a fragmented mass of grief and anguish. He pushed his hand into his pocket and took out his keys, knowing that at last it was over.

Hannah understood immediately that she had dealt him a fatal blow, stepped over the line and limits of his endurance. The magnitude of her words rose accusingly to confront her and she walked out into the corridor in search of him. But there was no sign of Lars, and she stopped to listen for his footsteps. When she heard the sound of the key in the lock she stood still, wondering whether he had decided to take a fishing rod and go to the river. Returning to the office she looked out of the window and saw him disappearing into a thicket beyond the lawn, where her father had built a seat for Lottie in the shade of a flame tree. As he vanished from sight, there was a sudden glint of sunlight on metal. The hair on the back of her neck and on her arms stood up on end as realisation burst into her consciousness.

'No! No!' She was screaming as she raced down the steps and across the grass. 'No, Lars! Lars! Please, no!'

He was sitting on the stone seat, staring down at the gun in his hand. 'I cannot go on.' His voice was already dead as he raised the revolver to his head. 'I want to die, because I cannot feel any more grief. Because I have lost everything and I can never make it right again.'

'Lars, oh God, I love you Lars! I'm so sorry.' Hannah flung herself across his body, pushing his arm to one side. 'I'm so terribly sorry. I didn't mean it. What I said. I have done so much wrong, so much harm. I can't survive without you, Lars. Please, please forgive me. Only forgive me. Give me the gun, Lars; give it to me please.'

His head drooped forward and he let the gun fall onto the grass as she buried her head in his lap, sobbing out words of regret until he lifted her face and took hold of her, and they wept together for all they had suffered. After a long time he pulled her up, placed his arm around her waist, and supporting one another they walked back to the house.

Chapter 32

Kenya, June 1978

As the trials of the two government ministers and Harjeet Singh progressed, Sarah became increasingly restless and apprehensive. The papers were full of the case, with daily headlines on the front page. Rabindrah's role in the events at the go-down provided gruesome copy, and Johnson Kiberu's determination to bring two of his powerful colleagues to justice caused widespread speculation as to his political future. Reminders of the fate of J. M. Kariuki, three years earlier, were unavoidable. The politician had been too outspoken in his criticisms of the government, stating that Kenya did not need ten millionaires and ten million beggars. When he was abducted from a hotel in the city centre, tortured and killed, Rabindrah had not minced his words on the dangers of pointing a finger at high-ranking individuals who flouted the law, while the President turned a blind eye.

Now Rabindrah himself was giving evidence in a highly publicised anti-corruption case, and supporting another outspoken critic of the administration. It did not seem that the two politicians accused in this instance had the support of the Mzee, or the henchmen who now ran the government, mainly in the President's absence. Still, Sarah recognised the dangerous position in which her husband and Johnson Kiberu had placed themselves, and Gordon Hedley's courage in publishing the story.

Rabindrah himself felt partly responsible for the fate of his uncle, and he had been unable to rid himself of the bloody images of Yussuf's death. As the days of the hearing dragged on he began to have nightmares, tossing and muttering, crying out in warning, waking in a sweat. He was also obliged to face Harjeet's relatives and members of his own family in the gallery, most of them hostile and convinced that he was a traitor to his own kin. Since Gulab's death he had been ostracised by the Sikh community, with the exception of Indar and Kuldip Singh.

'I'd like to come with you,' Sarah had said, on the first morning of the hearing. 'I can drop Suniva at school and then come to the courts. I want to be there, to support you.'

Rabindrah would not hear of it. 'Stop worrying, Sarah. The place is cordoned off by police. I'll be home as soon as the court is recessed. Relax. Take care of yourself and the baby. I'll tell you all this evening.'

The case had already run for the best part of a month, but now it was finally nearing judgement. The steps of the Nairobi Law Courts were thronged with spectators as Rabindrah made his way into the building. Cameramen, reporters, lawyers and politicians jostled for space under the arched portico. Security barriers kept the public at bay, and a heavy police presence had been deployed around the square. The evidence made for good copy and foreign correspondents were out in force. There was a buzz of anticipation on the front steps, and photographers raised their cameras as a black limousine with tinted windows drew up. Johnson Kiberu emerged into a barrage of flashbulbs and shouted questions. Flanked by bodyguards, he stopped to greet the journalists with an affable smile, advising them that he would be making a statement later. His escort closed ranks around him, and he moved inside.

Rabindrah was already seated in the court beside Gordon Hedley, waiting to be recalled to the stand, hoping that this would be his last appearance. The documentary evidence he had obtained from Manjit Singh's safe in Birmingham had been pivotal in the prosecution's case against Eliud Muruthi and Walter Ndegwa, which had come to a close the previous day. As predicted, Harjeet's counsel had argued that his client was not named in any of the documents pertaining to the laundering of money or the smuggling transactions in which the co-accused were complicit. His father's signature was the only one that appeared on any paperwork involving the company's business dealings in Kenya, and there were no further links to connect him to the other defendants. There remained only the matter of the events in the go-down in Mombasa, and the murder of the night watchman.

The court room was full, and the morning sun glared through the long windows, causing the temperature to climb rapidly in the crowded room.

The public gallery was crammed with people, whispering and fanning themselves, come to see justice administered, or mocked once again by the rich and powerful. Some had been paid and transported to the court, to lend support to the politicians on trial. Already the heavy smell of humanity, close-packed in a confined space, permeated the air. The sharp odour of nervous sweat blended with hair oil, the mustiness of black gowns worn by the lawyers and judiciary, women's perfume, and bare feet cracked and caked with dust.

The three accused were brought up from the cells, all of them handcuffed, blinking in the bright sunlight as they emerged into the well of the court. Harjeet looked ill. He was painfully thin, his suit jacket hanging in shapeless folds from his shoulders, his neck scraggy, rising out of the oversized collar. A navy turban was wound around his head, but the eyes under the heavy brows had a haunted look with dark circles beneath them, and hollowed cheeks. He was diminished, no longer the swaggering young man Rabindrah remembered from his cousin's wedding. As though the steel bracelets around his wrists had leeched his pride away. Even when the warder had removed them and Harjeet sat down, his shoulders were stooped, and he huddled in the corner of the dock, distancing himself from his co-accused, not wanting to be associated with them in any way. He did not look around the rest of the court. Heaven only knew what his life had been like these past months, in the prison.

The judge entered, taking his place on the raised dais, his dark robes a sombre contrast to the honeyed wooden panelling behind him. Rabindrah was called to the witness box, and reminded that he was still under oath. He answered questions about the circumstances of his presence at the warehouse on the night of the raid, and what he had seen. The photographs he had taken before he was discovered were put into evidence, and their significance explained. When the prosecutor had completed his direct examination Harjeet's defence counsel, Roger Cameron-Hall, rose to his feet.

Under cross-examination Rabindrah had to admit that Harjeet's role on that night was solely to make a record of the illegal cargo. He had not given any orders, or been directly responsible for the murder of the watchman. Surrounded at all times by armed guards he had simply followed his father's instructions.

Rabindrah had to stop and compose himself before he could describe Yussuf's death. When he related the grisly details of the beheading, sounds of surprise and horror erupted from the gallery, so that the judge was obliged to bang his gavel to restore order in the court.

'I want to be clear on one particular issue, however,' Mr Cameron-Hall insisted. 'Can you confirm that my client did not, at any time, offer violence towards you or the watchman.'

'He threatened . . .' Rabindrah stopped, realising that he could not go into the details of any threat without implicating his family. 'Harjeet did not personally assault anyone, but he was there, complicit in his father's operation. A part of it.'

'But the defendent has subsequently cooperated with the authorities, and furnished you with his father's papers pertaining to his business interests here, has he not? And there is nothing in these papers to implicate Harjeet Singh as being an active player in any of his father's illegal operations. Isn't that so?'

'Nothing written down, no.' Rabindrah spoke through a clenched jaw.

Cameron-Hall turned to address the court. 'It is my client's contention that he was forced to accompany his father to Mombasa on the night when the attempted smuggling of illegal trophies took place,' he said. 'He was there under duress, and his only involvement was a passive one.' He swung back to Rabindrah. 'He was simply standing there, checking an inventory. Not giving orders. Not wielding any weapon.'

'Not wielding a weapon but—'

'Thank you Mr Singh. That will be all.'

The prosecutor offered no redirect examination. Harjeet was sitting forward, his hand over his eyes. He did not look up as Rabindrah left the witness box, but Johnson Kiberu nodded to him as he passed.

By midday the prosecutor had closed his case, and the judge ordered a recess until two o'clock, when the defence would begin. As Rabindrah and Gordon made their way out of the court, the Minister's driver approached them.

'Mr Kiberu would like you to join him for lunch,' he said. 'I will drive you to the restaurant.'

'It is going very well, I think.' Johnson was in an expansive mood. 'Your contribution this morning was invaluable.'

'He might still get off,' Rabindrah said. 'I couldn't make my evidence strong enough to stick.'

'We will see what happens this afternoon, but you may well be right.'

Johnson's smile was sly. 'The other two will definitely receive long sentences, however, and that is the important thing.' He shrugged as Rabindrah leaned forward, startled. 'The son was never a major player. Not worth anything to us, except to bring us the evidence we needed for a conviction. Manjit Singh's papers were what we needed to prove the case against Muruthi and Ndegwa. And Harjeet will no doubt admit to being an accessory, and serve a shorter sentence.'

'But he is as guilty as hell,' Rabindrah said.

'I believe the court will be lenient.' Kiberu's laugh was mirthless. 'Harjeet is apparently pleading mitigation.'

'What mitigation?' Instinct told Rabindrah that a further deal had been struck, and that Kiberu knew it.

'We shall see.' Johnson ordered drinks and glanced at the menu. 'I believe we will have a quick result. Probably this afternoon. And you will have another good story for your paper. In addition the Mzee, despite his ill health, has been following the case. He will be pleased with the outcome, since the Government will be seen to be taking a tough line on corruption. It is a pity that we could not find anything concrete on Gacharu. The photographs that Manjit had were not specific enough, but he is a greedy man and he, too, will make a mistake one day. Now, we should eat.'

When the court reconvened at two o'clock, Muruthi and Ndegwa had changed their plea to guilty on all charges. They stood with their heads down, showing no reaction to the murmur that flowed from the crowd. One voice was raised in the back of the gallery but it was followed by a brief scuffle that quickly stifled any hint of dissent. When the judge handed down a sentence of ten years with hard labour for each man, there was a wave of noisy reaction through the court. Relatives and followers in the gallery wailed aloud, protesting the severity of the sentences as the two men were led back to the cells beneath the courthouse.

Roger Cameron-Hall rose to his feet. 'Your Honour, the defendant, Harjeet Singh wishes to change his plea to guilty of the lesser charge of aiding and abetting. However, I would like to call two witnesses who will give evidence on his behalf, of mitigating circumstances.'

'Is the State agreeable to this?' The judge raised his head, but he did not appear to be surprised by the sudden turn of events.

'It is, your Honour.' The prosecutor's answer caused a new stir amongst the crowds.

'Then you may proceed.'

Harjeet stood in the dock, and under the skilful guidance of his counsel's questions, recounted his years of terror growing up under the despotic rule of his father. From early childhood, he said, any refusal to do his bidding was met with severe beatings, so that even as an adult, he was afraid to disobey an order. Harjeet had hoped to free himself of Manjit Singh's influence once he married, but this had proved impossible. He and his wife had been financially dependent on the family business because he was employed there, and he had no other income of his own. When he was required to go to the warehouse in Mombasa, he felt he had no choice. But his only role was to take the inventory. The events of the night and the contents of the lorry had come as a terrible shock to him, and he had played no part in the murder of the night watchman.

At this point, Harjeet broke down. Holding the rail of the dock with both hands, he declared that he would never forgive himself for what had happened. But his father was dead, and he now wished to throw himself on the mercy of the court.

Rabindrah shook his head in disbelief, astounded by Harjeet's recital. This abject and humble prisoner, weeping in the court, bore no resemblance to the man he had known – the arrogant bridegroom, the confident bully who had threatened him in the go-down. It was a remarkable performance. The man was despicable.

'Your Honour, I would now like to call a new witness.' Cameron-Hall addressed the judge once more. 'A witness who can testify to the truth of what my client has said, who has known him since childhood, and can confirm his father's ill-treatment of him. I call Mrs Lila Singh to the stand, please.'

Rabindrah felt as though the breath had been knocked out of his chest. He twisted in his seat, and saw his cousin walking towards him, her face set, eyes on the ground. Lila wore a dark, tailored suit and her hair was tied in a severe chignon. She looked sophisticated, restrained, and older than her years.

'Lila! Why are you doing this?' He whispered the words as she passed him.

She paused for a second but made no reply. Then she was taking the oath. Her evidence was given in measured tones, confirming her husband's statement to the court, and finally asking the judge for leniency.

'He was a pawn,' she said. 'He had no power to disobey his father and he acted out of fear. I would ask the court to take that into account when determining his sentence.'

The prosecution did not challenge her statement. She stepped down, and went to sit at the back of the court, avoiding Rabindrah's gaze. Medical evidence followed in the form of a doctor's report and a series of photographs depicting the scars left on Harjeet's body by regular and severe beatings that had taken place over many years. Judgement followed quickly.

'While I find that the defendant was not actively involved in all of his father's illegal operations, he has admitted to being present when a crime was committed, and by his own admission, he did take part in that process, in however minor a capacity. I therefore sentence him to three years imprisonment.' As the words were delivered, Harjeet sank onto the bench.

'However,' the judge continued, 'I will take into account his history, as well as the corroborative evidence of his wife, and the fact that he has already been in custody for some time pending this trial. I will, therefore, suspend part of that sentence. He will serve eighteen months, and following his release, be deported immediately from this country.'

In the uproar that followed, Rabindrah searched for Lila, pushing his way through the newsmen at the door of the court. He was afraid that she would leave the building before he could demand an explanation of the extraordinary thing she had done. He saw her brothers trying to protect her from a gaggle of reporters, all calling out questions about her dramatic appearance.

'Lila – I need a word.' He reached out to take her arm, and was blocked by one of her brothers.

'It's all right,' she said, disengaging herself from his protective grasp. 'I want to talk to him. In private.' She turned to Rabindrah. 'Is there somewhere we can go?'

'Mrs Singh has nothing to add to her statement in court,' Rabindrah said to the noisy group of press colleagues. 'Give us a break, will you? I'll let you know when and if there is anything she would like to add.'

Taking her arm, he steered her into a quiet corner of the lobby. 'What the hell was all that about? Last time I saw you, you were making a life for yourself in London and my father was instituting divorce proceedings on your behalf. You never wanted to see Harjeet or any of his family again.

Have you any idea what you are doing? This man is partly responsible for your father's death. For the mess you are in. For the fact that no Sikh in Nairobi wants to hear my name.'

'He telephoned me,' Lila said. 'Mr Cameron-Hall. He said he had brought a psychiatrist to visit Harjeet. That he wouldn't survive a long sentence in jail. And after the trial his life would be in danger, because he would no longer be worth protecting.'

'And is he?'

'Sajjan begged me to go to court on behalf of her son. I couldn't ignore her, Rabindrah, so I decided to fly out and talk to him. Just once. Before making up my mind.'

'You came trotting meekly back to get him out of jail, because of family pressure? Is that what you're telling me?' Rabindrah could not believe his cousin had been so completely taken in.

'No. I only made up my mind yesterday, after I saw him in the prison. He has changed, Rabindrah. He pleaded with me to forgive him. Not to abandon him. And in the end, he is my husband.'

'Lila! Lila, he is manipulating you, can't you see that? He's just like his father . . .'

'No. Harjeet is a victim. He has been damaged both physically and psychologically and I've known that since we were children. I can help him to get through this, and when he has served his sentence we will try to make our marriage work. I will make it work.'

'But you don't love him, Lila. He and his family used you, and he will try to use you again. He can still destroy you, abandon you when it suits him.'

'Don't pour scorn on me, Rabindrah, or make me doubt myself. I'm going to stay with my mother until Harjeet is released. Then we will go back to England and begin again. In the meantime, what I need is your support and friendship. And Sarah's.'

'I'll do whatever you want,' he said. 'But don't ask me to agree with your choice.'

On the steps of the courthouse, Johnson Kiberu was making his statement.

'Today, we have taken a stand for honesty and integrity in government,' he said. 'There have been those who have used their position to gain wealth illegally, who thought they were above the law, but today, we have seen that no one is above the law. Every citizen, regardless of their status, must answer for their actions. We must work together to build a society that is just, and protect both our people and our wildlife, which is the basis of the tourist industry that brings in much of our vital foreign exchange. That is what we all want, from our great President right down to our youngest children. *Harambee!*'

Rabindrah and Gordon Hedley watched him leave, to the cheers of the assembled crowd.

'A brave man, that,' Gordon remarked. 'He needs to be careful, or he may end up in the morgue like Kariuki. He keeps telling us all that Kenyatta will be pleased with these convictions, but the Mzee is too old and frail to be aware of anything much. He hasn't played a real part in government for a while, and he won't be around much longer. His Kikuyu cronies are busy consolidating their positions and enriching themselves and Gacharu still has a lot of clout. Kiberu must have some fears about his own future, as long as that man is still on the loose.'

'There's no end to it.' Rabindrah was resigned to the verdict. 'This whole case was a stitch-up. I should have seen it coming.'

'At least they managed to put two major crooks away,' Gordon said. 'We can't hope to get them all at once.'

'I suppose you're right,' Rabindrah said. 'But from this day I am going to make it a priority to highlight any and every abuse of power that I see. In the meantime I need to find out what the hell my cousin is doing. Lila is not thinking straight.' He gave Gordon a slap on the shoulder. 'Thanks for your support, old man. Come to dinner with Maureen over the weekend. I'll ask Sarah to set it up, as soon as I get home. And if there is one single thing that I know, it is that I will never stop being grateful for the unyielding honesty and morality of my wife.'

'I can't believe it,' Sarah said. 'Why on earth would she go back to Harjeet? She had a new life in London, a job with Tom, even a possible romance. Harjeet's family would have had to give her a decent divorce settlement. They wouldn't want another lawsuit on their hands. Does Jasmer know what made her do this?'

'I don't think so,' Rabindrah said. 'And I sure as hell don't understand it. Maybe Lila will confide more fully in you within the next day or two. Meanwhile it's over. No, don't say anything about repercussions or future danger.' He placed his fingers over her lips and drew her close to him, filled with an overpowering sense of gratitude that she was there for him, that she loved him. 'I'm taking the afternoon off tomorrow,' he said, smoothing her hair, tucking a curl behind her ear. 'We are going to start looking for our new home.'

Two days later, as she walked into the house after dropping Suniva at school, the telephone was ringing. She picked up the receiver, rehearsing in her mind what she would say to Lila.

'Hello?'

'Sarah? I have to see you.'

She sat down, her knees turning to water. 'Hugo? Oh no. No, I can't.'

'I'm leaving tomorrow. For Edinburgh. I want you to meet me. Please?'

'Hugo, there's nothing to say.'

'There's goodbye. Face to face. You owe me that. I'm at the Norfolk. Room 26.'

In the early stages of her pregnancy it had been easier to pretend. Once the first three months had passed without the tell-tale danger signals, and her morning sickness faded, she had been able to bask in joyous anticipation. She watched her belly swell, felt the first feather-light movements inside her, and then the kicks of a healthy child. Then came Piet's accident and Hannah's premature delivery. All other considerations were pushed from her mind as she strove to support her friends, and to care for Suniva when she came to stay. During each day she spent several hours in her darkroom and at her desk, and took long walks with the puppy to stay fit and well. Most recently she had thought of little but Rabindrah and his growing determination to expose those who would overturn his country's fragile democracy.

The affair in the Mara had been buried. Something she need not deal with, could not afford to remember. When she had resolved to return to her husband she had written to Hugo, knowing it was a cowardly way to end things but unable to face him after what they had shared. He loved her, and she was not sure about her true feelings for him. There had been a blessed feeling of lightness in his company, a sense of acceptance, laughter, affection, and a depth of passion. But they were tangled up with the failures within her marriage. She had tried to explain this in her letter, to tell him how much he would always mean to her, to express how hard it had been to make her choice. But there was no easy way to say that it was over. His reply had been short.

Sarah,
*   You know how I feel. I said that I would wait for your decision, however long it took, and I can do nothing other than accept it. What we had was real and I believe that is still true. But it is, and has always been, your choice. I do not wish to make it difficult for you to visit Allie, who is so close to you. So I have decided to leave the Mara earlier than I had planned, and to take up the post I have been offered at Edinburgh University.*
*   Hugo.*

She had not seen him again. He had gone to Scotland to celebrate his father's birthday when she and Rabindrah went to the Mara in November. Afterwards, her pregnancy and her commitments to Hannah and Lars provided an excuse not to return. It was a relief to avoid seeing Hugo in person, not to meet the question in his eyes. But that question would not go away. As each month brought her nearer to the baby's birth, her foreboding deepened. Rabindrah was excited, loving, tender. Making plans, discussing names, coming home unexpectedly from work with a gift of flowers, a book, a basket of fruit. Each act of love increased her guilt. She could not tell him. And yet, if she did not and it became clear that the child was not his . . . There was nobody she could talk to.

After the phone call, Sarah sat staring at the patterns on the Persian rug until they began to swirl before her eyes. She was not ready to meet this man again, to resurrect what had happened between them. The effort to blot out the affair and its repercussions, in order to save her marriage, had created a black hole in her memory. But that denial had lain in wait for her, intruding unexpectedly, although she had tried to banish all thoughts of Hugo. There was no denying the distress she had caused Allie, however, and it had damaged their relationship. Sarah had been ashamed of her relief that they were talking on the radio, when she had confirmed that she was going back to Rabindrah. Allie's sadness resonated through the static, although her words were brief, and matter-of-fact.

'You've spoken to Hugo?'

'I wrote to him.'

'I guessed. He is devastated.'

'Has he . . . Has he said anything?'

'No. Except that he will be leaving for Scotland earlier than he originally planned.'

'Allie, I'm sorry. What happened between us . . . I realise now it was a terrible mistake. I never wanted to hurt him. Or you.'

'It takes two to have an affair, Sarah, and he knew the score. I only wish it hadn't been him, that's all.'

'Should I try to see him?'

'I don't think that would achieve anything. There is still a fair amount of detail to be finalised on the book, but I think it's best if you wait until Hugo is not around.'

She had followed Allie's advice, arriving in the Mara during Hugo's visit to Scotland, immersing herself in her work with the cheetahs, and observing the development of Hiba. The cub was growing fast, and the warden had arranged for a gazelle or impala to be shot by one of his rangers and delivered when necessary. He visited Allie and Erope often, intrigued by the young animal's progress. Allie herself was also enjoying the experience. Hiba was affectionate, mischievous, a joy to watch. They took her for long walks through the bush each day, to familiarise her with her future habitat. By tacit agreement, the subject of Hugo was avoided, but Sarah was conscious of his presence, brooding behind Allie's silence. Lying in her tent with Rabindrah, the echoes of her stolen passion crept insidiously through her dreams. They left before Hugo's return.

The crisis at Langani put everything else into shadow, and Sarah contacted Allie to tell her that she would not be able to come to the Mara for some time. She would work on the book from home.

'Tell Hannah and Lars my thoughts are with them,' Allie said. 'I hope the little boy will recover, and I'm terribly sorry about Lars's father.'

'I will.' Sarah cleared her throat. 'Allie . . .'

'Yes?'

'I'm pregnant.'

'I know. I heard it from Anthony when he dropped into the camp last week. I wondered when you were going to tell me. Congratulations. When are you due?'

'In July.'

There was a short silence. Allie was no fool. She had done the calculations. Sarah knew she should say something more, but she could not. And Allie did not probe further. Perhaps she did not want to know.

'You won't be travelling for a while, then,' she said.

'No. These first months are risky, and I have to stay put. Will you be coming to Nairobi? You could stay here and run a final check on all the material. I think we are almost done.'

'In the next month or so, yes,' Allie said. 'I'll let you know when I have a firm date.'

She had arrived for a few days towards the end of April, and they had worked on the text and the photographs, putting the final touches to the book. Hugo was still in the camp, but he would be leaving in June. He did not send any message. Allie had never chided Sarah for the affair, but her regret was evident. Hugo was the son she had never had. He had been deeply hurt, and the time she had hoped to share with him had been cut short.

Sarah did not believe that she would ever see him again, but now there was the telephone call, and she could not act as though he had never been a part of her life. Hugo was right. She owed him. Picking up her car keys, she left the house and drove into the city.

He answered her knock and she took a few hesitant steps into the room. The tousled hair and freckled skin, the grey eyes so sharp behind the tortoiseshell frames of his glasses, the sudden memory of his body, lean and muscular, beside her. She did not know how to greet him. A kiss would touch on the intimacy they had shared, and she could not do that. A handshake was too cold, too formal for what they had been. Their silence stretched across the ordinary, outside sounds of the day, muffling birdsong, the clink of coffee cups and the whistling of a cleaner.

'You're on your way to Scotland,' she said at last.

'Tonight. There will be a great deal of preparation for this new job. I haven't taught for a long time, and I'm not sure I will like it.'

'Allie will miss you. Is she here?'

'She doesn't like goodbyes. I left her with the cheetahs. And Erope.'

'Oh Hugo.' Her eyes filled with tears. 'I am so sorry. I ruined everything.'

'When is the baby due?' The question came out, staccato, like a gunshot.

'July.' Sarah avoided his gaze.

He reached out, gripped her arms. 'Is it mine?'

'No! I . . . I don't know.' She could not look at him.

'You don't know? Because you and Rabindrah were together right away? You went straight back to your husband's bed. Just like that. Christ, I can't imagine such a thing. You can't have left me and . . . God, I feel ill.'

'Please, Hugo . . .'

'I thought we had something exceptional. Sacred. But it didn't mean anything to you, did it, Sarah? Everything we shared, all the hours we talked, every time we made love? What was that? A way of getting yourself pregnant? Was that your real reason for taking me as a lover?'

She stared at him, horrified. 'How could you even think such a thing?'

'Then tell me. What did it mean?'

'Don't, Hugo. Please.'

'Tell me.'

'I tried to explain it in my letter. I truly believed, for those glorious days we were together, that I was free of all the troubles I had suffered. That you had made me so. And for a little while, I escaped from myself, from my responsibilities, from real life. We were in a fantasy world, you and I. You gave me back my ability to feel joy. Only it couldn't last, Hugo. Because I wasn't free. I didn't realise that at first. It was only when I went away that I knew I had been fooling myself. And lying to you, although I didn't mean to.'

'Does he know? About us?'

'No.'

'And what will happen when this child is born, Sarah? If it's mine? What will you tell him then? You can't really believe he will want it. Or you.'

'I don't know,' she cried. 'I can't tell him. I don't know what I'm going to do.'

'Come with me.' His voice dropped and he held out both hands to her, his expression radiating love and yearning. 'Come to Scotland and have our baby. Let me give you the life I promised you. I love you, Sarah. I asked you here to say goodbye, but I don't want to say goodbye. I want you to come with me.' He took her face in his hands, raising it so that she had to look at him. 'You say you don't know whose child this is. But you do know, and so do I. Years without a baby, two miscarriages, and then there was you and me. This is our child, Sarah, conceived during a time of incredible love. I want to raise it with you.'

She pulled away from him, and went to stand at the window, unable to bear the hope in his voice.

'You went back to Rabindrah out of a sense of duty,' he said. 'You told me so yourself, a moment ago. You couldn't escape from your responsibilities. That's what you said.'

'No, Hugo.' She turned to face him, her eyes full of remorse. 'You are wrong. For a while, I lost sight of my husband, got detached from the bedrock of our marriage. I was searching for happiness, for fulfilment in other things. And in other people, when I turned to you. But there is only one man with whom I can make my life. I am sorry, Hugo. So sorry that I have hurt you. It was utterly wrong, what I did. Selfish and unfair. I was unhappy, and I made a wrong decision, but I have no doubts now. I went back to Rabindrah because I love him. And even if the baby is not his, I will try to find some way for him to forgive me, and accept this child.'

Hugo sank down onto the bed, his head in his hands. 'You had better go,' he said.

'Forgive me, Hugo,' she whispered. 'Because I cannot forgive myself.'

He did not look up as she left the room.

Unable to face returning to the empty house, Sarah drove around for a while, hardly aware of where she was going. It was hot, and she heard a rumble of distant thunder. Impending rain made the air close and heavy, weighing down on her slumped shoulders. Eventually, she found herself outside the cathedral and she parked and went inside.

In the cool of the basilica she knelt in the shadows, willing away the turmoil. She closed her eyes, and tried to imagine a place of refuge. Somewhere calm, far away from the rending and tearing apart of her life. Somewhere she could find strength.

'I need a place to hide, Lord,' she whispered into the empty church.

There was a sound, and she looked up to see an elderly priest walking towards her. Thin, slightly stooped, his face lined. He stopped beside her bench and smiled, and she felt as though the sun had come out from behind the thunderclouds. She stood up, and on a whim spoke the words she had not thought of for a long time.

'Father, would you hear my confession?'

'Of course. Come with me.'

She thought he would go to one of the confession boxes flanking the benches on either side of the nave, but he led her to a small room off the sacristy.

'Kneeling can't be good for you at this time,' he said, pulling out a chair for her. He sat down himself. 'I am Father Andrew. And you?'

'Sarah.'

'You are tired, Sarah,' he said. 'In body and in spirit. I saw it when you came in. Tell the Good Lord what it is that burdens you, child. There is nothing you cannot say to him.'

'You are right. I am so very tired. And I'm living in a mess of my own making. Everyone around me is suffering, and I have added to their hurt instead of helping. I've failed as a wife. I've failed as a friend. I don't know what will happen when I become a mother.'

Stopping every few minutes, she told her story. The early tragedy of Piet's death, only a day after their engagement. Her halting recovery and the beginning of her feelings for Rabindrah. Then the slow-burning anger at her childlessness, the breakdown of her marriage, Camilla's abortion, the tragedy of Lars and Hannah and Piet, her own affair and her fears for the baby.

'Should I tell my husband? Oh God! How is it that every blessing I receive seems to carry some kind of retribution? You know, Father, I have been angry for so long, about so many things, that I feel a part of me has been completely destroyed. I don't know how to forgive, or to be forgiven. I've sat in judgement on others, while flouting every rule I should have followed myself. Now I am deeply ashamed. I want to reach out to Camilla, but I am afraid she will never see me as a friend again. I want to tell Rabindrah the truth, but I am afraid I will lose him. And if I don't tell him, I may lose him anyway. When we should be so happy. So full of hope. As for Hannah – she lost her brother and her father, and now her son has been crippled. Where is God in all this, Father? Because I am also tired of searching for any sign of him in my life.'

She stopped, remembering another time, after Piet had died. Then she had asked the same thing of Father Bidoli, the Italian priest who had been her friend and confidant. Who had married her to Rabindrah.

'There is no easy answer,' Father Andrew said. 'Suffering is often incomprehensible. Living through it humbles us. Makes us kinder, if we allow it to do so. It burns away the dross. Teaches us to accept and care for each other in our weakness, because one thing is sure — we will all be brought low at some time. Each of us needs consolation and support. The first thing, child, is not to judge. We cannot ever know for sure what makes people do what they do. Only God understands what we can never see. Leave judgement to him. He knows how to temper it with love. And do not judge yourself so harshly, either. Do you remember the story of the woman who was to be stoned to death?'

Sarah nodded. How could she not remember the adulteress awaiting her fate?

Father Andrew smiled. '"And which of you without sin will cast the first stone?" Jesus asked, as he wrote in the sand the sins of those who had gathered to execute her and watched as the crowd melted away in their shame. Then he raised her to her feet and asked her "Who is now left to condemn you?" And she answered "Only you, Lord." And he said to her, "I will not condemn you, my daughter. Go your way and do not sin again." Human weakness is universal, Sarah. But love heals, because it draws out what is good.'

'What do I do now?'

'Go and see your friend. Tell her what she means to you, say that you love her. Other words may not be necessary. And as for your husband . . .' He paused, and took her hand in his. 'Making your confession, that is good for you. It releases some of the burden. Telling him? How will that help him, or you? This other man is no longer a part of your life. It is over?'

She nodded, the rawness of their goodbye still fresh.

'Then let it go. Do not burden your husband with it. And as for the child . . . I am a great believer in the mercy of the Lord. Trust yourself to that mercy, and when the time comes and your baby is born, you will know what to do.'

She bowed her head for absolution, and walked away into the bright heat of the day.

Chapter 33

Kenya, July 1978

The Nairobi sky sagged, and the air turned damp and leaden. The fire in the sitting room had been lit and Sarah was searching for a sweater when Lila arrived.

'How are you feeling? Your ankles are so swollen, Sarah. Put your feet up on the sofa.'

'I've had them up for most of the day, but the baby starts a somersault programme each time I lie flat. I'm fine, though. Just impatient and a little scared, now that it's so close.'

'Rabindrah is over the moon,' Lila said. 'I've never seen him like this, even though we grew up together. Of course he is sure it is a son, but I know he will be just as thrilled if it is a girl.'

'I hope so,' Sarah said, somewhat disconcerted by this revelation. 'All we need is a healthy baby. My parents are arriving in two days, and I am so thankful they will be here. What's your news?'

'I've been to see Harjeet again. This morning.'

'How was that?'

'I don't know, Sarah. He is hopeful that I will stay with him and it has made him very dependent. It grates on my nerves, makes me feel claustrophobic, because I feel sorry for him. Sometimes I can almost believe that I love him, and at other moments it's repulsive and I'm more inclined to think it's sentimental pity.'

'Pity is not an ideal base for a marriage,' Sarah said.

'You're right. But either way, I won't abandon him while he is in that prison. It's harrowing, going to that place. Very frightening. The guards look at me in a certain way that makes my skin crawl.' She lit a cigarette. 'I went for another job interview, but no one really wants to take me on because of the hassle of obtaining a work permit. Now that I'm a British

499

citizen I have to have one, even though I was born here. I've found a lawyer who specialises in arranging these things – greasing palms in the Immigration Department, and setting up consulting companies for individuals like me, so that we are not officially employees. Of course he would take a slice of my first six months' earnings, and it costs a fortune to register the consultancy in the first place, but it seems to be the only way to get through the morass. Everything is a racket these days.'

'You are so right.' Sarah shifted her legs and tried to find a way to sit comfortably.

'And I'm a social pariah among the Sikh community because of the court case. It's ironic. I came back to help my husband avoid a long jail sentence, only to find that no one wants to know me.'

'Rabindrah is in the same boat,' Sarah said. 'An outcast in his family circle, despite all he has done to highlight issues of graft and fraud, and the necessity for wildlife conservation. The Vice President praised him in public last week, for his articles on corruption. Which is rich coming from Arap Moi. Still, he is going to be the next president when the Mzee goes, so it could be important for our future.'

'At least he has a job and you, and a child on the way. His own little community,' Lila said. 'I've got to the stage where I'm even thinking of going back to England. I could fly out to visit Harjeet every couple of months. It might be easier if I lived in Birmingham, although my mother would be devastated. She is the one person who is genuinely glad I am here. But I can't live my whole life to please all these needy people.'

'Would you think of going back to work for Tom?'

'God, no.' Lila laughed. 'I couldn't face him. Or look at that tart.'

'What tart?' Sarah frowned.

'Don't you know? No, of course not. You don't talk to Camilla. Oh, don't worry, I'm not going to ask.' Lila went on to describe Zahra's arrival in London and derailment of her own romance with Tom. 'It served me right, I suppose. I had no qualms about sleeping with him, but when he dumped me I felt used and sad.'

'I'm sure you could find another job in London that would allow you to be independent,' Sarah said. 'Instead of immersing yourself in a family situation that is a constant reminder of betrayal.'

'It's strange, you know, but I was brought up in a tight-knit community. Psychologically it is hard for me to break away. I can't seem to free myself of what is an old-fashioned Sikh mentality that I never thought applied to me. Or maybe I'm just not brave enough to strike out on my own. I don't know.' She switched subjects abruptly. 'Do you think Rabindrah would ever go to visit Harjeet in the prison?'

'I doubt it. He believes you would be better off divorced, and that Harjeet's family could still take advantage of you. And he will never forget what happened in that warehouse.'

'Where is Rabindrah, by the way?'

'Checking up on a breaking scandal regarding the disappearance of some German aid money. The usual lining of pockets. He's on another anti-corruption crusade and won't be side-tracked. He and Kiberu are like Rottweilers – they never let go once they are on the attack.'

'Brave but risky, I imagine.'

'I've tried to discuss that with him, but he waves me away.' She made a funny face, but there was no sign of humour in her eyes. 'We've had rows on this subject and I think he should let up for a while. It is dangerous, this constant spotlight that he shines on greed and fraud in high places. And there are key people in the government who have not forgiven him for exposing Ndegwa and . . . Oh, that might be Hannah,' she said, hearing a car in the driveway. 'She rang last night to say she was coming down. I suppose she has some shopping to do.'

She gathered up a selection of photographs and papers which were laid out across the table and over the sofa, and smiled a greeting as Hannah came into the room. 'Hello, Han. You'll have to excuse the mess. I'm sorting out the last details before the new book goes to press. Tea? I'm dying for some myself.'

'Yes please. It's good to see you, Lila.' Hannah put the baby's carry-cot down beside an armchair, and shooed away Sarah's puppy. 'Jorgen has only just fallen asleep and it would be a treat if we could talk in peace.'

'I'll leave you to it,' Lila said. 'Mother is taking me to the cinema. Bye, Sarah. Keep your feet up.'

'Poor Lila is having a rough time,' Sarah said, when Chege had brought the tea. 'She really doesn't know which way to turn and—'

'I have to talk to you.'

'What is it?' Sarah was alarmed. 'Has something happened to Piet? To Lars?'

'It's not about them. It's about Camilla.' Hannah plunged on. 'We three have had our disagreements and misunderstandings down through the years, but no matter what the circumstances, we always honoured the promise we made at school. Our friendship, the bond between us, it's beyond price and I cannot stand by and let that be lost. Life is too short for feuds. I have learned that through my own stupidity. This problem with Camilla is ridiculous. Anger is a terrible force for destruction if you let it rule you, Sarah.'

She stopped, her throat constricting at the horror of what had almost happened to Lars. She had never been able to tell anyone about that afternoon, but often in her dreams and at odd, waking moments she saw his contorted, despairing face and the gun raised to his head. The weapon she had placed there as surely as if she had handed it to him.

'When you accused me of concentrating too much on Piet and making the rest of the family suffer, I resented your interference. But you were right. I couldn't see the reality at the time, because I was too bogged down.' She paused, trying to find words that would penetrate Sarah's intractable stance. 'You have to bury this issue, no matter where it came from. Leave it behind for the sake of the people you love. The first step is the hardest, but the time is ripe, Sarah. The time is now.'

'I've tried to——'

'Hear me out. You and Camilla have held my family together. We would never have got through Piet's accident and all that followed without your love and support, and I will not accept that my dearest friends, my sisters, are permanently estranged. I know it must have been a serious matter, but you have to fix it. You have to. That is why I came down today. To bring you back together.'

'I've been trying to pluck up the courage for weeks,' Sarah said. 'But twice when I phoned, she was away. And the last time, when she picked up the phone, I chickened out. I want to heal the rift, but it's hard, even now.'

'What happened between you? Can't you tell me? If I understood what it was about . . .'

'I can't. But I will phone her. Ask her to meet me.'

'Do it.' Hannah went to the desk, picked up the telephone, and held it out. 'Now. She is at home today. I checked.'

Sarah dialled the number, her hands shaking. 'Camilla?' She spoke into silence. 'Can we meet? There are things I have to say.'

'I thought you covered everything pretty comprehensively last time.' Camilla's tone was not encouraging. 'I couldn't hear it again.'

'You don't understand. I want to make it right, if that is possible. Will you meet me? Please?'

'Here or at your house?' Hannah reached out and took the phone. 'And if you would rather I left the two of you alone, that's all right, as long as you end this.'

'No. I'd like you to stay,' Camilla said. 'I'll be there in fifteen minutes.'

When she walked into the room the atmosphere was taut, and beyond the windows the trees had turned black in a deluge of rain. Sarah looked at her, seeing her clearly for the first time since their meeting at Langani. On that day her feelings of outrage had blurred her vision, and she had lost her friend. There were so many things she needed to say. But Hannah still did not know what had happened.

'Forgive me.' Constrained by the secret, those were the only words that Sarah could offer. 'What you said to me . . . you were right. It was never my place to judge you. I am so sorry. For everything.'

'Hannah, you need to know the truth.' Camilla leaned against the door, looking into the past and its regrets. 'I had an abortion. In London.'

'Oh, God.' Hannah's hands flew to her face.

'It was a decision that almost killed me,' Camilla said. 'I was six weeks' pregnant but I knew I had to go on working. Without my contribution Anthony would have lost his business, and the life he had only just found again. So he came back here to salvage the company, and I went to a clinic in London.'

'He agreed to that?' Hannah was aghast.

'I told him I'd miscarried. He never knew the truth. I hope he never will.'

'Then how did Sarah know?' Hannah looked from one to the other.

Camilla's explanation was precise and brief. 'I don't know whether I could have survived without Rabindrah. I was so alone, my heart was so full of pain and guilt, and rage at what had happened to Anthony. I was close to the edge of madness and Rabindrah came and stayed with me for two days. That's how Sarah found out.'

'I'm sorry for the things I said.' Sarah closed her eyes in shame. 'All I could think of was that you had terminated a child's life, while I couldn't have a baby at all. And I was angry that you had excluded Anthony from your decision, but made my husband a party to it. Even if it was after the event.'

'I should never have put Rabindrah in that position,' Camilla said. 'It was unfair to both of you. I didn't think about it that way at the time. I was beyond thought. I needed a true friend and he was the only one I could trust.'

'You should have been able to count on me, but I let you down.' Sarah halted, needing to express a combination of honesty and understanding. 'I couldn't have done what you did, Camilla. Not even for Rabindrah. For me, brought up as a Catholic, abortion will always be wrong. I can't change my own feeling on that, but I should have been able to comfort you, even if I didn't agree with your decision. You acted to protect the person you love most, and I had no right to judge you. It makes me a hypocrite of the worst kind, after what I have done.'

'What does that mean?' Hannah was bemused.

Sarah turned away from them both, unable to look into their faces as she made her admission. It had become intolerable, finally, to face the imminent birth of her child alone, carrying the doubt of its true beginning. Hannah and Camilla knew the best and the worst of her. She sat facing the garden, her hands clenched in her lap, and told them about her affair in the Mara, trusting that they would show more mercy than she had offered either one of them. They listened as the whole story spilled out, including her last agonising encounter with Hugo.

'I should have told Rabindrah when we got back together, but it was over, and I was scared of losing him too. What good would it have done, to cause him such hurt? That is what I asked myself, how I justified not saying anything. And when I found out I was pregnant, it was too late.'

'Oh, Sarah, Sarah.' Hannah placed both arms around her. 'All these months, you've been living with this, not able to tell anyone. I know how that was, when Viktor left me pregnant. And you were the one who brought Lars back to care for me, and help me through.'

'My stupid arrogance made it impossible to tell the only two people I could confide in.' Sarah looked directly at her friends. 'Is it too late?' she asked. 'Can we start again?'

'Ach, look at us!' Hannah began to laugh. 'We've all nearly drowned in the mire, one way or another. Made terrible decisions, clawed our way up again. But one thing I know. We are still sisters. Blood sisters as we promised when we were young. We need each other more than ever, no matter what barriers we have to cross. We're all the same, heh? Stubborn and seriously flawed, like the rest of the human race. So we forgive, and we renew our promise to one another, and we go on together. Like we always did.'

And suddenly they were laughing and crying, holding on to one another, drawing comfort and strength from the bond that had sustained them since childhood. When Rabindrah arrived towards midnight he followed the sounds of celebration into the dining room, and found them sitting around the table with the remains of dinner and two bottles of champagne.

'Hello! What's the occasion?' he asked, surprised and delighted by the sight of Camilla in the house once more, decidedly tipsy and laughing.

'Come and join us,' Sarah said. 'We are drinking to the joys of reconciliation, and to the future.'

'*You* have been drinking?'

'Only two glasses.' She could not suppress a giggle. 'The others polished off the rest. I don't think either of them are very steady on their feet. They are both staying the night. God knows what effect the bubbles will have on Jorgen, but he might have his first hangover in the morning. Do you want some dinner? Chege is still around. I think he was keeping an eye on us. Where were you till now?'

'Writing an article about the latter stages of the war in Rhodesia. There have been rumours that the Rhodesian government has resorted to biological warfare – contaminating water sources with warfarin and infecting livestock with anthrax. Gordon might send me there to cover that.'

'Oh no,' Sarah said. 'It will be around the time when the baby is due. He can't send you away now, least of all to a contaminated area.'

'I can wriggle out of going down there for the time being,' he said, quick to placate her. 'I also had a drink with Johnson this evening, to talk about the latest foreign aid loan, supposedly to help small industry. But it seems that few people with a factory or workshop will ever see much of it. Anyway, I'm more than ready to forget all about it, and join your celebration.'

'Only happy topics are allowed tonight.' Camilla poured him a glass of champagne. 'To everlasting friendship. I love you all!'

*

Sarah stood with her arms outstretched as they came out of the customs hall, Raphael's smile lighting up the grey morning in spite of his obvious exhaustion after the long flight. Her mother made no effort to disguise tears of joy.

'Look at you,' Betty said. 'What a great day this is for us all. And you are blooming – just as you should be.'

'Including my swollen feet,' Sarah said. 'I'm ready. I'd rather carry this child around in my arms from now on. It's not very comfortable in here any more. I'll drive you home now, so you can rest after the flight. Then I'm going to Dr Roberts for my regular check-up. After that we will have time to talk. And talk, and talk.'

'Indeed we will, my little girl,' Raphael said. 'Indeed we will.'

'Sarah, we've run into a problem, I'm afraid.' Dr Roberts felt her abdomen again, probing gently, listening to the foetal heartbeat.

'What is it?' Sarah was immediately agitated. 'Is the baby in trouble?'

'Not at all. The difficulty is its position. Normally, in this last stage of pregnancy, your baby should be in the head-down position in the womb. But your child is what we call a breech. That means it is presenting the other way up, and would therefore be born feet first. Or bottom first, if you were to have a standard vaginal delivery.'

'Are you saying I won't be able to have a normal birth?'

'There are risks in breech births,' he said. 'The umbilical cord may be compressed during delivery, and that can cause nerve and brain damage due to lack of oxygen. I would prefer to deliver by Caesarean section. Of course, the procedure is more invasive for the mother—'

'That would be safer for the baby?'

'Yes. And in the light of your past history, it would be my advice. We can try to turn the baby around from outside the uterus, prior to birth. However, that may be difficult to manipulate if the placenta is low down. I want to do a scan, to check the exact position.'

'Is a Caesarean the only option now?' Sarah tried to slow down her racing mind, to ask a logical question.

'All breech births present some risk, including the possibility of the baby being trapped in the birth canal and suffering spinal damage.' The obstetrician pressed her hand encouragingly. 'I know you are disappointed that this first delivery may not be a natural process, but a healthy child is the only issue of real importance.'

'Yes. Yes, of course it is.' She wanted to cry, needed Rabindrah to hold her.

'I'll organise your ultrasound now, and we can book you into the hospital this afternoon for the rotation.'

'I have to be admitted for that?'

'I think that might be wise. You are close to term, and sometimes the procedure can trigger labour, or cause bleeding that puts the baby in distress. In that case we would have to be ready to perform the section immediately. Is Rabindrah here with you?'

Sarah shook her head, unable to speak, fear rippling through her.

'Have you any idea where you can contact him?'

'He said he would be out of the office for most of the day. I don't know where I could find him.' Lying on the examination couch, her body tense, she moved her hands slowly over her abdomen in an attempt to reassure her child. Tears spilled unbidden from the corners of her eyes.

'My dear, you and your baby are going to be perfectly safe.' Dr Roberts tried to ease her distress. 'There is no need to be afraid, but perhaps you would like to telephone a friend who could help you collect your personal things and bring you back to the hospital. Have Raphael and Betty arrived? Good. You have a great support team.'

'Yes, I do.' She waited while his secretary dialled Camilla's number.

'If you don't need me to drive you, I'll go straight to your house now,' Camilla said. 'Tell Raphael and Betty what has happened and pack everything you need. We'll be ready when you get here. And I'll ask Gordon to try and locate Rabindrah. Don't worry. You'll be all right. Both of you. All three of you.'

The ultrasound confirmed that the baby was in the complete breech position. Unless it could be turned successfully, a Caesarean section was essential.

'So I won't be awake during the birth?' She had come so far, and she had wanted above all else to see her baby as it came into the world, to hold it against her body and speak the first words of love and welcome.

'You will, within a half hour.' Dr Roberts smiled his encouragement. 'And Rabindrah will be there to see his child in its first moments of life.'

*

Camilla was waiting on the verandah and they embraced soundlessly.

'I suppose you can't have anything to eat?' she said. 'I thought not. We haven't found Rabindrah yet, but Gordon will send him to the hospital as soon as he tracks him down.'

'Dad?' Sarah stepped into the sitting room. 'The baby is a breech. Dr Roberts is going to try and turn it.' Her apprehension resonated through the room. 'Otherwise it will be a Caesarean.'

She stopped, and Betty came to hold her. In the silence, Raphael could hear his daughter's ragged breathing as she faced yet another crisis in her journey towards motherhood.

'Cliff Roberts is right, darling,' he said. 'I'm sure he has explained why this is necessary, and he is very experienced. I've known him for years. You couldn't be in better hands.'

'He keeps saying there's nothing to worry about, but I can't help it. I've waited and hoped for so long. If anything happens to this baby now . . .'

'What will happen is that you will have a perfect, healthy child, born safely,' Betty said. 'You might be groggy for a few hours, and sore for a day or two, but that won't count for anything. It's the joy of the new arrival that you must concentrate on.'

'Women have Caesarean sections all the time,' Raphael said. 'The baby is in good shape otherwise?'

'That's what Dr Roberts says. But Dad . . .'

'Tell me.'

'I'm scared. I'm falling apart here.'

'Don't be. Keep practising your breathing exercises as we drive to the hospital. It will help you to relax. And Rabindrah is sure to turn up any minute. It's going to be all right. Trust me.'

'Let's get going.' Camilla glanced at her watch. 'Your appointment is in half an hour. Look, I've put the baby's clothes in your bag. Oh God, Sarah, this is it! The arrival of the most wanted child on earth. I think I'm going to cry. By the way, Hannah is on her way down. If you are going to have this baby right away, we all want to be there.'

From her hospital bed Sarah could hear the murmur of voices in the corridor, as Raphael and Betty talked with Dr Roberts. Camilla pulled up a chair and sat beside her, holding one of her hands.

'What about when the baby is born,' Sarah said, her voice almost a whisper. 'I mean, if it's Hugo's child. If it looks like him and I'm still under the anaesthetic. Unconscious. What will Rabindrah do? Oh, God, Camilla, maybe I should tell him. But it's a terrifying idea. He could decide that he doesn't want it. Doesn't want either of us. He could walk away and there would be no one to welcome my child. No one!'

'Sarah, this baby is either going to be dark-skinned or light-skinned. If it is light-skinned then it takes after you. Suniva looked like Hannah from birth, but there is no real way to tell which parent a newborn baby resembles. It's just a squalling, snuffling little creature with its face all scrunched up and its eyes mostly closed. And they change every day. Rabindrah loves you and he will love this baby. And whatever happens, you won't be alone. We are here for you. Your parents and Hannah and me. So try and rest.'

Waiting for a decision on rotation, Sarah drifted into an uneasy sleep until a sharp pain woke her, making her cry out. Camilla was sitting beside her, reading. She looked up, concerned.

'What is it? Should I call somebody?'

'It was a twinge, that's all. Has Rabindrah phoned?'

'Gordon hasn't heard from him yet, but he is bound to check into the office soon. Raphael and Betty are down the hall, dozing in the waiting room. And Hannah has arrived. Do you want to see them?'

'No.' Sarah shook her head. 'I have to tell him, Camilla.'

'I wouldn't advise it. You're not thinking straight. Remember what the priest said.'

'I actually don't feel very well.' Another stab of pain hit her. The colour drained from her face and beads of sweat stood out on her forehead. 'I think I need to get to the bathroom,' she said, as the ceiling began to spin.

Camilla rang the bell and the room filled with sounds of loving encouragement. Dr Roberts appeared and smiled down at her.

'Looks like this baby has decided to make a move, rather than be pushed,' he said. 'The nurse is going to give you a little pre-med prick now. After that you will be on your way to the theatre.'

'Rabindrah. I need Rabindrah.'

'He is on his way. Gordon just phoned.' Hannah's smile shone like a beacon in the mist of Sarah's uncertainties. 'He'll be here in plenty of time.'

She barely felt the injection as another pain hit her like a sledgehammer.

She was lifted onto a trolley and doors opened and closed as she rolled down the corridor. In the theatre there were bright lights, and a smell of disinfectant, and she was surrounded by nurses in green gowns and masks.

'The placenta has torn, Sarah.' Dr Roberts was waiting for her. 'We are taking you in straight away, to prevent further bleeding and to deliver the baby safely.'

'Oh, God. Rabindrah . . .'

The anaesthetist had materialised and was checking her blood pressure. 'Don't worry, now,' he said. 'We will look after the two of you.'

'I need to speak to my husband. Please.' Her speech was coming out slurred, but somehow she had to make them understand. She had to stop everything, wait for Rabindrah. Why would nobody listen? The anaesthetist was smiling at her, making soothing noises. Lifting the syringe.

Then the door thundered open and she saw Rabindrah, wild, dishevelled, breathless, as though he had been running. Sarah clutched at his arm, desperate to speak.

'Don't be afraid, darling. I'm here now. I'll be near you all the time, and our baby will be with us soon. Don't cry, sweetheart. Relax. Relax . . .'

She felt the pinprick, and in the swirl and buzz the world flew away into the dark.

Someone was calling her name, insistent, the sound coming through the mist. She could see a light moving closer and she made an effort to open her eyes. In the blur above her, a face hovered and she concentrated on bringing the features into focus.

'She's waking up!' Rabindrah touched her cheek. 'Sarah? Can you hear me?'

Behind him, she could make out movement. Camilla and Hannah, smiling down at her. Her father and mother, beaming. And Rabindrah was turning to a nurse, taking something from her, leaning down.

'We have a daughter, darling. Look! The most beautiful child you ever saw.'

He laid the tiny creature beside her and the people she loved moved forward, to look, to kiss her gently, to murmur congratulations.

'She is the image of Rabindrah.' Camilla was smiling as she emphasised her message, and Hannah squeezed her hand.

'Well done, darling girl.' Tears were streaming down Raphael's face as Betty held her granddaughter for the first time. 'Well done.'

Then they were gone and Sarah lay with the child in her arms, flooded with joy and relief and thanksgiving as she examined the marvel of life she had brought forth. Olive skin, a shock of black hair, and as the baby stirred and woke, almond eyes that regarded her solemnly. They gazed at one another, enthralled. Rabindrah stood, looking down at his wife and daughter, brushing the strands of hair from her forehead, tracing the child's perfection with his finger.

'I love you, Rabindrah.'

So soft, he almost missed it. He leaned down to smother her with kisses, and to weep for joy at the gift of a miracle.

Chapter 34

Kenya, December 1983

The first year of university had been difficult for James. The faculty of Agricultural and Veterinary Sciences was located at Kabete, a Kikuyu farming area outside Nairobi. Many of the young men and women in his year had studied together since they were children. His unusual background made him lonely and aloof. He spent long hours reading in the library, a dusty place where the scrape of chairs and voices from the campus outside were the only sounds that broke the monotony. At night he lay in bed and thought about Suniva who was far away. He wrote to her often and her replies came regularly, describing life at school in Ireland and her own feeling of isolation. It was a place he could not imagine, and each letter made him more conscious of the distance between them. During his first days at the college the other students in his year had been curious, asking him questions about where he came from. Questions that proved difficult to answer.

'I live on a farm,' he had said. 'Near Nanyuki.'

'Does your family own the farm? How many acres?' A light-skinned girl from the Wakamba country moved closer to him in the dining hall. She leaned sideways, her smile inviting as she placed her elbows on the wooden table and hunched her shoulders forward, offering a clear view down the front of her dress.

'They are not my family,' James said. 'My parents died when I was young, and these people brought me up. On their farm.'

'Will you take me there?' The girl blinked dark eyes with curling lashes and giggled. 'My name is Katilo. My father has a good *shamba*, but I have managed to escape from it, although he still thinks it is a waste of money for a girl to be studying. And my mother grumbles because I am no longer at home to help her.'

'What is the name of the clan that brought you up?' Kimani was a year older than James. He was poorly dressed and prone to taking the bus from Kabete to the city, where he spent all night drinking beer and cheap, raw liquor from the bars in River Road. He had already made numerous snide comments on James's good clothes and the fact that he had a leather briefcase in which to carry his books and papers. When he had asked for a loan of one thousand shillings James turned him down politely, and had suffered constant slights as a consequence.

'Olsen. Their family name is Olsen.' He knew instantly that his answer would cause further problems, and silence descended on the table as everyone absorbed this revelation.

'If your mother was doing *jigi-jig* with the big bwana, how come your skin is so black?' Kimani had asked, causing raucous laughter.

James stood up, cleared his place and walked away before anyone pressed him for further explanations. After that incident he said that his mother had worked for a *wazungu* family who had taken care of his schooling after she died. Any other enquiries were deflected, and soon his peers left him alone, or made jokes at his expense when he ignored their questions and taunts.

Before he left Langani for his first term away, Hannah and Lars had given him money for clothes, and an allowance in addition to his fees and board, but he spent little and did not join in many of the activities enjoyed by the other students. Instead, at weekends, he made his way to Karen where he earned some additional pocket money working at Anthony's go-down. He enjoyed staying in the Chapman house where Camilla's tow-haired children ran wild in the large garden. He taught four-year-old Jack to ride his bicycle, and built a small go-cart for Annabel so that he could pull the toddler around the lawn and hear her shrieking with excitement as the dogs raced along in a frenzy beside them. At other times he returned to Langani to help on the farm and to be near to his memories of Suniva. These days it was Mike Stead who was often in charge of the day-to-day running of the place. It was four years since Lars's sister had divorced her husband, and she now owned the Olsen property in Norway where she lived with their old mother. This had enabled Hannah and Lars to join Anthony in the purchase of several acres on the beach at Msambweni, and the two families had built adjacent houses overlooking the sea, close to where Piet had started on his way to recovery.

'We will be going to Msambweni for Easter and you must come, James.' Piet's grin was lopsided and his speech still slurred, but his boundless enthusiasm for the coast had not diminished and he was constantly begging Hannah to take him back there.

'James has to study harder these days and he has agreed to work for Anthony for part of the Easter break,' Hannah said. 'Not everyone has a chance to go to the university, and he also needs the experience that your pa and Mike give him here at the farm.'

'It's better at Msambweni when he is with us. And Suniva, too.' Piet's disappointment was obvious.

'Of course it is. And next year we will have more time there, together. But you won't be so popular if you overturn Saidi's boat again.'

Hannah had placed her hand on her son's cheek and was laughing as she spoke, but she did not turn to include James in her response. She looked at him differently now, her expression strange and almost sad, but tinged with another emotion that remained a mystery. After a while James assumed that his love for Suniva was behind the change in her, and he shrugged off any hurt, knowing that those feelings were beautiful beyond censure.

Suniva. Her artistic ability was outstanding, and her teacher in Nairobi had urged Lars and Hannah to send her away for the last two years of schooling. Somewhere that would give her a chance of obtaining a place in a leading art college. It was Sarah who had suggested St Columba's outside Dublin, thinking that her parents' home in Sligo would be a good place for weekend exeats and half-term, and during the short Easter break. Sometimes, at night, James tortured himself with the idea that she would find someone to love, amongst the talented and affluent white boys with whom she studied every day.

Before she left for Ireland they had gone together to their place in the forest. He had turned it into a sturdy hut during the previous year, and Suniva had brought a low table and chairs, and an old divan that she covered with rugs and cushions. On their last day together James had kissed her soft mouth, and she had urged him to touch her breasts with the rose-coloured nipples, and to slide his hands down her stomach and inside her jeans where she was hot and moist. They lay close, each of them feeling the other's breath on their skin, kissing and stroking and whispering until he could bear it no longer.

'Let's do it now,' she whispered. 'You are already inside my soul, and I am in yours. Let's be a whole part of each other. Please.'

'No, Suniva. Not now.' His body was on fire, his heart thumping wildly and about to burst from his ribcage, but he felt that it was not right for her. 'I want to love you that way, but not now. Today is not the time, but it will not be long until the right moment comes. If you wait for me.'

'I will wait,' she said. 'I love you, James.'

'I love you, Suniva.'

He would never forget the smell and taste of her on that afternoon, her blue eyes and the wings of her brows, his fingers tangled in the gold of her hair. They had sworn their love for each other, and he had felt raw from wanting her. When she had gone, he hid himself away in the forest every day and tried to hold on to the last vestiges of the times they had shared there.

To begin with he had blamed Sarah for sending Suniva to such a distant place. But the Singhs had proved to be his salvation on many occasions during the first year in Kabete. When he felt particularly lonely he would go to stay with them, soaking up Rabindrah's tales of skulduggery in high places, helping Sarah in her darkroom, and playing games with Maya in the garden. Sarah understood his sense of alienation, describing to him the way she herself had felt when she first went to university in Dublin.

'It was cold and wet and dreary,' she said. 'Everything was grey. Like you, I didn't know anyone. I shared a pokey little flat with my brother, Tim. I thought it would be fun, but medical students are hopeless. He used to come in from his shifts exhausted, fling something on a frying pan that he left in the sink for me to wash, and then fall into bed. I imagined meeting the junior doctors who were his friends, but they were only interested in pubs and beer, and chasing nurses who were far more accommodating and less innocent than I was.'

'How did you survive?'

'I volunteered at a centre for homeless people,' she said. 'Drunks and drug addicts, and people who had fallen on hard times. There were some wonderful characters among them. Poets and dancers, and a former concert pianist. We fed them and gave them hot water and clean beds, and tried to keep them off the booze and away from whatever demons possessed them. That's when I started taking photographs. I won a competition with a series of portraits I made of those brave, ruined lives.'

'And then you came back here and joined the elephant study?'

'Yes,' she said. 'My parents were not at all pleased. Although I had my degree, they thought I should go on and get a Master's. Stay in Ireland. But all I wanted was to come home. To be in Kenya.' She paused, her head on one side, her smile sad. 'To be near Piet.'

James had never heard her talk like this before, perhaps because she had considered him as a child. Now she was speaking to him as an equal, and he was proud of it.

'Those were beautiful days,' she said. 'Being with Dan and Allie and Erope in Buffalo Springs, watching those great wise creatures and learning to understand their family structures. Then Piet was killed, and I wanted to die too, rather than to go on living without him. I was lucky, though. Lucky to have wonderful friends, and finally to meet Rabindrah.' She placed a hand on his cheek. 'Never give up,' she said. 'Suniva will be back soon, and she will be the same. In the meantime, you can come here whenever you like. Rabindrah is away so often, and both Maya and I enjoy your company.'

'Thank you,' he said, with humility. 'I work for Anthony on some weekends, at the go-down. And during the holidays I help in camp when he has a big safari. Also, Lars gives me jobs on the farm and at the lodge, and I like to spend as much time as I can with Piet.'

He tried to sound enthusiastic, but in truth all he wanted to do during his holidays was to be near Suniva. She did not return, however, for the first summer. Hannah and Lars decided to take Piet and Jorgen and travel to Italy, where Lottie had arranged for Suniva to do a course in the history of art and Renaissance painting. Her absence made a hollow in his heart, and although the flow of cards and letters continued, there were times when he was depressed by them. The images and words she used to describe her life and the art she had seen in Europe left him feeling inadequate and inferior, highlighting the changes between them, as he studied the basics of agriculture and the anatomy of cows. In the city library he took out books about painting and sculpture and studied them, memorising the names of the artists and the paintings that impressed him the most. But it was not the same as seeing the pictures or figures in their true setting, and he was disheartened by the fact that he might never have such an opportunity. It was Camilla who noticed him poring over a dog-eared book on Botticelli.

'I didn't know you were interested in art,' she said, and then laughed at herself for not guessing his reasons. 'I did a course in art history in Italy, when I was about Suniva's age. I have all my books and notes in a box somewhere, if you'd like to read them. They're not very scholarly, but I think my tutor helped me with some interesting observations.'

James took the package and at night when he had completed his university assignments he read each of Camilla's art books voraciously, until the painted figures blurred and danced before his tired eyes.

When Suniva arrived at Christmas he was awed by the vision that materialised out of the car. She was taller, her hair long and gleaming, her skin pale. The clothes she wore were different, and her shape had changed. The sight of her sent a jolt of desire through him and left him awkward and tongue-tied. He could not relate this new Suniva to the girl in torn dungarees who had raced him to their forest hideaway, built a fire to cook the trout they had caught with their bare hands, allowed him to kiss her sunburnt face.

On that first day he had remained in the background, as the family sat outside on the lawn and listened to her stories. His heart plummeted with the setting sun, still on fire but on the verge of extinction. Too shy to say more than a few words to her, he spent the early evening talking to Piet about the plants and flowers that had become his passion, and playing a board game with Jorgen. As Suniva moved past him, going in to dinner, he felt the pressure of her fingers and heard the whispered message. She would meet him at daybreak. In their special place.

He did not sleep, tossing in his bed, his body charged with longing and fearful anticipation. He left the compound in the dark and was waiting when she walked into the clearing, into his arms, so that he could feel her heart beating against him. They lay on a blanket he had brought, kissing, touching, murmuring, affirming their love for one another, the misery of separation, the rapturous joy of being together again. He did not ask for more than she offered and allowed, content to know that in spite of all the odds he had remained in her heart. From that morning they were inseparable once more.

Hannah watched helplessly, seeing each secret touch and silent message that flashed between them. The thing she had dreaded most was alive and growing, and she was powerless to stop it. She found it increasingly hard to look at James directly, to offer a gesture or a word of affection to the boy she had rescued and taken care of for most of his life. The boy who had now become a man, whose resemblance to his father caused a knot of fear to close her throat each time he appeared. The memory of Simon Githiri, buried for so many years, came back to haunt her.

'They are in love,' she said to Lars. 'She is almost eighteen years old and she has chosen James. It is my worst nightmare come true and I fear that he will bring a new kind of destruction into our lives. Just like his father did before him. It has to be stopped.'

'Hannah, I do not believe there is anything to fear from James.'

'Simon Githiri was a murderer.' Her statement was bald and held no hint of forgiveness.

'James is not his father. He is a responsible, serious young man and he has never given us cause for concern,' Lars said. 'He and Suniva have grown up side by side. If we try to prevent them being together now, it will only drive them closer. You know that. It is the same for all parents. They are young, Han, and each time she leaves, their paths and experiences will take them further from one another. It is inevitable.'

'You are wrong,' Hannah said. 'This will not go away.'

A week later Camilla arrived with the two children and their ayah, and later in the afternoon Anthony dropped his safari clients at the lodge and came to join them at the house.

'It's marvellous that we can do this,' Camilla said. 'We try each year to be together over Christmas and New Year, but it's the busiest time for Anthony. It was easier when there were just the two of us and I could join the camp, or bring our safari clients here to the lodge. But with Jack and Annabel that isn't possible. Do you remember last year, when Anthony had repeat clients for both Christmas and New Year, and they had no tolerance for children? We had to keep our distance, and I had to leave the Christmas tree up until the middle of January so that the children could share it with him.'

Jorgen and the two Chapman children had already disappeared into the garden with the ayah, and soon there was the sound of splashing in the swimming pool that had been built for Piet.

'Let's go down and join them,' Hannah said. 'It's beautiful out in the garden this afternoon.'

'Where is Suniva?' Camilla asked, lying in the grass, her head in Anthony's lap. 'She must be in seventh heaven, being home after all these months.'

'It's a disaster,' Hannah said. 'They are never out of each other's sight, and God only knows what they are doing when they are out of mine.'

'James?'

'In a word.' Hannah threw her hands in the air.

'He has turned into a fine young man,' Anthony said. 'Quick to learn. Soaks up everything like a sponge. I've been training him as a back-up safari guide and driver, each time he comes to one of the camps. He can spot a leopard as well as any tracker, and our clients love him because he is charming and highly intelligent. He will be an asset at the lodge, one of these days. And his agricultural degree will make him indispensable to Lars, if he wants to remain at Langani after his studies.'

'But I don't want him to become indispensable to my daughter,' Hannah said. 'I can accept most things, but not that. I know it sounds all wrong and I somehow never expected this, but he is the image of Simon and I find that distressing to deal with.'

'There is a strong physical likeness that has stopped me in my tracks a couple of times, and Sarah has found it unnerving too,' Camilla said. 'But I don't believe James has a bad bone in his body. Besides, Suniva is going to meet such diverse people over the next few years, especially at art school. I don't think James stands a chance in the long run. These are probably the last, bittersweet days of a childhood romance.'

'Lars doesn't seem bothered by it either.' Hannah sighed. 'But you haven't seen them yet, and you may eat your words when they appear. There is only one thing I know about this situation, and that is the absolute necessity to put an end to it.'

'You can't,' Anthony said. 'Opposition never works.'

'You are right, darling, Try to stay calm, Han.' Camilla was firm. 'Suniva is only here for another ten days, and then they won't see each other again until next summer. It's a long time, when you are seventeen.'

'What's the news from Sarah?' Hannah was too disheartened to pursue the subject of her daughter. 'She wasn't sure that Rabindrah would be around for the holidays.'

'He is here, fortunately, and they are spending Christmas and New Year in Tsavo,' Camilla said. 'In Allie's camp. She is completely absorbed in her lion project, man-eating or not. She has become so famous now, largely as a result of Sarah and Rabindrah's books. With steady funding and a stream of young zoologists competing for the chance to work with her. She is secure and happy.'

'Rabindrah himself has turned into a major force in journalism,' Anthony said. 'Starting with his articles on the Garissa Massacre three years ago, and then the book on corruption in independent African countries, he has become an international figure,' Anthony said. 'He seems to be spending as much time outside Kenya as in the country these days.'

'I know Sarah gets lonely sometimes,' Hannah said. 'Still, she has Maya, the light of her life. Fortunately she has been sensible enough not to spoil her, or build her existence around the child. It's a pity they didn't have one more.'

'Her books are deeply rewarding for her,' Camilla said. 'And I think this latest one on the migration is the best of all. She worries constantly about Rabindrah, though. Fears that he will become a target, because of his work. Look at the security system they have had to install at the house in Gigiri. Walls topped with barbed wire and shards of glass, and *askaris* at the gate, day and night. Still, when all is said and done, she has the one thing she wanted most.'

'She is almost as lucky as me, then.' Anthony kissed his wife and then rose to his feet. 'I'm going up to the lodge with these scallywags you call children. Jorgen, too, if that's all right. They are pretty good at being quiet, when there are animals around. I'll be back in about an hour.'

'What about Hugo?' Hannah asked, when Anthony had gone. 'He's not likely to turn up in Tsavo over Christmas?'

'No. He won't be visiting again until the summer,' Camilla said. 'Allie always tells Sarah when he is coming, and then there is a photographic trip or a lecture tour, or a safari with Rabindrah and Maya. Last summer they went to New Guinea to see her brother, and her photographs will probably be the subject of her next book. Tim's contract in Madang is almost over, and she is hoping that he might try for a job here. He has learned to fly, and he's particularly interested in the Flying Doctor Service. It would be wonderful for her if Tim found something in Kenya.' She trailed a tentative foot in the swimming pool and immediately retreated from the chilly water. 'Still, they are bound to run into each other one day, Sarah and Hugo. I don't suppose it would matter after all this time, but so far it hasn't happened.'

'When I think back to what we have seen and shared over the years.' Hannah burst into laughter. 'And we have survived it all. Look how well Piet is doing, with his love of plants and gardens and his ability to make anything grow. And who would have thought that Jorgen, who could fit into the palm of Lars's hand when he was born, would turn into a boisterous young whippersnapper with legs as long as a giraffe. And your two are *lekker* little people.'

'Always fighting and scrapping, although they defend each other fiercely from any outsider. Especially parents,' Camilla said. 'They say the "terrible twos" are the worst, but three- and five-year-olds seem to be infinitely more demanding. I have a strict rule that there will be no arguments between them until after nine o'clock in the morning, when they are at kindergarten, and I have left for my studio or one of the shops.' Her words and laughter were filled with a sense of peace. 'I don't know how I have deserved such happiness, but I am so deeply grateful for every hour of it.'

'I wonder how they will all turn out,' Hannah said, smiling. 'And whether they will create as much mayhem as we did in our time.'

When the last day came and Suniva's clothes were packed, she stole out of the house before dawn. James was waiting around the curve in the driveway, the engine of the old truck idling. She jumped into the cab beside him and they headed for the ridge. When they had climbed the path, they stood beside the cairn, watching the sun rise.

'I don't want to leave you,' she said, leaning her back against him as he placed his hands around her waist. 'I don't want to leave Langani either. I can paint and draw here, without years of lessons in faraway places.'

'Last year I was afraid you would forget me,' James said.

'Don't ever say that!' She swung around to face him. 'We belong to each other. Nothing will ever change that. We must never allow it to be changed. And although I am not supposed to be coming back for Easter, I am going to try and persuade them. I will find a way.'

'Look at the farm,' James said. 'You cannot see it like this from any-where else. It is more beautiful than all the paintings I have ever seen.'

'That is why Ma comes here,' Suniva said. 'To be near her brother. Come and sit on the stone seat at the edge. It is the place where he used to dream of the things he would do here. But Ma and Pa have done them instead so she climbs up here to tell him, and to talk to him when she has troubles.'

'Do you talk to him?'

'I never knew him when he was alive, but yes, I do talk to him,' Suniva said. 'Ma and Sarah say that he watches over us, and the farm, and we are going to talk to him now. Ask him to help us keep our love alive and strong, so that nothing can ever destroy it. Because I will always love you, James.' She picked up a small stone from the cairn and pressed it against his heart before he placed it in his shirt pocket.

'And I will love you, to the end of my days,' he said.

Chapter 35

'Daddy, do you like my shoes?' Maya skipped in front of him, demanding his attention, blocking his way to the study.

'Amazing,' Rabindrah said, his eye following her small, stick-like legs downwards to the clumpy footwear in green and pink leather with purple laces. 'Rather bright, though. Where did your mother find those?'

'Camilla brought them from London,' she said. 'They are the thing to wear now. Annabel has some too, but mine have more colours. I got them today, and I'm never going to take them off.'

'Potentially smelly,' he said, lifting her up and swinging her into the air, hugging her until she was breathless and squirming in his arms. He had to keep her innocent and carefree and safe for as long as possible. Never seeing the things he had seen. She was so perfect, with her large, almond-shaped eyes and black hair and full mouth. Fiery, too. Inherited from Sarah. And now turning into a fashion expert at less than six years old. 'Where is Mummy?'

'In the darkroom. I painted loads of pictures for you, while you were away. Do you want to see them?'

'I'd love to see them. And your homework, too.'

'You're back!' Sarah had heard the clink of his car keys in the bowl she kept on the hall table. 'I thought you weren't coming until tomorrow. This is great.'

'It's Jack's birthday tomorrow. Camilla is taking a picnic to the Ngong Hills and we are all invited for the day,' Maya said. 'Will you come, Daddy? In your car, with the hood down?'

'I will,' he said. 'If you show me your homework.'

She laughed and ran off to her room, and he reached for Sarah, her touch eradicating the pressure of travel and distance, and foreign hotels where he had spent too long at the bar with his fellow reporters, or lain in bed and watched television programmes in which he had no interest.

'Tell me about Ethiopia.' She scanned his tired face and looked forward to the quiet days ahead. He had been away for more than a week and although she was accustomed to his absences and she kept herself busy, instinct told her that this assignment had been different.

'A human catastrophe waiting to happen.' Rabindrah's voice was infinitely sad. 'A famine that will kill hundreds of thousands, but no one cares. I have seen children with normal size heads and bodies so thin and tiny that they look like aliens. Their little bones are poking through their skin, their faces are swarming with flies, crawling over hopeless eyes, open but not seeing. Children lying in their mother's arms, too lethargic to cry, dying of hunger. The Ethiopian government has spent most of its money beefing up its military budget, while the people they are supposed to be protecting are dying of starvation. Whatever I write now, it is already too late.' He threw himself onto the sofa and Sarah settled herself beside him. 'Sometimes I think I am burnt out, Sarah. That we should move on, bring up Maya away from all this poverty and violence that is growing around us like a devouring illness.'

'You always cover the worst stories,' she said. 'There are some good things happening here. All over Africa.'

He shook his head. 'Dark,' he said. 'What I have seen lately is the heart of darkness. No different from Conrad's vision.'

'There is progress,' Sarah insisted. 'It will take several generations for people to understand how to govern themselves better, and to prevent what is theirs from being stolen through corruption and greed. But there is hope. Education will do it eventually, even if it's slow. If you really feel you are burnt out, why don't you take a break. Let's do another book. Something that will restore your faith in the beautiful things around us.'

'That would take major inspiration,' he said.

'I have this idea about boats.' Sarah tried to illustrate her enthusiasm, to bring him out of his gloomy mood. 'A book on dhows and *ngalawas* and fishing boats. How those beautiful shapes came into being, the way they are built without drawings through knowledge handed down, generation to generation. The symbols carved on them, the shape and material of the sails, where they go, what they carry. We could start researching next week, when we go to Msambweni to join Hannah and Lars. I'm looking forward to our time down there, and Maya is thrilled to be staying with Camilla and her two rascals. What do you think?'

'I think you are the optimist I need, to keep me sane,' he said, smiling at last. 'But you need to make the dosage stronger.'

The call came in as they dressed for dinner. Sarah could hear the whine and static on the line.

'Someone out in the *bundu*,' she said. 'Asking for you. Can I say you're not here?' She was delighted when he nodded, putting a finger to his lips.

'Rabindrah is away,' she said. 'Can you try again tomorrow?'

'Mrs Singh?' The voice sounded Italian. 'I met your husband in Garissa four years ago. After the massacre at Bulla Karatasi. I need to speak to him as soon as possible. My name is Annalena Tonelli.'

Sarah recoiled at the memory of the barbaric incident when a village on the Tana River had been raided, in revenge for the killing of six government officials. The area was mainly inhabited by nomadic pastoralists of Somali origin who roamed the land with their herds of camels, cattle, sheep and goats, in search of grazing and water. In the years following Independence no attempt had been made to integrate them, or to provide the region with health or education services. Local security forces held unrestricted powers to imprison people and confiscate their property, and their power was accompanied by gross abuse of human rights. The inhabitants of Bulla Karatasi had been accused of harbouring Somali bandits. Rape, beatings and shooting had ended with hundreds of people being dumped into mass graves or thrown into the river. The government had denied any involvement, and promises of an investigation had come to nothing.

Standing close to the telephone, Rabindrah heard the name and remembered Annalena vividly. A diminutive Italian lawyer, she had worked for years to bring health and education to the forgotten people of the arid, sparsely populated district of Wajir. He had written several articles bringing international attention to her efforts, and now he took the receiver from Sarah's hands.

'Annalena. I've just returned from Ethiopia. What can I do for you?'

'Things are bad in Wajir,' she said. 'The government has cut off water supplies to the Degodiya people, and taken away their men. As prisoners. The excuse is fighting between the Somali clans. The security forces are saying they will only be released when they give up all their weapons.'

'How many Degodiya are being held? There isn't much room in the jail at Wajir.'

'About five thousand have been rounded up and taken to the airstrip at Wagalla, four or five miles from here.' Annalena faded for a moment as the radio hissed and then exploded into life once more. '*Wananchi*, businessmen, religious leaders, even government employees. It is like Bulla Karatasi, but worse.'

'When did this begin?' Rabindrah knew it was going to be bad.

'Two days ago. No one is allowed near the airstrip, not even to bring medical supplies. I have heard that the men have been made to lie face down on the tarmac in the blistering sun. There are reports of torture and killing. A few people escaped, but most of them died in the desert. I have found one or two survivors, delirious and telling appalling stories. Can you get this into the international press? And is there any way you could send me medicine for those who escaped?'

'I'll need eyewitness reports,' Rabindrah said. 'I will be there tomorrow.'

A pall descended on his homecoming. Sarah did not ask whether he really needed to go, if he would be in danger, or when he might come back. It would have been useless to protest. Sometimes she thought he might have stayed at home more if they had managed to have another child. A son for whom he would have wanted to be a more constant presence, as father and guide. It was a question she had never dared to put to him, although once she had asked Maya whether she missed having a brother or sister.

'Like Jack or Jorgen? Ugh! Who needs one of those?' Her daughter had screwed up her face and stuck her finger in her nose, as an indication of her feeling about the two boys. 'Always finding worms or snakes, pulling my hair, or making fun of me. Anyway, Annabel is my sister. We don't need anyone else.'

Rabindrah left before sunrise, having collected medical supplies from a list that Annalena had dictated over the radio. He took the Land Cruiser, filling the back with as many containers of water as he could carry, kissing his sleeping daughter and apologising to his wife. Sarah had long ago resigned herself to his absences, but this time a cold dread spread through her body and into her bones as he started the car. When she heard the gates closing she went into the sitting room and picked up a framed photograph of her husband, holding it against her heart.

'I wish you had stayed at home,' she said. 'You are needed here too.'

Arriving in Isiolo, Rabindrah spent an uncomfortable night in the run-down hotel as he made enquiries about reaching Wajir. A heavy military presence in the area indicated that something momentous was happening. In the morning he set out to find a policeman or an army officer to bribe. The hotel owner had told him the route was closed, that there were army checkpoints on all roads to the north.

'Many soldiers, no one let through,' he said. 'They shoot you. No *wazungu* or *wahindi* allowed there. Not even local people can pass.'

'Why? What are they doing?'

The man rolled his eyes. 'Wajir bad place now. Go home, sir. Much better.'

Outside the hotel, a young man in a threadbare shirt and a *kikoi* was sitting on the front fender of the Land Cruiser. He rose and walked towards Rabindrah, tall and painfully thin but graceful in his movements, with the high forehead and long neck of a Somali.

'I am Omar,' he said. 'You wish to go to Wajir? I have heard you saying this in the hotel.'

Rabindrah nodded, cautiously. If this was a police informant and they discovered he was a journalist, his journey would end in Isiolo.

'What you do there?' Omar was studying him.

'I want to visit a friend. To bring medical supplies.'

'What name this friend?'

'Annalena Tonelli,' Rabindrah said, after a second's hesitation.

'I know Mama Tonelli,' the young man said, reaching out to grasp Rabindrah's hand. 'Very good lady. Very holy lady. I take you to her.'

'The road is blocked.' Rabindrah shook his head. 'The army will not let us through.'

Omar made a sound of derision. 'We do not go on the road,' he said. 'I take you another way. The way of my clan.'

Rabindrah regarded him in silence, considering. This could be more dangerous than bribing his way though any army checkpoint. Driving into bandit country with an unknown Somali youth as a guide.

'Why do you want to go to Wajir?' he asked.

'I must find my family,' Omar said simply. 'All disappeared.'

There was an honest look to him, and he returned Rabindrah's scrutiny with a level gaze. It was crazy, but there was no other obvious way to get into the territory and Rabindrah motioned him into the vehicle. They left immediately, turning off into the bush before the first army checkpoint on the Mado Gashi road. The sun rose to its zenith as they juddered across sand and rock, following camel tracks used by Somali herdsmen through generations of wandering.

'I am Degodiya,' Omar said. 'They have forbidden us water and burnt our houses. The old people who could not move died inside. The army took my father and brothers away, and the women in my family have no home. No food or water. I work at the hospital, with Mama Tonelli, and when the soldiers came she hid me until dark and then she told me to run away. Only way to stay alive. But I must find my mother and sisters, and know what has happened to my clan. The government wishes to kill us all.'

They travelled through increasingly hostile terrain, arriving eventually at a place of brushwood shelters, set up in an area of half-cleared thorn scrub. Rabindrah stopped the car and got out. Hundreds of women and children huddled together in the stifling heat. Their clothes were scorched, and they stared at the ground, not speaking or looking at the car that had arrived. Omar moved among them, asking questions. Then he gave a shout of recognition as a woman and three young girls raised their arms to him, and began to weep. Through the blistering air, another figure was approaching, small, with a long cotton scarf tied about her head and thrown across her shoulders in the Somali tradition.

'Rabindrah! I knew you would get here somehow.' She drew near, raising her hand in greeting.

'Omar is a good guide,' Rabindrah said. 'Who are these people?'

'They are all Degodiya,' Annalena said. 'Their men have been taken away, their homes are destroyed, and they fear the soldiers will rape them and kill their children if they return to Wajir. International aid organisations are forbidden to enter the district, but I painted a red cross on the back and sides of my car and went looking for anyone who might have survived.'

'What about the men at Wagalla?'

'There are two here who escaped. One is beyond my help, but you can speak to the other.' She called Omar to accompany them.

Beneath the shade of a stunted thorn tree, Annalena had set up a medical tent. Two volunteers unloaded the medical supplies and stacked water containers that Rabindrah had brought. Inside the tent, a Degodiya tribesman lay on a blanket, face and hands beaten to pulp, his entire chest a raw, suppurating wound. His eyes were closed and his breath came in tearing sighs. Another man sat beside him, bearing the marks of torture, although the burns on his body were less serious.

'Lidan, this man is from the newspapers,' Annalena said. 'Tell him everything that has happened to your clan. Omar, you translate.' She sat on the ground beside her other patient, administering a dose of precious morphine to ease his passing.

'It was the army.' Lidan spoke with difficulty, his jaw swollen, gums bloody and toothless. 'They said we had killed some people of another clan. They put us in trucks, took away our identity papers, and brought us to the air strip at Wagalla. Many thousands of us, at gunpoint. Those who protested were shot. We were told to take off our clothes and lie with our faces to the ground. In the sun our skin stuck to the tarmac so that we were burned. They beat us with sticks and clubs. If we confessed and handed over the guns, we would go free, they said. They poured petrol on some men and burned them alive.'

Omar had begun to sob, but Lidan was determined to continue.

'There was no water.' Lidan's agonised delivery made the description even more horrifying as he began again. 'We drank our urine to stay alive. Some of us decided we would not lie down and let them kill us. We stood up together and ran to the fence. A few were able to climb over it but most were shot. We had to leave them hanging on the wires.' He was unable to continue and a trickle of tears crept from his closed eyes.

'I have been looking for more survivors, out in the desert.' Annalena stood up. 'I'm going out again now, Rabindrah. Will you come with me?'

They moved off slowly, searching the harsh landscape for signs of the living and finding only the dead. Men who had perished from hunger and thirst and dreadful wounds, lying where they had fallen, their sad remains summoning the scavengers of the bush. Near the airstrip, the stench was overpowering. Lorries were parked alongside the wire fence, on which many of the victims still hung. The tarmac was scattered with bodies, a pitiful few suffering the last hours of dehydration and fatal injury. The reek of death hung in the breathless air, making Rabindrah choke and gag as they approached the hellish scene. It was clear that orders had been received to release whatever prisoners were still alive, and to dispose of the remaining dead as quickly as possible. Under the direction of an officer, his uniform indicating superior rank, army personnel were lifting bodies and piling them onto trucks in a jumble of limbs. At the sight of the vehicle with the red cross, the soldiers became nervous and belligerent. The officer overseeing the detail strode over to Annalena's vehicle and stuck his gun into her face. He was not from any Somali clan.

'No one is allowed here,' he shouted. 'You are a spy! A spy! You will be shot!'

She turned to look him in the eye, his gun barrel trained to the middle of her forehead. Keeping her gaze on his face, her voice remained steady.

'You know me from Wajir,' she said. 'I am a woman of peace who takes care of all people. I have always given medicine to every man, woman or child in need, regardless of clan.'

His finger tightened on the trigger and Rabindrah knew that once he started firing, there would be no one left alive. Thoughts of Sarah and Maya rose in his mind, his terror coloured by the wrenching pangs of longing and regret. Then the man released his grip, and drew back from the open window.

'Go, Mama,' he said in a low voice. 'You have given my mother medicine some time ago, and it made her well. Go quickly.' Rabindrah barely heard the last words. 'And God go with you.'

They spent the rest of the day and most of the night driving in widening circles around the environs of the airfield, searching for survivors. The few they found were lifted with infinite care into the back of the vehicle, given water and kept as comfortable as possible until they could be treated. For two days they trawled the area, rescuing the living and burying the piles of dead that lay rotting on the scorching sand. There was no sign of Omar's male relatives, and Annalena encouraged him to take his mother and sisters and return with Rabindrah to Isiolo, to begin a new life.

Following nomadic tracks through the waterless terrain and dodging the rumble of army trucks and the danger of checkpoints, they reached the dusty sanctuary of Isiolo in the evening. As Rabindrah drove away he saw the young man take out a woven mat and place it on the ground, facing

Mecca and reciting a prayer to the God who had ordained the destruction of his family and clan.

'Every international paper has the story,' Sarah said. 'How can the government deny what happened at Wagalla? No one believes that they were trying to bring tribal fighting under control. That there were only a few dozen casualties.'

'These incidents are not going to end,' Rabindrah said. 'Violence is simmering all around us. I have been thinking more and more about Maya. I want her to grow up in a place that is not a ticking bomb of tribal animosity and corruption and ignorance. I cannot be an Annalena Tonelli, and I do not believe she will survive for long, in spite of the fact that her mission is to bring health and learning and peace. One of these days, someone like that soldier who threatened us will kill her. She will be a martyr, a headline for a time, but the butchery will go on. I want to see our daughter grow into a young woman in a safe environment. We should start thinking, Sarah. About where we might go.'

'He has been deeply affected by what he saw in Ethiopia and at Wagalla,' Sarah said as she sat with Hannah on the beach at Msambweni. 'I've never seen him like this. He has always held onto the belief that what he does can make a difference. Shine a light onto peoples' lives and alleviate some of their problems. Now he is hell-bent on leaving the country.'

'He will probably feel different after another day or two,' Hannah said. 'The coastal air cures everything in time. I'm so grateful that we built this house. It was mainly for Piet when we started, but I've found that I'm very happy coming down here with Lars, or just by myself. It is such a gentle, healing place. I'm sure it will lift Rabindrah's spirits. Make him less pessimistic. Anyway, where on earth would you go? This has been our home since we were children. Rabindrah too. You would find it hard to belong anywhere else.'

'I don't know.' Sarah was downcast. 'I only know I can't ignore such strong feelings in him.'

'I remember when Lars was riddled with guilt about leaving Kirsten alone on the farm in Norway. He became so depressed that at one moment I believed I would have to spend half my life there, in order to save our marriage.' Hannah looked back to the evening of Lars's lowest moment and felt cold inside. 'And then Ilse divorced that smug, ghastly husband and went home to the farm herself. It's perfect for her, and she saved us from making what would have been a very bad decision for everyone.'

'Here he comes,' Sarah said, as Rabindrah came down the path from the house to join them.

'No wonder you spend so much time here these days,' he said to Hannah. 'It's timeless and soft, with the ocean and the fishermen and the cleansing sight of an empty beach. Sarah is thinking about a book on boats.'

'Sounds like good material,' Hannah said. 'You haven't done a book together for some time. And you could stay here while you research it.'

'We'll see,' he said. 'I'll think about it for a while, and then we'll see.'

Chapter 36

Kenya, March 1985

'You are doing exceptionally well, here at Kabete.' The dean's praise was rarely forthcoming. 'I believe you should try for a scholarship, James. Cirencester College in England offers a degree course in environmental management and conservation that would suit you, and complement your present studies. If you come to my office later this afternoon, I'll help you to fill in the application forms.'

England. Not far from Suniva, in her Dublin school. James could hardly believe that fortune would smile on him so kindly. But it was the forms that dragged him back into the limbo of his origins.

'Your father's name?' The dean had his pen poised.

'Karuri.' James was immediately uncomfortable.

'First name?'

'I do not know. I was taken to an orphanage when I was very young. My parents were dead, and someone left me there. Then Mr and Mrs Olsen brought me to Langani. I do not have any other family that I know of.'

'Ah, yes.' The dean had heard similar stories before. Orphans were often unaware of the identity of the person or persons who had left them in an institution. Relatives frequently did not have the money to bring them up, or feed them, and were therefore reluctant to leave their names. It was, however, unusual for a white farming family to take in one of these children. 'Well, it doesn't matter, James. I am sure Mr Olsen can sign any other documents that might prove necessary.'

On the following weekend James took the bus to Nanyuki, and hitched a lift to the gates of Langani. It was a sweltering afternoon and drought had once again brought hardship and death. Cattle and goats wandered along the roadside, their protruding ribs and slow, plodding movements a symptom of hunger and thirst, as the herders drove them far from their normal territory in search of water and grazing. Spiky maize stalks rattled in the hot wind, their cobs withered away by the pitiless heat. Red dust devils spun across the cracked, dry soil, and on the farm the wheat crop had been reduced to half of its normal output. In the staff compound and at the main house, water was strictly rationed, and even at the lodge there were notices in the rooms asking the guests to use the precious commodity sparingly.

'It's good to have you home,' Lars said, looking at James with an expression that was oddly intense. 'You'll find Piet out in his vegetable garden, doing his best to keep the plants alive.'

He stood up and watched the retreating figure with a vague unease. James had certainly grown into a good-looking young man. Although Hannah had always celebrated his birthday on the date when he had arrived at Langani, they could not be sure of his exact age. Lars guessed that he must be about twenty-one, and his resemblance to his father had become unmistakable. It was a relief that Kamau and Mwangi had retired. They had both known Simon Githiri, but they had never been told of the relationship between Piet's killer and James, the orphan boy that Hannah had taken in. Only David knew the truth, and he had kept his promise never to divulge it.

James did not bring friends from the college to Langani, nor did he mention any of his peers except in passing. He was a loner, his tutors said. A dedicated and ambitious student who kept to himself and turned in carefully prepared work that was always on time. His only real friends were the siblings with whom he had grown up. Lars wondered whether James had a girlfriend. If he did, it would be a relief to Hannah who still feared the bond between her daughter and the boy whose hidden past she could never forget. However, the friendship between James and Piet was also deep and steadfast, and she understood its value.

Although he had made progress, Hannah refused to send Piet away to school. Instead, she had tutored him at Langani with the help of a teacher who came from the school in Nanyuki. Piet swam in the pool each day, even when the cold wind and leaden skies of July and August made the water too chilly for her own taste. His speech was sometimes indistinct, particularly when he was tired, and he still walked with a limp. The surgery that had eventually been performed on his damaged eardrums had been partially successful, and he could hear with the help of hearing aids. He had also mastered signing and could lipread, but his academic skills were slow and this had eroded his confidence. His true passion was for growing things. Everything Piet put into the ground burst into green shoots bearing flowers and seeds and fat, juicy fruit and vegetables that were used in the house and at the lodge. At the coast he had taken over a section of the garden behind the house and put it to the same use. Recently he had started to sell his home-grown produce to Anthony's safari company, and he hoped to expand his gardens so that he could offer the same service to other camps and hotels.

'What's up, man?' Piet held out a basket of vegetables for James's inspection, beaming with satisfaction. 'These are for dinner. You've never tasted anything so good. Pa shot an impala for roasting tonight. It's great that you are back for a few days. I'm done with the steady diet of Pa and Ma, and that little horror, Jorgen. It's a relief to have him at school every day, even if it is only for a few hours. Do you have any news of Suniva? I hardly ever hear a thing.'

'She has written a letter recently,' James said cautiously.

'Maybe she has other fish to fry, in that Irish school.' Piet laughed, unaware of the effect of his remark on James. 'Let's go to the Club in Nanyuki for an hour. Ma is there, playing tennis. She says she needs to lose weight, and she will sweat off a bucket of pounds in this heat. Ask Pa for the loan of the truck. He'll never refuse you anything.'

They spent the remainder of the afternoon in Nanyuki and on their way back to the farm they dropped Hannah off at the lodge.

'Pa can bring you up here later on,' she said. 'There are some interesting guests, and someone you know is coming in for the night. Oh, and ask him if he has told the *fundi* about the problem with the generator.'

But there was another question that James wanted to ask Lars, and when he had showered and changed his clothes, he knocked on the door of the office.

'I need to know about my family,' he said, aware of the change in Lars's expression. 'About what happened to my parents. The dean questioned me when I was filling in the forms for Cirencester, and I would like to have the answers. Not only for him, but for myself.'

'Your parents are dead, James.' Lars was gentle with his reply. 'We never discussed them with you, because you have always been part of our family. Ever since Hannah brought you here from Nyeri, when you were about two years old and a very bright little boy. You had a problem with one of your feet, so she took you to a doctor in Nairobi and had it put right.'

'What kind of problem?'

'You were born with something called a club foot, which means your right foot was twisted inwards.'

'Is that why my parents left me in that place?' James was well aware of the tribal superstitions often attached to deformities.

'No, that is not why you were in the orphanage,' Lars said, cursing himself for bringing up an unnecessary subject. 'In any case, a surgeon in Nairobi operated on you, and stretched the muscles over a period of time by using plaster casts. At night Hannah put a brace on the foot, and after a while you were able to walk normally. You were remarkably brave, but you probably don't recall any of that.'

'I think I remember the brace at night,' James said. 'But I would like to ask whether you knew my parents, and also how they died.'

'We never met them,' Lars said. He scratched his head and tried to sound vague. 'I think they were killed in a road accident. In a bus. You were a survivor, so you were taken to the orphanage until Hannah brought you here. We were lucky to have found you, James. You were always a good boy, and now you have turned into a fine young man. We are very proud of you.'

'Thank you,' James said, taken aback by the difference in Lars's answer, and the one that David had given him as a child. Which was the truth? He did not want to approach Hannah. He had tried to ask her a similar question some years ago when other boys in school had teased him about his lack of family. She had evaded the question, telling him that he should not think about what was past and impossible to recover. He had a bright future, she said, and that was all he needed. It was clear that no one at Langani had any real idea as to his origins, but now he wondered if he could approach Sarah on the subject. She might know why Hannah had selected him, an unknown Kikuyu child, from the orphanage. And if so, maybe she had some inkling as to what had really happened to his mother and father. If she knew anything, she would tell him. He had always trusted her.

'You have done well at Kabete from the beginning.' Lars interrupted his train of thought. 'When I went from my father's farm to the agricultural college it was hard for me, especially during the first year. But then I discovered beer and girls, and things became much brighter. Although I did less work.' He laughed and put his hand on James's shoulder. 'I hope you are accepted at Cirencester. Environment and conservation are two things that would be invaluable around here. It is a good course. Now let us find Piet, and we will drive up to the lodge.'

'It is the best place, up here,' James said, joining Hannah on the edge of the viewing platform.

'Yes, it's pretty special,' Hannah said. She turned to look at him, and her face contorted slightly as though she felt some kind of pain. 'Anthony has just arrived, by the way, with his clients. Why don't you go and say hello.'

'It is becoming harder to look at him,' she said to Lars, when James had moved away. 'Especially when I haven't seen him for a while.'

'I know. I noticed it this evening. And oddly enough he asked me about his parents. The dean had enquired about them when he was applying for Cirencester.'

'What did you say?' Hannah felt a deep disquiet.

'That they died in a bus accident.'

'That sounds plausible,' she said. 'There was a terrible crash on the Thika road only yesterday with twelve people killed, and more seriously injured. It's good you thought of that.'

'You are looking at the future of places like this,' Anthony said to his clients as he made introductions. 'James grew up at Langani and now he is studying agriculture at Nairobi University. Then he hopes to go on and learn conservation management at a college in England. An ideal way for all Kenyans to work together, and protect what you have seen during your safari days.'

They stood, talking quietly and surveying the procession of animals below them. There was more game than usual, since the surrounding territory was bone dry and the waterhole below the lodge was one of the few sources still viable. There had been complaints from subsistence farmers in the area. The white bwana had water that he was giving to elephants and buffalo and other *nyama*, they said, while their cattle and produce were dying from the drought. During the previous week Lars had been obliged to shoot a buffalo that had rampaged through the maize on an adjoining co-operative farm. The fallen beast had provided a good supply of meat for the family, but they needed water. Once again the herds were milling around the Langani boundaries, and people were stealing from the boreholes and what remained in the dam.

'I hear you spent a weekend with Camilla recently,' Anthony said, grinning at James. 'How were my *totos*? I think they are driving her mad, tearing around night and day when they are not caged up at school.'

James laughed. The children were as blond as their mother, and as wild and rugged as their father had always been. But it was a happy house to stay in, and he had been grateful for the invitation. Camilla had insisted on coming to Kabete to collect him, however, and the appearance of a white woman in a new Land Cruiser made for ribald comments as he climbed into the front seat beside her.

'I had a good time with them,' James said. 'We went riding in the Ngong Forest. We could hear a leopard and the horses were not happy. And we went to the cinema, to see *The Jungle Book*. Now Jack and Annabel are singing all the songs.'

'Piet will be coming to stay with us in a couple of weeks, so maybe you will join him,' Anthony said. 'I have a short break from safaris.'

'I'm sorry.' James looked for a way to turn down the invitation without causing offence. 'I have been invited by Sarah. She will be back from Ireland then.' He took a chance. 'She has seen Suniva, you know.'

'Ah! And Suniva will also be home for the summer, I assume.' Anthony could hear the powerful longing in James's statement. 'We will all be at the coast for August. Do you remember the first time we went? Just you and me with Piet and Otieno? That was when he began to grow strong again. We have all loved our times there since then.'

'It is a happy place,' James said, his eyes lighting up at the thought of Suniva swimming with him in the warm water, chasing their dreams along the edge of the waves. When he kissed her, she would taste of the sea as she kissed him back and put her arms around him. And perhaps more.

'I need to see young Piet for a minute, about the vegetables for our next safari. And to tell him I have a *rafiki* who wants to place an order, too.'

It was late in the evening by the time James located David with a moment to spare. He was standing at the back of the reception area, sorting and filing the chits and receipts of the day.

'Do you remember telling me about my parents?' James leaned on the desk, edgy and drumming his fingers on the polished surface. 'You said my father was robbed and killed in Nairobi, and my mother became very sick and died?'

'That was a long time ago.' David handed him a sheaf of papers. 'Here. Help me to sort these chits out, before Hannah comes to collect them.'

'Did you meet my mother?' James persisted. Something made him sure that David had seen her. 'Did she not come here, to the farm?'

'No. I can't remember. I don't think she ever came here. I'm not sure anymore.' David sounded flustered. 'It is a long time ago since they died. What is the point of knowing exactly when or how? You are alive and going to a university. Maybe even to England, I have heard. You have a good life before you. That is all you need to think about.'

'You have a good life, too,' James said, hearing the tinge of envy in David's remark.

'It is good, yes, but it will always be the same and it will always be here. I am married now and I have a wife and four children and a *shamba* to take care of. I was able to go to school, and Hannah helped with my training. I am better off than most. But my life will never change. And look at my father. Old Kamau retired from cooking, and now he sits outside his hut all day, and watches his wives till the few acres of land he has managed to buy. That is what he has, after forty years of service, and it is what he expected. But when *you* are my age, or as old as Kamau, you will be able to go anywhere, stand equal beside anyone. Remember that and forget the things that do not matter.'

'I need to drop Maya at Lavington,' Sarah said. 'She is spending the afternoon with a friend. And I'm going to the supermarket on the way home. I'm afraid Rabindrah won't be back until the day after tomorrow. Have a swim, James, when you've read the letters I brought. And later we will have tea and take the dogs for a walk, and I will tell you all about Ireland.' She smiled with mischief in her eyes. 'And Suniva.'

James spent a long time poring over Suniva's letters, and a selection of photographs that Sarah had taken. Suniva standing in front of some historic building, laughing into the camera. The long blonde hair had escaped from underneath a knitted hat and was blowing across her face, and her jacket collar and scarf were tucked up beneath her chin and her smiling, beautiful mouth. She looked happy, comfortable in this distant environment he could not share. He closed the envelope and put it into his pocket. For the next ten minutes he browsed the bookshelves, but he was unable to concentrate on anything and he roamed the verandah and the sitting room, hands in his pockets, impatient for the news that Sarah would bring. There was music playing on the radio, but he found it irritating and he reached out to turn down the volume. Above the stereo, the shelves were lined with old photograph albums and he took three of them down and began to leaf through the pages, reading the headings with interest. There were pictures of Sarah with her parents and brother, at the big house in Mombasa where she had grown up. Later in the book, she was standing on a quay beside a wide, grey river, surrounded by people whose faces were thin and haggard, and whose clothing was as threadbare as the beggars in Nairobi. This must be in Dublin where she had studied and looked after the poor. Dublin, where Suniva was. The next album featured Langani. There were pictures of Jan van der Beer, a tall, stocky man with a broad face and a leather hat. He was holding a rifle and there was a lion at his feet. On another page Lottie smiled into the camera, with Hannah and Camilla on either side of her, and her son Piet with his arm draped round her shoulders.

The last book contained a series of shots taken on safari, with Anthony and Camilla and Hannah looking like teenagers. Piet was in these pictures too, and there were outstanding images of leopard and elephant and buffalo, of Samburu *moran* and their women leaping and dancing in all their finery, and the wild magnificence of northern scenery, with the captions written in Sarah's steady hand, on each page. The final section showed the lodge under construction, and James studied it with interest, noticing the way in which the poles and the thatched roof and curved walls had been fastened to the existing rock to blend in with the environment.

When he turned the last page, he made a choking sound. Piet was standing in the centre of the picture, the sun highlighting his lithe body, his face filled with shining optimism. To his right was a *syce*, holding the reins of a horse. On the other side, a young man stared into the lens, his expression a little self-conscious, as though he did not feel comfortable being photographed. James gazed at his mirror image in disbelief. It was unmistakable. He calculated the years quickly and tried to slow his heartbeat and the rise of excitement rushing through him. He leaned closer to read the title. *Kipchoge, Piet and Simon.* Could this be his father? Had Sarah known him, and if so, why had she never told him, down through all the years of his childhood, or even since he had become an adult? Sarah, who had always seemed to be forthright and honest. He could ask her, but like everyone else she must be hiding some kind of truth. Perhaps he should search it out for himself. He took an army knife from his pocket, carefully easing the snapshot out of the album. Then he closed the book, put it neatly back in its place and left the house.

At the central bus depot James found a *matatu* to Nyeri. He bought a ticket and sat for hours in the overcrowded, swaying vehicle, arriving in the town late at night. Eventually he found a cheap hotel with a rickety bed and dirty sheets and paid a few shillings for the room. During the long hours before dawn he listened to the scuttle of cockroaches on the walls, and once he saw a rat scamper across the torn linoleum that covered part of the cement floor. In the morning he showered in ice cold water under a rusty spout, and ate a bowl of *ugali*, served with tea boiled in a large saucepan with milk and sugar. Then he set out for the Consolata Mission.

He was greeted at the door by one of the Italian priests who led him into a formal room where he sat down at a table surrounded by chairs with tall, straight backs.

'I am Father Guido,' the priest said. 'How can I help you? Do you need a job? Because I'm afraid we don't have—'

'I am not here about a job,' James said. 'I am here because I am looking for someone. You see, I have a friend whose father disappeared, and I know that the Mission takes in boys who have nowhere to go. Before he went away, this man left his son at an orphanage because his wife had died, and he had no money to feed the child. And now my friend would like to find his father. To understand what happened to him and why he was abandoned. So I am trying to help him.'

'I see.' Father Guido's smile was compassionate but he had lifted heavy brows in an unspoken question. 'Your friend is not here himself, however.'

'He is checking other places where orphans are taken in. We have divided them to make it faster.' James knew that the story did not sound right, that he was stumbling over the words.

'What is your friend's name?' Father Guido sat back in his chair, his fingers pressed into a steeple. 'Do you know approximately when he was left here?'

'James. His name was James Karuri. He is twenty-one years old now, and he believes that he was about two when his father went away. Later he was adopted by another family who took care of him, and sent him to school.'

'And does your friend know his father's name?'

'It was Simon. I have a photograph of him here.'

'Simon Karuri.' The priest looked down at the black and white print, clearly taken on a European farm. He could see the house in the background. And the striking resemblance to the young man making the enquiry was not lost on him.

'Even if there is documentation on Simon or James Karuri, I am not sure that I can release any information about him or his father. Particularly since you are not even a relative.' He rose to his feet. 'I will find out from the priest who keeps the records whether that is permissible. If you wait here, I will be back in a few minutes. May I ask your name?'

'Daniel.' James floundered and paused, trying to think of a family name. 'I am Daniel Waweru.'

When Father Guido returned he had an African clerk with him, carrying a stack of ledgers.

'These are the records of the boys who came to us over the last twenty-five years,' he said. 'You are welcome to look through them, but there is no one called James Karuri in the register. We have two boys with that family name, but both are younger than your friend and neither one is called James. I am sorry, but this is not the place you are looking for.'

'Thank you for your help.' James rose to his feet. 'Is there another orphanage in Nyeri?'

'Not for boys or young men.' Father Guido paused. 'But the nuns sometimes take in young women with babies they cannot look after, because of poverty or illness. You could try the convent.' He smiled and held up his hands to offer a blessing. 'I think that it would be better if you told them your real name. And who it is that you are really searching for.'

James muttered a few incomprehensible words and left the building, to make his way back to the town. At the convent the elderly nun he encountered was less forthcoming.

'Sister Maria Goretti.' She introduced herself and ushered him into a guest parlour dominated by a large statue of the Virgin Mary holding the Christ child, a bowl of roses at her feet. 'Please sit down. Father Guido telephoned and told me to expect you. I have been here for more than thirty years, so I can tell you the rules. When women bring their babies here, it is often to give them up for adoption. So I cannot disclose the names of those women to third parties, nor the identities of the people who brought those children up as their own.'

'I have not told the entire story.' James realised that half-truths would lead him nowhere. 'My name is Daniel Karuri and I am looking for my cousin. He is called James, but I do not know what family name he had. He is about twenty-one years old now, and I know that he was taken from an orphanage to live with a white family. He had a bad foot and these people brought him to doctors and fixed it.'

He knew at once that he had found his origins. The nun's face blanched and she looked at him with deep sadness.

'Why do you want to find this young man? And what could you bring to his life, if you discovered where he was?'

'He is a part of my family, and I would like to know him,' James said. 'My mother and father have a *shamba*, and they would also like to meet him. To let him know that he is welcome in our clan. Not alone in the world.'

Sister Maria Goretti came to sit beside James, her rosary beads clicking against her long skirt as she settled herself. 'Father Guido believes, as I do, that you have come to see us under false pretences,' she said sternly. 'We often receive visits from relatives who want to know where abandoned children were placed. Sometime it is a genuine desire to know one of their family or clan. But often it is because the child is now a grown man or woman who has been educated, and has a good job with a steady salary. Someone who could contribute to their financial situation. That is a sad fact, but true.' She watched James for a few seconds, recognising the turmoil in his mind. 'Would you like to tell me the real reason for your visit, and then perhaps I can help you.'

'I think I am James Karuri,' he said. 'And I have a right to know how I came to be placed in an orphanage, and what happened to my parents.'

'Do the Olsens know that you are here?'

'No.' James was astounded by the question.

'You do not live with them now? Have you had some disagreement?'

'I do not live there because I am studying at the University of Nairobi, in Kabete. I hope to go to England to complete my studies, and for this I need to know my father's real name.' James held out the photograph. 'I think the man called Simon was my father. I can see that I look like him.'

Sister Maria Goretti took the photograph in silence, and scrutinised it for a few moments before handing it back to James. 'I was here at that time. Your mother was very young and frightened when she arrived with Mr Olsen. She had been badly treated by an uncle with whom she lived. Beaten and starved. So she ran away, at great risk to herself. She walked all the way to Langani to find Lars Olsen and a friend of his, Sarah Mackay, whom she had met in the Kikuyu reserve where you were born. You needed medical treatment, and Miss Mackay had told your mother she could arrange it.'

'My foot. She knew about my foot.' James was mumbling to himself. 'She knew my mother. They all knew her.'

'Mr Olsen brought your mother and her child here, where she would be safe, and her uncle would not try to force her away or punish her. We were very fond of her and she was determined to make a better life for you. To have your foot healed so that you would walk normally. We baptised you here at the convent, and gave you the name of James.'

'Is she alive?' James whispered the words.

A silence opened out between them, punctuated at last by the nun's long sigh. She crossed herself before she spoke again.

'Unfortunately, your mother died soon after arriving here,' she said, turning to face the statue of the Virgin. 'That is when the Olsens decided to give you a home.' She stood up, abruptly. 'There is nothing more I can tell you. But it seems that your life has turned out well, and you have been more fortunate than most children in your position. You should give thanks to a merciful God, James, and to the Olsens who have taken care of you over the years. Prove your gratitude by doing well at your studies, and live the best life that you can. That is also the highest honour that you can offer to your mother for the love she gave you.'

'Is my father alive?' James had to know. 'And what was my mother's name?' He wanted to hear their names, more than he had ever wanted to hear anything in his life.

'Your mother came here alone. Your father had left her, and then he died. She gave her name as Wanjiru Githiri. That is all I can tell you. I should not have given you this information at all. However, you seem like a sensible young man, and it would seem wrong not to let you know that your mother was an exceptionally brave and loving young woman.' The nun took James's hands in hers. 'Goodbye, James. May God go with you.'

She opened the door and stood there as he walked away. Then she went to the chapel to ask forgiveness for her sin of omission. For the tragic facts that she had not told him. And she prayed that he would find a sense of peace in what he now knew, and close the chapter of his origins before it was too late.

Githiri. His parents were called Simon and Wanjiru Githiri. Yet he had been given the name Karuri after Esther, the ayah who had looked after him. He had always assumed she was a distant relative. Now he wondered whether she had ever known Simon and Wanjiru. His thoughts were in an uproar. He sat in the bus, barely noticing the exhaust fumes and the potholes on the road, as the ancient vehicle lurched towards Nanyuki.

Since her retirement Esther had lived on a small *shamba* outside of the town. He asked the way to her house and then began to walk along a rough trail, the dry, red soil rising with his every step to cling to his clothes and to the already dusty bushes on either side of the track. The huts were perched on the edge of a hillside, tucked in between vegetable patches and occasional stands of trees. Goats and chickens darted in between the mud walls, and thin plumes of smoke rose through openings in the thatched roofs. The sun was beginning to set and the air was cool. People looked at him with curiosity as he continued along the path, passing several women in leather aprons, their ears and arms and ankles decorated with coils of wire, their backs bent towards the earth under the loads of firewood they carried. Esther had retired two years earlier but James had never come to visit her. Now he was ashamed of his neglect.

She was sitting outside her house, wrapped in a cardigan that Hannah had given her, and stirring a pot of maize meal. She looked at her visitor with disbelief.

'Eehh! What are you doing here? Two years since I left Langani and you never thought of me. You, who slept in my house every night of your life, like my son. Even Piet has come, with David. And Suniva brought me warm clothes from Ireland, and a wool blanket for my bed. But not you.'

'I am sorry,' James said. 'I have been studying hard at the university in Kabete, so that I can finish my course in *Ulaya*. And during the holiday time I try to earn extra money working with Anthony, and on the farm. Also at the newspaper office where Rabindrah is. I will need money if I am accepted in the college far away.'

'Too important now.' Esther spat in the dust. 'Although I am the one who raised you like a mother, as much as Mama Hannah. That is what you have forgotten. You have been to Langani many times. I know this from Piet. There is nothing grateful in you, now that you have risen so high in the world. You have forgotten where you came from.'

'I never knew where I came from,' James said. 'I have only just found out my mother's name. Wanjiru. Did you know her? Were you related to her? Is that why I was given the name Karuri?' He was disappointed when Esther shook her head with vehemence. He tried again, holding out the photograph. 'Maybe you knew my father, then. His name was Simon Githiri.'

Esther stared at him, speechless, her face frozen with horror. Then she hauled herself to her feet, knocking over her stool, and walked away from him into her house, grasping the door handle in an attempt to close him out.

'What is the matter with you?' James put his foot in the doorway. 'Did you know my father and mother? Who were they? It is only today that I have found out their names. From the Mission in Nyeri.'

'Go back to your school,' she said. 'And do not go to Langani any more. Stay as far away from there as you can. For the rest of your life. Because you are cursed.'

She slammed the door and for some minutes he knocked and shouted until the neighbours began to gather around him, and a young man pushed through the crowd and grabbed James by the shoulder.

'What do you want? Why are you shouting, making a *matata* in this place? Get away from here, or I will find some of my friends and beat you up, so that no one will recognise you. Get out! *Toroka!*'

James looked around, and knew that he was in danger. He forced his way through the growing mob and ran down the path back to the main road. The sour taste of fear was in his mouth and he did not know where to go. If Esther's reaction to his words was a sign of some kind, it must be related to his parents. She had always loved him, cared for him when he was sick, given him a place in her house and in her heart. He stood alone in the impending darkness, trying to think in some logical way, to work out what to do. In the distance he could see the silhouette of the mountain, the place where the Great God N'gai reigned over his subjects from its icy heights. As he searched for inspiration he heard the rumble of an approaching lorry, and at the same moment a scrap of old newsprint blew across the road in front of him. A sign. He lifted his hand, thumb up, driven by some inner sense of compulsion. The truck slowed and came to a halt.

'I want to go to Nairobi,' James said, holding out some money.

The driver nodded, indicated that he should climb into the cab and pulled out onto the road again, heading south towards the city.

There was a message for James on the college noticeboard when he hauled himself out of bed in the morning. Mrs Singh had called. He should telephone her urgently. He took the paper down and shredded it into pieces before leaving the campus. Sarah had told him that Rabindrah was away, and he knew that Gordon Hedley would not be in the newspaper office during the lunch hour.

'I have been told by Mr Singh to check something out for him in the archives,' he said to Rabindrah's secretary. 'I'm doing some research on the treatment of stem rust in wheat, and he told me I could look up a couple of articles that appeared in the paper some time ago.'

'He isn't here.' The girl frowned, doubtful. 'And he didn't mention anything about it. You can't just go into the archives as a stranger.'

'I'm not a stranger. I have been here before to help Rabindrah with some research. You know me. Mr Hedley knows me. I am James Karuri from Langani Farm. I'm studying at Kabete.'

'Mr Hedley is not here either. He will not be back this afternoon,' she said. 'But I do recognise you now. I suppose Rabindrah forgot to tell me you were coming. I will take you in there.'

In the harsh fluorescent light he took out the old newspaper files and began his search, starting with the year 1965. Trawling through the front pages he spent an hour reading, not knowing what he was looking for, filled with the dread of the unknown. And then he saw the headline. 28 December, 1966.

Farmer, Piet van der Beer, Murdered at Langani

In a tragic turn of events, Mr Piet van der Beer was murdered last night on his property, Langani Farm. He had been slashed to death with a panga. He was found by his sister Hannah and Miss Sarah Mackay to whom he had recently become engaged. A night watchman, Ole Sunde, and Kipchoge Koech who looked after the stables at Langani, were also victims of the killer.

Suspicion has fallen on an employee at the farm, Simon Githiri, who disappeared on the night of the crime. Police would like to talk to Mr Githiri, and to anyone who may have information relating to his where-abouts or to these murders.

James's head was bursting with a pain so great that he could barely see, and his hands shook as he closed the file. Nausea swept over him in violent waves, but he could not contemplate walking through the busy newspaper office and out into the street. He sat with his head on outspread arms, alone with his horror, and waited for his mind to clear, for the pressure behind his eyes to ease. Finally, he straightened and with trembling fingers opened the files again, turning the yellowed pages slowly, not wanting to see or read any more. But it was all there. 7 June, 1967.

Killer of Farmer Piet van der Beer Gives Himself Up

Last night brought a surprise twist in the unsolved murder case of Mr Piet van der Beer in December 1966. At 8 p.m. Simon Githiri, a suspect and former employee at Langani Farm, walked into Nyeri Police Station and confessed to the killing.

'Simon Githiri has given himself up of his own volition, and confessed to this terrible crime,' said Chief Inspector Jeremy Hardy in an official statement. 'He is being held in prison and will now be indicted for murder.'

Mr van der Beer was found by his sister Hannah and his fiancée, Sarah Mackay. His body had been repeatedly slashed with a panga, his eyes gouged out of their sockets and his masculinity cut away. He was pegged out on the ground like a victim of a ritualistic killing. Two other employees on Langani Farm were murdered on the same night. The police have made no comment as to Mr Githiri's motive, or revealed the full details of his confession. A date for the trial is expected to be announced shortly.

James's windpipe seemed to have been squeezed shut and he gasped for air and clung to the arms of his chair, willing himself to breathe, to retain some measure of reason. After a time he returned to the files and skimmed several months, calculating the time it might have taken to bring Simon Githiri to trial. The paper did not have any further articles concerning the murder, either in 1967 or during the following year. He started again from the day on which Simon Githiri had given himself up. It did not take him long to find what he was searching for. The small paragraph sent shivers racing through his body.

Last night a man identified as Karanja Mungai ran amok in Nyeri township, attacking an elderly priest, Father Bidoli, from the Consolata Mission, and fatally wounding Wanjiru Githiri, a young woman working in the kitchen of the Consolata Convent nearby. The reason for the attack is unknown. The assailant was shot by the police, and Father Bidoli remains in intensive care, but is said to be in a stable condition. No one else was injured in the incident.

Two days later, the newspaper reported that Simon Githiri had died in Nyeri Prison, before his case could be brought to trial.

James pushed himself out of the chair and walked through the office corridors, trancelike, to stagger into the street. He had lost the self that he knew. He had lost everything. Traffic roared past, hawkers pushed their wares in front of him, and a horn blared as he stepped in front of a bicycle, causing the man to lose his balance and fall sideways into the stream of oncoming cars. He did not hear the screech of brakes or the shouts that followed him as he walked on. There was only one image in his mind. The one beloved likeness that would have to be erased forever. Suniva.

Chapter 37

The National College of Art and Design was situated in one of the oldest parts of Dublin, near many of the leading art galleries and museums. Suniva's art master, Michael Ryan, had suggested she attend a lecture which might interest her.

'It's being delivered by a visiting architect, and I rather think you would enjoy it.'

'An architect?' It was not a subject that Suniva had considered studying.

'A man called Viktor Szustak. He's speaking on sculptural themes in building design. His work is highly original, and he has a distinguished reputation. What might be of special interest to you is the considerable amount of time he spent in Africa.' Michael was reading from a leaflet in his hand. 'It says here that his years on the African continent "instilled in him a passion for structural fluidity, and informed his architectural vision". His speciality is the use of natural materials, locally sourced, and the design of buildings that blend into the contours of their surroundings. I suggest you go and listen to him. It will also give you an opportunity to look round your new college.' He handed Suniva the flyer, and hurried away.

As she walked through the arched gateway into the ancient cobbled courtyard, a sense of anticipation filled her. She watched the students thronging the Granary Steps, talking, laughing, arguing passionately, their arms full of rolls of paper or large portfolios, their clothing an eclectic mixture of trendy, whimsical and downright weird. There was a frenetic sense of energy in which she felt completely at ease. In each of the buildings students were putting the finishing touches to their work before the end of year assessments began. Painters at their easels, sculptors on ladders welding metal structures, hanging large organic forms from the ceilings. The library was full, the print studio awash with designs in bright colours, spread out on the walls, and on wide tables. This would be her base, her place of inspiration and discovery for the next four years. The tug of home, although still strong, was loosened by the prospect of this new life, and all it offered.

Suniva was jubilant about winning her place at the college. Despite stiff competition, she had been chosen from among three hundred applicants. The only disadvantage was the length of the course. Four years. An eternity, impossible to contemplate unless James won the scholarship to Cirencester. Then they would be able to spend time together – the occasional weekend, the Easter holidays. Away from her mother's watchful eye.

Ma came from Boer stock, and Suniva was convinced that her objection to James stemmed from inherent racial prejudice. She knew her parents both hoped that her feeling for James would fizzle out in time, but they were wrong. He was her first and only love and that would never change.

Her two years in Ireland had tested their relationship. She suspected it had been harder for James, as he did not seem to have formed any real connections with his fellow students in Nairobi, whereas she had made plenty of friends at school, while steering clear of romantic entanglements. Once, at a school dance she had allowed a fellow student to kiss her, but she found no pleasure in the experience. Afterwards she was filled with guilt, and she avoided any similar incidents by explaining that she had a steady boyfriend back in Kenya, waiting for her.

In the lecture hall she found a seat near the front, joining in the applause as Viktor Szustak was introduced. Dressed in black, and sporting a red silk cravat, there was a flamboyance about the man that demanded instant attention. He was tall and commanding, with a swarthy complexion and a shock of thick black hair peppered with grey at the temples. His nose was strong, lips full and sensuous, eyes deep set and very dark, framed by heavy brows. He emanated a feral passion and ferocity, like that of a predator stalking its kill. As he moved about the podium he used his hands with wide, expressive gestures to highlight his words, and his voice was heavily accented. Suniva found herself enjoying the cadences and tone of his sentences. Erudite and amusing, within minutes he had the rapt attention of his audience. He had brought slides of his building projects to illustrate his talk, and she was impressed by the beauty and harmony of the structures he had created. He seemed to have an affinity with the landscape on which his buildings had risen up, whether the site was urban or rural.

When he had shown them his most recent work in Europe, he began to talk about the fifteen years he had spent in East Africa as the true inspiration for his designs. There was a series of photographs showing a beach hotel outside Mombasa, and another collection of a ranch house on a coffee plantation facing Mount Kilimanjaro. Suniva gazed at the pictures, entranced, filled with nostalgia.

The next slide made her exclaim aloud, drawing glances from the audience as she stared ahead, unaware of their scrutiny. On the screen in front of her was a photograph of Langani Lodge. And Viktor was talking about its construction, how he had staked out the ground with wooden poles and twine, following the undulations of the *kopje* itself, the walls formed partly from the surrounding rock face. She sat gazing at Langani, mesmerised. Why had no one ever mentioned Viktor Szustak at home? She had always thought Uncle Piet had designed and built the lodge. Stunned, she hardly heard the rest of the lecture. The question and answer session drew to a close and Szustak began to gather his notes and slides together as the audience streamed out of the hall.

Determined to talk to him, Suniva rushed down the steps of the lecture hall and approached the podium.

'Mr Szustak?' She knew her voice sounded unnaturally loud.

'Yes?' He looked up and she saw something in his expression. Surprise. A flash of recognition that seemed unlikely. 'Can I help you?'

'Langani Lodge,' she said. 'You built it for my uncle. Piet van der Beer.' She waited for a smile of recognition, a sign of pleasure at the connection, but he said nothing. 'So, you must know my mother and father, Hannah and Lars Olsen.' She put out her hand. 'My name is Suniva.'

'Suniva Olsen.' His mouth twisted in a strange smile, but he did not take her hand. Instead, he reached into his breast pocket for a cigar and lit it. Still watching her. A college lecturer approached him.

'The dean would like you to join him, Mr Szustak,' he said. 'I'll take you to his rooms when you're ready.'

'Of course,' Viktor said. 'Goodbye, Suniva.' He strode out of the lecture hall.

She watched as the doors swung shut behind him and then she left the auditorium, emerging at the top of the flight of stairs. Keeping a safe distance between them, she followed Viktor, and when he went into the dean's rooms she chose a place to sit outside. And wait.

It was more than an hour before he reappeared and she drew back behind a column until he had passed her and was heading out through the gates and into the street. Then she ran after him, calling out his name until he turned, puzzled, frowning. He looked her over briefly, and then moved on once more.

'Can we go somewhere and talk?' She found it hard to keep pace with his long stride, but she was determined not to let him go, this man who was a part of her family history. 'Aren't you curious about how the lodge is doing? Did you know that Uncle Piet died? That he was murdered.'

He stopped and turned towards her with an enigmatic expression that she found disturbing.

'I need a drink,' he said. 'There's a pub right here.' He paused, with his hand on the door. 'Well? Are you coming?'

The bar was old-fashioned and frowsy, dimly lit with dusty wooden floors and faded posters tacked to the walls. The air smelt of stale cigarettes and beer, and a few older men sat hunched at the counter, nursing their afternoon pints and watching the racing on television. There was an empty booth in a corner away from the main entrance, and Viktor put down his briefcase and slid into the seat. Suniva placed herself opposite. When the barman came over to them, Viktor ordered a double vodka on the rocks, and looked at her.

'Gin and tonic, please,' she said, her face set, chin jutting forward as it always did when she was doing something risky.

He laughed suddenly, and took out another cigar from the leather holder.

'You look just like your mother,' he said.

'So you do know her, then?'

'Oh yes. I know her.' His face was almost hostile.

'And my father?'

'Only too well.' A faint smile.

The drinks arrived, and he downed his in one swallow and ordered another. Suniva sipped hers with caution, realising that she could not afford to get drunk. There was a tug, a connection with this man that she did not understand, but she sensed a darkness in him, a threat that he could do her great harm if he chose.

'I did know about your uncle,' he said into the silence. 'I'm sorry. He was a genuine friend and a man of enormous vision. The lodge was his dream. We planned it together. But the design was mine.' He had nearly finished his second drink.

'Then why . . .' She was not sure how to form the words. 'Why does no one talk about you at home? If he was your friend, and you . . .'

'What is it you want to know, exactly?' He watched her through the barrier of his cigar smoke.

'I always thought that Uncle Piet built the lodge on his own, and Ma took care of the interior decoration. When it burnt down, she rebuilt it in exactly the same way. I never knew there was anyone else involved. Why is that?'

'Does Hannah have other children?' His question cut through what she had been trying to say.

'I have a brother. Piet. He's two years younger than me. And Jorgen who is seven now.'

'Lars's children.' He laughed. 'What are you doing in Ireland?'

'A friend of my mother's, Sarah, fixed up for me to go to school here, so I would have a better chance of getting into art college. And I've succeeded. I'm starting at NCAD in September.' She felt the pride of her achievement, and smiled.

'Ah yes, Sarah and her photographs.'

'You knew her too?'

'When she was first working with Dan and Allie, although that was before the Indian husband. I know her books, of course. I always said she was a true artist.'

'She was here only a week ago,' Suniva said. 'I'm sure she would have loved to meet you again.'

'I doubt it.' Viktor's smile was sardonic, and she heard the bitterness in his voice. 'So tell me, Suniva Olsen, where does your artistic talent come from?'

'I've always thought it came from Uncle Piet.' Suniva stopped, remembering Lottie's words, a prickle of awareness making her swallow the rest of her gin. 'I once heard my grandmother say I had inherited it from my father, but he is too busy to sit down and draw or paint. He has always encouraged me, though, to develop the gifts I've been given. That's what he tells all of us.'

'He is a good father, then.'

'The best,' Suniva said, her smile wide with love. A silence grew between them until she tried to reopen the channel of conversation, not ready for it to end. 'Could I have another gin and tonic, please?' She waited as he signalled the bartender and ordered for both of them. When the drinks arrived, she began again. 'When you were giving your lecture, it sounded as though you loved Kenya particularly. Why did you go away?'

'You ask a lot of questions.' Viktor's tone was morose.

'I want to know what would make you abandon a place that gave you so much inspiration. I have to stay here while I am at college, in the hopes that I will become a fine artist. But once I finish my studies I will go home and nothing will ever make me leave.'

'You want to know why I left?' His eyes and his voice were full of darkness. 'Why your family never talks about the man who made Piet's dream into a reality? I can tell you about that. Oh yes.' He could find no trace of himself in the deep blue eyes, the blonde hair and fair skin. She was her mother's daughter, and the sight of her resurrected Hannah in his memory. Hannah lying naked beneath him at Langani. Hannah weeping when she found him in Nairobi, in bed with Johnson Kiberu's wife. Hannah, flanked by Lars and Sarah, standing on the steps of the farm, telling him never to set foot on her property again. He had guessed then that he must be the father of her child, but he had not cared. The only part of himself that Viktor could see in the girl was her burning creativity. Perhaps it was best that it was his only legacy.

'I was a drunk,' he said, draining another vodka. 'A real shit, if that is the truth you are searching for. I left your uncle in the lurch. Hannah was very angry. Never forgave me. Then I had an affair with the wife of a local politician, and the bastard set me up for tax evasion and had me deported. I can't go back. But since then I've made a lot more money in Europe than I ever did in Africa. So, what the hell. Tell me, what kind of artist do you want to be?'

She told him then about her aspirations, and when she had downed a second drink, he prised from her a portrait of life at Langani. She described it all, the gin dissolving any inhibitions as she talked about her childhood, the loving strength of her parents and the tragedy of Piet's accident and long recovery. And finally she told him about James.

He devoured her every word, drawn back to a time and place in his life that he had destroyed, gradually entranced by the fact that he was talking to his daughter. He had had his share of women in every place he went. Used them, amused them, left them laughing or crying, or cursing him, never caring about the consequences. But now he had come face to face with a girl he wanted to know, to be proud of, to acknowledge as a part of himself. As his own. He opened his briefcase, and took out the preliminary sketches he had made of Langani Lodge, all those years ago. Around the edges were notes he had taken down as he had discussed the project with Piet.

'You might like to have these,' he said. 'A memory of old times. Things that might have been.'

She looked down at the drawings he had given her, observing the fluid yet meticulous attention to line and form, to perspective. A mirror of her own work, as though he had taught her all she knew. In the margins his bold script, the spiky letters that hooked and swirled around the words, were like her own. If she followed the flow of the hand, it was almost as if she had written them herself. Viktor watched her, saw the gradual realisation dawning in her mind. He opened his mouth to tell her the truth. To even the score with Hannah, who had surely told Johnson Kiberu about his wife's affair. Suniva looked across the table at him, unsure, her stomach cramping with some unknown threat. He rose abruptly to his feet, throwing a handful of banknotes onto the table, staggering a little, his speech thickened by alcohol.

'Goodbye, Suniva,' he said.

Outside he hailed a taxi and collapsed into the seat, consumed by a piercing regret at not having spoken the words that could have gained him a daughter and a meaning for his empty existence. And he wept, knowing that he had accomplished the only decent thing he had ever done in his life.

Chapter 38

Kenya, June 1985

When she saw Lars waiting in the arrivals hall in Nairobi airport, Suniva knew at once that something was wrong.

'What's the matter, Pa? Is it Piet? Ma?'

'Suniva.' He took her into his big arms. 'I have to tell you right away. James has disappeared. We have searched everywhere, but he has gone.'

'Gone? Gone where? How could he disappear, when he knew I was coming home? What have you done to find him?'

But Lars could not give her any satisfactory answers. James had vanished from Sarah's house ten days ago, leaving no note of explanation. He was not in any of the Nairobi hospitals, and the police had found no trace of him. They had not told her because she was in the midst of her final exams.

'He must have left me a message. Something. Anything.' Suniva thought he might be dead and blocked the idea in her head. She would not allow herself to go down that road. But he could have been knocked down, or mugged. Nairobi was a violent city. The prospect of him lying in a ditch, beaten and unrecognisable, made her feel ill. The strangest aspect of the news was that he had disappeared from Sarah's house. Why would he have left there, without a word? There must be some reason. If they could discover that, it might be possible to work out where he had gone.

'Did they have a row?' She could not imagine such a thing. And Sarah had promised to give him her letters as soon as she got back.

'I have to talk to Sarah,' she said. 'Let's go there now.'

'We are going to Langani, Suniva. Your mother is waiting,' Lars said. 'You can phone Sarah when we get home.'

'I have to stay in Nairobi, Pa.' Her voice rose. 'I have to find James.'

Lars pulled the car off the road, and stopped. 'Suniva. Look at me.'

'Pa, we have to find him.'

'We have tried. Every day. When we heard nothing from him, we alerted the police. Rabindrah has a cousin in CID, Chief Inspector Laxman Singh. Believe me, he is doing everything in his power to locate James. There is no point in our trawling the city ourselves. We have no idea where to look, and the back streets are far too dangerous.'

It was a dark homecoming. Hannah could offer no insight into the disappearance. She embraced her daughter and tried to offer words of reassurance, but for the most part her face was closed and she spent long periods sitting in her study alone or taking walks with only the dogs for company. Not even Piet could elicit any response to his questions or needs. The news of Suniva's acceptance by the college of art was barely mentioned. She grilled Piet and Jorgen for information but they had nothing of relevance to tell, and she was afraid to voice her true thoughts. Would her mother have driven James away? Was Hannah glad, under her outward signs of concern, that he was gone? Each time the phone rang everyone froze, fearing to hope for positive news, listening for the dread words that a body had been found. James had been missing for more than two weeks now. Every passing hour made the likelihood of finding him alive and unharmed more doubtful.

After three days of unbearable tension at Langani, Suniva prevailed on Lars to take her to Nairobi. Both Sarah and Rabindrah were at home when they arrived.

'My cousin Laxman has sent out photographs of James to all his informants. He has every inch of the city covered, and the fact that he has not been found is hopeful,' Rabindrah said, trying to offer a crumb of consolation. 'There is no record of James at any of the hospitals, nor has he been arrested. And thankfully he is not in the morgue.'

Suniva felt tears of frustration rising and turned to Sarah, her voice wretched. 'What did you talk about when he came that day?'

'His work. The application to Cirencester. You,' Sarah said. 'I gave him your letters and some photographs of you. Then I went out to drop Maya and do some shopping. I left him listening to the radio.'

'You must have said something to make him leave!' Suniva's control snapped. 'Did you tell him there was no future for us? Was that it?'

'Don't talk to Sarah in that way, Suniva.' Lars stood up, and took her by the arm. 'It's inexcusable. She has been as worried as we are, and it is through Rabindrah that we have had the full cooperation of the police.'

'I'm sorry.' Suniva was close to hopelessness.

'Don't be. I understand how you feel. Anthony has had two of his staff looking in the Mathari area, but without any success.' Sarah looked away. 'Perhaps you should talk to Laxman. Rabindrah can ring and see if he is in his office.'

A few minutes later Lars steered his daughter out of the room. 'This may help you to realise that everything possible is being done.'

'This is all wrong, Sarah. However bad the truth may be, she should be told.' Rabindrah had waited until the car turned out onto the main road.

'I can't do that.' Sarah was wringing her hands. 'It should be Hannah who talks to her. Anyway we're not even sure that he went to search for his father.'

'What else could he possibly have been looking for, in the archives? I didn't give him any authorisation to go in there.'

'Hannah has to tell her,' Sarah insisted. 'It can only be Hannah.' She pressed her fingers to her temples, trying to soothe a throbbing headache. 'Will it ever end? Oh God, Rabindrah, when will it ever end?'

'They will find him eventually,' Rabindrah said. 'Poor James. I don't know how he will come to terms with this. Or what Hannah can say to him that will make it easier.'

'She will never be able to say the words that will let him know the whole truth,' Sarah said, as Rabindrah took her into his arms. 'I cannot go back to those times. I can't live it all again, suffer with the memories, frighten Maya by being unhappy. You were right last year, when you said we ought to leave this country. We should have packed up and gone, but then you got caught up in another story and I started working on my New Guinea book. It's not too late, though. Let's talk about it again. More seriously. Please, Rabindrah. It's time to go. To start a new part of our lives in a kinder place.'

As the days passed, Suniva and Sarah searched the streets, locking the car doors and rolling up the windows as they drove through the slums that had spread like a fungus on the edges of the modern city. Armed with photographs of James, they went into shops and bars and cheap hotels where they were frequently accosted and forced to leave in a hurry. No one recognised him. He had evaporated, like a ghost.

Rabindrah left on a second assignment to Ethiopia, where hunger had taken the lives of untold thousands. On his return, Gordon Hedley had some very different news to break to him.

'You've been invited to a concert,' he said, unable to keep an ear-splitting grin off his face. 'As a result of your reports on the famine in Ethiopia and the Sudan, Bob Geldof has asked you to join his Live Aid concert in London, on July thirteenth. A mammoth bash in Wembley Stadium, to raise money for the famine victims. Princess Di will attend, and every rock star you've ever heard of. You'll meet them all, and Geldof wants to give you a special mention and an award. I suggest you go home right now. Tell Sarah and Maya. The organisers are going to fly all three of you to London. Maureen and I are coming too. Wouldn't miss it for the world. This is history in the making. Your ship has come in, old chap.'

Rabindrah was elated and gratified. A break in London would allow him the time to talk to Sarah about a possible move, although he had no idea where they might go. Before his visit to Ethiopia, he had spent several days in Wajir, interviewing survivors of the Wagalla massacre. More than a year had gone by, and in spite of investigations by the police and statements from the government, no one had been able or willing to confirm the identities of the army officers responsible for the killings, and the Degodiya people were still living as refugees. Rabindrah had called for an official inquiry, although even Johnson Kiberu was convinced it was futile. Yesterday, however, he had received information that he thought might give him a lead. The name of a senior army officer who had been involved in the massacre and the cover-up afterwards. A name that he had begun to follow up through military records.

He walked out of the newspaper office on his way home, hands in his pockets, whistling one of Maya's favourite songs, smiling as he anticipated her reaction to his news. As he stood at the traffic lights, waiting to cross the street, someone called out his name.

'Mr Singh?'

An African man approached him, dressed in a nondescript suit. Rabindrah looked into his face. Hard eyes, bloodshot from smoking *bhang* and drinking cheap liquor, he thought. The sleeve of his jacket was too long, covering the arm and hand that he held close to his body, possibly due to an injury. He looked familiar, but Rabindrah could not pinpoint a time or place. Then, in a split second, he remembered. The officer in army uniform, his gun pointing through the car window at Annalena Tonelli's temple. The same innate cruelty in the eyes. The man brought his hand forward, and Rabindrah felt the muzzle of the gun against his chest. He never heard the explosion.

Sarah spent the night keeping vigil over his body, looking down into the coffin at the cold, still features that could not be her husband. Eyes closed, hands joined across the chest that had been ripped open by the assassin's revolver. She had never thought his nose so prominent, his lips so sculptured and fine. Death had stolen the fullness of life, the kindness from his face. When she bent to kiss him, he was like ice. Untouchable. Unreachable. A cold corpse, dressed in solemn dignity for burning. They had burned Piet, all those years ago. And now Rabindrah.

He had woken early on that last morning and left the house in a rush, blowing a last kiss to Maya, shouting a reminder to Sarah about their dinner date with Anthony and Camilla. Everything had been so normal. So ordinary. By noon his life was over. Poured out on a dusty pavement, as strangers stared and pointed. One more victim of violence. He had wanted to leave Kenya and she had not pushed hard enough. Why had they not gone away when he had first brought up the subject? Made a sanctuary in some quiet, ordinary place?

Everyone was talking in hushed voices, taking her hands, offering what comfort they could. But there was no comfort. No warmth. Only the memory of a vital man, reduced to ashes by this land that had taken everything. She gathered her daughter into her arms as the funeral car arrived. The coffin was placed inside, bouquets and wreaths heaped around it. At her side were Raphael and Betty, and her brother Tim who had come from New Guinea. Hannah and Lars, Camilla and Anthony, and all the children. Lila had flown out from England with her small son, but Harjeet could not enter the country. Allie, Erope, Gordon Hedley and Maureen, and Johnson Kiberu stood together, and behind them a sea of others. Solemn, subdued, some weeping openly.

There had been a memorial service at the Catholic cathedral, attended by huge crowds, with politicians and members of the press. Now the cortège made its way to the Sikh temple, for the cremation. And tomorrow, there would be nothing. The people who loved her would be there, anxious to help and console. They would encourage her to be brave and she would try. For Maya. Maya who was inconsolable, who could not understand where her daddy had gone. Sarah knew she must survive, for her daughter's sake, for the one part of her husband that remained since the moment when Camilla had come to the door, had asked her to sit down and spoken the awful words. Beyond anger, beyond grief, numb, she did not know how she would be able to move through the ashes of her life, to breathe or speak. To provide the haven, the future for their child, that Rabindrah had wanted. But it was the only reason she had for going on.

In the weeks that followed there was a deluge of cards, letters of condolence, praise for Rabindrah and his work, and cuttings from the press. One of the letters was from Hugo. She read them all, touched by the kindness of the many people who had sent messages of sympathy, and the articles by journalists who had known and respected Rabindrah, and sought to honour him. Suniva came to keep her company and to help with the deluge of mail. She was sitting at Rabindrah's desk when Sarah opened an envelope made of cheap, thin paper. Inside was a single sheet, written in a neat careful script.

Pole, Sarah, Pole sana,
I think of you. I am so sorry.
James

'He's alive!' Suniva leapt to her feet, hope blazing. 'Look, the envelope has a Nairobi postmark. And it's because of Rabindrah that we know it. It is his message to me.' She pressed the note to her heart, whispered his name.

For Sarah it was a moment of unbelievable pain. There was hope for Suniva, that one day she would find her love. But she herself would never again see her husband walk through the door and say 'It's good to be home.' Maya would never again run into his embrace, be swung up into the air, join her father's laughter.

'Pole, Sarah,' James had said. Like Simon, years before, in the dim green light of his prison cell. The same words. The same unbearable emptiness.

Chapter 39

Immediately after the shooting, Laxman Singh began an exhaustive search for Rabindrah's killer. Eyewitnesses gave descriptions that he hoped would result in constructing an identikit picture. There were too many differing accounts, and many were terrified to say what they had seen. All Rabindrah's latest articles and investigations were examined, and suspects who might have reason to want him removed were brought in for questioning. Gordon Hedley was convinced that the killing was linked to the Wagalla investigation, although there was no evidence to support his theory. The police started a sweep of the area around River Road and Grogan Road, and through the Mathari Valley and Kibera slum where guns often found their way to local criminals, but no one was willing to inform.

'I am sorry to say we have not found anything useful,' Laxman said when he called on Sarah late in the evening, two weeks later. 'People are afraid to speak. Between you and me, it is possible that the army is behind this, as Gordon believes.'

'If that's true, they will never find the man,' Sarah said with bitter resignation. 'You have been so kind, Laxman, phoning and coming here regularly with every small piece of information. Do you have time for a drink? You look tired.'

'That sounds good,' he said. 'A whisky, with a little water. On a linked subject, there is something we discovered this morning, by accident. That is what I have come to tell you.'

'Some kind of evidence in Rabindrah's case?' Sarah sat forward.

'Unfortunately not,' the policeman said. 'Do you remember that he gave me a photograph of a young Kikuyu who had gone missing? And then Lars Olsen and his daughter came to see me about the young man.'

'James. Have you found him?' Sarah put down her drink with shaking hands. 'Wait. Let me call Suniva. She has been keeping me company for the last few days.'

Suniva listened to Laxman, sitting opposite the policeman with her body straining forward and her head tilted, in case she might miss a syllable of what he was saying.

'My men have been questioning workers on all the building sites in the city. There is a fellow who seems to fit the description of James Karuri. He is working as a labourer on a new office block near River Road. He gave his name as Joseph Odinga, but the sergeant was suspicious because this Joseph was definitely not a Luo. And then my chap remembered the photograph. He thinks it is the same man. One of the *watu* on the site said that this Odinga lives on Grogan Road. Do you want me to pick him up?'

'No. I want to go there myself,' Suniva said. 'Right now. Please don't let the police arrest him. He hasn't done anything wrong.'

'Rabindrah told me that,' Laxman said. 'He is listed as a missing person. Along with countless others. But you cannot go to that area, especially at night. It is dangerous, out of the question for a white woman. Robbers, drug users, drunks, machetes and knives and guns. They drink *karara*, a very strong liquor, that makes them mad. Even the police do not go at night, unless there is a major emergency or a riot, and they are armed.'

'Can I go to the building site, then? To see if it is James.'

'I will bring you myself, in the morning,' Laxman said.

The neighbourhood in which James had been living was off River Road, a run-down area inhabited by criminals, pimps and prostitutes, and the detritus of the city. He had taken a room in a shabby building infested with rats and other vermin, but it was all he could afford on his meagre wages. In the first days after he had fled the newspaper office, he had wandered through the city streets, sleeping in doorways, eating at kiosks where cheap food was prepared on the roadside. Twice he narrowly avoided being picked up by a police detail, and as his money began to run out he went in search of a job. He was taken on as a labourer on an office building site, and one of the men he worked with had brought him to the lodgings on Grogan Road.

During the day he toiled through the heat and dust, hauling barrows of cement, loading the crane hoist and lifting the heavy steel girders, until the whistle blew and he dragged his blistered hands and feet and aching bones to a food stall. Then he made his way back to the dingy room where he lay on the lumpy bed beneath a single naked bulb that dangled from the ceiling. Trying not to think of his past life. Trying to forget that he no longer had a future.

All around him was the wreckage of poverty. As he had passed into his own building that night a man lay on the floor in the hall, a stream of yellow vomit running down from his mouth. There was a foul stench in the entrance hall and James moved on hastily, his nose wrinkling under an assault of odours – excrement from the open drains outside, and the sharp smell of urine. A mangy dog sloped along the street, and in the shadows down the alleyway, rats scurried over a shape on the ground and cockroaches ran across the floors and up the walls. He did not stop to see if the prone figure was human or animal.

His street contained a row of shoddy *dukas* and bars, paraffin lamps hissing on their counters, raucous music blaring out from radios. The customers standing around were shabbily dressed, smoking *bhang* and holding cans of beer, or tipping back glasses of *karara* and *pombe* that he remembered as forbidden in the Langani staff houses, because they ate away your brain. Near to despair, he was tempted to drink some of the vile brew and blot out his misery. But he was afraid that its effect would render him senseless and unable to protect himself, and result in his remaining money and few possessions being stolen. As he passed to and from work, the prostitutes called out to him, offering their wares, and jeering as he turned away. The nights were the worst as he tried to sleep through the noise of drunkenness and fighting in the street and on the stairs, and the scratching and scampering of vermin in his room. The shower room down the hall was covered in green slime that sickened him, and the water was freezing. But he braved it each day, determined to keep himself as clean as possible although his skin was now marked by bedbugs, fleas and lice. Cement dust had lodged in his hair and nose, and when he looked into the cracked mirror on the wall of his room he hardly recognised the man he saw.

When he heard about Rabindrah's murder, James was unable to remain silent. He longed to see Sarah and Maya, but knew there was nothing he could offer them. Why would she want a reminder of the man who had murdered her fiancé, at a time when her husband had been assassinated?

The news was on the television in all the bars on Grogan Road, and he stood out on the street, watching through the grimy windows. At his lunch break next day he bought a newspaper, scouring the pages for a mention of the people he had loved and lost. The photograph of Suniva, standing beside Sarah and Maya at the funeral, was like a knife in his gut. He wrote to Sarah, in the only words he could think of, and put the envelope in the post. Then he returned to the bleak drudgery of life on the building site.

It was the last day of the week and his pay packet was due. Rising at dawn, James scrubbed at his lice-ridden skin and hair and stood shivering in the icy trickle of water. Then he dressed and went out in search of breakfast. With a hunk of stale bread and a tin mug of tea from the kiosk, he walked to the site entrance. His shirt was torn under the arms now, his trousers were stained and his shoes had begun to wear away, but he was still better off than many of the other labourers. He looked up at the open storeys of the building, hoping that today he might be allowed to work on the upper levels. It was better than being on the ground, mixing concrete, choking in the dust raised by the delivery trucks as they churned in and out of the yard. Near the entrance to the site, he noticed a black car parked in the shadow of the hoarding. A uniformed officer was getting out of the front passenger door.

James froze. A policeman had questioned him recently, asking him where he came from, what he was doing in the city. Was he now going to be arrested? What had he done? He thought of running, but the police were notorious in this area, and flight would surely earn him a severe beating. His head drooped, and he stood, waiting for whatever would come.

'James?'

He raised his head. Looked into the blue eyes of the last person in the world he had expected to see.

'James, I've been searching and searching. James?' Her voice was so gentle.

She wound her arms tight around him, oblivious to the filthy clothes, the dust-clogged hair, the cracked nails and blistered hands. Her scent was sweet and clean and wholesome in his nostrils and she pressed herself against him, trying to absorb the pain he had suffered for reasons she could not understand. He stood in her embrace and listened to her words of comfort and wept, ignoring the whistles and cat calls from the site, and the lorries roaring in and out of the yard behind him.

'You must tell your parents,' Sarah said. 'Take James home now, to Langani. And then to the coast when they go down next week. Here is the phone, Suniva. Please ring your mother. Now.'

'Ma will never accept him,' Suniva said, her eyes blurred and ringed with red from weeping. 'I know it, and you know it Sarah, because you are her friend. James has told me everything, and he does not want to go to Langani. You knew why he went away, and you should have told me.'

'I have never understood why he left that day,' Sarah said. 'It was Rabindrah who thought he had discovered the truth about his parents, in the newspaper archives. But I don't know whether that is the case.'

'He found a picture of Simon Githiri in one of your photograh albums.' Suniva pointed to the bookshelf. 'A picture of himself. You all knew who he was, and why Ma would never let us be together. And you kept it from me. That was wrong.'

'I'm sorry,' Sarah said stiffly. 'I felt that only your mother could tell you the truth. I'm sure there have been times when she wanted to find a way, but it may have seemed pointless and impossible. You mustn't ever forget that it was Hannah who brought James to Langani. Gave him a home and a family and a chance at a secure life. She wanted to protect him from a terrible heritage over which he had no control. In which he and his mother had played no part. What good would it have done for him to carry that knowledge while he was growing up? She kept the secret down through the years for James's sake, and she deserves understanding and gratitude for that.'

'I'll speak to Pa. Tonight.' Suniva's voice was filled with confusion. 'This afternoon James is going back to Kabete. To see if there is any news from Cirencester. Then we will decide what to do.'

Sarah sighed as James appeared in the study, dressed in a pair of Rabindrah's trousers and one of his shirts. She could see no way in which Hannah would be willing or able to resolve this situation. 'You had better sit down, both of you,' she said. 'I know how much you love each other, and that is why you need to start out in the right way. Not hiding or living your lives as fugitives, hurting others, turning your backs on people who love you. I ran off with Rabindrah, because both of our families disapproved of our wish to be together, but we had to come to terms with them in the end. And they had to make compromises too. It is the only way, and you will have to do the same. Now let's get some decent food into James. I suspect it has been a while since he had lamb chops and potatoes.'

After lunch Sarah offered James her car, and he set off for the college while Suniva sat down to amuse Maya and draw pictures with her. It was not long before Lars arrived.

'You told him.' Suniva slammed her sketchbook shut and glared at Sarah.

'We need to talk,' Lars said, his voice firm. 'You and me and your mother. Thank God he is safe. And Sarah was right to let us know.'

'Ma does not want to talk,' Suniva said. 'Otherwise she would be here.'

'She wants you to come home now. She will talk to you there.'

'And James?' Suniva saw Lars shift his gaze away from her. 'Tell me what she has said about James.'

'Your mother and I know that you and James love each other,' Lars said. 'That one day you would like to be together. But you are both very young, and you need to finish your education. Without that, you have no chance of a stable future together. We want you to take up your place at art college in Dublin, Suniva. And we are willing to help James with whatever he needs financially, if the scholarship in Cirencester is still available to him.'

Suniva stared at Lars. The father she had loved and trusted all her life. The father she loved. Viktor Szustak had not told her the truth outright, but she knew what he had not allowed himself to say and she respected him for it. She would always keep the drawings he had given her, think of him sometimes, wonder where he was. Her parents need never know that she had met him, although she would tell James one day. In a strange way, her discovery would bring them even closer. For the moment she would go back to Dublin and James would be in England. They would see each other as often as possible, spend their holidays together, plan their future. In a swift movement she opened her arms to embrace Lars, barely noticing that he was still talking.

'In exchange, your mother and I want you to promise that you and James will not see each other again, until he has finished at Cirencester and you are twenty-one years old. At that time, if you still feel the same way about each other, we will accept your decision and move on together. For the rest of the summer you will come with us to Msambweni, and James will work full-time for Anthony who has a busy season.'

Suniva had opened her mouth to shout out her refusal, her outrage, when James walked into the room. Standing beside Sarah, confident and smiling, his head held high.

'Lars,' he said, suddenly unsure. 'I have been to see the dean at Kabete. They have offered me the place in Cirencester.'

Silence filled the room, as loud as thunder.

'We will do it, Pa.' Suniva spoke first. 'We will do what you and Ma want. If you wait here with Sarah, I will go into the garden and explain it to James, and then you can take me home.'

'You must agree to work for Anthony,' she said to him, his hands pressed between the palms of her own. 'He will have plenty of safaris to keep you busy, and he'll pay you well. I am going home now with Pa, but they will not separate us. In September you will fly to England first and go to Cirencester. I'll take the plane to London, but not the flight to Dublin. I will find a place to live near Cirencester and a job. Somewhere in the countryside where we will be together. Then I'll wait for two weeks and put an advertisement in your local Cirencester newspaper, with my telephone number.'

'How will I know it's your number?' he said.

'You will recognise it.' Suniva said, smiling. 'We will have to be very careful about seeing each other, but they will not find me or drive us apart.'

'You are giving up your chance at art school.' James held her hand. 'For a Kikuyu orphan boy, the son of a murderer. I love you, Suniva but I can't allow you to do that.'

'I love you, James. There is nothing else, and we can never be parted.' She kissed his lips, firm and full, touched the soft, tight curls on his head. Then she backed slowly away from him, her eyes locked onto his face until she disappeared through the doorway into the house.

Standing alone in the garden he heard the sound of voices, listened to Sarah's farewells, and watched as Lars drove her away.

Chapter 40

England, October 1985

It was James who arrived in London first. He was nervous about his new passport and the questions at the immigration desk, confused by the huge expanse of the airport with its different terminals and levels and yellow signs. It took him some time to locate the bus that would bring him into the city where he booked into a youth hostel for two nights. When he had put his bags in a secure locker, he took out the letters and postcards he had received from Suniva when they had first been separated all those years ago, and set out to visit each and every place she had described in her childish handwriting. Then he took a train and a bus to Cirencester, registered at the college, and waited.

Suniva flew in three days later. At the airport she posted the letter she had written to Lars and Hannah and took a train to Cheltenham. It was a beautiful town, gracious and imposing, large enough to absorb her and busy enough for her to find a job and a cheap place to live. In addition to her travel money, Lars had arranged for her to have an allowance that would see her through the first term at college, but it had been placed in a Dublin bank account and she did not dare to have it transferred, in case it would lead to her whereabouts.

The college questioned James on several occasions, and then the police arrived. He must know where Suniva was, they said. They could take him in for further questioning. James could only tell them truthfully that he had not heard from her or seen her, and he had no idea where she might be. His fellow students were curious at first, asking him if he had come into the country illegally, pressing him for information about the visits of the local police inspector. James told them that a student he had known in Nairobi had gone missing, and his new peers assumed it was another African who had come into the country illegally and lost interest in the subject.

Telephone calls came from Lars, from Sarah, from Camilla and Anthony, but he clung to his story, never wavering, never changing a word. During the first few days he thought he was being followed, but after a week he believed that it was his imagination. Lars telephoned again. He had received a letter from Suniva, mailed in London and begging him not to hunt her down. On the long distance line his voice shook as he implored James to divulge his daughter's address. Camilla would shortly be in London, he said, and she was willing to act as a mediator. But James had no idea where she was, except that he too had received a card assuring him that she was safe.

He threw himself into his new course with energy and focus, and his enthusiasm resulted in acceptance and popularity amongst his fellow students. In the forefront of his mind was a determination to obtain the best degree possible, as this would serve as proof that he would be able to take care of Suniva for the rest of her life. Beneath his cheerful exterior, however, impatience raged as he waited for Suniva to contact him. It was two weeks before he received a signal from her. Then, as they had agreed before leaving home, she placed her advertisement in the regional newspaper. It was in the personal section and she knew he would be waiting for it.

'Our House of Sticks 583 877'

He rang her from a call box and they chose a place to meet. She was laughing as he walked past her, not recognising the girl with the dyed black hair standing up around her head like a crown of thorns, and her eyes and brows defined by kohl. Dressed in drab clothes and boots with pointed toes, she was sitting on a park bench with a packet of sandwiches. She whistled at him and the familiar sound made him turn.

'I've got a part-time job as a waitress,' she said, staring ahead, not appearing to talk to him directly. 'Good tips and a room above the café. There is a frame shop down the street that might also take me on for a few hours a week. Wait ten minutes and then take the path through those large trees to the right.'

She left the park and he followed her at a safe distance until they came to a narrow lane that led out into the countryside. Then she held out her hand and they ran into the fields towards the river, leaping and laughing and running until they came to a place of shade, deserted except for the sound of birdsong in the trees that surrounded them. She had a rucksack from which she produced a rug and they lay down together, not speaking, palms pressed together, lips touching, her breath on his cheek.

'Love me,' she said. 'Love me completely, so I know we are bound together for the rest of our lives.'

The arrival of Lars's letter made him waver, and he read it several times.

James,

I believe you know where Suniva is, just as you knew her whereabouts when she hid in the forest many years ago, not wanting to be separated from you.

We need to hear that she is safe, and it is your responsibility as an honourable young man, to tell us what you know. Hannah and I have gone through torment over the past month. We love Suniva, and if you also love and respect her, you must realise that this is not the way.

Please write or telephone us — you can reverse the charges. But you must tell us where she is, James, so that we can all come to an arrangement that is in her true interests, and yours. If you can only trust me in this, I will come to England and talk to you both with an open mind.

Lars

'They are trying to make you feel bad, James. Promise me we will stay together, that you will not reply.' Suniva's look was intense, her voice hoarse. 'Promise.'

'I don't feel bad about us,' he said. 'And I will never let you go. It is only that I love them, too, and they are suffering.'

'You can't reply.' She was unyielding. 'They must not think that you have seen me, or it will be the same all over again. Ma will do anything to keep us apart. I've taken the train to London twice, and each time I have posted them a letter telling them I am safe and well. That I have a job and a shared flat, and I will not come home. I said I would never have made this decision if they had not tried to force us apart.'

'I will not reply,' he said, and they made love in the small room she had been given, wrapping themselves around each other with desperation, determined not to be parted again.

When the owner of the café objected to James remaining overnight Suniva found a tiny studio flat with a peeling linoleum floor and a bed that doubled as a couch. The north-facing window bathed the gas stove and the chipped sink in a watery light. A shower and toilet were tucked behind a flimsy partition and the gas boiler needed replacing, so that cold water was often the only option. Suniva used brightly coloured kangas that she had brought from Kenya, and made curtains and a bedspread. It seemed like heaven, a separate world that they had created for themselves alone. In addition she loved the city itself, with its magnificent Regency buildings and public gardens, and the museums and art galleries and bookshops in which she spent her spare time.

They decided it was not safe to meet more than once every two weeks and sometimes James would steal out at night, rather than have his absences noticed during weekends and daylight hours. Lars had paid for him to stay in the college residence for the first year, and he still had most of the money he had earned on safari during the summer months. Suniva was given some of her meals in the café and her wages paid the rent. She managed the rest of her needs with what she earned in the frame shop. It was clear that she would have to find a better job, however, and she had begun to worry about running out of funds when a stroke of luck changed her circumstances.

'I need frames for these.' The man was tall and well-spoken, and he was carrying a series of portraits that he rolled out on the counter. 'Simple and contemporary.' He frowned as the proprietor of the frame shop took down a selection from the display wall behind her. 'No, no. Wrong look,' he said impatiently. 'Not what I need. In fact, I don't see anything—'

'This one.' Suniva lifted down a sample and stepped out of the small display area where she was hanging a series of mediocre prints for sale. 'It won't argue with your colours or the strong lines you have created, but it's wide enough to define your subjects. And here is a matt. Very plain, but it adds to your clean style.'

'Smart girl. Can you measure them up and let me have a price for all six?' He was smiling as he turned to the owner. 'I'm working on a new show for the end of the year. If you're not too busy maybe you could send this young lady over to help me reorganise my exhibition space, and hang my pictures when the time comes.'

'Not a problem. This is Doris, by the way. Unfortunately we can't take her on full time right now, but she is a hard worker with a good eye.'

'Laurence Elkin.' He shook hands with her. 'I'm a painter and I also teach. Perhaps you would like to come along to my studio next week. To see the gallery space I plan to use for my show, and the pictures to be hung. Here's my card.'

It was not long before he discovered that she could draw. He gave classes to a carefully selected group of students and he offered to include her, in exchange for some filing and secretarial work. Finding that she was methodical and efficient he began to pay her on a part-time basis, so that she worked three afternoons a week in the small, untidy space that he called his office. For Suniva it was a godsend, and she was thankful that she had taken typing lessons in Nanyuki, at her mother's insistence. More than that, however, she had a chance to paint again, and she knew that her work was good.

'Where are you from, Doris?' Laurence stirred milk into the coffee she had brought him. 'And have you thought of applying for art college?'

'That's not an option,' she said.

He raised his eyebrows. 'You could try for a scholarship, you know. Talent like yours shouldn't go to waste, and you obviously had a good teacher at school. Where was that?'

'Birmingham,' she said, naming the first place that came into her head.

'Doris from Birmingham, eh?' His look was quizzical. 'Are your parents aware of your painterly abilities?'

'I ran away from home. They got divorced and my mum took in a boyfriend, so I left them to it.'

'Right.' He sighed. 'Well, I have a suggestion for you, Doris from Birmingham. From now on I'd like you to work for me on a full-time basis. Answer the phone and my minimal fanmail, look after the bills and the schedule for the pupils I have, run errands. Take care of all the chores I detest, and continue with your lessons. As you know, I'm putting together a show for Christmas, with some of my students' offerings. Better get to work if you would like to be included. How does that sound to you?'

'That sounds fair.' She nodded briskly.

He could see the relief and the excitement in her eyes, and he wondered where she really came from. Her accent was certainly not from Birmingham, and he guessed that she was not English at all. South

African, perhaps, or Australian. But she was talented and self-possessed and he did not believe her origins would pose a problem. Apart from which, he liked her and he wanted to give her a chance.

At Christmas she decorated the bedsitter with streamers and stars, and a tree with an angel on the top. It was her first Christmas away from her family and she celebrated with James, opening the champagne and a good bottle of red wine that Laurence had given her, and roasting a chicken with potatoes and vegetables in the small oven. The smell made her think of home and a vision of the kitchen at Langani lodged itself in her mind, with Hannah looking over Godfrey's shoulder as he basted the turkey, and her brothers sneaking past to steal crisp pieces of skin direct from the roasting pans, or to lick the mixing bowl from which the cake mixture had been poured into a baking tin.

'Christmas pudding next,' she said to James. And burst into tears.

More letters of entreaty arrived from Lars, and from Sarah. A brief note came from Anthony. Finally there was one from Camilla. The envelope was addressed to James, but the blue sheet of paper was not.

> *Darling Suniva,*
>
> *I know that you and James want to be together and I understand why. But it is hard to see your parents in such pain. I beg you to let them know where you are, and try to make peace with them.*
>
> *As a family you have always been so close, and I do not believe you will find real happiness by causing distress to those that you love best. We have shared secrets in the past, you and I. If you would agree to meet me in London at Easter, I promise that I will not tell anyone I have seen you. It might help, though, to talk. And maybe we could find a solution to all this sadness.*
>
> *With love to you both,*
> *Camilla*

Even Suniva felt her determination weaken as she read the letter and for several days she thought about Camilla's proposal as she typed and filed, and ran errands for Laurence. On the nights when James was with her they lay close together, clinging on to the world that they had vowed to preserve. He was doing well at Cirencester and his eyes lit up with satisfaction and pride as he described the courses that would one day be important in the preservation of Kenya's wildlife management and the utilisation of its rich agricultural soil. But on cold, winter evenings when Suniva was alone in the dingy room, with an electric fire that used too much of her modest salary, she was often wracked with sobs, and her longing for home made a hole like a cavern in her stomach. It was coming up to Easter and she had almost decided to meet Camilla, when Hannah precipitated a crisis that hardened her heart.

'I was called into the office yesterday,' James said, when he saw her next. 'My scholarship is still in place until the end of my studies. But there will be no more money from Langani for books or residential fees and food or other day-to-day expenses.'

'Ma is behind this. It's like a siege,' Suniva said. 'Another attempt to make us give up.'

'It means I might have to leave Cirencester.' James leaned forward, his head bowed so that she could not see the full extent of the blow he had received. 'And maybe you should try to win back your place at art school. I could return to Nairobi and finish my course at Kabete. Then I will look for work on a farm, until we can decide what to do. I'm holding you back, Suniva, and one day you will resent that. No, don't say it isn't possible. That is what could happen.'

'You won't leave Cirencester,' she said fiercely. 'You can find a weekend job somewhere, like plenty of other students who have to work their way through college. I saw a board outside one of the restaurants the other day, advertising for a waiter at night. And I can get extra work, too. Or try to sell more of my paintings. I could work one or two nights at the cafe, when I'm not in Laurence's office. Find another job that pays more. We can manage this between us, James. You will not leave, and they will not win.'

'Is this about winning now?' The idea saddened him. 'Maybe they are right, and it is time to find another way to prove ourselves. I feel that we are causing too much misery to Lars and Hannah who have always taken care of me, and who love you so much.'

'We cannot be parted.' She pulled him down onto the couch, sobbing and holding him so tightly that he could feel her body quivering with the fear of separation. 'I love you and we must stay together. That is the only thing that is truly important. And ours is the only way that will make them understand. Don't leave me James. Please don't leave me.' Her eyes were wild as she looked up at him.

'I will never leave you,' he said. But his heart was heavy.

'I have to find another job.' She could not look at Laurence directly, knowing she would be letting him down.

'And that would be because . . . ?'

'I need the money. I'm sorry, I really am, but I have to have more money. It's an emergency.'

'Well, I've been thinking of giving you a pay rise, Doris. And something more. As you know, I've been in my studio day and night recently, working towards a larger show in the summer. If you are prepared to work equally hard, I will put eight or ten of your paintings in the smaller room next to the main gallery, and give you a solo show on the side. Meantime, one of my buyers would like three or four pictures for a new house, so I'll take these along and show them to him.' He picked up a selection of her most recent paintings, and then turned to face her. 'You know, I think you're going to be a very fine painter one of these days. What did you say your name was?'

'Suniva,' she said, smiling through the tears running down her cheeks. 'My name is Suniva Olsen, and I'd like you to meet my friend James.'

When she knew they could earn sufficient money for James to continue, she wrote to tell Camilla that she did not think a meeting at Easter would be a good idea. Then she sat down and agonised over her letter to Lars. She would not come home, she said. She knew that life was hard for James, because he now had to earn the money to keep a roof over his head and buy food and books for himself. But she still had a job in London, and she would continue to work for the day when they could be together.

I know it was Ma who persuaded you to take away James's allowance at Cirencester, and we were not surprised by that. It has only made us stronger, though, and more determined to show you that we can make our own way and stay true to our hopes for the future. Please, Pa, do not blame James or try to hunt us down. It cannot bring any result that you would want, and you must try to explain this to Ma. I am safe and well, and I am painting as well as doing my job, so you need not worry about me.

I love you, but you have forced me to choose, and I could never have chosen anyone but James to be first in my life.

She took a train to London and mailed the letters. After that she made no attempt to contact her parents again.

'The races.' Camilla looked at Tom and sighed. 'I don't fancy the races, but I do love Cheltenham. Yes, I suppose I could go with you. You're getting a bit paunchy, by the way. I wouldn't like to suggest the word middle-aged, but it might be a look you should avoid. Where is your exotic companion?'

Zahra had left him, of course, and run off with an American oilman. He had seen her picture in *Town and Country*. 'It nearly killed me at the time,' he said to Camilla, a trace of his shattered ego still evident in his eyes. 'I've never been so hooked on any woman, or so screwed over, even though I knew what she was from the beginning. I suppose that made it all the more exciting. Kiss and make up?'

'Kiss and make up,' she said, laughing but feeling sorry for him, with his outwardly successful life that hid a loneliness he had not expected.

Rain fell, gentle and insistent, on the racecourse. After the main event of the day Camilla left Tom in a private box drinking champagne with friends, and escaped to visit the gracious town that appealed to her more. She had just ducked into a coffee shop and folded her soggy umbrella when she saw the gallery poster hanging on the wall. The colours were unmistakable, the style more refined but still the same. It took her fifteen minutes to locate the Laurence Elkin Gallery.

'The African paintings on your poster,' she said to the receptionist. 'Who is the artist?'

'Doris Brett. Mr Elkin is over there in the corner. He is the owner and a painter, too, and he can tell you more about her work. Here is the list of prices.'

'I'm very interested in Doris Brett's paintings,' Camilla said, when Laurence had introduced himself. 'Is she here? I'd love to meet her. And why does her work have this particular influence?'

'She is very talented. Also somewhat reclusive.'

'Isn't that rather unusual for someone so gifted?' Camilla moved closer to him, making full use of the power she could always exert over any man. 'I've lived in Africa myself, on and off, and I would like to buy one of the paintings.' She held out her hand. 'Camilla Chapman.'

'I know who you are. Doris has pointed you out in magazines,' Laurence said, his mouth twitching with amusement. 'She has been taking lessons from me. She is a wonderful young woman who is beginning to build a solid reputation, and I'm proud to say that she is my most gifted protégée. Disciplined and stable. Happy in her work. Happy and safe in her life. I wouldn't like to see her derailed.' His words were delivered with smiling courtesy, but his eyes carried a different message. 'I'll let her know you were here. Give her your contact number, if you have a card.'

'Thank you.' Camilla realised that they were both astute players in a game that had infinitely higher stakes than any horse race. 'Does she live in Cheltenham?'

'Would you like to take the painting now, or should I have it shipped?' The smile had vanished from his face.

'I would like it sent to my London address.' Camilla took out her cheque book and began to write in the amount, turning over in her mind the unpredictable, possibly disastrous consequences of discovering Suniva's whereabouts. 'And on second thoughts, there is no need to let her know I was here.' Her smile was sad. 'Goodbye Laurence. And thank you. I'm terribly glad to have met you.'

Chapter 41

Allie's camp was in Tsavo National Park, an area that covered some 8000 square miles, stretching from the verdant slopes of the Chyulu Hills in the west to the eastern plains bordered by the Yatta Plateau. She was already immersed in a study of Tsavo's lions with their legendary past and less certain future. Sarah had arrived there with Maya, hot and thirsty and covered in red dust, the child full of excitement after a close encounter with a rhino. It had burst out of the bush and chased the Land Cruiser for several hundred yards, coming within inches of goring the passenger door before disappearing into the scrubland as suddenly as it had emerged.

'What are you going to do? In the long run, I mean.' Allie sat back in her canvas chair. 'You can stay in Tsavo as long as you like, of course. But I know you too well, Sarah. Taking photographs of wildlife will not provide the salve you are looking for this time.'

'I would like to photograph the lions you are following,' Sarah said, training her binoculars on a monitor lizard as it emerged from the top spire of a termite castle. 'You are right, though. As usual.' She drank a fourth cup of tea, marvelling at the way the hot liquid remained the best thirst-quencher of any. 'I'll tell you what I have in mind, later, when I have Maya tucked up in bed.'

They took a game drive in the late afternoon, coming across a herd of elephant spraying themselves with rust-coloured mud in a waterhole close to the camp, meandering along the river and walking across the rocks to watch the rush of pounding water at Lugard Falls. There were lion prints in the sand, but no sign of Allie's subjects. After dinner, with the child asleep in the tent they would share, Sarah accepted a drink and sat on the edge of the river, listening to the hippos.

'What about Erope?'

'He is happy back in Buffalo Springs,' Allie said. 'With his family and his tribal surroundings. He has decided to set up as an independent safari guide, and he will work on a freelance basis with Anthony, and for one or two of the other top safari companies.'

'How did you feel when he decided to go home, after all these years? And aren't you lonely?'

'It was time,' Allie said. 'I'm grateful for what we shared, and we will always remain friends. And I'm not lonely here, with occasional students and people doing post-graduate studies joining me here for a few months at a time, which suits me well. Now tell me what you have decided. Are you going to leave Kenya?'

'I'm going to Wajir,' Sarah said, ignoring Allie's gasp of surprise. 'I have an agreement with magazines in New York and London and Germany, and I've talked to John Sinclair about a small book that covers the survivors of the Wagalla Massacre, and the history of the Somali clans in the area, good and bad. They are not all victims up there. Many of them are bandits – feudal warlords who are only interested in shooting up the world and stealing women and livestock from other tribes. But I want to show that the problems there should have been dealt with differently, and that innocent people were murdered or left to die by government officials.'

'Sarah, that is terribly dangerous.' Allie made no bones about her disapproval.

'I never thought of spending my life anywhere except here,' Sarah said. 'Now I have come to feel like Lottie did, when she left for Italy. This country has destroyed too many of the people and places I love. Rabindrah lost his life, trying to expose those who were responsible for the slaughter at Wagalla. I'm not an investigative journalist, but I can show the true situation up there. The danger of more and more firearms, and the neglect and privation still being suffered by the survivors of Wagalla. And generate help for them by doing it. It will be my tribute to Rabindrah. The only thing I can do to make his sacrifice worthwhile.'

'A book like that will take time,' Allie said.

'But I have to do it.'

'What about Maya?'

'I will do anything to protect Maya from potential harm,' Sarah said. 'When school starts, I am sending her to Msongari with Annabel. She will stay with Camilla whenever I am away, although I'll be home most weekends and during school holidays. We will spend the next month at the coast, and go to my parents in Ireland for Christmas. And probably Easter too. They are looking forward to that.'

'Will Annalena be able to help you in the north?'

'She's not there any more. The government revoked her work permit, because of her intervention. She has started a hospital in Somalia now.'

'I don't like this idea at all.' Allie's face was dark with dismay.

'My plan is to do the background research in Nairobi, take my pictures as quickly as I can, and then put it all together somewhere else. That will be safer.'

'Where will you go, finally?' Allie was still unable to come to terms with the plan.

'I don't know,' Sarah said. 'Somewhere away from Africa. Lottie has invited me to Italy for a few months, but I can't see myself there permanently. Or anywhere in Europe, with all the "when we's".'

'"When we's"?'

'The Kenyans who left, and now spend their time together saying "when we lived in Kenya we did things like this".' Sarah rubbed a hand across her eyes. 'Anyway, I can only manage one step at a time, and even that is a battle.'

'I saw Camilla and the children on their way to the coast.' Allie had heard the break in Sarah's voice and steered her away from her regret. 'Now you can fill me in on the Olsens and what is happening there.'

'They are also in Msambweni,' Sarah said. 'Hannah spends most of her time with Piet, helping with his vegetables and flowers. He has a good little business going now. She is sure that Suniva and James are seeing each other, but Lars has forbidden her to call in the police or a private investigator, and he is probably right. It would only make things worse if James had to leave Cirencester. I don't think they would ever see Suniva again if Hannah made that happen.'

'How on earth will this turn out? I feel for that young man, caught in something that is not of his making. But I feel for Lars and Hannah too. It must be an agonising thing, not to know where your child has gone, or whether she will ever come home again.'

'No one can predict how it will turn out. Hannah won't hear of any compromise, although that is the only way a solution can be found. If she does not relent, God only knows what the cost will be this time.'

For the next two months Sarah read everything she could find on the Northern Frontier District, and the Somali tribesmen and bandits who inhabited the area. Then, with Maya settled in school, preparations began for an expedition to Wajir. As she left her house in the city, Sarah struggled to suppress fear and a strong urge to abandon the whole project, but finally she delivered her daughter into Camilla's care and started out on the long journey north. Approaching the desolate country for the first time, a sense of her own madness overcame her. This was Wajir district, the place where Rabindrah had been in the months before he had been assassinated. The place that had cost him his life. Now she had followed in his tracks, at risk to herself and the daughter she treasured beyond all else in life. And yet she had come, against the advice of everyone who knew her.

Omar, who was acting as her guide, sat beside her, directing her across a white hot moonscape scribbled with fissures, scored here and there with deeper clefts where there had once been water courses, and dotted with withered thorn bushes. A land shrivelled by drought, where the bleached bones of livestock lay scattered as they had died, their herders forced to travel greater and greater distances in search of water.

The survivors of Wagalla, most of them women and children, were still living in destitution. Banditry was rife, and with the majority of their menfolk murdered there were few left to protect the diminishing herds from raiders. As their animals died of thirst, or were stolen from them, they became increasingly dependent on what little relief aid was being offered in the area. The Kenya government continued to ignore their plight, refusing to acknowledge their situation, or the violence that had brought them to the brink of annihilation.

Sarah had read Rabindrah's articles when they were published, talked to him about what he had witnessed, but nothing could have prepared her for the reality. With Omar as her interpreter, she stopped continually to photograph and talk to these forgotten remnants of humanity, still living on the rim of hell, existing in makeshift dwellings constructed of thorn sticks and spread with threadbare pieces of rag, or woven mats made of dried grasses and palm leaves. At first they would not speak to her, pulling their scarves over their heads, until Omar told them about Rabindrah and what he had done to publicise their plight.

'He died because of this,' he said. 'And this is his wife who has come to tell your story, with her camera and your own words.'

'They whipped us. Tore our flesh to shreds.' The man who spoke made a whistling sound through toothless gums. A survivor of the massacre, he looked about seventy. In fact, Omar said, he was only thirty-five. 'They hung us up by our testicles. Some were burned alive. Many died when they ran for the fence.' He pointed to his mouth. 'I have no teeth now, and my ribs were broken. I lay quiet, pretending to be dead. My brothers died, and my father.' A sob escaped his cracked lips. 'What happened to us there will never be known.'

'It will be known,' Sarah promised, her tape recorder whirring to a halt, clogged with dust so that she had to stop and try to clean the spools.

For days she moved amongst them, her lens opening up the barren landscape where families scrabbled for morsels of food so that they might survive for another day. Malnourished babies slept listlessly on their mother's laps, and youngsters with distended bellies and scabby match-stick legs sat in the dust through which animals trudged, ribs protruding, heads down. The women hid beneath tattered shawls that had once been full of colour, fingering their faded beads and ornaments, the legacy of a less cruel time. Men with rheumy eyes recalled the burnt corpses of their friends and relatives whose skin had melted into the bubbling tar on the runway, or fed the dust devils churning in the dry wind around Wagalla.

On this first visit Sarah had filled the car with *debbis* of water, knowing that this was the most precious gift she could offer, in addition to sacks of cornmeal, rice and sugar. But all too soon, the supplies were gone. There was a school, but the children could not leave their livestock to attend the lessons. When they did appear, it was because their few remaining beasts had died or had been stolen. And yet, in the midst of all the hopelessness, there was a spark of determination that made a woman smile and break into a high, reed-like song, or share a ribald joke with her sisters. Strong, proud people, they refused to be destroyed by the elements, or by their fellow men.

After five days Sarah returned to Nairobi, haunted by the images she had recorded, determined to find an aid organisation that would transport food and water into the district. And medicines. In her darkroom she wept as she developed the record of the lives she had seen, working all night, recognising the power of her camera to inform, to change. For the rest of the year, she went through all Rabindrah's notes and papers, extracting words and sentences from his earlier interviews to form the text of her book, transcribing the stories of the men and women to whom she had spoken herself. Returning to Wajir on later occasions, in the company of aid workers with food supplies, she felt an increasing fear of reprisal. But she forced herself to go on. Rabindrah had died giving a voice to these forgotten people, but now his words, and her pictures would allow the victims of Wagalla to be heard. That was the only fitting memorial that she could offer to her husband.

At Christmas time she took Maya to Ireland where they stayed with Raphael and Betty, and Tim who fell in love with his niece and took her everywhere with him. In January she travelled to London and handed over the first draft of her book to John Sinclair. Watched him weep.

'The tragedy of the Third World,' he said. 'You could not find such grief in our society.'

'Try taking a tour of Belfast,' Sarah said. 'Barbarity exists almost everywhere, simmering under the surface of our most venerated ideas and principles.'

Before leaving Nairobi she had written to James, asking if she could come to Cirencester to see him. Begging him to let Suniva know that she would be in England. There was no response.

Chapter 42

Kenya, July 1987

'She will be twenty-one at the end of the month,' Lars said. 'She is our only daughter, Hannah, and we have not seen her for three years. It must end, all this. If you will not relent, if you will not give in to love and acceptance, then I will go to England and find her. No matter what you say or feel. No matter what it takes.'

Hannah showed no sign of having heard him. She was sitting on the verandah, reading a book, the lines blurring as Lars made his plea.

'Sarah is going to leave soon,' he said. 'She has sold the house in Gigiri and moved into a rented cottage. The book she has dedicated to Rabindrah will be published in October. Did you even know this? You are isolating yourself from your friends, spending more than half your time at Msambweni these days, although I still need you here, at the lodge and on the farm. You cannot abdicate from our lives because the stubborn, unforgiving side of you has taken over. Eaten through the good memories and made a void in our family that I can no longer bear. Think, Hannah, about Piet and Jorgen. Do you know how many times they ask about Suniva? Where she is, when she will come home, whether she still loves us.'

He waited, hoping for some sign of surrender.

'Camilla will be here in an hour or so,' Hannah said. 'I'm going to look over her room, and see that everything is ready for dinner.'

'Will you talk to her? Isn't there something you can say that might make a difference?' Lars handed Camilla a drink.

She turned the glass slowly in her hand, her eyes focused on the amber liquid, her mind flying back to the days and nights of her childhood spent in this same room with Lottie and Janni. With Piet who was gone, with Sarah and Hannah. With Anthony. Laughing, singing, dancing, cowering under the attack of men with pangas. Hannah had been born in this house, married from it, brought new life into it. Suniva, Piet, Jorgen. She had brought James here too. To end the bloody cycle of attrition. And now she was caught in it herself. Lars was right. It was time to tell the truth.

'I know where Suniva is,' she said.

'What?' He rose and gripped Camilla's shoulders, his first reaction one of anger and betrayal. It was only the gaping wound his daughter had left in his heart that allowed him to listen.

'She is in Cheltenham. Safe and sound. Taking art lessons, selling paintings in a good gallery, and working for the owner. James must be finished in Cirencester, so they will have some choices to make now about coming back to Kenya. Or maybe going somewhere else to live and work, with his new qualifications.'

'Is there any way you can persuade Hannah to . . . ?' He listened as she told him how she had discovered Suniva's whereabouts, asked forgiveness for not having told him, knew that he understood.

'Please, Camilla, please help me to bring her home.'

'I'll try, Lars' she said. 'I'll try.'

'It's wonderful to think that we are going to the coast next week.' Camilla found Hannah in the room that had become her study. The space she had created in her determination, in spite of all the odds, to bring Piet to recovery. 'I'm looking forward to it. It will be different this year, though, because it may be the last time that we can all be there together. Sarah and you and me, Lars and Anthony, and the children. But there is one of us missing, Hannah.'

'You've been talking to Lars.' Hannah jumped up, spilling her drink, swearing under her breath as she made a production of mopping it up. 'I won't discuss this.'

'You will, Han. You must. What are you doing to yourself? To Lars. To all of us. How can you cut your daughter out of your life, out of your heart, because she loves the boy whose destiny you wanted to change? She is almost twenty-one. An adult. And James is a man now. A fine young man who has worked hard, studied hard, gained his degree. Done his best. It makes no sense any more.'

'What the hell are you talking about?' Hannah was shouting. 'Who knows whether they are still together, or what he has done to her. He may never have finished his course, having ruined her chance to paint and use the gifts she was given. I could never look at him again, or bring myself to reach out to her. We gave Suniva everything and she threw it back in our faces. Rejected us for that . . .' She knew she could not use the word.

'Oh, I know exactly what you were going to say.' Camilla's eyes narrowed. '*Kaffir*. That was the word, wasn't it, Hannah? The word that your Afrikaans forebears would have used. He is black. The love of your daughter's life is black, and that is a fact.'

'No, I was not going to use that word. The fact is that his father was a murderer.'

'The fact is that you have forgotten part of the story. The part we have all buried with our old nightmares. But James and Suniva are innocent except for the fact that they love each other. So it's time to ask yourself why you are heaping on them the sins of the fathers. His father. And yours.'

Silence fell on the room, eerie, like the eye of a hurricane. Then Hannah began to cry, her years of torment pouring from her in great gulping sobs. She could not stop the sounds, could not restrain the flow of remorse, remembering the weeks and months when she had longed to hear Suniva's voice and her footsteps running in the corridor, to smell her hair newly washed, see the blue of her eyes. When Lars came into the room he lifted her into his arms, rocking her like a child, murmuring endearments. When she was quiet at last he set her down on her feet, and together they left the room.

'What's wrong? What was that weird noise?' Jorgen had appeared with Piet in his wake, their faces frightened, eyes wide with dread.

'There's nothing wrong,' Camilla said, smiling. 'That was the beautiful sound of release.'

There were several telephone calls to Laurence Elkin and subsequently to Suniva. Two days later Lars flew to London, hoping that he would be able to bring them back with him. Camilla arranged the first meeting at her flat, and he had gazed in silence at his daughter before reaching out to gather her into his arms. To stroke the flaxen hair she had allowed to grow back, when she no longer felt threatened by discovery. At first she was stiff, fighting the joy of reunion, but within minutes her love for him had swept away the last vestiges of resistance.

James stood very straight as father and daughter embraced, saying nothing, his face guarded but composed. He had filled out, become a man, and although his sleeves were frayed and his clothes had been bought in secondhand shops, he was totally in command of himself and his surroundings.

'Your mother and I would like you and James to come home, now,' Lars said. 'It is time.'

'I don't know, Pa.' Suniva faltered, unsure and suddenly afraid.

'Yes, it is time.' It was James who made the decision. 'Suniva, we will go home and we will face the future together, and no one will try to force us apart. I believe we know this now.'

Later he sat close to Suniva, not touching but joined, listening to Lars's news of Langani and the family. When he held out Hannah's letter they read the single page at the same time, a fragile, fluttering symbol of reconciliation. A prayer. On the following night they boarded the aircraft for Nairobi.

As they rounded the last curve in the driveway Suniva saw the glory of the old house as if for the first time, rooted into the soil first cleared by her great-grandfather, surrounded by the colour and rhythm of Lottie's emerald lawn and the flower-filled borders that her mother had continued to tend. The chimney was wrapped in honeysuckle, smoke rising in a spiral from a tumble of flowers. In the hallowed light of evening the Great God N'gai commanded the golden land from his mountain peak. Hannah stood on the steps, waiting, her hand pressed to her throat. Dogs barked and jumped and ran in circles. Suniva took James's hand as they walked the last few steps, still not sure of an unconditional welcome until Hannah held out her arms to encompass them both. Piet and Jorgen emerged from behind her, shy and then boisterous in their greeting as the first tears of love and reconciliation began to fall.

It was almost midnight by the time drinks and dinner were finished. At first there were questions, tactfully posed, answered with careful reserve. But as the evening wore on the atmosphere changed, and the air was charged with the simple joy of homecoming.

When Jorgen had reluctantly gone to bed, and Piet had also taken his leave of them, Lars put more logs on the fire and brought out the brandy.

'Tomorrow is your birthday, Suniva,' he said. 'A day of celebration with your family and closest friends. But tonight your mother has something to say to you and James. About a part of our history that you need to carry with you into the future.'

'When I first saw you, James, it was because your mother brought you here.' Hannah's voice was shaky. 'Her name was Wanjiru and she had walked for days to bring you to a safe place. At first I did not know that she was the wife of Simon Githiri who had killed my brother.'

'Why do we need to go over this?' Suniva was on her feet, defensive and angry. 'Is that why you brought us back here? To drag James through a litany of his father's wrongdoings?'

'I have suffered for them and because of them, since the day I saw his photograph in Sarah's album,' James said. 'I cannot understand what he did or why, and there is nothing I can ever do to erase it. If I am here to be put on trial, then you should not have asked me to come back. Because I can't say or do anything that will make a difference to the past.'

'You are here because I want to make things right for you,' Hannah said. 'Because I have to tell you the whole truth about what happened to Simon Githiri, so that you and Suniva can share a future that is free and secure. I am the one who is on trial, James, because I gave you a home but I myself was not brave enough to live with the reality of the past, and I have made you suffer for it.'

She moved across the room to sit beside him, her eyes level with his as she began to tell the story in fits and starts, pausing when she could not find the right words or the strength to say them, wanting to portray a truth that would sweep away all misunderstandings and release them from the shackles of their shared history. She spoke of the Emergency more than thirty years before, of the days when the Mau Mau rebellion had begun. When Langani had become a different place, with bars on the windows and doors. With guns in every room and under her parents' pillows at night. The days when gangs had formed amongst the Kikuyu people, terrorising the members of their own tribe, and others who would not take the oath to drive the white man from their land. They had hidden in the forests and come down at night to raid the white farms, to kill and maim the livestock, to murder the bwanas and their families whose government and ancestors had cheated the tribal chiefs and stolen their land.

But the white farmers and other Kenyans had fought back, refusing to give up the territory for which they held title deeds under the law. Years of senseless killing and tragedy ensued. Although a handful of white people had been murdered it was the African population who had suffered most as more than thirteen thousand were killed by their own kind, or died fighting the British-led troops.

'My uncle died fighting up in the forests of the Aberdares.' Hannah's hands were shaking as she poured a second measure of brandy into her glass. 'His slashed remains were brought home for my father to bury. Some of the Langani cattle were slaughtered and their heads were left on the gateposts. Our dogs were poisoned. Several of the farm workers died because they refused to take the Mau Mau oath. Then Pa left to join the fighting. As part of the King's African Rifles, he went into the forests and lived there for months, tracking the gangs who had attacked his farm and his family, hiding, living on roots and berries, as close to starving as his enemy.' She stopped, and her sigh became a long, shuddering sound as she dug for the courage to go on to the bitter end.

'One night in the forest, my father was with some British soldiers. They surrounded and captured a group of men who had raided a farm outside Nyeri and were roasting a bullock they had stolen. One of the gang members was your grandfather, James. When he refused to give them any information, they trussed him up and tied him to the spit . . .' Hannah faltered and swallowed the remains of her drink before resuming the awful narrative. 'They roasted your grandfather until he died. Jan van der Beer, a loving husband and father, was responsible for that act. Your grandmother had been hiding nearby, hoping to keep her little boy safe, concealing him in the bushes. The soldiers found her and shot her dead, but the child had crawled away into the undergrowth and he was not harmed. His uncle, Karanja, found him the next day and brought him to the orphanage in Nyeri, because he could not feed the boy. The priests took him in and named him Simon Githiri. For months, he could not speak, because he was so traumatised by what he had seen. With care and kindness, he began to recover, but the memories of that night in the forest remained buried in his mind.'

Hannah lay back against the side of the chair, too distraught to continue. Suniva, her face white as a sheet, sat mute and rigid in her chair as her mother collapsed. It was Lars who finished the grim narrative.

'When the boy had grown into a man and completed his education,

Karanja reappeared. Now Simon was no longer an orphan. He had an uncle, an identity, a clan. Then he learned what had happened to his father. It was not difficult for Karanja to turn him into an instrument of revenge. There was a period of initiation when Simon lived for months in the forest. He took an oath and swore to kill Jan van de Beer, in order to avenge his parents' deaths. He was given a young girl, Wanjiru, to be his wife. When he turned up at Langani on the pretence of looking for a job, he found that Janni had left the farm and gone to Rhodesia. It was Piet who took him on. Liked and trusted him. And it was Piet who paid the price for his father's deeds. With his young life.'

'Both our families were part of a war,' Hannah said, talking directly to James. 'A deadly conflict that spanned generations, justified torture and killing on both sides, and resulted in the deaths of thousands of people. Many were innocent of any crime, like my uncle and your grandmother. Wanjiru, your mother, was a simple girl caught up in a brutal struggle she never understood. After Piet died, and Simon gave himself up, I wanted to end all that. To make some kind of reparation, I suppose you would call it.'

'So you brought me here. In spite of all that had happened.' James's words were strangled with emotion, with the enormity of what she had done for him, all those years ago.

'I could not forgive Simon,' Hannah said. 'Nor have I ever been able to forgive my father. What he did destroyed his life and it finally killed him. But I did not realise that in my own heart there remained a kind of hatred. An inability to let go of the past, and to have faith in a future that we could share as equals who love and respect each other.' She stood up and held out her hands. 'Tonight I can say that I have finally accepted this. I have learned its meaning from you, James, and from Suniva with your unswerving faith in what is right. And so I want to ask for your forgiveness and trust. And for your love.'

On the morning of Suniva's birthday the house was brimming with activity. James had risen early and gone with Piet to the garden, to select the best of everything for his sister's celebration. At noon the guests arrived. First Anthony and Camilla and the children. Then Sarah and Maya. Tables and chairs had been set out under the flame tree, Hannah gambling on the weather and winning the day. Allie arrived last, her small wiry form emerging from the passenger side of the vehicle as Maya ran out to meet her. Sarah stood on the lawn watching them, her arm linked with Hannah's, as Camilla brought glasses of champagne.

'Thanks for including my guest.' Allie was swinging Maya round in a circle, as Hugo eased himself out from behind the steering wheel.

'It's been a long time,' he said, walking towards the three women. 'I'm honoured to be here.'

'Hugo.' Sarah's reaction was drowned out by the sound of chanting as the dancers came round the corner of the house.

They streamed out onto the grass, dressed in their tribal finery, leaping and soaring, copper bracelets and anklets and earrings glinting in the sunlight, spears flashing, feathered headdresses quivering in the bright air. The women made high, ululating sounds of joy, their beaded collars bouncing on bare breasts as they formed a circle and danced to the pounding drums. David had organised the banquet that followed, taking his place at the table with old Kamau and Mwangi, Esther and Juma, all of them fussing over Suniva, exclaiming at James, rejoicing in their return, and the extraordinary news that they were going to have a child. It was Suniva who made the announcement.

'I am twenty-one years old today, and I'm grateful and happy that James and I are home. Langani was the place of my birth and my mother's birth, and my grandfather before that. It is a place of love, our farm, and soon it will be the place where the baby that James and I have created will come into the world. A new generation arriving with love, surrounded by love, ready to love in return. And that will be our family legacy, because that is all we truly need.'

Hours later, the setting sun had begun to skim the treetops and the cool of evening brought people into the house, to congregate around the fire. It was Lars who made the last toast of the evening to his daughter, and James who created a roar of approval as he asked Suniva to marry him. Allie seated herself beside Anthony, watching as Hugo moved slowly across the room, greeting people, easy and smiling until Maya tugged at his trousers, curious to know the newcomer, drawing him towards the place where her mother was standing.

It was mid-morning and the guests had finished breakfast and were preparing to leave.

'Suniva?' Lars beckoned her and motioned for James to follow.

In the study Hannah was seated at the desk that her grandfather had brought from South Africa at the turn of the century, hauling his favourite piece of furniture from the Cape to Nairobi, and then onwards towards the mountain and the high plains, cracking his whip, shouting as the span of oxen lumbered across the rich soil to reach the site he had carved out of the bush to make into his home. The place he would hand down to future generations who would work and love this land, far beyond his knowledge and measurement of time.

'Suniva, we are leaving for the coast today,' Hannah said. 'With Piet and Jorgen. The bags are in the car, and of course you will come down and join us when you are ready. Mike Stead will be here, to run the farm as he has done so well for so many years. To keep things going on a day-to-day basis. But before we go there is something I would like to give you both. It is a gift for which your ancestors and James's forebears fought for centuries.' She stood up and held out an envelope. 'These are the title deeds for Langani Farm. I have had them made over to you and James, because I believe that is how it should be. I hope you will love this place as the generations before you have loved it. As I have loved it. And I pray that your children will carry on its tradition.'

Suniva took the envelope and passed it into James's hands, watching as tears spilled unchecked down his dark face.

'I can't say the things I would like to say,' she murmured. 'I do not know the words.'

'When will you be back?' It was James who asked the question. 'When will we be able to welcome you home?'

But Hannah only smiled as she took Lars's arm and walked out onto the driveway. She stood very still for some moments, looking back at the house, taking in the scent of the garden, inhaling the woodsmoke that drifted in the thin highland air, bowing her head briefly before the proud silhouette of the mountain and its god.

And then she was gone, leaving only hope as a token of her passing.

Glossary

akili	cleverness, mental ability
asante sana	thank you very much
askari	policeman or guard
ayah	childminder, nanny
bariti	mangrove poles used for building
bhang	marijuana
bibi	woman, wife
boma	a fenced-in enclosure for dwellings and livestock
bui bui	traditional black garment covering a woman from head to foot
bundu	bushland, the wilderness
bwana	title of respect towards a white man
chui	leopard
dawa	medicine
debbi	metal container for liquid
duka	small shop
fisi	hyena
hapana	no
haraka	hurry
harambee	everyone pull together
hodi	Hello, anyone home?
inshallah	God willing

kali	fierce, cross, sharp
karibu	welcome, come in
kazi mingi	a great deal of work
kiboko	hippo
kikapu	basket
kikois	woven, striped sarongs
lekker	wonderful, fantastic
lugga	a dried-out river bed
makuti	roofing thatch made from palm fronds
manyatta	traditional dwelling of Maasai and Samburu tribes
mashua	boat
matata	problem
mbale sana	very far away
mbaya sana	very bad
memsahib	title of respect towards a white woman
mzee	term of respect for an old person
the Mzee	title given to Jomo Kenyatta, who became president of Kenya
mzungu	foreigner (usually white)
ndio	yes
ndofu	elephant
ngalawa	dug-out canoe
ngombe	cow
ngufu	energy, strength
nyama	meat
nyama choma	grilled meat
nyati	buffalo
pole	slowly, or sorry
posho	ground maize meal used as staple food
rafiki	friend
sasa hivi	immediately

shamba	smallholding, garden
shauri	problem, disagreement
shenzi	shoddy
stabbur	Norwegian farm building used for storage
tackies	canvas shoes
toroka	get away from here, get out
toto	child
Ulaya	a distant country
wahindi	an Asian person
wananchi	the common people
watu	men, labourers
wazungu	foreigners

www.vintage-books.co.uk